STRANGE ARE THE WAYS

STRANGE
ARE THE WAYS

Teresa Crane

Chadderton

HarperCollins*Publishers*

HarperCollins*Publishers*
77–85 Fulham Palace Road
Hammersmith, London w6 8jb

Published by HarperCollins*Publishers* 1993

1 3 5 7 9 8 6 4 2

A catalogue record for this book
is available from the British Library

ISBN 0 00 223851 9

Photoset in Linotron Trump Mediaeval by
Rowland Phototypesetting Ltd, Bury St Edmunds, Suffolk

Printed in Great Britain by
HarperCollinsManufacturing Glasgow

THIS IS FOR TONY,
WITH ALL MY LOVE AND MANY, MANY THANKS.

BOOK ONE

St Petersburg, 1908

CHAPTER ONE

'I shall go insane. You hear me, Anna? Quite insane, I tell you.' The words held a determined edge of agitation. Distractedly Varya Petrovna Shalakova applied a scrap of lace, cologne-soaked, to her forehead. Her soft-skinned and still pretty face puckered in child-like distress. She closed her eyes. 'Anna – I have a migraine coming on, most certainly I have. It had to happen, of course – all this trouble, all this fuss – it really is too much. Anna, darling – where is my Phenacetin?'

Anna, standing in the shadows by the window, her back to the room, turned, repressing sudden exasperation. How had she ever expected her pretty, senseless mother to survive these last stages of the move from Moscow to St Petersburg without a final and convenient migraine? 'I'm afraid the Phena tablets are packed with the other medicines, Mama. You gave them to me yourself. Please don't upset yourself. It's all right. The last sledge has arrived, and the things are being loaded. Papa is down there – he has everything under control.'

The small lace handkerchief fluttered again, faintly. 'Oh, I'm sure he has – well of course he has – but such a fuss! Lenka!' The light voice took on a sudden sharp petulance. 'Do sit up straight, child! How many times must I tell you? You slouch like a stable lad! You'll get a hump!'

Yelena, slumped in an armchair, her nose as always buried in a book, scowled ferociously but nevertheless shifted a little in the chair and after a fashion straightened back and shoulders.

Anna turned again to the window. Fine snowflakes whirled in the grey, still air and flew into the glass, clinging for a moment before reluctantly melting into beaded moisture on the outer window pane. Beneath her in the courtyard the foreshort-ened figure of her father, stocky, brisk-moving, fussy-looking

3

even at this distance, organized with obvious shortness of temper the late-come sledge. Two goods vans were well and truly booked, there was time and more than time to get to the station; but Victor Valerievich Shalakov was not a man who cared to have his well-laid plans disrupted. Anna, watching him, the sounds from below shut out by the heavy double windows that had as always been fitted for the winter, felt a mild but quite genuine twinge of sympathy for the tardy sledge-driver. Even she, always his acknowledged favourite, knew the sting of her father's tongue. The thought brought a too-familiar pang of unease and unhappiness. Her own recent battle with him, so stubbornly fought, so predictably, demoralizingly and utterly lost had left a scar still too raw to probe. Her rage at her father had been unnerving. The simple faiths and certainties of childhood upon which her life until now had been founded had failed her. Blind trust had been betrayed. Shying from the thought, she lifted her head sharply, looked out through the whirling haze of snow across the spires and domes that gleamed azure and gold, the endless snow-blanketed rooftops of Moscow. Holy Moscow. Little Mother Moscow. The city she loved, and was about to leave. She blinked, suddenly and rapidly.

Behind her, her mother's voice rose again, the edge of complaint setting Anna's teeth on edge. She leaned her forehead against the cold glass.

The eighteen years of Anna Victorovna Shalakova's life had been spent in Moscow, a city that had for centuries been the very heart and soul of Russia until, a mere century and a half before, the upstart St Petersburg – a city European in a way that a Byzantine Moscow with her roots firmly planted in the Middle Ages never could be – had ousted her.

Anna did not want to leave Moscow. She did not want to live in Petersburg: purpose-built, grand and gracious city of the Tsar. She loved the narrow, cobbled streets of Moscow, the bustle and excitement of her markets, the tolling of her bells, the tumbled variety of her buildings, the magnificence of her ancient Kremlin, the almost barbaric brilliance of her domed and gilded cathedrals and her old, spired churches. The pride of her ancient and sometimes terrible heritage. It was ironic that for all the fuss being made in the room behind her, for all her mother's petulance and Lenka's sulks, she, Anna, was the only one of them who truly hated the thought of the move the family were about to make. Mama from the first had been, insomuch as the words could ever be used about Varya Petrovna, unflaggingly enthusiastic; not least because it provided her with a chance to flout the will of her overpowering father-in-law – blessedly dead at last in his ninetieth year – against whom in life she had never dared to stand. Predictably, for Varya St Petersburg offered a will-o'-the-wisp glamour, a chance to be associated, however tenuously, with the great and the powerful of the land, a chance to share in the good fortune, always corrosively envied, of her elder sister Zhenia, already happily settled in the city. A chance above all to marry off her three girls to greater prospects than were to be found – or so she thought – in provincial, mercantile Moscow. Only the actual bother of the move itself had brought on this fit of the vapours; an affliction that could by no means be described as unexpected, but was no less irritating for that since it had been Anna who had, over the past weeks, taken most of the responsibility for the arrangements. As she almost always did when faced with her mother's vague and maddening inability to cope with anything beyond the complexities of the latest fashion or a gossip over glasses of tea with her friends. Lenka too, awkward, bookish Lenka, a year younger than Anna and usually her devoted follower in all things, had on this occasion shown a subversive tendency to think for herself. 'But Anna, the University in Petersburg is famous! When you persuade Papa – and I know you will! – think of it! St Petersburg! The very centre of all that happens in Russia!'

When you persuade Papa.

Anna looked down into the courtyard and the small, cold knot of anger and resentment tightened once again, a twinge of almost physical pain. What made Lenka so blithely sure that she, Anna, could persuade their father to allow them to attend the women's courses at the University? When her own dream, her own triumph, so short-lived, so apparently little valued, had been shattered by the man's adamant refusal to allow her to take the once-in-a-lifetime-chance that had been offered – that she had worked for and won – when she had gained the music scholarship? She heard again, as she so often had in the past weeks, the cold, horribly unexpected words, relived again her own disbelief, the rise of totally ungovernable rage as understanding had filtered into her bemused mind. 'You didn't think I could *do* it, did you? You didn't bother to stop me trying for the scholarship because it simply didn't occur to you that I was good enough to win it! You were humouring me! You thought you'd get your own way without having to do anything, without my blaming *you*! Well, I do blame you, Papa! I *do*! And I'll never forgive you! Do you hear me? Never!' Under normal circumstances Anna would have trembled to speak to her father so. But she had been beside herself with fury and with disappointment; this opportunity, so coveted, so urgently and exhaustingly worked for, had been against all seemingly insurmountable odds and competition hers. She had been offered the chance to study under one of the greatest violinists in Russia, the chance to discover and explore the worth of her own talent, always so deeply doubted. And curtly and out of hand her father had refused her. With neither debate nor discussion and so far as she could see with no understanding whatsoever he had crushed all her fragile, newborn hopes. No daughter of Victor Valerievich Shalakov would so demean herself and her family. To possess the talent to bring pleasure to friends and family in the decent privacy of their homes was one thing; to perform in public was, in Victor Valerievich's eyes – and in the eyes of many others of his kind – only one step from harlotry, and a short step at that. He would not allow it, and there was an end. The anger and outrage that each had felt at the other at what both had considered a betrayal, a rejection of understanding, had all but fatally damaged a relationship that had always been remarkably if undemonstrably close.

And now Lenka, with the old, unquestioning faith, had convinced herself that Anna could persuade their father to allow them to study at the University in St Petersburg.

Anna pushed a wiry lock of sandy hair from her forehead, looked unseeing into the swirling curtain that drifted across the rooftops. Perhaps, she thought, with a faintly cynical detachment that surprised herself, her sister wasn't so very wrong after all. Perhaps having imposed his will upon her over the music scholarship Papa would give way on this? She had had the feeling on more than one occasion that he had regretted, if not his decision, then the high-handedness of its implementation and the coolness that had fallen between them because of it. In his own stiff-necked way he had even attempted to make amends. It was certainly true that he had agreed with no argument to the idea of their sharing their cousin Katya's tutor when in St Petersburg. And – she turned her head, looked to where a battered leather violin case was propped in an empty chair – he had given her the violin. As a peace offering, which it undoubtedly was, though he would have died before admitting it, it had not worked. No instrument, however exquisite, however valuable in both sentimental and real terms, could make up for what he had taken from her; but as a straw in the wind perhaps it did not bode too badly for Yelena's own dream, held just as passionately Anna knew as had been her own. And Lenka could not speak for herself; her relationship with her father was such that if she so much as drew breath in his presence it could provoke irritation and rebuke. Awkward with most people, occasionally it had to be said almost to the point of rudeness, Lenka all too often became sullen and worse than tongue-tied when faced with the father who so clearly and openly disliked her. For all of their young lives Anna had stood as spokeswoman and champion to her younger sister.

'And Nina Pavlova says we'll all be murdered in our beds – the terrible riots –' Varya Petrovna's voice again, plaintive as a child's. 'The streets ran with blood so they say – a dreadful thing, dreadful!'

'Oh, Mama!' It was Lenka, of course, who could not hold her tongue. Anna lifted exasperated eyes to heaven. Dmitri, third of the four Shalakov children and the only boy, was sitting cross-legged beside his mother's chair, absorbed in a puzzle, oblivious to what went on around him; Margarita, at thirteen years the youngest child and only true heir to her mother's good looks, stood in dreamy and single-minded contemplation before a mirror, playing with her hair. Yelena's voice was edged with irritation. 'That was all over ages ago – three years or more! You know it! Anyway, it was certainly no worse in Petersburg than it was here in Moscow! And at least now we have the

Duma – a parliament of sorts – some say for the *people* in government.'

'The people? Government? Flying in the face of God!' Varya Petrovna turned her head a little, away from this incomprehensible daughter of hers. 'God will punish them. You'll see. Rita, dear, come to Mama a moment – your hair is really most dreadfully untidy – I don't know what Papa will say if he sees you in such a state.'

Margarita turned from the mirror, came obediently to her mother and sank prettily down beside her. Varya reached into a small crocheted bag and produced a comb. 'That's right, a little closer, my dear. Lenka, hand me that ribbon, would you?' She turned back to Margarita. 'Such lovely hair. A pity to let it tumble loose.'

Her youngest daughter smiled sweetly and hid her irritation. She knew well the effect achieved by the artless loosening of her thick golden mass of curls about her heart-shaped face. 'Seraphima didn't have time to do it this morning, Mama.' The lie tripped as easily off her young tongue as would the truth. It was one of Margarita's many undoubted advantages that she had never allowed herself to become enmeshed in the inconvenient net of absolute honesty. What Margarita wished to perceive of the world she perceived; and within minutes of reporting it so to others often quite genuinely came to believe it herself.

'That girl's as idle as the winter nights are long.' Varya expertly twisted the rope of hair, fastened it securely with the ribbon, and with gentle fingers brushed back the golden wisps that fell upon the wide, fair forehead.

Margarita stayed beside her, pulling the long plait over her shoulder, winding the curling ends about her finger. 'Mama, when we get to Peter –' she pronounced the word 'Pitta' in a studied and casually affected way that made Anna cast her eyes to the ceiling and turn back to her contemplation of the scene in the courtyard below. Lenka, hunched once more over her book, uttered a small snort of pure derision that earned her an icy glance from her mother. Margarita, as always airily indifferent to her sisters' reactions to her pretensions, continued with no break in the flow of her words. '– Won't you please persuade

8

Papa that I'm old enough to share Cousin Katya's tutor with the others? It really isn't fair –' a favourite phrase that brought the barest twitch of a smile to Anna's lips '– that I should have to go to that *boring* Gymnasium. Mama, please?'

Her mother, who a moment before had been totally absorbed in her most beautiful child, sat back in her chair, long fingers to her forehead. 'Margarita, please! As you well know this is your father's decision. It isn't kind of you to ask Mama to interfere with matters that are not her concern. Mother of God!' The lace handkerchief had appeared again, fluttering before her face. 'Anna, what in the world is happening down there? Are we never to leave?'

'They're nearly finished. They seem to be having some trouble with the hatstand.'

'Gymnasium?' Yelena's quiet voice came as close to amusement as it ever did. 'Are you sure you have that right, Rita dear? I thought you had to pass an examination to get into the Gymnasium? A real one, with questions and answers and things.'

Margarita, turned now from her mother's eyes, stuck out a long, furious tongue as far as it would go.

Dmitri's dark, slanting eyes flickered between them and he giggled under his breath.

The ghost of a smile lit Lenka's sallow face.

Margarita fairly glittered with temper, a becoming colour lifting in her cheeks.

'Anna, it's getting cold in here, fetch me the blue shawl, would you?' Varya put narrow white hands to her face. 'I really shouldn't allow myself to chill, you know.'

'Yes, Mama.' Anna moved the violin case and lifted the shawl that lay across the back of the chair.

'And that's another thing, Mama.' Margarita's aggrieved tone unconsciously matched her mother's so exactly that it might have been an echo. 'Why is Anna allowed to have her violin on the train with her when I had to put my theatre in that beastly box? I'm sure it will be damaged.'

'Don't be silly, Rita.' Briskly Anna cut across her mother's reply. 'I told you, your precious theatre is perfectly safe. I supervised its packing myself.' She walked back to the window, peered down into the yard. 'There, that's it from the look of it. The sledges are gone. Papa's coming up. It must be nearly time to go.'

'Oh, dear.' Her mother stood, brushing nervously at her skirt, flicking at the immaculate lace of her collar. 'The coats, Anna – and the hats and shawls – they haven't been packed?'

Anna shook her head, patiently. 'Oh, of course not, Mama! Seraphima will bring them when we're ready.'

'And our things will be safe on the train? The people at the station know where they're supposed to be going?' She had asked the same question at least a dozen times.

'They will be on the same train as we will, Mama! I've told you and told you! Papa has hired two goods waggons – he'll make sure that they're hitched to the right train, don't worry!'

'Well.' Victor Valerievich Shalakov, his wide-shouldered, substantial figure still dressed in fur-lined shuba with a tall fur hat upon his dark head, stood at the open door. 'At last we're ready. I think it best that we get to the station as early as possible. Anna, you'll get everyone organized?'

'Yes, Papa.' Anna reached for the bell. 'Nanny Irisha and Seraphima are waiting in the kitchen. Everything's ready.'

'Oh, isn't it *exciting*?' For one moment reverting to the child she actually was as opposed to the sophisticated young woman she liked to imagine herself, Margarita twirled into the middle of the room, calf-length skirts lifting and flying about her. 'I've never been on a train all night before! And Petersburg! Petersburg! I'm certain it's going to be wonderful!'

Even Lenka's lips twitched to a small smile at her young sister's sudden and infectious enthusiasm. 'Going hunting for a handsome prince, Rita?'

Margarita tossed her head, heavy plait swinging. 'And why not? Just because you spend your life with your nose in a book and couldn't care less if you look like somebody's kitchen maid doesn't mean I have to be the same! Why shouldn't I hope that St Petersburg will be wonderful?'

'No reason, child, no reason.' Victor Valerievich's tone was indulgent, the look he shot at Lenka was not amused. 'Though I trust you understand that times might be a little hard to begin with. It is a great step we are taking. It will take a good deal of hard work to make the name of Shalakov as well-known in the capital as it is in Moscow.'

'But the new shop's on the Nevsky, isn't it? Everyone's bound to come! And Uncle Andrei – he's famous already, isn't he? He and that new student of his?' Margarita struggled into the heavy fur-lined coat that Anna was holding for her, crammed a small fur hat onto her head.

'Was, dear. Was famous.' Varya's tone was waspish. 'Before the accident that is.' She shrugged her own fur shuba elegantly onto her narrow shoulders, adjusted the beaver hat to exactly the right angle, reached for her muff.

'Oh, Mama!' Anna's voice was scolding. 'You always talk as if poor Uncle Andrei hurt his hand purposely to spite you! And he is still famous, you know he is! Rita, do stand still a moment, or I'll never get you done up! Seraphima, where are the boots?'

It was a full ten minutes before they were ready. Booted, gloved and muffled to the eyes against the winter cold they stood for a moment in sudden silence. Even Margarita was still. The apartment that had been their home for so many years, left now with only the most basic of furniture, stripped of all personal possessions, all ornament, looked bleak and shabby.

Victor Valerievich cleared his throat loudly.

'Well.' Varya's voice wavered a little. 'Let us sit down for a moment, then we must go.'

Briefly and in silence they sat, the old custom made more poignant by the knowledge that this was the last time they would sit so together in this room. Then, with a last glance about her, Varya stood. Her husband offered his arm, and together they preceded the rest of the family out onto the landing.

Anna was the last to go. She turned at the door, stood for a long moment looking back into the room that had seen all of her childhood, then firmly she closed the door and followed the others down the stairs.

The women of the family had a small four-berth compartment to themselves, Dmitri and his father being next door and sharing with a couple of young officers who were on their way back to St Petersburg after leave. Seraphima and old Nanny Irisha, the only servants to accompany them to their new home, were travelling 'hard' in the public carriages, a fact that no argument of Anna's had been able to change. 'A servant is a servant, daughter,' her father had said, 'no matter how long-serving. They have blankets, and food. They could not possibly travel with us – think of the cost.' It was, however, not of the cost that Anna thought as she organized the stowing of their boxes and baggage and the serving of tea, but of poor Nanny Irisha's old bones and the long night ahead.

'Anna, where in the world is my blue shawl? I thought you said that –'

'It's here, Mama, here.' Anna produced the shawl, settled it about her mother's slender shoulders. Outside the early darkness of a northern January had fallen and ice crusted the glass as they sped through the winter night. The train moved smoothly, swaying a little, wheels clicking busily over rails that had been laid with especial and attentive care since this was a line over which the Imperial train ran often.

'Anna – the hampers – they're here?'

'Yes, Mama. Under the seat.'

'Oh, may we eat now? May we?' Margarita's eyes lit at the thought; she was at that stage in life when she was always hungry.

'In a moment, when the attendant brings the tea.' Varya Petrovna settled a cushion more comfortably behind her. 'My book, Anna?'

'Here, Mama.'

'And Anna – your father and Dima – please go to make sure they're comfortable. Remind Papa that Dima must not be made to sleep on the top berth, he'll most certainly fall out.'

Patiently Anna stood. 'I'll tell him, Mama.'

Dmitri and Victor were comfortably settled in the next compartment. Their companions, two young dragoon officers, booted and dashingly uniformed, looked up as Anna slipped into the compartment, then formally if a little awkwardly against the swaying movement of the train came to their feet, smiling.

'Oh, please – do sit down.' Anna was flustered, feeling warm colour lift to her face. The tendency to blush poppy bright at the slightest cause, legacy of her sandy colouring and fair, freckled skin, was and always had been a source of acute embarrassment to her.

The smile on the face of one of the young men widened. He was blond and slim and looked not much older than Anna herself. She felt herself blushing even more furiously. 'Papa, Mama wishes to know if you're comfortable? And asked particularly that you should not let Dima sleep on the top bunk. She thinks he'll fall out.'

Dmitri rolled his eyes and groaned theatrically. His father clicked his tongue a little impatiently. 'It's arranged, my dear, it's arranged. These young gentlemen have already offered to take the top berths. Tell your mother not to worry.' He went back to his newspaper, folding it precisely, pushing the pince-nez higher onto his nose.

'Yes, Papa.'

'Annoushka, Mama says –' the door behind her slid open and Margarita all but tumbled through. On meeting the amused eyes of the two strange young men she stopped, instantly aware, instantly collected, smoothing her skirts, smiling her most brilliant and beguiling smile. 'Hello. Sorry. Did I interrupt? Mama wants to know where the chocolates are.' Her wide and guileless blue eyes were fixed on the face of the fair young man. She laced her fingers in front of her demurely, tilted her head a little. His mouth twitched into a smile which she returned with interest.

'They're in the brown bag next to the hamper.' Firmly Anna caught her sister's hand and propelled her towards the door.

Margarita hung back. 'You're all right, Papa? You're comfortable?' Again she glanced coquettishly beneath long golden lashes at the fair young officer who was watching her in open amusement and some admiration.

'We're perfectly comfortable, thank you, my dear.' Astonishingly oblivious as always to his youngest child's precocious behaviour, Victor Valerievich bent forward to pat her hand. 'Back you go to Mama now, there's a good child.'

'Yes, Papa.' The lashes swept down against peach-smooth skin, stray golden curls escaped their pins and brushed the white, slender neck. With studiedly pretty care she leaned forward to kiss her father's cheek. 'Good night, Papa.'

'Good night, child.' Victor Valerievich nodded, pleased and

proud. Margarita smiled brilliantly. Anna could have slapped her. Firmly she ushered her through the door, but not before her younger sister had bestowed yet another dazzling smile upon each of her father's and brother's travelling companions, and received in return from each the silent homage of interest and admiration that she knew to be her due. In the corridor she gave Anna no time to speak.

'Annoushka, Annoushka? I need to go – you know –'

'What, again?' Anna eyed her suspiciously.

Margarita nodded. 'It must be the movement of the train.'

'But it's only half an hour since –'

'Please, Anna! I really must!'

'Oh, very well. Come on then.'

They set off along the narrow corridor, bracing themselves against the movement of the train as it swung around a curve in the track. Snow billowed against the windows. Margarita shrieked histrionically and staggered a little, falling against the door of a compartment in which it so happened that four young men, two in uniform, two in the garb of students, were intent upon a game of cards. One glanced up, grinned, winked a dark, laughing eye. He was as handsome a young man as Anna had seen and his smile was pure mischief. Grimly Anna tried to propel her younger sister forward.

'Annoushka, Annoushka, wait! My ankle – I've twisted it –'

Anna smiled, pleasantly. 'Your neck will be next. You want the lavatory? Go to the lavatory, and stop playing silly games.'

Margarita grimaced ferociously, sent a small, flirtatious glance towards the young officer who returned it in kind and then lifted interested eyes to Anna's.

Anna caught her sister's hand and hauled her down the corridor to the tiny room at the end. 'In,' she snapped. 'Here, let me do your buttons.'

'I'm perfectly able to do them myself, thank you.' Margarita was on her dignity.

Anna turned her back to the door, rested her arms upon the window bar, looking into the streaming, snowy darkness. Somewhere further down the carriage a man was singing, a deep and melancholy sound that mingled with the rhythmic rush and click of the wheels. In the tiny compartment next to the toilet the attendant rattled glasses upon a tray and a samovar hissed.

Anna rubbed at the streaming window, peered into the darkness, thinking again of Moscow; of home. Of the friends who grew further away with each turn of the hurrying wheels, of the Conservatory's teacher of music, the elderly and irascible Monsieur de Neuve to whom she knew she owed a debt it would be forever beyond her to repay, of the bustling markets and the fairy-tale domes and spires, of a certain brown-haired, blunt-faced young man, brother to a friend, whose nice eyes had smiled at her so warmly and whose attentions, slight as she had understood them to be, had nevertheless fostered the first small, private dreams of young womanhood. She blinked.

'Anna? What's wrong?' Margarita stood beside her, head tilted to look up suspiciously into her tall sister's face.

'Nothing,' Anna said. 'Nothing at all. Now do come on – Mama will wonder wherever we've disappeared to!'

She lay, much later, fully clothed except for shoes and jacket, upon the top bunk listening to her mother's slight and delicate snores beneath her. A few compartments along the noisy card game was still in progress. A balalaika played, and the same voice she had heard before lifted in song, deep, melancholy, vibrant with feeling; the sound, she found herself thinking, of the soul of Russia.

''Noushka? 'Noushka, are you asleep?'

She hesitated. Then, 'No,' she said.

She heard movement, dimly saw Yelena as she lifted herself upon her elbow to look across the gap between the two top berths. In the bed below, Margarita slept like a baby, a small smile upon her face. Her last words before sleep had concerned her most precious possession: 'Anna? You're *sure* my theatre is safe?'

Yelena leaned forward, speaking very softly, the words all but lost in the steady background noises of the train. ''Noushka, what's it going to be like? St Petersburg, I mean?'

Anna made a small sound, affectionate and exasperated. 'For heaven's sake, Lenka! How am I supposed to know?'

'I mean, it's going to be very different, isn't it?'

'I suppose so, yes.'

'It seems so very strange, doesn't it? To be leaving Moscow?'

Anna did not answer directly. 'We've always known it was Papa's plan,' she said. 'That's why Uncle Andrei stayed in St Petersburg. It was only Grandfather who prevented Papa from selling the Moscow shop ages ago. Now that Grandfather's dead –' she hesitated a moment. Could it be true, as she suspected it was, that she was the only one of the family that truly missed that crusty, impossible old man? Miss him she did, that was certain, more than she would have believed possible; a fact that would have drawn from the old man one of his rare cackles of amusement. 'Now that he's dead, and Papa has the money – well, off we go, willy nilly, to St Petersburg.'

'"Pitta,"' Yelena said, drily.

'Yes.' Her sister's voice was tart. 'Pitta.'

'And do you think that the new shop will be as successful as Papa hopes?'

'Lenka, truly, I don't know any better than you! Papa thinks so. He thinks that with the patronage that Uncle Andrei has already secured, and with a shop in the most fashionable street in the most fashionable city in Russia, the business is bound to do well. And I'm sure he must be right. Now, Lenka –'

But Yelena was not about to be quieted so quickly. 'And Uncle Andrei – do you remember him?'

'A little, yes. He's dark, like Papa, but much slimmer, at least he was, I think – it's years since I've seen him, I was just a little girl – it seemed to me, I remember, that he laughed a lot –'

'Papa's brother? What a marvel. Does he still, I wonder? How does he manage, do you think, since the accident?'

Andrei Shalakov, younger brother to their father, and even as a very young man a bow maker of immense promise and repute, had lost two fingers in the same accident that had killed his young wife and their unborn child five years before. Anna, a reserved but deeply emotional child of thirteen at the time, had had nightmares for months after news of what had happened had first reached Moscow. The horrors her mother had whispered to her friends behind her hand had appalled her. She still did not like to think of it.

'I really don't know. It must have been awful for him, the accident, but he still makes bows and they're still much sought-

16

after. Monsieur de Neuve at the Conservatory had one. Now –'
she wriggled in the narrow bunk. 'Lenka –'

'Oh, Anna, no!' Yelena, sensing what she was about to say,
broke in. 'You surely can't want to *sleep*? Talk to me for just a
little while? Please? Just a little while?'

Anna yawned, very loudly.

Yelena snuggled into her bunk, resting her head upon her
bent arm. 'I wonder, will we finish up living in an apartment
like Uncle Mischa's and Aunt Zhenia's?'

'Is that what you'd like?' Anna's sleepy voice was faintly
surprised.

'Oh, I don't know. I suppose so, yes. I've never forgotten our
visit there – so grand! So huge!'

'We were just children. It probably isn't so grand, nor so
huge.'

'P'raps not. I remember thinking it was like a palace! And
Katya, she'll have changed, won't she?'

'We'll all have changed.'

'But France, Switzerland! She's been everywhere! Anna?'
Lenka's voice dropped a little. 'Is it true, do you suppose, that
Katya was expelled from the Smolny Institute? Before she was
sent abroad?'

Anna yawned another huge, jaw-cracking and not altogether
convincing yawn. 'From what I remember of Cousin Katya it's
more than possible. Certainly Mama says that's why she has a
tutor – the Smolny apparently refused to have her back. Said
she was a subversive influence on the other girls, or something.'

'I don't suppose that bothers her one bit.' Lenka's one visit
to her cousin Katya and her family had made a lasting impression. She rolled onto her back, looking at the smoke-stained
ceiling so close above her head; sighed a little. 'Isn't it strange?
It seems that Katya can have anything – do anything – anything
at all that she wants, and we –' She stopped. 'Perhaps it will
be different in St Petersburg?'

Anna, keeping her doubts to herself, remained silent.

The train shrieked on through the night. The singer had
stopped, but the balalaika played still, softly and sadly. The card
players shouted. Margarita stirred.

'I don't want an apartment like Katya's.' Yelena's voice,

breaking the long silence, was very low but no less fierce for that. 'I don't want her pretty clothes, nor her silly friends, nor her prospects nor her fortune. I want – I want freedom! I want to attend the courses for women at the University. I want to learn! About real things! About the world! I want to meet people who know about politics, and art, and mathematics! I want to read, and read and read! I want to know everything! *Everything!* Oh, 'Noushka, you aren't laughing, are you? I mean it!'

'I'm not laughing. I know you do.'

'It's all I've ever wanted – it's all I'll ever ask! 'Noushka, you will persuade Papa, won't you? You do promise?'

'I can't promise, Lenka – you know that.'

'But promise you'll *try*! Papa will never listen to me. If he knew how much I wanted to go that would be enough in itself to make him say no.' Yelena's voice held nothing either of complaint or of self-pity. She stated a simple truth and they both knew it. 'But you – he'll listen to you.'

'Perhaps.'

'Oh, you know he will! Anna, please! You won't go back on your word?'

'Of course I won't! Of course not!'

'So.' Anna could hear the content in her sister's voice. 'We'll share Katya's tutor, and show him what an extremely silly pupil he's had till now –'

'Lenka!'

'– and then, the University of St Petersburg. Oh, how I wish we could be proper students, living in an attic, reading by candlelight till midnight, drinking cocoa out of tin mugs –'

Anna had to laugh. 'Idiot!'

Yelena snuggled into the thin blankets. Anna yawned again, genuinely this time, and sleepily. In the distance young men sang, with vodka-inspired cheer, of green fields and willing girls and the soft breath of summer. The silence of slumber fell. Anna's eyelids drooped.

''Noushka?' Yelena asked, suddenly and softly.

'Mmm?'

'Did you mind very much?' A moment's pause. 'The scholarship?'

Silence. The wheels clicked and turned.

Then, 'No.' Anna's voice was even, the single word closing the subject like the sharp click of a lock.

Yelena turned, burrowing into her pillow. Her voice was muffled. 'Oh, well, as Nanny Irisha is always telling anyone who'll listen, "Strange are the ways of God". Who knows? It's probably all for the best.'

'Yes. Very probably. Now go to sleep, Lenka, for heaven's sake. We have a long day ahead of us tomorrow.'

The song had changed, the voices quietened. *'Dearest, oh dear one, oh why do you deceive me?'*

Anna lay very still and stared into darkness.

The station, even at this hour of the morning, was teeming with activity. Rich and poor, master and servant, townsman, soldier and peasant swarmed upon the freezing, slush-covered platforms and into the lofty halls. The Shalakov women and the two servants found themselves a draughty but relatively quiet corner and stood surrounded by their belongings waiting as Victor, with Dmitri in tow, made the arrangements that would take them to their final destination in a street called Venskaya not far from the new shop on the Nevsky. Seraphima and Nanny Irisha, scarved and shawled, huddled stoically together, eyes downcast, saying little. That St Petersburg was a den of thieves, rapists and hooligans every good Muscovite knew; they waited with the fatalistic resignation of their race and class for the worst to happen. Anna and Yelena, both a head and shoulders taller than their tiny mother, took station one each side of her to protect her from the jostling of the crowds, Anna keeping firm grip of her violin case.

'Here comes Papa. See, he's waving – he must have managed to hire a sledge –'

In fact he had hired two, and it was in comfort that they drove to their new home, Victor, Varya and the two younger children in the leading sledge and Anna, Yelena and the two servants in the one that followed. Wrapped in rugs, collars turned up and fur hats firmly pulled down around their ears, Anna's arms wrapped protectively about her precious violin case, they strained their eyes into the darkness of the morning to see the city that was to be their new home. With the clean smell of fresh snow in their nostrils they bowled along the wide streets and boulevards to the sound of the bells on the horses' harnesses and the singing of the runners upon the packed snow. Braziers burned here and there on a corner, the ruddy glow of the charcoal warm and cheerful-looking in the morning darkness. The street lights gleamed upon large, well-proportioned, pastel-coloured mansions, upon slender spires, upon the graceful arch of a bridge across a frozen canal. Anna, tired as she was after an uncomfortable and broken night's sleep, was, despite herself, enthralled. Yelena, wide-eyed beside her, was struck equally to silence. Tall trees, leafless and still, etched in white, stood guard upon streets and squares of spacious and graceful elegance. Even in the darkness the city's special beauty was evident. A small troop of Cossack Cavalry rode past, harnesses jingling, the coats of their compact, muscular little horses gleaming, their officer, straight-backed and elegantly cloaked, looking like an equestrian statue come to life. Anna saw Margarita in the sledge in front turn in her seat and watch him with unabashed curiosity and interest. They skirted the huge square in front of the Winter Palace that even at this hour was ablaze with light. They followed the river a little way, past the Admiralty building with its slender golden spire, before crossing the Neva and moving into a quiet, respectable residential area of small houses and apartment blocks. Here there were more people to be seen; men and women, huddled against the cold, hurrying through the dark early morning to their places of work.

As they swung around a corner the leading sledge-driver called, the horses' pace slowed and stopped. An apartment house loomed above them. Victor stepped onto the pavement, and with some small ceremony handed his wife from the sledge. Anna tucked the violin case under her arm and she and her sister scrambled from the warm nest of their own sledge onto the icy road, Seraphima and Nanny Irisha grumbling down behind them. They found themselves before a large and gloomy doorway, dim-lit, beyond which a flight of wide, shallow steps led upwards into shadowed darkness. Bags and packages, the hand luggage they had carried with them on the train, were deposited upon the frozen road, the drivers swung back up onto their high seats and with musical, resonant calls urged the horses back into motion. Bells a-jingle, the two sledges swished away, leaving behind them a sudden quiet that held an edge of apprehension.

Victor craned his neck, looking up. He cleared his throat portentously. 'Well, this must be it. Andrei assured me in his last letter that the apartment that had fallen vacant above his was a roomy one, and could be made to –' He stopped. A figure had appeared on the shadowed stairs: a slight, lightly-moving silhouette that hesitated only for a moment before leaping down the last few steps and flinging long arms about the surprised Victor, saluting him upon each cheek with a kiss. 'Victor! Brother! You've come! Welcome!' The man stepped back. Anna saw the flash of surprise on her father's face and knew it must have been mirrored in her own and in the others' who watched. Her uncle – for surely this must be Andrei Shalakov? – turned, smiling warmly from one to the other. In the light of the single lamp above the door his hair, which Anna remembered as being thick and black as his brother's, shone, a shock of silver-white, bright as the snow. 'Come now, all of you, out of the cold. The stove's alight and the samovar's waiting. Come.' He scooped up the largest of the two bags and led the way up the stairs. A little wearily the small band followed, trudging up a long flight of stairs to the first floor, where a pair of battered double doors stood ajar.

'Wait.' Andrei set down the bags he was carrying and slipped through the doors. Beyond them the glow of a lamp beckoned and welcome warmth crept out onto the cold landing.

'What's he doing?' Margarita hissed in a whisper that could have been heard in Moscow. 'Why are we waiting?'

'Patience, child.' It was Nanny Irisha, who had, Anna suddenly remembered, been Andrei's nurse when he was a boy, as well as her father's. 'Patience.'

'Come in, all of you – come in!'

They filed through the door into a small hallway that led in turn to a large parlour, furnished simply; heavy armchairs and a sofa at one end, a round table upon which stood a simmering samovar at the other. By the table stood Andrei, his face, young-looking beneath its thatch of prematurely silvered hair, alight with warmth and welcome. He held a small icon of the Virgin and Child. On the table beside him was a tray upon which stood the traditional symbols of welcome: a loaf of black bread topped by a cellar of salt. Andrei raised the icon. With one movement the new arrivals went down on their knees as with it he made the sign of the cross above their bent heads. Then carefully he laid aside the icon and reached for the bread and salt, balancing it carefully as he again made the sign. It was as he turned to put them back upon the tray that the salt toppled. He made a swift grab for it and for the first time Anna saw clearly the maimed hand, which he was so skilled at hiding, looking claw-like in the half-darkness. She averted her eyes. The salt cellar flew through the air and clattered to the floor, spilling the salt as it rolled, stopping at the toe of Anna's boot. There was a small silence. Few things to the superstitious races of the Russias could be more badly omened than to spill the salt of welcome. Swiftly, filled with a sudden rush of sympathy for her uncle, Anna bent to pick it up. Nanny Irisha it was who took it from her, scolding gently, breaking that strange tense silence. 'Awkward is as awkward does! Always clumsy, the boy, always clumsy! Couldn't walk upstairs without falling over his own feet. It's a miracle he's survived to his thirty-fourth year, that it is! But there, but there – strange are the ways of God, they say, strange indeed are his ways!' She crossed herself once, twice, and then again; hobbled to the table to stand the salt cellar carefully back beside the bread.

They all began to speak at once; kisses were exchanged, coats, hats, boots and shawls discarded, exclamations made about the apartment – its size, its convenience, how very well the things that would be arriving from the station later would become it. Tea was passed around, and small sweet cakes. The stove in the corner of the room fairly glowed with warmth. The icon was set high in the corner where a small lamp burned beneath it. Tea glass in hand, Anna wandered to the window and drew the heavy curtain a little aside. It was growing light. She could see a spire in the distance glinting in the late-rising dawn. The street outside was busy; a tram clanked past the end of the road.

'Annoushka. I hope you'll be happy here.'

She turned. Her uncle stood beside her, smiling. He was of middle height, his head only just topping hers and, as she had remembered, slight. His face was both like her father's and yet, fascinatingly, unlike. The bones were lighter, the eyes a mild blue, yet something in the structure of the face, the slant of cheekbone and eye, that Dmitri too had inherited, stamped a family likeness that could not be denied. Andrei was fourteen years younger than his brother, these two the only survivors of eight children, six of whom had died at birth, and Anna had seen him only once since the day ten years before when he and his new young bride had left Moscow for St Petersburg. Anna had been eight years old then, and dazzled by the glitter and solemnity of the wedding service, the delicate beauty of the doll-like little bride. She had all but hero-worshipped her young uncle in those days; always he had had a kindly word, an ear to listen to childish woes. She had loved to watch him work, the deft, quick hands making wood and ivory and strong horse hair into a delicate, all but living thing that could draw music from the dullest of instruments. Andrei Shalakov's bows had been famous even then. Disconcertingly, now, she found it hard to reconcile her memories of a tall, dark, quiet-voiced uncle with this man whose height barely outreached her own and whose changed appearance – the shock of silver-white hair, the deep-etched lines about a mouth that she remembered always smiling – took her aback each time she turned her eyes to him.

He saw it. He flicked his head a little, genuine laughter in his eyes. 'A bit of a shock?'

She nodded.

He shrugged. Smiled a very little. 'Hard times, Anna. Hard times. But over now.'

She nodded.

His smile was warm. 'I hear great things of you.'

'Oh?'

His eyes moved to where the battered violin case lay upon the table. 'The scholarship.'

There was a small, sharp silence. 'Oh,' Anna said again, the inflection entirely different.

He moved, laid a light hand on her arm. 'Don't, 'Noushka. Don't ever despair. You never know –' He stopped, a flicker of pain clear and sharp in his eyes.

She had flinched. She could have chopped off her own arm

23

for its small, involuntary recoil, but it was too late. He had seen it. Felt it. He snatched the maimed hand away, still smiling. 'You never know what might come of such things. You did it. That's what counts. You beat them all. You must be good, more than good, to have done that. Hold on to that. Who knows what may happen?'

Cheeks bright with mortification, in the face of his composure she could behave no less well, for his sake. 'Strange are the ways of God, as Nanny Irisha so often tells us.' Her voice was very strained.

He nodded, and the smile was gone. 'Yes.' He watched her for a long, quiet moment. 'Strange indeed.'

'Uncle!' Margarita had appeared by their side. Her small, bright face, pretty and appealing as a kitten's, turned to Andrei. 'Mama says that you are to tell us about Petersburg – we are all quite lost. How far are we from the river? And the Nevsky? And have you seen Cousin Katya and her family?' She towed him away, laughing, to the centre of the room. Anna turned back to the window, cheeks still burning.

Outside full daylight was lifting, and it had started to snow again.

CHAPTER TWO

In crisp and sunny weather that made the buildings of St Petersburg glitter like so many prettily iced cakes, Victor Valerievich Shalakov strode through the streets of the city, collar turned against the wind, and contemplated the coming meeting with his brother-in-law Bourlov. He disliked intensely the thought of borrowing money from the man that Varya's sister had so shrewdly married, but the offer was there, and extra finance was essential if the new shop was to be brought to the standards demanded by the wealthy patrons he was determined to attract. He had worked his fingers to the bone over the years preparing for this day; the day when, his miser of a father dead at last, as senior partner he would have control of the business and make it his. Not that he felt any particular excitement or pleasure; Victor was a man to whom by nature disappointment came more easily than contentment. It was characteristic of him that surrounded by the beauty and brilliance of this lovely afternoon he should feel nothing but the bite of the wind. A successful businessman, always he saw only the greater successes of others. A respected family man, yet it could not be denied that privately he felt himself cheated by the Almighty in his brood of girls and his one weakly boy. Blessed with a shrewd brain and a pugnacious obstinacy that had stood him in good stead in his dogged fight to turn what had been a small and reputable family business into an expanding and profitable modern concern, yet always it had seemed to him that his brother's more artistic skills and talents had been greater appreciated and better thought of by the family and by the world. Since childhood he had been aware, with a practical lack of self pity, that no-one really liked him – a fact that accorded him no particular suffering, since in Victor's eyes to pursue the easy and worthless admiration of others was the surest sign of a weakness of character bordering on the insane. In consequence, however, any kindly interest, any unsolicited warmth had always been treated with the deepest of suspicion, and neither in childhood nor in adulthood could Victor Valerievich ever have been said to have had a true friend; the significance of this circumstance lying largely in the fact that he himself cared nothing for it, indeed might count it as reason for positive self-congratulation. Victor Valerievich could never be termed a self-indulgent man.

In no area of his life were these facets of his character more apparent than in his relationships with his family; a fact, perhaps, not so very surprising and made even less so since his marriage to Varya Petrovna was rooted in his one rash break with calm and self-centred common sense. Aged thirty, the sober and straight-laced Victor had made the fatal and irrational mistake of falling in love.

It had been Varya's sister Zhenia, now married to Bourlov, who had first caught his eye. At seventeen, thirteen years younger than Victor, she had been attractive, clever, practical and, with the family fallen into straitened circumstances since the death of a much-loved but irresponsible father, looking for a husband with ambition that matched her own. Victor might well have been that man, had his eye not lighted upon her younger sister. Tiny, helpless, kittenishly beautiful, Varya was the kind of woman that Victor had always abhorred. Spoiled and petted, brought up in surroundings that had always been beyond the family means, she had neither the stamina nor the wit of her sister; yet from the moment he saw her mass of golden hair, her wide, forget-me-not eyes, fell victim to the flirtatiousness that was and always would be second nature to her, Victor had been obsessed by her. And against all odds and despite all effort, was still, twenty years later. The marriage had been, at least outwardly and by the world's lights, a surprising success; she, child-like, dependent, still pampered, producing the healthy children that any good wife should, he the stern and reliable paterfamilias, a good provider, a strong protector. Only Victor knew the reality of his relationship with his wife; even Varya herself did not suspect the depths of his feelings, nor despite past troubles did she realize the agonies of possessive jealousy that still afflicted him when another man's eyes lit, casually appreciative, upon his vain, often silly but still beautiful wife.

There had indeed been a time, after Anna was born, when his suspicions of Varya might well have driven him to murder.

A young captain of hussars, handsome and highly-strung, son of a family friend and newly back from service in the south, had taken to haunting the apartment where they lived with Victor's father, ostensibly visiting his good friend Victor and his family, in fact all too obviously enslaved by Victor's lovely young wife. Varya, bored with life and perilously flattered, had done nothing to discourage him. On the contrary it had soothed and cheered her after the fearful and depressing shock of childbirth that this young man should press his attentions so sweetly and assiduously. Varya had married Victor, as she had done so many other things, because that had been what the world had apparently expected her to do; she had needed someone to look after her, Victor had been there ready and willing to do so. Both her mother and her sister – who by that time had been in determined pursuit of much bigger game – had each for her own reasons seen the match as desirable. Varya, as always, had taken the line of least resistance. At seventeen, for, in her own eyes, the very good reason that she had needed a relief from the uncertainties of sudden and appalling near-poverty, a home of her own, and something more than the company of women, she had married a man of thirty who scolded and bullied her as he might a pretty, half-witted child. Her feelings for Victor, or the lack of them, had not really entered into the matter at all. A year or so later, the mould of her life cast, the attentions of her handsome captain had been something else again; he had been a dream, a fantasy, a fairy-tale prince, a shimmering curtain of love, attention and above all uncritical admiration that hung between her and the true realities of her life. The joys of the marriage bed had passed Varya by completely. Quite simply and predictably, she had hated it; and married to someone who accepted that as normal and even becoming behaviour for a modest young female, the fumbling couplings with which she had paid for her home and her security had never become anything more than that: a furtive, incomprehensible and

27

humiliating exercise to be endured in darkness and banished from the mind at all other times. The thought of indulging in such disgusting behaviour with her young admirer would no more have occurred to her than she might have thought of sprouting wings and flying. Had Victor been a more sensitive soul he might have seen and understood that, but he was not. He had become obsessed with the thought that his wife was betraying him; which indeed she was but in a manner too subtle for either of them to grasp.

The ensuing fracas he preferred not to remember, though it did occasionally surface in the most disturbing of his dreams.

By a chance that had proved unfortunate for them all the young captain had turned up at the apartment when Varya was alone; an almost unique circumstance in itself. Victor had discovered them, together in the lace-draped boudoir of which Varya was so enormously proud, reading poetry. The strong and stocky Victor, righteous rage upon his side, had hauled his shocked rival by the collar and the seat of his fashionably-cut trousers out of the door and hurled him down a steep flight of stone stairs that might well have broken a back or a neck. Fortunately the young man's bones remained whole; a fact that did not at the time please Victor, but for which later, prudently, he thanked whichever gods had been presiding over his unnatural loss of control. Death or crippling would have brought scandal, and what might that have done for the respectable name of Shalakov? He had then taken primitive revenge upon his wife – the only time in a lifetime of marriage they were ever to couple in daylight – and the result, unfortunately for the child, had been their second daughter Yelena. That Yelena, of all of them, was in character the most like her father, that physically she resembled no-one, least of all the dashing young captain of the strikingly handsome looks, counted for nothing with Victor. His clever eldest daughter Anna was his pride, though he would have denied that indignantly if taxed. Dmitri was his boy, weakly perhaps and a disappointment in many ways, but nevertheless the one who would carry the Shalakov name into the next generation. Margarita, the pretty, frivolous image of her mother, held a special if sometimes grudging place in his heart. The very sight of Yelena enraged him. From the moment she was born, mute and helpless reminder of an act of anger and violence of which, had he been able to bring himself to honesty he would have admitted he was deeply ashamed, he had detested her. In his worst moments, despite all evidence to the contrary, he could convince himself that she was indeed the fruit of adultery, a cuckoo in his orderly nest, a stranger to his blood. That Yelena had grown up sullen and awkward was not surprising. Bewildered, resentful, a nature already darkened by melancholy and self-doubt had become very difficult indeed. Even her physical appearance angered her father; like her sister Anna she had grown almost as tall as her father but, unlike Anna who to her own private mortification was still skinny as a boy, Yelena's body had ripened to a sensual womanhood completely at odds with her pale, childish face and lank brown hair. Poor Lenka – even in this she was wrong; her breasts were full and heavy, her waist slender, her hips wide and seductively curved. Victor saw the look in men's eyes as this awkward daughter of his passed and, against justice, detested her the more for it.

He paused outside the building where the Bourlovs lived, in the fashionable boulevard of mansions and apartment houses that edged the Fontanka Canal, and looked up. The large windows of the expensive first-floor apartment glinted in winter sunshine, a chandelier gleamed behind heavily draped velvet. Not for the first time Victor wondered if he had been wise in agreeing that his daughters should be allowed to spend too much of their time in such surroundings; but then the offer of free education was hard to resist, and the Bourlovs had been very keen to have the companionship of her cousins for their daughter Katya; and at the moment the Bourlovs were to be cultivated. It would be only for a while. The girls were growing apace, husbands must soon be found for them. Perhaps Varya Petrovna was right at least in this; here in Petersburg their chances of an advantageous match might be better than in Moscow. Until then they might as well pick up as much polish and confidence as they could; it could do no harm.

Victor brushed the snow from his shoulders, straightened his hat and ponderously mounted the steps to the huge revolving door that led into the vestibule.

* * *

29

Mikhail Mikhailovich Bourlov, black eyes gleaming, eyed his brother-in-law with considerable if hidden amusement. Against all odds – and Victor himself would certainly never have believed it – Mikhail Mikhailovich harboured some rueful glimmering of something like affection for Victor. The man was a bore and sometimes a pompous one at that, but there was no doubting his intelligence, nor yet his strict and fussy sense of honour, at least where business was concerned. Mikhail Mikhailovich, known to friend and enemy alike as Mischa, found Victor's attitudes to business quaint in the extreme; and was aware that his brother-in-law's unease about Mischa's own somewhat piratical practices must disturb a tender conscience considerably. He could not be blamed, he considered, for taking a mild and graceless pleasure in the situation. 'I insist,' he said, smiling. 'The loan is interest-free for the first two years. After that, if repayments haven't been made, well, we'll see.'

'Mischischa,' Zhenia had said, glinting at him from beneath the mass of fair hair that was the only attribute she shared with her sister Varya, 'for me? Stupid Victor's solid gold, and you know it – he'll starve himself and everyone else rather than get behind on the repayments. To you it's such a little sum. The stock must be worth as much. Andrei says they have some very fine instruments. And there's some talk of a good contract in the offing. You can afford it. It will make Victor Valerievich happy. And if Victor's happy then Varya will be happy. And if Varya's happy –' She had laughed a little, and the attraction she still held for him had stirred, lazily, making them both smile, '– she'll be so very much easier for her poor sister to cope with!'

Victor was hard put not to show his relief. Low interest he had hoped for if not expected, but an interest-free loan would take much of the anxiety from these initial, difficult months. He felt, however, honour bound to protest further. 'I wouldn't dream of it, Mikhail Mikhailovich,' he began, stiffly. 'The normal terms of business –'

'Nonsense.' Mischa was brisk. 'I'm delighted to be a part of the new venture. Andrei has quite a reputation here in Petersburg, you know. Though it's generally accepted that his work will never perhaps be as good as it used to be he's counted still a great craftsman, despite his handicap. And his young apprentice – the young violin maker who has joined him – he too is making a name for himself and for Shalakov and Sons. I heard that the Princess Venskaya held a charity concert last week at which the young von Vecsey played his famous Stradivarius with a Shalakov bow. The Princess is a music lover and a patron of Andrei's, I believe. Such contacts can only bring great prestige, and in Petersburg prestige and success tend to walk hand in hand. So let's hear no more of it. You're satisfied with the premises in the Nevsky?'

'More than satisfied. The workshop is already in operation, or will be within the next few days. The shop will be open in a very few months I hope.'

'Good.' Mischa reached into his pocket and brought out a flat gold cigarette case that gleamed dully in the winter sunlight that slanted through the window. He offered the box to Victor, who refused it with a shake of the head. Mischa leaned back in his chair, extracted a cigarette and tapped it thoughtfully upon the box.

Victor threw caution to the wind. Really, he could not allow it to be thought that Andrei was the only one with influence in this upstart city. 'I too,' he said, a little stiffly, 'have acquired a patron. Of even greater worth, if I may say so, than the Princess Venskaya.'

Mischa had lit his cigarette. He blew a stream of smoke lazily to the ceiling. 'Oh?'

'I am as it happens about to sign a contract for the supply and maintenance of all stringed instruments to the Imperial Ballet School, the Music School and the Imperial Theatres both here and in Moscow.' The words came in a rush. Victor felt unbecoming colour mounting in his cheeks. He had told no-one of this; it was a secret he had nursed, through bribe and negotiation, close in his heart. Almost superstitiously he had refused to mention the possibility to anyone, as if to speak of it would be to break the spell of good fortune. He had not even mentioned the chance that they might get the contract to Andrei. To hear the words actually spoken was both frightening and exhilarating. He leaned back, studiedly casual, crossing his legs, firmly suppressing as he had suppressed all through this affair his own distaste for the established mores of business in the Imperial capital. He had long realized that the choice was between starving self-righteously and accepting, sensibly, that in Rome one must enter the market place in the Roman way. Conscience be damned; at least he could show this buccaneering brother-in-law that he was not the only one in the family who knew how to pull strings to his own advantage. 'As you know the schools and the theatres are subsidized by His Imperial Highness's own Privy Purse,' he said into the sudden, interested silence. 'A five-year contract is on offer it seems. Not a fortune of course, but a good steady income that should see us through the first difficult times, and a great honour for the Shalakov name.'

Mischa was eyeing him through a cloud of smoke, his expression a mixture of mild if gratifying astonishment and a dawning, knowing amusement. 'You actually have this contract?'

Victor shifted in his seat, a little uneasily. 'As good as, yes.' A slight edge of defensiveness sharpened the words.

'I see.' Mischa drew again, unhurriedly, at his cigarette, then added gently, 'And may I ask how?'

Victor waved a worldly hand. 'There have been – negotiations – in hand for some time.'

'Victor Valerievich, who have you been bribing?' There was open laughter now; laughter with a touch of friendly mockery that set Victor's teeth on edge.

'Most –' He hesitated, delicately, very much upon his dignity, '– contact – has been made through a man by the name of Pavel Petrovich Donovalov. He approached me originally in Moscow, when it became known –' He stopped at Mischa's sudden movement. 'You know him?'

Mischa had leaned forward, elbows on desk, his eyes sudden, sharp needlepoints of interest. He remained so for a moment, then sank back again into his chair, smiling through smoke. 'My dear Victor, in Petersburg everyone knows anyone who is bribable. And Pavel Petrovich is probably the most bribable of them all. He's got his sticky fingers into the Privy Purse now, has he? My, my! When I knew him he was a common or garden junior official in the War Ministry. Put a few contracts my way. For a consideration, of course. A weasel. Pure and simple. One of the nastiest pieces of work it's been my misfortune to do business with, I'd say. There's even talk – did you know? – that the death of his wife last year was not – how shall I put it? – not entirely lacking in questionable circumstances. But it was never followed up. The man has contacts in the most unlikely places. As I said: a weasel. Well, you've met him; I dare say I don't need to say more?'

'Indeed not.' Victor was abstracted. 'I wonder – since you apparently know the man?'

'Yes?'

'In your opinion –' Victor hesitated, embarrassed, then pressed on, 'will he deliver what he promises?'

Mischa shrugged. From the corridor outside a light and musical voice called. Laughter rang like a chime of bells and quick footsteps hurried upon the parquet floor. 'If it suits him.' Already he was turned towards the door, smiling. 'Just go through any contract with a fine-tooth comb and don't trust him any further than your pretty little Varya Petrovna could throw him. Oh.' He was already standing, moving towards the door. 'And keep him away from your girls. He has a reputation that would make a self-respecting dog retch. Katya, my dear. Is this the dress I've heard so much about? Well come, let me look at you – let me see the sight for which I've beggared myself.'

'Mischischa, darling!' The girl who burst into the room was of medium height, fair-haired, brown-eyed, tiny of waist and full of breast; as the dress she was wearing showed to every possible advantage. Of coral silk trimmed with green, it swirled about her in a shimmer of colour. She spun into a few dance steps, ended in a deep and graceful curtsy. 'There! Isn't it just lovely? Oh, hello, Uncle Victor. I didn't know you were here.'

Victor rose, stiffly and well upon his dignity. 'Yekaterina Mikhailovna.'

Her eyes brightened with laughter at the formality. With an openly mischievous glance at her father, she straightened, folded her hands and proffered a cool, equally formal cheek. She moved in a cloud of perfume, heady and sweet. Victor kissed her awkwardly. Then, the game palling, she spun away from him again, her eyes on her father. 'What do you think, dear Mischischa? Isn't it worth it? Isn't it?'

Her father stood, solemnly eyeing her. 'We-ell –' He hesitated, pretending a frown.

Katya laughed, threw her arms about him. 'You know it is! You know it is! Oh, Mischischa darling, it is quite the loveliest dress I have ever seen in my whole life! Thank you. Thank you so much!'

Victor found himself thinking that no business associate of Mikhail Mikhailovich Bourlov would have recognized the fond smile that softened his face and gleamed in his dark eyes. 'You look wonderful, my darling. Absolutely wonderful.'

'Thank you, Sir. Thank you kindly.' She broke away from him, dipped into another curtsy, openly impudent this time and coquettish. Then she swirled to where Victor still stood. 'Uncle Victor, when is Anna coming? And Lenka of course? I'm quite dying to see them.' If the expression and tone of the words were a little less enthusiastic than the words themselves Victor chose to ignore it. The girl was a minx and should have been taken in hand long ago. He was not alone, he knew, in his astonishment that his brother-in-law Bourlov, a man to be respected in most quarters – and more than a little feared in many – could allow himself such indulgence where this all but uncontrollable child of his was concerned. Some man was going to have the devil of a job when he took the girl to wife. If indeed anyone could be found to take on such a task, fortune or no fortune. Again he found himself wondering, was it wise to let Anna and Yelena spend time in this opulent house with this hoyden as companion? Then he remembered the loan, so important until the Privy Purse, always notoriously slow to open, actually started to pay out, and he smiled as best as he could.

'Whenever you like, my dear. Next week, perhaps? After we are well settled in the apartment? I know they're as anxious as are you for the reunion.'

'Next week.' Katya tossed her fair head, slanted a mischievous glance at her father. 'Good. Perhaps having Anna and Lenka here will stop Monsieur Drapin nagging me so. I do hope so. In fact I'm quite counting upon it. Anna and Lenka are so very clever.' The word was dismissively and unrepentantly amused. 'I'm sure they'll keep M'sieu happy for me whilst I pursue my own lazy ways. Misch', darling, Mama asked me to remind you

34

that you're due at the Kerelovs' this evening, and there isn't much time.'

Mischa sketched an elegant, apologetic gesture in the air in the general direction of Victor. Victor blushed furiously. 'I really must go,' he said. 'I've already taken up too much of your time.'

'You're sure you won't take tea?' The offer was polite, but far from pressing.

'No, no. Varya Petrovna will be waiting. My respects to your wife, Mikhail Mikhailovich. Good day, Katya, my dear.'

After he had gone Mischa turned to his daughter, only half-laughing. 'Katya, Katya! You really mustn't do such things, you know!'

'But he's such a *bore*!' Katya smoothed the coral silk, smiling as the gleaming, delicate material glinted between her fingers. 'It's really difficult to believe that he and the beautiful Andrei are brothers, isn't it?'

Her father shook his head, theatrically despairing. 'Katya —'

She kissed him, lightly. 'Don't say it, Mischischa. I know. I'm hopeless. A lost cause. I agree. Now, I'll go and change my beautiful dress and then you and I have time for a game of chess before Mama steals you for the evening.'

'Lenka, for goodness' sake — can't you move your idle self and *help*?' Anna stood, hands on hips, eyeing in growing exasperation her sister who lay slumped upon the bed, curled about a book.

Yelena grunted.

'Don't you want the room to look nice?' Anna hauled a heavy armchair close to the window, stood back looking at it critically. 'Just because three of us have to share it doesn't mean it has to look like a pigsty all the time! We might as well be comfortable!' She tossed a cushion onto the chair, plumped it up and looked around again. The large room held a big bed for herself and her sister and a small one, little more than a pallet, for Margarita, who needless to say had made herself very scarce at first mention of work to be done. A large black stove belched heat from one corner. Books were stacked in heaps upon the floor, and clothes were scattered upon the bed. 'Lenka, do move! You're lying on my best skirt!'

Yelena, grumbling, moved a fraction.

'What are you reading?' Anna peered over her shoulder. 'Dostoevsky? Again? Lenka, darling, you must know every word the man has written by heart!'

'Very nearly.' Yelena afforded her one of her rare smiles. ''Noushka, have you spoken to Papa yet?'

'Er, no.' Anna began to fold clothes, not looking at her sister. 'I haven't got round to it yet.'

'But Anna, when? When will you?'

'Just as soon as I can. Just as soon as the opportunity presents itself.' Anna threw the blouse she had been folding onto the bed and turned, arms wide. 'Oh, Lenka, you *know* how difficult Papa can be. If I catch him at the wrong moment –' She shrugged, pulled an expressive face.

'I know. I do know.' Lenka threw herself back onto the bed, her arms behind her head. 'It's just so important, so terribly important to me –'

'Yes.' Anna stood for a long moment watching the other girl who lay, head averted, looking sightlessly through the window into the light and faintly sunlit winter skies. 'I do know that, Lenka. Truly I do.' She sat beside her, touched her cheek gently with the back of her hand. Ever since she could remember she had been fiercely and protectively devoted to this difficult sister of hers. Even as a small child she had sensed Lenka's need of her; in their growing years the younger child, starved of affection from other quarters, had clung to her, looking to Anna for protection and for sympathy and rarely failing to find both in full measure. It had fallen automatically to Anna to mop her small sister's tears, soothe her angers, gentle the storms that had so often shaken her; Varya's motherly instincts barely extended so far to any of her children, and Victor, upon whom for most of the time Anna herself could rely, had been strangely and harshly impatient towards Lenka. And so a bond had grown between them, a bond that might have been irksome to Anna had she not been so deeply aware of her sister's unhappiness. She knew that it might be said that Lenka, difficult as she could be, was her own worst enemy. Yet Anna was sure that it was their father's inexplicable attitude to the child that had made her so. 'I'll talk to him, Lenka, I promise. Soon. Perhaps he'll agree – oh, good heavens, is that the time?' She rubbed at her forehead with a dusty finger. 'I promised Mama I'd fetch Uncle Andrei up for tea at three and it's ten past. I'd better go.' She jumped up, brushing down her skirt, peered into the mirror, decided against any effort at tidying the wiry mass of her hair, scrubbed with a handkerchief at a smudge of dirt on her chin and the other her dirty finger had left on her forehead. 'What a sight! Oh, do get up and do something, Lenka, please! At least get those books stacked on the shelves. I'll go down and fetch Uncle Andrei. Tell Mama I'll be back in five minutes or so.'

''Noushka?'

At the door Anna turned.

'Ask Papa soon? Please?'

'I will.'

As so often, as she hurried down the stairs, she found herself thinking that if only her sister would smile like that more often the world would perhaps think differently of her.

Andrei lived on the ground floor in two rooms, one of which was his work room. The door as always was on the latch. Anna opened it and peered around it. 'Uncle Andrei?'

The work room was still and quiet. A large and serviceable black stove occupied one corner and the air was warm. A single lamp burned above a narrow, padded workbench. Andrei's canvas apron was tossed across the bench, upon which rested a few long, straight batons of wood, neatly piled, and a selection of small planes and other tools. A second workbench, unlit, was clear except for some shavings and a few pieces of discarded wood and a lidless, all but empty varnish pot. From the ceiling hung a rack upon which were hooked several violins in various states of manufacture and repair. Above the bench still in use hung perhaps half a dozen bows, some finished, some not, and four or five hooks from which hung long hanks of horse hair.

'Uncle Andrei? Are you there?' Anna hesitated for a moment then walked through the work room and pushed open the door to the living room. 'Uncle Andrei? Mama asked me to bring you upstairs for tea.'

This room too was empty. A lamp burned upon the table and another before the icon that hung in the eastern corner of the room. In another corner a round table stood, covered with a long fringed cloth and upon it a samovar, empty and cold, and a small tray with tea glasses neatly ranged upon it. Upon a sideboard were set several photographs, and the wall behind the bed was lined with shelves that were neatly packed with books. More books were stacked beside a large armchair that stood comfortably beside the enamelled stove. There were several pictures upon the walls, and a rack of bows hung above the sideboard. The whole room was as tidy as the most virtuous housewife could have wished.

Anna had been in the work room before but never in here. On inquisitive impulse she slipped into the room, half-closing the door behind her, and walked to the sideboard. Several large silver frames were arranged upon the shining surface; and all of them but one contained a photograph of the same person, a wide-eyed girl, dark-haired, neatly pretty and in every picture laughing. Andrei's wife Galina. Courted at eighteen, married at nineteen and tragically dead before her twenty-third birthday. Much loved, never forgotten, never replaced. Anna picked up one of the smaller pictures and held it to the light of the lamp. The girl's dark eyes smiled into hers from a bright, suspended moment when life and love were all and the future stretched endlessly ahead. This smiling girl had died, Anna remembered, just a couple of weeks before the baby she had been carrying would have come to term. The child had died with her. Anna replaced the photograph very carefully, picked up the only pic-ture that was not of Galina. A tall, elderly, distinguished-looking man in formal dress, cane in hand, looked out upon the world with faint, quizzical amusement. The narrow face was deeply lined, there was a hint of humour about the eyes and the long, narrow mouth that Anna immediately liked. She won-dered who he was; obviously he must be someone of whom her uncle was very fond. Replacing the frame she noticed for the first time that lying along the back of the sideboard almost hidden in shadow was a bow, unhaired, the glowing polish of the wood almost lost against the surface upon which it lay. She picked it up; and in the instant her violinist's hands told her what she held. Even unhaired the thing was a wonder; perfectly balanced, perfectly weighted. Silver mounted and ornamented with mother of pearl, as were all of Andrei's bows – he dismissed with unusual vehemence the showy extravagances of gold and precious stones – yet everything about it from the smooth, polished curve of the wood to the shining ebony and silver frogs and the delicately opaque beauty of the mother of pearl ornament spoke of the genius of a true craftsman. Yet, oddly, for all its beauty and balance the thing was dead; no – she ran gentle fingers along the curve of the stick – no, not dead; but without the smooth tension of the hair to complete it, it did not yet live. She lifted it, hand delicately bent, as if to draw music from imaginary strings.

The soft closing of the door behind her made her jump so violently that she almost dropped the bow.

'Anna, I'm sorry – you were looking for me?' Her uncle stood by the door, smiling.

'I – yes.' The fair, freckled skin of her face warmed with embarrassment. 'Mama sent me to fetch you for tea. You weren't in the workshop; I came in to see –' She stopped, swamped in confusion. 'I'm sorry. I suppose I really shouldn't have –'

'Oh, don't be silly.' Still smiling, he dropped the bag he carried onto the bed. 'I've been over at the Nevsky, settling young Volodya into the new workshop. You haven't met him yet, have you?'

Anna shook her head.

'You should. He's a very nice young man. He shows enormous promise.' Her uncle sent her a sly, smiling glance. 'He's about your age I think. And you have a lot in common. I'm quite sure you'd like each other.'

The detested blush deepened.

He came to her, touched the bow lightly, without taking it from her. 'You like it?'

'Oh, yes! It's just marvellous! Why haven't you finished it?'

There was a fleeting moment of silence that drew her eyes to his face. The flash of pain, instantly hidden, was so fierce it was as if she herself had been struck by it. Then, easily and naturally, he reached with his undamaged hand and took the unfinished bow from her, running his fingers with capable competence along the length of it. 'It's the bow I was making when

Galina died. For obvious reasons I couldn't at the time finish it. When I could –' He laid the thing down, carefully, amongst the photographs, shrugged, smiling. 'I didn't. That's all.'

The desire to avoid this difficult subject at all costs warred with a sudden and human desire to know how that girl, so charming, so happy, so much loved, married when she was only a year or so older than herself, had died. Varya would never speak of it, shuddering with theatrical horror if the subject were raised. 'It must have been terrible,' she found herself saying. 'The accident, I mean.'

'Yes.'

'What happened?' She hesitated. 'Can you speak of it? I don't mean to intrude.'

Andrei turned from her, took off the heavy canvas working coat he was wearing and reached for a battered velvet jacket that hung behind the door. For a moment Anna thought that he would not answer, or would brush her curiosity aside, as she supposed it deserved. Then, still carrying the jacket, he came to the sideboard, picked up the small picture she had been look-ing at earlier. 'We had been for a trip on the river,' he said. 'Galina and I. A pleasure boat – with music, and a bar – you know the kind? It was a wonderful day – early spring, still cold, but the thaw was well under way. The river was turbulent, very high, very fast, full of the melted snows and ice of winter. Full of the new life of spring.' He stopped for a moment, put down the picture, slipped his arm into his jacket. Anna, in an instinc-tive movement born of serving her father, moved behind him to help him shrug into it. 'Galina was heavy with child, clumsy, dressed still in winter clothing against the cold. As she stepped onto the plank to disembark she slipped, and fell between the landing stage and the boat. I reached for her. She caught my hand.' A moment of quiet fell. Anna, behind him, brushed with sudden busy concentration at the dust upon the shoulders of the shabby jacket. 'There was nothing anyone could do. I held on – for as long as I could – but she was trapped – and my hand –' She felt the narrow shoulders beneath her hands hunch very slightly; the right hand, the maimed hand, slipped into the pocket of the jacket. 'There was nothing anyone could do,' he repeated.

Anna nibbled her lip; why in the world had she ever brought up the subject? 'It must have been awful for you,' she mumbled.

He turned, the untidy silver thatch of his hair shining in the lamp light. 'Yes it was. Of course it was. But it was a long time ago, Anna. And the world lives on. It would be wrong to mourn for ever.'

'I suppose so.' With a suddenly necessary but she hoped unobtrusive sniff she moved past him, looked again at the pictures on the sideboard. 'Who's this? The old gentleman?' Her voice was much too bright, much too obviously intent upon changing the subject. She winced a little. Honestly, little Rita would have handled this better!

Andrei gave a quite genuine snort of laughter. '"The old gentleman"! Oh, I shall tell him that, indeed I shall!'

'Well? Who is he? I must say he really looks rather nice.'

'I'll tell him that too.' Andrei was grinning like a boy. 'He's a very good friend of mine. Guy de Fontenay. He runs a most prestigious business in London, making and selling fine instruments.'

'Like you and Papa?'

He grinned. 'A little, yes. But rather better established and rather more splendid. The greatest players in the world go to Guy.'

'What's he like?'

The smile lit his face again. 'Guy's just about the best friend I ever had. He's a charming man, believe me – the most civilized man I know – the perfect English gentleman.'

'English? With a name like that? He surely must be French?'

'Half of him is. His father's half. But the important half,' he grinned again, 'his mother's half, is English. Believe me you'll never meet a more English English gentleman than M'sieu Guy de Fontenay.'

'How do you know him so well?'

Andrei bent to pick up the books that were stacked beside the armchair, carried them to the shelf and began to slot them neatly into their spaces. 'We met in Paris, while I was a student – seventeen? – no, eighteen years ago.' He shook his head, smiling. 'Half a lifetime!'

'All of mine,' Anna said.

He laughed aloud. 'Why yes, so it is! I was studying violin making, of course – I hadn't then become interested in bow making – but not, I'm ashamed to say, half as enthusiastically as I was studying the night-life of Paris! When first I met Guy my pockets were emptier than my head. He lent me money, watched whilst I squandered it then offered me more in payment for tuition in the Russian language.' He came back to the sideboard, with one hand and quick fingers rearranged the photographs, then walked to the table where burned the lamp. 'So, I taught him Russian and in return he taught me – oh, all manner of things.' His voice, and his laughter, were warm. 'That was how it started. As I said, Guy is the best and closest friend I ever had. I respect him more than anyone else I've ever known.' He turned down the lamp, pinched the wick to stop it smoking, stood looking down at it for a thoughtful moment. 'He's a very wise man,' he said, soberly. 'There aren't so very many people you can say that about.'

He ushered her out onto the stairs. The cold swept around them. Hunched against it they ran breathlessly up to the door of the Shalakov apartment. Anna rang the bell. Nothing happened. She leaned hard upon it, hearing it sound, shrill and insistent in the apartment. 'Honestly, Seraphima is so *slow*!'

The landing was chill. A single gas flare flickered in the gloom. Andrei was watching her. 'It was a pity,' he said quietly, and utterly unexpectedly, 'about the scholarship.'

Anna turned her head from him, pressed the bell again.

He would not allow her to ignore him. 'I haven't heard you play,' he said.

'No.'

'I should very much like to. You have an instrument?'

Still she would not meet his eyes. Beyond the door came the sound of shuffling feet. 'Yes,' she said. 'Papa gave me one of grandfather's violins. A very beautiful one actually.' She let a small, cold silence develop. 'A consolation prize, I think.'

'But you don't play it?'

She shook her head.

'You should,' he said. 'A great instrument lives only if it is played.'

She sucked her lip for a moment, turned to meet his eyes. He had, after all, shown no resentment of her questions; the least she could do was to return the compliment. To tell the truth she had desperately missed her music in these past weeks; it had been the stubborn resentment she still nursed against her father that had kept her from it. 'I know.'

The door opened. Plump Seraphima, breathing heavily, acknowledged their greetings in harassed fashion and scurried back into the apartment.

Andrei shut the door. They could hear voices in the parlour. 'You have a bow?' he asked. 'A good one?'

She shook her head. 'I have one, yes. But not one worthy of grandfather's violin.'

'Then what more appropriate than that I should make you one?' His voice was light, but his eyes were intent and serious on hers. 'Would you play then?'

'I –' She looked away. 'I suppose so, yes. Except – the apartment is so very crowded, there's never any peace.'

'Come downstairs to me,' he said, promptly. 'I've room and more than room. The workshop's always warm, and often empty.'

She had never had a place of her own to practise, away from Margarita's noise and Lenka's clinging presence. It was temptation beyond resisting. 'I shouldn't want to disturb you –'

'You won't disturb me. You'll come?'

She nodded. It was not, after all, that lovely violin's fault that her father had refused her the scholarship. Why should the poor thing suffer such silence?

He smiled, detained her as she turned away. 'Don't be too hard on your father, Anna. Life plays strange tricks sometimes. Perhaps – who knows? – it will all turn out for the best.'

Anna laughed. 'Oh, Uncle Andrei, no! You've been listening to Nanny Irisha again.' She lifted mocking eyes to the ceiling. '"Strange are the ways of God!"' She turned to the parlour door.

They walked into the light and warmth of the room. The samovar hissed in the corner. Heavy velvet curtains were drawn against the early evening darkness. Varya, fragile and pretty in velvet and lace, her fair hair piled upon her head, perched straight-backed upon a gracefully fretted wooden chair. 'Andrei, tea! And cakes of course. Margarita, bring your Uncle Andrei a glass. Anna, where ever have you been? Dima, come away now, let Uncle Andrei feel the warmth of the stove.'

Anna stood back, watching as her uncle was drawn immediately into the small, intimate circle of her mother's attention, aware that between one second and another she had lost him. It was Varya's talent to make almost any man who approached her a part of that charming, private world of hers. Anna, for a moment, could not suppress a surge of envy. Only recently, with the burgeoning of womanhood, had she begun to understand her mother. And, in part, to understand herself. This would never be her way, much as she might wish it otherwise. Yet Margarita, laughing and talking beside her mother, looking up teasingly into her uncle's face, already and effortlessly was a part of this female conspiracy. Uncle Andrei seemed to be enjoying it, as any man would.

Anna accepted her glass of tea from Seraphima with a smile and a suddenly heavy heart. The pleasure of the last half hour had all but fled. The world seemed, all at once, a confusing and oddly lonely place again.

The doorbell rang.

'Seraphima – for the good Lord's sake! – don't just stand there!'

At the sound of Victor's voice in the hall a small constraint fell upon the gathering. Varya looked up, anxious.

Victor appeared in the doorway, face flushed from the cold, dark moustache gleaming with moisture.

'Victor, my dear.' Varya stood.

'Vasha.' The endearing private diminutive, so little used, and usually only in the most intimate of circumstances, stopped her in her tracks. Her eyes widened. 'And Andrei! Well met! I have news for you all.' Victor beamed about him. Had Anna not known better she might have suspected that he had been drinking. 'I have news. I have news twice over! The shop will open on schedule the week after Easter –'

Margarita clapped prettily. 'Bravo.'

For once everyone ignored her. The air of excitement that trembled about Victor was so unprecedented as to be riveting. No-one moved an eye from his face.

'And –' Victor paused for further and quite unnecessary effect

44

'– I have just been informed that it is virtually certain that Shalakov and Sons have landed a five-year contract for the supply and maintenance of all stringed instruments to the Imperial Ballet School, the Music School and the Imperial Theatres both in St Petersburg and in Moscow.' He stopped, run out of breath. There was a small silence.

'Mother of God,' Andrei said, reverently.

'How lovely,' Varya said.

'The Imperial?' Anna stopped.

Victor looked at the glass of tea that Seraphima offered him, and shook his head. 'I think, Seraphima,' he said, complacently, 'that in this one instance a glass of something a little stronger is called for?'

CHAPTER THREE

The sudden shrill of the doorbell almost made Yelena jump
from her skin. She was standing by the parlour window looking
out into the steel-grey light of a late February day. A slight thaw
had set in, long icicles dripped from the eaves, patches of snow
had slid from the tiles and the snow in the streets had turned
overnight to slush. It was too early for the true spring thaw, but
after a month of bitter weather it was as if here was a promise
that winter would not always hold the city in its harsh grip.
'Seraphima! There's someone at the door!'

'Seraphima has a mouthful of pins.' Varya's light voice, calling from the bedroom, was quick with irritation. 'For goodness'
sake, Lenka, you know we're busy in here! Open the door
yourself.'

The bell rang again, a long, impatient-sounding peal.

Muttering under her breath Yelena went out into the small
hall and opened the front door. A man, tall and narrow-
shouldered, stood on the ill-lit landing, briefcase in hand. 'This
is the apartment of Victor Valerievich Shalakov?' The voice was
sharp and precise, chill as the draught that scurried about the
stairwell.

'It is, yes.' From downstairs came the muted and haunting
sound of a violin. The music tailed away, then started again,
the phrase repeated.

'I wish to see him, if you please.' The stranger moved forward,
arrogantly confident.

Yelena stood her ground. 'He isn't here. He's probably at the
shop on the Nevsky Prospekt.'

The man peered at her. In the half-dark Yelena caught an
impression of slanting eyes, long and black as beads of jet in a
face as sharp as a rat's. He shook his head. 'No. I've just come
from there. He left some time ago. I'll wait, if you please. I'm

sure he'll want to see me. My name is Donovalov. Pavel Petrovich Donovalov.' He waited for a moment, obviously expecting a reaction. 'I can assure you he'll want to see me, my dear,' he said again, insistently, his voice suddenly softer, almost intimate. With a surge of outraged embarrassment she realized that the black eyes had slid from hers and were openly and with slow deliberation appreciatively scanning her body. It was a long moment before he raised his interested gaze to hers again. 'Perhaps you'd tell your mistress I'm here?'

Yelena stepped back. 'I'm not –' Before she could finish he had brushed past her and into the hall; and as he passed she felt, with no shadow of doubt, the fingers of his lifted hand graze the fullness of her breasts. Rigid with indignation she glared at him. 'If you'll wait a moment,' she said, her voice not quite as steady as she would have wished, 'I'll tell my mother you're here.' She noted with some satisfaction the flash of surprise and understanding in his face before she turned from him; saw also to her mortification that it was swiftly followed by the ghost of an unpleasant and totally impenitent smile.

He executed a small and surely mocking little bow. 'Thank you,' he said.

She felt the black eyes, sharp and probing, like fingers upon her back as she left him.

Her mother was in her bedroom, standing upon a stool, the gown that Seraphima was altering pinned about her. A cup of chocolate cooled upon the table. Varya glanced up abstractedly as Yelena entered. 'What is it?'

'A man, Mama. He says his name is Donovalov.'

Varya shook her head absently. 'I know no-one of that name. Seraphima, a little lower here, don't you think? The fashions in Petersburg do seem to be rather more –'

'He's come to see Papa. I've told him he isn't here but he insists on waiting. Mama –'

Varya flapped her hand, not looking at her. 'Lenka, dear, you can see I've no time at the moment. I'm hardly dressed to entertain gentlemen callers, am I?'

'This,' Lenka said, a little desperately, 'is not a gentleman, Mama. He's positively horrible.'

Varya was barely listening. 'Make him tea or something. Papa

47

won't be long, I dare say. Seraphima, do be careful! You scratched me with that pin, clumsy girl!'

Seraphima, kneeling before her, mumbled apologies, caught Yelena's eyes and turned her own to heaven and sighed in a parody of patience.

'Mama, must I? Can't I go downstairs and fetch Anna? She spends more time down there than she does up here lately – and I really don't want to –'

'Lenka!' Her mother jerked her head, sharply and impatiently. 'Nanny Irisha is in the kitchen. Fetch her if you must. Now for goodness' sake – go and make some tea.'

In the kitchen the old woman was settled comfortably in a battered chair by the warm range, sound asleep. 'Nanny? Nanny, please,' Yelena hissed, shaking her. 'Nanny, wake up!'

The old woman grunted, shifted, snored the louder.

'Nanny!'

'Let the poor old monster sleep for heaven's sake.' The cold voice was amused. Yelena spun round. The man Donovalov leaned in the doorway, watching her. Her hand flew to the buttons of her high-necked blouse, suddenly certain, from the look in his eyes, that they must be undone.

He laughed. 'Do you consider that I owe you an apology?' He let a small, suggestive silence grow before adding, 'For taking you for a servant, that is?'

She backed away from him, collided with the table. 'I – suppose I do. Yes.'

'Then I apologize.' His smile was the most unpleasant thing she had ever seen; it invested his thin, rat-like face with an almost demonic ugliness. Instinctively she sensed cruelty in the man. The intent black eyes roved about her face and her body with a relentless intimacy that almost paralysed her with embarrassment and terror. The openness of his regard made her feel as if she were allowing him to handle her, as if she were in some way encouraging him deliberately to humiliate her and, even inexperienced as she was, she saw from his smile his pleasure in her obvious fear and confusion. Sweat broke out on her skin; clammy on her back, prickling horribly between her breasts. She hunched her shoulders, crossed her arms before her, tense as a spring. 'My – my mother is busy at the moment I'm afraid. Perhaps you'd like to come back later – I'm sure Papa will be –'

'You haven't told me your name.'

She stood, trapped and helpless. 'Yelena,' she whispered. The probing eyes stripped her, assessed her, shamed her; worse, they touched knowingly upon hers, as if the man sensed precisely the terrible treachery of her body, the lush, woman's body that she hated so much.

'Yelena,' he repeated. 'Well, Yelena Victorovna, are you not going to offer your guest a glass of tea?'

Tea, samovar and glasses were in the sitting room. On trembling legs she started towards the door. He did not move. A foot from him she stopped, her head raised defiantly, refusing to pass so close. The slanting eyes in the narrow face watched her steadily. Fierce colour stained her neck, her face, blotched the white skin of her arms.

He stepped back.

As she passed him she heard the sound of her father's key in the lock.

'Papa!' She all but ran along the corridor to the sitting room, dashed across it to the door that led into the small hall. Clumsily she threw it open, all but fell through it. 'Papa, a man is here to see you –'

Victor, in the act of removing hat and gloves, looked up sharply, frowning, mouth tightening in irritation. 'For God's sake, child, must you always behave like a bull in a barn? What man?'

Sullenly Yelena glared down at her feet. 'A man named Donovalov.'

Her father stilled, eyes suddenly very sharp. 'Donovalov? What in the world is he doing here?'

'I don't know. He –'

Her father ignored her. Still wearing his heavy shuba he brushed past her, hand outstretched. 'Pavel Petrovich – what an unexpected pleasure. What brings you here? No problems, I trust?'

The other man shrugged. 'Nothing that can't be dealt with swiftly and to both our satisfaction, I'm sure, Victor Valerievich,' he said, smoothly.

49

Victor rubbed the flat of his hand upon the heavy fur of his coat. 'I thought –' He stopped. 'Lenka!' he snapped. 'For heaven's sake, what have you been about? Light the samovar. Pavel Petrovich, make yourself at home – you'll take tea, of course – I'll take off my coat.'

In amazement Yelena heard the slight trembling of her father's voice, saw a faint anxious sheen of perspiration bloom upon the skin of his face. Heavily she moved to the table where the samovar stood. Donovalov watched her, that faint, hatefully sardonic smile upon his face again. Clumsier than ever beneath his eyes she lit the silver samovar, set out the glasses. 'All right, Yelena. I'll do the rest. There's no need for you to stay.' Her father had re-entered the room. 'Where are the others?'

Yelena hunched her shoulders, avoiding those questing eyes. 'Mama's in the bedroom – Seraphima's altering a dress for her. Dmitri's at school, and Rita's gone to the tutor.' To Margarita's huge disgust a tutor had been engaged to ensure her passage through the examination that would take her to the local Gymnasium. 'Anna's downstairs, practising.'

'And an elderly monster is snoring by the kitchen stove,' Donovalov put in. 'Is that the roll call of your household, Victor Valerievich?'

'Indeed it is, indeed it is.' Yelena was amazed at her father's almost eager acceptance of the man's effrontery. 'Very well, Lenka, perhaps the best thing would be for you to join your sister downstairs. Pavel Petrovich and I have business matters to discuss.' He shot a faintly questioning glance at the other man who inclined his head, smiling. 'I'll send Seraphima for you when we're finished.'

'Yes, Papa.' With enormous relief Yelena started towards the door.

'A moment, my dear.'

She froze.

Donovalov came to her, reached for her hand, bent to brush it with dry, hard lips. 'I must thank you for –' he hesitated for long enough to bring further furious colour to her cheeks '– entertaining me so well.'

She tried to pull her hand away, but it was trapped in strong, bony fingers whose grip was harsh enough to bring pain. She stood quite still, fingers rigid in his. After a moment he straightened, dropping her hand, turning back to her father, dismissing her.

She shut the door behind her, leaned against it, grateful for the clean, cold air that brushed her cheeks and cooled her skin. The sound of Anna's violin drifted up the stairwell. She stood quite still for a moment, breathing deeply. Sweat was drying on her body. She could feel it. Smell it. She felt dirty. She remembered those slanting, brutally questing eyes; what in the name of God was her father doing associating with such a man? A blisteringly cold draught gusted up the stairs. She shivered suddenly; but whether from cold or from the disgust and fear brought by the memory of those eyes she could not tell. Hunched against the cutting cold she ran swiftly down the stairs to Andrei's rooms.

As she reached the door the music stopped, and she heard Andrei's quiet voice, then Anna's. She pushed open the door. 'Anna –'

Anna did not look up. She stood, instrument and bow poised, beside Andrei, whose varnish-stained long finger marked a place upon a sheet of music propped upon a music stand. As Yelena shut the door quietly behind her Anna brought bow to string and played again, the same haunting phrase Yelena had heard earlier. Andrei's face relaxed and he smiled, watching her. Anna's eyes flickered to his, and her own brief answering smile was as sure a communication as words. They stood together, enclosed and encircled by the music, as Anna, fierce with concentration, played the difficult phrase through to the end and then stopped, the last, unfinished note hanging in the air like a promise unspoken.

'Wonderful,' Andrei said, quietly. 'That was truly lovely, Anna. You've got it.' His right hand, as usual, was in his pocket, his left lying relaxed upon the music stand.

'Anna,' Yelena said again.

Anna flicked an absent smile at her. 'Oh. Hello, Lenka. Do you really think so?' The question was not addressed to Yelena.

'Absolutely. It was that middle phrase, there –' Andrei pointed, hummed a few notes. Anna picked up the tune on the violin and played again, easily this time, the timing perfect.

'Papa sent me down,' Yelena said, too loudly. 'He's got an absolutely horrible man up there with him. I can't think what he's up to doing business with such a rat-faced pig.'

That did the trick. Two pairs of startled eyes were turned to hers. Andrei's dark eyebrows shot almost to his silvered hair, eyes gleaming with surprised amusement. Anna was not so restrained. She exploded into laughter at the childish phrase. 'Lenka! Honestly! What a thing to say!'

'Well, he is.' Obscurely gratified to have shattered that odd, almost palpable, magic circle of music that had for those few moments stood between her and her sister Yelena pulled a fearsome face. 'He's the most awful man. Horrible! And Papa's drinking tea with him! Ugh!' She shuddered exaggeratedly, rather enjoying the drama and attention. 'I'd as soon drink tea with – with the devil himself!'

'What's this gruesome creature's name?' Andrei had gone into the other room, there was the clink of tea glasses.

Yelena wandered into the room, stood behind her sister looking over her shoulder at the music on the stand. 'Donovalov,' she called, in answer to her uncle's question. Then, 'Goodness, that looks difficult. I'm not surprised you were having problems.'

'Donovalov?' Andrei had appeared at the living-room door. 'Hasn't Victor mentioned his name in connection with the Imperial contract?'

Anna shook her head, abstractedly, her eyes still thoughtfully upon the music score. Yelena shrugged. 'I don't know.'

Anna lifted her head. 'Why has he come to the apartment, do you think? Could there be some kind of problem?'

'Who knows? Probably not. Come on, you two – tea and cakes. Lenka, I found an article in a magazine the other day that I thought might interest you –'

It was an hour before Seraphima tapped on the door to tell them that they were expected upstairs. 'Such goings on!' she giggled to Anna. 'The young people are home and the poor little lamb is in a great taking about these examinations she must pass. Varya Petrovna has burned the rice again and is in a great temper and demanding to employ a cook, and your Papa is asking to know if she thinks that the money for such things grows on trees – '

'Is that dreadful man gone?' Yelena demanded.

Seraphima shrugged. 'I fetched his coat and hat before I came down. Now, I must run back – heaven only knows what state the kitchen will be in.' She lifted her skirts and hurried back up the stairs.

The others followed more slowly. As they reached the front door it opened to reveal Victor and his visitor. They stepped back to allow the man through. He nodded politely, smiled at Yelena. She dropped her gaze to the scuffed toes of her boots. 'There!' she hissed at Anna as they went into the warm hallway. 'You see?'

Anna laughed. 'He was no oil painting, certainly, but he didn't seem such a monster to me.'

Yelena's lips tightened. Just the sight of the man had brought the rise of instant fear, instant loathing; and something else – something unnatural, and most certainly shameful. And he had seen it. She was certain of that. She kicked off her boots, slipped her feet into the slippers that stood waiting. 'Go help your mother in the kitchen, Yelena,' her father said, sharply. She glanced at him. He was watching her, unsmiling; something in his face made her hesitate for a moment, thinking he was about to say more. But, 'Go on, go on,' he said, testily, and turned away.

Anna tidied the boots, slipped her own slippers on. Her father did not immediately follow the others into the sitting room but stood for a long moment, staring into space, lost in thought.

'Papa? Is anything the matter?'

He turned unfocused eyes upon her. 'What? Oh – no, my dear, of course not.'

'Uncle Andrei thought the man Donovalov had come about the Imperial contract. Is that right?'

'Yes. Yes, that's right.'

'And is all well?'

'Yes, yes. I've said. Everything is fine. It's just – ' he hesitated for a moment '– just going to be a little more costly than I anticipated, that's all. Now, Anna, do run along and see what you can do in the kitchen. I greatly fear that dinner will be ruined again.'

'Prague.' Katya propped her chin upon her hand, looked with every appearance of deep thought down at the map spread before her. 'Dear M'sieu, I'm sorry – I have no idea where it might be.' She added after a moment, candidly cheerful, 'I've been there of course –' her French was every bit as polished as her tutor's '– it's an enchanting city.' She sent a sly, laughing glance at Anna. 'But for heaven's sake, one doesn't need too much know-ledge of geography to board a train, does one? Paris, now.' She cocked her fair head. 'I just might be able to find Paris on your tiresome little map.' Then, with mocking honesty, 'Though to be truthful I doubt it. Dear M'sieu Drapin – can't we dispense with Prague and Paris for the day?' Her smile was winning. 'Just look at the weather, it's just perfect for skating – and it may be the last opportunity of the season. It isn't often we get such a cold snap so late. Easter's only a couple of weeks away. It will be spring soon, with all that dreadful slush and mud – no oppor-tunity to exercise at all – and you know Papa is very keen that I should get as much exercise as possible.'

'Mam'selle! Please!' The much-tried Monsieur Drapin held up two small, perfectly-manicured hands in dramatic gesture.

Katya subsided, grinning.

'I am employed, Mam'selle Katya,' the Frenchman said, in his precisely-accented French, 'to educate you. To instil some knowledge of the world into that pretty head of yours.'

'Oh, I think you'll find there's plenty of that in there already,' Katya assured him, brightly.

Anna nibbled her lip, trying not to laugh. In honesty she felt a touch sorry for the little Frenchman – Katya had behaved abominably all morning, chatting affably to her cousins over Monsieur's attempts to explain, in French of course, the basics of English grammar, dismissing his attempts to extract from her the dates of the reign of Peter the Great with an airy 'Oh, Lord, how on earth should I know? Really, my dear, it was all so long ago, wasn't it? Papa says that history is best ignored, and I'm quite sure he's right.' Now, with no by-your-leave she got up from the table around which they were all sitting and wandered to the window. She was right; it was a most beautiful day. Overnight the temperature had dropped like a stone, and fresh snow had fallen. Now sunlight glittered upon the golden spire of the Admiralty that soared in the distance into the bright sky like a needle of light. The frozen Fontanka glittered. A few flakes of snow still drifted in the quiet air. Sledges, the sound of the harness-bells muted by the winter windows, flew down the wide street below that edged the riverbank. Katya tapped her fingers restlessly upon the window sill.

'Mam'selle Yelena.' Monsieur Drapin, very creditably Anna thought, held precariously to his patience. 'Perhaps you could oblige me by pointing out the approximate situation of Prague upon our small map?'

'Oh, fiddle to Prague!' Katya turned from the window. 'M'sieu, dear M'sieu –' there was, surprisingly, real if exasperated affection in her voice '– I insist. You cannot expect us to sit about a table in a stuffy room playing silly games with maps when we could be out skating. Now can you?' She smiled again, dazzlingly.

'Mam'selle Katya –'

'If Papa were here I'm sure he'd agree. He doesn't expect you to stuff us full of facts like the Easter goose, you know. Lenka and Anna have worked far harder than I have this morning – they deserve a rest.'

'We haven't any blades with us,' Anna began.

'Oh, don't be silly.' Katya shrugged, hands wide. 'There's a houseful here! So, it's settled. We go to the river. And, my darling Jean Pierrovich –' with cunning she used the teasing, Russified version of his name that she well knew, privately, he rather liked '– I'd be very greatly obliged if you'd take a message for me to Ludmilla Gavrilovna. She's in my dressing room, I believe, mending the ball gown that was torn last week. Tell her please that I've changed my mind about this evening – ask her to have the dark blue ready for six. Oh, and I'm perfectly sure she'd be happy to share a pot of chocolate with you, if you should order one. Tell her I said she's working too hard.' She opened wide, earnest eyes. 'Like my cousins here she deserves a rest, don't you think?'

There was a brief, telling silence. Monsieur's pale, plump face had pinkened very slightly, and his ears, Anna noticed with interest, had turned a fiery red. 'Mam'selle –' he began again, doggedly, and then stopped.

'That's right,' Katya said, kindly. 'As Papa always says, never enter into battle unless you're certain of victory. Best to give in gracefully, don't you think? I really am quite determined. I tell you what – I promise to discover the whereabouts of boring Prague by tomorrow. There, does that satisfy you? Now, off you go, there's a pet. If you don't hurry Ludmilla may well have finished and be gone.'

The little man folded his map, collected his books, bowed stiffly to the girls and left the room.

Katya, not bothering to hide her laughter, danced across the room behind him and shut the door. Yelena was watching her, wide-eyed and with a trace of awe. To treat an adult so – and in particular an adult in a position of some authority – was so far beyond her that she could barely believe her eyes and ears. 'Who's Ludmilla Gavrilovna?'

'My maid. Poor M'sieu is very sweet on her. He pursues her with Gallic enthusiasm. And she, bless her, torments him to death. It's all very entertaining. Now – goodness, look at the time! Let's go and find the skates.'

Anna eyed her suspiciously. 'What has the time got to do with it?'

Katya smiled, innocently. 'Nothing at all, of course, cousin dear. Nothing at all.'

They arrived at the frozen river half an hour later, escorted by a young male servant called Yuri who was obviously so over-awed by his young mistress that he jumped nervously every time she addressed him. After he had helped them strap the blades to their boots Katya deposited him near one of the bonfires that had been lit on the banks of the river. 'There,' she said, briskly. 'You can stay here and keep warm. There's no need to come with us, we'll be perfectly safe. Come on, you two, off we go.' She flew onto the ice like a graceful bird, cutting her way through the laughing skaters with enviable ease. Rather more gingerly – neither of them had ever become particularly accomplished skaters – Anna and her sister followed.

They had come to that part of the river that stretched, almost a mile wide, between the Winter Palace and the Fortress of St Peter and St Paul. Here on New Year's Day the Tsar, in a solemn and brilliant ceremony, each year blessed the waters of the Neva, the Imperial troops parading on the ice in colourful splendour, watched from the windows of the Winter Palace by the Imperial Court and its honoured guests. Now those windows glittered, giving back the fiery light of the low winter sun, and bonfires and braziers glowed ruddily upon the banks of the river. Near the Island bank sledges were racing. A band played upon the ice and skaters, singly and in pairs, swooped and spun in time to the music. Spectators leaned upon the Palace Bridge, watching. Vendors of chestnuts, of Lenten pancakes dripping with cream and honey, and of hot drinks moved amongst the crowds; there was an air of holiday. Anna and Yelena, holding hands, smiled at each other as they skated across the ice towards the spot where Katya had disappeared into the crowds.

'Where is she?' Anna skidded to a halt, put her hand up to shade her eyes. 'Can you see?'

Yelena shook her head. 'She can't be far – oh, look, isn't that her? Yes, there she is –' Yelena craned her neck. 'Who's that with her?'

The young gentleman with Katya proved to be a very tall and improbably handsome young captain of hussars. He and his friends, a half-dozen or so boisterous young officers in scarlet and blue, had quite obviously been waiting for Katya to join them. Her cousin's anxiety about the time, Anna thought a little ruefully, now made rather more sense. As, a little shyly, they skated up to join the group, Katya broke away from her companions, laughing, and skimmed across the ice to her cousins, stopping neatly beside them in a dashing spray of ice. She was dressed in burgundy and white, dark skirt swirling as she moved, white fur cape and muff brilliant and soft, the tiny collar standing up about her bright face. A small white fur hat was set at a becoming angle upon her fair head. She looked quite breathtakingly lovely. 'Anna – Lenka – come and meet Kostya – and Oleg, and Tolya and all the others whose names I've entirely forgotten and so shan't be able to introduce to you! I suppose it must be terribly bad form to skate with someone to whom you haven't been introduced?'

Fleetingly Anna considered her father's possible reaction to such light and lax social arrangements, then hastily put it from her mind. She knew perfectly well that just the sight of these glittering young men within a mile of his respectable daughters would very possibly be enough to cause an explosion that would be heard back in Moscow. She allowed Katya to seize her hand and draw her to where the young men stood, nodded and smiled, vaguely, through the confusion of introductions. The ease and laughter within the group told of long-standing friendship. The jostling and horseplay had but one inspiration; an obviously highly-prized place at Katya's side. Anna allowed herself to be squired about the ice by a dark young man rather quieter than the others, thankful that he did not apparently expect from her the kind of perilous verve that Katya and her partner were displaying as they swooped and whirled across the ice. She saw that Lenka too was skating with a young man, albeit a young man whose eyes were for the most part openly fixed upon the graceful burgundy and white figure of their cousin. She answered the polite questions of her escort; yes, she was new to St Petersburg, yes, it was indeed a most wonderful city, and no, she had no invitation to the Kirolski ball the following week, nor was she expecting one.

The red sun slid across the sky, dipping towards the islands and behind the vast bulk of the Fortress, the slender, improbably beautiful spire of its cathedral spearing the darkening sky like a glinting rose-gold needle. Suddenly, with the walls shadowed and mysterious, Anna remembered the whispered stories she had heard of the place; imprisonment, torture, death. Tales to curdle the blood and chill the soul. One could disappear into the Fortress's granite heart and be gone for ever, so people said, with no redress and no comfort for those left behind. What kind of person would you have to be to torture another human being? She shuddered a little. Her well-mannered escort was immediately all attention. 'You're cold?'

'A little.'

'Come, a warm drink –' He guided her with a firm hand upon her elbow towards the bank.

It was there, perhaps half an hour later, that a slightly anxious Yelena found her. 'Anna, it's getting late – we should go.'

'Yes. Where's Katya?'

'I don't know.' Yelena glanced a little nervously at the young officer beside Anna. 'She – seems to have disappeared.'

'Disappeared? What do you mean?'

'Gone. I think she might have gone on a sledge ride. With that young man – Kostya something I think his name is.'

'Oh dear.' Quite suddenly it was getting dark. Flares had been lit around the ice and lamps glowed warmly in windows. They should, Anna knew, have been home some time since. It really was too bad of Katya.

'Please, I'd be happy to escort you home.' Her skating partner, in all his brass-buttoned and braided glory, very properly, had straightened beside her, bowing a little, though it could not be said that his offer had been delivered with any degree of real enthusiasm.

'Oh, good heavens no!' The words were out before she could stop them. 'That is, thank you, but no. We really don't have far to go.' The thought of the consequences of turning up at the apartment squired by this handsome young peacock produced in her alarm and laughter in about equal degrees. A glance at her sister's face showed the same emotions in slightly different proportions. Poor Lenka, with good reason, always automatically expected trouble. 'Honestly, we'll be perfectly all right. Lenka, we really should go.'

Yelena, balanced precariously on one foot, was already unstrapping her skating blades. 'And Katya? What about her?'

'We can't wait, she must know that. Yuri is waiting to escort her home. She'll be all right. Oh, yes – goodbye – it's been very nice meeting you –' Anna lifted a hand to the dark-haired young man who was obviously anxious now to be gone, watched as he struck out across the ice with strong, sure movements. 'She'll be all right,' she repeated, drily. 'I have the strongest suspicion that our Katya is more than capable of looking after herself. I don't think she'd want us to worry about her.' She slipped her hand through the crook of her sister's arm, and dropped her voice, reflectively. 'I very much doubt if she's worrying about us.'

*　*　*

They hurried through the freezing, darkening streets. It had started to snow again. By the time they reached the street called Venskaya it was drifting quite heavily around them. They paused at the entrance to the apartment building to brush it from their shoulders, kick and stamp it from their boots and shake it from their scarves and hats.

'Anna! At last! I've been waiting for you.' Andrei's door opened, and warm air gusted into the dark hall. He was dressed, as he often liked to when at home and relaxing, in full-sleeved peasant shirt belted over baggy trousers that were tucked into soft leather boots. His silver hair was tousled. 'I've found that piece by Paganini that we were talking about – Lenka, hello, how are you?'

'I'm well, thank you.' Yelena accepted his brief kiss, crushed the sudden rise of swift resentment as he turned to Anna, face intent.

'Have you got a moment or two?' His arm was linked in hers. Anna was laughing. 'Just come and have a look – see what you think –'

They disappeared into the work room, and the door closed behind them. Yelena stood for a long moment, alone in the cold darkness of the hall. The stairs were dirty, grimed by melted ice and snow. The air was bitterly cold.

Slowly, very slowly, and with a suddenly heavy heart Yelena climbed the stairs to the apartment. It wasn't possible – it wasn't right! – that she should be jealous of the relationship between her sister and their uncle. It was perfectly natural that Anna and Andrei, the two most musically talented of the family, should have discovered such a rapport. But – she paused for a moment, between one step and another – but Anna was *hers*. Anna was her only friend. Her only ally. The only person in the world who understood her, who cared about her. She couldn't share her. Couldn't lose her! Her young heart almost stopped beating at the thought. For a brief, almost frightening moment she allowed the floodgates of her soul to open; she'd hate anyone who came between her and Anna. Hate them from the bottom of her heart. She'd hate Anna herself if she allowed it to happen, for then she – Yelena – would be alone. Totally alone. For ever.

From behind her, lifting from the darkness of the stairwell, came the sound of Anna's violin; light and happy, played with a sure and confident touch. Yelena knew how long it was since Anna had played like that. She mustn't resent it. She mustn't! Young and utterly confused as she was, even she could see the seeds of disaster in that.

She rang the doorbell. 'Hello, Seraphima.'

'Yelena Victorovna. You're very late? And where's your sister?'

'She's downstairs with Uncle Andrei. I don't think she'll be long. Is Papa home?'

'Yes, he is.' Seraphima was busying herself with Yelena's coat and boots. 'He's in the parlour, with your Mama and the others.' The girl smiled a little, mischievously, leaned towards Yelena. 'Your Mama has just spoiled the dinner again. Your Papa has finally agreed to hire a cook.'

Yelena almost smiled. 'Thank the good Lord for that.'

In the parlour, now comfortably furnished with the pieces brought with them from Moscow, Dmitri sat opposite a scowling Margarita at the big table, both of them with notebooks and pencils, whilst on the small round table in the corner the samovar sang its comforting song. Her mother and father sat in the overstuffed armchairs that were set in the corner near the stove. Her father was reading a newspaper which he set aside as she entered. 'Lenka. You're home.'

'Yes.' She was surprised and made immediately wary by the use of the diminutive, the determinedly pleasant tone. 'I'm sorry we're late. Cousin Katya couldn't decide where Prague was. Anna's downstairs. Do you want me to fetch her?' There was a decidedly unappetizing odour in the air.

'No, no. Don't bother her. We won't be eating for a while yet.' Victor shot a significant glance at his wife who, impervious, worked with neat dexterity at her crochet. Victor steepled his fingers, looked at Yelena over the tips. 'Prague,' he said, heavily thoughtful.

Yelena pushed her hands into the pockets of her skirt and hunched her shoulders defensively. Never so long as she could remember had her father taken the slightest interest in anything she had ever said or done, except to criticize or to punish. This conversation was making her extremely uneasy. 'Cousin Katya said she didn't need to know geography to get on a train.'

At the table Margarita pushed back her mass of hair and grinned. She had set aside her notebook and was carefully colouring a tiny cardboard figure of a king, complete with crown and trailing robes, a key actor in the new play she had written for her beloved theatre.

'Hmm. Too clever by half, that cousin of yours.' Victor picked up the newspaper, folded it neatly. 'And you? Did you know where it was?'

Yelena was growing more wary by the moment. 'Not absolutely exactly,' she said, carefully. 'I mean, I know it's in Czechoslovakia, and I know where that is –'

'But can you spell it?' Margarita asked, smartly, from the table.

'Quiet, Rita,' Victor said, then, to Yelena, added expansively, 'The atlas is over there, if you want to check.'

'Thank you, Papa.' Embarrassed at being the focus of attention she caught her foot on the chairleg as she passed. Her father's lips tightened, but he said nothing. There was a moment's silence as Yelena pulled out the big old atlas and ran her finger down the index.

Her father craned his neck. 'Found it?'

'Yes, Papa. It's here. On the river –' she strained her eyes '– Moldau. I shall know if Monsieur Drapin asks tomorrow. Thank you.'

'Ah. No.' Her father withdrew rather suddenly behind the wings of his chair, like a turtle drawing into his shell. 'Not tomorrow, Lenka. I'd like you to stay at home tomorrow.'

In the act of replacing the book Yelena turned, surprised. 'At home, Papa?'

'Yes.' A hand reached out, picked up the newspaper again. The paper too disappeared into the armchair amidst much rustling. 'Pavel Petrovich is coming to lunch. Your mother is otherwise engaged. I was going to ask Anna to stay but Pavel Petrovich particularly asked that you should be here.'

The long moment of appalled silence was so obvious, so dense with sudden terror that Yelena was amazed to see that the other occupants of the room continued with their separate occupations as if nothing had happened. She stared at the back of her father's chair. 'I –' Frantically she fumbled the atlas back onto the shelf, all but ran around the chair to confront her father. 'Papa – must I?'

He was apparently absorbed in his newspaper. 'Yes. If you please. It is important to me.'

'But –'

'No buts, Yelena. You are to stay at home tomorrow and help Seraphima with the lunch. There's an end to it.' The familiar edge of ill-temper was showing in his voice, but his eyes avoided hers.

'Papa, please.' Desperate, she caught his hand. 'Couldn't Seraphima manage on her own? You know I'm not good at such things.'

He disengaged his hand with a look of such distaste that she stepped back from him, biting her lip. 'You must become good at such things, my dear.' His voice was cold. 'What kind of a wife will you make if you don't learn the social graces? This is as good an opportunity as any.'

'Papa – please – I can't! I –' She hesitated, plunged on. 'I don't like Pavel Petrovich, he frightens me –'

Margarita had lifted her head, perched her chin upon her bunched fist and was watching and listening with avid interest. Varya's head was bent absorbedly over her work.

Victor crushed the paper into his lap, eyes fierce with anger; with anger and with something else, some edge of understanding, almost of guilt, infinitely bewildering, infinitely frightening. 'What nonsense! Enough of this, girl! You'll stay, and you'll do as you're told. There's an end.'

Blindly Yelena turned from him and walked from the room. Out into the hall. Through the front door. Down the stairs. Her jaw was clenched, her lower lip caught painfully between her teeth. Why? In God's name, *why* had Ratface insisted that she be there? And why was Papa so adamant that she should stay? She shook her head fiercely. She couldn't do it. She wouldn't! Anna would understand. Anna would know what to do. Anna would help her.

She stopped on the last flight of stairs that led to the door of the workshop, standing quite still, arrested in her flight, one

63

hand clasping the smooth, cold banister. From within came the soft murmur of voices. A small, dashing phrase of music, gypsy-like and full of laughter. Another, as a second instrument joined in with the first, a game, a laughing duet, the music glittering and dancing like sunshine on running water. Faster and faster they played, to a climax that brought a peal of laughter from Anna.

Yelena stood there, listening; listening to the music, and to the laughter in which she had no part. Then, shoulders drooping, she sank down onto the filthy stairs, her knees drawn to her breast, her arms folded upon them. She sat so for a long time, shivering in the gnawing cold, staring into the darkness, barely blinking. At last, in a small, helpless gesture of unhappiness she bowed her head, resting her forehead on her arms. It was the only movement she made.

Inside the room Anna slipped the violin carefully into its battered case, together with the bow that her uncle had given her. She was breathless with laughter. 'I really must go. It's past dinner time. Are you eating with us tonight?'

Andrei, packing away his own instrument, shook his head, smiling. 'No. I'm dining with a friend.'

Anna was surprised at the surge of disappointment his answer brought. 'Oh.' She slipped her arms into the coat he held for her. 'Tomorrow perhaps?'

'Almost certainly tomorrow, yes.'

'Good.' She stood for a moment, reluctant to leave. In this room over the past weeks she had unexpectedly discovered a haven, a place of music and laughter, of relaxed companionship and of understanding. Here she was not the eldest daughter, eldest sister, responsible, capable, reliable; dull. Here she was simply Anna; here she could live her music with someone who through ties of blood and of shared interest could understand it and her. Each time she left this room to return to the apartment upstairs it was with regret.

Her uncle was watching her, questioningly. He had a disconcerting way of guessing what went through her mind. Briskly she turned away from him – too briskly, for as she did so her heel caught in the frayed edge of the rug that lay upon the uneven floor. She was standing very close to the hot stove.

Caught off balance she nearly fell, hands automatically out-stretched to save herself. Andrei reached for her quickly, grabbing her arm, swinging her away from the searingly hot metal and steadying her. To save herself from falling she clasped the hand that held her. They stood so for a moment as she regained her balance, and clearly in his eyes she saw him flinch from her, expecting rejection. The hand that had saved her, the hand she held in her own, was his right hand. The maimed hand, distorted, scarred and ugly. The hand he had as far as was possible hidden from her since that first day when she had so clearly shown her horror of it. Abruptly he tried to pull away. She held him. Then with deliberation, her eyes on his, she brought the hand to her face, rested her cheek against it.

His face changed.

'Thank you,' she said.

He smiled.

The scarred skin was warm and oddly smooth against her face. She closed her fingers upon his. She did not want to let him go. Not now. Not ever. And in his eyes too she was sure that she saw –

Startled, they stepped apart. Andrei shoved his damaged hand deep into his pocket. Anna gathered her coat about her, busily buttoned it and tied the belt, not looking at him. 'I'll see you tomorrow, then.'

'Yes. Tomorrow.'

She grabbed her hat and hurried to the door. Opened it. Yelena had come stiffly to her feet when she had heard the music stop. 'Lenka!' Anna's voice was too high, sounded false and silly. She cleared her throat. 'What are you doing here?'

'I came – to tell you it was time to eat. And to –' She stepped clumsily forward, caught at her sister's arm. ''Noushka, I need to talk to you –'

'Not now, Lenka.' Anna turned back, caught Andrei's eyes upon her, ducked her head and headed for the stairs very fast.

'But – Anna, please! It's important!'

'Lenka, for heaven's sake! It's freezing! Look at you – you're shaking!' Anna herself, she realized, had begun to tremble; it had been too warm in her uncle's room, she was feeling the sudden cold. She rounded upon her sister. 'Stupid thing!' she

65

snapped. 'Fancy coming down here without even a shawl! Honestly, Lenka, haven't you the sense you were born with? Come on, now!' Anna lifted her skirt and fled up the stairs as if the devil were behind her.

Later that night, lying with her back to her sister, her head buried beneath the bedclothes, determinedly feigning sleep, Anna dismissed that ridiculous surge of panic as absurd. Whatever had got into her? What, after all, had actually happened? Nothing that could not be explained by her natural affection for her uncle and his for her. The incident, such as it was, had happened so quickly – it was vague in her mind now, a scene flashed upon her brain like the flickering magic lantern pictures Papa had taken them to see last Christmas. She had held his hand, his poor, maimed hand; and she was glad of it. It was surely the least she could do to repay his kindness to her? Nothing else had happened. Nothing.

Yelena, beside her, feeling her sister's warmth, hearing her low, steady breathing, stared grimly into darkness, unhappy, afraid, and utterly alone.

CHAPTER FOUR

The shop on the Nevsky opened on time, two weeks before Easter, and attracted immediate and distinguished custom.

Anna loved it. The decor was discreetly and fashionably opulent, the mahogany and brass counters and display cases gleamed, religiously polished each day, as was the wooden floor that was laid with large and extremely expensive softly-coloured rugs. The bevelled and etched glass and mirrors reflected every image and glint of light with sparkling clarity. The best of the instruments were exhibited with loving care, the magnificent sheen and depth of their colour, the masterly craftsmanship that had gone into their making complementing perfectly these surroundings that had been created to display them to just such advantage.

Varya, eyeing the splendour with a jaundiced eye, complained – predictably, Anna thought – that Victor's customers enjoyed far greater luxury than did his wife and family.

'But, Mama – can't you see? This is the Nevsky! It's important that the shop be comfortable – and beautiful. The customers that Papa wants to attract wouldn't settle for less. You remember when we visited Monsieur Fabergé's shop and workshop the other day? You loved that, you know you did. It made you feel special. Well – that's what Papa is trying to create here. The people who will come to such a shop expect to pay more for the privilege.'

Varya looked around her, sniffing. Vague and future profits were, to her, much less important than present apparent extravagance; unless of course the extravagance be lavished upon her. 'With such expense I should hope so!'

The work rooms above the shop were very much less luxurious. The building fronted the Nevsky with its coffee houses, its confectioners and its fashionable luxury shops, and three large windows looked out across the wide, elegant and always busy avenue. At each window stood a padded workbench, to catch the best of the light, and already the benches were littered with pieces of wood, tools, half-made instruments and those in the process of being renovated or mended. Violins and violas hung from racks on the ceiling, a big old cello leaned against the wall, awaiting attention. There was a large wooden cabinet with what looked like hundreds of tiny drawers, and several wooden boxes containing various pieces that Anna knew had been salvaged from old instruments damaged beyond repair, to be used to restore others. The atmosphere was comfortably warm and dry, and there was a strong smell of varnish. Bags of polishing cloths hung from the benches and there were shavings upon the floor that rustled as she walked through them. Andrei, conducting them around, introduced them with unconcealed pride and pleasure to his craftsmen, perched upon their stools, rough aprons varnish-stained, big, clever hands handling tiny gouges, chisels and planes that looked more suited to a doll's house than to this great room.

The oldest of them, introduced as Pyotr Pyotrovich, did not look up from his work as Anna murmured greetings. She watched, fascinated, as with gnarled fingers he used a tiny, gun-metal plane no bigger than the top joint of her own thumb, smoothing and shaping the bleached-looking wood. Beside the man lay an instrument in the process of being varnished and polished. The wood, beautifully grained, glowed like a living thing; Anna longed to touch it, to pick it up and test the weight, the balance. She extended a finger, and then drew back without touching the instrument. 'It's very hard to believe,' she said, voicing a thought that occurred to her not for the first time, 'looking at this – that it's true that old instruments sound better than new.'

The old man still did not look at her, nor did the steady, delicate movements of his hands falter. 'Don't you believe it, mistress,' he said. ''T'ain't so.'

Andrei slanted a look at Anna, smothering a grin.

'An' what's more –' The old head lifted at last. Anna found herself, disconcerted, looking into a pair of alert and piercing eyes. 'Don't be fooled by the pretty varnish. God forsaken things'd be a damned sight better off without it.'

'But – I thought –'

'Thinkin' doesn't make violins. Hands makes violins. And you can take it from me – the more you tamper the more you spoil.' The grey head turned again, back to his work.

Andrei laughed outright. 'Anna, you of all people must know that there are as many theories about violin making as there are violin makers! Pyotr would have his played –' he spread his good hand, strong and slender '– raw! Looking like a packing case.'

'But –'

'But don't worry, little mistress.' The man did not take his eyes from his work. 'Won't happen. Can't happen. Pretty. That's how they want 'em. Pretty. So I makes 'em so. But they'd sound better if I didn't. Take it from me.'

'Andrei, Victor said something about tea in his office?' Varya lifted the hem of her skirt, shook it delicately to dislodge shavings and sawdust.

Anna blushed, embarrassed. 'Mama, there are others to meet yet.'

Varya sighed.

The lutenist at the middle bench was a shy man in his middle thirties who specialized in intricate repairs. Absorbed, Anna watched him, complimented him on a restored instrument that he showed her, modestly proud. 'But – you'd never *guess* it had been repaired! And such a violin! I'd be scared to touch it!'

'A Lupot,' Andrei said. 'French, 1800. Lord knows where it's been, that it should have been so badly treated. Now, come and meet Vladimir. Volodya, here's Anna Victorovna. I've told you of her –'

The tall young man at the third workbench bowed his head a little and smiled shyly. This, Anna knew, was the young man in whom Andrei had such faith. Already his instruments were spoken of in the same breath as the best of the contemporary Italian and French makers. He was fair, long-legged and thin-faced, his narrow shoulders slightly hunched.

Andrei laid a light arm across his shoulders. 'We expect great things from our Volodya. One day you'll be proud to have met him, you mark my words.' Again the shy smile. The young man glanced at Andrei from beneath long blond lashes, obviously delighted with the praise, and Anna was struck again by that quality in her uncle that made the most dour of people warm to him. She found it hard to believe that anyone could resist his quiet and good-natured charm; for herself she knew that the move to this new life in a strange city would have been much harder had he not been there. The still slightly uncomfortable memory of that moment of disturbing intimacy in his work room had faded. At first, oversensitively, she had been certain that he, too, was embarrassed – she had feared for the few days that followed that he was avoiding her. But gradually they had slipped back into the old, easy camaraderie and in the end she had almost persuaded herself that she had imagined the whole silly episode. Except that sometimes she found herself watching him: the turn of his head, the slight, crooked smile, his defensive habit of keeping his right hand hidden, and was aware that the depth of feeling that these small things roused in her might be frowned upon by others who might not understand their source. She was not, of course, attracted by Andrei as a man; he was her uncle, such a thing simply was not possible. But, surely, it was perfectly natural that she should love and admire him: as a truly great craftsman, as a courageous man who had outfaced tragedy, as a wise and kindly friend whose affection she treasured. His loneliness – for he was, she somehow instinctively guessed, lonely – touched her, his strange vulnerability aroused her tenderness. That was all. They laughed together, and they shared their music. His rooms were a haven of quiet away from the apartment that lately always seemed riven with squabbles and tensions and Lenka's sullenness. That was all. She watched him putting the awkward young man at his ease, and smiled.

'Tea,' Varya said, with patience. 'Please?'

'Tea, certainly. In Victor's office.' Andrei smiled. 'This way.'

He led the way into a corridor that was part balcony, overlooking the shop downstairs.

'Where do you work?' Anna asked.

'Still at home at the moment, but I'm thinking of having the little room next door here converted to a workshop.' He sent her one of his laughing glances, half-apologetic. 'I'm not very good at working in company. Ah, here we are. Victor's office.'

The room into which he showed them was small, comfortable, one wall booklined and another entirely taken up by a large wooden filing cabinet, its drawers precisely labelled and lettered. The papers on the large desk were tidily stacked, as were the magazines on a nearby table upon which also stood a small samovar. Everything was neat and well-ordered. Anna thought that if she had been shown into this room anywhere in the world she would have guessed that it belonged to her father.

Andrei was busy with the samovar and tea glasses. 'Where's Lenka?' he asked. 'I thought she was coming?'

Varya, settling herself with charming effect into the only comfortable chair, apart from Victor's, in the room, shrugged irritably. 'Don't talk to me about that girl! She really is becoming impossible lately. She decided she would rather stay at home with Seraphima and the children, and to be perfectly frank with you I didn't try to dissuade her. She walks around with a face like a wet Sunday; I can't get a word out of her. I really don't know what's got into her. Even Anna's out of sorts with her – aren't you, dear? – and you know how unusual that is.'

Anna fiddled a little uncomfortably with her gloves.

'Oh?' Andrei handed her a glass of tea. 'What happened?'

Anna shook her head a little brusquely. 'Nothing. Lenka was being stupid, that's all.'

Andrei's dark eyebrows lifted. He said nothing, but his look was shrewd and questioning.

'You're just the same as everyone else!' Yelena had stormed. 'You won't listen to me! You don't care about me! You promised – *you promised!* – to speak to Papa about the University! When? *When?* You spend all your time downstairs with Uncle Andrei and your *wretched* fiddle! Or giggling with Katya, like stupid children!'

'I don't! I don't!'

'Yes, you do! And you don't see – you don't see what's happening right under your nose! You don't *see* what they're doing to me!'

'Lenka, for heaven's sake! What are you talking about? You're hysterical.'

She accepted the tea, not looking directly at her uncle. Only once or twice in their lives had she and Lenka quarrelled, and on each occasion the hurt had been exacerbated by the breaking of a bond usually so firm as to be unquestioned. The problem for Anna this time was that she suspected that right was to a certain extent upon Lenka's side. It was true that she, Anna, had promised to approach their father about the possibility of the women's courses at the University. She was aware, too, that of late her attentions had been drawn away from the narrow confines of her home and her sister's troubles. But wasn't that natural? They weren't children any more, after all. She had discovered, a little surprisingly, in these past few weeks that she was tired of this role that had been forced by circumstance upon her; daughter, sister, capable organizer, ever-present help – housekeeper to her father, companion to her mother, stand-in nanny to her brother and sisters – she was *tired* of it. Just lately she had become aware of a restlessness that until now she would have considered totally alien to her nature. It was as if she stood on the threshold of an exciting and unknown room, or perhaps on a mountaintop waiting for the sun to rise and to reveal – what? 'I'm sorry?'

'I said that you and Lenka have barely spoken in the past few weeks,' Varya repeated.

'Oh. Well, I wouldn't put it quite like that.' In fact, if she had forced herself to honesty, that was indeed exactly the way she would have put it. She and her sister had, in the course of the days, exchanged common or garden words, had passed the butter and the sugar, had complained about Monsieur Drapin's fixation upon the geography of Europe, had agreed that Cousin Katya had the very easiest of lives of anyone they knew or could imagine – but they had not actually spoken together, not in the old way. Lenka over the past couple of weeks had become more and more sullenly withdrawn, less and less apparently interested in breaking down the barrier that had grown so frighteningly quickly between them. And as for Anna – her secret dreams and fears, her quietly awakening womanhood, were not to be discussed and dissected; she was happy with silence.

But Lenka? The one thing that Lenka was not was happy,

Anna knew that with the certainty that came of love and long association. She sipped her tea. She would talk to Papa about the University. She would. Soon. And perhaps at the same time she might mention how much her sister disliked the attentions of the man Donovalov? Lenka had not actually mentioned the man's name, but with sure instinct Anna sensed it; twice now Papa had insisted that Lenka be at home when Donovalov visited, and after each occasion her sister's withdrawn and sullen mood had deepened. There couldn't possibly be anything in it – the man was at least twice Lenka's age and a relatively recent widower – but if she could catch Papa in the right mood at least it might help Lenka if she mentioned it?

'You are of course coming to the performance tonight, Andrei?' Varya trilled laughter like a pretty bird, accepted her glass with a smile and a dip of her long lashes. She could not, Anna noted with some exasperation, resist flirting even with a man who was brother to her husband. 'Rita will be so disappointed if you don't. She's worked so hard at her little play – and the scenery she's painted – it's absolutely wonderful.'

'I think little Natalia painted most of the scenery, Mama,' Anna murmured, scrupulously fair. They had all spent the past three evenings listening to Margarita ordering her quiet and unassuming schoolfriend about and scolding her like a recalcitrant servant; the child surely deserved the credit for the hard work she had done. Credit, Anna guessed, that in the light of her devotion to Margarita she would never claim for herself.

Varya waved a dismissive hand. 'Oh, fiddlesticks. The child's like a little mouse. I can't imagine what Rita sees in her. So, Andrei – you will come?'

'Yes, I'll come. Of course. On one condition.'

'Oh?'

'That you all join me to watch the midnight procession at St Isaac's on Easter Eve. It's the most wonderful sight – something not to be missed on your first Easter in St Petersburg.'

'Oh, Mama! May we?'

Varya tilted her head prettily to one side. 'We should ask your Papa.'

'I'll ask him,' Andrei said. 'And if he agrees, you'll come?'

Anna's mother smiled her most charming smile. 'Of course. We'd love to.'

Margarita's play was to be performed that evening after supper – a supper that, as it had for the past Lenten weeks, consisted of fish and vegetables only. The Shalakov household was not a particularly religious one, but Victor insisted upon the outward observance of traditions that he considered to be a mark of decency and respectability, so during Lent there were no eggs, no butter, no meat, and during the week that led to Easter the family would live upon vegetables only; a hardship for which, as in almost every household in Russia, high or low, the feast to be mounted upon Easter Sunday and Monday would more than compensate.

The little theatre was set upon the table in the parlour, draped tablecloths hiding the human participants in the drama, a cunningly placed lamp set to illuminate the tiny, colourful cardboard characters as they moved about the stage on their lengths of wire. The audience – consisting of the entire family plus the conscripted Nanny Irisha, Seraphima, and Sonya, the somewhat forbiddingly efficient new cook – sat obediently quiet upon the chairs that Margarita had persuaded, or to be more exact ordered, Dmitri to set into a row across the room. Margarita was in her element. 'No, no, Natalia! The princess doesn't begin the scene there, stupid thing! Do read the notes! There, that's right. And do make sure the curtains lift right back when you open them. Are we ready?'

Her faithful acolyte nodded, meekly.

Margarita lifted her voice a little. 'All right, Anna. We're ready –'

Anna, standing in the shadows at the back of the room, lifted her violin, settled it snugly upon her shoulder and played softly the pretty tune that her sister had chosen as the overture to her play.

Andrei glanced around at her, his smile warm. He loved the way she played the instrument; even soundless the very picture she made, the delicate line of hand and arm, the poise of instrument and bow, held for him a perfect beauty.

And in Anna's heart at the sight of that smile sudden and

tender happiness lifted. It showed on her face, the narrow, high-boned and usually serious face beneath its cloud of bright hair. It shone with innocent serenity from her eyes and softened the line of her mouth. Their eyes held, for the briefest of moments, a natural and secret communication across the overcrowded, darkened room. The music linked them like a fragile strand of silk.

Very abruptly Andrei turned away.

Upon the table the artfully-contrived curtain lifted to reveal prince, princess and a charmingly-painted walled garden in perfect miniature. There was a smattering of applause; the play was under way.

Andrei sat, very straight and very still, seeing nothing. The bright cardboard figures jerked, their lines proclaimed with verve and vigour. Behind him Anna's flawless touch upon her instrument sent the music rippling towards him, silken ribbons to bind his heart. He knew she was watching him, with that shocking, unwary happiness shining from her face. He could feel it, like the bruising aftermath of a blow. He closed his eyes, took a deep slow breath, forcing himself to face at last the shattering thing that had happened to him; the monstrous thing that had been lurking beneath the conscious surface of his life for weeks.

The gaudy figures were propelled stiffly back and forth across the stage. 'Betrayed!' the princess cried dramatically, her cardboard face smiling blankly. 'My heart is broken! I shall never love again!'

I shall never love again.

That, indeed, was what he had believed. In the years that had followed Galina's death nothing and no-one had touched him. So great had been the pain, so harrowing the torment, that he had truly believed himself crippled by it, as surely inwardly in the mind and heart as outwardly in the mangled hand. No-one knew – no-one would ever know – the despair he had suffered at her loss. That there could be anyone who could touch that same chord in him, who could rouse in him the same aching depths of love and tenderness had seemed a simple impossibility.

The brokenhearted, if practical, princess had decided, with commendable speed, to marry for money. '– And to the man who can fill this garden with gold, I shall give my hand –'

God Almighty. The breathtaking cruelty of fate. Almost he laughed aloud. Not more pain, surely? Was it possible?

Anna had stopped playing, awaiting her carefully rehearsed cue towards the end of the scene. Andrei could see her young face as if, illuminated by a torch's flame, she were kneeling before him. Not, measured by the world's standards, what might be called a pretty face. But arresting; and unique. The pale skin, freckled like a child's, the light, clear eyes, lucent as water, the straight, uncompromising mouth, the patience, the humour, the hidden glimpses of a character fuelled by a passion as yet unacknowledged, released only through her music. He felt again her impulsive grip on his ugly, damaged hand, the warmth of her soft cheek against the scarred skin.

The violin played a brisk fanfare to herald the end of the first act and was followed by an enthusiastic round of applause. A bright-faced, tousled Margarita appeared from beneath the enveloping tablecloth looking bewitchingly pretty. 'The second act takes place at night, so Dmitri has to fetch a smaller lamp.' There was a short period of activity then, the lighting suitably dimmed, Margarita disappeared again.

He must, of course, take serious steps. They must see less of each other. The child must be discouraged from coming to visit him. He should perhaps spend more time at the workshop; unhomelike as it was, the empty room beside Victor's office would be just as good a place to work as the room downstairs. He must at all costs keep her from hurt.

Exotic suitors by the dozen were appearing on stage, gold – in the form of the gold-leafed walnuts left over from the decoration of the Christmas tree and begged from Varya as being essential to the plot – appeared in cardboard wheelbarrows, in a cleverly contrived troika, in a sledge drawn by awkward-looking cardboard reindeer. The princess dismissed all as unworthy. When the handsome young peasant appeared – his paper rags barely concealing the princely garb beneath – Dmitri, upon hissed instructions from under the tablecloth, scrambled for another lamp.

'I'll fill your garden with gold, my princess – with the gold of the early morning sun – see, the sunrise!'

76

'Oh, lovely! Victor, look! – how clever!' Varya clapped her hands like a child.

The last scene showed the obligatory wedding, during which the humble peasant was revealed to have been a handsome prince all along and everyone was declared to be certain of living happily ever after. Anna played a spirited finale with a flourish and the whole thing ended in applause and congratulations which Margarita accepted with becoming modesty. Victor, expansive, enjoying for however brief a moment this role as head of a contented and talented household, suggested, as lamps were turned up and the chairs moved back to more normal positions, that Anna might play for them a little longer.

'Of course, Papa. What would you like to hear?'

'You choose, my dear.'

'Glazunov. You'd like something by Glazunov?' She knew him to be one of her father's favourite composers.

'Most certainly.' Victor settled into his chair. 'A small recital; and then I must take our little Natalia home to her mama.'

Andrei stood. 'I'll take her.'

'No, no. Stay, Andrei.' Victor waved a hand. 'I'll walk her home in a little while. It isn't far.'

'I – rather feel the need of a breath of fresh air.' Andrei studiously avoided catching Anna's surprised eye. 'And it's a little late, you know. If Natalia will have me then I'll escort her.'

Dmitri, with unusual energy, bounced from his chair. 'May I come? I feel like a walk.'

'Oh, no, dear – I don't think –'

'Mama, please! I've been sitting here for *hours* watching Margarita's –' Dmitri hesitated, thought twice about the word 'silly' '– nice play. My legs are quite cramped. 'Talia doesn't live far. She won't mind if I come. Will you?'

Thus directly addressed, the girl blushed furiously, ducked her mousy head and then shook it.

Anna, amused at the telltale affectionate diminutive – Dmitri, harassed by three sisters, was not usually known for his attentions to or interest in the opposite sex – tried unsuccessfully to catch her uncle's eye, to share the affectionate laughter. He, however, did not glance her way. 'Let him come,

Varya. A walk will do him good. Please, relax and enjoy your evening. I'll see you tomorrow at the shop, Victor.'

'You won't come back for a small glass of something?' Victor was surprised. 'I thought you said –'

'No.' The word was abrupt. 'I won't come back. I'll send Dima up as soon as we get back. Seraphima, could you get the children's coats and hats, please? Dima, if you're coming with us you'd better put another jumper on. It's still quite cold out –'

Dmitri ran with alacrity from the room. Natalia's eyes followed him shyly. Margarita snorted. 'What's got into our Dima? He's usually as idle as a bear in winter!'

Minutes later, muffled against the cold, the three of them left the apartment. The door shut firmly behind them. The stairs were dimly lit and cold. 'Come on, 'Talia.' Dmitri caught the girl's hand and they started down the stairs. 'I'd better help you. It's a bit dark.'

Andrei stood for a moment, watching them, collar turned up around his ears, hands deep in his pockets. He had not bothered to wear a hat to come up to the apartment. He ought to stop in at his rooms downstairs to pick one up.

He tried not to think of the untroubled light in Anna's eyes as she had kissed him, lightly, on each cheek in unthinking and formal farewell.

Dmitri's voice came to him from below. 'Mind this bottom step – it's a bit uneven,' and then, as they reached the heavy door and the boy struggled to open it, 'Sunday is Palm Sunday, isn't it? I'm sure Uncle Andrei will know where we can find some pussy willow. If I ask him, would you like to come to collect some with me?'

Slowly Andrei started down the stairs. From the apartment above came the sound of Anna's violin, pursuing him, gently and faultlessly beautiful. He hunched his shoulders; against the cold, and against that soft, haunting sound.

Face set, he followed the children, bareheaded, out into the bleak night.

The week leading up to Easter was, as always, the busiest of the year. All of the food for the Easter Table – the feast to be eaten by family, servants and friends on Easter Sunday and

Monday to break the Lenten fast – must be prepared almost wholly in advance, for on those two days no-one must be made to work. Almost everyone was dragooned – mostly by Anna – into helping with the preparations for the great festival. The Easter ham had been brought with them, months ago, from Moscow and had been hanging in the cold larder beside the strings of dried mushrooms and herbs that had also travelled with them from the Moscow kitchen. Chickens and joints of veal were bought from the market, cheesecakes and cakes were prepared; the whole family held the strongest conviction that Nanny Irisha's 'koulich', an iced fruit cake upon which, with great care and ceremony, the first letters of the words 'Christ is Risen' had been beautifully enscribed, was the best to be found in St Petersburg. The traditional 'pashka', a sweet, soft cheese, was prepared, under the eagle eye of the new cook, who, Anna noticed, did not herself do much of the hard work of mixing. Salmon too was cooked and cooled, and caviar bought from a shop on the Nevsky, together with more vodka than was usually seen in the Shalakov household, and several bottles of a liqueur known as 'ribinovka', flavoured with rowan berries, of which Varya was particularly fond. Dmitri, professing a masculine disinterest in the affairs of the kitchen, spent most of his time painstakingly dyeing, colouring and decorating eggs. Throughout the week, the whole household went at one time or another separately to church for their confession. And all before they left went to the other members of the household to ask and accept forgiveness for any wayward sin that might have caused hurt during the past year.

Anna, reciting the formula to Lenka and receiving equally automatic pardon, resolved with a little unease and in good faith once more to speak to her father about the University just as soon as the opportunity arose.

Victor, of course, took little part in these domestic arrangements. The initial success of the shop on the Nevsky had gratifyingly continued, though first interest, inevitably, fell off a little. The contract with the Imperial theatres and schools was all but signed and sealed; with that solidly behind him he knew that the future could be considered assured, and in a much shorter space of time than he had ever dared to dream. In

St Petersburg where the Tsar or his representatives led the whole world gladly followed.

'So, Pavel Petrovich –' he poured another glass of vodka for Donovalov, left the bottle within easy reach of the other man's hand '– we are agreed, I think? Shall we drink a toast?'

Donovalov picked up the small glass, turned it in his hand. He sat at his ease in the chair opposite the desk in Victor's office. His dark and narrow face was impassive. 'I – see no reason why not.'

His tone stopped Victor in his tracks. The glass half-raised, he stilled. 'There is a doubt?' There couldn't be. He had given everything – everything! – the damned man had asked.

Donovalov smiled, lifted his glass a little. 'No. Of course not.' He made a slight movement towards Victor's glass. Victor, relieved, clicked his against it and tossed the drink back. Donovalov did not move.

There was a small, tense silence. 'What?' Victor asked, quietly, aware that for all his efforts something like despair edged his voice. 'You want more?'

The dark, level glance held his. Then, 'No,' the man said. 'No, of course not, Victor Valerievich. Of course not,' and with a single movement he lifted the glass and emptied it.

Victor sat down, rather too suddenly for dignity. It was done, then. The contract was his. The gamble had paid off. He had spent a great deal of money on the shop on the Nevsky, more than his original careful planning had foreseen; his dealings with Pavel Petrovich had cost him dearly too. But the prospect of the Imperial contract and the advantages it offered, dangled so temptingly, had overcome his habitual prudence. 'The agreement,' he said, indicating the impressive-looking document that lay upon his desk. 'Shall we sign it?'

'Of course.' Donovalov reached for the bottle, refilled his glass to the brim. 'Of course. And then –' he lifted his head, letting a small silence draw out between them '– there is perhaps another little matter that I would like to discuss.'

'Oh?'

The other man reached into his pocket, pulled out a cigarette case, extracted a cigarette and lit it, unhurriedly. 'Your daughter Yelena,' he said. 'She interests me.'

Victor reached for the bottle.

The contract lay, unsigned, between them.

Donovalov smiled, not unpleasantly.

'She's – very young,' Victor said. The man's reputation was barbarous.

'But my dear Victor, of course she is. That's one of her charms.' The man leaned forward and pulled the contract and the pen and inkwell towards him. He picked up the pen, toyed with it, put it down.

'I'm not sure that –' Victor stopped.

Donovalov's face hardened a very little. He was tired of street girls. Tired of living alone. Since stupid Olga's unfortunate death there had been something missing from his life; lately he had become aware of that. The initial thrill of freedom had long worn off. The small, vicious adventures of the streets, bought and paid for, had quickly palled. He had become sated. Yelena's instant, instinctive terror of him had awakened an excitement he had thought lost to him, had sharpened his jaded senses delightfully. Just the thought of her young, lush, heavy body even now brought a slight moisture to the palms of his hands, a stirring of his body. And she was his for the taking. For nothing. The look on Victor's face told him so. He leaned back, drew on his cigarette, waiting.

Anna loved Easter. She was not in any true sense religious but, encouraged by her grandfather, who had taken her from babyhood to the magnificent cathedrals of Moscow's Kremlin, she had for as long as she could remember been fascinated by the rich and ancient rituals of the Orthodox Church. She loved too the settings – those dark cathedrals, extravagantly gilded and bejewelled, their shadowed spaces lit by the candles of generations of the faithful and scented by the incense of centuries of worship. The opulence of vestment and altar, the glimmer of gold, the grave-faced icons bedecked with a king's ransom of precious metal and stone, induced in her a feeling of awed wonder; not it must be admitted simply at the glory of the sacrificed God to whom they were dedicated, but at the human and artistic achievement that these vast and lavishly decorated fantasies of faith represented. And then, of course, there was the music. Whilst Lenka and the others had fidgeted from foot to foot, or traipsed to the benches at the back where the very young and the very old were allowed to rest, even as a child she would stand like a statue through the longest liturgy, enthralled by the haunting beauty of the voices that lifted, like the voices of angels, to the vaulted, domed and ornamented ceilings in the solemn and intricate chants and harmonies of the Church.

On Thursday of Holy Week she went to the evening service of the Passions of Our Lord with her mother, father and a grumbling Margarita who looked the very picture of an angel with her lighted candle shining upon her fair and pretty face. Lenka and Dmitri had both come down with what Anna suspected were very convenient chills.

Spring, at last and quite suddenly, had arrived. The combination of an early Easter and a late cold snap had disguised it until now, but the ice was all but gone from the river, the wind had lost its cutting winter's edge, and the smell of hyacinths was in the air.

'Papa, we may go to see the procession at St Isaac's with Uncle Andrei, mayn't we?' Anna had seen little of her uncle since the night of Margarita's play, but his invitation was firmly lodged in her mind, and she did not entirely trust her mother to pursue it. She was well aware that Varya's idea of civilized amusement probably did not include watching a religious procession in St Isaac's Square in the middle of a still-chilly night.

'What? Oh – yes, I suppose so.' Victor's voice was abstracted. The service, unexpectedly, had awakened his conscience, and it was a more uncomfortable experience than he cared to admit. 'Yes. Of course.'

Anna tucked Margarita's hand more firmly into the crook of her arm, smiling.

Margarita wrinkled her small nose ferociously. She glanced back at her parents, lowered her voice to a fierce hiss. 'Anna! I don't have to go, do I?'

Anna shook her head. 'Of course not. No-one has to, if they don't want to.'

They walked a few steps, Margarita trying to adjust her step to her taller sister's strides. Suddenly, unexpectedly and infectiously, she giggled. 'Anna?'

'Mm?'

'Do you want to know a secret?'

Anna sent her a small, suspiciously quizzical look. 'Whose secret?' She knew better than to believe that her younger sister would give away a secret of her own.

'Dima's.' Margarita's brilliant blue eyes gleamed with mischief.

'If it's Dima's secret you shouldn't tell me.' But Anna could not resist laughter.

'He's in love with Natalia!' Margarita let out a small squeal of laughter, quickly subdued. 'Natalia! That little mouse! Can you believe it?'

'Oh, Rita, come! You shouldn't –'

'It's true! I promise! I've seen them.'

Anna's eyes widened. 'Seen them?'

Rita tossed her head, irritated. 'You know – seen the way they look at each other.'

'Ritashka!' In appalled amusement Anna resorted to the teasing baby name that she knew her sister heartily disliked. 'What ever can you mean? They're children!'

Margarita's chin came up. 'Natalia,' she said, with a certain ominous dignity, 'is the same age as I am.'

'Oh, Margarita!' Anna gave in at last to open laughter. 'No-one is the same age as you are!'

Her sister smiled, pleased. 'You just wait and see,' she said. 'You just wait and see.' They walked on for a few moments in silence. Then Margarita spoke again, an edge of petulance to her voice. 'You'd think that Uncle Mischa and Aunt Zhenia would have invited us for the whole of the Easter feast, wouldn't you? I mean, they have that lovely house, and *plenty* of room.'

Anna, having seen at first hand the grandiose preparations that were going on in the house on the Fontanka, was only too pleased not to be too closely included in the Bourlovs' Easter celebrations. 'We're going on Monday. Be satisfied with that.'

'I shan't be satisfied with anything.' Margarita's young voice held a note of adult and steely determination that might to a more experienced ear have been disturbing. 'One day, you'll see, I shall have my own Easter celebrations. The best in St Petersburg. And I shall be the one to decide whether Cousin

Katya and her friends come on Monday –' she skipped a little, to keep up with her sister '– or on Tuesday!'

Saturday was a day of frantic activity. There was last-minute shopping to be done, the final touches to be put to the Easter food, the apartment to be rearranged to accommodate family and guests. By many standards the Shalakov celebrations were very modest indeed; there was only the immediate family, Andrei, and from the workshop Pyotr Pyotrovich who, widowed, lived alone and Andrei's young protégé Vladimir, whose family were in Archangel, too far to travel for the festival. Late in the evening the Easter Table was laid, with the best china, cutlery and glass, the centrepiece a pyramid of Dmitri's eggs: sapphire and vermilion, gold and emerald.

Anna stepped back, hands on hips. 'There. That looks lovely. Now, come on everyone – Uncle Andrei said to be downstairs by a quarter past eleven.'

In the event almost everyone had elected to go to watch the procession; even Margarita had decided that she could not resist the opportunity to stay up so late. So everyone but old Nanny Irisha – who had declared that God would well understand that her old bones were better off by the kitchen stove than galivanting about St Petersburg on a chilly spring evening – and the cook Sonya, who, duty done, was spending the next few days with her own family in the Vyborg district, trooped down the stairs to collect Andrei before stepping out into the street and making their way to the great cathedral in St Isaac's Square. Others were heading in the same direction, in couples and in groups. The streets of the city held a muted excitement. Anna slipped through the group until she was walking next to Andrei. She linked her arm with his. 'Thank you for having such a lovely idea.'

He smiled faintly, but did not reply.

'It will be very beautiful, I should think?'

'Yes.'

'You've been before, I suppose, often?'

He nodded.

'Did you – did you used to come with your wife?'

There was a moment's pause. 'Yes. Yes, I did. Excuse me a

moment, Anna. Victor – a word with you –?' With a firmness that was all but brusque he disentangled his arm and lengthened his stride to where Victor and Varya walked in the front.

The small incident was over in seconds. Anna tucked her hand back into her muff. The rebuff had been unmistakable. All the small suspicions that she had been trying to dismiss over the past busy days crystallized, suddenly, into bitter conviction. He *was* avoiding her. She had not imagined the constraint that had fallen between them, the faint coldness in his manner on the few occasions they had spoken. But – what had she done? Why had he changed so? They had been such good friends – what in heaven's name had happened to change that? She swallowed, but the lump that had suddenly grown in her throat refused to budge. She clenched her jaw.

'Just look at all the people – the whole of Petersburg must be here!' Margarita was fairly dancing with excitement, but her voice was hushed.

Literally thousands of people were massed in the square, still and quiet, most heads bowed in prayer. Each held a lighted candle, making the huge square a sea of glimmering light, and in the centre of the silent congregation stood the great cathedral, lit and decked for this joyous festival. From within came the sound of music.

Anna's happy excitement had evaporated. Exaggerated by hurt every small, and until now disregarded, incident of the past days was moving in angry procession through her mind. She took the candle Seraphima handed her, folded it in her hands, bowed her head, her eyes riveted, unseeing, upon the flame. Why? Why was he behaving so? She was not imagining it; his attitude to her had changed utterly. What had happened to those happy times of laughter and music? What, oh what, had she *done*?

The candle flame blurred suddenly. Terrified someone might notice her tears, she turned her head, blinking. And found herself looking straight into the eyes of her uncle, standing a little behind her, his gaze, over the candle he held, steadily upon her, and in his eyes, usually so mild and so merry, a look of such clear anguish that it all but stopped her heart. In that moment, lit by candlelight, it seemed to her that the image of his face would be branded upon her memory for ever. Bareheaded he stood, the shock of silvered hair catching the moving light, the planes and angles of his sensitive face shadowed. So sudden had been her movement that he had had no time to turn away, no chance to hide that unguarded look of hunger, which even in her inexperience the woman in her could not help but recognize. Eyes locked, they stood like statues, unsteady candlelight flickering between them.

The midnight chimes sounded. Heads lifted. A murmur ran around the vast square. The heavy cathedral doors opened and the glittering head of the Easter procession appeared at the top of the steps above the crowd.

In a dream, Anna turned to watch. In all its stately and ceremonial splendour the great procession moved down the steps into the square, voices lifted in magnificent song. '*Khristos Voskryese!* – Christ is Risen!' Choir and clergy carried high the breathtakingly beautiful jewel-encrusted icons for which the cathedral of St Isaac's was famous, which glittered and gleamed in the light of the massed candles, each one of them a gift of thanks from someone recovered by the grace of God from serious illness. Jewelled and embroidered vestments shimmered, aglow with colour, as their wearers moved with measured tread around the cathedral, the Easter Anthem swelling again – '*Khristos Voskryese!*' Incense lifted into the still air.

Tears were running quite openly down Anna's face; though whether their cause lay in the overawing and emotional scene before her or in the intolerable confusion of her own feelings she could not herself have said. She saw the gleam of tears on other faces, brightness in other eyes. It was hard to resist such splendour and such fervour.

'*Khristos Voskryese!*'

And '*Voistinu Voskryese! –* He is risen indeed!' responded the crowd, joyfully. The procession had returned to the steps, was moving slowly back into the great building. The bells of St Isaac's and of all the other churches and cathedrals across the city had begun to ring, peal upon peal, a carillon of rejoicing. Easter greetings were being exchanged, as stranger saluted stranger in the brotherhood of the Resurrection.

'Christ is Risen!'

'He is risen indeed!'

Kisses were exchanged. Anna dashed her hand across her eyes, bent to kiss Margarita, proffered her cheek to her mother and then her father, turned at last to where Andrei had stood, watching her.

Her uncle had gone.

'Where's Andrei?' Victor's voice was surprised, a little testy.

Anna's eyes searched the crowd, hunting for the unmistakable thatch of silver, but could catch not a glimpse of it.

'Anna? Have you seen your uncle?'

'He – he was here. A short while ago.'

Varya shrugged. 'He must have got lost in the crowd. Never mind. We'd better be off. Andrei is perfectly capable of finding his own way home. Time the children were in bed. Goodness, those bells are enough to give one a migraine! Seraphima, take Dima's other arm please, we mustn't get separated. Anna! For goodness' sake, what are you dreaming about? Do come along – we have a busy day ahead tomorrow –'

Anna took one last long, urgent look across the heads of the milling crowds, but there was no sign of Andrei.

'Come on, Anna.' Sleepily Margarita took her hand. 'Mama's waiting.'

Obediently Anna turned, her arm about her younger sister, and followed the others out of the square.

Behind them the bells pealed, joyfully, as if for the wedding of princely lovers.

CHAPTER FIVE

Anna was not entirely surprised when Andrei did not turn up at the Shalakov apartment on the following day at the agreed time; nor, in her confused state of mind, could she honestly decide in her heart between relief and bitter disappointment at his absence. After an all but sleepless night, in the dark hours of which her emotions had seesawed alarmingly between an overwhelming and indisputably reckless elation and something uncomfortably close to guilty terror, she was not unhappy to have a little more time to collect her thoughts and feelings before facing her uncle again.

'He'll be here, Mama, don't fuss. There –' Her heart all but jumped from her breast at the sound of the doorbell. She was astounded that her voice remained perfectly calm. '– that's probably him now.'

But it was not. It was Pyotr and Vladimir, each carrying an Easter gift of eggs – Pyotr's a small but very pretty porcelain one for his hostess and chocolate eggs for the children, and Vladimir's made of papier mâché and decorated with pressed flowers, the largest and most elaborate of these pretty novelties presented shyly to a surprised Anna; a gift that caused Margarita to open wide, interested eyes full of graceless speculation. The formal Easter greetings were exchanged. Neither man had seen Andrei.

'*Voistinu Voskryese.*' Varya nodded, with an absent smile, to Vladimir's greeting. Then, 'It really is too bad of Andrei. He should have been here an hour ago.' She was vexed. Andrei was, after all, the link between the family and their two guests; the atmosphere without him here to bridge these first few awkward moments was stiff with formality. 'Anna, run downstairs and see what's keeping him, would you?'

88

Anna froze. 'I – I – was just going to the kitchen to help Seraphima – '

'I don't see why Seraphima needs any help – everything's done.' Victor was handing round small glasses of vodka. 'Off you go, my dear. Run down and tell your uncle that we're waiting.'

It was of course the most natural request in the world; still she hesitated, biting her lip. Yelena's glance was enquiring, her mother's impatient.

Anna, with no possible excuse to offer, snatched her shawl from the back of a chair and went.

The door to Andrei's work room was unlocked. She pushed it open. The work room was empty, and unusually chill. The stove had gone out. Almost certainly that must mean that Andrei had not come home at all last night; Anna had never known him let the stove go out in this room – except on the warmest of summer days he kept it going, she knew, to keep the even temperature and dry atmosphere necessary for his craft. The door to his living room stood ajar. Literally weak-kneed with relief, she had turned to leave when a stirring of movement arrested her. Glass clinked upon glass.

Very, very slowly she turned back, moved quietly to the half-open door.

Andrei sat in an armchair beside another cold stove. On the floor beside him was a bottle, almost empty. In his hand, lax upon the arm of the chair, was a glass, filled to the brim.

Anna pushed the door, and let it swing inwards, creaking, until it stood wide open. There was a moment's silence in which neither of them moved. Then he lifted his eyes to hers for the briefest of seconds before, with no word, tossing the drink back in a single swallow, and reaching for the bottle again. There was another bottle, Anna saw, completely empty, lying on the floor by his foot.

She watched him as with surprisingly steady movements he poured more vodka into the glass. His hair was tousled, his shirt and breeches a little crumpled, but beyond that he showed small evidence of having been drinking all night; which she could not help but assume was what he had been doing. The room was very cold.

She could not think of a single thing to say.

He was watching her with apparent unsurprise and unnerving intentness.

'Mama –' she began, and had to cough to ease her dry throat. 'Mama sent me down – to remind you –' the words tailed off.

'Ah. Yes.' Carefully he tipped the last of the contents of the glass down his throat, stood the glass precisely upon the floor beside the bottle. 'The Easter Table. Pardon me. I had forgotten the time.' He stood up. In silence she watched him as he reached for a cravat that hung over the back of the chair, walked to the mirror that hung on the wall and with steady fingers expertly tied it. His velvet jacket hung behind the door. Anna stepped to one side, still watching him, as he took it and shrugged it onto his shoulders, ran his hands over his untidy hair, slicking it down. For the space of several breaths they stood, unmoving in the cold, quiet room.

'Andrei –' Anna began.

His good hand moved, swiftly, a cold finger lifted and laid briefly upon her mouth. 'No, Anna. No. Say nothing.' He was, she sensed now, though nothing in his voice or his demeanour proclaimed it, very drunk indeed. 'That's best, isn't it? Say absolutely nothing. That way you're safe. And that's what we must do, above all things. Keep Anna safe.'

He turned abruptly from her, went into the work room, walking quickly towards the door.

'Andrei!'

The tone of her voice stopped him in his tracks. He stood for a moment, quite still, his back to her, his hand on the door handle, his narrow shoulders slightly and defensively hunched before, slowly, he turned back.

Her eyes searched his face and for that one moment he allowed it, making no attempt to shield himself. 'What are we going to do?' she asked after a very long moment, softly.

'Nothing.' His obstinate calm was totally at odds with the tension that rang between them like a bell. 'Absolutely nothing. We're going to say nothing, and do nothing. That way –'

'Anna will be safe,' she finished for him, bleakly.

'Yes.' He turned again, leaving her.

She lifted her chin, sharply. 'And if I don't want to be safe?'

Never in a long life did she know what prompted those quick, defiant words.

She heard the break in the rhythm of his footsteps upon the stone stairs, heard it resume again, steady and clear. She ran to the door. He was already a flight above her.

'Andrei!'

He turned; slight, poised, graceful, distant. 'Come, Anna,' he said, 'Christ is risen. Indeed He is risen. They're waiting for us.'

He led the way up to the apartment, Anna following silently behind.

'Volodya's in love with you!' Margarita squealed with laughter and ducked as Anna shied a cushion at her, half-heartedly. 'He *is*! Anyone could see it! He mooned around behind you like a – like a lovesick calf!'

'Don't be ridiculous, Rita. Go to sleep.'

'I can't. I'm not in the least bit tired. Wasn't Uncle Andrei funny? I didn't know he could do silly tricks like that.'

'No. Neither did I.'

'It was a shame he couldn't stay to hear you play. Is he coming to Aunt Zhenia's tomorrow?'

'No. He has other plans.'

'You should ask Volodya.' Margarita giggled from beneath the bedclothes. 'He'd come like a shot.'

'Rita!'

But it was true. That poor Vladimir appeared to have lost his heart and his good sense all at one go had been painfully obvious to everyone. He had trailed behind Anna all day; she had fallen over his feet every time she had turned around. He it had been who had prevailed upon her to play for them all; with the predictable result that Andrei had excused himself, gracefully and perfectly believably, and left. And with him the light had gone from the day. Whatever she felt for him – however wrong it might be – she could no longer lie to herself. A room without Andrei in it was empty indeed, and held neither joy nor laughter.

But he was her uncle. Her father's brother. It was wicked to feel so. Wicked! She brushed her hair fiercely, tugging painfully.

'I suppose Katya has some marvellous new creation to wear

tomorrow?' Margarita leaned on one elbow, her head propped on her hand. 'And I'll have to wear that silly childish sailor dress that I wore today!'

'Lenka and I will be wearing the same as we wore today as well.'

'Yes, but you don't *care*!' Margarita threw herself back on her pillow, fair hair spread becomingly about her face, looking up at the ceiling. 'Oh, I do so wish I could grow up! I sometimes think it'll just never happen!' She stretched, hands clasped above her. 'One day I shall have so many pretty things that I'll be able to wear a different outfit every day for a month! I bet Katya could do that now, the lucky thing! And I'll bet she has loads of young men just queuing up to marry her. I wonder if she has a lover? I would if I were her. I'd have two. An old one and a young one.' She was eyeing her older sister slyly, waiting for the shocked reaction.

Anna refused to rise to the bait. 'Margarita, you don't know what you're talking about. Now do be quiet and go to sleep.'

'Where's Lenka?'

'She's helping Seraphima tidy up. Now, you want to look your best tomorrow, don't you? Well, you'd better go to sleep then. Or you'll have bags under your eyes.'

Grumbling still, Margarita tossed onto her side, burying her face in the bedclothes.

Anna continued brushing her hair, counting the strokes – one – two – three – four – anything to prevent herself from thinking –

In the parlour Lenka picked up the last of the glasses, dropped one, saved it before it rolled off the table. Her father, sitting comfortably in an armchair reading a news journal, stirred, peered over the top of the paper. 'Ah. Yelena.'

'Yes, Papa. I'm just helping Seraphima to clear away.'

'Ah,' he said again, then, 'Yes.'

Lenka, his eyes upon her, promptly dropped the glass again. Her lank hair had fallen free of its pins and straggled about her face. She tried to tuck a strand behind her ear, and almost lost the other glass. He winced. Where in the world did this awkward, overblown cuckoo come from? Her gracelessness appalled him. The very look in her eyes – half-fearful, half-defiant, wholly troubled – was enough to try the patience of the most reasonable of men before she ever opened her mouth. What Pavel Petrovich saw in her he simply couldn't understand.

The thought brought a nasty twinge of conscience; more than a twinge. Even a father could see the purely physical and sensual attraction of Yelena's full breasts, her strong and supple waist, the curve of her wide hips, all so much at odds with that plain and unremarkable face. In rare moments of honesty he had to admit that he was not altogether easy in the bargain he had struck with Donovalov; but then – life being what it was, what could a man do? And in the world's terms the man was a catch for such as Yelena; where else would she get such an offer? This was no fly-by-night boy but a grown man, of some substance and with a Government position. He'd be good for her; of course he would. The disquieting matter of reputation, and of some vague gossip about a dead wife, all that was pure nonsense. Hearsay. Any man made enemies as he fought his way to success. Lenka would have her own establishment, a husband with some little wealth and much ambition. There seemed small doubt that Donovalov would go far. The thought brought a wry twist to Victor's mouth. Oh, yes – Pavel Petrovich would certainly go far. And, with any measure of luck, his father-in-law with him. He was surely entitled to some return on the outrageous sums the man had extorted from him? But – perhaps he should in fairness prepare Yelena? Her eighteenth birthday was at the end of July, and upon that day she was to become betrothed; the wedding, Donovalov was insisting, should be no more than a couple of months later. Sooner or later – for reasons as much practical as emotional – she must be told.

'Lenka, my dear –'

'Yes, Papa?' The girl turned that closed, wary face to him.

'Your eighteenth birthday – it's this summer, isn't it?'

'Yes, Papa.' Lenka eyed him. His square face was unusually benign, his eyes held hers, smiling a little. Could it be? Had Anna kept her promise after all?

'We have to talk about the future, don't we? Such a big girl you're becoming –'

The jocularity rang false. She hesitated, and then could

hesitate no longer. 'Anna's spoken to you? She's asked about the University courses?'

There was a long and uncomfortable silence. 'I beg your pardon?'

Lenka was still clutching the glasses. She scowled down at them. 'Anna – said she would speak to you – about the University –'

Victor shook his head testily, rattled his paper. 'In the name of God, girl, what are you talking about now? No. That isn't what I meant at all. Of course not. I was going to –' He stopped. The glasses clinked nervily in Lenka's hands. His customary irritation reasserted itself. 'Oh, for heaven's sake, child, go to bed. I'll talk to you another time. And send Seraphima in here; the stove needs making up.'

The bedroom was dark, and quiet. One lamp still burned, left for her. 'Anna?' Lenka hissed. 'Anna!'

Anna's breath was as even as a child's, the bedclothes tucked to her chin, her wiry, reddish hair spread about the pillow.

'Anna!' There was a thread of miserable anger in Lenka's voice. But even she could not bring herself to wake the sleeping Margarita with a lifted voice. Rita, once awake, was no easy customer to persuade back to sleep again.

Anna, with difficulty, kept her breathing level and quiet. Whatever grouse Lenka had now could most certainly wait until morning. She – Anna – couldn't – she wouldn't! – be soothing, rational and conciliatory. She felt none of those things. She felt, at this moment, utterly confused and wretched. And there was worse. So desperately at this moment did she herself need to talk to someone that she knew that just one word, one gesture of enquiry or affection from her sister would open floodgates that must at all cost be kept clamped shut. She gritted her teeth.

Lenka, preparing for bed, blundered about the darkened bedroom, muttering to herself, her movements angrily sharp. Anna tensed a little as her sister slid into the bed beside her, but Lenka did not attempt to wake her.

In the hall outside the bedroom the tall clock melodically struck eleven.

*   *   *

94

The apartment on the Fontanka was full of flowers, crowded with people and bursting at the seams with food and drink. There were bowls of hyacinths everywhere, filling the rooms with their sweet and heady perfume. With every moment it seemed to Anna that other guests arrived, calling and laughing as they swept through the great revolving doors and mounted the graceful sweep of the stairs to the front door of the Bourlovs' home; the formal Easter greeting rang through the magnificent rooms with laughter and with kisses.

'Oh, Anna, isn't this just *wonderful*?' Margarita looked about her with eager, fascinated eyes. The apartment was indeed a grand one. The small but charming ballroom in which the Easter tables had been laid had two tall windows with balconies that overlooked the road and the glittering waters of the canal. The room was already crowded and abuzz with conversation. Anna recognized hardly anyone. She smiled at her young sister who was standing on tiptoe gazing about her with avid curiosity and all but jumping up and down with excitement. 'Whoever do you think that lady over there might be? She looks *terribly* grand! Are they real diamonds, do you think? She's got an awful lot of them if they are. And – Anna, look! – isn't that someone famous? I'm *sure* I recognize his face!'

'Rita, for heaven's sake, don't stare at people so – it's really very rude!'

'And the handsome gentleman with the splendid moustache – I know him! It's Scriabin, isn't it? Papa took us to see him. Do you think he'll play for us?'

Anna followed her sister's gaze. 'Yes, it is.' Her heart sank like lead. Her father had agreed with what had seemed to Anna to be ironic enthusiasm to Uncle Mischa's genial suggestion that she should play for his guests after lunch. Anna herself had agreed readily; not for a moment had she expected such a huge and august gathering; still less had she expected one of the city's most respected musicians and composers to be in the audience.

'Uncle Mischa must know just about everyone in St Petersburg.' Margarita bestowed a winning smile upon a portly gentleman, who returned it with delighted interest. 'I'm going to find Dima.' Before her sister could restrain her she had disappeared smartly into the crowd.

Anna stepped back a little, into the shadow of a spreading palm, stood alone, watching the greetings, the flicker of fans, the colourful movement of the throng. Dresses were sumptuous, jewels gleamed, brilliant uniforms studded the room. Everyone seemed to know everyone else. The noise, echoing to the high, ornate ceiling, was almost deafening. In her green woollen dress, demurely cut and, she was aware, just a little short, she felt dowdy and out of place.

'Tea, Mamselle? Or liqueur?' An immaculately-dressed young manservant hovered at her side, a silver tray in white-gloved hands.

'Oh, yes – tea please.' She took a glass of tea, stood clutching it as the man moved away leaving her alone again.

'Anna! Darling, what on earth are you doing drinking that beastly stuff?' Cheerfully and unceremoniously her cousin Katya, appearing at her side like an extremely pretty and animated Jack-in-the-box, took the glass from her hand and deposited its contents into the palm. 'Come and get some food – there's champagne over there. Never drink tea when there's champagne on offer – it's terribly bad for you, you know!' Laughing, her cousin caught her hand and towed her through the crowds, gaily returning the greetings of her parents' guests on the way. Katya was wearing the coral silk that rustled and swirled about her as she moved. Margarita's eyes had almost fallen out of her head when she had seen it. Anna felt like the dying tail of a glittering comet as she allowed herself to be drawn in her cousin's wake. She acknowledged introductions with nods and smiles, Katya giving her no time for any more elaborate courtesy.

'Here we are. Food. Thank goodness. I'm starving.'

They had arrived at the far side of the room where stood three long tables spread with the most astounding array of food that Anna had ever seen. Dishes of caviar, grey, black and orange, smoked and marinated fish, pâtés, hams and chickens. There were pickled mushrooms and cucumbers, whole cold salmon, baby sturgeon in aspic. An entire table was devoted to a variety of cakes, pastries and sweetmeats. Iced bottles of champagne and of the inevitable vodka were set in clusters at intervals along the tables.

'Champagne.' Katya handed her a tall glass filled to the brim with the sparkling liquid. 'The very best.'

'Katya, I'm playing later on! I'm already terrified enough!'

'All the more reason. Nothing like a glass of this to soothe the nerves and boost the confidence!' Katya stood back, eyeing her a little critically. 'Have you brought another dress?'

Knowing her cousin as she did, and in the light of the quite surprising affection that had grown between them in the past months, Anna could not take offence at her outspokenness. She laughed. 'Katya – of course not! I haven't *got* another dress!'

'What a pity. A pity too that you're so much taller than I – you could have borrowed something.' Katya sipped her champagne pensively. 'I know! I've got a very pretty scarf, and some earrings – you ought to wear something more dramatic, you know.' She scooped the champagne bottle from the table, took Anna's glass from her. 'Tell you what, I'll take charge of this, you get a couple of plates of food – plenty of black caviar, please, and some of that smoked salmon – and we'll nip along to my room and see what we can find. It'll be more comfortable anyway – I hate eating standing up. Oh, Mother of Angels, look out! Here come the two mamas. Hurry up, Anna, or they'll nail us to the floor in the cause of good manners!'

Anna scrambled some food onto the plates and the two girls fled through the crowd, laughing. Katya's mother, watching her daughter's disappearing back, shook her head, smiling. 'What is the girl up to now? Not more mischief, I hope.'

'Anna's with her,' Varya said, as if that simple fact made any such notion highly unlikely.

Which, Zhenia thought, with a twinge of sympathy for her young niece, it very probably did. One did not somehow associate Anna with mischief. A pity really. The child did not seem to get much fun out of life. 'Well, little sister – we haven't seen much of each other over these past weeks. Are you enjoying St Petersburg?'

Varya set down her empty glass, tried unsuccessfully to keep her eyes from widening at the sight of the laden tables. 'Well enough, thank you. The apartment is a little small of course – but then it's only a temporary arrangement, Andrei found the place for us and he really has very little idea of the needs of a family. Just as soon as Victor is settled on the Nevsky we'll start to look for something a little better.' Her eyes flickered to the luxury that surrounded her. She lifted her small, pretty chin. 'Nothing too ostentatious, of course.'

Zhenia smothered a smile. Her younger sister's envy of her own better fortunes, expressed often in small, sanctimonious pinpricks of apparent disapproval, amused rather than dismayed her. Varya's greeting to her that day: 'My dear – what a very pretty dress! It must have cost a fortune! I've noticed that shade of blue is very popular this season, isn't it? Absolutely *everyone* is wearing it!' had already been relayed to a grinning Mischa, who found his sister-in-law, in small doses, highly entertaining.

'Zhenia Petrovna – and your charming sister! Two lovely little birds on a single branch, so to speak! What luck! Come, ladies, allow me to serve you. The caviar I must tell you is absolutely delicious.' A large man, flamboyantly uniformed, bowed extravagantly before them, took Varya's extended hand to his lips.

'General Stonberg,' Zhenia acknowledged, with a small smile.

Varya, tiny beside him, sent him her most alluring look.

Zhenia, gracefully, disentangled her hand from the General's hard grip. 'I really should see to my other guests. General – I may leave my sister in your capable hands? Varya, as the General says, do try the caviar – it really is very good. And General – may I suggest a small glass of that excellent cherry brandy for my Varya Petrovna?' With some relief she left them together. Give Varya a solid gold, prettily-uniformed General to charm and she'd be well occupied for the rest of the afternoon. And so would he.

Margarita, installed a little grumpily beside her brother upon a pair of intricate, gilded chairs, watched the proceedings with avid eyes. 'Dima, honestly, aren't you in the least bit interested in what's going on?'

Dmitri shrugged. 'I'm hungry, if that's interested. Come and get some food. I saw it earlier. There's absolutely *everything*.'

Margarita's eyes were upon a group of young men in uniform who lounged elegantly, short furred jackets slung with negligent grace from epauletted shoulders, vodka glasses in hand, surveying the room with a kind of arrogant disinterest and laughing a little too loudly at their own jokes. 'You go,' she said, absently.

'Aren't you *hungry*?' Her brother looked at her, startled. 'Do you feel all right?'

Margarita tutted irritably. 'Of course I'm all right. We don't all live for our stomachs you know – good heavens! Look at Anna!'

Their Uncle Mischa, Anna smiling shyly beside him, had appeared at the door. 'Ladies and gentlemen –'

'What's she done to her hair?' wondered Margarita. 'And where did she get that scarf? And the earrings – goodness, they look like a gypsy's!' She laughed a little, understanding. 'A gypsy with good taste. They must be Katya's. Well, who would have believed it?'

Anna's coppery hair, usually pulled severely back to reduce its wiry mass, had been piled softly upon her head. Tendrils escaped, artfully casual, tempering the severe lines of her face. Swinging golden earrings glinted, emphasizing the graceful length of her neck. Her narrow shoulders and the stark neckline of the green woollen dress were softened by a scarf of silken blues and greens. The effect was striking. She carried in her hand the violin her grandfather had made fifty years before her birth. Her father's peace offering.

'Please – if you would find a seat?' Mischa's pleasant voice lifted again. 'I'm delighted to announce that my charming and talented niece, Anna Victorovna, has agreed to entertain us. It is our hope that afterwards –' dark eyes gleaming Mischa bowed a little to where his most famous musical guest stood, smiling '– Alexander Nikolayevich – the great Scriabin – will also play for us.' A small, excited murmur rippled around the room. There was a buzz of activity as chairs were pulled out from the perimeter and set into groups. Ladies spread their skirts gracefully, fluttering their fans. Gentlemen settled the tails of their morning suits and hastily replenished glasses.

Considering the circumstances Anna played well, and she knew it. As she gained in confidence, and as she caught the wandering attention of her audience, she found herself playing not so much for them as for herself. Deliberately she had decided to play, for this most Russian of festivals, the music of only Russian composers – music that she and Andrei had studied, analysed, discussed, until their music came to her as naturally as breathing. Rimsky-Korsakov, Glazunov, Tchaikovsky; and the members of her audience loved it. When she finished with the wild Tsigane melody that Andrei had taught her, the most bored of them came to their feet clapping, stamping and laughing delightedly. Flushed and smiling, she bowed and made to leave the stage to the revered Scriabin. Whatever else, she had not disgraced herself. And for those fleeting moments she had been entirely happy; confusion had fled. The great pianist captured her hand, led her onto the floor again. Flowers flew, pulled from Zhenia's careful arrangements. Katya winked. Her parents were looking at her with slightly bemused pride. Margarita and Dima clapped enthusiastically. Only Lenka sat, still and unsmiling; Anna caught a brief glimpse of her before being swept into Uncle Mischa's enthusiastic arms. 'Anna, my love, what talent!'

Scriabin was settled at the piano. An awed hush fell. As the first notes lifted into the quiet air Katya appeared at Anna's side, slipped an arm about her waist. 'Well done,' she whispered. 'You were splendid!'

The master played Chopin. Even the most restive guest stilled. The applause at the end was deafening. The short and intricate virtuoso piece he chose as an encore brought an even greater clamour.

Katya leaned to her father's ear. 'Anna needs a breath of air,' she shouted through the uproar.

Mischa turned surprised eyes upon his niece who was standing composedly beside her cousin. Anna, who had not heard Katya's words, smiled.

'Perhaps a stroll along the canal?' Katya's face was the very picture of innocence. The applause was dying, chairs were being scraped back against the wall, conversation was lifting again. 'We won't be long, I promise. We'll be back for tea and the dancing.'

'Of course, my dear. But please – not too long, eh? You really mustn't neglect our younger guests you know.'

'Yes, darling Mischischa, I do know. But I can't leave poor Anna to take the air alone, can I?' She kissed him, lightly. 'It must be a great strain you know, playing to such an audience.'

Mischa nodded, patted the surprised Anna's arm solicitously before turning away.

'What was that for?' Anna asked.

Katya giggled. 'In sympathy for the vapours you are resisting so valiantly.'

'I don't have the vapours! I'd go so far as to say I've never had the vapours in my life! Katya, what are you talking about?'

Her cousin slipped a firm hand under her elbow, steered her rapidly towards the open double doors. 'I thought –' she nodded sweetly to an elderly couple, side-stepped them smartly '– that you might enjoy a breath of fresh air. A little stroll. Along the canal.' She held on as Anna tried to release her elbow. 'Half an hour, that's all. It will do you good.'

'Katya!'

'You look a little pale,' her cousin said, solemnly. 'And it was very hot in there.' She was still steering Anna firmly, down the hall towards her bedroom where their outdoor clothes were. 'All that cigarette smoke –'

Anna stopped. Katya, perforce, had to stop too. Anna disengaged her elbow. 'What are you up to?' As always she could not help but smile as her pretty cousin lifted fair, innocent eyebrows.

'Up to? Why, what could I possibly be up to? Oh, come on, Anna. Do let's go for a short stroll? If I have to smile and be polite for a single moment longer I shall burst! There's hardly anyone worth talking to, now is there? And if one other ancient dowager tells me how very grown-up I've become and how amazing it is that I'm not already married with a string of brats about my skirt I shall pull someone's hair out by the roots. Now, you wouldn't want that to happen, would you?'

Anna, still laughing, shook her head. 'All right. No, I shouldn't want that to happen. A stroll it is.' She followed Katya into the large and airy room that was almost the only thing of her cousin's that she truly envied her. 'But – they're right, aren't they?' She caught the short cape that Katya tossed to her, picked up her hat from the bed. 'I suppose you will have to think about marriage?'

'Sooner or later I suppose.' The words were airy. Katya slipped her arms into a neatly fitting green jacket, perched a small feathered hat on her mass of hair, skewered it expertly with a pin, pulled a pair of green kid gloves from a drawer. 'But if I have anything to do with it, it will be later.' She leaned to the mirror, tweaked a few curls about the brim of the hat, caught Anna's eye in the mirror. 'Much, much later!'

They strolled in the early spring sunshine, watching the activity on the canal. The ice was gone, the grip of winter was loosened, and the water flowed again, bright as new-minted coins in the sun. The trees were in bud, a small boy bowled a hoop along the pavement.

And a couple of young men in uniform leaned in apparently casual conversation upon the embankment wall. Anna recognized them both instantly. 'Katya!'

'Isn't it amazing,' her cousin asked, with a bland, disarming smile, 'the people you can come across on the Fontanka on an Easter Monday afternoon?'

'Where did you *go*?' Margarita asked, fiercely. 'I looked *everywhere* for you!'

'Katya wanted to go for a walk,' Anna said. 'We strolled along the canal, that's all.'

Margarita eyed her suspiciously.

Anna returned the look unblinking, suppressing the desire to laugh. I, she thought, am becoming as bad as Katya herself. She had enjoyed the past hour. That both young men undoubtedly had their eyes on the same prize – Katya – had not prevented them from courteous and entertaining conversation with Anna. Katya had flirted outrageously with both of them, Anna had watched, astounded and entertained. Altogether it had been an extremely diverting interlude. She had not even taken Katya to task for her quite shameless scheming; not, she was aware, that it would have done an iota of good if she had.

'Well, do come on, now – the dancing's starting.'

Anna allowed herself to be towed back into the ballroom.

'Oh, Anna, do look – Mama's dancing with that General – he looks like the bear we saw at the circus in Moscow!'

'Rita, honestly!' But her sister's description of the man really was so accurate that she found herself bursting into laughter.

'Oh, and look at Katya! Doesn't she dance well?' There was such longing in the young voice that Anna put a sympathetic arm about her shoulders.

'Rita, darling, don't fret so! And don't wish away your childhood. You'll grow up soon enough, I promise you.' In a second the light-hearted mood engendered by the occasion and her cousin's escapade deserted her. The line of her mouth was suddenly sombre. 'And it isn't that easy, you know. Being grown up.'

Margarita shook her head impatiently. 'Oh, don't be silly, Anna! You sound like Sister Maria at school! And you know what a bore she is! I wonder – could I make a set for my theatre like this room?'

The afternoon passed quickly into evening. To her own surprise Anna was squired onto the dance floor twice, under Margarita's envious eyes, once by an elderly gentleman with twinkling eyes who barely reached to her shoulder and whose paunch was rather more than a slight disadvantage to graceful movement, and once by a nervous young man with vague, short-sighted eyes and spots who said not a word during the whole proceeding. As darkness fell and the older guests began to leave or to repair to the drawing room, where card tables had been set up, a balalaika band in peasant dress took over from the orchestra and the pace of the dancing changed. Young men swept their chosen partners into line as the rhythmic and vibrant traditional melodies of Russia were played. Small circles were formed; the dancers wove in intricate pattern, hands touching and dropping, the girls' eyes demurely downcast. People around the floor turned to watch. Several began to clap in time to the music as the tempo speeded up. As the girls still wove their pretty circles the young men, one by one, leapt to the centre, whirling, stamping, clapping, spinning like tops, heels clicking, booted feet flying, each vying to outdo the other. Many were officers of the Cossack regiments and no strangers to such displays; as many a café owner in St Petersburg whose table tops had been used to stage such competition would have testified.

Margarita was ecstatic. She clapped until her hands hurt, eyes glued to the handsome, arrogantly athletic figures who cut such a dash. One in particular caught her eye; a lithe, dark-haired young man in Cossack uniform who leapt higher and with more grace than any other. She stopped clapping, her gaze riveted upon him.

'Really – it's time we were getting home.' Victor appeared fussily beside Anna and her young sister.

'Oh, Papa, no!' Margarita was agonized.

Her father cast a disapproving glance at the goings-on on the dance floor. 'Anna, where's Yelena?'

'I don't know, Papa. I've hardly seen her all afternoon.' Anna had sought her sister out just once during the day, but her reception had been so cool that she had shrugged and left her to herself. She knew Lenka of old; once the sulks had set in there was little to do about it but to let the mood run its course. Obviously Lenka was annoyed with her; Anna guessed she'd find out soon enough what, if anything, she had done to upset her.

'Well, do find her then. And Dima too.' Victor was not in a good mood. Not only had he had to spend the day surrounded by the all too clear evidence of his brother-in-law Bourlov's material and social successes but his empty-headed wife had made a positive exhibition of herself with that gold-braided hulk of a General. 'Anna! Hurry up!'

'Just a moment, Papa – look – Katya's dancing.'

The music had changed. A man playing an accordion stepped forward. A dozen or more girls, led by Katya, had formed themselves into a line, hands linked, coloured scarves floating from their fingers. They moved sedately, heads poised, feet hidden beneath their long skirts as they glided smoothly into a traditional village dance, weaving and bobbing, ducking beneath the arches of their own lifted arms, their line like a colourful ribbon enlaced about the dance floor. One of the group of young officers began to sing in a deep melodic voice, one or two others joined him, their lighter voices mingling with his in that harmony that was so deeply and so especially Russian. The music changed subtly. The line broke into two, came together, broke again and then linked, scarves drifting gracefully about it. And now the girls were laughing; their tiny steps were as sedate, their backs and shoulders as straight, their heads as haughtily and gracefully lifted. But eyes gleamed from beneath lashes, there was a certain movement of the hips, a seduction in the gestures of scarf-draped hands. Katya, mischief written in every line of her pretty face, eyes downcast in a modesty so false as to be in itself a challenge, led them on. She moved with a grace that brought a smile to the sourest face, gliding like a swan upon water, back straight, arms poised above her head. Several of the card players had come to the door, crowding around to watch. One of the balalaikas began to play, lifting the rhythm, the deep male voices urged the dancers on. They moved faster, the smoothness of their movements unbroken. More instruments took up the challenge; the young men could stand it no more. They swept with a whoop onto the floor, chose a partner – most of whom turned a haughty shoulder in charming pretence of offence – and were off again, on knee and heel and pointed toe, some with more grace than others, all with an infectious energy and vitality that had the onlookers stamping and shouting with them, until in a final crescendo of sound it finished.

Margarita was standing, hands clasped in front of her, as if in a trance.

Victor was rigid with disapproval. 'Anna. Find the others please. Margarita, come. Find your coat please. Margarita!'

His daughter blinked. 'Yes, Papa.' With one long last look at the laughing dancers she turned and preceded her father from the room.

The family walked home almost in silence, each wrapped in thoughts it seemed they did not care to share with others. Varya, dazzled by dreams of conquest, innocently certain that every other female in the room must have envied her her triumph, failed utterly to notice that the quality of her husband's silence was, to say the least, ominous. Yelena, pointedly walking as far from Anna as she could, answered any question addressed to her with a monosyllable. Dmitri's thoughts centred mostly on his regret that he hadn't been able to eat more, whilst both Margarita and Anna, walking together, each had more than enough to occupy her mind and imagination.

It was dark by the time they reached the apartment building. As they approached it Anna could see light glowing from the two windows that were Andrei's. All day she had told herself that she must not see him. That she did not want to see him. That he most certainly would not want to see her –

'Papa – might I pop in to see Uncle Andrei for a moment? I think I left some music in his room.' The words were out with no conscious thought before she could prevent them; it was as if someone else had spoken.

'What? Oh, yes. Of course.' Victor's face was set in forbidding lines. He hardly looked at Anna. He held the outer door open, glowered at the oblivious Varya as she swept past him with the poise of a queen.

'Lenka, would you take my violin?' Anna held out the case.

Lenka shrugged, took it in silence.

Anna turned from them and tapped lightly on Andrei's door. As she pushed it open she heard Margarita say from above her, her voice soft, '– And the uniforms, Mama! Oh, weren't they just the most *handsome* things?'

Andrei was sitting upon his stool at his workbench. He was dressed as he liked in loose shirt and trousers, belted peasant-style about his slight waist. He was intent upon the strong and slender wand of wood upon which he was working, planing the curve of the bow. He glanced up as Anna entered the room, his hands stilled for a moment, then resumed their skilful, sure movements. 'I told you not to come,' he said, quietly.

'I know. I'm sorry. It's just – it's been such a lovely day – I wanted to tell you –' She did not finish the sentence; the words trailed to nothing.

The room fell to a silence broken only by the small sounds of the tiny plane Andrei was using.

Anna crossed the room to stand quietly beside him, watching. She flicked a quick glance to his calm face. Apart from a certain pallor he showed no sign of yesterday's excesses. His eyes were steady upon his work. 'You've changed your hair,' he said.

She was startled. She had, in fact, forgotten. 'I – yes. I suppose I have. Katya did it.'

'How was it? The day?'

'Lovely. It was such a shame you couldn't come. There were hundreds of people, and mountains of food. Mama flirted with a General and I'm afraid Papa isn't best pleased with her. Rita,' she smiled faintly, 'fell in love with a soldier, I think. Dima didn't stop eating all day. He'll be lucky if he isn't sick.' She stopped abruptly. She was babbling, and too well she knew it. 'And you? What did you do?'

'I visited some friends.'

She felt a sudden, irrational and completely unjustifiable surge of jealousy. Friends. Andrei's friends. People who knew him, probably better than she. She picked up a small piece of ebony that lay on the bench, ran her fingers over its smooth and glassy surface, forced lightness into her voice. 'What did you do?'

He shrugged. 'We drank a little. Talked a lot.'

'What about?'

He turned his head, looking at her, a question in his eyes.

'I just wondered,' she said, defensively.

He laid down the baton on which he had been working, swung his feet down from the bar of the stool. 'What do Russians ever speak of? Politics. Religion. The meaning of life.' His long mouth turned down at the corners in a small, half-mocking smile. 'And as always to no avail whatsoever.'

She watched him cross the room to the door that led to the living room.

At the door he turned, poised and impassive. 'Tea?'

She felt the rise of such a conflict of emotions that for a moment she feared she might scream.

'No,' she said, very quietly. 'No tea. Thank you.' The slight, still figure blurred before her eyes. 'Andrei,' she said, hearing her own voice, too loud, childishly out of control. 'Please! I can't bear it that we shouldn't be friends. I can't – bear it.' The tears spilled hot down her cheeks. She did not bother to hide them, nor to brush them away. The lamp light shone on his face as he moved swiftly towards her. A single step took her into his arms. All control lost, she was sobbing furiously now, her body shaking, her head buried in his shoulder. His arm tightened about her; she felt his hand, gentle in her hair. He was murmuring quiet, soothing words that through the storm of her emotions meant nothing; the only thing she was aware of was the feel of his body against hers, the warmth of his skin, the brush of his crisp, thick hair against her cheek. She could not move. She wanted to stay for ever there, pressed so close to him she could hear – feel – the beating of his heart as if it were in her own body.

She lifted her head. And gently he kissed her; tenderly, thoroughly and for a very long time.

At last they drew a little apart. His eyes were open, honest and steady upon her face. Anna could not sustain the look. She bent her head a little. He waited. 'Now you see what's happened to us,' he said, at last.

She said nothing.

'And now you see why we *must* stay away from each other.'

'*No!*' The word was agonized. '*No!* I can't! I've – I've never had anyone – never known anyone –' She stopped, confused, angry with herself at her inarticulate outburst. She took several long, steadying breaths. 'I've never had anyone to love before,' she said; and believed it. She lifted her chin, suddenly sure, suddenly brave. 'You want us to run away from it. You want us to pretend it hasn't happened. Don't you see that we can't do that? We have to face it. Face it!' She stopped, not sure of herself enough to continue.

His expression had changed. He watched her intently, listening.

She stepped a little further from him, her hands still linked in his. 'You're right of course; we mustn't allow this to happen again. But – Andrei – how can we deny our friendship? Our –' she hesitated '– our love?' Her face was still tear-streaked, the fragile skin fiercely flushed. 'The world is such a loveless place,' she whispered, and the tears overflowed again.

'What are you suggesting?' he asked. His warm fingers gripped hers firmly, a lifeline in stormy seas.

'That we don't – can't – throw away something so precious. I don't care what others might think. We know ourselves; we know that something so wonderful can't be wrong. We must be careful, yes. Of each other, and of others. But Andrei – surely that doesn't mean that we must cut ourselves off from each other? You wouldn't harm me – I know you wouldn't. But I'll die, I mean it, I'll *die* if I don't have you to come to. To talk to. To make music with. Andrei, please!' In her innocence the words were spoken in perfect faith and honesty. 'We can be friends, can't we? Loving friends? You can't deny me that?'

He dropped her hand and turned from her.

'Andrei!'

He took a long breath, exhaled very slowly. 'Yes, Anna, of course. We can be friends.'

'And I can come and see you?'

'Yes. You can come to see me. But Anna – bring Lenka, or one of the others. Don't come alone.'

'No. I won't. I promise I won't.' She stood for a moment uncertainly. He did not turn. There was a long moment's silence. Anna turned towards the door. Stopped. Waited.

Andrei neither moved nor spoke.

Longing to touch him, longing to ease the awful tension that she sensed in his grim jaw and tensed shoulders, the feel of his mouth still upon hers, she turned and left. 'Good night,' she said quietly from the door. 'God bless.'

He did not reply.

A moment after the door had shut behind her he began to curse, savagely and steadily. In nearly thirty-five years of life he had acquired a breadth of expression that surprised – and in other circumstances would have amused – him. After a few colourful moments he stopped, walked purposefully to the door, taking his jacket from the hook on the back of it as he passed and flinging it about his shoulders. He did not bother to shut the door, but left it swinging open behind him.

Upstairs Anna excused herself swiftly on the grounds of tiredness and went to bed. Hardly anyone noticed. Dmitri was being excessively sick, attended by the stoic Seraphima and a Varya who, the nursing of the afflicted not exactly being her forte, looked about to join him at the bowl. Lenka was sitting hunched in a chair in the parlour, her nose determinedly in a book, ignoring the world; Anna did not even bother to bid her good night. Margarita was blissfully asleep, her expression seraphic.

Anna hurried into the big bed, pulled the clothes over her head. Only then did she allow herself to think about what had happened downstairs. She could not recall a word that either of them had said. She remembered only the feel of Andrei's body against hers, and above all the touch of his lips. Exhausted, she slept surprisingly quickly.

Andrei tipped the dregs of the bottle into his glass. A dark-haired girl with gypsy eyes snaked an arm about his waist. He shook his head, smiling. She pouted, and left him. On the far side of the room a girl stood with a sailor, laughing. She was tall, and thin, and her hair glinted copper in the light. Andrei crooked a finger at the man who served behind the bar. The man leaned to him. A couple of glittering coins changed hands. The man slipped from behind the bar and crossed the room.

Andrei tipped the glass, and drained it.

The red-headed girl turned disdainfully from the barman, stopped, took something from him, lifted her head and looked across the crowded café.

Andrei watched her.

She spoke to the sailor, shook his hand from her arm and began to move through the crowds to where Andrei sat, waiting.

CHAPTER SIX

Lenka returned the respectful greetings of her father's two dapper young assistants as she walked through the shop and mounted the wide staircase that led to Victor's office. The walk from the apartment had been a pleasant one; before she returned home she would be able to stroll along the Nevsky and look in the shop windows. Perhaps it wasn't such a nuisance after all that Anna had not been available to carry her mother's message to her father.

She tapped on the door; had pushed it open before she had had time to register that the voice that had answered was not Victor's.

Pavel Petrovich turned from the window, smiling. The chair behind Victor's desk was empty.

Lenka stopped in the open doorway as if struck. 'I – was looking for Papa –'

'So am I, my dear Lenka. So am I. Or, should I say, I'm waiting for him. I have to leave Petersburg for a little while and we have some unfinished business to attend to before I go. They tell me downstairs that he'll be back at any time. Come in, child, come in. It's draughty with the door open.'

She trembled quite literally upon the verge of turning tail and running like a frightened child; and she could see that he knew it. His smile widened. The rapacious eyes flickered, and the skin of her body crept, raising the hairs on forearms and neck. 'I'll come back later,' she said.

'No.' He crossed the room in a couple of quick strides, took her arm and drew her into the room, pushing the door shut behind her. 'Oh, no, my dear. I'm certain your father would rather that you stayed to keep me company until his arrival. Don't you think?'

She did not reply.

He stepped away from her, perched himself upon the corner of the desk, arms crossed, one leg swinging, watching her.

The familiar, paralysing panic rose; she could barely breathe. His gaze quite deliberately dropped to her breasts, lingered there. When he slipped from the desk and moved towards her she stood petrified, rooted to the spot. 'There are many things I shall teach you, Lenka,' he said, softly. 'Oh, yes. Many things.'

'Wh-what do you mean?' His face, with its slanted bones and narrow eyes, seemed to her to be the cruellest thing she had ever encountered. Everything about it terrified her; the eyes, though lit with that venomous light, were cold, the line of mouth harsh. She felt as an insect must feel, pinned live and helpless to a table top. When he lifted his hands to her breasts she turned her head sharply from him, her face twisted in fear and in disgust. His touch at first was surprisingly light; expertly he roused her. She clenched her teeth. He laughed. And then he had her nipples between his fingers, pinching viciously, deliberately hurting. She gasped with pain, tried to pull from him, but in a quick movement he had her wrist in his hand, her arm pinned behind her arched back. Easily holding her he bent his head, closed his lips and then his teeth upon her nipples through the material of her dress, deliberately biting. At first she felt only the pain; and then the sensation of warmth, the wetness of his spittle as it soaked through the thin material and, revulsion overwhelming her, she found the strength to throw him from her. Taken by surprise at the sudden strength of the movement he laughed aloud; in her inexperience she failed utterly to see that her resistance, far from deterring, afforded him a delight that, jaded, he had thought long lost.

She retreated clumsily to the door, watching him fearfully, groping behind her for the handle. She knew as well as anyone how important this beast was to her father. She knew that if she screamed, if she caused a scandal – if indeed anyone believed her story, which was in itself probably doubtful – her father would never, ever, forgive her. She fumbled for the door handle.

He had straightened and was upon her in a stride, a hand over her shoulder, upon the door, holding it shut fast. 'Bare your dugs, Lenka,' he said, softly, into her ear, a fierce edge of excitement to his voice. 'Let me touch them, naked. The first – I am the first, aren't I? Come, Lenka – open your dress and bare them. Let me see your naked breasts. Your big, soft, naked tits – what harm? A small favour, before I leave.'

She was shuddering with disgust and terror, beyond tears.

'Bare yourself, Lenka.' His fingers were working upon the buttons of her dress. 'You'll enjoy it. I promise you. You'll see –'

'No! *No!*' She pushed him from her, wriggled from his hold, flew to the desk, banging her hip painfully upon it as she ran behind it, putting its solid bulk between them. 'I'll scream,' she said, desperately calm. 'Believe me. I'll scream this building down if you touch me again. The whole of Petersburg will hear me.' Her breath was choking her. Her fingers fumbled frantically with the buttons he had undone. 'I'll – I'll tell Papa.' She knew as she spoke the emptiness of the threat.

The already harsh line of his mouth tightened. He stood tense for a moment, then stepped back, leaving the way to the door open. She finished buttoning her dress, stood in silence, warily watching him.

'You want to go?' he asked, the contemptuous quiet of his voice a menace in itself. 'Go. You want to play the outraged innocent? Please yourself. But know this, Lenka – you won't escape me. When you're mine I'll have you serving at my table barebreasted if I so desire. Best to please me, Lenka. Always best to please me. I can be a loving master or a cruel one. A bitch is brought to heel as well by a beating as by kindness. The choice is yours.'

She stared at him. The words made no sense to her. All she knew was that she had to get away, away from those merciless eyes and from the filthy threat of the man. Very slowly she sidled around the desk, moved towards the door. He watched her mockingly. 'Naked to the waist, Lenka,' he said, quietly, smiling, the very normality of his voice as he spoke the monstrous words almost the most shocking thing about them. 'Think about it. Serving at my table. And – my friends perhaps? Would you like that, do you think? Serving us naked – offering yourself to be fondled – you know you could enjoy –'

'*Stop it!*' Her hands over her ears she made a dash for the door. He made no effort to stop her. She flung it open, turned on him. 'You're mad!' she said. 'You hear me? Mad!'

As she turned and ran along the open balcony to the stairs she heard his soft laughter behind her. Blindly she clattered down the stairs, ignoring the surprised looks of assistants and customers alike as she ran through the shop, blundering into a table, stumbling over a rug. Outside she took several great gulps of air before turning to run down the wide avenue, skirts lifted, feet flying. Anything – anything! – to put distance between her and that foul tongue, those disgusting eyes, those groping, twisting fingers.

She did not stop until she reached the river, where she leaned against the parapet of the bridge, panting for breath, fighting a humiliating need to retch. Slowly, slowly, her breathing calmed.

The waters of the river moved beneath her, shining and serene.

She leaned her elbows on the parapet, bent her face into her cupped hands, stood so for a very long time. Images flickered behind her closed eyes, Donovalov's voice sounded in her ears. Her breasts were horribly sore. Words were pounding in her head, repeating themselves, over and over. Terrible words. What had he meant: 'When you are mine'? *What had he meant?* She closed her eyes, struggled to calm her breathing. He had said it to frighten her of course. Everything he said, he said to frighten her. He could not possibly have meant it literally. How could he?

She could still feel his hands on her body, still hear the sound of that aroused and vicious voice in her ear. Still sense that tiniest and disgusting quiver of reaction that she knew her treacherous body had imparted to him.

It was her fault. It must be. He did not look at Anna like that; would never dare to lay a finger upon her sister, Lenka knew. No. Her father was right. The things that happened to her were always her own fault. Somehow, Donovalov knew; she was as bad as he was. The surge of self-disgust that accompanied the thought brought another stirring of nausea.

She lifted her head, feeling the gentle breeze on her wet face.

The river – cool, smooth, clean – swirled quietly about the pillars of the bridge. It was deep here, and very wide. She stood for what seemed to be an age, staring down into it. Here perhaps was an answer? A swift, cold shock – the quiet of the dark waters – and then peace. She let the thought float in her mind for a moment and then in despair she turned away. She did not have the resolve to kill herself. Even in that she would fail, she knew.

Workers were hurrying across the bridge, back to the cramped maze of streets on the other side of the river where most of them lived. Several glanced at her curiously. She was suddenly aware of her tears, of her hair blowing untidily in the wind. She scrubbed at her wet eyes with the back of her hand, tried largely ineffectually to tuck the long wisps of hair back into its pins. A little calmer, she turned back to the river. Great pied crows hopped heavily upon the muddy strand, scavenging. The spire of the Admiralty gleamed in the afternoon sun. The old, sullen resentment was rising. Why should the rest of the world be always right and she, Lenka, always wrong? Why could she never achieve the content that others apparently took for granted? Under what miserable star had she been born that her life should be so blighted?

Her young spirit was as sore as her abused body, her uncertainty and her fear of the future crystallized suddenly into a near-hatred of the busy, normal, apparently happy world about her. Always difficult, always lonely, she now felt totally isolated, utterly miserable.

And it was Anna's fault.

The thought came from nowhere, settling into her mind like one of the huge, ungainly birds that flapped and cawed along the shore. Anna's fault.

She pushed herself away from the parapet and began to walk, slowly, across the bridge, in the direction of the apartment, eyes blindly upon the pavement at her feet.

Anna had not spoken to their father about the University as she'd promised. As she had faithfully promised.

Anna had not even attempted to break the strained silence that had fallen between them in these past weeks. She had been too involved in her new friendship with their cousin, too absorbed in her stupid music, too busy running up and down the stairs to Uncle Andrei. Anna did not care. Anna had never cared.

Hot tears blurred her eyes again. Self-pity rose, not unnaturally, to smother self-disgust. Disappointment and hurt merged into self-justifying hostility; whatever the world might think, Lenka's unhappiness was not her own fault; it was Anna's.

Anna had not even noticed Donovalov's horrible and unwelcome attentions to her sister. Or – worse – if she had, she had ignored them. She had not listened when Lenka had tried to tell her; had not wanted to listen. Always before she had been there, encouraging Lenka to run to her, reassuring her, supporting her, loving her. Or so she had pretended. Where was she now? Where had she been these past weeks? Anna had deserted her, and now she had no-one, no-one at all to turn to.

And through the miserable anger, through the resentment a question nagged at the back of her mind, too terrible, too frightening to be faced, and answered.

What had Donovalov meant by those confident words 'When you are mine'?

Grimly she hunched her shoulders and, head down, walked on.

The first thing she heard when she reached the apartment building was Anna's voice, coming through the half-open door of Andrei's work room.

'– Honestly, Rita! Whatever you do don't let Papa hear you saying such things! He'll put you under lock and key!' The words were warm, light-hearted.

Lenka stopped at the foot of the stairs, turned, leaning against the newel post, listening.

Inside the room Margarita shrugged an airy shoulder. 'I mean it. I do! I'm going to marry a soldier. And not just any old soldier, either, I can tell you! An officer. In one of the Cossack regiments, probably. The uniforms are so very dashing, don't you think?' Her voice was completely composed and matter-of-fact, her sister's open laughter notwithstanding.

'With a title thrown in, I presume?' Anna enquired, grinning.

Margarita shrugged, blandly. 'Why not? Stranger things have happened, you know.'

Anna laughed again. 'Not a lot stranger!'

'What do you think, Uncle Andrei? Don't you believe that I

could make a handsome young officer fall in love with me?'
Margarita cocked her head in the almost unconsciously coquettish way that so brought to mind her mother.

'I have no doubt at all, my dear, that you could twist any
red-blooded man around your little finger,' her uncle agreed,
soberly.

Margarita was not to be fooled. 'You're laughing at me too,'
she said, undisturbed. 'I don't care. I'll do it. You'll see.' Her
young voice was perfectly confident.

'How are you going to meet this dashing young man of
yours?' Anna was still teasing. 'You can't exactly walk up and
introduce yourself to him on the street, can you? And I don't
somehow see Papa allowing you to frequent the restaurants on
the Islands!'

'Why, at Cousin Katya's, of course. You'll be silly yourself,
Anna, if you don't take advantage of Uncle Mischa's connections. Mama says it was just about the only worthwhile reason
for coming to Petersburg.' Ignoring the quizzical look that
passed between her sister and her uncle she added imper-
turbably, 'I've quite made up my mind. You just wait and see.'
Looking like a fresh spring flower in pale lemon sprigged cotton
she moved about the room with her small, dancing steps. It
always seemed to Anna that her younger sister moved to a
music that no-one else could hear. Margarita had picked up the
half-finished bow that Andrei had laid upon the bench and
was inspecting it with some interest. 'What funny wood. It's
sort of red, isn't it? And it's so heavy! Where does it come
from?'

Andrei relieved her of it, gently but firmly. 'Brazil. It's called
pernambuco. It was originally used as a dye wood – if you put
it in water, the water turns red.'

She picked up a small, heavy block. 'I know what this is. It's
ebony, isn't it?'

'That's right. From Mauritius.' Andrei was watching her,
amused at her butterfly interest, fully aware that her questions
were simply to keep his attention upon her. Anything he told
her would go in one ear and out of the other; tomorrow they
might well repeat the self-same conversation, and she would be
as disarmingly ignorant again. 'And the horse hair,' he added,

pulling a slim hank of it through his fingers, 'is our own Russian horse hair. From Mongolia.'

She leaned against the workbench, with a slender finger gently tilting the finely balanced scales that he used to weigh the bows. 'Uncle Andrei, if your bows are so famous, why do you still only use mother of pearl and silver to decorate them? If you used proper precious stones and gold, couldn't you charge a lot more for them?'

'Rita!' Anna was torn between despair and laughter.

Andrei laughed outright. 'My dear little Philistine! A Shalakov bow is not valued by its content.'

'What is it valued for, then?' Now she was being deliberately pert.

Exasperation won. 'It's valued for its weight, its strength and its balance,' Anna said, shortly. 'As you well know, I think. No amount of gold and diamonds could make them better. Ostentation isn't everything, you know. Oh, Rita, for heaven's sake, do be still for an instant! Now where are you going?'

Margarita had danced across the room and disappeared into the living room. Andrei and Anna exchanged glances again, smiling, unconsciously conspiratorial. Andrei bent his head once more to the unhaired bow he was oiling and polishing. Anna watched the practised movement of his hands, resisted the impulse gently to touch the thick silver hair that gleamed in the light that fell upon him through the window.

'There's a bow that isn't finished in here,' Margarita's voice called from the other room.

'I know,' Andrei said.

Anna marched into the living room. Margarita was standing by the sideboard with the unfinished bow in her hand.

'Rita! You really are the limit, you know! You've no business to poke about in other people's rooms!'

'Uncle Andrei isn't other people, he's Uncle Andrei,' her sister said with irrefutable logic. 'He doesn't mind. Do you, Uncle?' She did not wait for an answer; she was leaning forward, peering at the photographs. 'Is that Aunt Galina? I suppose it must be. I've never seen a picture of her before. Wasn't she pretty?'

'Margarita, please!' Anna hissed.

Andrei spoke from the door, his voice easy. 'Yes, she was. Very. And as good and gentle as she was pretty.' He moved to where Margarita stood, removed the picture from her hand and stood it back in its place. 'Which is more than can be said for some.'

Rita laughed delightedly, enjoying herself. 'Uncle Andrei, what can you mean? Oh – and who's that distinguished-looking gentleman with the silver hair? Isn't he handsome?'

Andrei regarded her with over-innocent eyes. 'That's me.'

She giggled. 'No! Not you – the picture!'

'Ah. The picture. That's Guy de Fontenay. A very old and dear friend of mine who lives in England.'

'He looks nice,' Margarita said.

'He is nice. Very nice. Something you'll have a chance to discover for yourselves in a few weeks. Now, my dears, much as I love your company if I'm to finish what I'm doing I really think –'

'He's coming to visit?'

'Indeed he is. He comes most years – partly business, mostly to see his many friends in the city, of whom I'm proud to count myself one. He never comes in the winter, for he detests the cold. But he loves the white nights, so usually he comes in June.' They had turned and were walking back into the other room.

'My birthday's in June,' Anna said, 'and Mama says we may have a midnight picnic by the Gulf. Will he be here for that, do you think? Would he like to –?' She stopped.

Yelena stood in the doorway. Her hair was dishevelled, her brows a straight, glowering line. She greeted no-one. 'Anna,' she said, abruptly, 'I want to talk to you.'

'Lenka? What's the matter?'

'Upstairs,' Lenka said, and turned on her heel.

Three pairs of eyes watched her departure in astonishment, and, on Anna's part at least, anger. 'Lenka!' she called, sharply.

Yelena did not reply.

Margarita grimaced ferociously. 'You'd better go, Anna. That's Lenka's absolutely grousiest face. If she bumps into Papa in that mood there'll be the most awful trouble!'

Anna's anger was rising. 'She really shouldn't –' She stopped.

'Oh well, I suppose you're right. I'd better find out what's the matter.'

Lenka plodded miserably on up the stairs, ignoring her sister's voice calling behind her. She knew she was behaving badly; but in those moments when she had stood, an outsider as always, listening to that silly, light-hearted conversation the grudge against Anna conceived in the past hour had hardened to resolve. Anna had broken her promise; in the walk from the river Lenka had convinced herself that there lay the root cause of her unhappiness. She had trusted her sister to talk to their father, to persuade him; and Anna hadn't even tried. Nor had she listened when Lenka had tried to articulate her fears about Donovalov. She'd have it out with her. She would!

They faced each other in their shared bedroom, the sound of Seraphima singing about her work in the parlour down the hall an incongruously pleasant background to their low, angry voices.

'Lenka, honestly, your manners get worse with every passing day!' Anna was furious. 'It's no wonder you make people angry with you!'

'At least I keep my promises! At least I don't give a person my word just to keep her quiet and then break it!'

'What are you talking about?' The thin, pale skin of Anna's face had flushed suddenly.

'You know very well what I'm talking about! The University! You promised – you *promised* – to talk to Papa –'

'Lenka, I haven't had the chance –'

'You should have *made* the chance!' The floodgates were opened; all of Yelena's misery and confusion, her anger against an unfair world, were vented upon her sister. And Anna, knowing in her heart that there was at least some justice in the other girl's accusations, took refuge in anger. Furious, they faced each other; neither guarded her tongue. Small spites and small irritations were flung like wounding stones. Their voices rose. Both said things they did not mean; either one of them would have died before admitting it. The bitter quarrel was broken up eventually by a flustered Varya, afraid that the newly-arrived Victor would hear the raised voices.

With a wary but interested Margarita in her narrow pallet

bed still awake and with ears cocked, they went to bed that night with a stony silence lying between them like a blade; a silence that was hardly to be broken, except for the most imperative and unavoidable of communications, in weeks.

The northern spring turned to temperate summer, and as the balmy evenings lengthened for a time at least the interminable dark days of winter were forgotten. Katya and her parents were preparing to spend several weeks, as they did each year, at their dacha in Finland, fifty miles or so north of the capital.

'Oh, Anna, do come! I asked Papa, and he said you could. It really is such fun! We swim in the lake, and there's riding and walking in the forest. The Molinskis always take the house on the other side of the lake – we get together for parties, and picnics – oh, do come?'

Anna shook her head. 'I can't, Katya, really I can't. Mama needs me here.'

'Oh, fiddlesticks! Sometimes, my chicken, you act as if you're thirty years old. Do you know that? Come, oh, do come, at least for a time.'

'I don't think Papa would ever agree, Katya.'

'Mischischa would get him to agree if I asked him.' Once with her teeth into something Katya held like a terrier. 'We have paper chases, and hay rides – and it's so quiet and beautiful –'

'Not for long after you arrive from the sound of it.' Anna's voice was amused.

Katya pulled a face. Then, impulsively and affectionately she took her cousin's hand. 'Do come, Anna? My parents could persuade yours, I'm sure they could. Won't you let me try?'

Anna shook her head, gently obstinate. 'No. Really, Katya – not this year. It's best that I stay in St Petersburg.'

Katya eyed her, suddenly and astutely thoughtful. 'Anna Victorovna! What are you up to?'

'Up to?' Oddly flustered, Anna disengaged her hand, set about tidying the desk that was littered with paper and books. 'Whatever do you mean? Why should I be up to anything?'

Her cousin was still watching her with a disconcertingly shrewd interest. 'What's keeping you in St Petersburg when you could come to Finland?' A sudden smile tilted her pretty mouth. 'Oh, Anna – surely not? A man?'

Anna straightened, hands on hips, facing her. 'For goodness' sake, Katya! This is me you're talking to – Anna – remember? Not one of your fly-by-night friends! A man indeed! How very silly!'

Katya shrugged a little, reluctantly surrendering the intriguing but she had to admit unlikely suspicion. 'It was just a thought.'

It was indeed. It was a thought that occupied Anna on and off for the next few days. Just a few months ago she knew she would have been very tempted by the opportunity to spend the summer in Finland with the Bourlovs. Margarita, hearing somehow through her own obscure channels of the opportunity her sister had refused, had been openly consumed with envy and as openly incredulous. 'Anna, how *could* you refuse? Oh, Lord, if only I were older! If they'd only ask me I'd go – like a shot I'd go! Just think of all the people you'd meet.'

'I'd rather stay in St Petersburg,' was all Anna would say.

Because of Andrei.

For her own peace of mind she came up with many other quite credible excuses. Her mother did need her; though she could certainly have managed without her for a few weeks. Her father would undoubtedly have disapproved of his eldest daughter gallivanting about Finland with what he quite openly perceived as an irresponsible and 'fast' – if not worse than 'fast' – set of young people; but with Mischa on her side she knew he could have been persuaded to let her go. She would have been an outsider, at least at first, and her meagre wardrobe and possessions might have marked her apart from the others; but with Katya to champion her not many would have cared to make too much of such social distinctions. And anyway for Anna it would have been the opportunity to explore the lovely, tranquil countryside of Finland that would have been the attraction rather than the social life offered. No. In her heart she knew that her reason for staying in the city was Andrei. The only thing she knew with any certainty was that the mere thought of being away from him for a matter of weeks, perhaps months, was something she simply could not contemplate. The disturbing depths of which feeling she did not care – or perhaps more honestly did not dare – to plumb too deeply.

That it might have been better for Andrei had she taken this opportunity to part them was something that did not occur to her until much, much later. She was, after all, very young; and first love is never easy.

There was, she assured herself in the spirit of her self-deception, a lot to be said for St Petersburg at this time of the year. Bands played in the parks and gardens: waltzes and military marches, operatic arias and popular songs from the stage. Small sails swooped about the wide river and across the sea-water Gulf, graceful as birds in flight. The days grew warm enough to be, for northern blood, almost uncomfortable; but the evenings were, though still pleasant, fresh and magically lit. In the enchantment of those white nights in which the sun hovered dimly upon the horizon as if reluctant to leave the beauty of the lovely summer's twilight, the Gulf of Finland to the north of the city was a still and limpid lagoon, the salt sea air mingling with the sweet fragrance of flowers.

Together with half the population of the city on one fine Sunday the Shalakovs took the train to Peterhof, where the Court of the Tsar spent the summer months and where, in a Versailles of gardens, palaces and pavilions set against the glittering backdrop of the sea, fountains played constantly, and the rich, the aristocratic and the ambitious vied for favour or simply enjoyed themselves. The common populace almost to a man came to watch, to wonder and often acidly to comment; whilst in the rides and parks those who ruled them rode, took carriage, paraded their riches with apparently little thought and much ostentation.

'Oh look! Look! The lady in the black victoria! Isn't she *beautiful*? I wonder who she is?' Margarita was in her element. In honour of the season she had persuaded from her father a new outfit, quite the most grown-up she had ever worn, if for her own taste a little lacking in colour. Yet inadvertently the soft dove grey of the demure silk gown with its darker braid edging set off her blossoming good looks to perfection. Many a head turned as Margarita danced by; as for all her apparent indifference Margarita well knew. 'I wonder if we'll see the

Grand Duchesses? Or the little Tsarevich? And oh, Mama –
look at the gentleman on the grey horse, isn't he splendid?'

'A tailor's dummy whose boots would feed a family for six
months,' Lenka muttered, scuffing along behind her.

Her father shot her a sharp, frowning glance.

'I shouldn't like to eat his boots,' Rita said, sweetly, and was
rewarded by her mother's silvery trill of laughter. Margarita had
not quite mastered that pretty sound, though not it must be
said for want of trying. She smiled delightedly at Varya and
resolved to try harder. She had seen men's heads turn at the
sound of her mother's laughter.

'There's a concert in the gardens by the sea this evening,
Father. May we stay for it?'

'Why not?' Victor was expansive. Things were going well,
business was picking up very nicely and the Imperial contract
was at last his, signed, sealed and delivered just before Donovalov had left the city on unspecified business of his own a couple
of weeks before. 'We can catch the later train back if you'd like.
Andrei, you'll stay with us?'

Andrei nodded. 'Most certainly. I'd like to.'

Anna caught his eye, and smiled. The first few days after that
emotional scene in the workshop had been difficult for both of
them. Andrei, despite his promise, had avoided her, and she for
that short while had been content to allow it. She had had much
to think about. Every word they had spoken, every gesture,
every touch she remembered. Treasured. He loved her; impossible it might be – even wicked perhaps – but the knowledge
was a small flame of joy that could not be extinguished. Again
and again she told herself: something so wonderful could surely
not be wrong. Even Andrei had admitted that they could be
friends; devoted friends. The words had a romantic, almost
poetic ring to them. The memory of his kiss and the frightening
emotions it had roused in her she buried deep, afraid to examine
it, to confront the dangerous truth of her real feelings for her
uncle. At last, unable to stay away, she had taken to visiting
him again – though as he had suggested almost always in company of one of the younger children. And as these enchanting
summer weeks had progressed, the tensions between them had
seemed to drop away. There was an ease between them now, a

shared but unspoken intimacy that delighted her. How perilous was this intimacy she, unlike Andrei, did not in the least understand; nor did she know the effort it cost him to sustain this apparently calm and easy friendship. While Anna in her youth and innocence happily deceived herself, Andrei could not. She would have been shocked had she known that his fiercest and most heartfelt prayers were that she should find another love, as young and innocent as herself, for only in her loss, he knew, could his own agonizing dilemma end. His own desires and feelings he could handle; but the look in those clear eyes, the perfect trust in her warm and ready smile, above all the music that she played, he knew, for him alone, sometimes all but broke him. At such times the vodka bottle was not enough. Anna would have been even more shocked to know of the red-headed young prostitute in the dockland café.

'When does your English friend arrive, Uncle Andrei?' Margarita had skipped up beside him and slipped her arm in his.

'On Wednesday.'

'Will he stay in one of the really grand hotels?'

'Most certainly. He usually uses the Hotel de l'Europe.'

'Goodness! Will he invite us there, do you think?'

'He might. If you smile at him very nicely.'

'You must bring him to dinner, Andrei,' Varya said. 'On Thursday, perhaps. Or Friday. Do you think he would like to?'

'I'm most certain he would, Varya Petrovna.'

'Anna shall play for us,' Victor said. 'Does your English friend like music, Andrei?'

Andrei smiled again at Anna. 'Guy loves music – more than almost anything else, I think. I have already promised him that our Anna will play for him.'

'Oh, heavens! That sounds terrifying!' Anna did not look in the least bit terrified; in these past months her confidence had grown, and she was, for many reasons and in many ways, no longer a child.

Andrei shook his head. 'Guy isn't terrifying. He's the most amiable man you could wish to meet. You'll like him, I'm sure.'

'If he's your friend,' Anna said simply, 'then I know I shall love him.'

★　★　★

The words in a way were prophetic; for if Anna did not exactly love Guy de Fontenay on sight she certainly liked him immensely from the moment he walked through the door. Tall, lean and distinguished-looking, he was indeed exactly as Andrei had described him: engaging, courteous, highly intelligent. But he was more. With sure feminine instinct Anna sensed that here was a kindly man, his warmth and charm no empty facade. And even had his personal qualities not won her, his obvious and open affection for Andrei would have been enough to ensure him an immediate place in her heart. Forewarned by Andrei, he came bearing gifts for everyone – flowers for Varya, cigars for Victor, a pretty brooch for Margarita, a handsome, lacquered bilboquet for Dmitri, whose pride at his expertise at this game, which entailed deftly catching a small ball in a cup on one end of the stick or impaling it on the spike at the other, was matched only by the irritation of most of the rest of the family at the clicking, clattering noise it made. For Lenka there was a book and for Anna a pale green silk scarf.

The evening was a great success. Sonya the cook outdid herself in honour of the foreign guest; the inevitable but tasty soup was followed by a selection of cold meats and fish and then by Sonya's speciality, the delicious meat and vegetable pies known as 'pirozhki'. Although normally dessert in the Shalakov household was eaten only on a Sunday, thinly sliced oranges sprinkled with sugar followed. The conversation was entertaining, Guy proving more than happy to satisfy his hosts' curiosity about England and the English. His Russian was excellent, if strangely accented; he had had, as he pointed out with a smile, a very good and enthusiastic teacher. A bottle of vodka had been emptied and a new one started before the meal ended around the table upon which the steaming samovar was set. Even Lenka had been charmed from her usual reserve to question and even to laugh at the dry humour in which most of the answers were couched. Anna was then prevailed upon to play, and a little nervously she took the lovely old violin from its case and settled it upon her shoulder. Guy steepled long, bony fingers, leaned forward, watching her intently. His eyes, set in a lean, deeply-lined but not unhandsome face were the brightest blue Anna had ever seen. She played Mozart and Vivaldi; finished with

126

Andrei's wild gypsy tune. Their guest's reaction was gratifying.

'Wonderful, Anna Victorovna, wonderful! Andrei, you didn't do your niece justice! Such sensitivity, such great maturity in one – if I may say so without offence? – so young!'

The small party broke up with warm thanks and an invitation for the whole family to join him for dinner the following Monday at the Hotel de l'Europe, an invitation that set Margarita's pretty eyes glowing.

Some little while later Anna, having supervised the clearing of the table and the work in the kitchen, came into the parlour to find her father alone enjoying a last small glass of vodka and one of Guy's cigars. He was reading the newspaper, his pince-nez perched upon the tip of his nose. 'I came to say good night, Papa.'

He nodded a little absently. 'Yes indeed. Good night, my dear.'

'It was a lovely evening, wasn't it? I liked Mr de Fontenay very much.'

'Charming man. Charming.'

Anna plumped up a cushion, moved a chair back into its accustomed place. 'It will be nice to go to the hotel for dinner, won't it?'

'Most certainly it will.'

'I was wondering – perhaps Mr de Fontenay would like to come with us on my birthday? The picnic? Since the Bourlovs can't be there it would be fun to have someone different, don't you think?' The midnight picnic to be held in honour of Anna's nineteenth birthday had been the subject of much discussion and much excitement over the past days, for all it was a full fortnight away.

'By all means invite him, if he's still going to be in St Petersburg.' Her father closed the paper, folded it very neatly.

'Oh yes, he will be. He's here for a month, Andrei –' she stumbled a little '– Uncle Andrei said so.'

'Good.' Her father carefully pinched out the cigar. Anna hesitated. Over the past few days, Lenka's irritating sulks notwithstanding, her conscience had not been entirely clear. If she were going to try to persuade her father to allow her and her sister to enrol on a course at the University as Lenka so desperately wanted the subject would have to be broached at some time between now and the autumn. Several times she had been on the point of speaking to him, but each time somehow the occasion had not seemed exactly right. She remembered all too clearly the dreadful quarrel after his refusal to allow her to take up the scholarship; whilst outwardly their relationship had returned to normal she knew all too well – probably better than her father did – its true fragility. But still, sooner or later, the attempt would have to be made; perhaps this evening, convivial as it had been, was as good a time as any. 'Papa?'

Victor was fussily folding his glasses, putting them into their small leather case, placing them precisely upon the folded newspaper. 'Yes, my dear?'

Varya's voice sounded in the hall outside, talking to one of the others. Victor turned his head, listening. Varya had behaved quite well this evening, he was willing to admit. She had graced his table prettily and played her role of hostess admirably. Possibly the stern talking-to he had given her after the Bourlovs' party had paid dividends after all. Possibly too the headache of which she had been complaining ever since might have been cleared by such a pleasant evening. 'I'm sorry?'

Anna hesitated. 'I was just saying –' Perfectly obviously her father's thoughts were elsewhere. Perhaps now was not the time after all. 'Nothing, Papa. I was just saying good night.'

'Yes. Of course. Good night, my dear.' He kissed her cheek perfunctorily, inclined his head absently in the direction of the icon above its steadily burning lamp in the corner and left the room.

After plumping up the cushions of her father's chair and turning down the lamps, Anna followed. There really had been no point in trying to talk to him this evening. There'd be another chance soon. Perhaps on her birthday. He'd surely be readier to accede to such a request on such a day than at any other time? Lenka would just have to wait a little longer. It served her right for being so grumpy.

She stood in the darkened hall for a moment, alone. She heard her parents' voices from behind their bedroom door, heard the click and rattle of the new bilboquet from her brother's room. Margarita's trill of laughter rang out, dishes clattered in the kitchen. Downstairs, just one floor below her, her uncle would be alone in his neat and quiet room. What was he doing? Reading perhaps? Asleep already? She pictured his face, calm and relaxed in sleep and fought a sudden, wanton impulse to slip out of the front door, down the stairs and –

She pulled herself up, shaking her head. Devoted friends. That was what they were. She must never forget that. Devoted friends. The line was set between them and as long as neither overstepped it both were safe. She found herself thinking suddenly of Guy de Fontenay, of the obvious affection he and Andrei felt for one another. It was good that Andrei should have such a friend. Anna remembered Guy's intent enjoyment of her playing, recalled his warm praise, and smiled. Even on such short acquaintance she felt strangely certain that if she needed it he would stand friend to her too.

She stood for a moment outside the bedroom door, her fingers upon the handle. From within she heard Rita's laughing voice and Lenka's low reply. For one second longer she stood, savouring this small, solitary moment in a life in which such times were few. The evening had been lovely. She had played well. Andrei, she knew from the look in his eyes, had been proud of her. She was after all glad that she had not spoken to her father about the University; with a sudden uncharacteristic lift of light-heartedness it came to her that, despite all, for tonight she was as happy as she had ever been. It would have been foolish to spoil it. She would speak to him on her birthday. There was plenty of time.

CHAPTER SEVEN

In the two weeks that led up to her birthday only the continuing ill-feeling between herself and Lenka clouded Anna's happiness; yet even that could not truly blight those days of delight. That her high spirits might be ill-founded she refused even to consider – the sun shone, her precious 'loving friendship' thrived and grew and made each day a new adventure. The world, for that short, light-hearted time was hers, and resolutely she would see nothing in it but the good. The weather held, and as one long, warm day followed another the gilded city showed herself to her very best advantage. There was an air of holiday as people promenaded through the bright evenings along the banks of the rivers and canals or in the wide avenues and tree-filled squares. The Shalakovs dined with Guy de Fontenay at his hotel – an experience which set Margarita dreaming pre-occupied and glamorous dreams – and he in his turn accepted with pleasure Anna's invitation to her birthday picnic, insisting over Victor's polite objections that as his contribution to the evening he would provide the transport to take them the few miles to the shores of the Gulf, arguing with self-mocking solemnity that if they took an elderly gentleman like himself on such a trip they could not expect his old bones to survive the buffeting of public transport. Laughingly Anna pointed out that those same elderly bones had managed quite happily to transport themselves halfway across Europe by train; unruffled, he seriously assured her that such a feat had only been made possible by large quantities of vintage champagne and a kindly conductor. Anna took leave to doubt that; Guy de Fontenay was by no means a young man, but his vitality and energy belied his years. An almost immediate warmth had grown between these two, their shared passion for music linking them, their obvious enjoyment of each other's company encouraged by

Andrei, their mutual regard for whom created yet another bond.

Guy was not the only outsider to be asked to the picnic. To everyone's mild astonishment and mostly hidden amusement Dmitri had announced with some bravado that he had invited Natalia to accompany them.

Margarita was derisive. 'Oh, Dima, what on earth for? She's such a dull little thing!'

Dmitri's face reddened. 'Just because she doesn't shriek and shout the way you do doesn't make her dull.'

'I thought you liked Natalia?' Anna asked her sister.

The girl shrugged dismissively. 'She's all right.' In fact Margarita's pretty nose had been put considerably out of joint by her brother's friendship with the quiet girl who had originally been her own devoted acolyte. What was Natalia doing attracting masculine attention – even such insignificant attention as Margarita considered her brother's to be – when she, Margarita, had as yet no beau? Though she would have died under torture before admitting it, Margarita was jealous. Whenever Natalia was in the house Dima always contrived to be nearby. Many a time Margarita found herself the odd one out in their quiet conversations and soft laughter. Not that Natalia's attitude to Margarita had changed; on the contrary, she was as devoted as ever. But there could be no doubting the sincerity of the shy smile that lit her face when Dmitri entered the room, nor the fact that she looked for him the moment she entered the apartment. Margarita was not used to sharing attention with others and she was not particularly enjoying the experience. Her chagrin was complete when Dmitri, never known for his interest in or application to his school work, adapted a scientific experiment involving wire, water, salts and much patience to produce a small, sparkling crown that glittered like diamonds, which he proudly presented to Natalia. It really was an exquisite thing, and Margarita coveted it, though crossly she denied even liking it. 'If it were real diamonds, well, that would be worth something.' As for Natalia's invitation to the picnic, Margarita, had she thought of it, would happily have invited the girl herself. It was not poor Natalia's presence to which she objected, it was the fact that Dmitri had been the instrument of it. No girl's brother had invited Margarita to his sister's midnight birthday picnic this summer, and the thought that dull and mousy Natalia had succeeded where bright and lively Margarita had apparently failed rankled; and her treatment of her long-suffering and patient friend had deteriorated accordingly.

A few days before the picnic Guy announced what he called his own small birthday treat for Anna. He had obtained two tickets for the Italian Opera, who were performing 'La Bohème', at the Mariinski and he would be more than honoured if Anna Victorovna would accompany him. He addressed his request formally through Victor, of course, who had no qualms about allowing her to accept. Had Guy been a younger man then a chaperone would have been necessary. But Guy was several years older than Victor himself, and in these past days had firmly established himself as a family friend, so there could be no question of impropriety in such a thoughtful gesture. When he stretched the invitation to include dinner afterwards however Victor hesitated.

'Oh, Papa, please!' Anna had never been offered such an outing. As a family they went of course to concerts and operas, as did almost every other family they knew, but their seats were never in the fashionable part of the house and such extravagance as supper afterwards was unthinkable. 'It is my birthday after all; and if Guy has offered it would be terribly rude to refuse, don't you think?' She held her breath.

Victor relented. 'Very well. But I must make it clear that you should be home no later than eleven.'

'Of course, Papa. Thank you.'

Even though Anna did not nurse the kind of social aspirations that were almost an obsession with her younger sister, the thought of such an evening could not but excite her. St Petersburg was famous for its glittering social life – the theatres, the restaurants were counted amongst the best in the world. There was just one problem; what in heaven's name should she – could she – wear?

It was the one and only time that Varya took motherly charge of her eldest daughter's affairs to any effect. This, after all, was a real crisis. Poor, plain Anna – which was the way Varya privately thought of her daughter – must not be allowed to attend such a glittering occasion in drab and well-worn cotton. A dress must be found.

And indeed, a dress was found. A short and decisive interview in which Varya made it clear to Victor that this was a matter that might, if not resolved, be the cause of the severest of headaches, was followed by a visit to Zhenia's dressmaker. Through a combination of coaxing and bullying which left Anna herself open-mouthed a dress of pale watered silk in which only the slightest flaws were detectable was hastily put together to fit her tall thin frame. During the one fitting in the hurried timetable she had to admit that she much enjoyed being described as 'slender'. Within twenty-four hours the dress was ready.

Varya stood back and surveyed her with a critical eye. 'Do stand up straight, Annoushka! Shoulders back – so –'

'But Mama –' Anna fluttered a nervous hand about her all but bare shoulders '– it feels so odd!' She glanced again into the mirror, hardly believing what she saw. The dress, perforce, was simple, too simple she knew for her mother's taste, the almost severe lines emphasizing her height, the pale, oyster silk bringing out in hair that at its worst could look like a mass of copper wire a soft marigold sheen.

'Wait.' If there was a skill that Varya possessed it was the art of adornment, of producing an effect, and her memory had served her well. She delved into a drawer, brought out the green and blue filmy scarf that Katya had given Anna. 'There. That's better. Poor Annoushka, you are so very –' she hesitated '– angular. Softness is the thing – such a pity that there wasn't more material – the skirt is a little skimpy –'

The family assembled to inspect her as she waited for Guy to collect her. Only Lenka, eyeing her, still sullen, said nothing.

'My little Annoushka! How lovely you look!' Victor was uncharacteristically emotional. 'A grown-up lady!'

'Oh, Anna, you lucky thing! What a pretty dress!' Rita's eyes were like saucers.

Dmitri grinned in grudging admiration. 'Not bad,' he conceded. 'Not bad at all.'

Margarita was at the window. 'Oh, look! Look! Guy's here! In a car! A hired car! With a chauffeur!'

There was a stampede to the window. Anna stood, excited as a child, breathing evenly, apparently calm.

Margarita flew to the door, opened it. They heard her voice, her laughter, Guy's reply. He appeared at the door, tall and distinguished in impeccably-cut evening suit, bright blue eyes twinkling. He smiled to see her, a ready, admiring smile that warmed her heart. 'Anna, my dear, you look lovely.'

Minutes later they were on their way, Guy's hand firmly beneath her elbow as she picked her way carefully down the stairs.

The door to Andrei's workshop remained firmly shut.

Anna suppressed her feeling of disappointment. She had so much wanted Andrei to see her in her new, grown-up finery. Until this last moment she had expected to see him appear.

'A pity,' Guy said, as he reached for the outer door and held it open for her, 'that Andrei could not postpone his visit to Moscow. I told him – I'm certain the Embassy could have obtained an extra ticket for him.'

Anna opened her mouth. Shut it again. Andrei was not in Moscow, she was certain of it. He had been with them for dinner the night before, and had mentioned nothing of such a trip. Allowing herself to be handed into the splendid, leather-upholstered interior of the car, aware of the faces pressed to the window above, settling herself comfortably beside her smiling, avuncular escort she quite carefully allowed the words to sink into her mind. Andrei could have been with them. He had chosen otherwise. He had lied to allow himself that choice. The blow was painful, she could not deny it.

The car purred softly away down the empty street.

Andrei's deception was the only shadow to darken an otherwise wonderful occasion, and even that disappointment could not spoil Anna's enjoyment of it. She lost count of the number of 'firsts' that the evening produced. Never before had she ridden in a chauffeur-driven car. Never had she sat in the isolated splendour of a velvet-curtained box with a view of the stage uncluttered by the silhouetted heads and shoulders of other members of the audience. Never had a gentleman bought her a corsage, a whole box of chocolates, champagne for the interval.

Never had she been so cosseted and cared for; indeed, when the family visited the theatre it was invariably she who spent the best part of her time organizing the comforts of others.

Guy for his part watched her with a quiet amusement and delight, more than happy to be the source of her fresh and artless pleasure in what had come to him to be quite unremarkable things. The invitation had been upon impulse. He liked Anna very much; he enjoyed the company of young people, especially of intelligent young people, and Anna reminded him in some indefinable way of her uncle in those first years of their friendship so many years before. He found, too, her total lack of artifice and sophistication refreshing. She possessed an odd mixture of ingenuousness and self-sufficient maturity that amused and touched him; an attractive mixture that he had already identified and appreciated in her music. In a long lifetime of extremely eligible bachelorhood he had learned a considerable amount about the more designing side of feminine nature. There was an openness, a sense of honesty about Anna that beguiled him. When all about them lace handkerchiefs fluttered prettily upon poor Mimi's theatrical demise, tears poured unashamedly down Anna's cheeks and, sniffing, she accepted the man-sized handkerchief he offered, mopped her eyes and blew her nose like a child.

They took supper at the well-known Restaurant L'Ours, Guy's original plan to take her out to the more fashionable Villa Rhode on the Islands having to be changed because of Victor's insistence on Anna's being home by eleven. Anna cared not a jot about the change of plan. L'Ours seemed to her to be the very height of comfort and luxury. She ate oysters – another 'first' – and caviare and drank altogether too much champagne. Her one and only moment of real discomfort came when she realized that she needed the Ladies' Room, and that, having in an agony of embarrassment ascertained through Guy its situation, the trip there and back involved walking alone across what looked like acres of deep red carpet and up a sweeping staircase beneath glittering chandeliers, reflected in myriad mirrors and under the admittedly disinterested but nonetheless intimidating gaze of what seemed like half of St Petersburg. Until now everything she had done, she had done with her arm tucked well and truly into Guy's. With remarkable rapidity her head cleared, and she quailed.

Guy smiled, gently. He covered her hand with his, dry, warm and strong, sensing her sudden terror with sure instinct. 'My dear. Look at me.'

She lifted her clear, nervous eyes to his.

'Listen to me. There is absolutely no reason to worry. You lift your head, so –' he tilted her chin with his finger '– and you walk, back straight, head up. When you come back, you find me – you watch me – and you won't be afraid. Go.'

She went. And it worked. With possibly champagne-induced assurance she wove between the tables, mounted the stairs, found herself in the most luxurious room she had ever seen, all velvet reds and golds and gilded mirrors, elegantly lit and deeply carpeted. As with everything else she had seen and done this evening, she did her best to memorize the look of the place; Margarita she knew would be far more interested in the Powder Room of the Restaurant L'Ours than in the merits or otherwise of the Italian Opera. When she rejoined Guy at the table he was paying the bill. Regretfully she followed him out of the restaurant to where the car awaited them, the door held open by a respectful doorman. Her ingenuous smile and bright 'thank you' brought a genuine return; the man's face lit, and the automatic touch to his cap was jaunty. 'Madam. Excellency.' As the car glided through the summer twilight of the streets of the city she turned to Guy. 'Oh, thank you! Thank you so much! I have so enjoyed the evening.'

He patted her hand, pleased. 'And so have I, my dear. So have I.' It was, he reflected, more than a simple good-mannered pleasantry. He had enjoyed the evening immensely. Guy de Fontenay counted himself, with very good reason, a lucky man. His life had been long and varied, his bachelorhood was a matter of choice occasioned in the first instance not by a dislike of women but by a genuine love of them. In his younger days it had seemed to him that only a fool would tie himself to one delight when so many others were on offer; and he had never seen the attraction of a marriage based upon infidelity as it seemed were the unions of so many of his friends and contemporaries. The simple answer, therefore, was not to marry. And as he got older he had seen no reason to change his mind. The family business in London was a well-founded and prosperous one; the small but exceptionally attractive estate that the de Fontenays owned in Sussex had become over the years the centre of an urbane and intelligent group of artists, writers and most especially musicians, all of them renowned in their field, all of them true friends of Guy de Fontenay. His life was full and happy, he pleased himself and followed his own wide-ranging and civilized interests and inclinations; on balance he had seen no reason to disrupt things by acquiring a wife. In his time he had squired some of the richest and most beautiful women in Europe, yet the simple pleasure of watching Anna's open, unforced enjoyment of the evening had been a real and surprising delight to him. He smiled to himself as he watched her sharp, decisive profile. Perhaps he had indeed become a little blasé over these past few years. Anna had been good for him, her youth and freshness like a breeze through the opened window of a warm and perfumed room. The small conceit pleased him. 'I'm greatly looking forward to your picnic.'

She turned. 'Oh, so am I! Sonya's been baking for days – and Papa says we may have real champagne! I do so love these summer's nights – I always think I'm so lucky to have been born in June, when the white nights are here.'

He smiled at her enthusiasm. 'Lucky indeed. Ah, here we are.'

The car purred to a halt at the kerb. Anna turned to face him and, shyly impulsive, leaned to kiss his cheek. 'Thank you, Guy. It's been the most wonderful evening.'

'It's for me to thank you,' he said, gently. 'It's been a very long time since I enjoyed anything so much. Now, we must return you to your papa before you turn into a pumpkin.' He smiled again, enjoying her laughter. 'That would be a poor end to such an evening, would it not?'

The day before Anna's birthday it rained. Sewing in the parlour with her mother, Anna watched from the window, anxiously. It would be too bad if after these past lovely days the weather broke now. In the afternoon, however, the clouds cleared and the evening was a fine one. 'It'll be a good day tomorrow, Anna

Victorovna,' Seraphima, who was looking forward to the trip as much as any of the family, assured her with peasant certainty, 'you'll see. A good day.'

The birthday did indeed dawn a little cloudy but with the air of summer about it. The atmosphere was warm, a little heavy. On the breakfast table lay a small pile of gaily-wrapped presents. To Margarita's incredulity – she could no more have left a present unopened than she could have skated on water – Anna waited until after their breakfast of hot chocolate and buns before opening them. Victor had breakfasted earlier and left for the shop. His and Varya's present to their eldest daughter was a small trinket box that tinkled a pretty tune when opened. Margarita and Dmitri had clubbed together to buy her a pair of silver earrings. There was a slender gold bracelet from Katya and her parents, entrusted to Varya before the Bourlovs had left for Finland. And from Lenka there was a book of Chekhov short stories. Warmly Anna kissed her, genuinely pleased with the thoughtful present. 'Thank you, Lenka. Thank you.'

Lenka shrugged a little, but at least she smiled.

From Seraphima and Nanny Irisha came a length of green ribbon to tie up her hair, and Sonya had cooked a special cake. Anna clapped her hands delightedly. 'We'll take it with us tonight!'

But for Anna the best present of all was the one that Andrei gave her, when he arrived that evening to help with the preparations for the picnic.

She knew what it was, as did everyone else, from the long and slender shape of the parcel. 'I promised to make you a bow,' he said, with a small, deprecating movement of his hand. 'But I thought – perhaps this one would suit you better than any –?'

She opened the long case. There was a small silence. With every eye upon her she assured herself of complete control before lifting a shining, smiling face. 'It's – beautiful. Thank you.' She took the bow out of its case, weighed it, marvelling, in her fingers. Silver and ebony and mother of pearl gleamed softly. The wood was oiled and polished smooth as silk. Once handled it could not be mistaken; this was, she knew beyond doubt, the bow she had seen on that first visit to Andrei's rooms; the bow he had left unfinished after the death of his beloved Galina. A magnificent thing it would have been, made by any master; but this was the last Andrei had made with his two good hands; the final illustration of a genius maimed. He had haired it now, and, complete at last, it was his birthday gift to her. A gift beyond price. Unable to speak she stepped lightly to him and dropped a swift kiss upon his cheek. She felt his body tense very slightly as she touched him. Quickly she stepped back. 'Thank you,' she said, quietly, 'it's lovely.'

'Play us something, Anna!' Margarita said. 'The gypsy song! Play us the gypsy song!'

Anna fetched her violin, raised the bow, gracefully and steadily poised. It was the most exquisite thing she had ever held; strong, balanced, the perfect weight. She tested it, lightly and with care, her face absorbed. Magically, it was as if the thing were a living extension of herself, a bridge between nerve, mind and heart and the instrument she held. Tentatively she played the first phrase or two, stopped, stood absolutely still for a quiet moment, her eyes half-closed, then she launched into the gypsy tune that Andrei had taught her. The music was joyous. Victor beamed. Margarita clapped and stamped her feet, her body moving with instinctive grace in time with the compulsive rhythm. Even Lenka's head lifted, her eyes brightening almost to a smile.

Andrei watched her, his face masked.

Only Seraphima heard the doorbell. It was a moment before Guy appeared in the doorway. He stood quietly, watching and listening. Anna saw him. The music stopped in mid-flight. 'Oh, please –' he raised expressive hands '– don't stop.'

'But we must!' Varya's attention was immediately upon more practical things. 'Come – it's getting late!'

'M'sieu de Fontenay!' Margarita breathed from the window. '*Two* hired cars!'

Guy beamed upon them all. 'I thought we should be comfortable,' he said.

Comfortable they were. The hampers and the rugs loaded into the boots of the long, gleaming cars, they distributed themselves between the two vehicles, settling amidst laughter and exclamations into the luxuriously sprung leather seats – Seraphima sitting straight as a ramrod, an expression of pure terror on her face; she had heard that these dreadful contraptions could travel as fast as a galloping horse. The train she had found trying enough; this she had not bargained for. Fatalistically she crossed herself; strange were the ways of God.

They were borne smoothly and swiftly through the streets of the city and out into the flat, wooded countryside. The sun dipped and swung low along the wide horizon. The ride here was not so smooth, nor was progress so fast. There were few other cars on the dusty roads, though they passed one or two carriages and several parties of young people on horseback. A family wobbled along upon bicycles, mother and daughter in voluminous bloomers that had Varya staring and Seraphima, shocked for a moment out of her fright, blushing furiously. Margarita spent a few interesting moments wondering if it might be worth the effort of learning to master one of those silly machines in order to be given the opportunity to wear such a scandalous garment. A moment's thought, however, and a glance at her father's face convinced her, reluctantly, that the likelihood of a Shalakov female bicycling in bloomers was slim indeed.

Peasants leading donkeys, or carrying loads piled high upon their own shoulders, stopped to stare as they passed. Margarita was in her element. Sitting next to the window she preened and tossed her head, chattering and laughing vivaciously, apparently unaware of the attention she was attracting, in fact acutely conscious of every glance. The waters of the Gulf glittered through the trees, reflecting the fire of the sunset through stands of graceful birch and larch, and tall, dark pine. Small gabled wooden houses, many of them brightly painted, stood in the clearings of the forest, chickens pecking about the yards. Dogs sprang to life as they passed, barking furiously and chasing the wheels of these strange, noisy vehicles. They turned at last down a sandy track and came to a stretch of shingle that edged the vast, still waters of the Gulf. The trees here were predominantly birch; they stood almost to the water's edge, their silver trunks straight as wands, their small glittering leaves shimmering in the faintest of breezes. The vast expanse of water, glimmering through the trees, gave back the tranquil colours of the evening sky.

'It's perfect! Perfect!' Anna clasped her hands, looking about her. Seraphima, openly relieved to be out of the infernal and dangerous automobile, fussed with the hampers, Varya arranged herself decoratively upon a rug. The cars moved back to the road to await the time of return.

'Come on, Dima. Firewood.' Andrei caught the boy's hand and, laughing and calling, they disappeared into the shadowed woods.

'I'm going to paddle! Come on, Natalia.' Margarita kicked her shoes off, turned her back as she wriggled out of her stockings. Then, skirt lifted daintily, she stepped into the gently lapping water. 'Natalia, do hurry! It's lovely!'

Some little way along the curve of the beach another family party was already settled to a picnic. A young man played a balalaika, and a girl sang, a sweet and soulful sound that echoed across the still waters.

Bottles of vodka were opened. The men sat in shirtsleeves – even Victor for once wooed to informality by the magic of the soft evening air – elbows on knees, glasses in hand. Dmitri sulked a little at first when Andrei watered the clear spirit before passing him his glass, but soon regained his good humour as he sipped the still-strong spirit. Varya, the girls and Seraphima sipped thimble-sized glasses of rowan-berry liqueur; Rita maliciously delighted when Natalia, unused to such sophistication, became openly giggly after embarking upon her second small glass. The picnic was spread; the inevitable and delicious 'pirozhkis', smoked sausage and chicken, the doughnut-like rolls called 'kalachi' that were one of Sonya's specialities, cheesecakes, spiced biscuits and fruit. The picnic samovar had been set upon Andrei's fire; woodsmoke drifted, fragrant, in the air. It was a moment of the most utter perfection.

'A feast!' Anna said, happily. 'The Grand Duchesses themselves couldn't possibly have a better! Lenka, do try these lovely mushrooms – they're your favourites, I know.'

Lenka accepted the plate Anna held out to her. Her mood was lighter than it had been for some time; on such an evening it was hard to harbour a grudge, though still her spirit was sore at what she saw as Anna's betrayal, and still worry gnawed at her like a rat at a packing case. What had he meant? How had he dared to handle her, to talk to her so?

They ate, drank tea, cleared the food, opened the bottles of champagne that Guy had insisted on providing. Andrei shook his head in refusal, laughing. 'I'm going for a swim – coming, Dima? Victor? Guy?'

The two older men shook their heads. 'Are you trying to kill me off entirely?' Guy enquired mildly, smoke from his cigar wreathing about him.

Andrei and Dmitri moved off up the beach, for privacy, for as was the norm they would bathe naked. Victor lay back, arms behind his head, yawning. Varya had produced a pack of cards. 'Come, girls – a game. Anna, you'd like to play?'

Anna had been sitting very straight and still, head turned, listening. From beyond a small stand of trees came male laughter, and a loud splash. Dmitri laughed again. Out through the still, silvery water a sudden dark shape cut, graceful and speedy. Andrei was a powerful swimmer. Strong arms lifted rhythmically, hardly disturbing the glimmering water through which they sliced.

'Anna?'

'I'm sorry, Mama?' Anna's voice was abstracted.

'A game?'

'Oh – no, I think not if you don't mind. I'd like to walk a little. I'm quite disgracefully full of Sonya's lovely cake.'

'Very well. But don't go far.'

'No, Mama.'

'Lenka, you partner Rita and I'll take Natalia – come, Natalia dear, you play bridge of course?'

Anna stood up, shook out her skirts. Guy, sitting propped with his back against a log, another cigar between his long fingers, saluted her with a lazy smile as she passed, quite evidently content and enjoying himself. Her father was beside him, head on his chest, pince-nez dangling, snoring very gently.

She walked into the woodland. The sandy ground was soft beneath her slippers. The sky was light and milky, a pale, lingering dusk cloaked the trees and the water.

A white and silver night, she found herself thinking, mysterious and exciting – a night for enchantments and for the weaving of spells.

Behind her she could hear the voices of her family. Varya laughed her pretty, bell-like laugh. The girl along the beach was singing again, her voice not strong, but soft and haunting. The small path Anna was following turned back towards the water, led down onto the shingle to a tiny, enclosed beach. Trees edged the strand, stooping gracefully as if to admire their own perfect reflections. Oars splashed, and some way out into the Gulf a narrow skiff sped across the sky-lit, lustrous mirror of the water. Further still away from the shore a small sail swooped like a sea bird. She leaned against the straight, paper-barked trunk of a huge silver birch, tilting her head back, closing her eyes. The world rustled about her.

She never knew what told her that he was there. Certain she was, though, before she ever opened her eyes. He stood poised a few paces from her, watching her. He carried his jacket slung over his shoulder, and his boots in his other hand. His feet were bare. His silver hair was dark and slick with water. His skin was still wet, the loose white shirt sticking to chest and shoulders, open at the collar to reveal the pale skin of his throat.

She did not move. Even breath seemed suspended.

In the distance the girl sang, a siren sound in the whiteness of the night.

He was smiling at the sight of her, a small, unwary smile of love.

She pushed herself away from the tree. Stood straight, her eyes almost on a level with his.

The smile died. Almost reflexively he shook his head sharply, his wet hair falling across his face. But he did not move. He stood as if rooted there beneath the rustling trees.

She it was who moved to him, slowly, as if in a dream. The bones of his face looked sharp and fragile, shadowed in the strange, unnatural light. He smelled of the water; his skin was cold with it. He stood unmoving, his hands by his sides, as she touched his face, very gently, with her warm finger.

He swallowed. Fascinated by the movement she ran her finger along his jaw, gently lifting it, then with neither thought nor consciously formulated intention she leaned to him and kissed the wet skin at the base of his throat. He stood for a moment longer like a statue, head thrown back, tensed against movement. Then he broke. His hands were in her hair, his mouth on hers. As suddenly, instinctively savage as he, she arched her body into his; felt the hardness of him against her belly, only half-understanding. He kissed her with brutal unrestraint, all the pains and frustrations of these past months released into this one moment. They stumbled back against the tree. His hands lifted to her breasts. Wild with delight and desire she lifted her arms, braced against the tree behind her, offering herself to him. He fumbled with the buttons of her bodice; she felt the cool air against the naked skin. He bent his mouth to her bared nipples. The most exquisite sensation she had ever experienced flared through her body. She dropped her arms, buried her hands in the thick, springy damp hair, holding him fiercely to her. In that moment, in that perilous and wonderful moment, so wholly and unguardedly did she love him that she thought she might die of it; would have been happy to have died of it. In that swift, single moment there was neither right nor wrong; the rest of the world with its narrow ways and strictures simply did not exist. She flung back her head again, arching her back, feeling for the first time in her life beautiful; glad that the faery light was bright enough to display her nakedness to the man who, despite all, must surely be her first and only destined lover.

In the oddly shimmering depths of the woodland beyond the tiny clearing a shadow flickered, indefinable yet unmistakable. The pale blur of a face was there, and then it was not. Ghostly, it melted and was gone.

It took a moment for her to understand what she had seen. He felt the change in her. Straightened, grasping her shoulders. 'Anna? Darling, what is it? – I'm sorry – Oh, my God, I'm so sorry! – I shouldn't –'

'Someone was there.' Her voice despite all efforts shook like the leaves above their heads. 'Someone was watching. Andrei, *someone was watching us!*' She clung to him, trembling, the woman fled, a child again, caught in wrongdoing. Caught in a wrongdoing so great as to be beyond forgiveness. The world, held at bay for those few transcendent moments, had its revenge. She shook with terror.

He soothed her, as best he could, his own face taut with worry and with self-repugnance. Disgrace for himself was nothing. But for Anna? The thought was unbearable. 'Who was it?'

'I d-don't know. But it was *someone*, I tell you! And he – she? – I don't know! – was watching, Andrei, watching us! Oh, it's horrible!'

He put his arms about her as she leaned, trembling, to his shoulder. 'Come now, Anna. Come now. Try not to distress yourself. It may be no-one – no-one who knows us, that is –' No-one who understands what they saw. The thought was with them both, though neither spoke it. Uncle and niece. A man caressing and suckling the bared breasts of his brother's daughter. They could not look at each other. What had been clean and beautiful between them now was dirtied, broken beyond mending.

Back in the picnic clearing nothing appeared to have disturbed the peace. Victor still snored. Guy sat now upon the fallen tree, smoking and watching Varya play patience. Seraphima busied herself packing the last of the hampers. Dmitri and the three girls were at the water's edge, playing with the small, lapping waves. No-one so far as Anna could see paid the slightest extra attention to the new arrivals. 'Ah. Here you are. Time to go home, I think.' Varya stood up, packing the cards neatly with a practised hand into their box. 'I trust you have enjoyed your birthday, Annoushka?'

Anna forced a smile, too brightly. 'Certainly I have, Mama.'

'Good. And now I think we shall truly appreciate M'sieu de Fontenay's contribution to the evening – a walk to the station or to the landing stage I fear would be entirely beyond me! Dmitri, do wake your father up. Come, everyone. Andrei, give Seraphima a hand with the other hamper, would you?'

The drive back was quiet, the hour late, everyone drowsy. Anna sat in a dark corner, head turned to look out of the window, her mind and her heart in a turmoil. Despite herself she had felt a twist of bitter disappointment when Andrei had opted to travel in the other car. Despite all, as she leaned to the window, watching as they sped through the glimmering woodlands in the pale light, she could not forget – did not want to forget – the feel of his hands, his mouth, upon her body. Horrified as she had been to know that they had been spied upon, much as that knowledge had flawed that perfect moment, yet some small part of her clutched at the straw of hope. Perhaps, indeed, it had been a stranger who watched. Who in the family could have observed and not in outrage spoken? Perhaps, still, their secret was safe.

Her nerve was steadier now. She could face what they had done. The dreadful flood of guilt and shame was receding, to be replaced by this small, defiant flicker of hope; perhaps, after all, all was not lost; perhaps somewhere, somehow, they would together find shelter, and happiness, if only for the odd stolen moment such as tonight's? He loved her, of that she was now utterly certain; right or wrong she would hold to that. She had nothing else.

The cars purred over the gleaming river and into the just-stirring city. Dogs barked. In the half-light small groups of ill-shod and inadequately-clothed early workers walked the pavements, slow-footed, hardly lifting their heads as the polished limousines glided by.

Andrei stood tense, his hands upon his workbench, his back to his visitor, shoulders hunched. 'So,' he said, after a very long, quiet moment. 'It was you.'

Guy looked tired. His face was drawn. For the first time that Andrei could remember he looked every year of his age. 'Yes. It was me.'

The silence that stretched between them was not a happy one. Andrei refused to turn, refused to face his old friend and mentor.

'Do you realize,' Guy asked at last, 'how lucky you both were that it *was* I who saw you? Jesus Christ, Andrei –' his voice, though so low as to be almost inaudible, was rough with angry emotion '– it could have been *anybody*. What in God's precious name are you thinking of?'

Andrei shook his head, unable to answer.

Guy waited for a moment. Someone ran, calling, down the

146

stairs outside, and the entrance door slammed. 'She's a child,' Guy said, very quietly. And then, 'Your brother's child.'

Andrei rested his elbows on the bench and buried his face in his hands, the shock of silver hair covering his fingers.

'Even if you can ignore the hurt you will do to her.' Guy was remorseless. 'Even if you can be that blind, that selfish, think of the scandal. Incest, Andrei, that is the name the world will put to it. Incest.' He saw the other man flinch from the word; his even voice did not falter. 'Anna will be ruined. You will be ruined. The scandal will besmirch Varya and the other girls. And your brother's business? What of that?'

'I'll go away.' Andrei's voice was muffled.

'On what pretext?' Andrei had never heard his friend's voice so cold, so harsh. 'And to what purpose? For now Victor's business depends much upon your contacts, your reputation. You know it. You'll abandon him now, just as he's struggling to establish himself? And what of Anna? Would she accept such a solution? From what I know of infatuated young women and from what I saw last night I take leave gravely to doubt it. Could you prevent her from following you? From throwing her life away for you, and in doing so ruining her family? Ruining you? I ask you again, Andrei Valerievich, what in God's name have you been thinking of?' The controlled tenor of his voice broke at last and it lifted, edged with disbelief and with something that Andrei could only recognize as revulsion.

He straightened and turned, his back to the bench, his face pale as bleached bone. 'What am I going to do, Guy? Tell me!'

Guy neither moved nor spoke.

'You're right. I know you're right. Anna's the one who'll be hurt. And, sweet Jesus, I can't stand the thought. I love her, Guy. I love her!' There were tears in his voice. 'I tried to warn her! Tried to stay away from her! I did! But –'

The man he respected above all men watched him in sombre, ungiving silence. Andrei's shoulders slumped. He shook his head, tiredly. Guy watched him. His first reaction when he had stumbled upon the scene by the lake had surprised him; it had been so long since he had experienced anything so barbarous as the stark fury that had assaulted him that he had barely recognized the emotion. He had stood rooted to the spot. Anna's face, fragile and radiant in the milky light, the gleam of her naked skin, the swell of her young breasts, had burned itself into his memory; it haunted him still. He had left the scene fighting revulsion, disbelief, a savage and destructive rage of which he would have said until that moment he was no longer capable. He could in that first moment have beaten Andrei bloody with his bare hands. It had taken a long, sleepless night of brutal self-examination to reveal the astonishing basis of these violent feelings. 'Andrei,' he said suddenly, after a moment. 'How far has this gone? Have you –?' He stopped.

There was no mistaking the genuine and swift horror in the lift of the other man's head, the widening of his pale eyes. 'No! I swear it! Last night – was as far as –' He could not go on.

Guy despised himself both for the impulse that had made him ask the question and for the small lift of relief that eased the tensions in his muscles and the tightness in his stomach at the answer. The decision would not have to be made then; she was whole in body, if not in heart. And if she had not been? Who in God's name was he to judge her? Or, in honesty, to condemn Andrei?

'Andrei,' he said, very quietly, 'I have a suggestion to make.'

'Marry you?' Anna said. And then again, the emphasis different, 'Marry *you*?'

'Is it such a strange idea?'

The three – Andrei, Guy and Anna – were in Andrei's living room. It was evening. Anna had come gladly, summoned by a brief note from Andrei; had found herself facing a formidable Guy and an Andrei battered by emotion almost to dumbness. She understood well how he felt. The knowledge that it had been Guy there in the shadows last night inflicted upon her a greater humiliation and shame than she had ever believed might be possible; yet to her own surprise she had not cried, nor had she attempted excuses. She had gritted her teeth and lifted her chin; tried not to see the attitude of utter defeat in Andrei's bowed head. For him Guy's involvement had been insupportable. Literally insupportable. She could not fail to notice that he had hardly met her eyes from the moment she had entered the room. 'We've done nothing wrong,' she had said, stubbornly, not once but several times. 'We've done nothing wrong. You won't make me think we have.'

Still Andrei had not spoken.

'Anna.' Guy had been stern. 'You are an intelligent woman. You aren't a child, to lie to yourself and to others. You cannot outface the world! You cannot be so recklessly stupid. It is not you alone that will suffer. Have you thought of that?'

'We've done nothing wrong.'

Guy's eyes had flicked from one to the other. 'In thought and in deed,' he had said, softly. 'Pure as the driven snow?'

She had flushed, painfully. Had refused to answer.

'Oh, Anna, Anna! I say again – you can't take on the world! You'll lose. You'll be destroyed. And not you alone. Don't you see that? Andrei could be prosecuted. Sent to jail. Your family would be ruined. What of your sisters' prospects, your father's business, your mother's –' he paused, turned the knife quite deliberately '– your mother's sanity? For you know, I think, that that is what it would amount to? You'd jeopardize them all for your own selfish ends?'

'No-one needs know,' she had said, sharply, battling still, holding his eyes defiantly with her own. 'If you say nothing, no-one needs know.'

'Not now, perhaps. Nor even tomorrow. But the next day? Or the next? You haven't behaved exactly with restraint.' His voice was dry, renewing the colour in her cheeks. 'Anna, in God's name, anyone – *anyone!* – could have come across you last night! How long before someone else, someone far more dangerous, discovers what's going on between you?'

She had turned from him. 'Nothing is going on between us,' she had said, quietly and obstinately.

'I see.' He had let the quiet hang heavily in the room. 'You regularly put on the kind of performance that I accidentally witnessed last night?' he had asked, gently.

Even Andrei came out of his self-absorbed misery to protest at the cruelty of that. Guy had ignored him, his eyes steadily upon Anna. At last, chin still defiantly high but with anguished eyes she had turned to him. 'What should we do?'

'One of you must leave,' he had said.

149

She watched him, wary and unblinking.

Andrei lifted his head. 'Guy –'

Guy did not waver. His eyes were steady upon Anna. 'That one should be you.'

Anna waited for a very long time. At last she asked, very softly, 'Is there a way?'

'There's a way.'

His proposal had been made calmly and unemotionally. Anna's outraged reaction had been far from either. He let the storm blow. She stood finally silent, turned at last to her uncle, hands stretched in a gesture very close to pleading. 'Andrei –?' She stopped.

Andrei determinedly would not look at her. He had picked up a piece of ebony and was smoothing it with regular, compulsive movements between his fingers. In that single, sharp moment she understood; it was already all but agreed between them. 'You've already talked of this?' she asked, calmly, her voice still ragged and hoarse with tears. She was speaking to Guy. Her eyes were upon Andrei.

'Yes,' Guy said.

Something was happening to her, something almost physical, so strong was its effect upon her mind and upon her emotions. Suddenly and absurdly she was reminded of Monsieur Drapin's science lessons, little appreciated, of – what were the words? Mutation? Transmutation? Metamorphosis. Yes. That, surely, was it. Metamorphosis. An immutable change.

The men waited. Her eyes were straight and steady upon Guy's, searching. She saw for the first time the tiredness in his face. 'Why are you doing this?' she asked, suddenly. 'To save Andrei from me?'

He waited for a moment, his handsome, grave face pensive. 'Say rather to save Andrei from himself,' he said, quietly. And then added, 'And, eventually, to make you happy, I hope. I'm making no sacrifice, Anna, believe me. We could do well together, I think.'

'Was ever a proposal couched more reasonably?' She cast one last look at Andrei. Turned back, chin up, to Guy. 'All right,' she said. 'If you think it's best, I'll marry you. I suppose – you should speak to Papa?' She could not believe her own composure. Andrei had dropped into an armchair, bowed his head into his hands.

'Yes.'

'Very well. We'll talk again afterwards, I dare say.' And, turning, and with no word for Andrei, she left them.

She walked very straight and rather carefully up the stairs. Smiled at Seraphima as she opened the door, commiserated with her over a spoiled stew. She mouthed greetings to Varya, Dmitri, Margarita and young Natalia who was patiently painting a tiny set of clothes for one of Margarita's more exotic actors. She waited, painfully, for a full half an hour before, with no word of a lie, complaining of a crashing headache. She allowed herself the rare luxury of being ushered to bed, cosseted, soothed and made much of.

Then, alone, at last gave way to her tears and wept as if she would never stop.

Across the city Guy de Fontenay stood at his hotel window looking into the light summer's night, pondering the wayward impulse that had led him to propose to a girl young enough, almost, to be his granddaughter. And yet – was it truly that wayward? He had always been a man of swift decision, a man who trusted his instincts. Anna Victorovna Shalakova was a rare young woman; the challenges she was likely to set him would enrich and enliven the years that were left to him. No, in honesty not such a wayward impulse after all. Nor an entirely selfless one. It would be no bad thing to see the world through those young, clear eyes. He'd take her to Salzburg. To Vienna. And to Paris. Anna would like Paris – and what's more he'd hazard a guess that Paris would like Anna. Then there was Italy, and the blazing, lovely shores of Greece –

He shook himself, bemused. Moon madness. The insanity of these pale white nights. He most certainly must have taken leave of his usually well-ordered senses.

He reached for his cigar case, lit a cigar, blew smoke to the ceiling. Forced himself in a long, thoughtful moment, to honesty.

'After all these years,' he said, aloud, wryly and quietly

mocking. 'Guy de Fontenay – ensnared at last, it seems, and by something very close to love!'

In her room across the city, curtains tight closed against the pale twilight, Anna cried quietly on.

CHAPTER EIGHT

The outcome of Guy de Fontenay's interview with Anna's father was never in doubt, clearly dumbfounded though Victor was at the older man's approach. What father could turn down such an unexpected offer for a favourite daughter whose assets both physical and material he had always known would by many be considered to be rather less than adequate? The difference in age, though great, was by no means unusual. And there were many far more important things to set against that small disadvantage; Guy offered stability, respectability and no mean fortune. What more could a girl of Anna's station possibly have asked? That Anna herself appeared suitably agreeable to the match, if perhaps a disappointing and surprising touch subdued in her pleasure at this undoubted triumph, made things easier still; any misgivings Victor might have had could be soothed by the knowledge that his daughter was happy. She had, he thought, typically of her, made a most sensible decision – she would be secure, well cared for, and financially independent, since she would more than probably outlive her elderly husband and be then in a very advantageous position indeed. Guy's age was in some ways a positive advantage; too many girls in Victor's vehemently-held opinion put too much store on a strong young body and a pretty face, and lived heartily to regret it. He had, to be honest, been harbouring thoughts about the young violin maker – the one Andrei called Volodya, who had so obviously been interested in Anna – for he had never really expected her to attract a great number of suitors, and the thought had been in his mind to bind the young man to the family at not too great a cost. But that plan he shelved with no regret. There was no doubt; Guy de Fontenay was a catch, and his Anna had caught him. He was delighted.

If Victor was pleased, Varya was rapturous. Astonished, but

rapturous. What a very clever child her elder daughter had turned out to be after all! And how devious! Anna endured her mother's mindless and excited chatter — how *envious* her friends would be, how *surprised* the Bourlovs — for the most part in silence. The strange and devastating decision taken, she found herself drifting in an odd state of unreality, as if the world, with its intrusive comment and opinion, lived and breathed and moved without her. She supposed herself, when she could bring herself to think of it, to be in a state of shock. Neither her father's smug pleasure nor her mother's unnerving excitement meant anything at all to her. Margarita, on hearing the news, swung in very short order and with predictable ease from appalled disbelief that her sister could contemplate marrying a man so dreadfully old to an unflattering amazement at the mention of Paris, Rome and an estate in the country. Anna accommodated her young sister's ensuing and undisguised envy and her young brother's equally undisguised indifference with equal lack of effort. She simply did not care. Her main — almost her only — desire was just to get away; from the city, from her family, above all from Andrei; to get this odd business over and done, and to leave. She found it hard to look any further than that. She agreed docilely to almost every suggestion put to her; yes, she perfectly well understood that Guy would have to return to England for a couple of months to settle some affairs, yes, September would be a perfectly acceptable month in which to marry, no, she had no objection to a Paris honeymoon. Nor, Guy observed wryly, did she have any great enthusiasm for it, but sensibly he did not pursue the point. He, above all people, knew the strain she was under; he, he frankly admitted to himself, had the most to lose if she cracked and refused to go through with it. For, as he had begun to suspect on that first night, the most unlikely circumstance in the world had arisen. Guy de Fontenay — urbane, experienced, ever wary — was in love. Anna stirred him — her innocence, her unexpected passion, her quiet intelligence, her musical talent excited him as he had not been excited for longer than he cared to remember. Anna was a canvas, fresh and intriguing, waiting for the brush, clay unmoulded, a book with as yet no words. He knew the chance he took, leaving her here with Andrei; yet sensed too that if he could not trust Anna, he could most certainly trust Andrei, who had stood at the edge of the abyss and had withdrawn, trembling. He had seen – had actively encouraged – the lack of communication between them, seen Anna's hurt at her uncle's apparent coldness. Dispassionately he watched, and doubted that even Anna would have the reserves of strength to breach that wall now.

Meanwhile Anna, perfectly composed and in the eyes of her female acquaintances quite ridiculously self-deprecating about her triumph in snaring the rich if elderly Englishman, drifted on in her self-preserving dream. Since thinking always seemed to take her in a swift and vicious circle from whatever point she chose to start to the memory of that night in the woodland by the Gulf and its humiliating aftermath, she tried, quite simply and on the whole fairly successfully, not to think.

Only Lenka, with the brutality of fury at a perceived betrayal, broke through that shell.

'So. This is what you've been up to?' Lenka's voice was low and bitter. 'How could you? *How could you!*' They were in the Summer Gardens, Lenka having despaired of getting her sister to herself in any more private setting. The gardens were lovely, planted by the Tsar's own gardeners for summer greenness and beauty, dotted with statuary that spent the winter cocooned in shuttered boxes filled with straw. In the distance a band played a waltz by Strauss. The Fontanka gleamed and rippled in wind-blown sunlight that glinted on the windows and domes of the small stone-built Summer Palace of Peter the Great. Wearily Anna turned her head away from her furious sister. She was tired. And she was afraid. Her life had careered, out of control, like a sledge ill-driven on a river's winter ice. She had no strength for others' problems, not even Lenka's.

'You promised!' They were sitting on one of the ornate iron benches that edged the wide path through the gardens. Elegant ladies and their escorts strolled by, families took the air, the children made bright and fractious by the summer wind. Lenka leaned forward, strands of her straight brown hair blowing across her face. She pushed them back impatiently. 'You can't have forgotten?'

'What?'

'The University! You promised!'

'Oh, for heaven's sake!' She had promised. She knew it. She shook her head.

'You've sold yourself!' There was a harrowing bitterness in her sister's voice. 'That's what you've done! But, worse, you've sold me too! Have you even *thought* of me in these past months? Have you ever considered your promise – the plans we made?'

Anna had not. She could not pretend that she had.

'It's this damned, *damnable* city!' Lenka's voice shook with sudden, furious tears. 'Oh, God! How I wish we'd never left Moscow!' She jumped up, awkwardly, walked to the nearby railings, gripped them with gloved hands as if she would wrench them from the soil.

Anna watched her for a moment, tempted simply to stand up and to leave; to walk away from this difficult and self-centred girl. Guilt kept her. The band had broken into what seemed to her to be an entirely incongruous polka, as bright and gay as the sunshine and the wind. She came quietly to stand beside her sister. 'Lenka –' She could not go on. She had nothing to say.

'What?' Lenka turned, watching her fiercely. '*What?*'

Anna shook her head.

'Why are you marrying him?' The question was granite-hard, giving nothing.

Anna looked to the blaze of a summer flower-bed, the petalled heads dancing in the breeze. The music played on, relentlessly cheerful.

'Why?' Lenka asked, more quietly; and if Anna had had the ears to hear, it was the last appeal, the last chance to mend a wound so deeply felt, a hurt consisting of so much long-brooded misunderstanding, that its consequences could only be fatal to the love they had always and so deeply shared.

Anna shook her head, helplessly.

Lenka stared at her for a long moment. 'I shall speak to Papa myself,' she said, her voice suddenly clear and sharp. 'And Anna, please – don't ask me to attend you at your wedding. I shall be there, because I have to, but I won't be an active part of this –' she hesitated, choosing her word with unusual and cruel care '– this farce. You understand?'

'I understand.' She wanted to get away. She had to get away. She thought of Andrei, of the deceits, the exhausting emotions; she thought of Guy, tall, quiet, commanding, kind. 'I'm marrying him because he is kind,' she said. 'And perhaps – because he is like Grandpapa – he knows so many things – he cares about so many things –'

But Lenka had gone, striding through the gardens as if they and their summer splendour did not exist. Seething with anger and with bitterness; and with a buried fear she had shared with no-one. What had that brute meant: 'When you are mine'? Why hadn't she been able to share her terror with Anna, why hadn't she been able to calm herself, as she had always done before, through a confidence with her sister?

Because Anna had betrayed her, finally and lastingly. Not only was she incomprehensibly to marry this rich and elderly Englishman, she was to leave Russia. Apparently without a thought. Leave Lenka, alone.

A small child cannoned into her, his nurse, flustered, apologized. Lenka scowled and strode on.

Anna returned to the bench, sat down, watched the glimmer of the canal through the shimmering, tossing leaves. Tried, wearily, not to imagine what might happen – and what might be her own responsibility – if Lenka, in this mood, finally decided to confront their father.

'University?' Victor, in his astonishment that this subject should be broached again when quite clearly he remembered scotching it some weeks before, all but laughed into his daughter's earnest face; cleared his throat portentously instead. 'No, Yelena. Of course not. There can be no question of University.'

'Why not?' Lenka stood rigid before her father's desk, hands clasped fiercely to prevent their trembling. She had deliberately chosen the impersonal venue of his office for the interview. 'Papa, why not?'

Victor eyed her sharply; surely the girl did not actually expect him to take her seriously? 'Because the very idea is ridiculous. That's why.' He was dismissive. He ostentatiously reached for some papers, leafed through them.

'But –'

With studied patience he tapped the papers back into order, laid them neatly before him, squaring them with the edge of the desk. Then he looked up, his face stern. 'Yelena, even you can surely not seriously have expected me to entertain such a preposterous notion? A daughter of mine at the University? Part of that –' he allowed himself a small grimace of distaste '– vulgar mob of layabouts and subversives who choose to call themselves students?'

'Papa – please, if you'd only listen –'

'They have the morals of a pack of alley-cats.' Victor's voice was quiet and even, but betrayed an edge of barely-controlled anger that Lenka recognized all too well. 'Their politics are disgusting. They openly support murder, treason, the overthrow of our lawful government –'

'Not all of them, Papa –'

'Yes. All of them.' Real anger showed now. 'The place is a pit of subversion. And if it were not –' He waited until she lifted her head and met his eyes; now was as good a time as any. It was time for this unloved and importunate daughter to face reality. He softened his tone a little. 'Even if it were not there could be no question of your attending. I should never under any circumstances have allowed it. And as it happens –' he shifted in his chair, sitting back, spreading his hands expansively '– I have made other plans for you. I've been waiting for an opportunity to speak to you of them. You are a lucky child, Yelena my dear. A very lucky child. You need not look at your sister Anna with envy –'

Lenka stared at him, willing him not to continue, suddenly knowing what he was about to say. 'No,' she said, flatly.

He ignored her. 'A lucky child, as I said. I'm delighted to tell you that my good friend and colleague Pavel Petrovich has approached me –'

As he spoke she became very still. It was as if every vestige of life were draining from her, a dreadful haemorrhage of warmth and of feeling. The chill of it made her shiver. She shivered for what seemed like a long time, teeth clenched to prevent their chattering, whilst, as if totally unaware, her father droned on. '– He has connections in the very highest quarters and will very probably go far –' It was then that, quite suddenly she began to shout. She threw back her head and screamed like a demented fishwife; she used words she did not know the meaning of, words she had heard only in whispers, read in forbidden books, the only words to express her outrage and her terror. Her father stared at her in horror. Still she howled at him, herself appalled at what she was doing, what she was saying, crying now, trying to tell him what he had done, to what viciousness he had condemned her. After a moment's frozen immobility her father thrust back his chair, moved very fast from behind the desk and slapped her face, very hard, holding back none of his man's strength, rocking her back on her heels. She stared at him in utter hatred. He slapped her again, backhanded. She snarled, lifted her hand. He glared at her, daring her to strike him back.

She could not. Crying uncontrollably now, unable to control her fear and her hatred, she broke. He watched her with distaste; the heaving shoulders, the blotched and twisted face. 'In God's holy name, pull yourself together, girl,' he said coldly. He pulled a clean and folded handkerchief from his pocket, shook it out fastidiously, handed it to her. Her sobs quieted a little. She blew her nose. 'Since the unfortunate day that you were born I have had occasion to wonder,' her father said, his voice icy, 'if indeed you are my true child. I find nothing in your behaviour, now or ever, to convince me that you are not a scoundrel's byblow. Only my faith in your mother, the need to protect her feelings and reputation, prevents me from denying you absolutely.'

She lifted her head. In silence they stood, the gulf of misliking and misunderstanding yawning to hatred between them. Any tender conscience Victor had had about his acceptance of Donovalov's offer was gone. Good riddance to the girl; Donovalov was welcome to her.

In silence Yelena turned and walked to the door. She opened it. Stepped out into the corridor beyond that was edged along one side with the balcony from which Victor could watch the comings and goings in the crowded shop downstairs. She lifted her voice, still hoarse and ragged with tears, pitching it to sound above the murmur of conversation below. Faces turned upwards. She saw her father's eyes widen, saw him move sharply towards her. She stepped back from him, repeated what she had said. 'You hear me, Papa? I said I'd *rather* be a bastard than a daughter of yours!' She had reached the head of the staircase, stood trembling, daring him to come and get her, to stop her. Victor stood like a statue in his office doorway. All movement and all noise in the shop had ceased. 'A father from the gutter would be a better father than you are or have ever been to me! I wish I *were* a bastard! Then I'd be the lucky child you tell me I am!' Battered and untidy, yet with an odd dignity she turned and marched down the stairs, ignoring the stares and the whispers. Her cheek throbbed from her father's blow, her eyes were swollen from weeping, her nose red.

'Yelena! *Yelena!*' Her father's voice cracked like a whip above her. She ignored it. What could he do to her that had not already been done? She pushed through the door and out into the street.

The two weddings were celebrated within a few days of one another, and the two occasions could not have been more different.

Anna and Guy were married in the Church of the Resurrection, a pretty church with many golden domes, its walls encrusted with brilliant mosaics that glinted in fitful September sunshine. The dark interior gleamed with candlelight; the bridal candle that Anna held burning as straight and as bright as any. When the rings were exchanged her hand was cool and steady; the only tremor came after that, when the bride and groom were led by the priest, as tradition demanded, three times around the lectern, the golden crowns of marriage held above their heads by two groomsmen. It had been as impossible for Guy not to ask Andrei to be his groomsman as it would have been for Andrei to refuse. Equally, since the other groomsman was a friend of Guy's whom Anna did not know it was logical that Andrei should carry the heavy crown above his niece's head, carefully sidestepping the long, silken train that swept the floor behind her. It was the moment Anna had been dreading. As he took her hand Guy squeezed it, very gently, and smiled, his wise, brilliant eyes gleaming in the dancing light. And that was the moment that Anna realized, at last, that given the total impossibility of her forbidden love for Andrei she had made no mistake in agreeing to marry this man, however odd the circumstances, however disparate their ages and their backgrounds. She remembered, as she walked in stately procession beside him, behind the chanting priest and in a sweet cloud of incense, that her first impression of Guy had been of a kindly man. And she had been right. Now she was certain of it; certain too that, passion and the hot blood of youth notwithstanding, kindness could be considered no mean gift to bring to a marriage.

The reception was held at the Hotel de l'Europe, where a suite had been reserved for bride and groom, since they were staying in St Petersburg for the first few days of their married life in order to attend Yelena's wedding before leaving for Paris. On hearing of that betrothal Anna had at last understood something of what her sister had been suffering over the past months and had attempted to make amends, to break the terrible barrier of anger and hurt that had grown between them. But Lenka had rejected outright every overture. Bitter and sullen, she had withdrawn entirely within herself. She had, as she had threatened, refused to attend upon Anna – a delighted and amused Katya and a radiant Margarita filling that role – and throughout the reception she sat beside her fiancé silent and unsmiling. Nor at any time did she offer good wishes to the newlyweds. But despite her sister's graceless behaviour, Anna enjoyed the occasion. It would have been difficult for any normal young woman not to. Guy had many friends in the city, both from the considerable English colony and from the Russian business and musical world, and all seemed genuinely delighted that the 'crusty old bachelor' as he was described, in laughter, more than once had at last succumbed to the siren call of marriage. Her pleasure was enhanced by the fact that, even set beside her cousin and her sister in their wedding finery – and no-one would have contested that these were the two prettiest girls in the room – she knew she looked coolly, and to her own mind astoundingly, elegant in the dress that, to Varya's outrage, Guy had insisted on helping her to choose. Pale, simple and of sumptuous silk, it had cost a small fortune, cunningly cut to emphasize her height and her narrow waist, sweeping to a slim, stately train behind her. Even Varya, whose taste had run originally to flounces and heavy, swaying skirts, had to admit to its beauty.

Katya had insisted upon her coming to the Bourlov apartment to have her hair dressed by the Bourlov women's personal hairdresser. The result was a soft red-gold cloud folded to the top of her head and threaded with real flowers. She did not need the easy compliments of others to tell her that she looked, if not exactly beautiful, certainly striking and by no stretch of the imagination plain. She sat through the endless courses, the even more endless toasts beside Guy, distinguished and handsome in his formal dress suit. As the party became rowdier the younger elements about the tables began the odd custom – that Anna herself had always thought faintly ridiculous – of complaining, each to his neighbour, of a bitter taste to the food, the wine. The buzz of the repeated word grew into a chant: 'bitter, bitter, bitter!' At this point the newlyweds were expected to kiss, to sweeten the day and chase away all signs of ill-omen. Smiling, Guy turned to her, and very gently he kissed her. Tables were thumped, a roar of applause broke out, more toasts were drunk. Anna turned back and found herself looking directly into the drawn face of Andrei some way down the table. For one moment their eyes held, then he lifted his glass to her, unsmiling, and toasted her before turning to his neighbour, apparently absorbed in their conversation. For a single second she allowed herself to watch him; the fluent gestures of his good hand as he spoke, the shock of prematurely silver hair that even for a formal occasion such as this refused to be tamed but sprang in unruly curls across his forehead. Then Guy turned to her. 'My dear, Ivan Ivanovich here apparently heard you play at the Bourlovs' earlier in the year – and in front of the great Scriabin –'

She cast one last look at Andrei and then turned, smiling steadily, back to her husband.

That night, in the biggest bed she had ever seen let alone slept in, in the most luxurious room she had ever occupied and after more champagne than she had ever drunk in her life, Guy gracefully and with great care made love to her. She did not dislike it, though tired and overwrought as she undoubtedly was, she was happy when it was safely over and she could sleep.

Guy, beside her, leaned on the huge frilled pillows, lit a cigar and watched her as she dropped into the instantaneous slumber of the young, her face smooth as a child's. He would have been less than human not to wonder if Andrei had been in her mind as he had made love to her. He reached forward, brushed a lock of hair away from her sleeping face. The irrevocable step was taken; only time now would tell whether his instinct had been right.

By contrast Yelena's wedding was a dour and charmless affair. The ceremony was held in a small church on Vasilievsky Island and the reception in the Shalakov apartment. Given the bride's lack of enthusiasm for the whole affair – that she made no effort to disguise – it was not surprising that the celebrations were stilted, the gaiety forced. Donovalov watched his new young wife's sullen and graceless behaviour with an expression, not entirely lacking in pleasure, that promised a later reckoning. Lenka, seeing it, promptly and perversely behaved worse than ever, glaring her defiance, daring him to stop her.

Anna's outstanding and uncomfortable memory of what could only be described as an outstandingly uncomfortable occasion was, almost certainly deliberately she realized later, the only words her sister addressed to her during the whole day. Standing tense and unsmiling, an untouched glass of wine clenched between strong and ill-manicured hands and with a face all but expressionless, Lenka watched her husband as he moved from group to group about the crowded room. Only when she turned to Anna, looked with fierce and unblinking accusation directly into her sister's face did Anna see the despair in her eyes. The look was like a blow.

'I'll never forgive you for this, Anna.' Lenka's voice was low, perfectly calm. 'Never. Not for as long as I live. Understand that. Remember it.' And she left her, rejecting with sharp contempt Anna's small, pleading gesture, refusing for the rest of the day to speak to her, even to say farewell when she left.

The next day Anna, with Guy, boarded the train for Paris with those words echoing still in her ears.

INTERLUDE: 1909–1911

Those first months of Anna's marriage opened to her a world
of which until then she had not even been aware. In Paris she
was welcomed – as Guy had guessed she would be – as 'la
p'tite Russe', discovering to her astonishment that simply to be
Russian at that moment in that most modish of cities was the
very height of chic. That spring the Russian impresario Serge
Diaghilev had arrived in Paris and had taken the city by storm.
Russian music, Russian opera, Russian ballet was the rage. Russian names were upon every tongue – the genius designer Bakst,
the fabulous and adored Nijinski and the young composer Igor
Stravinsky were the darlings of the Parisian fashionable world.
Guy de Fontenay was already a well-known and popular figure
in the salons and dining rooms of this blithe and brilliant place:
his unexpected arrival with this very new, very young, charmingly unspoiled – some would go so far as to say incredibly
gauche – Russian wife sparked off enough speculation, interest,
and gossip – and consequent invitations – to keep them fully
occupied, had they desired it, every moment of the day for
several months at least.

Anna, to begin with, was all but paralysed with nerves.

'No need, my dear, no need!' Guy said, firmly, when first she
brought herself to voice her fears. 'Remember our first evening
together? Your first visit to a Ladies' Room alone? You survived
that, did you not?' And then, enjoying her sudden burst of laughter, 'Then what in the world has Paris to offer that is so very
intimidating? Come – find your hat and gloves. We go to visit
M'sieu Paul Poiret. No knight worthy of his spurs would go
into battle without armour – a few days of the master's attentions and you, and your wardrobe, will be ready, I promise, to
take on not just this wicked city, but the world!'

With Guy at her side there was indeed little for her to fear.

With great enjoyment and infinite patience he coaxed her into his world – and with equal care he kept from her less pleasant aspects of it.

And, as he had hoped, overlaid by the trepidation, excitement and fascination of this new life, week by week and month by month the painful memories of Andrei began, a little, to fade.

They visited the Louvre and the Grand Palais, they attended the theatre, the opera, the ballet and the music hall. They dined at the most expensive and fashionable restaurants in company with the most expensive and fashionable people. They attended a few small private dinner parties at which, at Guy's gentle instigation, Anna was prevailed upon to play; it was not long before de Fontenay's little Russian wife was almost as much in vogue as M'sieu Poiret's gowns and the exotic designs of art nouveau amongst the discerning and competitive hostesses of the city.

She made mistakes, and she learned by them. Always she watched Guy. Always he was ready with a smile. And almost always, with those bright, confident eyes upon her, the nerves and the shyness could be overcome. He educated her palate and guided her untutored tastes. He delighted in buying her clothes – elegant and expensive things that made her feel, and therefore in a strange way become, a different, a more poised, a more confident person.

St Petersburg began to seem a very long way away.

She wrote to her family religiously once a week, to Katya and to Lenka less frequently but at least once a month. From her father she received short and stilted replies equally regularly. From Katya she would hear nothing for weeks and then receive anything from a scribbled and all but indecipherable two lines to a scrawled and mammoth screed of such diverse and often amusing subjects and so many pages that Guy came to refer to them as 'Katya's novelettes'.

From Lenka she heard not at all.

Between her father and Katya she kept abreast of affairs in Petersburg: Margarita's somewhat volatile progress through the Gymnasium, young Dmitri's utter indifference to any girl but his first, childhood love Natalia, the birth of a child, a girl, to

Lenka, and subsequently and far too soon a miscarriage seven months later.

In the new year they moved on from Paris to Vienna and then in the summer from Vienna to Rome. For those with the funds and freedom to enjoy it the Europe of those years was a gay and opulent playground. Few saw the dark perils that, like quicksand beneath sweet grass, lay just beneath the glittering surface: the ever-growing gap between rich and poor engendered by the industrial revolution and the unrest that such persistent injustices were bound to cause, the growth of nationalism and the consequent struggle for power that was bound to threaten the peace and stability of this confident and all too often thoughtless world. It was a time of great, intriguing and far-reaching technological advance – Louis Bleriot's flight across the Channel heralded a new age of air travel, telegraph and wireless revolutionized the world of communication, and the first mass-produced motor cars were rolling off industry's first assembly line in Detroit. That all of these advances had military as well as peacetime application did not fail to register with those who cared about such things; for others it was all simply part of the fun and helped to make a good life even better.

It was the autumn of 1910 before Guy decided it was time to take his young wife to that place that was closest to his heart; the place he had kept as all the best things should be kept, until last; the place that was, for him, truly home. It was a different Anna, outwardly at least, who stood beside him on the steamer's deck and watched the gleaming cliffs of Dover loom out of a September mist than had boarded the train at St Petersburg with him just over a year before. He watched her, wondering a little. For all the closeness of their relationship they had never, by mutual consent, spoken of Andrei nor of the odd circumstances of their marriage. He had watched in these past months as she had grown – as he had known she could – from uncertain child to apparently confident and happy woman. He loved her more than ever he would have believed it possible; he was diverted to discover that now it was he who was nervous. Sythings awaited its mistress. What a disaster it would be if Anna could not find it in her heart to love the place as he did.

His anxiety was misplaced. Anna, more than ready to love

Sythings for Guy's sake if for no other reason, took one look at the lovely old house set within its peaceful garden in the veiled green of the Sussex countryside and was enslaved. She ran from room to room like a child, exclaiming and laughing delightedly. 'Oh, Guy! – Guy! – It's beautiful!' She spoke, still, in French, her newly-learned English deserting her in this moment of pleasure and excitement. 'And look! A music room! A real music room! What a lovely piano! What a wonderful view!' She flung open the tall french doors that led out onto the terrace and thence to the wide green lawns of the garden. 'Oh, Guy, my dear –' she was absurdly close to tears '– it's quite the loveliest house I've ever seen!'

The house became their true home from that moment on, though still they travelled often, and as often used Guy's small London flat for business or for the pleasure of concerts and the theatre.

The letters from St Petersburg continued to arrive. Dmitri had served the first months of his obligatory national service in the army of the Tsar before Victor, in the accepted way of such things, had bought him out at what he gave Anna to believe was enormous expense and set him to work in the business. Lenka had miscarried yet again. Katya was mildly and amusedly taken with the growing Margarita: 'What a child! Are you quite sure your mother didn't play fast and loose nine months before she was born?'

Anna wrote once more to Lenka, expressing her sympathy at the loss of this second baby.

And, once more, Lenka did not reply.

BOOK TWO

1911–1913

CHAPTER NINE

'My papa,' Katya said, lightly, but with a faint, wry edge to her voice that belied her laughter, 'is not pleased with me.'

Margarita turned, startled. 'Your father? Good heavens, how in the world have you managed that?' For Mischa to express real disapproval of his indulged daughter was all but unknown. 'Have you murdered someone?'

'It's not so much what I've done,' Katya gave the vase of flowers she had been arranging a last tweak and set it upon a nearby table, 'as what I haven't. And what I don't, if I can possibly help it, intend to. At least for as long as is possible.' They were in the ballroom of the Bourlov apartment. Around them the frantic activity that necessarily accompanied the preparations for a coming-of-age ball was reaching its climax. A small army of floor polishers skated about the gleaming parquet floor, soft cloths on their feet. A low stage upon which the orchestra would sit was being decorated with swathes of gold and green silk and set with huge potted plants and flower arrangements. In the centre of the floor a ladder was set precariously beneath the chandelier, which was being painstakingly cleaned, its swinging crystals jingling like sleigh bells on a winter's night.

Katya led the way out onto one of the balconies. Margarita followed; watched as Katya produced a long cigarette holder and a packet of cigarettes. Katya proffered the packet. Rita, fascinated but reluctant, shook her head. 'Papa would kill me.' Katya laughed, lit her cigarette, blew smoke into the clear autumn air. It was September, and there was a chill in the almost imperceptible breeze that was all too familiar. Summer was over. Winter, inexorably, was approaching.

'So. What is it that you haven't done?' Margarita, as ever, could not contain her curiosity.

'Can't you guess?' Katya waved her empty hand eloquently, as if the whole of St Petersburg must surely know of her misdemeanour. 'I haven't married. I haven't, God help us all, even become engaged. And consequently I haven't produced, or am not imminently to produce, the Bourlov heir that poor Mischischa so desires. And neither will I if I can help it!'

Margarita raised fair eyebrows. 'What's so wrong with being married?'

Katya turned on her a look of such pained astonishment that the other girl could not help but laugh. In the three years since Anna had left the city these two, each for her own reasons and despite the difference in their ages, had developed a mutually advantageous relationship that could at a casual glance be taken – mistakenly – for close if light-hearted friendship. Margarita unashamedly and for reasons she made no attempt to hide preferred the Bourlov home to her own and determinedly spent as much time there as was humanly possible. She was sixteen years old, and she had plans; plans whose natural starting point was here, with her wealthy relations and their contacts, not at home on the Venskaya with her mother's migraines and her father's sober and grinding respectability. For her part Katya enjoyed having the younger girl around, and would have been less than human not to have enjoyed the open hero-worship that her cousin was all too ready to bestow upon her; though, shrewd as her father, she was perfectly aware that the basis of that apparently artless admiration owed as much if not more to envy than to any warmer emotion. Margarita coveted everything about Katya's life, from her pretty clothes and her father's money – that in these past years of industrial boom in Russia had grown to no mean fortune – to the relaxed indulgence with which her parents treated her. Katya did little to discourage or disabuse her; it suited her admirably to have this pretty, malleable youngster in tow – for Margarita, chatterbox that she was, was nevertheless astute enough to know when to keep her mouth shut and could be quite remarkably and cheerfully devious when it came to the small intrigues and adventures of which Katya was so fond.

'What's wrong with being married, my dear, is just about everything. The idea of handing oneself over lock, stock and barrel to some – *man* –' Katya pulled a mockingly ferocious face '– who, quite absurdly, will take it upon himself to lecture you, order your affairs, make sure you behave yourself for the rest of your life – it's abominable! What's wrong with marriage? You might as well ask what's wrong with prison!'

'But I thought you liked men?'

'I do. Oh, I do. In their place.' Katya slanted a small, wicked glance over her shoulder. 'I've come to the conclusion that our smart and sneaky Anna had it right all along, you know. Marry a man old enough to be your grandfather, and rich – then the one thing you can guarantee is he'll pop off and leave you a free and wealthy widow. What bliss!'

Rita's pretty laughter pealed again, delightedly scandalized. 'Katya!'

'But a *young* man? God, no! Noisy, bossy, opinionated folk are young men.'

'Your father doesn't approve of your plan to marry a rich old man?' Rita picked a petal from the flower she still carried and dropped it over the edge of the balcony, watching as it fluttered brightly through the still air to the ground.

'I'm afraid not.' For a moment the shadow of real gloom showed in her cousin's face. 'I told you. He wants a grandson. Two. Three or four if possible. He's absolutely fixed upon the notion. What a perfectly terrible idea! And there's worse!'

'There can't be.'

'Oh, yes there can. He's actually found someone!'

That caught the younger girl's attention. She turned, her laughter dying. 'You mean – someone he wants you to marry?'

'Exactly. Can you imagine? I've refused of course. The idea's monstrous.' Katya leaned back, drew on her cigarette, blew smoke into the air.

'And – that's why your father is annoyed with you?'

'It is.'

Margarita cast mildly caustic eyes to the room behind them. 'He can't be too angry. It hasn't stopped him giving you a most splendid party for your birthday.'

'Ah, but that's all part of it, you see. This beastly man is going to *be* at this blessed affair tomorrow. We're supposed to –' Katya shrugged '– get to know each other.'

173

Her cousin was watching her, bright-eyed and interested. 'Who is he? What's he like?'

Katya stubbed out her cigarette. 'It's immaterial, Margarita, my pet. I plan to make myself so utterly objectionable that he'll refuse even to consider me as a future wife, money or no money.'

'He's marrying you for your *money*?' The words were openly astonished.

Katya smiled again, that singularly wicked smile that Rita, having observed its effect on several young men, spent much time emulating in front of her mirror. 'You aren't listening, Rita. He's not going to marry me at all. I've quite made up my mind.'

'Before you've ever met him?' Rita was doubtful.

'Oh, I've met him. Once or twice, in Finland. His sister's married to Turnakov, the industrialist – he's a friend of Mischischa's. She isn't bad, actually.'

Margarita waited. Katya said nothing more. Exasperatedly Margarita gave in and asked, 'Well? What's *he* like?'

'Turnakov?' Katya asked, innocently. 'Oh, he's just the kind of person I was talking about – a very great catch – old, and rich, one foot in the grave almost – but I told you, he's already married.'

'No! The other one! The one your father wants – oh, Katya, don't be so trying! What's his name? What's he like? Why does your father want you to marry him?'

'His name is Johannes Lavola. Everyone calls him –' she paused, spoke the next word with flawless disdain '– Jussi. He's Finnish, for God's sake!' She lifted unbelieving eyes to heaven at the very thought. 'Finnish! He's tall. Fairish. Not very good-looking. And most assuredly not very well off.'

'But – why would your father –?'

Katya shrugged. 'He's a Count. Or something.'

'A Count?' The word was hushed. 'A real one?'

'No. A Finnish one.' Dismissively Katya dropped her cigarette to the floor, crushed it with her foot. 'But that's the problem, you see. Mischischa wants this fictional grandson of his to have a title, even if it is only a Finnish one. He also wants closer ties with Turnakov, family ties. It's all very complicated and if you ask me rather greedy; Mischa already has far too much money for his own good, and I told him so – but he won't listen; he wants grandsons, he wants the title and he wants to tie Turnakov to him; so I'm to be sacrificed on the cold stone altar of marriage.' She smiled, very sweetly. 'Except that I won't be.' She moved back through the doors into the busy ballroom.

Margarita followed. 'But – what are you going to do about it? How can you stop it?'

Katya pulled a long fair curl across her mouth, nibbled at it. 'Watch me,' she said, and all trace of laughter had left the blue eyes. Then, 'Now, let's get out of this shambles, it's worse than a circus ring! Come and have some tea. I forgot to tell you, I've had a letter from Anna –'

Margarita dodged across the dance floor behind her, missing a skating polisher by inches. 'We had one a couple of weeks ago. From Vienna. Guy paid for her to study under some famous teacher for the summer – I've forgotten his name –'

'She's back in England now.' Katya led the way into a small but extremely elegant parlour, reached for the bell pull. Her face was suddenly pensive. 'It's interesting, isn't it? I mean, Anna of all people! Well, she seems remarkably happy, I must say.'

Margarita settled herself decoratively into a chair. 'You're surprised?'

'Yes. I think I am. Didn't it all ever strike you –?' She stopped.

'What?'

'– as a little – well, odd? Anna and Guy – it was all very sudden?'

Margarita shrugged, disinterestedly. 'Guy's not young; once he made up his mind I suppose he reasoned that he didn't have much time to lose. And Anna – well, I suppose she must have seen her chance to get out and took it.' She rolled expressive eyes. 'Just give me such an opportunity; you won't see my heels!'

Anna was indeed happy; and her cousin Katya was not the only person to be surprised that it should be so. Anna sometimes wondered herself at the twist of fate that had brought her to Guy and to a life richer and fuller than she had dreamed could be possible. It had been hard at first – harder than she had ever conceded, to herself or to Guy. The world to which she had so precipitately fled had been an intimidating place to start with. She had been desperately homesick, and the wound of the brutal break with Andrei had been a longer and more painful time in the healing than she had allowed herself to admit or to show. But of course always there had been Guy; with patience and, she later realized, love, Guy had been her guide and her protector; he had neither hurried nor tried to dominate her. He had introduced her to his world, and his world had welcomed her; the world of the artist, the writer, the musician. She could not fail to have been seduced by it; more extraordinary had been the slow but sure awakening of her deeper feelings for Guy himself. For his generosity, his kindness, his understanding, she could not help but love him as a friend; as time had moved on and the memory of Petersburg and of Andrei had begun to dim, she had come, to the delighted surprise of them both, to love him wholeheartedly as a man. Now, three years after the wedding the unlikely union had become a joy and a pleasure to them both. And if still, sometimes, a ghost stood between them, a phantom that neither would admit to seeing, and if Anna rarely if ever played the music of the Russian composers that Andrei had taught her to love, it in no way diminished their pleasure in each other.

'It's Katya's birthday.' She stood at the window of the small flat in Westminster that Guy used for his trips to the capital, looking out across the busy river. 'Tomorrow. Her twenty-first.'

Guy lifted his head, looking at her. Tall, slim and graceful, she was dressed in the colours in which he most loved to see her, soft greens and blues, the narrow tunic skirt tapering to her ankles, matching jacket fitted to her small waist, the shirt-like collar turned up to frame her sharp-boned face. Her hair was the colour of the first of the autumn leaves that moved in the breeze outside the window. No longer a child, no longer the gauche, artless, defiant Anna who had faced him in Andrei's work room, this was a woman of confidence and of style. His wife. The thought still had the power, sometimes, to startle. 'Are you missing St Petersburg?' he asked after a moment, with that quick intuition that could be so very disconcerting. 'Would you like to go back – for a visit, perhaps?'

The silence maybe lasted just a shade too long. Anna, her back still to him, did not move. He watched her, quietly, waiting. Saw the sudden sharp, negative movement of her head. 'No.' She turned. She was smiling a little, her face serene, though he fancied that a shadow lay somewhere in her eyes. 'No. Not yet. Soon, perhaps. But not yet.' Her English was clear, slightly but not unattractively accented. She came to him, stood beside him, her narrow hand upon his shoulder. 'Is your business in London nearly finished? Could we go back to Sussex? The garden at Sythings is so beautiful at this time of the year.'

He smiled, nodded. 'We'll go tomorrow.'

She touched his cheek with her finger. 'Home,' she said. 'We'll go home.'

Katya's coming-of-age ball was nothing if not ostentatious. More than two hundred people packed into the Bourlov apartment to take advantage of Mischa's lavish hospitality. The evening began at seven, decorously enough, with tea and cakes. Maids moved through the glittering, chattering throng with trays of cups and small sweet cakes. A serious card game was already in progress in the large parlour, the stakes high, the protagonists – two dowagers, a crusty General and a member of the German Diplomatic Corps – old and shrewd enemies, the game undoubtedly set to last into the small hours. Tea finished, and with more guests arriving by the minute, tables containing vast dishes of fish and meat, pâtés, hams and cheeses, the inevitable caviar, vodka, liqueurs and champagne were wheeled into the ballroom. A string quartet – the best available in Petersburg, naturally – played upon the stage, fighting a losing battle to be heard over the hubbub of talk and laughter. Bejewelled fingers fluttered, bare shoulders gleamed in the light, diadems and coronets glittered upon elaborately-coiffed hair and peacock shades of silk, satin and shimmering velvet, reflected in the tall, gilded mirrors, turned the ballroom into a kaleidoscope of shifting light and colour. Katya was everywhere, vivid in sapphire-blue silk, her bright face the centre of any group she joined, her laughter ringing clear and gay. This was her evening, she intended no one to be in any doubt of that; and she was going to enjoy every single second of it.

Margarita stuck to her cousin like a burr. Where Katya was, there was Rita, arm in arm, laughing with her, basking in reflected glory. She had wheedled a new dress from her father for the occasion and, with shrewd and new-found subtlety, had had the wit to opt, over Varya's pained objections, for dove white, artfully simple, with a rose-pink sash. In the hothouse opulence of the ballroom the dress stood out like a splash of pale innocence against a swathe of scarlet sin. She looked young, fresh and enchantingly pretty, and she knew it. She wore pink and white flowers in the mass of her hair, pinned high upon her head, and upon the bodice of her dress; lacking decent jewellery she had decided, again to her mother's consternation, not to wear any at all. The effect was striking; calculatedly so. Margarita knew exactly what she wanted; tonight was the night she intended to take the first steps towards getting it.

'Rita, my dear, how very lovely you look!' Her uncle kissed her soundly upon both cheeks, put his arm about his daughter's trim waist.

Katya leaned back from him, laughing up into his face. 'You look remarkably handsome yourself, Mischischa darling. Quite the best-looking man in the whole room! I insist you start the dancing with me! I've kept the first dance free for you.' She laughed, mischievously, knowing he would not be able to refuse her. To grant any young man the first dance on this most special of occasions would be to give him a public advantage over his fellows, something she had no intention in the world of doing.

Her father, knowing perfectly well what she did, laughed. 'How can I refuse? But –' his arm tightened a little as she made to slip from him '– only on condition that you come and make yourself extremely pleasant to my friend Turnakov and his young wife. They're over there by the window. Come.' He caught her hand and began to weave between the tables, acknowledging greetings, stopping for the odd polite word, never relinquishing his firm grip upon his daughter's hand. Perforce, the rebellious Katya followed, and quite shamelessly so did Margarita.

'Yuri Alexeievich! Welcome! And Elisabet.' Mischa bowed

over the hand of a tall blonde girl dressed in deep red velvet. Rubies picked up the same vibrant colour at ears and throat, and her fair hair was simply dressed. Her face, whilst by no means beautiful, was strong and clear-boned.

Her smile was warm, her blue eyes cool. 'Mischa. What an extremely grand party.' The appraising eyes moved to Katya, assessing her; the smile was apparently unaffected and genuine, though still those cool, intelligent eyes weighed and measured, oddly severe. 'Katya, you look lovely, as always.' The steady blue eyes moved to Margarita, questioning.

'Margarita Victorovna, my niece,' Mischa said. 'Rita, this is Yuri Alexeievich Turnakov and his wife Elisabet.'

Margarita smiled dazzlingly, and was rewarded by a twinkle in the older man's eyes as he bent over her small hand. There was a brief, slightly awkward silence. Elisabet made no attempt to acknowledge the introduction. Around them the talk and the laughter rose and fell like the sound of waves beating upon a sanded shore. 'I'm afraid,' Elisabet said, calmly, 'that my brother Jussi hasn't arrived yet.' She smiled at Katya, frank and unapologetic. 'I can't think what's happened to him. He'll be here directly, I'm sure.' There was a small, sharp edge to her voice that boded ill for the missing brother. Her Russian was smooth, only slightly accented.

Katya had disengaged her hand from her father's. Her smile matched the other girl's for brightness, and for wariness. 'Don't worry,' she said, and waved an airy hand at the gathered guests, 'we really aren't missing him. It's been so nice to meet you again, thank you so much for coming – I'm sorry, there really are so many people that I should –' and she was gone, slipping into the throng like a fish into water. Margarita cast a single look at her uncle and followed; Katya was her touchstone, her talisman for the evening; she must not lose her.

Mischa turned a look of quick and exasperated enquiry upon Elisabet.

'I'm sorry,' she said. 'He should be here. I can't think where he is.'

Beside her, her husband laughed, and raised experienced eyes to heaven.

*   *   *

'Such a pity that Lenka couldn't come.' Zhenia Petrovna Bourlova linked arms with her sister and guided her towards the card game. They stood for a moment, watching.

Varya managed a faint, becoming blush. 'She's – indisposed.'

Neither Zhenia's look nor the faint snort that accompanied it could have been described as ladylike. 'Pregnant again, you mean! Honestly, Varya, how you could have allowed her to marry that – that rat of a man!'

'Zhenia, please!' Varya was very much on her dignity. 'Pavel Petrovich is our son-in-law.'

'He's a rat,' Zhenia said, calmly. 'And as for poor Lenka being with child again – how many times is this?'

Varya nibbled her lip. 'Since Tonia – three I think, all ending in –' she cleared her throat '– that is, ending in unfortunate circumstances. This is the fourth.'

'Do you see anything of her?'

Varya, suddenly apparently absorbed in what was happening at the card table, shook her head vaguely. 'Not much.' She allowed a small silence to develop. 'She was always a difficult child,' she said, plaintively.

Zhenia took quick breath to speak, held it, exhaled it slowly. Even a sister could go only so far. 'And Dmitri? He and his little Natalia are to marry?'

Varya nodded. Another disappointment. That her only son, so soft, always so very *manageable*, should have taken this one stand against her was a sore point. Not that she had anything against young Natalia – unless one counted her looks, her lack of vigour, her personality. She sighed.

Zhenia smiled. 'Made in heaven, that one,' she said. 'Be thankful. They love each other – well, goodness, they've been like Siamese twins ever since they met – oh yes, think yourself lucky, Varya. They'll be happy, those two, together.'

Varya said nothing.

'And your little Margarita – you have your hands full there!' The words were indulgent. 'Such a pretty child.' Zhenia slanted a not unaffectionate look at her younger sister. 'Very like her mother. How well I remember you at that age.'

That pleased Varya, as Zhenia had known it would. She glanced into a mirror that hung upon the far wall of the room, noted in the soft glow of the candles how her eyes still gleamed, her golden hair shone, with not a trace of grey.

'I was wondering?' Zhenia hesitated. Varya looked at her. 'Perhaps she might like to spend more time here, with Katya? She's such a lively child. A positive delight. We could perhaps be of some help –' she waved a vague hand '– introductions, and such?' She let the words trail to nothing, knowing the unspoken offer would be well understood. Each time Zhenia Petrovna Bourlova looked at her bright-faced niece she remembered the sister she had manipulated into marriage with a safe, stolid, boring man, and conscience, very slightly, gnawed.

'I'm sure she'd love to.' Varya was positively proud of the calm understatement; of all of her children Margarita was the only one she truly understood. Margarita, she knew, would kill to stay at the Bourlovs'.

Zhenia linked her arm again into her sister's. They strolled back along the crowded corridor and into the ballroom. The dancing was about to begin; tables had been moved to the side of the room, a full orchestra had taken their place upon the stage. Guests stood in groups about the floor, laughing and talking. 'And Anna,' Zhenia said. 'Katya received a letter from her the other day. She seems happy?'

Varya turned surprised eyes upon her. 'Well, of course she is,' she said. 'Her husband has money.' They walked on into the busy ballroom. 'I still can't think how she managed it,' Varya added, a little vaguely; and wondered why her sister laughed.

More guests arrived; the party gathered momentum. There was dancing, more food, dancing again and yet another feast. Vodka and champagne flowed, loosening tongues and lifting laughter. Katya flitted still, like a bright and restless butterfly in a field of flowers, and Margarita followed. Followed, that is, until, at last, a pair of particularly bright eyes met hers, eyes set in a young and handsome face above an equally handsome dress uniform. He was slim, slightly built, moderately tall and of more than moderate good looks. The vodka bottle that stood on the table before him was empty. But where others had been loud, he was quiet, where other advances had been harshly confident, his were diffident, almost gentle. She settled beside him, a dove come to rest.

Her brother Dmitri, eighteen years old, slim, pale, tall now and habitually serious, hovered by Natalia's side, uneasy in his cheap, ill-fitting evening suit, his whole attention upon his love. Natalia, equally out of place in this gathering, smiled at him, a calm, motherly smile, and held his hand. They did not dance, nor often did they speak. There was no need. Together they sat upon a curved sweetheart chair, in silence, hands clasped, a small, still core of quiet that waited for this silly storm of celebration to pass. Varya, catching sight of them, clicked her tongue and shook her head. 'Those two,' she said to Victor, 'they're like an old married couple already.'

Katya whirled from the dance, extracted herself from her partner's enthusiastic embrace, took another glass of champagne from the tray proffered by a smiling manservant.

'Women in Finland,' a clear, self-confident voice said, somewhere close by, 'have been voting since 1906. It doesn't seem to me that the Duchy has exactly descended into depravity and chaos.'

Diverted, Katya turned. It was the Finnish girl Elisabet, of course – she had recognized the voice and the accent immediately – who smiled with utter self-possession into a florid face. 'Women pay taxes, do they not? To refuse them a say in the spending of their own money is surely the height of injustice?'

'Stuff and nonsense, girl!' The florid face empurpled further. 'Yuri Alexeievich, you surely don't agree with this rubbish?'

Elisabet's husband smiled, mildly. 'My wife's views are her own, Sergei Sergeiivich, she needs no brief from me to hold them.' His voice was amused.

Elisabet turned her head and caught Katya's eyes upon her; then her gaze moved beyond her, and her usually well-schooled face changed slightly. Katya turned. A tall, very fair young man was advancing across the dance floor, talking as he came, a group gathering about him. His pale hair was tousled, the jacket of his formal evening suit unbuttoned, his tie not quite straight. He wore a bright but lamentably wilted flower in his buttonhole. Leaving a buzz of conversation in his wake, he moved with long strides to where his sister and her husband waited; stood before them, bright-eyed and slightly dishevelled. 'Someone's tried to assassinate Stolypin,' he said cheerfully. 'In Kiev. Word is they've probably succeeded.' He looked around, relieved a servant of the last glass of champagne on his tray, drank thirstily.

Elisabet's mouth snapped shut. She stared.

Her brother put the empty glass back on the tray. 'The news has just come in. It's all over the city. He's in a bad way, it's said – he isn't expected to survive. Sorry I'm late.' His eyes rested, belatedly, upon Katya. Unabashed, he came laconically to something approximating attention, took her hand, bowed over it. 'Yekaterina Mikhailovna – my apologies. My late arrival is, I know, absolutely unforgivable.' His formal use of her name contrived somehow to sound faintly mocking; he made not the slightest attempt to inject into the words the smallest part of repentance, nor did he seem aware of the disturbance and stir his news had brought to the room. Pyotr Stolypin, the Tsar's Prime Minister, was as admired by some as he was detested by others. Dubbed 'Stolypin the Hangman' for his brutally efficient crushing of the Revolution of 1905, yet few would in honesty doubt his integrity, and his recent attempts to break the growing and sinister hold of the monk Rasputin over the Empress and through her the whole of the Imperial family had met with wholehearted support in many quarters.

Katya looked coldly down at the bent fair head. 'Do you make a habit, Jussi Lavola, of arriving at other peoples' celebrations – as you say yourself – unforgivably late, and looking as if you've come from a street fight?' she asked crisply, and loudly enough for a great many people to hear. The orchestra had stopped playing, dancers stood together on the floor, discussing the news.

'Katya.' Elisabet was beside her, a hand on her arm, surprisingly conciliatory. The look she shot at her brother was a flash of blue steel. 'Jussi didn't mean to –'

Katya, firmly, shook her arm free. 'What Jussi meant or didn't mean to do is immaterial.' Jussi was watching her, and, infuriatingly, he was smiling, genuinely amused. There was a faint smell of alcohol about him, he rocked gently on the balls of his feet, balancing. 'He's drunk,' Katya said, in her voice an unfeigned and steely anger that anyone who did business with Mischa Bourlov would have recognized.

Elisabet shook her head. 'Katya –'

Her quiet words were drowned by Mischa's lifted voice from

183

the stage. 'Ladies and gentlemen, please – if I might just give the little news we have? There has apparently been an attempt to assassinate Prime Minister Stolypin this evening in Kiev. He is reported shot, badly injured. That is all we know. Now, sad as the news is, might I suggest that there is little or nothing to be gained in abandoning our small celebration?' He moved back, nodding to the conductor who stepped once more upon the podium, baton raised. Music lifted, the sweet, lilting strains of a Strauss waltz.

'How is it,' asked a man's voice, deep, oddly disembodied, 'that we Russians can find no way forward, except in violence?'

'Forward?' Another voice took up the challenge, fiercely. 'You call it a step forward to murder such a man?'

The music, thankfully, drowned out any reply. Dancers took again to the floor.

'Yekaterina Mikhailovna.' Immaculately formal, his expression still gracelessly and unflatteringly full of laughter, his stance still far from stable, Jussi Lavola extended a long and startlingly grubby hand. 'May I have the pleasure?'

Katya surveyed him, her swift temper gone, calmly smiling. She knew a winning game when she saw one. 'No,' she said. 'You may not.' Coolly she nodded to Elisabet and her husband and turned away, hiding the sudden lift of laughter. The idiot had played right into her hands. A smile lit her face as a young Cossack officer bowed over her hand. 'Good heavens, my dear, is it our dance already?' No-one, least of all her father, could now expect her to entertain the thought of accepting this provincial boor – this Finn! – as a husband, title or no title. And it would take time to find another suitable applicant for the post. Meanwhile – she smiled up into the ardent dark eyes of her Cossack officer – she could not, for the moment remember his name – meanwhile, she was free.

'You fool, Jussi.' Elisabet's voice was tartly conversational. 'You damned fool! Will you never stop playing games?'

Jussi laughed. Despite every effort the sound was not easy.

She turned her head to look levelly at him. 'You've been with that woman again.'

He shrugged. She waited. 'Yes,' he said.

Elisabet took a long, slow breath, containing fury. 'Jussi. You simply can't be so irresponsible! We agreed. All of us. What you do with your private life is, I suppose, your own business. But this marriage is essential. The money is essential. Yuri is becoming suspicious.'

'She's a spoiled brat,' he said. 'Indulged. Arrogant. And with as much intelligence as a moth. And apart from anything else it isn't fair to involve her –'

'Jussi – she's rich.'

He looked out across the glittering, shifting sea of dancers. 'I don't like her.'

His sister's hand clamped upon his arm. 'You don't have to like her. You have to marry her.' Her voice was flat.

He shook his head, as if to clear it.

'Jussi, listen.'

'I know,' he said, sharply, and then again, 'I know.' But the smile had gone from his face and the expression left in his eyes was rebellious.

Margarita was in a seventh heaven. The young man was dark, and very handsome. He was an officer in the Preobrajensky Guards; the uniform was magnificent. He was the incarnation, the very picture, of her dreams. And he was looking at her as a starving man might look at a banquet. His name was Alexandr Feodorovich Kolashki; he had already begged her to call him Sasha. He had utterly refused to relinquish her hand to the young man who had had the forethought to book the supper dance, but had whirled her himself into a dashing and light-footed mazurka that had attracted satisfying attention from the onlookers about the dance floor before escorting her himself into the supper room. This was the one. She wanted him.

She smiled, dazzlingly. 'Alexandr Feodorovich –' she hesitated, blushing, dipping her head shyly '– Sasha, it's so very warm in here –'

'The balcony,' he said, drawing her small hand into the crook of his arm. 'It's cooler out there. Come.'

Varya watched from across the room, smiling a little. How lovely Rita looked tonight; the very image of her mother all those years ago. And how very clever she was. Varya slipped her arm into her husband's, gently manoeuvring him so that his back was to the tall window towards which the handsome young officer was so attentively escorting his youngest daughter. One could never tell with Victor; he could be the most dreadful spoilsport. For a moment she stood, allowing the small blade of envy to cut at her heart. If she had had such opportunity, what might her life have been? If she had married such a one instead of dull, respectable Victor – 'I'm sorry, my dear?'

'I said,' Victor repeated, testily, 'that we really should begin to think of leaving. It's one o'clock in the morning – really far too late for the children to be up.' He glanced about him. 'Where are they? Where's Margarita?'

'I believe she's resting, in Katya's room, with the young Lubachova girl. She's perfectly safe,' Varya said, smoothly, steering him towards a group that contained a face she had been looking out for all evening. 'Come now, Victor, the party goes on until two – we really can't be so ill-mannered as to leave now. Look, the girls are lining up for the cotillion – just see how many ribbons Katya has collected! It is her birthday, of course, the young men are bound to try to please her – why, General – how very nice to see you!'

No fairy waved a wand, no magician arrived to turn back the clock; inevitably the party had to end. At three the last of the revellers left – a group of young men in the midst of whom Katya spotted Jussi Lavola, heading she guessed not for home but for the delights of the shadier side of the night-time city. Jussi had not been near her for the rest of the evening after his unconventional entrance, except formally to take his leave. She stood at the window, watching the young men in the street below, rowdy as schoolboys, pushing and shoving each other, laughing and talking with no regard whatsoever for those more sober citizens abed and trying to sleep. As they passed beneath a lamp the light struck upon the pale, untidy thatch of the young Finn's hair. He had his arm about the shoulders of another of the young men, though who was supporting whom was impossible to guess. With any luck they'd both fall over. Katya smothered a smile and turned back to the wrecked ballroom. She had a strong and satisfying feeling that she'd seen the last of Jussi Lavola.

* * *

She was wrong.

He called the next day, to her utter astonishment, asking first for her father. Katya, pale and feeling by no means well in body or in temper after the excesses of the night before, was outraged. She prowled the floor of her room, refusing to come out, forcing her father to send for her which, in due course, he did. On entering his study she was quite spitefully pleased to see that Jussi, standing tall and excessively pale by the window, looked even worse than she felt. She pitched her voice just a little higher than usual as she returned his subdued greeting, smiled very brightly and watched in satisfaction as he winced.

Her father regarded her repressively, but could not for long keep the amusement from his eyes. 'Jussi thought you might like to take a stroll in the sunshine with him. Unlike most young men he had the good sense to ask me first.' The amusement was open now. Katya scowled at him. He sustained her glare with equanimity; nodded towards the door. 'A breath of air will do you good, child.'

She opened her mouth. 'I don't —'

'You do. Yes, you do, my dear.' Her father smiled again, with firm purpose.

Katya subsided. Even she could not best or deflect her father when he was in this mood and she had the sense to know it. With ill grace she fetched cape, hat and gloves, jamming the long hatpin into her mass of hair as if she could think of many better uses to which to put it. With some care Jussi took her elbow and negotiated the stairs without jolting his thumping head too much, flinched as they stepped out into the windy September sunshine.

'What a wonderful idea,' Katya said, heavily scornful. 'Thank you so much. I can't think of anything I'd rather do today than take a stroll in the biting wind. With you.'

He did not respond, at least not verbally, but his grip on her elbow tightened and his long-legged strides lengthened until she was all but running to keep up with him.

'Let go of me!'

'Oh, do shut up,' he snapped.

She wrenched her arm from his, glared at him.

He stopped, put a hand to a head that felt as if it might split.

She waited, watching him fiercely. His face was thin and at the moment quite translucently pale; unusually he was clean-shaven, the line of his mouth straight. He could by no means be described as handsome, though she supposed some might find him attractive. For herself she preferred dark men. She thought she might tell him so.

'I'm sorry,' he said, ruefully. 'I'm not handling this very well, am I?' He laughed a little, too obviously self-deprecating. 'I really do feel quite dreadful.'

Katya raised fair, scornful eyebrows. 'A self-inflicted injury, I think?' Wild horses would not have dragged from her a confession as to the state of her own head.

He grinned suddenly, appreciating the jibe despite himself. 'Quite the worst kind, don't you think?'

They turned, began to walk together along the wide boulevard that ran alongside the canal. 'I don't understand,' Katya said, abruptly. 'Whatever possessed you to come to the house today? What is this – this charade?'

He slanted a glance down at her, a small appreciative gleam in his eyes, but said nothing.

They walked on in silence. Beneath trees that tossed in the chill, strengthening wind stood a wrought-iron bench. He stopped, wiped the seat with his handkerchief, settled her upon it. She sat bolt upright, as far from him as she could possibly manage without actually falling off the end of the armless bench, watching him.

'Is it possible for you to stay quiet for two minutes while I explain?' he asked with a sudden spectacular smile.

Beyond a tightening of the lips she did not deign to answer.

He played with the handkerchief, folding and unfolding it. He had long, thin fingers, and good nails. 'The world,' he said at last, 'for its own reasons, seems to be determined upon our marrying – or at least our giving the thought some consideration.'

'Over my dead body,' she said, venomously pleasant.

'Quite.' He lifted his head, regarded her steadily and thoughtfully. 'My sentiments exactly. Except that if my sister gives me one more lecture upon the benefits of marriage and a secure and steady life I fear it might be over her dead body; and since

I'm really rather fond of her I'd like to prevent that if I can.'

She refused to be tempted to laughter.

'So. It occurred to me that –' He hesitated, shook out the handkerchief again.

Composedly Katya leaned forward and removed it from the fidgeting fingers. 'It occurred to you?' she prompted.

'– that we might come to some –' he shrugged '– some arrangement that could be to our mutual advantage.'

She eyed him warily. 'How?'

'If we gave them the impression that we were – how shall I put it – at least *trying* to accommodate them all, that is, if they thought we were meeting on occasion, spending some time together –'

Light had dawned. Pensively Katya put a finger to her mouth, her blue eyes intent, though still wary. 'Except – that we aren't?' she asked, softly.

His smile was beatific. 'Exactly.'

She tapped her lip, still watching him. There was a very long silence.

'There is, I assume, another –' she hesitated '– lady involved?'

'Yes.'

'A married lady?'

He nodded.

'And you want time – shall we say that doesn't have to be accounted for? Furthermore,' she laughed a little, genuinely amused, 'you want your sister to stop nagging you?'

Jussi's smile was bland. 'Put simply: yes.' Time, he told himself, that was all he was buying; a little time. Convictions and causes were one thing; tying oneself for life to a flibbertigibbet who no more wanted you than you did her was quite another. Anyway, as he had said to Elisabet, it simply wasn't fair. The thought made him feel positively virtuous; an unaccustomed feeling that he took a self-indulgent moment to enjoy.

The wind caught a strand of her hair and whipped it free. She turned her head to look at the rippling water, remembering the ardent look in the eyes of her young Cossack captain last night, remembering too his last, whispered words –

'What an extraordinarily good idea,' she said.

CHAPTER TEN

Sasha Kolashki would have been the first to acknowledge that neither by nature nor by inclination should he have been in the army at all, let alone in the crack Preobrajensky Guards; and he was all too aware that he was not the only one to know it.

His reluctantly acknowledged call to arms had come about through the sudden, tragic and predictably spectacular death of his older brother, thrown by a recklessly-ridden, half-broken horse, compounded by Sasha's own total inability to stand up against a world that was ready, neatly, to slot him into that same dead brother's shoes. His second misfortune – the Guards' Commission – came through the well-meaning interference of a family friend whose influence in high circles was matched by a complete misunderstanding of, or indifference to, Sasha's own needs and character. To say that Sasha was no soldier would be to state but half the case; he was unsuited to such a life in almost every possible way. Artistic – he had, in his youth, been much given to the composition of poetry – imaginative, easy-going beyond the point of positive weakness, he had been per-fectly happy as a second son of whom little was expected and to whom little of his fearsome father's attention was paid. Until, that is, the day that a wild and unmanageable horse had thrown his equally wild and unmanageable brother into a ditch and rolled on him.

The family, old, respected, severely and constantly short of funds, lived in a quietly decaying house on an estate a few miles outside Moscow that had for the past hundred or so years steadily shrunk in size and profitability as each generation turned a few more hectares into cash in order to keep body, soul and ancient name together. His education had been haphazard, mostly at his gentle, long-suffering mother's knee; for his father, possessing as he did in the bone-headed Grigor a son and heir in his own image, had been content on the whole to leave his second, prettier but less belligerent boy happily attached to the apron strings of the mother who adored him together with the sister whom he so resembled. Grigor's untimely death had shaken the whole household to its not very firm foundations; but to no-one had it come as such a blow as to Sasha. Not that he had loved his brother – quite the contrary, having since childhood been subjected to the heavy-handed, sometimes downright vicious torments that Grigor considered it fitting to visit upon a younger brother – but with his death, suddenly, there was no-one standing between Sasha and his father. Between Sasha and the harsh real world. Worse; between Sasha and the Tsar's army. In each generation for as long as their ancient and now crumbling house had stood at least one Kolashki son had served his ruler; sometimes, indeed, whole families had served and died together. Sasha's great-grandfather had lost his life in the defiant stand against Napoleon, his grandfather, a little less valiantly in Sasha's opinion, had been fatally wounded in the Polish patriot uprisings of the 1830s. There had been a Kolashki at Sebastopol, and his own father had, to his eternal shame, been part of the defeated Russian army routed by Japan in 1905. With Grigor gone there was no-one but Sasha to carry on the immutable tradition; and, ironically, he did not have the strength to stand against the pressures and expectations of this world into which he had been born. Because he did not have the courage to do anything else, he became a soldier.

When his mother had first seen him attired in the vivid and dashing dress uniform of an Ensign of the Preobrajenskys she had shed tears, both of sorrow and of pride; for in one circumstance alone did Sasha surpass his overpowering brother – he had his mother's looks, and in uniform he was a sight to see. In truth Sasha had not been far from tears himself, but for very different reasons; for by then he had already discovered the horrors of barracks life. Only the natural skills acquired throughout a pseudo-military country childhood had saved him. He was lean and fit and fairly strong despite his light build; he knew an order when he heard one and rode as naturally as he walked. His excessive good looks, at least some were ready to concede, were hardly his fault. They even, to his horror, attracted a certain amount of interest in some quarters. His books of poetry had been burned by callous hands before his eyes within the first week. He had been – as was any newcomer as a matter of course – abused and brutalized; he had had many an occasion to remember his brother Grigor, and to wonder if here even he might have received a taste of his own peculiar medicine. Yet by the skin of his teeth, through a practised combination of stoicism and sycophancy that he himself despised, he had come through it all, though he knew too well that there were those he fooled – usually his fellow officers – and those he did not – all too often those he was supposed to command. And more often than not those he did not deceive were those he respected most. Nevertheless the young Lieutenant Sasha Kolashki who attended Katya Bourlova's coming-of-age ball with a group of acquaintances he had met in a brothel the night before had achieved at least some degree of comfort and acceptance in a world that was not and never could be his own. His simple prayer, each day and more particularly in the dark hours of a lonely night, was that he should never be required to see action; he knew himself too well. Privately he thought of himself as a lead soldier, brightly painted, a toy. In fact he did himself injustice; he was a sensitive man, and a man of imagination; such a man sees too well what might be asked of him, what might be visited upon him, in times of violence.

Margarita Shalakova saw none of this, neither then nor it must be said at any later time. Margarita, as always, saw what she wanted to see. Heard, too, what she wanted to hear. She saw a handsome young man with instant interest and attraction in his eyes. She saw a brave uniform, a pair of wide shoulders, a neat turn of leg, narrow, well-made hands. She saw dark and ardent eyes and what to her inexperienced eyes looked like a small fortune in soft leather boots, gold-braided, bright-buttoned tunic, casually slung fur-edged jacket; she saw a foil for her own bright beauty. She heard laughter and a pretty turn of phrase, whispered compliments, a passing mention of an estate near Moscow; heard too a small, delightfully disturbing note of real desire in the well-modulated voice, saw it reflected in those warm dark eyes.

For his part Sasha was enchanted. Whilst by no means sexually inexperienced – aged fourteen he had happily surrendered his virginity to a mercilessly practised kitchen maid and even given a natural discrimination since then his good looks and his station had guaranteed a steady supply of compliant bedfellows – he had had surprisingly little social contact with respectable girls. No contact at all with respectable girls who looked as Margarita looked, who enticed as she enticed, who combined that devastating mixture of innocence and pure carnality of which she herself seemed unaware. The kiss – the two kisses – that she had readily surrendered upon the balcony of the Bourlov apartment that evening had intriguingly demonstrated two things; first, her utter inexperience, tantalizing in itself, and second, an unstudied wantonness that had him leaving his fellows to carouse without him whilst he wandered alone along echoing, gaslit streets remembering the feel of her eager body against his and composing small, fragile verses to her beauty.

As the sun rose that morning he stood upon the Dvortzovi Bridge watching the light play upon the moving waters beneath him and against the grim walls of the great fortress of St Peter and St Paul, and determined – as she, unknown to him, already had – that he must see her again. She had steadfastly refused to give him her home address, but had hinted that Katya and her officer friends might be the contact between them. He pinched out his cigarette, tossed the end into the river, watched it pensively, a tiny scrap, born away on the current.

Katya's small conspiracy with the young Finn Jussi Lavola worked even better than either of them had expected. That Margarita was more than ready to be drawn into their light-hearted deceptions made the sport all the easier. Jussi would call at the Bourlov apartment; Katya would be awaiting him, chaperoned by her young cousin. They would depart, demurely and with parental blessing, for carriage-ride, concert, afternoon walk or, as the first frosts came, perhaps a skating party on the river, or a sleigh ride in the countryside along the Gulf. At a given spot they would split up, to meet again at an agreed time and return innocently home. The scheme was neat and all but flawless. That it was also wildly irresponsible Katya knew but chose to ignore. Although far from stupid, she was all but incapable of thinking in such terms. She had been far too indulged to put Margarita's well-being before her own; she saw what she wanted, and she took steps to ensure that it would be hers. Margarita, her unflagging acolyte in all things, learned this particular lesson very soon and very well.

Margarita had in fact little idea how fortunate she was in Sasha Kolashki; instinct had served her more than well. Despite his profession, despite the undoubted brutality of the world in which he lived, Sasha did not have it in him to harm anyone, let alone an innocent, and a beautiful one at that, whom he perceived as trusting him. Margarita was every heroine of every romance he had heard at his virtuous mother's knee. To take advantage of that artless innocence would have been to run counter to everything in his nature. The added excitement of the deceits they practised in meeting, the flattering way her face lit when she saw him, the to all appearances ingenuous naivety that at one moment blushed like a poppy at a compliment and at the next warmed the brilliant blue eyes with the most ardent desire enslaved him. For the first time in his life Sasha lost his good sense entirely to infatuation, a not unpleasant experience for a young man with romantic inclinations.

Margarita, as ever determined upon perfection, liked to think she, too, was hopelessly in love. She certainly thought about Sasha most of the time, as she fetched and carried for her mother, sat beside her plying a dutiful needle and letting Varya's often petulant voice flow over her like a bubbling stream, unheeded. Her sisters' departure had left these two virtually alone together and unsurprisingly this had slightly soured the relationship, on Margarita's side at least; no longer the pampered youngest, she found her mother's demands as wearying as Anna had before her. They still, despite plans and promises, lived in the apartment on the Venskaya; after the splendours of the Bourlov apartment where she spent as much time as she possibly could, Margarita found it drab, dark and depressing. Sonya, after a positively operatic row with Varya, had departed the year before and Victor, given the reduction in the household numbers, had thriftily insisted that Seraphima and Varya manage the cooking between them; a decision, Margarita was convinced, much aided by the fact that, with the business flourishing, Victor himself ate out with clients most of the time. So, yes, Margarita spent a great deal of time thinking about Sasha Kolashki; and more particularly about how to entice him – or if necessary force him – to marry her. She was quite set upon it, the fact that despite his protestations of penury, which she did not believe anyway, his station was a great deal higher than hers notwithstanding. On the contrary, she had always known this to be her destiny. She had come this far; all that remained was to ensure that the besotted young man remained so entangled in her web that he had no chance of escape. At some point soon she planned to confide in her mother. But not yet. Not quite yet.

The weeks slipped by, and Christmas was approaching. Once again the city and the countryside wore their winter finery of silver and white. To worker and to peasant the bitter cold was a punishment to suffer, to be endured, on occasion to die under; but for those with the means, the time and the energy to enjoy the skating, the sledging, the sleigh and troika rides it was a time of magic.

The days were very short, dusk falling in mid-afternoon over the snow-cloaked city. Still Katya, Margarita and the feckless Jussi continued their clandestine expeditions. There was unrest in the city, mostly in the workers' suburbs: the odd strike, the odd meeting broken up by soldiers and police – a few heads cracked, a few people ridden down by the Cossack ponies that were bred for such work, but nothing more disturbing than that. In Switzerland, in London, in Berlin and in Helsingfors, called Helsinki by the Finns, sedition was hatched by a few trouble-makers best left to themselves. There were rumours that the unhealthy and venomous influence of the monk Rasputin upon the Empress, and through her upon the Tsar, was greater than ever; people shrugged and went about their business. Strange were the ways of God, and of the ruling classes: what did such goings-on have to do with ordinary folk? That a combination of circumstances was at work which was conspiring to create a gulf of epic, possibly unbridgeable, proportions between the rulers and the ruled occurred to very few; to those who did see it even fewer wanted to listen. Equally ignored on the whole were the rumblings in Europe, where the dogs of war, chained for a generation, were snarling greedily as nations jostled for position and power, jealously guarding their own interests. What had that to do with Mother Russia, secure as ever behind her snow-protected boundaries?

Margarita and Sasha snuggled together beneath heavy furs as the troika flew over the packed snow, a barking dog scampering beside the singing runners. The tall, straight trunks of birch and fir flashed by, the slanting sun glimmering in the pale and shadowed depths of the woodland and falling in bright bars of light across the track they followed. Every so often the trees thinned to reveal the frozen Gulf, snow-covered and beautiful, stretching into the infinite, ice-hazed distance. They passed a small village of wooden buildings set haphazardly, like the play-things of a child, within a clearing in the forest. In the silence the bells on the harness rang like crystal, sounding clear above the muffled sound of the horses' hooves and the high song of the runners.

Margarita disentangled a small hand from her muff and slipped it into Sasha's. 'How much further?'

He smiled down at her, dark eyes warm. She looked quite dazzlingly pretty, her fair hair curled about the white fur hat that had once been Katya's, cheeks bright with colour in the cold air. 'Not far.' His heart, as he looked at her, beat uncomfortably fast. They would stay just an hour at the dacha. That was all. And nothing would happen. Nothing. He would show her the house. And then they would leave. She smiled again, trusting and happy; and again his heart lurched uncomfortably.

Margarita, well-satisfied, snuggled deeper into the fur, aware of and amused by the fact that Sasha had no inkling that it had been she who had contrived this trip, she who had chosen the time and the place, she who knew exactly what would happen, and how. When he had first mentioned that a cousin several times removed – a fellow officer in the Preobrajensky – owned a small dacha on the wooded shores of the Gulf, she had clapped her hands with pleasure, knowing how her child-like enthusiasm delighted him. 'Oh, but how lovely! I'd so like to see it!' She had allowed a small reproach to dim the brightness of her smile. 'Sasha, darling Sasha, I haven't seen anything that belongs to your family.'

He had been awkward. 'It – isn't exactly ours. That is, I think it used to be, but, well, like so many other things at some point or other it had to be sold –'

'But still –' she had bestowed another warm, glowing smile '– wouldn't it be fun to visit it?'

'I – yes, I suppose so – one of these days.'

And here, sooner than he had ever anticipated, the day had come; and he found himself desperately doubting his own motives in having brought his pretty love here to the loneliest and most beautiful spot imaginable. He drew away from her a little, turning the collar of his heavy greatcoat up about his chin. Laughing she followed him, laying her head against his shoulder, the fur of her hat tickling his nose.

The dacha stood in a small clearing; it was not a big house, but long, low and verandahed, the gables decoratively carved, the windows shuttered. The troika driver pulled up in an unnecessary but spectacular spray of fine snow. 'There, Excellency – this is the place?' His small eyes were knowing, his smile faintly unpleasant. He was so wrapped about with rugs and blankets that he looked like a small, shapeless haystack topped with a tattered fur hat.

'Er – y-yes. It is.'

Rita had sat up, leaning forward eagerly. 'Oh, Sasha! It's so pretty!'

'There's a village a little further on, my man.' Awkwardly Sasha leaned forward and a coin changed hands. 'There's an inn there, I believe, where you'll find a meal. Come back in –' he glanced at Rita '– an hour.'

Margarita pouted a little. 'Oh, two hours I'd say. We have our picnic, don't we? And see – the shore is only a step away. After I've seen the house I'd like to go out onto the ice a little way. It's so delightfully terrifying to feel that you're walking over an ocean, don't you think? Two hours, Sasha?' she wheedled. 'At least? We have time. We don't have to meet the others until five.'

Stiffly Sasha nodded. 'Very well. Two hours.'

The driver helped them unload the basket containing the picnic, and drove away, his last look, cast over his shoulder at Sasha, a distinct mixture of salacious envy and a kind of knowing contempt. For one moment the pacific Sasha found himself wishing that the man served under him, specifically in the company of a sergeant by the name of Marakov, whose well-deserved reputation for impeccable discipline achieved by a particular brutality was the source of much squeamish if ineffective disquiet for his superior officer.

Beside him, skirts lifted above the deep snow, Margarita waited impatiently. 'You have the key?'

'Yes.' He stepped in front of her, clearing the way as he walked for her to follow to the front door.

The house was like an icebox, and dark. Furniture loomed in dust-sheet shrouds. Icy draughts scurried like mischievous sprites, moving curtains, stirring the air.

'Goodness!' Margarita ran to the window, opened it, flung open the shutters then closed the tall window again. Sun streamed through, slanted low, already almost at the horizon. Sasha watched, bemused, as she ran, laughing, from room to room, letting in the light, exclaiming and examining. 'A stove! Here, Sasha, in the kitchen! Oh, may we light it, do you think? We could eat in here. What a pretty little house! Just look at this view – Sasha – do come and look!' But before he could join her she was off again, throwing open doors, lifting sheets, playing like a kitten, exploring every room.

Smiling, he set a match to the ready-laid stove, went back out into the snow to pick up the picnic basket. It was growing colder. The sun was dipping fast, half lost to the western horizon.

Back in the kitchen the efficient stove was already roaring and the fragrant and comfortable smell of woodsmoke drifted in the air. Still dressed in fur-lined cloak and becoming hat, Margarita perched on a wooden chair beside the table. 'What have you brought? Caviar? Darling Sasha, I do hope you've brought caviar?'

He had indeed. And smoked meat, and cheeses, and fresh-baked bread. And champagne. Lots of champagne.

The kitchen was a large and comfortable room, flagstoned but made warmer with rugs. The furniture was fairly primitive, a heavy wooden table with huge matching dresser, a couple of armchairs and a battered settee set by the stove. As Sasha fed the already glowing fire from the stack of logs that ran along one wall the air, chilled as an icebox when they had first entered, warmed to soporific comfort. Margarita, cheeks flushed, shrugged out of her cloak, flung her hat after it into a corner. Sasha too had doffed fur hat and greatcoat. He was dressed this afternoon not in uniform but in well-worn country clothes, riding breeches and an English tweed jacket; even Margarita, disappointed at first that her peacock officer had chosen to become a sparrow, had to concede that he looked every bit as handsome thus attired and in this setting as he had that first night she had seen him at the Bourlovs' ball. She had drunk just enough champagne not to have to masquerade, as so often she did. When, as the sudden dusk fell, he bent to light the candle that stood upon the table she reached a hand to him perfectly naturally, and as naturally his mouth touched hers, gently at first, then much more fiercely, his fingers in her hair. She closed her eyes, enjoying the sensation, arching her back to brush her body against his as he bent over her. He pulled her to her feet, crushing her to him, kissing her again and again, mumbling foolishly into her hair. Who first made the move towards the settee beside the stove would have been hard to say.

Beyond the window the sun continued its steady descent, a bright slither of red against the dark-drawn horizon, and the sky was aflame.

'I'll die! Oh, my God! I'll die of shame!' Margarita sobbed heartbrokenly into a scrap of handkerchief, shoulders shaking, tears streaming down her face. 'I'll kill myself! I swear it!'

'Darling – darling Rita – please don't say such things – please don't upset yourself so.' Sasha was aghast, at what he'd done and at this inevitable but distressing consequence. The light had gone from the sky, the troika and its unpleasant driver would be back at any moment, he was due back on duty in under two hours and Margarita, hair a tangle about her distorted, weeping face, was all but hysterical.

'Upset myself?' She lifted a tragic face. '*Upset myself?* Sasha, how could you? I'm ruined! Sweet Mother of God! Ruined! How will I ever face poor Mama and Papa? I'll die! I will! I want to! I – want – to – die!' She went off into another paroxysm of weeping. In truth she had worked herself up into such a state that the tears and the hysteria were all but real. 'I won't go home! I won't! They'll – they'll see! They'll know! They'll know what I've done! Oh, it's horrible! Horrible! They'll hate me! Sasha – oh, Sasha – what am I going to do?' She folded her arms upon her knees and laid her face upon them, sobbing.

Uncertainly he laid a hand upon her shoulder. Last time he had touched her she had screamed at him and pulled away. Now at least she allowed the hand to rest where it was. A little encouraged, he leaned gently to stroke her hair. 'Rita – please – don't worry. I'm sorry. I'm so sorry. I didn't mean to –' He stopped.

Her noisy sobs had subsided a little. She waited, not lifting her head.

He was bemused. How in the world had this happened? He had been so determined to behave himself, so determined not to take advantage of her. 'What a beast I am,' he said. 'Rita, don't cry so, darling. It will be all right. I promise you.'

She let a small, dramatic silence develop before she lifted her head. Her kittenishly pointed face was set, the sapphire eyes gleamed still with tears. She lifted her little chin bravely. 'What? What do you promise, Sasha? What *can* you promise? Now?' Her voice broke on the word. 'Can you give back what I've lost? Can you undo what we've done?'

He drew back, stood up, turned from her looking out into the darkness. Through the trees he saw the lamps of the troika as it sped through the darkness towards the house. 'The – the sledge is coming.'

She shook her head sharply. 'I'm not coming. You go. Leave me here.'

'Rita, don't be absurd! You can't –'

She flew to her feet, face blazing, small fists clenched. 'Don't tell me what I can and can't do! What do you expect me to do? Face my father? My family? Knowing –' she bit her lip, tears surged again '– knowing I've betrayed them? It will break their hearts, Sasha. As it has broken mine!'

'No!'

'*Yes!*' The shrill word echoed between them. She turned from him, shoulders hunched against him. 'Yes,' she said again. 'Everything they've taught me, everything they warned me against – I wouldn't listen. Oh, how wicked I've been! I thought they were wrong. I thought – with you – it would be different. I thought I knew better. They didn't know you, you see.' She lifted her head, allowed pain to quiver in her voice. 'I thought I did.'

Truly distraught now, he came swiftly to her, gathered her into his arms, holding her close, rocking her like a child as the tears came again. 'Rita, Rita, no! Don't say such things. I love you. I love you!'

Mutely she shook her head against his shoulder, her face buried in his jacket.

'But yes! I do! I love you more than anything! More than life!'

The troika came out of the trees and into the clearing in front of the house. Sasha had to get back to Petersburg. The colonel himself was due in barracks tonight. Desperately gentle, he pushed her a little way from him, peered into her face, lit by the flicker of candlelight. Tearstained and dishevelled, he thought she had never looked lovelier, nor more vulnerable. 'Margarita, we'll talk later – but we must go.'

She shook her head stubbornly. 'No.'

'You can't possibly stay here alone.'

She said nothing, watching him.

His heart was beating unpleasantly fast. 'Rita, what are you thinking of? You can't stay here. You know it. Why won't you come back with me?'

Still she did not reply. Her small mouth was set. So immersed was she in her role that for the moment she had come to believe it. 'I can't go home,' she said, at last, very clearly and quietly. 'I simply can't, not now. Not ever. What is there for me? I can't live with you, it's unthinkable. And – I can't live without you. So –' she bowed her head, her voice a whisper '– so I don't think I want to live at all.'

'Rita!'

'I mean it.' She was suddenly quite convincingly calm. He looked at her in horror, utterly taken in. 'I mean it,' she said again, and managed a small, sad smile. 'Leave me, Sasha. It's best. I know you won't marry me. I know you can't. I know I'm not good enough for you. I suppose I've always known it. I've been stupid. So stupid. But I loved you, loved you more than anything.' She smiled that small, sweet smile again. 'Love you, that is. Still. You know that.' She blushed deeply, but kept her eyes bravely steady upon his, turning the knife. 'I've shown you that, today, haven't I? And now –' she took a tremulous breath, shook her head '– what is there for me now?'

He caught her cold hand. The stove had burned low and the air was chill. 'Margarita, listen to me. I'll find a way. I promise you. What do you take me for? I love you. I love you! I'm a grown man – I can marry anyone I want.' He shut out, flinching, the too-clear memory of his father's heavy, scowling face, his roar of anger when crossed. 'Please, dry your eyes, my love. Stop talking such nonsense. Come home with me. And don't worry. I'll work something out. I promise.'

She searched his face with despairing, tear-wet eyes.

'Please? Please, Margarita?'

'I –' she spoke hesitantly, wavering, shook her head. 'I don't think –'

'Rita!' He used as assertive a tone as he could manage. 'This is ridiculous! Of course you must come back with me. You have to!'

She punished him with silence and a defiantly-lifted chin. Then, 'Supposing,' she said at last, controlling with an obvious and courageous effort the tremor in her voice, 'supposing there's a –?' She stopped, ducked her head in an apparent agony of embarrassment. She glanced at the rumpled settee. 'What we just did – isn't that the way –' she swallowed '– the way children are made?'

His heart sank further. Oh indeed yes, that was the way that children were made. 'Darling, I told you – I'll work something out.'

'You keep saying that. But what do you mean?' Impatience was growing. There was a chill, shrewish edge to the words.

'I – I told you. I'm not a child, I'm a grown man –'

'You'll marry me?' she asked sharply. 'Is that what you're saying? You'll marry me?' Belying the stubbornly pressing tone of the words she was looking at him with wide, innocently trusting eyes that were still swimming with tears. 'You really mean it?'

He hesitated for just a moment too long. Temper stirred. Her face crumpled. She took a swift, trembling breath and opened her mouth.

'Yes, I mean it,' he said, hastily. 'Of course I mean it.' Again the spectre of his father hovered; again he pushed it from him. 'We'll be married, my darling. Of course we will. What do you take me for?'

A question best left unanswered. 'You swear?' she asked at last. 'You swear on your honour?'

'I swear. Of course I do.'

'On your honour.'

'On my honour.'

She watched him for another long, level moment. Then she allowed him to drape the cloak across her shoulders, picked up the muff that lay upon the table. 'Very well. I accept your word,' she said. 'Now – we should hurry – Katya will be waiting.'

It was an odd trick that fate played upon Sasha Kolashki that day. When he arrived at his quarters in the barracks near the Winter Palace, having with some relief handed over a calmer if still edgy Margarita to Katya and Jussi, a telegram awaited him, lying upon the table of the small, bare room. He was halfway to the press where his uniform hung before he saw it. He stopped, arrested in mid-movement. Then he snatched it and tore it open. Stood for several long moments, all movement frozen.

His mother begged to inform her beloved son that his father, Feodor Alexandrovich Kolashki, had died of a seizure two days before.

After a stunned moment of silence, appallingly, he found himself laughing. To his relief however the laughter did not last long. By the time he had flung himself onto the bed, his face buried in his arms, he was crying.

★　★　★

It was her mother in whom Margarita chose to confide first, trusting, with good reason, that here was her best ally. The simple but carefully-constructed story she told was convincing, if only half the truth; if Varya suspected the omissions she did not pursue them. Margarita told her mother that she had met Sasha at the Bourlovs', that he was a friend of Jussi's and had joined them once or twice on their afternoon expeditions. They had fallen in love at first sight; despite the obvious difference in their stations he was determined to marry her. She made no mention of the deceits they had practised and in particular no mention of the afternoon at the dacha. There was, she reasoned calmly, no cause to bring such things into the open now that Sasha had declared his intentions with no further pressure.

Everything had gone exactly according to plan. Better, in fact, for not even she had foreseen or could have contrived Sasha's father's convenient death. What remained to be done was relatively simple. She could, she knew, safely leave it to her delighted mother to break the news to Victor; and once her parents met Sasha with his handsome face, delightful manners and ancient name and holdings they would of course both fall over themselves to give their permission for the marriage.

Which should take place, she had decided, just as soon as possible.

With the steely determination that had been the hallmark of her campaign to possess Sasha, Margarita to everyone's surprise refused utterly to entertain thoughts of a large and extravagant wedding, which necessarily would take time to plan. The fragile, baited hook was taken; only a fool would play the fish for too long.

She was marrying a soldier, she informed them all with a sober, charming, and self-deprecating maturity, and with his father newly dead and his mother and sister needing the income from the estate, they must learn to live on his pay. This was, of course, as so often with Margarita, only half the truth. She intended, at some time in the near future, to take in hand this high-minded eschewing of the estate's income. Meanwhile her reasons for – regretfully but shrewdly – deciding against a splendid wedding did indeed involve those shadowy figures of Sasha's mother and sister, but had rather more to do with their unfortunately predictable reactions to Sasha's new wife than anything else. By the time she met them she intended to be firmly married; under no circumstances, having come this far, would she run the risk of Sasha being talked out of his commitment. Appearances notwithstanding, Margarita was far from foolish – she knew, or guessed, at the doubts her intended must on occasion entertain about her suitability as a wife for a Kolashki. She simply gave him no time to think about them, and certainly no chance to express them. Her future in-laws might be less easy to manipulate. Again circumstances conspired to help her; after the shock of her husband's death Sasha's mother had, according to his sister Galina, virtually gone into seclusion, hardly leaving the house. Sasha had returned home for his father's funeral, but at Margarita's gentle and concerned suggestion had made no mention of their plans. He must not, she had insisted, worry his mother with such things at such a time. Always ready to take the easy way Sasha, with some relief, had concurred.

The moment Sasha returned from the funeral Margarita set about ensuring that their marriage took place just as soon as possible by the simple means of assuming his agreement and steadily forging her plans. She spent much time with him, re-enchanting him with her pretty ways, teasing him light-heartedly, infecting him with her own enthusiasm. She refused point blank to sleep with him. Indeed, she displayed tremulous hurt and shock at the very suggestion, making him feel such a villain even to have considered such a thing that he was contritely ready to do anything to bring the smile back to her pretty face. Of course they would marry, and of course it would be soon. He truly believed that he could not live without her; what choice did he have?

He wrote a letter telling his mother and sister of his plans. Margarita offered to post it; and post it she did. Two days after the wedding.

Dmitri and his Natalia through all this quietly planned their own nuptials, long awaited, happily and securely certain of their love. It seemed to Varya, who had little to do with the organizing of this wedding, since the task had naturally fallen to

Natalia's oddly unpleasant mother, that these two had lived virtually in a world of their own since they had met in child-hood; their actual marriage would be no great novelty, it was simply a calm and inevitable step along the road they trod together. And so it fell out, coincidentally, that Dmitri and his sister Margarita were wed within a few days of one another, as Anna and Yelena had been, both weddings celebrated in the middle of a dark and viciously cold January. But if the cere-monies were the same, the participants were very different. Dmitri and his new wife had planned their union since child-hood, together and with no deceit; their future was clear and calm, a certain road, as they saw it, to quiet, endless happiness. That Margarita and Sasha had known each other for exactly three months was the least of the differences between the two young couples. When Margarita Victorovna Kolashkova stepped out into the bitter January day, her hand tucked firmly into her handsomely-uniformed husband's arm, she felt like a General who has seen his battle plan work down to the last detail. All that was left to do now was to ensure that she won the war.

And, having come so far, she had no reason whatsoever to doubt her ability to do that.

Like Anna, who reluctantly decided against travelling to Russia in the face not just of the fierce winter but of a faintly alarming downturn in her husband's usually entirely dependable health, Yelena attended neither wedding, but for a different reason; in her bitterness she had little or no contact with her family, and anyway, she was pregnant again. She was in the fourth terrible year of her marriage, and in that time she had produced one living child, her daughter Tonia, born just nine months after the wedding. There had been four other pregnancies; this was her fifth. On the day in her seventh month that with cold-blooded lust her husband attempted the rape that, pregnancy or no, invariably followed the more savage of his beatings, she produced a knife, long, thin and deadly, which she had procured with bleak forethought from the kitchen. She held it out before her, braced in her two hands, steady as a rock. 'Get away from me, you pig,' she said, calmly. 'Or I swear I'll kill you.'

He stepped back, startled.

'I'm carrying this child to its full term.' She moved carefully around him, putting the bed between them. 'You've murdered four. You aren't having this one. Nor any other. If you ever touch me again – ever, you understand? – you'll never sleep safe again. Sooner or later, somehow, I'll kill you. Believe me.' The apartment in which they lived, more roomy than their original home since Donovalov had acquired – by less than salubrious means, Yelena suspected – a fairly senior post in the euphemistically named Ministry of the Interior, was empty, apart from Tonia, sleeping in her own bedroom down the hall. Though Donovalov was ready to pay for the couple of servant girls that he felt that his station demanded he would not have them sleep in; servants were notorious gossips. What he did in his own home was not for the eyes and ears of others. He recovered himself now. Eyes narrowed, bony hands spread, he moved, albeit warily, towards Lenka.

She did not give an inch, only brought the knife up a little in a sharp, threatening gesture. 'Back!' she snapped. Years of sullen subservience, of pain and indignity, of terror and humiliation, were made almost worthwhile by the look on his face at that moment.

'I mean it,' she said. 'It's finished. Go and play your filthy games somewhere else. If you touch me again I promise I'll kill you.'

'You're my wife,' he said, his thin, precise voice, so detested, almost a whisper.

She made no attempt to disguise her revulsion. 'Your – what?' she asked.

There was a long, tense moment of silence. She could see him measure the distance between them, measure equally her resolve. The well-honed, narrow blade held steady. Her jaw throbbed from the last blow he had dealt her. The last blow.

He straightened, contempt on his face. 'You're mad.'

'No. On the contrary, I'm sane at last.' She was astounded at the steadiness of her voice; she held his eyes with her own. 'And I'm not about to fall downstairs, either,' she added, very softly.

The narrow face tightened. Fury flickered in the sharp, dark eyes.

'Another – accident – might be difficult to explain away, don't you think?' she asked.

'Fat bitch.' The words were low, slow, vicious. 'Sow! Look at you! Ugly bitch! Who'd want you anyway? You're not worth pissing on.' His voice rose a little, suddenly and horribly threaded with excitement.

She took a steadying breath. This she had expected, but it made it no easier to bear; his tongue was as depraved and as brutal as was his belt and his favourite knotted leather harness strap.

A movement by the door caught her eye. A small figure stood silhouetted against the light in the hall.

'Stop it!' she said, sharply.

The venomous litany droned on. He told her in infinite detail what unspeakable punishments should be visited upon her now, and every day until she crawled to him for forgiveness.

'*Stop it!*' she shouted.

Tonia ran to her, dodging around her father, scrambling across the bed to where her mother stood. It said much for the child's presence of mind, to say nothing of her instant understanding of the situation, that she did nothing to deflect her mother's concentration. The knife gleamed still and steady between them and the husband and father who stood beyond the barrier of the bed. Very carefully the little girl slid closer to her mother, one small hand automatically reaching for a handful of skirt, the other thumb as automatically and firmly in a small, thin-lipped mouth. Her hair was the colour of marigolds in the sun. Her pale blue eyes watched her father with a fixed expression of hatred.

Faced with the two pairs of eyes his voice died.

Lenka stood, straight and still despite the heaviness of her body, one hand on her daughter's tousled red-gold head, the other holding the razor-sharp symbol of her final desperate revolt. 'Go,' she said. 'I know you have places to go. I know there are people – women, God help them! – who are ready to pander to your –' she let a small, blistering silence take the place of words '– unusual tastes. Go to them. Leave me alone. I'll have none of you. Never again.'

He resisted for a moment longer, glaring belligerently at her.

Then he turned. Over his shoulder he said, 'You've had an easy life until now, Yelena Victorovna. Money in your pocket. Food in your belly. Servants to light your fires.' He went into the hall, reappeared in the doorway carrying hat, coat and scarf. 'I think you might find things get a little – difficult – from now on.'

'Just leave me alone,' she said, simply. 'That's all I ask. Leave me alone.'

He let his eyes run up and down her bloated figure, her shoulders broad almost as a man's, her breasts huge, her belly sagging, her ankles puffy and swollen. He smiled into her plain, sallow face. 'With pleasure,' he said, and the malice could have been cut with a knife. 'With very great pleasure.'

For moments after the outer door slammed she stood quite still, Tonia still clinging to her skirt. The silence in the apartment was absolute; it sang in the ears like an invasive external sound. Outside, a dog barked.

Very, very slowly she lowered the hand that held the knife. As slowly the muscles of her body relaxed.

Tonia made a small sound.

In a sudden and swift movement Lenka dropped the knife and swept the child up into her arms. Tonia clung to her, soundless, her small body bunched, her head buried deep into her mother's shoulder. Crooning, Lenka rocked her a little, then moved around the bed to the door. Tonia clung tighter. In the child's bedroom Lenka had to disentangle the tiny clinging fingers in order to tuck the little girl back into her bed. She sat beside her, holding her hand, murmuring words that were worse than meaningless, singing the songs of childhood, the silly, innocent songs that bore no resemblance whatsoever to this child's life, until she slept. Then at last, stiff, exhausted, overburdened, she stood.

Back in the bedroom she bent, picked up the knife that lay upon the floor, straightened to find herself looking into a mirror.

A grotesque figure looked back at her. The wasted pregnancies had indeed taken their toll; it had not needed Donovalov's malice to tell her that. The figure that had been statuesque was now, even distorted as it was by yet another pregnancy, gross. Worse, her face, drawn and bitter, was all but lost in rolls of fat. The knife glittered, ridiculously menacing, in her hand. She stood for a small, harsh moment, watching herself in the glass. Then she tossed the knife onto a table and made to turn away. Stopped.

Beside the knife a letter lay, unopened, an English stamp fixed upon expensive stationery, with a small crest in the corner. Anna's writing, as always, was clear and concise.

Lenka picked up the letter, walked to the stove in the corner of the room and dropped the still sealed envelope into it.

She had shut the ornamented lid of the stove almost before the paper had caught.

CHAPTER ELEVEN

Sasha Kolashki discovered the flint beneath his young wife's kitten softness within a very short time of their marriage. The first shock came when he broached the subject of resigning his Commission and retiring to the country to run what little was left of the estate.

They were on the train to Moscow on the first leg of their journey to Drovenskoye, the village some miles north-west of Moscow near the town of Sergiyev Posad, lovely seat of the Russian Orthodox Church, where the Kolashki estate was situated. Since he had not had the heart to disappoint the pretty little thing he had married so precipitately they were travelling in style, despite the cost, in a first-class Pullman sleeper with electric light, comfortable velvet chairs that would become beds when they were made up for the night and a bell to call the attendant. He had bought her chocolates from the Nevsky, silly fancies shaped like mice with bright glass eyes and long silver tails, which were at the moment the rage of young St Petersburg. The box lay, discarded, its contents half-eaten, upon the table. Rita sat idly turning the pages of a magazine, ignoring the drear and endless winter landscape through which they travelled, the lines of telegraph poles that flickered past the window with monotonous and mind-numbing regularity. She looked quite delightful in deep blue fur-trimmed velvet, a matching hat perched upon her fair curls, tiny blue leather boots peeping from beneath the hem of the well-cut skirt. She had bought the outfit, together with two others equally pretty, equally expensive, the week before. She had also purchased an extremely becoming dove-grey mourning dress to wear at Drovenskoye, a house still grieving for its master. He could in no way criticize her for that; but he must, he really must, have a word with her about their expenditure.

He shifted a little in his seat. She looked up, caught his eyes upon her, smiled vaguely and turned back to her magazine. The new higher waistlines really were very flattering, especially to someone as slight and slim as she – and she would truly die if she didn't acquire a couple of these hobble skirts that seemed to be so much in vogue in Paris and London. St Petersburg, for the normal shopper, could be so very *provincial*. At Madame Barry's, where she had bought her new outfits last week, a charming girl with whom she had entered into conversation had been telling her of the shops in Paris. She lifted her head again. Sasha had spoken. 'I'm sorry?'

He stretched his long, well-shaped legs. 'I was just saying that I must have a word with Mama about the running of the estate before I can take it over properly. If I resign my Commission it will still –'

'What?' The word was sharp. The magazine closed with a snap.

He shrugged, avoiding her eyes. Weak Sasha might be but he was far from stupid. It had not passed him by that Margarita would not be happy about this particular idea. 'I said – I was thinking I might resign my Commission – take over the estate –' He had thought of little else since the death of his father. Nevertheless the words were tentative.

Margarita was not. She stared in flat amazement. 'Resign your Commission? Oh, Sasha, don't be so utterly silly. Of course you are not to resign your Commission. I wouldn't hear of it.'

'But –'

'But, Sasha, darling, there can be absolutely no question of it. Surely you can see that? Goodness, whatever would people think? The moment your father dies you leave the army to run back to Mummy with your tail between your legs?' She ignored his half-hearted attempt to interrupt. 'Oh, certainly not, my dear. You shouldn't make such jokes.' She laughed a little, turned to catch her reflection in the window, pushed at a fair, stray curl with her finger. 'Bury us in the country with nothing but pigs and chickens for company?'

To say nothing of your mother and sister – oh, no! Margarita had plans, and those plans most certainly included the

Drovenskoye estate; but not now, not yet. Not until she had her hands firmly upon the reins and had entirely vanquished the opposition she knew she was about to encounter. She was married to an officer of the Preobrajensky Guards, albeit at the moment a very junior one. She lived in St Petersburg, the very centre of the empire's government. Sasha's fellow-officers had welcomed the pretty little bride to their midst with quite charming enthusiasm; just the night before they had thrown a party for the newly-weds at which a young Uhlan officer had paid her quite the most extravagant compliments – oh, no. Margarita was not about to give this up to become a dependent daughter-in-law in the country. She would go to Drovenskoye when Drovenskoye was hers, and not before.

'Absolutely not, my dear. And I'm quite certain that your mother will agree with me – why, surely, your poor father would turn in his grave to think of his son deserting his duty so?' She smiled her sweetest smile. 'I'm so very proud of you, my darling, you know that, don't you? Do you know, that nice Vitaly Petrovich was saying last night that you're quite the best horseman in the regiment –'

Sasha opened his mouth, shut it again, returned her warm smile. Wondered what it would be like to make love in these narrow beds on a moving train. The matter of the Commission could wait, he supposed; army life wasn't anywhere near so bad with a wife to come home to, despite the grim warnings of his commanding officer who had taken a terrible amount of persuading to grant his permission for the union.

Margarita opened the magazine again. That was that. She would have no more of such nonsense. The very idea! She reached for a chocolate, with sharp teeth bit the head very neatly off a mouse.

Sasha settled back in his chair and, a little gloomily, surveyed the bleak white landscape beyond the window. In truth he wasn't at all sure if he could afford to leave the army; the pay wasn't much, but it was better than nothing. The small allowance Victor had been persuaded to give to Margarita barely kept her in shoes and stockings the way she spent it. And he had no real idea of the financial standing of the estate, though he had his darkest doubts. His father had been no farmer, that he did know; they had lived off his pension and what little the home farm produced. The pension now presumably had stopped and he wasn't sure there was any other source of income. He supposed he'd have to get in touch with that dry old stick Malenkov, the family lawyer.

Margarita shut the magazine, tossed it onto the seat beside her. 'I've had a wonderful idea.' She smiled, dazzlingly, leaned across between the seats to kiss his cheek, lightly.

'Oh?' He could not resist that smile. He trapped her small hand in his. 'What's that?'

'Instead of going straight on to Drovenskoye, why don't we spend a day or two in Moscow? There are some wonderful shops – and we do so need some new curtains and furniture for that dreary little sitting room of ours, don't you think? I do so want to make it just perfect for you. And it would be such fun. Sasha darling – do say yes?'

'I – we promised Mama we'd be at Drovenskoye tomorrow –'

'Oh, surely she wouldn't mind?' Margarita pouted prettily. 'We could send a telegram, tell her we've been held up. Just a day or so, Sasha dear; it is our honeymoon, after all, isn't it?' She dropped her voice a little, leaned to him to whisper in his ear, 'We could stay overnight in an hotel. We could dine by candlelight, and then –' she blushed a little, dropped her eyes '– go to bed.' She almost laughed at the spasmodic movement of his hand upon hers at that; almost, but not quite. She flickered a glance at him, half-shy, charmingly daring. 'We could pretend that we aren't married at all!' She threw back her head, covering her face with her hands, gurgling with laughter. 'Oh, how wicked! Do say we can, Sasha. Please?'

They stayed in Moscow. They shopped in the Gostini Dvor, and in Muir et Merilese, the first department store to have opened in Russia. They browsed among the stalls and street traders, they ate at the famous, and outrageously expensive, Slavianski Bazaar. Sasha spent money like water, rewarded amply by his bride's unassumed delight and happiness, the open affection with which she cajoled and teased him. It was, after all, he kept telling himself, their honeymoon.

Only with Rita sleeping like a tired and contented child beside him after they had made love in the huge bed in the luxurious suite that the hotel manager, to Margarita's delight, had insisted was the only fit accommodation for the Excellency and his young wife, did he lie looking into darkness, counting the cost of their extravagance, and trying to ignore a small, gnawing anxiety.

The following afternoon the long, wood-burning train pulled slowly to a stop at a ramshackle country station, stood puffing impatiently for just long enough for two passengers and their luggage to disembark, then, shooting sparks into the gathering dusk, chugged and clanked away along the long, curving track towards Sergiyev Posad.

Margarita, who throughout the uncomfortable ride from Moscow had made absolutely no attempt to curb her growing nervy bad temper, tapped her booted foot upon the icy platform and pulled the collar of her fur shuba up about her face. It was bitterly cold. Flurries of fine snow flew in the chill wind. 'Where the devil is everyone?' she asked, peevishly. 'Surely there should be someone to meet us? You did send the telegram, didn't you?'

'Yes. Of course I did. You know I did. The train's very late – perhaps –'

'That's a reason to be here, not a reason not to be.' She turned and marched towards a small wooden hut that stood at the end of the deserted platform, leaving Sasha to pick up the luggage and follow. As she approached the door opened and a wizened man in a battered sheepskin coat peered out, his eyes going past Rita to Sasha, his lined face almost splitting apart in a gap-toothed grin. 'Master Sasha! Hey, Yuri! It's them!'

'Pavel, you old bear!' Sasha dropped the cases, slapped the man on the shoulder, laughing. 'And Yuri!'

'Young master.' A huge man in moth-eaten fur shuba and a ragged fur cap appeared at the door of the hut, grinning hugely. 'You're late.' To Margarita's astonishment the man used the familiar 'thou' in his speech.

'The train, Yuri, the train! When did you ever know the Moscow train to arrive on time?' Sasha stopped. Both men's eyes were upon Margarita, polite, sharply curious. 'My wife,' he said, the words still novel enough to bring simple pleasure in the saying of them. 'Margarita Victorovna. Rita, this is Pavel, our station master and Yuri Petrovich, an old friend and comrade.'

The big man laughed delightedly at the description. Margarita frowned a little, nodded stiffly. She had never expected such informality – not to say familiarity – in the introduction of servants, which, after all, was all that the man Yuri could be.

Yuri bent, lifted the cases as if they were a featherweight. 'The sledge is outside, young master. Your mama waits with great impatience.'

Margarita's frown deepened. Did she detect a trace of reproach in the words? Had the dark eyes that had flickered in her direction shown a shadow of resentment?

Sasha was laughing. 'Come then, home!' He threw his head back and breathed deeply of the cold air. 'Why does the snow always smell so much *cleaner* in the country? Margarita, tuck yourself into the furs here – I'll ride up front with Yuri.'

Margarita sulked thoroughly, and to no avail at all, during the long ride. Huddled in furs that smelled none too clean, she allowed her apprehension and self-pity full rein. Sasha was ignoring her. It was thoughtless and unkind of him not to be sitting with her, warming and reassuring her. The first few moments within the sphere of his family and already she had been relegated to a back seat, both literally and metaphorically. Well – her small mouth tightened a little – they'd see about that.

The deserted, seemingly endless road wound through mile upon mile of all but featureless woodland, passed through a few scattered, poor-looking villages, crossed an unimposing frozen river. The rhythmic jingle of bells, the sound of the horses' hooves upon the snow thrummed monotonously on, constant and unvarying. Margarita seriously considered screaming. Holy Mother! Would they never get to this God-forsaken place? Then at last, two long hours after leaving the station and with full darkness upon them, the horses, harness and bells jingling, swung through a large, open, wrought-iron gate and onto a narrow, winding drive that sloped into a small valley. As it did so two small dogs, barking hysterically, hurled themselves upon the sledge, snapping at the horses' heels, leaping about the runners. 'Petya! Melya! Here!' Sasha bent, held his arms open. The two little dogs leapt like monkeys onto the moving sledge, climbing all over Sasha, licking his face, tails wagging wildly, still yapping in an ear-splitting frenzy of delight. Sasha laughed over his shoulder at Margarita. She smiled thinly back. Her heart was racing, her stomach churning. In the distance she could see faintly glowing lights and what looked, so far as she could tell in the darkness, to be a long, low house, two storeys high and with many chimneys. Drovenskoye. They had arrived.

On first impression Drovenskoye was, to Margarita's inexperienced eye, every bit as imposing as she had expected and hoped it would be. The sledge swept in a wide semi-circle and drew up in a three-sided courtyard formed by the long, low housefront and two stable wings, at the foot of a flight of wide, shallow steps leading to a great, ancient-looking wooden front door. That the steps were quite obviously crumbling, the sweep of drive packed with dirty, uncleared snow, the lamps that glimmered on either side of the door rusted and smoking she did not notice. Nor did she see the peeling paint or the unhinged shutters. She saw a childhood dream; a country house, a private house many times larger than any she had ever set foot in; than she had ever dreamed of setting foot in, let alone owning. For a moment, looking up at the crumbling facade, she saw brilliantly-lighted rooms, shining floors, gleaming crystal, heard music and gaily-lifted voices. Saw herself the lovely chatelaine, greeting her guests with kisses and with laughter. No painted set for a toy theatre this. No cardboard cut-out prince either, standing beside her, but a tall and handsome young man who was her husband. For one brief moment she almost loved him; for bringing her here, for owning this. Then she remembered the women who waited beyond this door – the women who belonged here – and the moment died. 'For heaven's sake, Sasha, where is everyone? Do you want me to freeze to death?'

Sasha had leapt down from the high front seat of the sledge. Yuri swept the yelping, struggling dogs into his arms, tossed them back into the sledge, where they worried the fur wraps, shaking them like rags. Like a boy Sasha bounded up the shallow steps, pushed open the great door. 'Hello? Mama? Galina? We're here!'

More slowly Margarita followed, found herself standing in a

large hall, completely empty but for a carved wooden settle and a tall marble torchère upon which guttered a smoking candle lamp. More candles were set in wall sconces, reflected in small, triangular, smoke-darkened mirrors.

Sasha snatched off his hat, shrugged out of his heavy fur coat, tossed them carelessly upon the settle. 'Mama? Galya?'

'Sasha!' A door opened. A light-footed, dark-haired girl dressed in shabby black ran across the hall, hands outstretched. Margarita would have recognized her anywhere. She was the living image of her brother. 'Sasha!' she said again, and in a swift movement took him into her arms, kissing him on both cheeks. 'Oh, how good it is that you've come!'

Sasha hugged her, laughing. Margarita stood like stone in the shadows. When brother and sister drew apart at last she stepped forward. Sasha held out a hand. 'Rita, darling, come and meet my Galina. Galya, this is Margarita, my wife.'

The two girls looked at each other, the smallest comprehensive flick of a glance taking in everything from the crown of fair or dark head to Margarita's shining boots and Galina's shabby shoes. Then dark eyes met blue and in that long, cool moment, war was declared. Galina smiled, very brightly, held out a slim, cool hand. 'Welcome.'

And, 'Thank you,' Rita said, equally warmly, equally falsely, and kissed her new sister upon both smooth cheeks.

Sasha, watching, beamed. 'I know you two are going to be very great friends. Galya, where's Mama?'

'In the drawing room. Come. She's waiting to greet you.' Galina led the way into a square, cold, lofty room, candlelit, as was the hall. Margarita had a swift impression of heavy old furniture, darkly panelled walls, smoke-stained portraits. Then her attention was held by the tall, slender woman, not young but fraily beautiful in the shadowed light, who stood awaiting them. She was dressed, in honour of the occasion of welcoming the heir of the house and his new wife, in a formal dress of a shining gold stuff so old and so fragile as to be almost transparent, the train spread upon the threadbare carpet behind her. In her hands was a lovely and obviously ancient icon of the Virgin and Child. On the table beside her stood a tray, upon it a round loaf of black bread topped by a small silver salt cellar.

Sasha caught Margarita's hand in his, led her forward, dropped to his knees in front of his mother. A small stir of rebellion kept Margarita on her feet for a moment longer than good manners demanded before she, too, responding to the pressure of her husband's hand in hers, knelt. Sasha's mother made a reverent sign of the Cross with the icon above their bowed heads, then she took the bread and the salt and again blessed them. Rita glanced sideways at her husband. He knelt like a child, head bowed, eyes shut. 'My children,' the woman said, gently, 'welcome.'

For some strange reason Margarita found that her teeth were locked, vice-like, fast together, her jaw rigid. As she rose gracefully to her feet she made a purposeful, physical effort to relax them. She smiled her most beguiling smile. 'Mother,' she said, shyly. And saw Galina's dark, sardonically-lifted brows as she stepped forward to accept the butterfly embrace of her mother-in-law.

The visit could not by any stretch of the imagination have been called a success, which was no more than Margarita had expected; what did surprise her was how little, in the end, it actually mattered. She had known from the start that Sasha's family, not unnaturally, would view with some disapproval and caution the upstart nobody who had so unceremoniously arrived in their midst as his wife; oddly, what she had underestimated was her own hold on her besotted young husband and the consequent lessening of the influence of his devoted mother and sister. That devotion, too, told against them; they treated him like a favoured child, still. What Sasha wanted must be given. And Sasha undoubtedly wanted Margarita. A lifetime of defending a sensitive younger child against the depredations of an intolerant and overbearing father and brother had ingrained habits that were hard to change. That Galina disliked her intensely Rita knew; she reciprocated in full. It irritated her beyond belief that the other girl, dressed as shabbily as any servant, on cheerful, first-name terms with every ostler and kitchen girl – not that there were many such at Drovenskoye – yet with her clear, clipped voice, her infuriatingly natural, aristocratic bearing achieved a cool self-possession that

Margarita positively ached to emulate, and could not. Even in the smart, dove-grey mourning she had been so careful to buy she felt out of place, almost vulgar compared to Galina in her rusty black and Sasha's mother in her unfashionable, heavy gowns and woollen shawls that might have come from the back of any peasant woman, and in which Varya, Margarita knew, would not have been seen dead. Galling it was too when Sasha and his sister rode out each morning – Galina, to Margarita's scandalized surprise, dressed in breeches and heavy sheepskin against the cold – on the horses that had been theirs since childhood. Margarita had never learned to ride a horse, was positively afraid of the great, bad-tempered beasts, so it was impossible to accompany them. She was left alone with Sasha's quiet, gentle mother in whose company she felt as clumsy as the most inept servant girl and as out of place as a pebble in a jewel box.

She spent long hours avoiding everyone by exploring the house, at least half of which had apparently been shut up for years, fascinated by the endless rows of portraits, many of them recognizably Sasha's ancestors, upon the damp-stained walls, the ancient, heavy furniture, the old fabrics and rugs that looked ready to fall apart at a touch. Well-wrapped against the cold she would wander from room to room, enthralled as a child at this strange new world she had entered. It astonished her that the Kolashkis, an ancient family of what seemed to her wealth and standing, should live in such relatively primitive conditions; the Shalakov apartment on the Venskaya boasted running water, warm and comfortable rooms, and recently-installed electric light. In this decaying house it was a constant struggle to keep warm, curtains and wallcoverings were mildewed, and – most astonishing of all – all water had to be brought by cart or by sledge each day from the nearby river. The toilet facilities were of the most basic kind, the great beds, to which they repaired by candlelight, cold and damp. Margarita developed a chill within hours of arriving. Yet, living in conditions not unlike those that held sway in the Vyborg and other working-class districts of St Petersburg, these people retained an air of superiority, of unquestioned and unquestioning authority, of unshakable self-confidence in themselves and their world that made Margarita feel an outsider, worse, an interloper. That her father in his new-found prosperity probably possessed more disposable income than did the entire Kolashki family, let alone her Uncle Bourlov who could undoubtedly have bought this estate several times over if he had had a mind, made not the slightest difference. The divide was there, and no amount of well-mannered effort could disguise it. And as the days went by, certainly on the part of Galina and of Margarita herself, less effort, well-mannered or otherwise, was made. The two girls had disliked each other on sight and made little beyond the slightest polite attempts to disguise it. Yet in a way, far from harming Margarita, Sasha's sister's hostility was a positive advantage. Sasha was no fool; he sensed the undercurrents and knew their cause; knew also that in this alien place his young wife had no champion but him. Margarita, whose chief talent was manipulation, took full advantage of this.

After a series of skirmishes she won a final and significant battle over the speaking of French at the dining table.

As was customary in such families the Kolashkis conversed, fluently and easily, only in French at table. Margarita's education falling rather short of her protagonist's – her application, it must be said, falling even shorter – her smattering of the language was in no way good enough for her to keep up with the rapid-fire talk and laughter that Galina, recognizing her advantage, immediately instigated. Sasha, slipping into old ways with ease, at first satisfied himself simply with laughing translations for his smiling, prettily gracious, inwardly fuming wife. A short and fiery interview before bed one evening, however, followed by a cold, inexorably turned back quite decisively restored his sense of husbandly duty. When he and his sister returned from their morning ride the following day Galina's face was set; in the afternoon Sasha sat with his mother in her small parlour – virtually the only warm room in the house – recalling the past, talking of the future, and making a reasonable to say nothing of well-mannered suggestion.

That night, with no comment made, they spoke Russian at table.

They stayed for a week; a strange week for Margarita. Though disappointed at the degree to which her husband's inheritance had run to ruin, yet still she could not rid herself of the sense of excitement that the old house with its sense of history, its aristocratic connections aroused in her. Indeed she understood well that had Sasha's family been as well-off and as well-connected as once they had been her marriage to the son of such a family could never imaginably have taken place, whatever her charms or his weakness. All the childish romance to which she still clung – the very first thing she had done upon moving into their far from large apartment had been, to Sasha's delighted disbelief, to set up her small toy theatre on the tiny sideboard in the living room – was fed by this house with its empty, echoing rooms, its faded glory, its unkempt and run-down fields and garden. Yet the bourgeois in her was impatient to the point of contempt; how *could* they have allowed it to happen? For all their airs and their undoubted graces, what good were they, to themselves or to those who depended upon them? More than once she found herself thinking of her Uncle Bourlov – whom above all people she admired – his energy, his shrewd business brain, his single-minded ambition. He would never in a million years sink into the genteel, mostly self-inflicted poverty in which the Kolashkis found themselves. And if by any ill chance he did, he would not sit idly by twiddling aristocratic thumbs and speaking French at the dining table while the world continued to crumble about him. She'd speak to him – ask his advice. If they could marry Galina off – there must be *someone* who would want her? – and perhaps farm Sasha's mother out to some distant relation, surely something could be done to restore at least some comfort and prestige to the Kolashki estate? Anna, by all accounts, was living a life of landed luxury in England – the photographs she had sent of her husband's Sussex house where they now spent most of their time showed a small but exceedingly pretty country house set in lovely gardens and rolling parkland – why should not her youngest sister achieve the same end in Russia?

Thus dreaming Margarita sustained herself through the last few uncomfortable days before they could leave and go back to life in St Petersburg.

On the day before they were due to leave Sasha's mother,

gently but very firmly, suggested that she and her new daughter-in-law spend the morning together.

Margarita, who had quite cleverly avoided any such intimacy up until now, could do nothing but agree. She joined her mother-in-law in her parlour, poured water from the bubbling samovar into the tea glasses and prepared for the inquisition.

It did not come.

Olga Mikhailovna Kolashkova was by no means stupid. The marriage was made, nothing could be done about it. It was unlikely, anyway, that anyone of their own station would have looked at poor Sasha with his debts, his dependent female relatives and his millstone of an estate. The problem was not Margarita's lowly birth, it was her character. Above all Sasha's mother was concerned for the happiness of her beloved son; nothing she had seen of Margarita had convinced her that this was in safe hands. 'My dear,' she said, after the everyday courtesies had been carefully observed, 'it occurs to me – Sasha has never been happy in the army. He took his Commission only to please his father. Might it not be an idea now for him to leave, to come home? The estate needs a man, someone with a strong hand, to run it, to get it back on its feet.' She tried hard to make that sound like a positive premise rather than a hope.

Rita, already sitting ramrod straight, stiffened further. She took a long moment to sip her tea, very composedly to replace her glass in its small saucer. Then, 'Oh, no,' she said, very sweetly and reasonably, 'I really don't think that will be possible. Not for a while, anyway.' She lowered her eyes, hiding the sharp gleam of anger. 'Sasha has his way to make in the world, Mother-in-law,' she added, quietly, her young voice edged. 'He's changed. Of course he has. He's no longer a little boy. He's a man. He knows what he has to do.'

Olga lifted a narrow, elegant hand. 'He was never suited to the army,' she repeated, doggedly. 'Never.'

Margarita lifted her head, fixed the older woman with a wide, confident, apparently innocent stare. Faded, astonishingly uncertain eyes met hers. There was a long silence. The eyes dropped. Margarita let out a small, satisfied breath that had been pent in her throat. In such a short moment, they both knew who had won.

The silence lengthened. Olga sighed. She had, she supposed, known it would be useless. This vital, exhausting, self-centred child would never think of anyone but herself. Her mother's heart bled for gentle, incredibly silly Sasha. She remembered her own marriage, not in the beginning the penance it had later become, and flinched from the knowledge that history, inevitably, seemed to repeat itself. 'You're leaving tomorrow?' she asked, conversationally, in her voice not the slightest sign of despair.

'Yes.' Margarita was watching her warily.

Olga sat still and graceful upon a straight-backed chair, the thick and softly-curling grey hair that was drawn up upon her head making the slender neck look fragile as the stem of a flower. She turned her head, looking out of the window to where Sasha and his sister, the excited dogs at their heels, rode up the snowy drive, returning from their last morning ride. 'Tomorrow,' she repeated. 'How very fast time flies, does it not?'

Margarita said nothing. The week had seemed an eternity to her.

The following day they left to return to St Petersburg. Sasha did not broach the subject of resigning his Commission again.

Katya was bored. Bored with dancing. Bored with the endless, senseless flirting. Bored with young men who, it seemed to her, all looked and sounded alike, the only noticeable difference between them the colour and cut of their uniforms. She was also aware that her small deceptions were on occasion coming perilously close to discovery; indeed, if it had not been for the fact that her father had been involved in major business negotiations that had involved a great deal of travelling to and around Germany, she doubted she would have got away with her light-hearted prevarication regarding the progress of her relationship with Jussi Lavola for as long as she had. Further, she knew that her father, indulgent or no, was likely to take a terrifyingly dim view of his daughter's escapades if they came to light. But an odd, unsettled and unsettling dissatisfaction drove her. She was looking for something, she did not know what. She suspected, in her more morbid moments, that it was something that did not exist.

On the evening that she met Major Kostya Illyarovich, an officer of the Volinsky Regiment, in Felicien's Restaurant, a fashionable eating place reputed to be the most beautifully situated in Europe she was, unusually, actually with Jussi. For each of them it was on occasion politic to appear in public together, though neither took any great notice of the other and the company – all young, all perfectly aware of the 'arrangement' – accepted the situation with equanimity.

In the moment of introduction Katya recognized Kostya Illyarovich as quite clearly the most dangerous man she had ever met. Jussi himself introduced them, one eye on a red-headed gypsy girl who was moving from table to table with a basket of flowers, selling her wares to the highest bidder. As the girl reached them he slid a long arm about her waist, his smile angelic, and skilfully steered her away from the next table and into a curtained alcove.

Katya was left facing a pair of coal-black, appraising eyes in a flat, brown face, scarred from jaw to eyebrow on the left side. A heavy black moustache gave the man the air of a bandit, and no fancy uniform could disguise the arrogant power of his stocky body. He was the oldest of the company, in his late thirties, perhaps, or early forties. His features had a mongol cast; he looked a barbarian. She had watched him all evening, and she knew that he knew it. He was not tall, but strong, and his stance was easy; experience showed in every line of his square, all but impassive face. In some odd way, without so much as moving an eyebrow, he had about him an immediate aura of violence that repelled and attracted her in absolutely equal measure. His eyes took mannerless and only slightly interested stock of her face, her jewellery, and then, more slowly, her body.

She should, she knew, walk away now.

'Good evening, Major,' she said, and returned a level look with one of her own. Her father was away. When he returned she was certain he would require an accounting; he demanded a son-in-law, and a grandson. He would not wait too much longer. The trap was closing.

The man nodded. Grinned suddenly. Took her hand and carried it to his lips, but instead of the usual formal brushing of lips against the back of the hand he turned it to kiss the palm. His moustache was strong and wiry against the sensitive skin. She opened her fingers, surrendering to the small, outrageous intimacy; shivered a little. 'Good evening, lady,' he said. 'Would the lady care for a drink?'

She was playing with fire. She knew it. But that, she told herself, altogether too smartly, was better than not playing at all. 'Yes. Thank you,' she said. 'The lady would very much like a vodka.'

It was the most entertaining evening she had spent in a very long time. Secure in this most crowded of public places, stimulated in equal measure by vodka and an excitement not unmixed with a quite delicious if very real trepidation, she teased and tempted the man in a manner not unlike the child who will poke a stick through the bars of a wild animal's cage knowing that retribution cannot possibly fall upon it. And exactly like that same animal, he watched and he waited, allowing her her moment, his square, mongol face impassive, an expression flickering occasionally in the hot eyes that sent a shiver of warning through her, and then served simply to provoke her into greater indiscretion. When the restaurant dimmed and the spotlighted gypsy singers and musicians appeared, he was sitting next to her at the table. As if to get a better view she moved her chair a little, closer to him, leaned forward, her elbows on the table. Almost casually, quite openly, he reached a hand to her breast, cradling it in a strong hand, his thumb moving over her nipple. For a moment she allowed it, trembling, sudden fire in her veins. Then abruptly she sat back, folding her arms across her bosom.

She heard his laughter in the darkness, above the music. He turned from her then, his broad, insolent back to her, eyes and attention on the gypsy girl who stepped into the circle of light, arms raised, fingers clicking.

She burned with humiliation. And with something else. Something she recognized as being very dangerous indeed.

In the sledge on the way home Jussi, unusually, attempted a warning. 'He's a dangerous man, Katya. He isn't a child, to be played with. He's not one of your pretty boys who'll dance to your tune and thank you for it.' He was unwontedly serious.

Katya cocked her head provocatively. 'Oh? You think I can't manage him?'

'I know you can't,' Jussi said, simply. 'He's –' He stopped.

'What?'

'There have been – stories.'

'What kind of stories?' She was innocently and deliberately obtuse.

He turned to face her. The runners hissed on a new fall of snow, bells jingled on the harness. 'You know well what sort of stories. For heaven's sake, Katya, don't pretend to be stupid! Just believe me, Kostya Illyarovich does not play this game by the same rules as most of the rest of us. He has no fear, no respect for anything or anyone. He is a law unto himself. He's a gambler. He's a born fighter. He cares about nothing and no one but his regiment and his men. And he's a brute with women.'

She settled back into the furs. 'How very interesting,' she murmured.

'Katya!'

The vodka and the cold air were making her dizzy. She giggled a little.

'Please. Don't be any sillier than is absolutely necessary.' Jussi was more brusque than she had ever heard him. 'Stay away from Illyarovich.'

'But, Jussi – you introduced me to him yourself!'

'A mistake,' he said, grimly, his pleasant face for once unsmiling.

She let a small silence develop. Then she turned. 'Jussi, we have an arrangement. You remember?'

He nodded. 'I remember.'

She pointed a gloved finger an inch from his nose. 'You look after your sheep,' she turned the finger to point to herself, 'and I look after mine. That was it, wasn't it?'

He held out for a moment longer, then relaxed, laughing more than a little ruefully, into his seat. 'Yes, Katya. That was the arrangement.'

The sledge glided on through the snow-sculpted countryside of the Islands towards the lights of St Petersburg.

*   *   *

Illyarovich did not contact her, though for those first few days she looked minute by minute for some kind of message, so certain was she that he would. A week went by. Another. She was furious. The more he ignored her the more she thought about him; the more she thought about him the more fascinating he became. She would lie in bed at night and build his image before her; the bull shoulders, the strong, stocky body, the flat, terrifying mongol face. She looked for him at the skating parties, the sledge rides, the concerts and the parties; but he did not come.

Her father arrived home, busy and distracted, left again. Her mother was involved with a new charity, a smarter and more demanding set of friends. Katya danced and skated, laughed and flirted, kept up the pretence of her association with Jussi Lavola, watched constantly for Kostya Illyarovich.

And in the end, of course, the fish played to perfection and begging to be caught, he came.

The occasion was Jussi's sister's birthday.

It was late March, still cold, the river and Gulf still ice-locked, and likely to be for a month or more longer, but with the faintest suggestion of change in the air. Snowstorms still swept from the wastes of Siberia, the bitter wind still sliced down the streets of the city, cutting through clothing like a sharp-honed blade, but on occasion in the lengthening days the sun shone, glittering on the iced and frozen world with a tentative springlike suggestion of warmth. Elisabet's birthday fell upon such a day, and so the sport that Jussi and his friends had arranged in her honour was the more flamboyant, the more enjoyable for the bright beauty in which it was couched.

First there was the inevitable splendid luncheon at the Turnakov mansion, situated in a small square off the Nevsky, early so as to leave as much time as possible for the races and games on the ice that Jussi had arranged for the short afternoon. Jussi had his own small apartment in the west wing of the mansion, a privilege obviously available only on the grounds of his sex – a sister, Katya had often pointed out, tartly, would have been allowed no such freedom – and one that Katya much envied. The luncheon was for the selected few, and Katya was resigned to the fact that necessarily she was seated next to Jussi with Elisabet's eyes uncomfortably sharp upon them.

She smiled a small, wry smile at him over her crystal glass. 'How's your plump little widow?'

He grinned. 'Plump. And very widowed. On Tuesdays and Thursdays, at least.'

Katya could not prevent a small, spluttering shout of laughter. 'Poor man!'

Jussi was injured. 'Not at all. It's preferable to being dead every day of the week, isn't it? And, by the Cross!' He rolled his eyes. 'That's what he'd be if I didn't relieve him of some of his – husbandly responsibilities.'

Her laughter was genuine. The one thing, possibly the only thing, she had to admit to liking about Jussi Lavola was his sense of humour. His lean face was the picture of put-upon innocence. She caught her mother's eye upon her, lifted her glass in salute, breathed a small word of thanks that she could not hear what the two supposed love-birds were talking about, then laughed again at the thought.

'And you?' Jussi asked.

Katya shrugged. 'All right. I suppose.'

He affected surprise. 'But – didn't I hear that young Marushki and Ivan What's-his-name of the Corps de Pages were on the point of a duel over you?'

It was an exaggeration, and more than an exaggeration, as he well knew. She grinned her appreciation. 'As I said: all right, I suppose.'

The many courses finished, more and yet more food packed into sledges and taken to the banks of the Neva to feed the wider party invited to the afternoon's celebrations, they repaired to the ice. Braziers were lit. Passers-by hung over the bridges, watching. Wooden benches and seats were provided, with foot-warmers, handwarmers and blankets for the knees. There were sledging races and skating races. There was what seemed to Katya to be an excessively silly game involving officers from two rival regiments and the bladder of a pig, which unfortunately ended with at least one broken leg, a near-serious challenge to a duel the following day and – uncounted – several black eyes. The climax of the afternoon, to be followed by fireworks and skating, were the horse races; and if what had gone before, broken leg and all, had been comparatively light-hearted, there was no pretence here at anything but a deadly resolve. The young men, dashingly uniformed, expensively horsed, milled about the starting line, pushing and jostling for position.

Katya, standing by a brazier on the ice, sensed someone behind her, turned to find Jussi, towering above her, his eyes on the riders. 'Why aren't you out there?'

He shrugged without looking at her, smiled his disarming smile. 'I am not an army man.' He paused for a moment, flashed a quick grin. 'And I can't ride. Not in the way that is necessary to keep body and soul together out there, anyway.' He slanted a laughing glance down at her. 'My soul is very precious to me. I don't want to part with it. Not yet.'

She laughed outright. 'I sometimes forget you aren't a Russian –' She stopped.

There he was. On a sturdy Cossack pony that he rode as if he were born into the saddle. A single rein, a light bit. That same careless, arrogant stance; she would have recognized him anywhere. The pony was smaller than most other horses in the race. She saw him speak, remembered the things she had heard about these animals; that they were controlled entirely by the knee and by the voice of the rider. Despite the uniform, the gleaming decorations, the trappings of civilization, here was a rider from the steppes, a Mongol of legend. A disciple – a reincarnation – of Genghis Khan. She watched, suddenly, with bated breath.

He turned the pony with perfect timing, was on his way like an arrow just as the signal shot was sounded. No man saw anything of him but his back.

Two heats he ran, two heats he won, with the rough-coated little horse barely blowing. Katya neither cheered nor waved, as others, newly discovering an outsider, did. She stood like a statue, watching intently. The final race involved half a dozen horses, each the winners of the heats. Two in particular were splendid beasts, aristocrats ridden by men who knew both their own worth and their animals'. Their riders exchanged good wishes, leaning from their saddles before they raced, shaking hands, laughing.

Kostya Illyarovich circled his small beast away from the milling contestants, some of whom it must be admitted had partaken quite copiously of the hospitality on offer. Katya watched. Saw him lean to the little horse's ear, short, powerful legs lifting him in the saddle. Restless, eager to be off, the animal pawed the ground. Its rider, watching the starter, wheeled to the line.

One of the contenders was down before the race was truly begun. How such an unfortunate accident occurred was impossible to tell. In these icy conditions, anything could happen. Even Katya, who saw the incident from start to finish, since it quite clearly involved the rider upon whom the whole of her attention was focused, could not for her life have sworn to what happened. Certain it was that the little Cossack horse, apparently avoiding the falling animal, leapt clear of the melee and was off in pursuit of the race leader like a hound on scent of the prey.

The onlookers on the bridge suddenly decided to take sides. 'Come on, the Volinsky!'

The Volinsky, a fascinated Katya saw, came on, and with a vengeance. He streaked up behind the bigger horse, dogged him for long enough to unsettle the beast, then shot past him like a bullet out of a gun to pass the finish line a good two lengths ahead.

'Well,' Jussi said behind her, very dry, 'justice is done again, I see.'

The prizes were presented. The fireworks began, a spectacular show. Katya waited, watching the sparkling, jewel-like colours reflected in the snow. Sure enough a solid, stocky figure detached itself from the crowd and came to stand beside her. Jussi had gone.

'Congratulations,' she said.

Kostya shrugged.

She could see her mother, fur-draped, elegant as ever, chatting animatedly to an acquaintance. She stepped back a little, into the shade of an overhanging tree.

'A prize for the winner?' he asked.

As she had expected his arms and his body were strong, overwhelmingly so. His kiss took the very breath from her body.

She struggled free. 'Stop it! For heaven's sake! Are you mad?'

He laughed, very quietly. Out on the ice flares were being lit against the darkness, a band struck up. He kissed her again, very fiercely, forcing her back against the treetrunk. There was a soft sound behind them. They jumped apart. Jussi stood there, in his hands a pair of skating blades, that without comment he handed to Katya. As she bent to put them on he said, coolly, 'People are wondering where you are,' and was gone.

She straightened. Kostya stepped back, a shadow in the shadows. 'Meet me on Thursday,' he said, quietly. 'Two o'clock. By the bandstand in the Summer Gardens.'

She hesitated. Prudence, or perhaps fear, unexpectedly won. 'I – can't,' she said. 'Not Thursday.' She could not see his face. She wanted, immediately, to deny the words, to tell him she'd meet him anywhere, any time –

'Katya? Katya – there you are! We've been looking for you everywhere!' A group of laughing youngsters were skating towards them. 'Come on, do! Come and skate.'

He looked at her for a long, calm moment. 'You meet me Thursday, or you meet me not at all,' he said, and turned and left her.

She met him. She told no-one, not even Jussi. He had hired a sledge and a driver; they drove out along the shores of the Gulf, into the winter forests. They talked a little, but only a little; she questioning, he replying with laconic brevity. Yes, he had seen active service, both in Japan and in the Ukraine. No, he had no family. And no, he had no interest in possessions; what above a good horse, a sword and a gun did a soldier need? She resisted neither when he kissed her nor when, beneath the furs, his strong, hard hand slid beneath the bodice of her dress to caress her breasts: nothing in her life had ever excited her so. The sheer brute strength of the man both fascinated and repelled her. As unlike the young men who usually danced attendance upon her as he could possibly be, he drew her like a magnet; yet at the same time if she were honest she had to admit that he truly frightened her. And what frightened her more was that at that moment, absurdly, she knew that had he asked she would have gone anywhere with him, risked anything for him, done anything, absolutely anything that he required of her.

But he did not ask. He delivered her back at the Summer Gardens punctiliously two short hours after they had left, lifted her hand briefly to his lips and left her, watching after him, confused, angry, near to tears. He had not suggested another meeting.

That night, restless, she could not sleep, could not get the image of the man out of her head. Almost for the first time in her life she longed really to talk to someone, to confide in someone who might understand the strange and painful clash of emotions he roused in her.

At midnight, with the house asleep around her, she lit her candle, settled by the stove in her room and wrote a long overdue letter to her cousin Anna.

Anna received the letter as the soft green bloom of spring was turning to the lusher verdancy of early summer in the Sussex countryside. She stood by the open French windows of the music room reading Katya's impatient scrawl. A cuckoo called distantly from the woodland. The garden, which she had grown to love so dearly, lay tranquil and beautiful in fitful sunshine, a breeze rustled the bright new leaves.

Guy sat behind her in a deep armchair, watching her, waiting for her to finish.

She turned to him, smiling a little. 'Poor Katya. She's found her match at last from the sound of it. She's fallen in love, she says, with a barbarian.' For all the extravagant extremes of emotion in the letter – so like Katya – she could not help but laugh a little. 'Poor Katya,' she said again. 'It had to happen, I suppose. She's such a reckless soul.' She dropped the letter onto a small table, went to stand behind her husband, her hand gentle upon his shoulder, stood looking out into the lovely garden. By the open windows a thrush sang.

He covered the hand with his own, turned his head to look up at her. His bout of ill-health had taken its toll. He looked, she thought suddenly, frail and a little tired. 'Would you like to go for a stroll in the garden?' she asked.

He shook his head. 'Later, perhaps. I have some work to do. If you seduce me into your lovely leafy domain I'll never shake myself free. I'll come in an hour or so, and you can show me all your latest labours.' He smiled, his still bright eyes warm. 'A green-thumbed gardener indeed! Anna, my love, you've become more English than the English, do you know that?'

She laughed, picked up a wide straw hat that lay upon a chair. 'An hour. No more. You mustn't wear yourself out. And I want you to see the bluebells in the woodland garden before they fade.' As she moved to the window she picked up the letter before she stepped into the sunshine.

She read it again sitting on a stone bench set against a huge clipped hedge of yew. The leaves scented the air in the sunshine, bees buzzed busily in a nearby flowerbed. She lifted her head. As a brief and haphazard postscript to her main letter Katya had appended news of the family; Lenka had had a little boy, but hardly anyone saw her any more since she seemed to have withdrawn entirely from the family. Margarita seemed blissfully happy with what Katya termed 'her handsome toy soldier', Dima and Natalia were living 'like the most ancient of old married couples', and Natalia was expecting a child. Anna sat quite still, her eyes distant. St Petersburg. The domes and the spires. The great river, locked in winter's ice, turbulent with the spring thaws. The northern winters. The long, rose-gold days of summer. The white nights. Katya. Her family; suddenly she realized that almost without her noticing it a strange thing had happened. St Petersburg was no longer home. She looked around her. This was her home. When first she had come to England to read such a letter would have brought on a bout of homesickness that she would have had to fight for days; now she felt no such sadness. 'More English than the English' Guy had called her; and it was true. England suited her. This life, with its friendships, its music, the utter delight of this garden, suited her. She no longer wanted to go back, not to live. Recently she had been tinkering with the idea of going to visit, and that she thought she would enjoy, though even the vaguest of plans kept being postponed, casualties of a filled and busy life. The point was that she could contemplate it with no fear; the danger was over; she would not, she knew, find it hard to leave that other life to come home. As for Andrei: perhaps sadly, she hardly ever thought of him now. That wild young passion

234

had died. When Varya mentioned him in her letters, which she did, infrequently, there was now no unsettling stirring of emotion. She was happy. She smiled suddenly. That was it; she was happy, here, with Guy, with her music, with her garden.

Strange indeed are the ways of God, she found herself thinking, the words coming to her, unusually, in her own native tongue. She sat for a long quiet moment looking about her, trying to hold the moment, savouring the discovery of her contentment. Then she stood up and strolled back towards the house, to answer Katya's letter.

Not, she admitted to herself with a sudden, rueful smile, as she bent to tug at a stray weed in the flagstoned path, that she believed for a moment that anything she might say would deflect her cousin in the least from her own flamboyant and wayward path. God alone knew who or what would do that.

CHAPTER TWELVE

There was little to distinguish the summer of 1912 from any other St Petersburg summer, except of course in a personal sense when events scarcely noted by the world at large changed the course of a private life. The weather was, as always, variable. The only significant political event was the election of the new Duma – a body regarded on the whole as a toothless watchdog of the peoples' rights, leashed and held in check by the overwhelming power of the Tsar. Beneath the surface, the political cauldron seethed: revolutionary bodies, their leaders, exiled almost to a man to the various capitals of Western Europe, plotted, as always, against the State and against each other and the workers and students of the city, stirred up by the agents of these same political agitators, relieved the tedium of life's dreary, hand-to-mouth struggle by a series of strikes and demonstrations. In the middle of July the Okhrana – the Tsar's hated secret police – found a new recruit in Pavel Petrovich Donovalov, Lenka's husband, who embraced his new responsibilities with predictable enthusiasm. Lenka did not care how unsavoury was her husband's new occupation, it mattered only that he had ceased to torment her. Meanwhile polite society, equally predictably, retired to the summer delight of Peterhof, there to ride, to dance and to pay court to its ruling family. And in a Europe regarded by most Russians, ignoring the lessons of history, as an alien world totally separate from their own, the great powers snarled and jostled for power in an undeclared contest of strength that grew more dangerous every day.

Sasha Kolashki's thoughts were far from such weighty matters as he made his way from the regiment's headquarters near the Winter Palace towards the tiny apartment he shared when he could with Margarita in a narrow street behind the Liteini Prospekt; an apartment that, though cramped and far from

236

comfortable, was nevertheless beyond their means. He had had to borrow yet again from his mother this month, a thing he hated to do. Sasha was thinking, as he so often did these days, of two things; money, or the lack of it, and his wife. He was thinking, too, of the very real possibility that far from being given the opportunity to leave the regiment of his own accord, if he displeased his senior officers further by his inability to sustain the social life expected of a Preobrajensky Guard he might well be required to make way for someone who could, connections notwithstanding. His immediate commanding officer had been more than unhappy at the marriage of his least well-off junior officer; it had been made clear at the time that the joys of marital bliss must not be at the expense of the regiment. This brought him to the matter of the Princess Vasselevski's ball. Should he mention it to Margarita? If he did then certainly, between her and his displeased Major, he would not be able to escape attending. All officers of the Preobrajensky and of the Semeonovsky had been invited – the Princess's father having served in the one regiment, her husband serving presently in the other. But to attend would mean a complete new outfit for Margarita and, even more expensive, a new dress uniform for himself, the old one – handed on from his father – having finally faded beyond even reflected glory. Such things did not come cheap.

He sighed, gloomily, shouldering his way through the crowds on the Nevsky, crossing the great Fontanka Canal with no glance at its swirling waters or the grand houses and palaces that lined it. Nothing came cheap. Especially when your pockets were for most of the time empty. Not even love.

As he turned into the Liteini a tramcar clanged by, trailing blue sparks into the faint summer drizzle that drifted in air that was, despite the time of year, uncomfortably chill. A cool wind blew from the water.

No, most certainly not love. Where Margarita got her spending habits from he really could not imagine. He hunched his shoulders beneath the shabby English jacket that he favoured when off duty. He had a two-day pass after having been in barracks for almost a week. At some time during those two days the unpleasant subject of their expenditure would have to be tackled. He flinched a little at the thought. Whilst it could not be denied that Margarita's enchanting, child-like prettiness with every passing day matured towards true beauty, at the same time her tongue seemed to be sharpening with every passing hour. Graceful, the most beguiling of creatures when she cared to be – with Margarita on his arm he knew himself to be the envy of many of his young fellow-officers – yet crossed she could be a termagant, the storms of tears and torrents of passionate, accusing words exhausting in the extreme. But still, as he thought of her, he had to admit to the fact that with Margarita docile and lovely in his bed the doubts and fears that beset him when he was away from her dissipated like mist in the sun. He hoped she would be in a good mood. He thought of her, kneeling as she so often did before the tiny, intricate toy theatre that had been his first gift to her, absorbed as a child in the small conceits and fantasies she so loved. At those times, watching her, he believed he loved her more than life itself.

Almost unconsciously he lengthened his stride. If only she would curb her extravagance a little. And if only she would respond with a little more decorum to the light-hearted but flagrant advances of his friends. Frowning suddenly, he paused to cross the busy street, tramcars and motor cars vying with horse-drawn traffic to make it as dangerous an operation as any skirmish on a battlefield. Finding a gap he dodged across. One couldn't blame her, he supposed; she was such a pretty little thing, it was hardly her fault that she attracted such attention – 'Oh, I'm sorry.' He had cannoned into a young man hurrying from the sidestreet into which he, Sasha, was turning. The boy was dressed in the virtually uniform student garb of blue flat cap, rough blue shirt and baggy workman's trousers. The lad muttered something, brushing off Sasha's steadying hand, and hurried on. Behind him another group of youngsters surged out of the sidestreet. Sasha stepped aside. He heard now what his preoccupation had prevented him from hearing before; the growing, ragged chant of many voices – 'Bread! Justice! Freedom! Bread! Justice! Freedom! Workers of the world unite! Bread! Justice! Freedom!'

Another of those absurd demonstrations. In the narrow street he pushed against the running tide of humanity until it became too difficult, then with an impatient grimace stepped into a doorway, allowing the growing flood to pass him. It was useless. He'd have to wait until the thing was past.

It was not a very big demonstration, as these things went; mostly students, some working men and women, the inevitable banners and placards. The faces on the whole were grim, though here and there a young couple walked with swinging step, arm in arm and smiling as they chanted. Though most were dressed in the inevitable shabby dark blues and blacks of the working classes, some of the girls had thrown bright scarves about their heads to keep from the rain. He glimpsed one, bright scarlet and green, flower-like in the dimness of the narrow street, bobbing towards him. He glimpsed something else too, at the very moment when his practised ear picked out the sound of horses' hooves on cobbles. At the far end of the street a small squadron of horsemen had appeared – Cossacks from their uniforms – and were riding steadily towards the demonstrators, herding them before them. People cast swift looks over their shoulders as the sound reached them, and the pace of the march quickened a little, the people behind pushing at those in front, treading on their heels. But still the chant, defiant and rhythmic, continued: 'Bread, Justice, *Freedom*!'

Sasha felt a sudden and extremely odd surge of something close to envy as he watched them; here were comrades indeed, united in their pathetic crusade, and, yes, in their courage. Their lives might be hard, but he sensed about them a shared fervour, a fraternity that went beyond mere friendship. He drew back into his doorway as they streamed past, driven almost to running pace by the oncoming riders. He saw a man snatch a child as it fell and swing it onto his shoulders, saw a young man anxiously clasping the arm of a heavily pregnant girl as he helped her along.

The Cossacks were riding easily, something unpleasantly like mischief in the dark, moustachioed faces; they were deliberately riding just that little bit too fast, nudging into the rear of the column, grinning at the signs of panic their presence was causing.

Most of the marchers had reached the end of the narrow lane and were spilling into the Liteini. The Cossacks spurred on.

239

Sasha saw the girl in the bright headscarf again – nearer now. She was towards the back of the column, walking with a thin young man and another girl. Her narrow face within the brilliant framework of the scarf was a blaze of defiance. Her mouth moved as she chanted. The three were arm in arm, marching steadily, refusing to be pushed. Behind them the muscled, curbed Cossack ponies pranced, bits jingling. Sasha frowned. The Cossacks had their whips out.

What triggered the charge was very hard to tell; he saw a horseman jostle a marcher, a huge young man carrying a banner upon which the single word 'ISKRA' had been painted – the word, meaning spark, was he knew the battlecry of one of the many workers' parties. The young man turned, angrily. The banner flapped in the pony's face. It reared. Its rider, knowing well what he did, wheeled the animal, dancing it flamboyantly on its hind legs, to bring its flailing hooves crashing down upon the marcher. Blood spurted. A girl screamed, shrill, fearful and distraught. The riders, as one man, whips raised, clapped their heels to the impatient ponies' sides.

What remained of the march broke in panic. People ran, shrieking, from the oncoming riders. Whips rose and fell. There was another high, pain-filled scream. A girl reeled from a galloping horseman, her hands hiding her face. Sasha saw the girl in the red and green scarf, running like a hare, her skirts lifted to her knees, long legs flashing. Behind her a stocky pony bore down on her, its rider obviously having picked his target. Run! Sasha found himself thinking, and then out loud he shouted. 'Run!'

She ran. And on the rain-slick cobbles opposite Sasha's doorway she slipped, reeling, arms flailing, unable to keep her balance. Instinctively he was moving before he knew it, leaping out in front of the Cossack rider, arms waving into the pony's face, screaming his throat raw, 'Away! Get away!'

It was over in a moment. The horse, startled, shied. The rider, furious, fought it down. Sasha, dodging the hooves, had grabbed the girl's hand and was hauling her back into the doorway. He saw the raised whip, could do nothing to avoid it. He jerked his head sideways and the lash intended to catch him full in the face sliced instead across his jaw. The blow sent him sprawling in a helpless heap on top of the stumbling girl. By the time he had scrambled to his feet the rider had gone, spurring after his fellows, and the street was empty but for the still form of the trampled marcher that lay, ungainly in death, on rain- and blood-slick cobbles, a weeping girl crouched beside it, and a few others, shocked, battered but alive, who stood or leaned in small groups along the length of the narrow lane. It was very quiet. Even the roar of the traffic from the main street seemed muted. Nearby a woman sobbed, quietly, and a man swore, viciously and ferociously.

'Thank you.' The girl's voice was light and commendably calm, though a slight tremor shook it and she had to clear her throat before she spoke. 'You saved my life, I think.'

He shook his head, embarrassed. The side of his face throbbed terribly. Something dripped from his chin onto his jacket; he put up his hand. It came away crimson with blood.

'The Pharoes!' someone called, urgently, from the Liteini end of the street. 'The Pharoes are coming!'

The girl caught his hand. 'Come! Quickly!' She pushed him out of the doorway into the street. 'This way!' She turned.

'Wait!' He pulled away from her, though her hand gripped his firmly. 'I'm all right. You go.'

She looked at him in impatient astonishment. 'Don't be stupid. You heard what he said – the Pharoes are coming –'

'I don't know what you're talking about –'

The look deepened to exasperation. 'The police, stupid! They're coming to arrest us!'

'But I wasn't part of the demonstration –' He stopped.

She had raised her eyebrows. He put his hand to his face again. The cut inflicted by the Cossack whip was bleeding copiously. 'Try telling them that,' she said, brusquely. 'You'll have worse than that to show for it before you've convinced them, believe me! They'll beat you half to death before they ever get around to asking your name. Now stop buggering about and come on, for heaven's sake. That cut needs seeing to, and I know someone who'll do it, no questions asked.' She grinned, quickly, the smile lighting her dirty face, a sudden, lively flicker of interest in her dark eyes. 'He won't spoil that handsome face, I promise. Now, do come on – run!'

He ran with her, down the street, round a corner, away from the direction he should have taken for the apartment and Margarita. He allowed himself one small prayer of thanks that neither his wife nor his commanding officer could see Alexandr Feodovorich Kolashki, last son of that name as, face streaming blood and clothes wet and muddy, he allowed his brusque and shabby guide to tow him into the back streets of St Petersburg. Once in relative quiet she stopped, turned to him, pulling her own long woollen scarf from about her neck. 'Come here.'

Obediently he bent his neck. She wound the scarf about it, then up across his jaw and the lower half of his face, hiding the bloody gash. 'Keep it up high. If anyone sees it we're gonners. We'll catch a tram – tuck your head down and sit still.' A tram clanked around the corner, ground to a halt. She pulled him by the hand. 'Here we are – hurry, do –'

She took him to the Vyborg district, to the north of the city, an industrial area of mills, factories and working-class slums through which Sasha had come many times by train whilst travelling to or from Finland but in which, in common with many of his class, he had never before set foot. They jumped from the tram as it slowed to turn a corner. It clanked on, leaving them alone in a wide and dirty thoroughfare flanked by what looked like warehouses and a huge factory wall.

Sasha's companion took his hand. 'This way.' She led him across the road and down a narrow alley, dark even on this midsummer's evening. The drizzle had stopped, though the sky was still milky with cloud. The walls between which they passed were black with soot and with grime, Sasha's boots squelched on God knew what kind of rubbish that was strewn across the cobbles. He heard the rustling scuttle of what could only be rats. The girl turned a corner, and another. They passed the open doorways of neglected tenements; dark and squalid stairways reached into shadow. The smell was abominable.

Sasha's jaw was throbbing. Blood had congealed and hardened upon the scarf; too late he wondered how clean the tattered thing might have been. Too late also he began to feel apprehensive. What in God's name was he doing in a place like this with a girl he'd never seen in his life before and surrounded by presumably hostile strangers? Not that anyone took any notice of the hurrying pair. The rain had stopped. Men lounged about in groups on corners, smoking and talking; women, shawled and scarved, sat on the stairs or on battered chairs outside the tenement doors gossiping and watching the children play in the filth of the streets. Occasionally someone called a greeting to the girl and she replied, brusquely as seemed her habit, but did not stop. No-one showed the slightest interest in Sasha. On the contrary, backs were turned, eyes averted; only later did he realize that in this district a hurrying man with blood on his face was best ignored, for what a man did not know could not be beaten out of him.

They turned a corner into a small, dirty square, almost a courtyard, surrounded on three sides by tall tenement houses. The girl towed Sasha across it to a door. As they entered, the smell enveloped him, suffocating, disgusting, like filthy water closing over his head. He put his hand to his face, covering his nose, pretending to rub his eyes. The girl glanced at him, her grin telling him that she was not fooled. Boiled cabbage, rotting food, the rank smell of urine; he held his breath for a moment. How could people live like this?

The girl had led him along a corridor and was tapping at a scarred wooden door. 'Nikita? It's Valentina. Open the door.'

Silence.

The girl rapped again, impatiently. 'Nikita! Open the door!'

There was movement. The door opened. A slight young man in shapeless woollen jumper and trousers and wearing wire-rimmed glasses peered into the shadows. Valentina pushed past him. 'The march was broken up. Bloody Cossacks. We've got a casualty. I think he needs sewing up.'

Sasha flinched.

'It's all right.' Valentina was shrugging out of her muddy coat. 'Nikita's a medical student. A very good one.' She laughed a little, with no great humour. 'And he's had a lot of experience of this kind of thing.'

The young man had taken Sasha's chin in his hand and turned his face to the light of a flickering gas jet. 'It's not too bad. Valentina's right. A couple of stitches will do it.'

Sasha pulled away from him. 'Perhaps – if I could just clean

it? It seems to have stopped bleeding. The hospital, perhaps –
or my own doctor?'

The young man stepped back.

'Don't be daft.' Valentina was reaching up to a shelf, obviously
knowing her way around. 'Get near one of the city hospitals at
the moment with a wound like that and you'll be arrested on
sight. As for a private doctor – you can't trust any of them, you
know. They're all informers. Didn't you know that?'

She turned. She was tall and very slim. Her narrow, dirty face
was pale and freckled. She had pulled the bright scarf from her
head; her light brown hair, thick and wavy, was cut short, her
eyes were dark and very bright. It was a striking face, by no
means pretty, but alive with intelligence and with a certain
rueful, almost mocking, laughter. He remembered it as he had
seen it as she had marched bravely in front of the Cossack
ponies, chanting defiantly.

'Well?'

'Sorry?'

She clucked impatiently. 'Your doctor. Are you sure you can
trust him? They aren't exactly known for their sympathy
towards us, are they?'

'Us? But –' He stopped.

She came to stand beside him, smiling into his face that was
almost on a level with his. 'I promise you, Nikita can do it, and
with no danger. He's done dozens worse. You'll be as good as
new. I owe you that. Trust me.'

The operation was brief and exorbitantly painful, yet certainly, to Sasha's relief, the young man Nikita did seem to know
his business. As he worked Valentina talked, telling him of
the demonstration and its bloody end, of Sasha's intervention.
'Have you seen any of the others? I lost sight of Lev when I
started to run, though I saw Christina get away. The Pharoes
must have been waiting on the Liteini. Bastards.' She said the
last word with no particular rancour. Sasha swivelled his eyes
to look at her. He had never heard a woman swear before.

'Keep still,' said his tormentor, sharply. 'Can you manage?
Valentina can hold your head if you can't.'

'No.' Sasha spoke through gritted teeth. 'I'm all right.'

'There's a meeting next week. Are you coming?' Valentina

was tidying the bloodied rags of sheeting that Nikita had used to clean the gash.

'Yes.' Nikita was preoccupied with his task. 'Sorry. Did that hurt? If you could just keep still for a moment longer? Valentina, pass me the bowl and swab, will you?'

The girl handed him the implements. 'Goodness, what a lovely neat job. You could get employment as a seamstress!'

The young man laughed, went to the bowl on the table to wash his hands.

Sasha, to his embarrassment, was trembling. The effort to sit still, not to cry out, had taken more strength than he had realized. He stood up.

With an easy camaraderie Valentina came and slipped an arm about his waist, supporting him. 'Are you all right? You're awfully pale.'

'I'm all right.'

'He needs a cup of tea,' Nikita said. 'Or something stronger if you've got it.'

She nodded briskly. 'Tea I've got. And I think Lev left some of that dreadful brew we were drinking the other night. Coming?'

Nikita shook his head. 'Exams tomorrow. I have to study. I'll see you later, perhaps.'

'Fine.' Valentina turned to the door.

'Wait.' Sasha put his hand into his pocket. 'I haven't paid you.'

The young man cocked his head. His eyes looked tired behind the glasses, his face was thin, his clothes as shabby as any Sasha had seen that day. He shook his head. 'Buy Valentina some flowers,' he said.

'But –'

'Medicine should be for all,' he said, quietly. 'Not something to be bought and sold by those who can afford it. The day will come when it is so. Until then I try to practise what I preach.'

'But – you have to live –'

'My friends keep me,' he said, simply.

'And in exchange he patches us and sews us up,' Valentina said, cheerfully, from the door. 'And stops hotheads from getting hotter. Oh, do come along – I need a cup of tea if you don't.'

*   *   *

245

She took him to the room, two floors up, where she lived. She shared it, she explained, with another girl called Nina, who came and went in her own time and with no questions asked. Valentina had not seen her for the past three days. They both worked part time in the mill up the road. Valentina had come to St Petersburg as a student but when her father had died the money had stopped coming. 'So, I had to keep body and soul together. I went to the mill.' She handed Sasha a glass of tea, turned to rummage on a cluttered shelf. 'I've got some biscuits here somewhere, I think.'

'Oh, please. Don't bother. I'm not hungry.' In fact he was starving; he had intended to eat with Margarita that night. But the ill-furnished room with its bare floorboards and dirty curtains that were worn ragged illustrated well its occupier's finances.

She turned, hands on hips. 'You know your trouble?' That mocking laughter was back.

'No?' He was wary.

'You're too good-mannered for your own good. And from that, and the fancy accent, I surmise –' she put her head on one side, narrowed her eyes, pointed a finger '– that you aren't what you appear to be.'

Ridiculously he felt himself blush to the roots of his hair. 'I don't know what you mean.'

She laughed, went back into the curtained alcove that concealed what passed for a kitchen. 'I think you do.'

The table at which Sasha was sitting was covered in heaps of papers. Deciding on silence as the most sensible answer, he started to clear a space for his tea. A page, battered, much scribbled-upon, caught his eye. He cocked his head to read it.

> In painful moments often I've believed
> That no God lives, no order rules our world.
> But then the sound of laughter,
> The sight of tears,
> Touches me.
> Is He there?

'What are you doing?' She had come back into the room; moved swiftly around the table towards him.

'You wrote this?' he asked.

'Scribbled it, more like.' She snatched it from him, screwed it up and tossed it back upon the table.

He watched her. The little poem had not been scribbled; it had been written and rewritten, minutely and carefully. 'May I see the rest?'

'No,' she said, shortly. Then, less abrasively, 'Have some more tea. Unless you can stand Lev's concoction?' She held a bottle in her hand, half full.

He grinned, suddenly enjoying this odd adventure. 'Why not?'

She put two chipped glasses on the table, poured two hefty tots. 'You're going to look like a pirate, you know, with that scar on your face. How will you explain it?'

The liquor hit his stomach like fire. He managed, just, not to choke. Moments later an absurd feeling of well-being spread through him. 'A duelling scar,' he said, lightly.

'Aha!' She pointed a thin, bony finger. 'Like I said! Not what you seem.' Her dark eyes flickered to the well-worn but far from inexpensive clothes he wore. 'I don't suppose you work for a living by any chance?'

Without analysing the thought, he knew he had not the slightest intention of admitting to a profession that he was certain would come between him and this surprising girl like the edge of a sword. His gaze flickered back to the heaps of paper. He raised innocent eyes, toasted her with his already half-empty glass. 'I'm a poet,' he said, solemnly and carefully, Lev's concoction having had a somewhat surprising effect on his tongue. 'Like you.'

He kept telling himself – and Valentina – that he must leave. But he did not. They talked for hours; talked the night away. They talked of poetry and of literature; she adored Tolstoy, disliked Dostoevsky – the amicable argument that followed saw the clock tick on inexorably past midnight. They talked of music, and found themselves united on Glazunov and Tchaikovsky, at odds on Rimsky-Korsakov. Oddly, they did not speak of themselves. A little hazily Sasha thought it was like being cast upon an island, remote from the world, two people with nothing, and yet everything, in common.

'You remind me of my sister,' he said.

'Your sister's an anarchist?' she asked, pulling a small, funny face.

He frowned a little, concentrating. 'No. Of course she isn't. Is that what you and your friends are?'

She measured him with narrowed eyes, playing with her glass. 'It's the label others fix upon us sometimes.'

'Explain,' he said.

The clouds had cleared, a smudged sun had rolled around the horizon and was lifting again through the fog of smoke and industrial haze that hung permanently over the district when Valentina walked him through the streets to the tram stop. The cobbles echoed to the boots of the workers. People hurried by. A factory whistle sounded. Girls ran past them, calling to each other and laughing.

She stood with him, waiting for the tram. 'I don't think I've convinced you,' she said, smiling.

'You've convinced me of many things.' His mouth smiled. His eyes were deadly serious.

She looked away, gave her head a small shake that moved her thick, short hair about her face.

The tram wound its noisy way towards them, blue sparks cascading from the wires, bright in the early morning gloom. 'I want to see you again,' he said.

She shook her head again, sharply this time.

'Please.' He had vowed he would not ask her.

She hesitated. The tram stopped. She leaned quickly to him, brushed her lips across his cheek, light as the touch of a butterfly. 'Go away,' she said, and turned, leaving him. The tram clanged, started to move. Swearing, Sasha scrambled aboard. Valentina did not turn. He watched the tall, narrow back, the jaunty stride, until the tram turned a corner and she was lost to his sight.

It was ridiculously easy; Margarita had not been expecting him, so she had not missed him. She accepted his explanation of the wound on his face – an accident during over-enthusiastic sword practice – with no question. Why would she not? She even

248

declared herself impressed with the change to his appearance: 'Sasha! How very terrifying you look! Quite the bandit!' and did not object too strenuously when, for the first and last time in their married life, he made love to her not in darkness and beneath the bedclothes but in the broad light of day on the living-room floor.

He tried to forget his meeting with Valentina, and when he could not he tried to trivialize it. It had been an aberration. An odd accident. There had been no magic in that small, filthy room, no joining of souls. Shock and cheap liquor had combined to produce a fantasy. His life was with the regiment, and with Margarita.

Alarmingly there was a small part of him that refused to play the game.

His jaw healed, leaving only a faint, straight thread of a scar. Nikita had done his work well. Sasha wondered about him, sometimes. There were one or two more demonstrations as the summer wore on; Sasha thanked his God that he was not, in his official capacity, detailed to break them up.

And still he struggled to forget her, and could not.

The first time he went back to the Vyborg Valentina was not there. He hung around the landing for a while, sustaining questioning and unfriendly glances – even the shabby clothes he had deliberately donned for the visit stood out like the gleam of gold in these surroundings – before running down the stairs to tap at Nikita's door.

Nikita blinked, understandably not recognizing him.

Sasha turned his jaw. 'I came to show you your handiwork.'

That amused the young man. He grinned.

Sasha put his hand into a capacious pocket, produced a bottle of vodka, held it up in silence.

Nikita, still grinning, stepped back, inviting him in.

Perched on rickety chairs beside a tiny stove they drank the vodka, and as they drank they talked. Of the campaign of civil disobedience in Finland, of the growing unrest in St Petersburg, of the Russian character and of Russian history and its strange habit of swinging from tyranny to chaos and back again. They did not speak of Valentina until the bottle was nearly empty.

Then, 'Stay away from her, Sasha,' Nikita said, in calm and friendly fashion. 'You don't belong together. Anyone can see it. You'll only hurt her.'

'Will you tell her I came?'

Nikita shook his head.

There was a long silence. 'You're right. It was stupid of me to come. I won't come back.'

Nikita picked up the bottle, tilted it, peered intently. 'Have another drink.'

But it was no use; he could not stay away; though in conscience he tried, and for weeks succeeded. Yet there was a sense of something unfinished, of something left unsaid, a nagging ache, like toothache, that would not leave him.

The Vyborg in late autumn was a dreary place. There was sleet in the rain and a razor's edge to the wind as Sasha stepped from the steamy warmth of the tramcar into the bleak cold of the street. This was it. If Valentina was not there this time he would take it as a sign; he was not meant to see her again.

She opened the door, eyes and mouth round with surprise, her short thick hair limned in the light of the lamp behind her. For what seemed a very long time neither of them spoke. She stepped back, holding the door open for him. He walked past her, into the room he remembered so absurdly well. He heard the door shut behind him. Turned. She was leaning against the door, watching him. She had not smiled. 'I'll make tea,' she said.

They made love, later, in her tiny, freezing cold bedroom on a mattress laid upon the floor. Despite the surroundings, despite the cold, their lovemaking was fierce and warm and utterly satisfying.

They lay afterwards, thin blankets pulled up to their chins, limbs still entangled. Valentina's face was on Sasha's shoulder. 'You have a wife,' she said, quietly. 'Don't you?'

'Yes.' He stroked her hair. She said nothing. His hand strayed to her cheek. He wiped the tears with his finger. 'Don't cry. Please don't cry.'

'I'm not crying,' she said. 'Don't come again. Please don't.'

'No. I won't. I promise.'

But, of course, he did.

Major Kostya Illyarovich did not actually dislike Katya Bourlova, though it could hardly be said either that he particularly
liked her. But then, on the whole Kostya liked very few people
and of those he did not one was a woman. Women were pretty
things, but useless, diverting on occasion, talkative always,
emotional to the point of boredom. Their best – in Kostya's
opinion their only – useful purpose was served in a man's bed;
the measure of a woman's worth in his case was the amount of
trouble to which he would be willing to put himself to get her
there. Katya's infatuation amused him; he actually enjoyed the
torment he knew he could inflict upon her. His indifference to
her feelings was far from assumed. He played her throughout
that year like a fish upon a line; a very small fish the escape of
which would not be much rued and which, if caught, would
merely be tossed back without a thought. The girl was a virgin
without a doubt. For his pleasure Kostya did not like virgins;
they cried and mewled and had no idea of how to serve a man.
But for his pride, that was another matter. A woman, they said,
never forgot her first lover; there were many women who
remembered Kostya Illyarovich. And this one burned for him.
He saw it in her eyes. Her young flesh was warm and smooth.
Her teeth were sharp. Perhaps she might be worth a try. The
woman with whom he had been carrying on an until now
extremely satisfactory affair was becoming a bore; worse, her
husband was returning to the city. Sitting one early winter night
in the gaming room of his favourite drinking den on the Islands
he tossed a coin.

Laughed, and bought a round of drinks when his Tsar's head
glittered at him from the table top.

The note was delivered a day or so later. Katya's hand shook as
she slit the envelope; the writing could only be his. She had
not seen him for weeks, had all but given up looking for him.
Throughout the summer and into the brief transition of autumn
he had flickered in and out of her life like a flame, tormenting
her half to death. She had not, of course, been able to escape

the long summer trip to Finland. Beside Kostya how gauche, how very *young* the young men had seemed. How safe. How boring. Back in St Petersburg she had sent him a note to which he had not bothered to reply. Then he had turned up at a party and danced with her all evening before disappearing again – on manoeuvres he had said, but much as she had wanted to she had not believed him. Now here it was, the invitation she had looked for; a small supper party, with friends, at their apartment. He had never introduced her to any of his friends, never indeed bothered to take her anywhere that might be thought of as personal. She looked at the address, laughed a little, softly. How very convenient! Just a stone's throw from the Turnakov mansion where Jussi lived! She experienced a moment's twinge of worry; was it perhaps too close? Might she ruin their convenient arrangement by bumping into someone who could put two and two together to make an uncomfortable four? She dismissed the thought. Re-read the note. Nothing would stop her from attending. Nothing. She ran to her room. Outside the window it was snowing steadily. Winter had come early this year, the river was already frozen, the stoves in the apartment had been roaring for weeks and the winter windows had been fitted. She settled herself at her small desk, reached for a sheet of perfumed paper.

It snowed heavily all week with hardly a break. She could not, to her annoyance, contact Jussi. She had told her mother that she was going to the theatre with him that night and that they would have supper with friends afterwards. 'I've told him not to bother to pick me up,' she said, airily. 'We're having drinks with Elisabet and some friends first – old Zhorik can take me in the sledge. Jussi will see me home.'

'Not too late, young lady.' Her mother was sitting at the mirror, her maid plaiting and twisting the gleaming lengths of her hair. She had found herself wondering more than once lately if, with Mischa so often away, she was too lenient with Katya.

'Of course not.' Katya leaned to drop a kiss on her mother's bare, smooth shoulder. 'You're looking very nice. Where are you going?'

'The Princess Starovich has asked me to join her committee

for the care of disabled soldiers. At least, I think that's what it's in aid of. There really are so many of these good causes! I'm to have supper with her.'

'Aha!' Katya winked, gracelessly. 'Aren't we going up in the world?'

Her mother smiled, easily. 'We do our best, my dear. We do our best.'

'Right.' Katya danced to the door. 'I'll tell Zhorik to hurry home after he's dropped me at Jussi's. We can't have you being late for the Princess, can we?'

It was all almost too easy. She had, she told herself, faintly alarmed, become so adept at deception that she no longer had to think about it. 'You can drop me here, Zhorik, then you won't have to turn in the Turnakov courtyard. Mama particularly asked for you to get back quickly. She's waiting.'

Grumbling as always the man did as he was bid. Katya stood on the swept pavement, shaking out her skirts, watching as the sledge moved off into the darkness. Then, uncomfortably aware of a heart that was beating rather faster than normal, she slipped around the corner, away from the mansion and towards the building in which Kostya's friends lived.

There were no friends.

She knew it the moment he opened the door. No friends. No servants. Just Kostya. He was dressed in soft, baggy trousers tucked into flat leather boots and a sumptuous dark silk shirt, full-sleeved, embroidered in gold thread, belted at the waist, that emphasized rather than concealed the broad, barrel chest, the muscled arms. Behind him a table was laid for two, dishes of caviar and of smoked fish, a bottle of champagne, a bottle of vodka already broached. For a fraction of a second she stood quite still, the words of greeting silenced on her lips. Black eyes in a flat, barbarian face challenged her. 'Welcome,' he said, and took her hand, brushing it with his lips.

She stepped across the threshold. The winter windows were in place, muffling sound; the apartment was very quiet, and very warm. A tiled stove occupied one corner of the room, in another was set the dining table. At the far end of the room comfortable chairs and settees strewn with cushions were set upon softly-coloured rugs. There were bronze statues upon a shelf, the curtains were of heavy gold velvet. It was a perfectly lovely setting, warm and luxurious.

But there were no friends.

And at the far end of the room a door stood open; in the dim room beyond could be seen a bed, heaped with furs.

'I think,' she said, a little shakily, 'that I should leave.'

He shrugged, careless, gestured with hands outstretched, his eyes, exasperatingly mocking, still upon hers. 'You won't even try the champagne?'

The champagne was good. The food was good. The setting was seductive. 'Where are your – friends?'

He reached for the bottle – the champagne was for Katya, he was drinking vodka. 'Regrettably –' he grinned his wolf's grin '– they had to go away.'

'Rather suddenly?'

'Rather suddenly.'

As always he fascinated and repelled her at the same time. His strength all but hypnotized her; his very ugliness attracted her. The dress he had affected for the evening, obviously – almost mockingly – deliberately, emphasized the barbaric nature of the man. He made no attempt whatsoever to disguise his intentions.

She must leave before things got out of hand.

She knew, beyond doubt, that if she did she would never see him again.

The champagne swam in her head. Stupid, stupid! What was she doing here? And yet she stayed, a lamb in the lair of the wolf, willing victim.

From outside, despite the muffling effect of the windows, came a faint, violent crackling. She lifted her head. 'What's that?'

'Nothing. It's nothing. A demonstration, perhaps. These vermin should be put down.' He stood up, came round the table towards her. 'I'd put them down. Personally. Every man, woman and tit-sucking brat of them.'

She had no single doubt that he meant what he said.

He stood behind her, slid his hands over her shoulders, down onto her breasts.

'I think – perhaps – I should go home,' she said.

'Oh, no.' The corded, horseman's arms were like iron bands about her shoulders. 'Not now. A while ago, perhaps, I might have let you go. But not now.' She could smell the vodka on his breath. She turned her head away.

He laughed. Lifted her like a doll from her seat.

The unchecked violence of the man dazed her, his strength was overwhelming. He laughed as she struggled. In his own brutal need he took no care, no heed of hers. Savagely he violated her, with his mouth and with his fingers and with the ramrod of his body. When at last, sore and weeping, she gathered her torn and soiled clothes he watched her, stretched upon the fur covers of the bed, his hands behind his head.

'M-my father will kill you,' she said, torn between sobs and a storm of fury. 'I'll have you c-court martialled! Pig! You're nothing but a pig!'

The flat, Tartar face smiled. 'Perhaps, little sow. Perhaps, yes, I'm a pig. But your father won't know.' He left a small, intent silence. 'Will he?'

Tears of rage, of pain, and of sheer, awful humiliation streamed down her cheeks. In God's sweet name, what had she done? She snatched her heavy cloak from the chair where he had thrown it, leaving hat and muff where they lay. All she could think of was to get away. She fled from the apartment, stumbling in a tangle of feet and skirt as she flew down the wide, circular staircase, praying she would meet no-one. Outside it was bitterly cold and a winter fog had settled, swirling from the river, drifting moisture that froze as it settled onto her clothes and her loosened hair. Her mouth was sore, she could taste blood. Great God, what a sight she must look! How could she go home like this? The pig had been right, of course, bitterly, faultlessly right. She would die before she would admit to her parents what had happened. But now – what was she to do? What refuge, however temporary, was open to her?

The first thought was the only one. In the hazed light of a street lamp, fog choking her, tears all but freezing on her cheeks, she turned in the direction of the Turnakov mansion.

The lights in Jussi's apartment, on the ground floor across the courtyard, glimmered against the fog. The relief was so great

255

that she stopped for a moment, leaning against the wall, grateful for the sheltering, swirling mist, breath hiccoughing in her throat. She was aware of a burning discomfort, there was a foul wetness between her legs. She felt filthy. She stood perfectly still, and very straight, breathing deeply. Katya Bourlova might be spoiled, she might on occasion be downright stupid, but she was her father's daughter and she did not lack in spirit nor in strength. She needed a moment's respite, she needed a helping hand. Instinctively she knew that if Jussi were here he would offer both. From there she could manage alone.

She slipped along the wall, avoiding the main gate with its fussy watchers and wardens, moved into a sidestreet where she knew there to be a small garden gate that Jussi, for his own reasons, made it his business to see should be left open. It gave easy access to the back yard of his suite of rooms, which were totally independent of the rest of the house. She lifted the latch. As she had expected, the gate opened soundlessly. She gathered her cloak about her, sidled through, shut it behind her. The back wing of the house loomed before her. The light from Jussi's windows glowed softly in the smothering fog, which was thickening with every minute.

The back door was unlatched. Afterwards she wondered at their lack of care, could only think that the pressure of emergency had led to the oversight. She stepped into a small room that housed harnesses, fishing tackle, skis, skates, a small sledge. She followed the glimmer of light into a shadowed hallway, up the stairs into the living quarters. At the sound of voices she stopped. Damn! Jussi had company. The door to his living room was ajar. She flattened herself against the wall. Froze.

The first thing she saw were the guns. Not sporting guns, not the guns that accompanied any gentleman on a trip to the country, but fearful weapons, heavy and deadly-looking. Machine guns, and rifles. Carrying them several young men and one young woman, roughly dressed, stood in a group, their concerned faces all turned to where Jussi stood, propped against a table. His head was thrown back, his fair face very pale, his right shoulder a bright and bloody mess of ragged material and torn flesh, at which a young man picked with tweezers, quickly and efficiently and with a face clamped against sympathy as his patient flinched beneath his ministrations.

The sheer shock of the tableau took the breath from Katya's lungs and set her trembling, cold as death. She stood for a moment, still as an animal that scents danger. Then, very slowly, she began to inch silently backwards.

The voice that arrested her came from behind her. 'Prying, Katya my dear?' Elisabet asked, coldly. 'My goodness, if you're that inquisitive, perhaps you should find out exactly what's going on?' A firm hand propelled her along the corridor and with a small push into the lighted room.

Every eye turned to her; and every eye was hostile. She stood clutching her cloak about her, looking from grim face to grim face. She saw the movement of hands towards guns. 'Jussi,' she said, faintly, and then again, louder and more firmly, 'Jussi? What – what in heaven's name is going on?'

Jussi had pushed himself from the table, shaking off help. 'God Almighty, Katya,' he said, helplessly. 'What are you doing here?'

'I – I came – to –' Her voice tailed off. She cleared her throat. 'Jussi – what's happened? Who are these people?' Her dazed brain, belatedly, started to work. 'The shooting – earlier – it was *you*? You're one of these – these terrorists?'

'No, Katya.' Elisabet stepped into her line of vision. Her voice as steady and as firm as the small but lethal-looking pistol that was held in two competent hands and levelled unwaveringly at Katya's head. 'Jussi isn't a terrorist. Jussi is a Finn.'

'Lissi!' Jussi's voice was edged grimly with pain, yet carried more authority than Katya had ever heard in it before. 'No!'

Elisabet turned a calm face to her brother. 'It's a pity,' she said, coolly rational. 'But she's seen us. Seen you. She has to die. Doesn't she?'

The silence that followed the words rushed in Katya's ears like water. Nothing in the world had prepared her for this. She swayed a little. Elisabet's knuckles whitened as she tightened her grip on the gun.

'Oh, Katya!' Jussi smiled, painfully. 'Trouble just follows you around like a little lapdog, doesn't it?'

'Stand still, Jussi! You'll start the bleeding again!'

'I'll go,' Katya said, desperately calm. 'Just let me go. I won't say anything. I promise.'

Jussi shook his head.

Elisabet clicked her tongue impatiently. The gun was steady as a rock. 'Jussi?'

Pain flickered in his face. He bowed his head for a moment, grimly fighting it. When he straightened his face was very white, yet the gleam of a smile showed in his eyes. 'Katya likes Finland,' he said. 'Don't you, Katya? So – why don't we just take her with us?' He looked at Katya. 'I'll just let Heimo here finish digging out the bullet he's making such a mess of finding and then we'll please everyone, my lovely. We'll elope.' He laughed a little, stopped abruptly, coughing.

She shook her head, dazed.

His face hardened. 'You'd rather die?' he asked. 'For a sensible girl I can't say that you appear to be thinking very clearly?'

'Jussi, don't be ridiculous. It's going to be hard enough to get you out of the city, without taking her –'

'Shut up, Elisabet.' For the first time Jussi appeared to take in the details of Katya's appearance. Her cloak had fallen open revealing the torn and dirtied dress. A massive blue bruise discoloured the whiteness of her bared shoulder. Blood still smudged her lip. His eyes narrowed, something like distaste flickered in his face. 'You look as if you've been in a war of your own,' he said. 'Lissi – get her something more sensible to wear.'

Katya tried once more, desperately. 'Jussi, please! Just let me go! I swear I won't tell –'

'Jussi, for God's sake let me get at this thing. Half the city's looking for you and you can't travel until I've finished and got you patched up –' The man who had been treating Jussi's shoulder laid none-too-gentle hands on him and forced him back against the table. 'Stand still, or by Christ I'll tie you down!'

Jussi turned his head to look at Katya. 'Katya – this is no game. You come, or you die. That is the only choice.'

'I'll come,' she said.

With no sound and little grace, Jussi fainted.

CHAPTER THIRTEEN

Jussi Lavola's sister, fiercely wary, fiercely protective, did not trust their unexpected and troublesome guest an inch further than she might have been able to throw her, and she made no bones about showing it.

'One move,' she said, expressionless, tossing a dark woollen riding suit upon the bed, 'just one – and I'll kill you. I'm a very good shot. And I'll do it. You understand?'

Numbly, Katya nodded.

'Get yourself cleaned up and changed for God's sake.' The pale eyes raked her with sudden unfriendly scorn. 'You look like a refugee from a whorehouse.'

A bowl of water stood beside the bed. Trembling with shock and with an all but unendurable humiliation Katya hastily splashed her face. Dispassionately her captor stood and watched her, not allowing her the boon of even a pretence of privacy. Close to tears, Katya tried with shaking fingers to unhook the fastenings of her wrecked dress, the dress she had chosen with such care and such excitement earlier in the evening, the dress that now, torn and dirtied, fairly shouted her stupidity and her guilt to the cold-faced young woman who watched her.

'Oh, for heaven's sake – here!' Elisabet laid the small, lethal-looking pistol upon the dressing table for a moment. 'We haven't got all night.' With austere efficiency she began to unfasten the dress.

'Elisabet – please – what exactly is going on? What's happened to Jussi? Where – where are they taking me?'

The other girl stepped back, retrieving the gun. For a moment her face remained hard as granite, and Katya thought she would not answer. Then she shrugged a little. 'You don't need to know exactly what's going on. Jussi and the others went on a mission tonight, that's all. Things didn't go quite the way we had hoped.

It could have been worse – we don't think Jussi was recognized
– but he was hurt –'

'What sort of mission?'

There was a small silence. 'An assassination,' Elisabet said,
calmly.

Katya's fingers stilled. 'An –' She stopped. 'You mean Jussi
and the others – they *killed* someone?'

'I sincerely hope so, yes.'

'Who? Who did they kill?' Katya's voice was a whisper.

Elisabet turned on her fiercely. 'One of the men responsible
for the arrest and exile of half my country's judges, her provincial governors, her doctors, lawyers, national officials. One of
those – Russians –' she invested the word with a blistering
scorn that turned it into an epithet '– who believe they can
keep the people of Suomi in slavery by sending our leaders to
Siberia to die of cold and of hardship. For God's sake, Katya,
don't you know *anything* of what's going on around you? Are
you so self-centred – so stupid? Don't you ever read a paper?'

'Well, yes, of course – I –'

Elisabet turned from her in undisguised and weary disgust.
'Get dressed. Hurry.'

Katya scrambled as best she could into the borrowed riding
suit. It was uncomfortably tight across her breasts, and the
heavy skirts swirled a little too high about her ankles. 'Does –
does your husband know about all this?' she asked. Oddly, she
was recovering her equilibrium a little as she adjusted to the
strange circumstances.

Elisabet shook her head. 'No. Of course not. Poor old Turnakov would have a fit – several fits – if he knew the use to
which his roof and his money have been put.' She smiled a
small, humourless smile. 'The old man uses my body; I use his
money and his name. A fair exchange I think. You'll need some
boots. And a coat. It will be cold out on the ice.'

Katya, who had been struggling into the fitted woollen jacket
of the suit, stopped, eyes startled. 'The ice? You mean – the
Gulf? We're going across the Gulf?'

'Well, what else do you think you might do? Arrive at the
Finland station in the Turnakov sledge to catch a train? With
Jussi with a bullet wound in his shoulder and half the city

260

looking for the group responsible for tonight's activities? Do try not to be any more stupid than you can possibly help, Katya.'

'But – the ice? Isn't it very early in the year to try to cross the ice? Is it – is it safe?'

Jussi's sister gave her a long, cool look. 'For Jussi it's a lot safer than St Petersburg is at the moment,' she said, tartly. 'They have no choice.' For one moment her composure faltered. She clenched her fist and banged it upon the dressing table. 'If only he hadn't been hurt! We had it all so well planned. He had a perfect alibi –'

'He had two,' Katya said, miserably.

Surprised, Elisabet glanced at her and then, astonishingly, laughed in sudden genuine amusement. 'Oh, my poor Katya! What an evening this has been for you! And – you had used Jussi as *your* alibi?'

Katya nodded.

'All the better then. Your parents won't be surprised to hear that the most brainless and irresponsible pair of young people in St Petersburg have decided to run away together, will they?'

Katya was not so sure. Nor did the idea of remaining tangled in this confusing and violent web into which she had so appallingly blundered appeal. She tried once more. 'Elisabet, please! Won't you take my word that I won't breathe a word of what I've seen and heard tonight? Won't you please let me go?'

The fair head shook. The faint warmth that had flickered in the other girl's eyes died. 'No. Absolutely not. There's more at stake here even than simply my brother's life – though that alone would be enough for me to kill you, whatever Jussi said.' The words were totally matter-of-fact. Katya fought the uncomfortable and worrying squirming of her stomach. 'We have to get him away, and quickly, and we have to do it with no possible suspicion falling upon him or upon me. It should be easy enough – he comes and goes so frequently no-one will question it. But his wound can't be treated here. We can't trust anyone. We don't even have the contacts that most of the revolutionary groups do. And under no circumstances must our association with the freedom fighters be discovered. Our connections in St Petersburg are invaluable to our country as things stand;

discovered, we would be less than useless. I will not allow my brother and my cause to be jeopardized by a stupid and irresponsible girl who spreads her legs for a man and then runs screaming for help when he does as nature – and presumably she – intended. I don't know why men bother with girls like you, Katya. Whores are much better value.' She had turned towards the door, but stopped, turned back, shaking her head, passing a hand across her eyes. The gun hung by her side in a suddenly limp hand. 'I'm sorry,' she said, quietly. 'That was unforgivable. I should not have said it.'

Katya was staring at her, white-faced, the flat cruelty of the words taking her breath. Then, 'You're right,' she said, bleakly, and blinked at the sudden rise of frightened tears. 'You're right,' she repeated, her voice a whisper.

Elisabet shook her head again. 'I'm tired. Overwrought. I apologize. These past few days have been – difficult. And now, to see Jussi hurt –' She made a small, vague gesture with her hand. 'I can't tell you how it makes me feel.' For a moment the cool possession dropped from her; she looked young, tired, close herself to tears. She made a visible effort, straightened her back, lifted her head. 'Come. We're wasting time.'

Katya did not move. 'Elisabet?'

'What?'

'Wh-what will happen to me?' She could not for her life control the trembling of her voice.

The pale blue eyes met hers, serious and direct. 'I don't know. I'm sorry, but there it is. It's up to the others. It's up to Jussi. He's saved you so far. But there are others involved. One thing I promise you –' the words were dispassionate, but by no means entirely unfriendly '– a false step and you're dead. An – unfortunate accident; they are easy to arrange. So behave yourself. Perhaps, for us, you are a blessing well disguised; at least his "elopement" with you will in the short term explain Jussi's absence if embarrassing questions should be asked.'

'My parents?' Katya's voice wobbled precariously again.

'You'll write them a note, of course. The note of a scatter-brain. A note they will recognize as yours. You've eloped with your handsome Finnish prince.' Even Elisabet smiled, wryly, at that, remembering Jussi's far from princely looks. 'Another thoughtless, silly escapade. A whim of the moment. Make it good. They have to believe you.'

'But –' Katya stood like a bewildered child, uncomfortable in the slimmer girl's clothes, her face blotched with tears, her cut lip swollen.

Elisabet leaned to her, her face deadly serious. 'Take it, Katya. It's all there is. The alternative you've been told. This is not a game we're playing. We risk our lives and our liberty, and the lives and the liberty of those we love. Every day. Every hour. I'm afraid that makes for a certain – lack of sympathy – for others.'

And for the first time the true peril of the situation in which she found herself struck Katya like a blow. Pale and silent, unable to control the slight, frightened trembling of her limbs, she followed Elisabet from the room.

The city was still wreathed in a freezing fog that drifted and swirled about the gas lamps and braziers, hung above frozen river and canal, cloaked and muffled the city and its sounds. Midnight was well past when two ordinary and unremarkable sledges set out from the Turnakov mansion, their occupants wrapped to their ears in furs and blankets, their booted feet resting uncomfortably upon hastily concealed guns. In a tense and wary silence they sat, as the horses picked their careful way through the fogbound, snowy streets. There could be no question of speed.

Katya sat crammed between a huge young man in a shabby and remarkably pungent sheepskin jacket and the man called Heimo who had doctored Jussi's shoulder. Opposite were Jussi, his face in the dim light drawn to the bone with pain, and a girl dressed in the clothes of a student, though she looked indefinably misplaced in the part.

The city was surprisingly quiet, though once at a hissed instruction the two sledges drew to a halt in a quiet sidestreet as a company of soldiers rode beneath the lamp that lit an intersection some fifty yards away.

'The bridge will be the key. There's bound to be a guard,' Jussi said, quietly. 'Remember – let me do the talking.'

263

'Can't we go further upriver?' It was the girl who spoke.

Jussi shook his head. 'No. They'll all be guarded. It'll look far more natural to take one of the larger ones. We'll try the Dvortsovyi; and don't forget – you're off to enjoy yourselves – make it good!'

The young man beside Katya, whom she had heard addressed as Kaarlo, produced a bottle from beneath his dirty sheepskin jacket. 'We'll make it good,' he said, and tilted his head back to drink.

'Not too bloody good,' Jussi said, only half humorously.

'Take it easy, Kaarlo,' the man called Heimo said.

'Piss off,' Kaarlo said, gently, and drank again. Katya could smell the spirits mixed with the unpleasant odour of the filthy coat. She huddled into her cloak, arms tight across her breast, leaning away from him. He felt her movement, watched her with bright, callous eyes, grinning.

'Watch it. Here they come.' They were at the bridge. Faintly the huge bulk of the Winter Palace loomed in the darkness. A road block had been set up. Several soldiers huddled about a glowing brazier, rubbing their hands and stamping their feet, their fog-smudged figures vague in the opaque light. Others stood beside the barrier, rifles slung across their shoulders. A mounted officer slouched, bored, in his saddle some small distance away. He straightened and walked his horse forward as the two sledges drew to a halt.

Katya was shivering. How many times had she seen this? How many times had she impatiently waited as her carriage or sledge was waved respectfully through just such a checkpoint? How could it possibly be that she was sitting here, helpless, amongst assassins, her feet upon the barrel of a machine gun? Oh, God, she prayed, desperately, if I ever get out of this I swear I'll never misbehave again. Never!

'Keep still,' Kaarlo said, conversationally. 'One word. One movement. That's all it would take.'

'Well, well.' It was Jussi, very quietly, a trace of satisfaction in his voice. He raised it a little. 'Ola! Malinski! It is you, isn't it? What are you doing stopping respectable citizens from going about their legitimate pleasures?'

The officer leaned in the saddle, peering into Jussi's face.

Then he straightened, laughing. 'Lavola! You dog! Where do you think you're going at this time of night?'

'Out to the Islands of course. For a bit of fun. What in Hell's name are you doing stuck here? Come and join us, why don't you?'

Kaarlo stirred beside Katya. The knife he held beneath the furs touched her hand. She drew back.

The young officer shook his head ruefully. 'You trying to get me court martialled? They'd shoot me for a lot less, you useless article.'

'Why? What's going on?'

'The usual. A bunch of bloody lunatics have shot up Kanoviev's carriage as he drove to the theatre tonight. Why the bastards always have to choose a night when I'm on duty I don't know.'

The girl beside Jussi leaned forward. 'Is he dead?' she asked, eagerly.

Through the drifting mist Katya saw Jussi's quick frown.

'Very,' the officer said. 'And so's his driver. But they got one of the terrorists, so they say. Badly hurt from the sound of it. They won't get far.'

'Neither will we at this rate,' Jussi grinned. 'You sure you won't join us?'

The horse danced in the snow. Fog billowed from the ice-locked river, rolling about them; frost gleamed and glittered in the pinpricks of lamp light. 'Better not.' The young officer threw back his head and laughed. 'For more reasons than one. The way I recall it you nearly got me knifed last time we went out to the Islands together. Remember the girl at the Angel?'

'How could I forget her?'

'All right. Let them through.' The young man raised his hand to the men by the barrier. Leaned forward to Jussi again. 'Have one for me,' he said, and slapped his shoulder in friendly salute before wheeling the horse and moving back onto the bridge.

Jussi's fair head went back in an agonized spasm of pain. How he had resisted crying out Katya could not imagine. She watched, appalled, as the sledge began to move forward. Jussi swayed, white-faced; lifted his good hand in an answering wave to the young officer.

'Hold him,' Heimo said, sharply.

The girl grabbed Jussi, her arm about his waist, supporting him. As they passed beneath a lamp Katya saw the savage pain that bleached his face; and still he made no sound. Once off the bridge and away from danger Heimo called for the sledge to stop.

'No.' Jussi, who had slumped forward, straightened. 'No. We can't stop now. We have to get on.'

'But –'

'You can do whatever needs to be done once we reach Finland.' Jussi's voice was quiet, husky with effort and with pain. 'Thirty miles. That's all. Just thirty miles, and we're safe. But we can't stop now. There are still the forts.'

The fog thickened, and so did the silence, as they reached the forest that edged the marshlands of the coast. There were few lights now, their own lamps were like glow worms smothered by the blanket of the freezing mist that drifted between the trees in wreaths and ribbons that seemed imbued with an unearthly life of their own. Katya's eyes ached from straining them into the eerie, shifting darkness. They passed the occasional house or cabin, barred and muffled against the cold. Woodsmoke mixed sometimes with the fog; the smell brought visions of small, often all but unnoticed comforts. Suddenly Katya was overwhelmed with misery. She wanted to go home. She wanted things to be normal, ordinary. She wanted to be the girl she had been that morning. She wanted her room with its pretty things, its warmth and safety. She wanted her mother.

'How far out are the forts?' It was the girl who spoke, her voice small and unnerved in the quiet that was broken only by the faint jingling of harness.

'Six miles.' Jussi eased himself in the seat. He had appeared to sleep for the past few miles. His voice was stronger, his face more alert. 'Once past them we're safe. At least the fog will be some protection against the lights.'

'But no protection against losing our way,' Heimo said, softly.

Jussi shook his head. 'We're in safe hands. Our drivers aren't only Finns. They're – shall we say more than usually experienced with this crossing? They won't lose us.'

'Smugglers,' Kaarlo said, and tilted his bottle again.

'Gentlemen of the free trade,' Jussi said, and in the darkness there was the shadow of a smile in his voice.

'But the ice?' It was almost the first time Katya had spoken. 'Is it safe?'

She could all but feel the silence about her.

'Trust you to ask a bloody silly question like that, Katya my love,' Jussi said, mildly.

Ahead, faintly through the trees, could be seen a cluster of lights, as they approached a small community of cabins set along the frozen quiet of the shore. Figures moved in the misty darkness. Words were exchanged, quietly. Coins chinked. Men bent to the horses' hooves, worked upon the harness. 'What are they doing?' Katya asked.

'Deadening the sound,' Heimo said. His voice and his face were tense. 'The sailors in the Kronstadt tend to fire first and ask questions afterwards at this time of night. Or at any other time come to that.'

A man, muffled to the eyebrows, came to the side of the sledge and offered tin mugs of sweet, strong tea. Katya sipped it gratefully; she was shaking with cold and nerves. Kaarlo shook his head, swigged from the bottle again.

'Give Jussi some of that,' Heimo said.

Kaarlo lifted his eyebrows.

Purposefully Heimo leaned forward, forcibly took the bottle from him and splashed some of its contents into a mug of tea. 'Drink that.' He thrust the mug into Jussi's hand. Katya was shocked to see how it shook.

Five minutes later, amidst whispered good wishes, the two sledges, runners swishing quietly, swung down off the shore and through the flat, frozen marshes that led out onto the wide, quiet ice of the Gulf.

It was a journey Katya would never forget. As they left the land the fog closed about them, claustrophobically dense, brutally cold. In virtual silence they moved through a lightless world, their breath and that of the horses clouding about them, freezing as it settled, as they moved with tense care towards the line of forts, dominated by the Kronstadt, that guarded the sea approach to St Petersburg.

Katya ached all over. Her head, her shoulders, her back. There was an uncomfortable burning between her legs that she tried to ignore. Her lip was swollen and sore. She felt utterly wretched. Yet not even she could sink so far into self-absorbed misery that she could not sense the taut nerves of the others as the first searchlight swept through the fog, reflecting uselessly back into itself against the shifting wall of mist. The sledge stopped – they had long since lost contact with the second one – the driver scrambled from his seat and walked quietly forward to take the horse's head. Heimo slipped from his seat beside Katya to join him. Together, dim figures in the foggy darkness, they led the horse on, trudging one each side of the beast's head, hands ready to muffle the slightest sound.

The frozen Gulf stretched about them, empty, an icy waste-land swept by those probing fingers of light. At least it seemed that the ice was safe. Or was it? Even as the thought occurred Katya fancied she felt a small movement, heard the faintest of sounds. She caught her breath.

'Katya?' Jussi's voice, calm and cool in the darkness. She could not see his face.

She swallowed. 'Yes?'

'Are you all right?'

'Yes,' she said again.

He said no more. But the small contact had been a comfort. Beside her she sensed movement, saw a faint shift in the darkness as Kaarlo lifted the bottle again and drank.

She was having difficulty in breathing – each small breath sounded so loudly that she was sure it must be heard for miles. Yet any attempt to control it made her feel as if she were suffocating. She fought down a lift of panic.

The light swept around again, an impersonal finger, probing, arrogant in its assumption that the ice was its own domain, that no-one would dare defy or try to evade it. They were level with the forts – they were slipping past them – the light swept again, and again, baffled by the wall of mist. Katya waited for the challenge, the burst of gunfire.

Nothing happened.

Slowly, slowly, led on by Heimo and the driver they moved through the line and on towards the distant coastline of Finland, that its people called Suomi. The sweeping lights were swallowed by the fog behind them. The driver climbed back up onto the seat and clucked confidingly to the horses. They picked up speed, running smoothly and quickly now. Kaarlo chuckled. Jussi laughed, too, relief clear in the sound.

'We've done it,' Heimo said, almost reverently. 'By God and all his angels, we've *done it!*'

'Not quite.' Jussi had sobered. 'There's half of occupied Finland between us and Kuopio, remember.'

'Where's Kuopio?' Katya asked and was rewarded with a silence that was suddenly thick with hostility.

'Bloody Russian,' Kaarlo said.

They met up with the other sledge and its occupants at a pre-arranged spot when they made landfall at a small fishing village on the Finnish side of the Gulf, near the little port of Kotka. Katya was exhausted. She huddled into a blanket, hearing the murmur of voices, unable to understand what they said, hardly caring. Her head drooped; she slept, fitfully, a flawed sleep of dreams and terrors. She jumped awake, frightened half to death, as a hand touched her.

'It's all right. It's me.' The late dawn of winter had not yet found them; but at least the fog had lifted. In the cold winter darkness Jussi looked drawn and ill, but his faint smile cheered her a little. 'We're going to have to move on. The others are going to Helsinki. You'll come to Kuopio with me, Kaarlo and Heimo. For now we need some rest.' He smiled again, obstinately, a ghost of his usual cheerful grin. 'Have you ever slept in a barn before?'

Her eyes widened. She pulled the blanket to her chin. 'In this weather?' she asked, appalled.

He shook his head. 'It's all right. This is no ordinary barn. It's been –' he hesitated '– adapted. It's warm and it's as safe as we'll be until we get to Kuopio. And I can get some first aid.'

She bit her lip, her eyes searching his face. He looked awful, the blue eyes shadowed, the wide mouth a straight line of pain. 'How is it?'

'It's all right. It'll be all right. Don't worry. Katya –' He stopped.

She waited.

He was unsmiling now, his eyes held hers, and at the look in them fear stirred again. 'I'm sorry. Truly sorry. I never in the world intended to get you mixed up in this. I'll never forgive myself if –' The words tailed away abruptly.

Katya had had time to think on the long cold journey across the Gulf. 'It's not your fault,' she said, bleakly. 'Not entirely, anyway.'

He put his good hand on her shoulder. The small, kindly gesture all but destroyed what composure she was managing to maintain. She looked away quickly, unwilling for him to see her sudden, frightened tears.

'One thing,' he said, very quietly.

'Yes?' Still she did not look at him.

'Stay close to me. All the time. You understand?'

'Yes.' She understood all too well. She had already registered the unwelcome news that Kaarlo of the pungent breath, the filthy sheepskin coat and the too-ready knife would be a companion on their journey to the unknown Kuopio, was in no doubt at all what the man thought of their uninvited passenger and what his solution to the problem she posed would be.

'Good.' Jussi swayed a little, caught the side of the sledge to steady himself.

Katya closed her eyes. The man did not look capable of protecting himself, let alone her. 'Jussi?'

'Yes?'

'What's at Kuopio?'

'Friends,' he said, and clambered into the sledge beside her, laying his head back tiredly on the worn upholstery. 'Friends.'

The journey to the small town of Kuopio, in the north-eastern part of the country, through almost two hundred miles of all but trackless forest took days. It was bitterly cold. They travelled through blizzards or under leaden skies on the ice of the lakes and rivers that laced the flat forest lands and were at this time of the year the only passable highways. They moved from village to village, were passed from guide to guide. Katya could not help but notice that everyone, from the local mayor to the smallest child, seemed to know Jussi. Whenever they could stop for long enough his wound was dressed; but nothing could hide his rising fever or the steady erosion of his strength. Yet he would not stop. Where they could they avoided villages; in the one in which they did stop, a pretty place of painted wooden houses and small, snow-covered barns, Katya saw Russian soldiers, huge and arrogant in their greatcoats and fur hats, patrolling the streets, guns slung across their shoulders, and understood, a little, Kaarlo's hostility, Heimo's reserve. She watched Jussi worriedly, for her own sake as well as his. God alone knew what would happen to her if he should die. She did not dare think of it. The sight of his wound, when Heimo dressed it, sickened her; she turned away, unable to watch – but not before she had seen and smelled the putrescence, registered the flicker of agony in his eyes, the contempt upon the faces of his companions at her squeamishness.

The time came when Heimo said, 'You have to stop, Jussi. You're killing yourself.'

Jussi's eyes flickered to Katya. 'No. One more push. One more day and we're there.' His face was thin and flushed, his eyes sunken. Numb, exhausted, frightened, Katya could not believe he would find the strength to survive.

But he did, if only just. And when they reached the haven towards which he had pushed himself so ruthlessly, Katya understood why he had so determinedly persevered. In a blessedly solid, cream and white painted house that smelled of polish and the smoke of pine and birch logs, competent but gentle hands received and tended him. With a minimum of fuss and a maximum of efficiency there was food, drink, hot water, clean clothes. It was the house of a doctor and his wife, sympathizers to the cause and old friends of Jussi's family. It stood in a respectable street that ran down, as did almost all of Kuopio's straight, criss-crossed streets, to the water that nearly surrounded the town, frozen solid now and drifted with snow, island windmills dotted across it like so many scarecrows etched against the winter sky. Jussi held grimly to slipping consciousness for long enough to issue a few urgent orders. Then, gratefully, he abandoned the struggle and the grinding pain and slid into insensibility.

'You'll come with me, please?' The doctor's wife, plump,

brisk, not unkindly-looking, took Katya's arm. Wordless, Katya followed her, scarcely capable of putting one foot in front of the other. She thought she might well die of tiredness. Even the fear that dogged her still was distanced by her exhaustion. All she wanted to do was sleep.

The woman led her along a corridor to a solid wooden door. Opened, it revealed heaven; a warm and pretty room, lamplit and cosy, containing bed, chairs, a table. The shutters were up against the weather, a stove was set in a corner that was lined from floor to ceiling with shining blue and white tiles. Everything else was wood; floor, walls, ceiling, warm and lovingly polished. There was a scent of fresh herbs in the air. Katya stood for a moment, speechless.

'I'll get you some night clothes,' the woman said, gently. 'You're exhausted, I think. Jussi says you are to be treated as his guest.' Curiosity flickered for a moment in the faded blue eyes, and was gone. 'Please – make yourself at home. You're quite safe here.'

'Thank you. Th-thank you so much.' Katya reached out to the bed. It looked soft and infinitely inviting.

'I'll bring warm water. You'll want to wash.'

'Yes. Thank you.'

The woman turned and bustled from the room. Katya turned, fell back onto the bed, arms spread. She closed her eyes.

Very clearly, very sharply, she heard the key click in the lock.

That she should be treated as his guest was obviously not the only order Jussi had given.

CHAPTER FOURTEEN

'There's a child, of course. You mark my words.' Varya, eyes bright with malice and something close to satisfaction, stirred her tea. 'There can be no other reason for such foolishness.'

'It certainly seems strange.' Margarita was standing by the window looking down into the snowy street. It was bitterly cold. People hurried past, muffled against the icy wind. The small sitting room was cosy and warm. She turned. 'How have Uncle Mischa and Aunt Zhenia taken it?'

'My dear, Mischa is positively *furious*. And as for Zhenia – she simply refuses to discuss it. Well, after all, it makes them look so very silly, doesn't it?'

Margarita returned her mother's smile. 'Yes. It does rather. And I must say that I'm surprised. I mean, when you think of the wedding Katya could have had –'

'There's a child,' Varya repeated, with sanctimonious certainty. 'It's the only possible explanation.'

'What did Katya say in her note, do you know?'

Varya shook her head. 'Not exactly. Some rubbish about it being more romantic to elope, I believe.'

'Where are they, do you know?'

'Somewhere in Finland is all anyone knows. Mischa has set investigations in train, of course, but at the moment I don't think he's trying all that hard to find the young people.'

'In case your theory turns out to be true?' Margarita's face was lit with the same malicious mischief as her mother's.

'My dear, it isn't just my theory. Everyone's saying it. Just everyone.'

Margarita laughed. 'Then it must be true, mustn't it?' She came back to the table upon which the samovar stood. 'More tea?'

They settled back into their chairs. Margarita enjoyed these afternoons when her mother came to call. They shared a love of gossip that could be indulged to the full and would talk for hours – as they had this afternoon – dissecting other people's lives, affairs and motives with the kind of absorption and interest that others might expend on politics or the more arcane and intricate facets of religion. Neither had been able, nor indeed had felt the need, to disguise her mildly spiteful satisfaction at Katya's not unexpectedly disgraceful behaviour and the consequent embarrassment to her parents. Both safely ensconced in complacent respectability, they had tutted and shaken their heads, delightedly scandalized; Katya, they had assured each other, had always been a hoyden, and a spoiled one at that – who could be surprised at what she did?

'Mama thinks Katya is having a baby,' Margarita said, later that evening, to Sasha, who was home for the first time in several days. 'What a scandal! I wonder if it's so? It would certainly explain her running away, wouldn't it?'

'I suppose it would, yes.' Sasha's reply was absent. He was watching his wife as she busied herself arranging a bunch of dried flowers. She looked quite remarkably pretty as she stood back to survey her efforts. The time had come. He would have to say something. Tonight. He pushed the thought of Valentina from him. This was his wife. His life was here. A family – he needed a family, to hold to and to protect. To keep him from what he knew to be madness. 'They're very nice.'

'Mama bought them for me this afternoon. But how wonderfully wicked if it's true! Katya, I mean, and the baby. Goodness, I should never be able to hold my head up again if it were me.' Margarita, he noted ruefully, had long ago affected to forget their afternoon together in the dacha on the shores of the Gulf.

'Rita –'

'And to think of the wedding she could have had! Can you imagine what Uncle Mischa would have been prepared to pay? Mama says he's absolutely *furious* –'

Sasha stood, came up behind her, turned her to face him. 'Margarita, I'm not in the least bit interested in what your cousin Katya has or hasn't done –'

'Oh, but I am!' Laughing, she stood on tiptoe to kiss his nose, then ducked beneath his arm, slipping from him. 'Most certainly I am. There hasn't been anything half so much fun to talk about for years! Oh, by the way, Mama asked us over to dinner at the weekend. Will you be here?'

He shook his head, still watching her. 'I'm on duty.'

'Oh, bother!' She did not, in fact, sound bothered at all. 'Oh, well, I suppose I shall just have to go alone.' She had gone into the kitchen. He heard the sound of running water. He followed, stood by the door. She stood at the sink, her back to him, still talking. 'Mama tried to persuade Lenka to come, but she wouldn't. Since this last baby she really has been very strange. She doesn't seem to want anything to do with anyone. Mama said she was quite sharp with her the other day when she called; more or less told her to mind her own business, when Mama really was only trying to help.'

Sasha made a small, wry face that Rita, perhaps fortunately, did not see.

'Lenka's marriage really does seem a strange one, doesn't it? But then – I never did like Pavel Petrovich very much. I don't envy poor Lenka a bit –'

'Not even her two children? You don't envy her those?' The words were very quiet, but given their effect they might have been shouted. Margarita's movements stilled. She did not turn. Silence fell.

'Margarita? I said –'

'I heard what you said.' Margarita's voice was clipped and cold. 'And really, Sasha, it's most indelicate of you to –'

'Margarita!' He cleared the space between them in a stride, took her by the shoulders, forced her to face him. 'I know,' he said, his voice very quiet, 'I know that you take – precautions. I know you are preventing us from having a child.'

'Stop it!' She had flushed a fiery red. Angrily she wrenched herself free of his hands. 'Stop it! You're disgusting!'

'It's true, though. Isn't it?' A child. He wanted a child. Margarita's child. His child. A bond between them that would be unbreakable, that would split him for ever from Valentina whom he knew now he loved and to whom he could do nothing but harm. A child was the answer, he had told himself in desperation, a child was the only answer. The only way to make sense of this suddenly senseless marriage. 'Isn't it?' he asked again.

She would not reply.

'Margarita, please – don't you want a child? Our child?'

'Of course I do.' The words were stiff, her soft mouth was set in a straight, sullen line. 'What do you take me for – some kind of unfeeling monster?'

'Of course not! But Rita, I'm right, aren't I? You are – preventing it from happening?'

She lifted her chin, stalked past him. 'I don't have to listen to this. I'm going to bed.'

He caught her arm, not gently, as she passed. 'Margarita, I am your husband. I have the right to expect that you bear my child –'

She stood quite still in his grasp, her face cold. 'I don't have to listen to this filthy talk,' she said, with dignity. 'Really, Sasha, I'm surprised at you. You aren't in the barrack room now, you know.'

'But we have to talk about it, don't we? We have to sort it out.'

'There's nothing to sort out. If I have a child it will be in God's good time. And there's plenty of that.'

'You deny that you're taking precautions?'

She turned her head, looked him straight and coldly in the eye, and lied, as only she could. 'Yes,' she said. 'I do.' Then, straight-backed and offended, she left him. He heard the bedroom door slam, the key turn in the lock.

He reached into a cupboard, brought out a bottle of vodka, splashed a large amount into a glass and returned to the sitting room. Margarita's treasured theatre was standing upon the sideboard. She had carefully arranged the tiny figures into a tableau depicting a royal party; the prince and his princess stood at the top of a flight of cardboard stairs, their courtiers beneath them. With a sharp movement Sasha shook the thing; the bright figures tumbled, lay with fixedly smiling expressions in a tangled heap upon the stage. 'God damn it,' he said, quietly and bitterly. 'God *damn* it!' He tilted his head, tossed his drink back, strode out into the kitchen for more.

Rumours of war; they trembled in the air of Europe, rumbled in the distant Balkans like the echo of gunfire. In the quiet winter peace of the English countryside Anna heard them and tried to dismiss them; it was easy to do so as gentle day followed gentle day, days full of music, laughter and quiet content. News of Katya's escapade reached her through a letter from her mother, and explained the lack of communication from Katya herself. She shook her head, affectionately exasperated. 'Wouldn't you know that Katya would do something as outrageous as this? Whatever possessed her?'

Guy smiled. 'Katya, as I remember her, is one of those people who could make a drama out of eating breakfast. You're surely not surprised?'

'No. I'm not. But Mama says that Uncle Mischa is terribly angry.'

'He would be, of course. It certainly seems to be a very silly thing to have done.'

'Guy?' Anna walked to his chair, laid an arm about his shoulder, resting her cheek upon his still-thick hair. Beyond the windows a drifting rain veiled the gardens. 'I'd like to go home, for a visit. Perhaps next summer?'

'Of course, my dear.' His voice was calm. 'But – home?'

She laughed a little, hugged him again. 'You know what I mean. And, of course, this is home. But – Papa isn't getting any younger. And I have nieces and nephews I've never seen.' She counted them on her fingers. 'Lenka has a girl and a boy, Dima a little girl and another baby on the way – I'd like to see them, that's all. I've never even met Margarita's handsome husband. Yes, I should like to go back.' She had not in her four years of marriage once heard from Lenka. The news she had received from her mother had been sketchy at best. But surely – surely! – her sister could not still be harbouring the childish grudge that had caused those last distressing words that had passed between them? And Andrei – she could face him now, she was certain, the pain, the destructive and dangerous emotions behind them; indeed, she realized suddenly, she needed to face him, needed to prove to herself and to him that it was truly over. 'Next summer,' she said. 'I'll write to Mama and tell her. I'll visit them all next summer.'

'We,' he said. 'We'll visit them.'

'Are you sure? You of all people know how trying the journey can be, and you know you haven't been terribly well.'

'Nonsense.' His hand reached out for hers, still strong, still warm. 'You're not getting away from me that easily, my girl!'

She touched his cheek, suddenly serious. Andrei's name hovered between them, unspoken. 'You don't have to,' she said. 'I promise you don't.'

'I know,' he said, and smiled. 'But I'll come anyway.'

It occurred to Katya to wonder, uneasily and more than once in the days that followed their arrival in Kuopio, if the locked door were not almost as much for her protection as for her restraint. 'Stay close to me. All the time,' Jussi had said; but now? What control had he, on a sick bed fighting for his life? And supposing he died? The thought brought nightmares. On the first morning of her captivity she heard Kaarlo's voice outside the door, persistent and angry, and with it a woman's voice, calmly arguing, the voice of the woman who had greeted and sheltered her. Since they spoke their native tongue she could not understand exactly what they said; but the man's voice was fierce and far from friendly, and she stood listening by the door, her heart beating in fear.

Later the woman came to her with milk and porridge, cheese and coddled eggs. Her face was grave, she said little. Katya waited until the last moment, until the woman was at the door, before she could bring herself to ask, 'Jussi? How is he?'

The woman, who had told Katya she was called Tilda, hesitated. Shook her head. 'He isn't good. He's fevered.'

Katya stared at her. 'He won't –' Her voice cracked a little. She cleared her throat. 'He won't die, will he?'

The woman did not hesitate. Her face was calm. 'We can't tell yet. I'm afraid he might. The wound was left for too long.'

Katya pushed the tray away, her appetite gone. The woman turned to the door. Stopped. Came back to the bed. 'Eat it,' she said, gently.

'I can't.'

Shrewd blue eyes measured her. 'Don't be afraid. August – my husband – and I won't let anything happen to you. For our own sakes as well as for Jussi's. This is our home. You're safe here.'

Katya thought of Kaarlo's dark, unfriendly eyes and could not help but doubt that. She said nothing.

Tilda laid a plump, firm hand upon hers. 'Eat. I'll bring you some clothes. We have nothing very suitable, but something of my daughter's might fit you, with a little adjustment. She's in Helsinki. She won't mind.'

'Thank you.' Katya's voice was dull. Her brain was dull. She could not think.

'You've had a hard time. Sleep.'

She thought it impossible, but strangely sleep she did, on and off, for all of the day and most of the night. The exhausting journey had taken its toll; her rest, in the feathered nest of the comfortable bed, was far from peaceful but it at least defended her from thought, from the need to face the bizarre situation in which she found herself.

She woke to a warm and lamplit room, shadowed, strange; for a moment she could not recall where she was. Then recollection hit her and her stomach churned. She sat up.

The figure in the armchair, set by a lamp on a round table that held a bubbling samovar, lifted her head. 'You're awake,' Tilda said, calmly, setting aside her needlework.

Katya dragged her tangled fair hair from her eyes. 'Jussi?' she asked.

The woman shrugged a little. Her eyes were shadowed. 'Still bad.'

Katya lay back on the pillows.

'Would you care for tea?'

'Yes. Please.'

With neat and composed movements Tilda mixed the tea, brought the glass to the bedside on a small tray. 'I've been sitting with Jussi. Heimo's taken over. I couldn't sleep. I – ' she hesitated ' – I thought it a good idea to sit with you for a while?' Her voice was oddly tentative.

'Thank you. That was kind.' The tea was strong and lemony. For a devastating moment it reminded Katya of home, of safe and blessed normality. She took a deep breath, nibbling her lip, fighting the weak tears. The brew cleared her brain of the fog of too-long, too-deep sleep. Tilda had settled back into the chair, sewing. Silence settled about them for a while, calm and not unfriendly.

'More tea?'

'Yes. Thank you.'

Katya accepted the tray. Looked up into the lined and weathered face. 'I don't understand,' she said. 'I've been to Finland. I've been often. I've read of course about – about the extremists. But Jussi? You?' She shook her head. 'I don't understand.'

'That's because you are a Russian.' The words held no animosity. Tilda sat upon the bed, watching her, her face serious. 'My dear, what you have to understand – what the world has to understand – is that Finland is not a part of Russia. She never has been. Finland is a Duchy, an independent state, with her own laws, her own Constitution. Since the early part of the last century we have simply been – it is an irony I think to say it – under the protection of the Russian crown. That's all. We had guarantees. Treaties. But now, in the past thirty years, the Russian monarchy has abused the power that has been vested in it. The Tsar outlaws our language, our culture, our Constitution. He mistreats our people, our public servants. We are to be –' she spread square, expressive hands '– Russified.' She shook her head. 'He misunderstands us. The world misunderstands us. Badly. Finns are not by nature passionate people perhaps, but they are determined, they are not lacking in courage, and they are strong for justice. They are slow to anger, slow to react, as damp kindling is sometimes slow to burn; but once roused, once burning, the fire is deep-seated and impossible to extinguish. Unrest has been smouldering for years. Our young men refuse to serve in your army. We demand that once again our courts, our schools, our cities should be run by Finns, not by Russians. Our language is precious to us. We are not a subject nation; your government acts illegally and unconstitutionally in trying to subject us. We will be free. There are those who counsel caution still – those who rely on the good will of Britain, France, Germany, who all pay lip service to our cause but do nothing to aid us for fear of angering the Tsar – many of our older folk detest and fear the thought of violence. But there are others, like Jussi, who seek the direct way. I don't know who is right. My own nature bends to caution and to the way of the law –' she smiled a little, gently '– I fear I am a typical Finn! But I love Jussi dearly. His mother was my closest friend, closer than a sister. And even I, and many like me, are becoming tired of waiting. Perhaps the young people are right. Perhaps it will be necessary that we fight.'

'Fight?' Katya asked, faintly. 'Fight the Tsar? And all his army?'

The rosy, weathered face smiled. A shoulder lifted. 'Perhaps. Who knows? There is no more just cause than ours, and no more corrupt regime than the one we face. Change is coming. But enough.' She smiled her kindly smile. 'I didn't mean to lecture. For now, rest, my dear. And try not to worry.'

The shadow of Katya's usual bright smile lit her face. 'Hard to do with Kaarlo on the other side of the door. He doesn't like me.'

'I have told you; you are a guest under our roof. And as such you are safe.' Briskly the woman moved to where she had been sitting, shook out the material of the skirt she had been sewing. 'There. I had to guess the size – our Milja is rather bigger than you – but I think it will fit. Sleep now, and in the morning we'll talk again.'

'My parents,' Katya said. 'May I write to them?'

Tilda turned. 'We spoke of it,' she said. 'Kaarlo and Heimo thought not. For fear you sent some secret message, betraying us. I suggested that a brief note, scrutinized by all of us, could do no harm.'

Katya watched her as she folded her sewing. 'Who won?'

Tilda's smile was serene. 'They may be young men, and strong, and they may, to their eternal glory, be challenging the strength of the Tsar himself.' She laid the skirt tidily over the back of the chair, collected the tea glasses. 'But in Tilda Heikkala's house Tilda Heikkala rules. I'll bring pen and paper tomorrow.'

'Thank you.' A little comforted, Katya lay back upon the pillows. The sound of the key in the lock disturbed her not at all.

⋆ ⋆ ⋆

Her comfort did not last. The next day she knew from the tension that pervaded the house and from Tilda's quiet that Jussi was sinking. That night, after concocting a bright and deceitful note that would at least serve to relieve her parents' worry, or so she hoped, she sank to her knees by the side of the bed and prayed more fervently than she had in a very long time, for his life and for her own; she could no longer look any further than those simple needs. There was another tension too; that afternoon she had heard a disturbance in the street outside, shouts and cursing, a shot. From her window the view of the street was restricted, but she saw Russian uniforms, heard the hammering at a door, saw a young man dragged struggling away. The Heikkala house quietened; it was as if no inmate breathed, for fear of attracting attention. A young maid brought her meals, which on the whole she left untouched. Tilda brought her books and magazines, shook her head when Katya enquired after Jussi. 'He's bad. But there's still hope.'

The day was endless, the night that followed worse. Heimo came in the morning to replenish the stove. Tilda, he told her, had been up all night with her husband, nursing their patient.

'How is he?'

Heimo shrugged. He looked tired and drawn. 'Not good.'

She could settle to nothing. She spent long hours at the window, which looked onto a small courtyard garden, surrounded on three sides by the immaculately painted cream-boarded walls of the house and on the fourth by the stables. It was through the stable arch that she could see a little of the street. The courtyard was kept clear of snow and was neatly swept each day. It contained a single tree and a few bare, tidily-clipped bushes against the far wall. The sky was stormy and dark; often it snowed. The house was of one storey, as were its neighbours. The tall, shuttered windows, their surrounds and sills white-painted, were double-glazed against the fierce chill of winter, the protection cutting off sound as well as cold. She saw movement through the arch; sledges passed, people hurried by, but all in utter silence. And behind her too the house was still.

She went to bed in the early darkness, miserable and afraid.

Tilda came the next day. Katya was sitting by the window when she heard the key turn in the lock. She jumped up, facing the door, scanning the woman's face anxiously as she came into the room. Tilda smiled, tiredly. 'The worst would seem to be over. August thinks he'll be all right. He needs rest now.'

Relief overwhelmed Katya. She sat down, very suddenly, in the chair again. 'Might I be allowed to see him?'

'Perhaps. Later. But for the moment, no. It's best you stay here, I think.'

Katya glanced at her, sharply. 'You think? Or Kaarlo thinks?'

'For the moment Kaarlo has gone. There are arrangements to be made. Jussi cannot go back to St Petersburg with an unexplained wound. He must regain his strength. Even Kaarlo has been brought to see that you are an advantage in this. Elisabet has written to tell us that no-one has questioned the story of the elopement. Your parents are angry, but they have no fear for you.'

Katya nibbled her lip.

Tilda put out a sympathetic hand. 'Try not to worry.'

'How can I help it?' Katya pulled away, turned back to the window. The sky was leaden with snow; in the dreary half-light the already familiar view looked depressing and restrictive. 'I'm not stupid, whatever you might all think.' Her tone was bitter. 'I'm convenient, yes. For the moment. But afterwards? Will Jussi be content to keep me locked up for ever? And if not, then what?' She turned again to face Tilda, chin up. 'An even more convenient "accident"? "Madcap young bride falls into lake?" "Tragic shotgun accident"?' It was the first time she had allowed herself to articulate her fears; the very sound of the words brought a rise of panic. She folded her arms tightly across her breast, gripping her upper arms fiercely, fighting it down.

Tilda could not disguise the fact that she had no reassuring answer for her. She could only say, quietly, 'I don't believe that Jussi would allow that.'

The memory of Elisabet's cool eyes, steady above the levelled pistol, the awareness of Kaarlo's undisguised hostility, were too strong to accept that as comfort. 'Are you sure that Jussi will have the last say?'

The woman did not reply.

Katya turned away again.

'When Jussi is strong enough they'll go into the forest for the winter. His family have some land – the house is small and almost derelict, but it will serve. Kuopio isn't altogether safe. There is a big Russian garrison here, and there are people who are not friendly to our cause. August and I have made enemies, for we are outspoken and have brought some small trouble to some. Jussi and the others will be safer away from here.'

'And I?' Katya asked, bleakly. 'Where will I be safe?'

The silence behind her was telling. 'Try not to worry,' Tilda said again, quietly, after a moment. Katya heard her move to the door. Stop. 'I'll do my best for you,' she said.

Katya said nothing until the door had closed behind her. Then she threw back her head in sudden miserable frustration of cooped energy and fury. 'Damn it!' she whispered. And then, again, '*Damn it!*'

In the event she did not visit Jussi, he visited her, three days after the start of his recovery. Those days had been a strange time for Katya, a time of boredom broken only by Tilda's visits and by her own fiercely-recurring fears; yet there had been one small relief when her monthly period arrived, flooding and uncomfortable but infinitely welcome. It had been overdue, a circumstance which had further deepened her misery and fear, and its arrival lifted at least one worry from her overburdened mind. It was in the dying light of the early afternoon of the third day that she looked up, hearing the key turning in the lock, and saw him there, leaning in the doorway. His tall, always slight frame had shrunk to skin and bone. His right arm was in a sling. His face was thin, his eyes dark-ringed, his shock of pale hair tousled as straw. But the smile, the graceless, mocking smile that had so often infuriated her was the same. And still it infuriated her.

'Well,' she said, tartly. 'The bridegroom. How nice.'

His grin widened, though he winced as he closed the door very quietly behind him and walked cautiously into the room, lowering himself into a sitting position on the bed. 'As a matter of fact that's what I've come to talk to you about.'

'What?'

'The wedding,' he said, straight-faced. 'I really think I ought to make an honest woman of you, don't you?'

'Oh, for God's sake!' Furiously she turned away from him. 'Can't you *ever* be serious?'

There was a very short silence. 'Just for once,' he said, very quietly, 'I am.'

The silence that followed was much, much longer. She turned. Studied his face. Almost laughed aloud in sheer disbelief. 'You mean it,' she said at last. 'You – you actually think I'll *marry* you!'

'I don't think you have any choice.'

It took no time at all for the truth of that to sink in. Katya's soft mouth tightened angrily.

'Katya, listen to me.' All humour had gone; without the smile his face was sunken with pain and tiredness. 'You must realize the difficulty – the danger – of your situation? Through no fault of your own you know things that could destroy us all. That could have us all arrested, tortured, executed. That could endanger our friends and our families –'

'But –'

'I know. It wasn't through choice. But it happened.' Jussi put a long, pale hand to his forehead, rubbed it absentmindedly. 'We have to go on from there. I can't think of any way to protect you but for us to marry. At least then perhaps I can take responsibility for your silence. But – I have to tell you – even that isn't guaranteed to work.' His voice was sombre. 'There are those, you must know it, who simply think that your knowledge is too dangerous to us for you to live.'

She was white-faced. She watched him with lifted chin and in silence. She would not cry. She would not beg. She would not show her fear. She would not! But she could not speak.

'It will give us a breathing space at least.' He shrugged, a little helplessly. 'It's the best I can think of for now.'

She was aware of his weakness, his deadly tiredness. He looked perilously frail.

'Jussi Lavola!' The door opened with a sharp click; Tilda stood in the doorway, hands on ample hips, an expression of not entirely assumed outrage on her face. 'For goodness' sake, what do you think you're doing? Back to bed with you! This minute! Or I'll tell the Russians about you myself!' Behind her Heimo stood, grinning.

Jussi lifted his undamaged hand, laughing. 'Don't be such a bully, Tilda! You know what I am when it comes to a pretty girl! Go take your own dreadful medicines and leave me to mine!'

'Out!' She bustled to him, took his arm to help him from the bed; and for all her briskness she did it with infinite care. 'Out with you! It's a good job August isn't here to see this – he'd wash his hands of you, that he would!'

They left the room. Before Heimo shut the door to lock it after them he sent Katya an amused and not unfriendly wink. Obscurely comforted by the small gesture, she settled herself, thoughtfully, by the window to ponder this strange new development.

They were married a week later in the lofty pine-panelled sitting room of the Heikkala house, with Heimo, Tilda and her husband August, a tall, stooped man with a gaunt but kindly face, as witnesses whilst a returned – and scowling – Kaarlo looked on. The simple ceremony was performed by a trusted cleric dressed severely in black and white. There was neither music nor feasting. The groom's voice was firm, the bride's less so; they did not kiss. Anything further from the kind of celebration that Katya Bourlova might have expected for her nuptials could not have been imagined. The groom was still grimly pale. The unexpected bottle of champagne that Heimo produced afterwards was drunk awkwardly and almost in silence. Then the bride was escorted back to her imprisoning room and the groom was ushered to his bed.

For the first time since her arrival in Kuopio Katya cried herself to sleep that night.

At least, on Jussi's insistence, from then on she was not kept so closely confined. With the ever-watchful eyes of Jussi's friends upon her she was given, more or less, the freedom of the house, which made her captivity at least a little less irksome. Tilda's home was warm and spacious and beautifully kept; not a speck of dust marred polished floors and furniture, the stoves gleamed in their tiled corners as did the pots and pans in the whitewashed kitchen and the shining brass knobs of the wooden doors and the iron bedsteads. The only part of the house that was closed to Katya was August's office and surgery, where strangers came and went without disturbing the peace of the rest of the house. She was not allowed outside. A week passed, and then another. Jussi grew stronger; already he spent more time in a chair in the sitting room than in his bed. With a shock Katya realized that Christmas was approaching. She spoke to Tilda about the possibility of writing to her parents again – perhaps of giving them some address so that they could write back. Even her father's fury, her mother's disappointment would be easier to face than blank silence. Tilda promised to have a word with the others. It was significant, and they both knew it, that Katya had not approached Jussi.

It was in the first week of December, with the initial tentative preparations for the coming festive season being made, that the bombshell burst.

Katya was woken in the middle of the night by raised and urgent voices, quickly hushed. She sat up in bed, straining her ears. A small night-light burned on the table by her bed; grotesque shadows loomed on wall and ceiling. She slipped from the bed, walked on bare and silent feet to the door, eased it open a crack. Kaarlo and Heimo, fully dressed, stood in the hall, outside Jussi's door. Tilda, in dressing gown and shawl, her grey-brown hair loose and untidy down her back, was with them. Jussi leaned in the open doorway, clad in a nightshirt, his right shoulder still bulky beneath it with dressings and bandages.

'One at a time!' he snapped. 'How did you hear this? How reliable is it?'

Kaarlo gestured at Heimo. 'Totally reliable,' Heimo said, quietly. 'There's no question. They don't know who we are, but they suspect – more than suspect – what we are. They're coming at dawn. My informant works in the Okhrana office. It isn't we who have been betrayed – it's Tilda and August. Someone has laid information that they are harbouring terrorists.'

'Then we leave. Now. At once.'

'You can't –' began Tilda.

'We can't do anything else.' Even now, Jussi was gentle with this brave and staunch supporter. Gentler, some remote part of

Katya noted, than he had ever been with her. 'Come. Tilda, we need clothes, food, and the loan of a sledge. Thank God Kaarlo had the sense to go to Pikku Kulda. Kaarlo, the house is stocked?'

'Yes.'

'Then that's it. We go to the forest. Now.'

Kaarlo jerked his head. Katya drew back, alarmed. 'And her?' he asked, the old animosity edging his voice.

Jussi eyed him very levelly. 'She's my wife, Kaarlo. Don't forget it,' he said. 'She comes with us.'

CHAPTER FIFTEEN

Margarita was surprised but not particularly disturbed the first time her brother-in-law Donovalov called upon her. He was not the only man to use what she perfectly well perceived to be the feeble excuse of having been in the area – of 'all but passing the front door' – and of being overcome by a pressing urge to check that Sasha's pretty but presumably unavoidably neglected young wife was not in dire need of assistance or company. Her husband's unattached fellow-officers – indeed even one or two of the indisputably attached ones – remarkably often had the same charitable thought; far be it from Margarita to discourage such gentlemanly instincts. Never in the habit of looking beneath the surface of her own or others' actions and long accustomed to taking for granted the attentions of the opposite sex, it did not occur to her to think it strange that a man who though related to her by marriage had barely bothered to pass the time of day before should suddenly take it into his head to call upon her.

Donovalov perched upon her pretty chintz chair, his tea glass balanced upon his knee. They discussed the weather – there had been a sudden unseasonal thaw in the city and the streets ran unpleasantly with mud and slush, making any but the shortest of journeys all but impossible – and the dying but still delightfully spicy scandal of Katya's elopement. He mentioned neither Lenka nor the children; Margarita, never more than marginally interested in the affairs of her older sisters, barely noticed the omission. Generalities over, and a second glass of tea offered and accepted, he enquired politely and interestedly, if a little unexpectedly, about the possibility that Margarita and her husband might be visiting the estate at Drovenskoye this summer. It was a question that Margarita found a little disconcerting since she always found some difficulty in treading the fine line between her delight at being able to speak in casual vein of her husband's landed background – after all who but she was to know of the impoverished land and the strange, dilapidated house? – and avoiding any direct commitment to going back to a place to which she had no intention of returning except as undisputed mistress. She answered his apparently aimless questions about the family and the estate vaguely and with charming if assumed diffidence. Donovalov, a skilled interrogator, did not bother to pursue the subject too far. He had learned enough; certainly just such a background had bred more than one earnest, pseudo-intellectual would-be revolutionary. As for this silly child – she'd be easy enough to break if the necessity ever arose. He allowed himself one intriguing moment to savour the thought of that before getting up and walking to the sideboard where the little toy theatre stood. 'Charming! How charming! It's yours?'

'Yes.' The odd, veiled and speculative look, indefinably unpleasant, that Margarita had surprised in his eyes had discomposed her; she found herself, for no discernible reason, drawing her lace-trimmed collar a little closer about the low-cut neckline of her dress. The movement drew his eyes and she flushed. 'Sasha bought it for me. I – I make up plays –' The words sounded ridiculously childish in her own ears. Her colour heightened further. Her brother-in-law apparently noticed nothing. 'Charming,' he said again, absently, reaching in through the curtained proscenium arch to touch the tiny figure of the princess, dressed on this occasion in ruby red and sequined gold. 'You mean you write these little plays yourself?' He managed to inject just exactly the right shade of admiration into the words.

'Yes.' Her defensiveness was gone. Eagerly she joined him. 'Mostly, anyway. Fairy stories, you see – often I take fairy stories – embroider them a little, if you see what I mean? – Cinderella – The Sleeping Beauty – but not always. I write my own too.'

'How very clever.'

She shook her head, pleased. Surely she must have mistaken that strange, fearful moment of threat? 'Oh no, not really. But I do love it. I make up plays for Sasha and his friends –'

'Which I'm sure they enjoy immensely,' he interrupted smoothly. 'Sasha must be very proud of you.'

She laughed, the special, pretty laugh that she no longer had to practise. 'Oh I'm sure that half the time he must be bored to death – they all must! But of course they're far too gallant to admit it!'

'Surely not?' He was looking at her directly now, and again she was suddenly aware of that odd frisson of fear. 'Surely nothing you could say or do would bore your handsome husband?' The words were exaggerated, heavily playful; yet strangely she sensed a question; a disturbing question to which she was not certain she knew the answer. 'A man who has someone as lovely – as talented – as you to come home to couldn't possibly be bored.' He left a small, deliberate silence. 'Could he?'

'No.' She laughed a little, annoyed with herself that the sound was uneasy. 'Of course not.'

'And he comes home often, of course?' He had turned back to the theatre, was apparently absorbed in the brilliantly-coloured cardboard figures.

'Yes. Whenever he can.'

'Ah. Yes. Whenever he can.' He nodded. Turned. 'Might I trespass upon your good nature and ask for another cup of tea?'

'Oh – but of course.'

He stayed by the theatre whilst she poured it, watched her as she carried it to him, thanked her pleasantly as he took it. 'Sasha's friends,' he said, turning back to the theatre, 'for whom you perform your little plays – they're his military friends, I take it?'

'Why, certainly.' Margarita looked at him in surprise. 'Sasha doesn't have any other friends. Heavens – he doesn't have time!'

'Of course not.' She was utterly and transparently guileless – in this at least. He allowed himself to acknowledge for a moment what a pity that was. Certainly he would have to look elsewhere for his informant; and for his information. He'd leave this soft-skinned little chicken alone. For the moment, at least. Patently Margarita was not the author of the obliquely-worded note that had brought him here. He could not, however, resist a last sly shaft. He had long ago discovered that a little mischief could sometimes go a very long way. He turned back to the

291

theatre, picked up the tiny figure of the prince, aware of and amused by Margarita's small start of annoyance as he did so. 'A handsome lad,' he said, thoughtfully, and lifted dark, sardonic eyes to hers. 'But something of a scallawag from the look of him. Tell me – does he mistreat his poor little princess? Does he love her truly?' He smiled, gently. 'Dare I ask it – is he faithful to her?'

She was affronted. And, again, indefinably uneasy. She stepped forward and took the tiny figure from him. 'Faithful? Yes. He's utterly faithful.'

'You're sure?'

'Of course I'm sure. I made him up. I invented him.'

'Why, so you did.' The words were mild. 'So you did.'

He left a few minutes later, bowing over her hand.

When he had gone she went to the window, looking down, waiting for him to appear in the street below. Something about the man – something about his quiet, probing questions – had been infinitely unsettling. She heard her own voice, clear and sharp: 'Of course I'm sure. I made him up. I invented him', and then his: 'Why, so you did. So you did.'

Her brother-in-law had stepped out into the filthy slush of the street below. He looked up. She drew back sharply, but not before he had seen her. He lifted his hat in an exaggeratedly, almost mockingly chivalrous gesture. She turned from the window, stood leaning upon the sill, looking at the tiny figure in her hand, the figure with a small, dashing scar upon the left side of his jawbone. *Of course I'm sure. I made him up. I invented him.*

They had had the most dreadful row again last night. About the same wretched thing; the lack of a child. It seemed to her that Sasha had become positively and unhealthily obsessed with the idea, and she had said so. He had stormed out, gone back to the barracks. At least – that was where she had assumed he had gone.

'Does he love her truly? Is he faithful to her?'

Ridiculous. Absurd. But yet?

She replaced the cardboard prince upon the stage, for once did not stand and rearrange the figures, nor carefully redrape the pretty curtains as usually she would. Very thoughtfully she moved to the chair by the stove, dropped into it, fingers drumming a faint abstracted rhythm on the arm. If she for a moment could be brought to believe that Sasha was anything but totally and utterly devoted to her she would, quite simply and quite coldly, wish him dead, she knew it. She would if necessary kill him herself with no hesitation and no compunction. Except that of course there could not for a moment be any truth in such silly speculation, so there was no need to think such nonsense. She was uncomfortably aware that it made much more sense to think about this abominable business of the baby, which was causing so much trouble between them. She had to face it; Sasha was absolutely set upon it. Not for the first time the thought occurred – if Sasha so much wanted a beastly child, then why not have one? She supposed that sooner or later she would have to give in, why not now? Of all things, this was the one that would be guaranteed to tie him irrevocably to her. How remorseful he would be as she suffered bravely to produce the child he wanted so much. She saw herself, beautiful, great with child, valiantly hiding her pain and discomfort; saw Sasha beside himself with guilt and worry, dancing attendance on her, telling everyone of her gallant, self-sacrificing courage. She felt a stir of excitement at the idea. It couldn't be that bad, could it? Everybody did it, after all – even Mama had managed it, and four times at that! And Sasha, then, would truly be hers. She would have his child and he would adore her for it, slavishly and for ever. Cinderella would indeed live happily ever after.

Suddenly bright, she stood, and in a swirl of skirts went back to the sideboard, where carefully and with utter concentration she took out all of the bright characters from the stage of the toy theatre and set about rearranging them in a significant and complicated pattern that meant nothing to anyone but herself.

It was a hard winter at Pikku Kulda. The small house, not much more than a log cabin with a large verandah, scarcely suited to and certainly not intended for winter living, stood on the shores of a lake deep in the forests south of Kuopio. Above all things the memory of those strange months for Katya carried with it the memory of silence; the waters of the lake, which in the summer would ripple and lap against the shores, were petrified to solid, snow-covered ice, the forests were shrouded and carpeted in white. Except when the storms came, whipping the wind and snow through the darkness, battering door and window and wooden wall, the trees themselves stood in glacial silence; no bird sang. They saw tracks – of fox, hare and occasionally of wolf or moose – but those creatures that made them did so soundlessly. Only when Kaarlo took his axe into the woods for firewood did the quiet bowl of the sky ring with noise; even their voices sounded small, lost in the winter stillness.

The cabin had three rooms, the smallest of which, upon arrival, was immediately allocated to Katya by Jussi. It was tiny and all but bare, its furnishings consisting of a simple, low wooden bed, a chest of drawers, a table and a rickety chair. There was a small oil-lamp and a paraffin stove that smelled abominably but without which the room would have been untenable. The furs that served as bed clothes were far from clean but welcome for all that. Not for the first time Katya found herself reflecting upon the bizarre change in her circumstances and the perhaps not so surprising change in values that had accompanied it. A couple of months before she would have thrown a fit rather than sleep in such a room; now it seemed a haven, and above all things she was thankful to Jussi for preserving her privacy.

The rest of the house consisted of a large room which Jussi, Heimo and Kaarlo shared as a bedroom and an equally large kitchen which served as living room and dining room as well. Obviously in the summer most if not all of the living was done on the huge verandah, almost as big again as the house itself, that faced the lake. At this time of the year such a prospect seemed improbable to the point of absurdity; all that the verandah was used for was to stack the wood for the stove and to shelter a battered sledge and several pairs of elderly-looking skis and skates. There were outhouses, including servant's rooms, two water closets, unused in the winter, and, at the lakeside, the inevitable sauna. The main source of warmth was the wood-burning range in the kitchen, and since wood was the most readily available fuel that was where they spent most of their time.

Katya's first problem might, under other circumstances, have struck even her as being funny; it became apparent within a very short time of the party's arrival that here, unlike in the Heikkala house in Kuopio, she was expected to work her passage. And since, after all, she was a woman it seemed natural to the three men to expect her to cook.

'I can't,' she said, flatly.

Jussi's lips twitched. Kaarlo frowned. Heimo paused, a half-open sack on the table in front of him from which he had been pulling cheeses, salted fish and a ham, bread, a bag full of root vegetables. 'What do you mean?'

'I mean exactly what I say. I can't. Cook. I wouldn't know where to start.' She looked at the ancient iron range. 'I've never so much as boiled a saucepan of water.'

'And she's proud of it,' Kaarlo muttered behind her.

She swung on him. 'I'm not proud of it. But I'm not ashamed either. Why should I be? It's a simple fact. Can you play the piano?'

Kaarlo scowled.

Heimo laughed. 'Fair enough, Kaarlo – answer her.'

'No.'

'Why not?'

'Don't be so damned smart.'

Katya smiled, very sweetly. 'Because you never learned. Exactly. So if you want to eat the equivalent of boiled bootleather and stewed socks then force me to cook.'

'We'll eat it to the accompaniment of Kaarlo's piano,' Jussi said, soberly.

'I'll cook,' Heimo said, returning to his sack. 'I'm actually quite good –'

'And modest,' Katya said, carried away by her success against Kaarlo.

'– and Katya can clean,' Heimo continued, placidly. 'How's that for a bargain?'

Jussi could not contain his laughter at the outraged look on Katya's face. 'We can always hope,' he said.

In fact Heimo did indeed turn out to be a more than passable cook, though the fare he provided was on the whole unfamiliar to Katya. When she and her family had summered in their

295

Finnish dacha they had eaten Russian food prepared by Russian servants; now she was introduced to traditional Finnish dishes – mashed potato or turnip baked in the wood-burning oven for a long slow time until it became sweet as a pudding, an egg and fish dish, a favourite of Jussi's, called 'kalalaatikko', the salted Baltic herring that was a staple diet of the people. She began too to notice other things; the difference, for instance, between Jussi's accent and the accents of Kaarlo and Heimo. Questioned, Jussi grinned, and Heimo, good-humoured as always, laughed aloud.

'He speaks Russian with a Finnish accent and Finnish with a Swedish one,' he said. 'Isn't that so, Jussi?'

'That's right.' Jussi was undisturbed.

'Why? Why don't you speak the same as the others?'

Jussi shrugged.

'Because he's an aristocrat,' Heimo said, solemnly. 'Eh, Jussi? And our little aristocrats are brought up to speak Swedish, not Finnish.'

'Were,' Jussi said, through a mouthful of sweet potato. 'Were brought up like that. Not any more. You'll see.'

'When Suomi is free,' Kaarlo said, 'no-one will be brought up like that. Our language will be our own again.'

Jussi rolled his eyes. 'Perhaps in sympathy with coming generations I'll give up the fight after all now I come to think about it.' He grinned. 'All those damned verbs! Words as long as a dictionary! What a language! And the *Kalevala*, Kaarlo – you'll have all the poor little beggars chanting that from beginning to end, will you?'

Kaarlo slanted a dark look at him. 'It isn't funny, Jussi.'

'Everything's funny, Kaarlo.' Jussi was mild as a lamb. 'To one degree or another. Or life isn't worth living.' In that moment his eyes touched Katya's and he smiled; and for one instant she saw that the Jussi Lavola with whom she sat now under such strange circumstances was not so far removed after all from the Jussi she had known in St Petersburg. He believed what he had just said; it was his philosophy. She smiled back. At least they shared something.

Later she asked him about the conversation. 'What was it you said? About a Kaleva-something? Kaarlo seemed quite angry.'

'Kaarlo's always angry, you've surely noticed that?' He was easy. They were washing and wiping dishes. Kaarlo had taken his gun into the woods, Heimo was off on an errand of his own. 'The *Kalevala*,' Jussi said, 'is our national folk epic. Fragments of it have been handed down, orally, through many centuries. In the last century a man called Elias Lönnrot collected the fragments together and published it as an epic poem. It came at a time when Finns needed inspiration, needed an identity. The *Kalevala* gave them what they needed. To someone like Kaarlo to joke about the *Kalevala* is to commit the worst of blasphemies.'

She had stopped wiping, was watching him in open curiosity. 'And to someone like you?'

He appeared not to be disconcerted by her interest. 'As I said: not to joke is the blasphemy to me. It doesn't mean, you understand, that I take things less seriously –' he carefully balanced a plate on the board to drain, flicked her an innocent blue glance '– it just means I get to laugh more.'

That surprised a small gurgle of laughter from her. He grinned approvingly. 'You see? And others get to laugh more too. It's surely better?'

'It's better,' she said.

He turned, leaned against the wooden sink, still favouring his wounded shoulder. 'Why? Why do you ask?'

She reached for a plate. 'Just being a good wife,' she said. 'Isn't that what a good woman's supposed to do? Whither thou goest –' She stopped, hearing the distinct and bitter failure of the attempt at light-heartedness. She ducked her head and would not look at him, rubbing at the plate as if her life depended upon it.

The silence was long, and significant. 'Katya,' he said at last, and his voice was deadly serious, 'I'm sorry. I'm more sorry than I can say. Believe me, if there had been another way – another possibility – I'd have taken it. It was just such damned bad luck your walking in just when you did – I had to do *something*.'

'It doesn't matter,' she said, tensely.

'It matters. It matters to you and it matters to me.'

She lifted her head and turned to look at him. In the past weeks she had lost weight, her face had thinned, her body lost some of its softly-rounded curves. Her soft brown eyes were

297

shadowed, palely ringed from all but sleepless nights and the fair hair that was such a contrast to those dark eyes was loosely pinned away from her face, dirty and untidy as an urchin's. 'It matters to the others too,' she said. 'They don't like me.'

His eyes remained riveted to her face for a strange, long moment before he said with a small shake of his head, 'It isn't that. They don't trust you. You're a Russian.'

'That isn't my fault.'

'No.'

'I'm afraid.' The words came from nowhere, unheralded and unsought, the voice that spoke them small and shaky. 'Jussi. I'm *afraid*! What's going to happen to me?'

'Nothing. Nothing! I promise you.' He had stepped towards her and she towards him with no thought. He caught her to him, hugging her hard and comfortingly, heedless of his damaged shoulder. 'I promise you,' he said again, fiercely.

Silence fell. She trembled against him. Felt his face brush the top of her head. Then, in a single movement, as if at an unheard signal, his arms dropped from around her and she stepped away from him, turning, nearly running across the room to the window where she stopped, gripping the sill, looking through the misted glass to the quiet, magical winter landscape beyond. 'I know it's hard,' he said after a moment. He had not moved to follow her. 'But try not to worry. I'll think of something.'

She nodded, shakily. Knowing that he no more believed it than did she.

The weeks moved on. Kaarlo mysteriously disappeared and just as mysteriously returned a few days later with supplies and two newcomers, who stayed for a couple of days, slept a lot, spoke hardly at all except to Jussi in low, secretive tones and then left.

This was the first of many such comings and goings; sometimes it was Kaarlo that guided the fugitives to them – for that certainly was what Katya felt them to be – and sometimes Heimo. She was not slow to note that those who came with Kaarlo regarded her with rather more suspicion and hostility than did those who arrived with the more affable Heimo. Jussi remained at Pikku Kulda and now day by day his strength was returning.

But spring was coming. There was time yet, the snow still lay deep, the ice thick, the trees bare of green, yet coming it must be. And with it, Katya sensed, a decision would have to be taken, a decision that concerned her above all others and over which she had no control whatsoever. She had served her purpose. With the spring she could become nothing but a liability; her parents, who had not tried the impossible task of pursuing the runaways into the frozen depths of a Finnish winter, would surely question now if no word came. And questions were dangerous. Sometimes she would catch the eye of Kaarlo as he sat, wrapped still in the filthy sheepskin jacket, picking his teeth with the long and wicked-looking knife with which he had threatened Katya in the sledge what seemed a lifetime ago on the bridge at St Petersburg; and more and more often he would look away, unable it seemed to meet her eyes.

Nothing yet had frightened her as much.

It was on a grey day in March as she walked along the frozen lakeside that she overheard a furious argument between Jussi and Kaarlo. They spoke their own language; she could not understand a word, except her own name, repeated more than once by both of them. She drew back into the shadowed woodland as they passed. Gesticulating, intent upon their quarrel, they did not notice her. She saw and heard the fierce anger in Jussi's face and voice, saw too the lack of conviction on Kaarlo's as he listened. At last he threw up a hand, shook his head and said something very short and very sharp. Again, Katya heard her name, understood too the single adjective, that Kaarlo spat as he might have spoken the name of the devil – 'Russian'. Jussi stood tight-lipped and silent before turning swiftly on his heel and striding away towards the house. Kaarlo slouched, watching him go, then turned, shrugging, to make his own way down towards the lake.

A bitter wind blew across the ice-bound countryside. Katya, chilled suddenly to the bone, turned and hurried after Jussi towards the warmth and shelter of Pikku Kulda.

Margarita's last hope – that she would find it difficult to become pregnant – failed signally to be fulfilled. Within three weeks of her reluctant decision she knew herself to be with child.

Predictably Sasha was delighted; equally predictably Margarita took almost at once to her bed. 'I feel so *ill*, Sasha! You simply don't understand.' He hired a girl to come each day – the last one having left in a flurry of tears and high-tempered recriminations when Margarita had slapped her for knocking the theatre scenery askew when she dusted – petted and cosseted her as if she had been an ailing child. She did indeed suffer from morning sickness, a misfortune which was excuse enough to make her pettish for the rest of the day.

Sasha complained not at all; it was enough that she was bearing his child. To Valentina he sent a brooding and heartfelt letter, explaining why he could not see her again; he was unexpectedly mortified when his high-minded impulse came to nothing, the letter being returned, unopened, by Nikita, who had recognized his handwriting and who explained that Valentina had gone from the apartment and had left no forwarding address. So the break was mutual and, he told himself sternly, for the best. Now he must make it up to the suffering, unsuspecting Margarita.

Margarita, actually suffering very little though she would have died before admitting it, settled herself in to enjoy the attention; it seemed to her that given the circumstances it was no more, after all, than she deserved. She was secretly pleased to see how her pale skin glowed, how the initial loss of weight suited her, how her hair shone as she brushed it. Sasha told her she had never looked so beautiful and she knew it to be the truth. Of the birth itself and what might come after she tried not to think. She entertained her mother and her aunt, and various of her friends, declaring herself far too delicate to venture out into the city; others must needs come to see her. Sasha spent every available moment with her, though as influenza struck the barracks he was on duty rather more often than not. For two or three weeks she was almost content. It was a full month before the novelty of this new role started to wear off and boredom began to set in. Another virtually unprovoked loss of control saw the new servant girl leave, sullenly forgoing a month's pay rather than stay a moment longer.

'Good riddance, you lazy little cat!' Margarita was scarlet with temper. 'Go! See if I care! Starve on the streets – that's all you're good for! Be sure you'll get no reference from me!'

The girl gone, the apartment seemed still to echo the sound of the angry voices, the air strung with tension and ill humour. Restlessly Margarita roamed from room to room, picking things up, putting them down, plumping cushions, kicking bad-temperedly at a ruckled rug. In the bedroom she paused in front of a long mirror, eyeing herself, turning sideways, sucking in her stomach. Her breasts were fuller, her belly rounded. She suddenly remembered seeing Lenka pregnant; lumpish and slovenly, dragging her bulk about the house, hand to her aching back. What had she done? What in God's name had she *done*? A wave of self-pity engulfed her. She didn't want this child. She was afraid. She was most terribly afraid.

It was as if the thought opened a floodgate of terror. All the distorted stories she had ever heard, whispered old wives' tales repeated with salacious and lovingly-embroidered horror by girls who in fact knew no better than she did herself, suddenly were there to haunt her. Blood and agony. Death in childbirth. She heard a whimper, pressed her hand to her mouth in case it had been she that had made that small, animal sound. She looked into the eyes of the white-faced image in the mirror; looked away, hating what she saw. A shawl lay tossed across a chair, where she had thrown it the night before. That damned girl! She'd dared to leave before she'd cleared up the bedroom!

She snatched the shawl from the chair, flung open the wardrobe door. The big cupboard was packed with clothes.

She ground her teeth in rage. Rags! Just look at them! All rags! She wouldn't be seen dead in most of them! Just wait – after this – this thing was born – Sasha would have to buy her a whole new wardrobe. Everything! Simply everything!

She had to vent her fear and her temper upon something; she reached in to the deep wardrobe and snatched from its hanger a pale blue dress, ruched and dainty, decked in rosebuds. She tossed it onto the bed. That could go! And so could the red. God Almighty, how had she allowed herself to be *seen* in some of these?

In a sudden irrational frenzy she began to drag the clothes from the cupboard, tossing them in a sprawl of crumpled colour

301

on the bed. A fine blouse tore as she pulled at it; in rage she ripped it, flung the two pieces upon the pile. All her pretty clothes; was this all they had been? Tawdry rubbish? Sasha would have to pay – oh, yes! She savoured the phrase – Sasha would have to pay for a suitable wardrobe for his wife. Mistress of the Drovenskoye Estate. Mother of its heir. She paused for a moment at that, lifted her head; saw a tall, handsome son, who smiled possessively and proudly as he bent to his beautiful mother's hand –

She took a long, slow breath, the fierce fit of energy dying. She pulled another dress from the wardrobe, looked at it, held it to her, pulled a face, tossed it on the heap on the bed. Her side of the deep cupboard was all but cleared. There were still the hats, of course, and the shoes. She would tell Sasha when he came home tonight – it must all go. She pulled the other door. Compared to hers, Sasha's side of the wardrobe was militarily ordered. Two dress suits, two dress uniforms, his slightly shabby and well-worn English tweed jacket, a couple of pairs of trousers, precisely hung. Beneath them, shining shoes and boots, neatly paired, stood as if on parade. And behind them, tucked in the shadows at the back, the battered old leather bag that sometimes he carried when he went to and from the barracks. The catch had been snapped shut awkwardly; a piece of dark, rough material showed. Her curiosity aroused, with not the slightest compunction she reached for it, dragged the heavy bag out onto the carpet, snapped it open. Frowned, puzzled, at what she saw.

A cheap, heavy, worker's jacket. A rough, homespun shirt. Shabby trousers. A pair of well-worn boots. A flat, navy-blue peaked cap. And a creased letter, tucked into the folds of these strange clothes that had no possible place in her husband's bag, in her wardrobe, in her bedroom.

She picked the letter up. It was addressed to Sasha, at the Preobrajensky barracks, in a sharp, impatient-looking hand, and it had been opened. She shook the envelope, pulled out the single sheet of paper, opened it.

Sasha – the new address – I'm sorry, my love – I swore to myself and to the God in which we both know that I don't believe that I wouldn't send it. But you knew I would. Didn't you? Why, oh why do I love you so much? Valentina.

She sat back upon her heels and stayed very still for a very long time. Then, shockingly, she made one small noise, wordless, a savage sound of rage, and smashed her clenched fist painfully upon the floor before silence fell once more.

Sasha got away early that evening. He bought flowers, and a magazine that he knew Margarita liked. Though the evening was dark and the air still cold, spring was in the air; the ice was moving, the first breakers had been upriver. During the day there had been a faint sunshine. He had to go back on duty later that evening, but from the day after tomorrow he had a twenty-four-hour pass. Perhaps he could persuade Margarita to come out for a walk with him – she had no need to be embarrassed – she really didn't show yet.

Whistling, he took the last few steps two at a time, let himself into the apartment. 'Rita? Margarita? Are you there?'

The apartment was apparently empty, and cold. Puzzled, he dropped flowers and magazine onto the table in the hall. The stoves had burned low. There was no light except for a faint lamp light that came from the bedroom. Suddenly apprehensive, he flung open the door. 'Rita? Are you there?' He stopped. She had stood as he entered. Her face was in shadow. It was expressionless, utterly still.

'Margarita? What in the world is wrong?'

She had sat in that room for nearly three hours, waiting. Long enough for cold hatred to fill the vacuum when the fires of fury and pain had died. 'Who's Valentina?' she asked, her voice quiet and firm, as she had planned it. And then, when he did not answer, 'Sasha?' Her control was not as absolute as she had thought; she could not contain her rage. Her voice rose, shrilly accusing. 'Did you hear me? I asked – who's Valentina?'

The words had hit like a hammer blow. He stood, shocked and silenced, knowing his guilt to be written upon his face, utterly unable to disguise it.

She advanced upon him. In her hand she held a crumpled and grubby piece of paper. He recognized it; closed his eyes for a second in an agony of self-castigation. In the name of God! Why hadn't he thrown the damned thing away? Once only had he used it, once only since it had arrived. He had gone one day to see the run-down apartment house where she now lived – where she had moved, he knew, to escape him, despite the later weakening of her resolve. He had gone simply to see it; he had not been able to bear the thought of not knowing where she was, of not being able, in those secret times when he could not keep her from his mind, to fit her into her surroundings, however squalid they might be. He had to know where she was. Like a stupid, love-lorn boy he had stood outside the dismal, dilapidated building, almost the twin of the other, for five, perhaps ten minutes; then he had left. He had not communicated with Valentina.

'Answer me!' Margarita stood very close to him, glaring up at him, face taut and fine-drawn with rage. 'Answer me, damn you!'

'Margarita –'

'Who is Valentina?'

He did not, could not, answer.

She stepped back from him. 'You pig,' she said, suddenly unnaturally calm. 'You disgusting animal. No! Get away from me – don't touch me. Don't dare!' He had stepped towards her, hand outstretched. He stopped as she recoiled from his touch. She shuddered theatrically, white-faced. 'Get away from me,' she said. 'Go to your whore. Do whatever filthy things you do with her.' She saw the flinch of pain in his face that he could not hide, and laughed. 'Filthy!' she spat again. Quite suddenly and absolutely silently tears were coursing down her cheeks. With an oddly abrupt movement she sat down on the bed. For the first time he noticed the chaos around them; the torn and crumpled clothes, the shards of a broken mirror upon the floor. 'I'll never forgive you,' she said. 'Never. Not for as long as I live.'

'Margarita, please – listen to me.' All too aware of her condition, he was frightened by the look of her. Careful not to touch her, he went down on one knee beside her. She turned her head away, refusing to look at him.

'Valentina is – is just a girl I met – a working girl – she means nothing to me – believe me, Margarita – nothing.' He heard the words and he despised himself; an emotion he saw reflected in his young wife's face. Whatever else she was, Margarita was no-one's fool.

She turned, looked coldly into his face that was on a level with hers. 'Oh?' She lifted the paper she still held clutched in her hand. 'Yet she doesn't seem to feel the same way?' She had read it so often in the past hours she did not have to look at it. She kept her eyes steadily and fiercely upon his face. '*Sasha,*' she said, '*The new address – I'm sorry my love – I swore to myself and to the God in which we both know I don't believe that I wouldn't send it. But you knew I would. Didn't you?*' She stopped, watching him. '*DIDN'T YOU?*'

He said nothing.

'This is – just a girl you met? A girl who means nothing to you? A little whore you visit, use and leave? Leave to come home to me – to lie to me – to force me into your bed – to risk my life to have your child?' Her voice was bitter, full of malice.

He did not guard his face. He let her hurt him, let her see she hurt him, in the hope of placating her; in the comfortless hope of absolving himself.

'Then "*why, oh why does she love you so much*", Sasha?' The words were unnaturally quiet, totally at odds with the blaze of her eyes and the trembling of the pale, small-boned hand that clutched the note. 'Why, when she means nothing to you? That is what you said, isn't it?'

He tried to preserve his refuge of silence.

'Sasha? That is what you said?'

'Yes.'

'Say it again.' She leaned to him, her low voice savage. 'Sasha. Look at me and say it.'

He sat back on his heels. Lifted his dark head. In both movements there was an odd submission, a surrender. 'She means nothing to me,' he said.

'But you've – you've known her. Known her body.' It was not a question. 'You've rutted with her. Like the animal you are.'

He bowed his head.

'Sasha?'

He knew what she wanted, knew what she was doing. 'Yes,' he said. 'I've known her.'

'So. It's as I thought. She is a whore, this "girl you met" – this Valentina?'

After a long moment he lifted his head again and met her eyes. 'Yes.'

'Say it,' she said, softly; mercilessly.

'She's a whore.' In the few heartbeats of silence before he spoke her face had hardened further.

'A filthy whore,' she said.

He shook his head, flinching from the words.

'Say it!'

He turned his face from her.

With raging strength she buried her fingers in his hair and dragged him back to face her. Face wrenched in pain, he made no attempt to defend himself. *'Say it!'* she screamed.

'She's a filthy whore.' The words, deservedly, almost choked him.

She twisted her hand in his hair once more, deliberately cruel, before letting him go. 'And what,' she asked then, once more savagely quiet, 'does that make you?'

A coward. As I have always been. As I have always known. A coward. You cannot shame me more than I shame myself. He said nothing.

She stood, moved past him to the door. 'A brute,' she said. 'That's what it makes you. A worthless, faithless, disgusting brute. Get out. Leave me alone.'

'Margarita!' He came to his feet, took a step towards her.

She turned from him, walked from the room across the hall and into the sitting room. He followed, stood by the door, watching her. She walked to the sideboard, swept the small theatre from it with one fierce motion of her hand. The little structure splintered, the tiny cardboard figures flying in all directions. 'Get out,' she said again, her voice rising, a dangerous edge of hysteria in it. 'Do you hear me? *Leave me alone!* Go and play your squalid games with your – disgusting – Valentina –' She was sobbing now, yet managed to invest the word with a grotesque mimicry of passion.

He stood helpless. A step towards her brought another piercing shriek. *'Get out, I say! Get away from me!'*

He went. He stood for a long time, tensely, outside the door listening to the sounds of destruction within; the smashing of glass, the fierce, emotional sobbing. Then he moved slowly down the stairs, shoulders hunched, and out into the chill night air.

It was a very long time before Margarita's passion spent itself. She smashed everything she could pick up, throwing glasses and ornaments at walls and mirrors, stamping upon the remains of her precious theatre, flinging herself down like a child in a paroxysm of rage to beat her fists upon the floor. At last she ran back into the bedroom, threw herself upon the bed amongst the pile of ruined clothes and abandoned herself to loud and ugly sobbing, crying as if she would never stop.

Later, at last, she calmed. She stood for a long while in front of the tall, cracked mirror, looking at her distorted reflection.

A voice sounded in her head, mocking, insinuating. *'Does he love her truly? Is he faithful to her?'*

And: *'Of course I'm sure. I made him up. I invented him.'*

Her eyes were puffed and swollen, her face blotched and unsightly with crying, her hair dull and tangled. She looked with loathing at the swell of her breasts, the firm lift of her belly. She thought of Sasha.

He must be punished for this. Punished and punished and punished again.

In the building next door, in the basement apartment with its discreet side door and its eerie, darkly-curtained rooms lived the woman who had been so understanding – so very understanding – about Margarita's reluctance to become pregnant. She had, so rumour had it, many other skills.

With firm and determined movements Margarita went to her dressing table, opened a drawer, took out a key, unlocked with it another, smaller drawer and extracted a small, chinking bag of coins.

She miscarried three days later. Sasha, sent for by his worried parents-in-law, flew home to the apartment to find Margarita abed; beautiful, transparently pale, patently and appallingly ill, and terrified. His fault. He knew it. Saw it in her eyes as she looked at him, flinched from him, turned away from him eyes from which all fire had flown, driven out by the terror of the

307

moment. She was bleeding badly. The doctor tutted and sent him from the room.

'In God's name, lad.' Victor, waiting in the sitting room, feet astride, stocky form bristling with anxiety and indignation, was gruff. 'What's been going on here?' All the best efforts of Varya and her daughter-in-law Natalia had not been able to eliminate the signs of violence from the room. A broken picture was propped against the wall. A bucket of shattered glass and porcelain stood by the door. The pathetic wreckage of Margarita's theatre was stacked in a cardboard box.

Sasha dropped to his knees beside it, sorting through it, handling the silly, brightly-coloured cardboard pieces as if they had been spun glass. 'We – we had an argument, Victor Valerievich –'

'An argument? Indeed?' His father-in-law looked with lifted eyebrows about the room.

Sasha stood up. 'Margarita was – very upset – distraught –' He stopped as he heard the bedroom door open, the doctor's voice in the small hallway. Both men waited.

'She's to rest.' Quiet Natalia slipped into the room.

'But – she'll be all right?' Anxiously Sasha stepped forward.

His sister-in-law moved a little away from him. The look she sent him was wary. Natalia was not used to the kind of passions that produced a near-wrecked apartment and – it surely had to be deduced? – a miscarriage. She was uncomfortable with them. 'Yes. The danger is past. She's lost a great deal of blood and she requires careful nursing, but the doctor thinks she'll be all right.'

'May I see her?' Sasha was humble.

She cast a small, sideways glance at him. 'I'll ask Varya Petrovna.'

Margarita lay exhausted upon her pillows. Had she known the terrors of the trial she had brought upon herself she would never have dared to undertake it; but it was done, and triumph was hers. With a small sigh she turned her head from Sasha's desperate and guilt-ridden face and settled herself to sleep, the sound of her mother's voice in her ears.

Sasha Kolashki spent the following few weeks neglecting his duties in order to scour St Petersburg for the best designed, most splendid and beautiful toy theatre that the city could produce. On the day that, not without qualms, he presented it to his recuperating wife, the same day that she offered him the first ghost of a smile since Valentina's name had fallen between them like a sword, he swore, with every best intention, never to see Valentina again.

'Why Pikku Kulda?' Katya and Jussi were sitting on the verandah, well wrapped but appreciating the pale sunshine. 'What does it mean?' Through the trees the still ice-fringed lake glimmered.

'It means –' he thought for a moment '–"little darling" – "sweetheart" – literally, "little gold one". It was my grandfather's nickname for my grandmother. He built this place for her. It was their retreat. She loved it.'

Something in his voice drew her eyes to him. 'What happened to them? Your grandparents?'

'My grandfather was exiled to Siberia, and died there. My grandmother was never strong. Grief killed her.' He spoke with little emotion, but she did not miss the narrowing of his eyes as he looked out across the quiet vista of lake and forest.

'I'm sorry.'

He shrugged. 'There's no need to be. It's hardly your fault.'

'Kaarlo would say it was. I'm Russian.' She turned on the bench to look at him. 'Or am I? I am, after all, married to a Finn.' Her voice was very quiet.

He turned his head. The silence that fell between them was neither inconsequential nor empty. Neither looked away from the other. In these past, strange weeks a friendship – a companionship – had grown between them that neither would deny, and that the others, even Kaarlo, had come to accept. What had begun as an enforced intimacy had grown into a true enjoyment of each other's company. They joked and they argued, she had asked to be told more of this unknown struggle in which she had found herself so unexpectedly embroiled, and with quiet and unexpected passion – and the unasked help of Heimo and Kaarlo – he had told her. Despite the odd circumstances – perhaps even because of them – a camaraderie had grown between the four of them, marred only by Kaarlo's obviously ingrained though at least now marginally less obvious distrust of her.

And then, yesterday, all had changed.

She had seen him naked, and with a shock that had been like a blow she had wanted him. And he had known it.

The three young men had gone to the sauna – a habit that Katya, in this still freezing weather, had resolutely refused to acquire. Her bathing was done, amidst much on the whole good-natured grumbling, in decent privacy and warmth before the big stove in the living room, the men excluded firmly for the duration. The Finnish passion for steaming themselves into a stupor in order to shock themselves awake by plunging through the broken ice into the bitterly cold waters of the lake struck her as being mildly demented, to say nothing of masochistic, and nothing the others could say would persuade her. Usually she stayed within the house whilst the peculiar communal ritual took place; yesterday however, in the first of the spring-like sunshine, she had been walking on the lakeshore, delighting in the fresh green that showed where the snow had melted, the amazing delicacy of growth that in defiance of the still freezing temperatures was beginning to appear. In a few weeks, she knew, the lakeside would be a tangle of wild flowers – coltsfoot, buttercup, harebell and clover, marguerites turning their pretty faces to the sun. Later there would be lilies on the lake and the tall spikes of Rose Bay waist-high beside the water. And where, as these flowers greeted the summer beside the stretch of water she had come to know so well, would she be? Deep in her own thoughts she had hardly heard the shouts, the splashing, the strong male voices of the others as with whoops and laughter they had fled like high-spirited boys the small, log-built sauna and leapt naked into the waters of the lake. Some minutes later, still thoughtful she had come from the trees and there he had been – tall, slender, winter-white as marble, the pucker of the healed scar dark and still a little inflamed upon his smooth shoulder, his skin slick with water, fair head glittering as he laughed in the sunshine. As the others had splashed and shouted in horseplay in the water he had seen her. And had known, she was certain of it, the almost frightening shock of physical desire that had jolted through her at the sight of that bright body. She had turned and all but run from him. Neither had mentioned the incident. Yet now, eyes locked, it was in both their minds, and both knew it.

'Married to a Finn,' he repeated, softly, as if testing the words.

'And yet – not married at all,' she said.

He smiled.

She was finding it oddly difficult to breathe normally.

'This isn't the time,' he said.

'No. I know.'

'I have nothing to offer.' He waved a hand, encompassing the cabin, the lake, the countryside surrounding it. 'I'm committed.'

'I know that too,' she said. And then, 'But so am I, aren't I? You married me, after all – it was legal, I assume?'

'It was legal.'

'The winter's over.'

'Yes.'

'Something has to happen. Something has to change.'

'Yes.'

'Would you let me leave?'

The silence was a thoughtful one. 'Yes.'

'You trust me? Not to betray you all?'

'Should I?' His eyes were very bright.

'Yes.'

'Then I do.'

'And –' She could sustain that clear blue gaze no longer. She looked down at her clasped hands. '– And – if I don't want to go?'

This time the quiet lasted so long that she was forced to lift her eyes to his again. He was watching her intently. 'You don't have to be afraid of Kaarlo,' he said, carefully.

'I'm not afraid of Kaarlo.'

He smiled. Put out a hand.

She took it. 'One thing.'

'Yes?' The other two were coming. They could see them toiling along the track from the lake, fishing tackle in hand, the enticing gleam of silver glinting from the basket Heimo carried.

'That night – in St Petersburg – when I came –' She stopped, blundered painfully on. 'You know – you can guess? – what had happened to me – what I'd – what I'd done?'

He nodded. 'It isn't important.'

'It is.' She had been struggling with this ever since yesterday, ever since that strange, irrevocable turning point had been reached. She had to say it. 'Jussi, I may not be a wife. But I'm not a virgin either.'

He grinned then, half at her, half at the other two as they called from the edge of the clearing. His hand was hard and warm and reassuring upon hers. 'It's a wicked world we live in, my Katya,' he said. 'Who is?'

She was still laughing as Kaarlo heaved a basket full of small fish onto the wooden verandah. 'Come on, woman,' he said, unsmiling, but with a glint in his dark eyes that was not altogether unfriendly, 'you've shown us often enough that you've got a fishwife's tongue – let's see what you can do with these.'

That afternoon the soldiers came.

Almost they were taken by surprise, for so long in this winter fastness had they felt themselves secure. One moment the peace of the forest was undisturbed; the next there came the faint jingling of harness, the equally faint but unmistakable crunch of feet upon the still-frozen mud of the track that led to Pikku Kulda.

'Jesus! Russians!' Kaarlo, sitting upon the verandah whittling at a piece of wood with his lethal-looking knife, leapt to his feet. Through the tall bare trunks of the woodland distantly a flicker of colour showed, and the dull glimmer of metal. As Kaarlo spoke Heimo appeared, running, gesticulating as he came.

'In! Get in!' His low voice was urgent.

Kaarlo had grabbed Katya's arm, was dragging her with no ceremony through the door to the darkened interior of the house. Jussi grabbed the chairs in which they had been sitting, all but threw them after them, frantically scraped with his boot at the fresh woodchips Kaarlo had left on the boarded floor.

'Russian soldiers!' Heimo was holding onto the verandah rail, gasping for breath after his sprint through the forest.

'How many?' Jussi was still clearing the verandah of the all too obvious signs of life – the ancient book Katya had been reading, culled from a shelf in the living room, his own fishing tackle that he had been mending.

'Not many. But enough. And armed to the teeth. What in God's name are we going to do?'

'Get inside. Shut the door.'

They stumbled into the darkness, slammed the door behind them. Katya stood like a statue in the centre of the room, Kaarlo's arm about her waist, his knife at her throat.

'For Christ's sake, Kaarlo!'

'She's a Russian,' Kaarlo said, and did not move.

There was a moment of tense silence. Jussi tensed; his hands came up.

'Jussi, no!' Heimo moved between them. 'God Almighty, are we to kill each other before they even get here?' He jerked his head at the door.

They all heard the sharp call, the whinny of a horse.

'Kaarlo, let me go.' It was Katya, her voice very quiet, very reasonable. 'I can talk with them. I can make them go away.' Only the faintest tremor betrayed her fear.

The knife pricked her throat.

'Kaarlo!' The warning in Jussi's voice was fierce.

'Hello? Hello the house? Anyone there?'

'We'll fight them off,' Kaarlo said.

'We can try.' Heimo's voice was grim.

'Please! Kaarlo, believe me – I can get rid of them. At least I can try!' Braving the knife, Katya turned her head.

'Let her go, Kaarlo.' Jussi's voice was flat, totally devoid of emotion. 'Harm her and I'll kill you.'

Kaarlo lifted a bitter face. 'Well you would, wouldn't you? You're besotted. You have been from the start. You think I haven't known?'

Katya threw a swift, startled glance at Jussi. His face had not changed. 'Let her go.'

'She's a *Russian*! She'll betray us without a thought –'

Jussi launched himself. Katya, seeing it coming, threw herself to one side. The two men went down.

'For God's sake, you two!' Heimo reached for the struggling men.

Katya slipped past him to the door, opened it and stepped

through, shutting it firmly behind her. She blinked in the light, pushed a hand through her dishevelled hair, straightened her bodice a little, smoothed her skirts.

The silence that her appearance had imposed upon the gathered men in the clearing lasted for a full and valuable minute. Long enough for her to gather her thoughts, to take in the scene before her. An officer, young, fresh-faced, inexperienced-looking, sitting his horse, fur-lined cape draping its flanks. Perhaps a dozen fierce-looking, moustachioed soldiers, booted, great-coated, fur-hatted, stamping their feet, pulling off gloves, blowing upon their hands. A sense of impatience and of boredom. A great many weapons, slung across shoulders, tucked under arms. The young officer carried a pistol, unholstered. 'Goodness, Captain,' she said, laughing a little, yet keeping a little hauteur in her voice and in her level glance. 'I don't think you'll need that.'

The sound of her unmistakably educated and equally unmistakably Russian voice threw him completely. He stared. Coloured. Hefted the weapon uncomfortably in his hand.

Katya laughed again. Behind her, through the door, she felt rather than heard a crash. Brightly and briskly, chin high, she stepped forward, offering her hand. 'Yekaterina Mikhailovna –' she allowed herself to hesitate a little, willed a blush '– Lavola. How may I help you?' She was as composed as if it had been a St Petersburg salon.

The young man scrambled from his horse, removed his heavy gauntlet. Took her hand, bowed over it. 'Stasski. Captain Branislav Stasski. At your service, Madam.'

'Captain.' She inclined her head gracefully. Almost she could have laughed at the look on his face. Almost. She waited, politely enquiring.

'Yekaterina Mikhailovna – forgive the intrusion.' The young captain glanced around him, bemused. 'We have information –'

She allowed her eyebrows to climb a little.

'– information concerning a certain nationalist terrorist group –'

'I beg your pardon?' She allowed a chill to creep into her voice.

'Of course I realize –' His voice tailed off. One of the soldiers nearby coughed, none too delicately, swung his hands across his torso, thumping them to restore the circulation of his blood. As Katya glanced at him he hawked, and spat. Here was one who was not impressed by a gentle voice and an upper-crust accent.

Katya made a small, impatient gesture with her hand, 'Captain, I appreciate that you have a job to do – but terrorists? Do I understand you to mean –' she paused, as if searching for the word '– assassins? Here? At Pikku Kulda?'

'N-no. Of course not. That is – not here, especially. But in the area. We were told to check, to discover if there might be anywhere where fugitives might be sheltered. Some have been traced to hereabouts.'

This time Katya allowed her laughter to peal into the cold quiet. 'Shelter fugitives? At Pikku Kulda? Why, Captain, look for yourself – there is scarce room for the two of us, let alone for –' she laughed again '– for *fugitives*? By all means, search the outhouses if you wish. Climb the trees. Drag the lake. Who knows what you might find? Fugitives indeed! Captain, I may be married to a Finn, but I am a true Russian, as is he. Long live the Tsar! You'll find none of your fugitives here.'

Still he looked uncertain. The soldier hawked again. Spat again. His eyes roved the clearing.

'Now,' Katya said, glinting a sudden laughing glance, moving a little further away from the cabin as she did so, 'if you were to abandon this silly story of terrorists and tell me that you were in the pay of my papa – then I'd believe you!'

The young captain showed every reasonable sign of bewilderment.

'Tell me, have you been in Petersburg this winter?'

'Why yes. At Christmas.'

'And had the scandal already died?' Again her look was arch, laughing. 'The Bourlov heiress and her Finnish Count?' She waited.

He thought for a moment. Then, 'Oh, good lord! You're –'

'Yekaterina Mikhailovna Lavola,' she murmured and dropped a sketchy, mocking curtsey. 'As I said. And truly, Captain, do you think my husband and I have had nothing better to do this winter than to shelter fugitives?'

He laughed with her, his acceptance of her story instant and unreserved. 'Many apologies Countess. If I had known –'

'If you had known you might have told my father,' she said. 'But now it is too late, for we plan to return to the fold anyway. So – you have uncovered one set of fugitives, but sadly I cannot help you with your more important task. Now, may I offer you and your men tea? You have time, I think, before getting back to the village? Though –' she lifted her head, sniffed the air '– the weather is far from settled. Even at this time of the year a blizzard can set in with very little warning.'

He lifted a hand. 'No. We won't impose upon you. We have good billets in the village, but it's a long march. The sooner we get back, the sooner the men will be satisfied. I apologize, Countess, for the intrusion.'

She nodded her head politely. Her knees felt absurdly weak.

He pulled on his gauntlets, walked to his horse, took the reins from the waiting soldier.

'And, Captain?'

'Countess?'

She smiled beguilingly. 'I can trust you to keep our little secret? In a month or so we'll be back in Petersburg. I should like to keep our whereabouts a surprise until then?'

'Of course, Countess. Of course.'

His very expression belied his words. Katya had every confidence that within days the world would know the whereabouts of Jussi Lavola and his impulsive bride. Safe. She was safe. It was an extraordinarily odd feeling. She smiled. 'Thank you, Captain.'

She watched them out of the clearing, the men shuffling behind their well-mounted officer. At the edge of the clearing he turned, lifted a hand. She waved brightly back. When the last man had disappeared from view she turned to the house.

The door stood open.

Suddenly trembling, she walked slowly to the steps, climbed them, went on into the shadowed room, walked unthinking into Jussi's arms, open and waiting for her, hugging her, fiercely and possessively. For a very long time no-one spoke.

'We have, I think, another fighter for Finland,' Jussi said at last, over her head.

'For Suomi,' Kaarlo corrected him. His nose was bleeding.

'I had quite forgotten,' Katya said, her voice muffled by Jussi's none-too-clean sleeveless sheepskin jacket, 'that I had become a Countess. It seems after all that I must be my father's daughter. I find I rather like the idea. You'll not get rid of me now, Jussi. Don't dare try.'

INTERLUDE: 1913–1914

Katya and Jussi returned to face the music of St Petersburg late in the spring of 1913, and were received by her father, to no-one's great surprise, with the relief and celebration so often reserved for prodigals.

Anna heard of the runaways' return in the summer, in a letter from her mother that arrived confirming the arrangements for Anna's long-planned trip to St Petersburg.

Three days before the arrival of the letter, Guy suffered a severe stroke.

She sat at her husband's bedside, the letter in her hand, her eyes upon his face, usually so lean and so vital, now thin, pallid and distorted with the paralysis that drew down one side of his mouth and made his left eyelid droop. Beyond the window a soft summer shower drenched the garden, misting its glowing colours, drifting through the heavy verdant canopies of the trees. 'A letter from Mama,' she said, softly.

He attempted a smile. She steeled herself to smile back, not to betray her own pain at the sight of his. He could not speak, not yet, though the doctor was hopeful. His good hand squeezed hers.

'Katya's come home, complete with husband and – to Mama's intense disappointment I suspect – no child. There goes the winter gossip out of the window! Katya was, it seems, simply being Katya after all and livening up a dull world with a bit of outrageous behaviour. Now there's to be a "proper" wedding – all the trimmings, all the expense – and as usual she's achieved the best of all possible worlds! Dmitri, Natalia and the children are well. Margarita is recovered, though sadly there seems to be no sign of another child.' She saw the flicker in his open eye and hurried on, 'She says nothing of Lenka.' She sighed a little. 'I wonder why she doesn't answer my letters? I had so hoped –' Her voice died. His hand squeezed hers again. Gently she reached to smooth the silver hair from his high forehead. 'Are you comfortable? Do you need anything?'

His head moved very slightly upon the pillow.

'I'm not tiring you?'

Again the small, negative movement.

'Mama speaks of my visit. I shan't go, of course. I shan't leave you. No!' He had made a small, protesting movement with his hand. 'No! Absolutely not. I shan't go, and you won't make me. It's out of the question. We'll go to St Petersburg when we can go together.' A small smile glimmered upon her tired face. 'I can't trust you – how can I leave you?' Her voice was gently scolding. 'When you're better, then we'll both go.' She forced brightness into her voice, firmly suppressed misgiving. 'Now, would you like me to read the paper to you?'

She fetched the paper, settled down again in the chair. War in the Balkans again – Bulgarians and Serbs, Greeks and Turks, all at each others' throats. The dangerous antagonism of Muslim and Christian, the even more dangerous tangles of alliances and ententes, the desperate weakness of a dying empire. She read with only half her mind concentrated upon the content. She had not realized how much she had been looking forward to seeing her family again. To seeing the new generation, the children she had never met, who knew little or nothing of their Aunt Anna who lived in the strange country of England across the sea. To Dmitri's and Natalia's children she sent presents on Name Days and birthdays; to Lenka's also, though she suspected they never saw them. Certainly she had never received a single word of thanks or acknowledgement. Poor Lenka evidently nursed her grudge still. If she could have seen her – met the children – the children, again. She remembered the flicker of pain in Guy's eye as she had mentioned Margarita's childlessness. She did not know how he knew, but he knew. They had never discussed the matter of children. Yet somehow he had sensed that in this past year or so her own longing for a child had been the single grief in a happy – a very happy – life. And now – too late. A price she had always known she would have to pay for her precious marriage to this most precious of men.

But – if he died? What then would she have of him but memories?

'The woman who threw herself under the King's horse has died. What a strange thing to have done. Does she really believe that such actions will influence Parliament to give the vote to women? They choose to fight with strange weapons, these women. Though the new law that allows them to be rearrested after they have recovered from their hunger-striking is harsh I think. Whatever else they are, however misguided, one cannot doubt their courage. I don't think I'd have it in me to do such brave and painful things.'

The good side of his mouth twitched a little. The one, bright blue, intelligent eye glinted. How could he bear it, this silent prison of flesh in which he was trapped? What would he do if the none-too-confidently predicted improvement did not materialize? She could not bear to think of it. Briskly she rustled the newspaper. 'The editorial is about the Irish troubles – you'd like me to read it to you?'

Later, the rain stopped, she wandered the soaked garden, rubber boots squelching in the mud, the hem of her skirt sodden and disregarded as it flapped about her ankles, in her hand the inevitable pair of secateurs. The air was fresh and beautiful. She worked her way through the rosebed, letting the simple task of deadheading distract and calm her mind and emotions. Once she turned towards the house, lifted her hand in greeting, in case he might be watching. Rain shimmered upon the rosebuds like diamonds upon the smooth skin of a beautiful girl. She thought of Katya and her strange escapade, and smiled a little. She would write to her cousin. Perhaps she could persuade the newlyweds to visit her here? What fun that would be, and some recompense for the disappointment of not being able to go herself to St Petersburg after all. Next year. She would go next year. Guy would grow strong again – he would, of course he would – and they would go together. If they travelled slowly and with care he could manage it, she was sure. Anna was young still, and in the young hope truly springs eternal.

Guy did indeed improve, though he walked with a shuffling gait and a stick, the clear voice was hesitant, a little blurred, his words slow, and the left side of his face sagged, marring the fine, patrician looks. In the year that followed he fought his own battle with a quiet courage and determination that surprised Anna not a jot. By the following spring he was indeed as recovered as he ever would be, and dignity and that gentle delight in life were his again. But there could be no question of his undertaking the journey to Russia, and they both knew it.

Resolutely she refused to leave him; as resolutely he insisted that she should. But then reports began to reach the outside world of violent unrest in St Petersburg, of marches and demonstrations, of strikes and barricades, of confrontations between unarmed workers and the Tsar's all-too-well-armed army. There was talk of incitement, of *agents provocateurs*. There was talk of revolution. Since Guy's illness, Anna had continued the pleasant habit of reading *The Times* to her husband each day; but increasingly as that hot summer progressed, as the bees bumbled in business-like fashion about the splashed colour of Anna's herbaceous border, as friends came and went and long, lazy afternoons were spent in discussion and in making music, the news became steadily worse. Not just Russia, but the world in turmoil.

It was in June that a Serbian student discharged the bullet that was to send the world to war. In the tense and confused weeks that followed there could be no question of travelling to Russia. In July the Austro-Hungarian Empire declared war on Serbia; Russia immediately mobilized her troops along the German border and Germany declared war on Russia and her ally France. It could only be a matter of time before the conflagration spread to the rest of Europe; optimistic souls thought still that Britain could remain aloof.

But at the beginning of August – a month given in memory to holidays, to sunlit mornings and hot, dreaming afternoons, to laughter and the roll of waves upon a beach – Germany marched into all-but-undefended Belgium and the flames of war took hold. As guarantor of Belgium's neutrality, Britain could not stand by and see her crushed. The youth of a nation rushed to join the fun, fearful it would all be over before they got there. Singing, they marched to war.

In that strange quiet time after they had gone, when the

321

country watched and waited, Anna received two letters. One was from Katya; a strange letter, guarded and somehow, Anna felt, oddly unforthcoming when compared with her cousin's usual warm and impulsive outpourings. Katya and Jussi it seemed had returned to Finland. There had been some trouble with the authorities, who had not appreciated the fact that Jussi was not burning to become an officer in the Russian ranks. It would blow over. Meanwhile Katya offered no address, but promised to write when she could.

The second arrived a day later and was from her brother Dmitri. Like Katya's it had taken more than a month to reach her. The contents stunned her.

Her father and her Uncle Andrei, on their way to the shop on the Nevsky, had been caught up in a violent demonstration. The soldiers had come. The killing had been cold-blooded and indiscriminate. Victor and Andrei had been caught first in the crossfire and then in the charge that had cleared the street. Victor had died at once, shot through the head. Andrei had died a short while later, with a Cossack bullet in his lung.

BOOK THREE
1914–1917

CHAPTER SIXTEEN

The shock of the deaths of Andrei and Victor on that sultry July day in 1914 was a blow that so numbed the Shalakov family that, for a time at least, they were shut both from the seething intrigues of the city and from the increasingly dangerous concerns of the world at large. The tragedy was hardly to be comprehended. During that tense and scorching summer such violence had become alarmingly commonplace in St Petersburg; but how could it happen that two quiet, law-abiding men could be ridden down in cold blood, slaughtered where they stood, with no compunction and for no reason? As the city lay in an all but exhausted, heat-induced torpor beneath copper-coloured skies and the drift of smoke from vast fires that blazed like omens of evil to the north in the forests of Finland; as rumours flew; as one report followed fast upon the heels of another concerning the assassinations in Sarajevo, the righteous anger of Austria, the threat to Russia's ally Serbia, the Shalakovs mourned, confused and isolated by shock and by grief, their personal tragedy overshadowing for them all the significance and hazard of outside events. But not for long could this hold true; for as they grieved Europe moved, slowly and steadily, towards bitter conflict. On the day that the crowds gathered on the streets of the city to cheer their country's official entry into the communal mania of a war that was to encompass the world, Varya was lying, as she had for days past, in a darkened room in her sister's home overlooking the Fontanka, deep in the drugged sleep that was her only refuge from terror and an unventable fury that those around her understandably mistook for inconsolable grief. The touching and spontaneous demonstration of the following day outside the Winter Palace, when ten thousand people fell to their knees, the national anthem lifting from ten thousand throats, at the sight of their Tsar and his family upon the palace balcony, was reported to her by an excited Margarita – the first of the family to realize that momentous happenings were afoot and to recover her equilibrium enough to want to partake in them – but made no impression. Even when, some days later, her son Dmitri received his papers as part of the country's mobilization for war the fact barely registered with Varya. Victor had dared to leave her, alone and defenceless. The foundations of her world had been swept away; the structure that was left was fragile indeed, and Varya had little or no time for the troubles of others, large or small.

A wave of patriotic fervour swept the city; the name that had been proudly borne for two centuries was abandoned, judged to be too Germanic. Whilst Varya slept and her family woke to realize the enormity of the events which had overtaken them, St Petersburg overnight became Petrograd. The clamour of protest that during that sweltering summer had come so very close to the articulate roar of revolution for the moment died, smothered, as a flame might be smothered, by the blanket of need to unite in common cause and against a common enemy. Almost the entire Opposition in the Duma, with the exception of the Social Democrats – Bolsheviks and Mensheviks alike, sworn enemies though they were – declared its support for the Government and the war. Mother Russia was threatened; as always, her sons and daughters would defend her to the death. The streets filled with endless columns of soldiers, khaki-clad, stoic-faced, marching to the stations where waited the long requisitioned trains that would carry them to the front to face the enemy. Beside them often walked the wives, the families, the mothers and the sisters, tear-stained and valiant, wishing their menfolk 'Godspeed and a safe return', and blessing their Little Father, the Tsar.

Meanwhile, those that had kindled the flame of revolution that had come so close to causing an inferno now bided their time, tended the spark that still glowed, and waited.

Whilst poor bemused Dmitri, torn so unexpectedly from his little family, remained, for the present, in Petrograd for training, Sasha was one of the first to go to the front. A combination of ill luck and bad management saw him on a train south just three weeks after the declaration of war. Margarita, dressed in a becoming new outfit for the occasion, was at the station to see him off. Quite overcome by excitement she cried prettily, noted with pleasure that her husband was beyond doubt the most handsome of the young officers waiting to board the train, and assured him and herself that the newspaper just that morning had prophesied that the war would last no longer than six weeks. She then visited her mother and Aunt Zhenia, enjoying, in the absence of much interest from her mother, the sympathy of her aunt, before going home to her toy theatre with its new cast of dashingly uniformed men and their brave and valiant women.

Sasha, wrapped in unusual silence in a corner seat of a carriage that had turned immediately into a vodka-drinking card school, sped south-west, towards East Prussia, and a place called Tannenberg.

He had not known that such terror existed; had he known, would certainly never have believed it to be endurable. The anticipation was bad enough – the night before his first action he lay awake, exhausted with fear, his stomach like foul water, his head throbbing from the vodka with which he had vainly attempted to drown the abject and degrading terror that he found himself, to his disgust if not to his surprise, entirely incapable of controlling. And then, harrowingly, he found that the reality of battle was worse than the worst of his imaginings. After the first brief experience of coming under fire he knew with certainty that he would never be able to face it with the courage or fortitude – or the sheer bravado – that so many others showed. Before, during and after action, in his flinching imagination he died a thousand times, and horribly. He simply did not have it in him to endure the nightmare in which he found himself. He hated it all, from the bottom of his soul; the barbaric, earsplitting noise of the bombardment, the wicked, slicing chatter of the machine guns, the snipers' bullets that sang like vicious insects about his head, searching, he always felt, for bone and for blood; the truly awful effort entailed in leading his men out of the comparative safety of their bunkers and trenches into the field of fire, the field of death, that awaited them, and him. And – almost the worst thing of all – he knew beyond doubt that they knew it, these men whose lives were entrusted to him; they recognized his cowardice – for that, undoubtedly, was the only name he knew to put to it – and despised him for it, some of them openly. Yet not even that humiliation could stiffen his backbone; he could not face the carnage, the dreadful threat of death, could not harden himself against the madness and the suffering around him. During the first deceptively successful push into East Prussia – successful only because German arms and efforts were at that moment concentrated upon Belgium and France on the Western Front – Sasha found himself in the field, leading men for the first time. On the second day the non-commissioned officer walking beside him was obliterated by a shell, nothing left of the living man, whom in fact Sasha had detested, but ragged and bloody flesh and bone and one boot, ridiculously all but undamaged, the foot still in it. Sasha leaned from the saddle, gagged and was sick. Again and again he was sick. A young officer with whom he had been drinking the night before caught at his horse's reins, hauling him along beside him; 'Ride, Sasha, ride on! Don't think of it.' But how could he not? Then, and later in nightmares, until other, far worse images took its place? He found himself incapable of courage, even of the spurious kind that showed itself in the recklessness, often vodka-inspired, of many of his young fellow-officers. Friends died about him, and his fear, his terror of death, grew like a cancer within him. It was worse still after the initial advance – characterized from the start by a military ineptitude that on occasion amounted to crass stupidity – ground to its inevitable halt; for then, slowly and relentlessly, the reinforced German army led by Marshal Hindenburg outwitted and divided the Russians and began to push them back – back across those rivers, through those same fields and forests for which so many men had needlessly died, and in which the bones and the ruined flesh of man and horse still lay, stinking, half-buried in the churned and defiled earth like so much discarded offal. Sasha was haunted by the thought of pain, hag-ridden above all by the fear of dismemberment, of becoming one of those screaming wrecks who shrieked their lives away in the blood-spattered hospital tents or in the night-dark horror of no-man's-land, too far from friend, too near to foe, to be helped with a kindly bullet or blade.

The German advance picked up momentum. Two entire Russian army corps surrendered. Their General, helpfully, committed suicide. The Tsar and his Administration pontificated, from well behind the lines. In Sasha's section – and not only there – the ordered retreat became a rout. Sasha abandoned his men who had been ordered to defend a heap of stinking rubble on a totally indefensible mountain track, and fled openly at last, urging his tired horse away from the merciless guns and bayonets, the marching feet and the grim, battle-hardened faces, away from the threat of death, of mutilation. He was fortunate that he was not alone. One man's panic-stricken collapse hardly showed in an army in full retreat. He joined a party of Guards officers who, cut off from their units, were making for the railway. Nothing was left of the early Russian successes; weeks of carnage had gone for nothing. The Tsarist army had lost three hundred thousand men.

The Russian forces were regrouping, overrunning a small town the name of which Sasha never bothered to discover. The title of this nameless, faceless shambles of a place in which he found himself did not concern him; he had one obsession, and one only. And within hours of arriving in the chaos of a fragmented and for the moment defeated army, dirty, hungry, and determined, he had located the salvation for which he looked.

General Alexis Nicholaev Sevronsky had known Sasha from childhood; indeed it had been in the drunken company of the General's son that Sasha's brother Grigor had met his end. It had been Alexis Sevronsky who had secured for Sasha his inappropriate captaincy in the Preobrajensky, one of the Tsar's own crack regiments of Guards.

And the General was here, in the chaos of the retreat, making concise and efficient arrangements to evacuate himself and his staff to his distant cousin the Grand Duke Nicholas's general field headquarters, known as Stavka, in Baranovici, in the safety of the middle of the Byelorussian countryside, well away from any further uncomfortable prospect of action. Sasha went to him ready to beg; in the event such a self-betrayal proved unnecessary. In an army in which who you were and who you knew had always counted for more than military valour, knowledge or experience, the General was more than happy to add the son of his old friend to his personal staff. The boy was a handsome lad, a good hand at the card table and a splendid rider; what else could one ask? Brusque messages were sent to Sasha's commanding officer, another old friend of the General's, and the deed was done. Within twenty-four hours Sasha Kolashki was on a train heading north to safety, carrying within him a quite ferocious determination never to approach a field of battle again. Despite the defeat in East Prussia the news from the south and from Poland was good. The Allies were holding in the west. Confidence was still strong; Britain, France and Russia between them would defeat the Hun in weeks, then they could all go home and get on with their lives. Until then, Sasha had contrived to ensure his own safety.

Margarita heard the news of her husband's new appointment in a letter that arrived some few weeks later, and was far from displeased about it. To be attached to the personal staff of a General related to the Grand Duke Nicholas himself sounded very grand indeed; she wasted no time in spreading the news. The first hard frosts of the winter had arrived; the snow would not be far behind. The river slowed, muddily, and froze, the icebreakers crashed upstream to keep the waters open for as long as possible. By the time Sasha's letter came the optimism that had invested the city had dissipated; no-one thought any longer that the war would be over before Christmas. But then, reasoned Margarita, with all those poor young men being killed at the front, and with Sasha having access to the ear of a real live General, who knew what might happen? There was nothing like a war to advance a young soldier's fortunes, even she knew that. She studied newspaper pictures with care and designed several bright new uniforms for her favourite tiny cardboard character.

Dima, home on a short leave before being sent to the front, shook his head at his wife's question. 'No, my love. I won't be home for Christmas. Don't set your heart on it. Go with the others to Aunt Zhenia's. Or perhaps to Sofia Petrovna's?' This last was spoken hesitantly.

Natalia, at the sound of her mother's name, shook her head. 'She doesn't like the children, Dima, you know she doesn't. She says they make her head ache.' Calmly she ironed, folded and packed, as if her heart were not breaking, as if the joyous secret she had kept from her husband had not become a lead weight upon her spirit. At her feet little Natasha played, fair-haired and blue-eyed as her Aunt Margarita, whilst at the table solemn Nicholai doggedly attempted the intricacies of a simple wooden jigsaw puzzle. Dima watched his small, composed, brown-haired wife helplessly. Since childhood he had loved her; there were no words to tell her how much. And as for the children –

He bent and picked 'Tasha up, throwing her in the air, making her squeal. Natalia stopped for the briefest of moments, watching them, then she turned her back, busying herself again. 'I truly don't know what you do with your socks, Dima – do you chew them to produce such holes?'

He smiled wryly from behind his daughter's uninhibited giggles. 'The food we get, I might as well.'

It did not occur to Dima to complain. Like so many of his countrymen he was a fatalist; like all of them, he was a Russian. He did not want to leave his home, his much-loved wife and family, but his country called and he must answer. It had always been so. The needs of his small family must be submerged beneath the needs of the larger family that was his country. The Tsar, father of his people, asked it. These past weeks had not been so bad, stationed as he had been close to St Petersburg – Petrograd as it now was, though he could never remember to call it so – but the time had come now for him to leave. So leave he must, and it did not occur to him to question that. He bent to stand his small daughter upon unsteady legs. Last week an agitator had appeared in the camp; leaflets had been passed from hand to hand, the man had appeared and disappeared, talking to small groups, whispering, inciting. Dima supposed he must be a brave man; for certainly he would have been shot had the authorities caught him. In the end there had been no need; the men themselves had tired of him and taken it upon themselves to throw him in the river and leave him to freeze or to sink. A separate peace with Germany, he had preached. The overthrow of the men who perpetuated this filthy war; a capitalist's war, nothing to do with the needs and lives of the workers; a war to preserve the rich and their riches, a war fought with the blood and the guts of the underdog to keep the underdog down. Dima had understood not a half of it. Things were as they were, and that was it. He needed no upstart Bolshevik to tell him that he was closer to a German worker than he was to his own officers; how could that be? A German worker was a German; Dima's officer, however young, however arrogant, was a Russian, and the argument ended there. He swung his young daughter onto his shoulders and galloped clumsily about the small room. Natalia ducked her head and ironed a shirt for the second time, rubbing with painful vigour at nonexistent creases. Nicholai scowled beneath lowered brows at both of them, then diligently applied himself to his jigsaw.

Christmas came, and Christmas went, the first of the war, subdued and quiet. The Tsar in his wisdom had banned all sales of alcohol for the duration of hostilities; not an edict to which many paid much heed, except in public, but one that certainly affected the more common places of entertainment. The first, fragile successes of Russian arms were celebrated privately, and with a confidence born of a lack of understanding. In the field, though it had yet to be fully demonstrated, the Tsarist armies were ill-equipped, ill-led, and ill-founded. All that the Tsar of All the Russias had to expend was men, souls counted in millions. And, for the moment obedient, those souls fought like demons, and like demons were destroyed in the fire.

Varya was living, more or less permanently, at her sister's house on the Fontanka. Nanny Irisha, with the far from princely sum provided for her in Victor's will, had been pensioned off to her somewhat reluctant family in a village near Moscow. Strange, she had bitterly informed anyone who would listen, were the ways of God. Seraphima had been given simple notice to quit.

Delicate and lovely in her mourning – for black, as she knew, suited her well – Varya, with drooping head and bravely held back tears, tyrannized the household. Wartime shortages notwithstanding, her delicate appetite must be tempted. Frail and desolate as she was, she could not be expected to take part in the bandage-rolling sessions that Zhenia organized, nor the fund-raising activities, nor the hospital visits. Her indisposition however did not prevent her from holding court with friends and family in Zhenia's small private sitting room, that Varya with steely enterprise had taken firmly and indisputably as her own. She held always a delicately-embroidered, lace-trimmed handkerchief, snowy white, with which to dab at her still-lovely eyes each time the names of 'my precious, martyred Victor' or 'poor dear Andrei' could be produced, or when bewailing – as she did at length and with pious resignation – her poor widow's lot.

Lenka, inevitably, was the first to lose patience with her.

'Mama, for heaven's sake! Anyone would think that Papa had got himself killed just to spite you! It's been seven months! There's a war on! I know it doesn't make it any easier, but people are being killed all the time!' Why not Donovalov? The thought was never far from her mind. Please, God, make him die. The thought was as automatic as a 'bless you' after a sneeze. 'Don't you think you should try – just try? – to go back home, to manage the shop – at least to attempt to pick up the threads? You'll never feel any better while you sit here doing nothing but brood and eat those damned chocolates!'

Zhenia, sitting behind her sister, a heavy woollen balaclava taking shape beneath her competent hands, cast a wryly amused glance at her niece but held her tongue.

Varya lifted a pale, affronted face. 'Brood, child? Whatever can you mean? My health is not good, that cannot be denied – but then what else could be expected in the circumstances?' The pretty handkerchief fluttered, dabbed. 'But brood? I don't think that's at all a nice word to use to your poor mother, do you? It does smack so of self-indulgence.' Her eyes, sharp and clear, lifted challengingly to her daughter.

Lenka sighed, and looked away.

The long lashes drooped, triumph hidden. 'Of course, if I felt for a moment that I were a burden, if I felt there were no room for me here –' She turned her head a little, veiled gaze still on Lenka, but inclining head and body towards Zhenia.

On cue, resignedly, Zhenia shook her head. 'Of course not, Varushka.' The words, despite effort, were brusque. 'Don't be silly. There's a home for you here for as long as you like, as you well know. Didn't you ask Mischa the self-same question just yesterday?' It was a small barb she could not resist. 'Lenka dear,' she added, mildly, 'do you think you could persuade Tonia to put down that pretty thing she's taken a fancy to? I wouldn't normally mind, but it is Fabergé, and a particular favourite of Katya's.'

Heavily Lenka turned. Varya averted her eyes from her daughter's untidy bulk. 'Tonia,' Lenka said, sternly, but with a caressing note in her voice that was used for no-one but this first-born daughter, certainly never to her small, placid son, 'put it down, little one. It's very fragile.'

'I won't break it.' The child, thin as a rail, freckled and with a mop of marigold hair that her Aunt Anna, had she ever seen her, would have recognized, scowled.

'I know. But Aunt Zhenia thinks you will.'

Adversity, Zhenia reflected ironically, had taught Lenka little of tact.

'And since it's hers, I suppose you should put it down, don't you?'

The child, still scowling ferociously, replaced the gleaming crystal thing upon the table, but reluctant to leave it she clasped small hands behind her back and leaned forward, studying it, rapt.

'What is it?' Lenka asked. And, as she so often had been, Zhenia, watching, was struck by the rapport between these two. The look on Lenka's face, whose very structure was lost now in rolls of fat, was intent, almost hungry, as she watched the spare, small figure of her daughter.

'It's a little tree. It has apples. And golden pears.'

'And a little bird.' Relenting, Zhenia set her knitting aside and went to join the child. 'Would you like to hear him sing?'

'Yes.'

Zhenia waited, glancing at Lenka.

Lenka said nothing.

'Yes what?' Zhenia asked, mildly.

The child lifted her small, pinched face. The wide pale eyes held an intelligence – no – Zhenia groped for the word – an awareness far beyond her years. 'Just yes,' she said, flatly. And would, Zhenia knew instinctively, have sacrificed tree, bird and life itself before she said more.

'That child,' Varya said, clearly and coldly, 'has the manners of a peasant.'

Zhenia was winding the tiny golden key.

'What a pretty thing.' Margarita who, bored almost to tears, had been standing by the window looking down onto the frozen canal, wandered across the room, her interest caught. 'Fabergé, you said?'

'Yes.' Zhenia was watching Tonia. The child stood, still and intent, listening to the sweet trilling of the bird, her rapt face free of its usual fierce scowl. 'Lenka, I swear your little Tonia is getting more like her Aunt Anna every day!'

The effect on the child was startling. She threw back her head like an animal suddenly challenged. Stepped back from Zhenia and Margarita. Turned fiercely to her mother.

'No, Tonia,' Lenka said. 'You're nothing like your Aunt Anna.'

There was an odd and indisputably awkward silence. Only Margarita was apparently unaware of it. 'That reminds me,' she said, almost absently, still watching in fascination the tiny jewelled bird that warbled so musically, 'I have a letter. From Anna. I keep forgetting to tell you. It came last week.'

'Last week.' Zhenia looked at her in exasperation. 'Last week? Is it too much to hope you've brought it with you?'

'Of course I have. Well, at least –' Margarita was scrabbling in the small wrist-bag she carried. 'Ah, yes. Here it is. Would you like to hear it? It doesn't really say much.'

Zhenia picked up the little tree, clicked it to silence with a sudden sharp movement, and placed it back upon the table. 'Yes, Margarita. We'd like to hear it.'

Margarita shook out two pages of flimsy paper. Screwed up her eyes a little. Read rapidly and with little emphasis.

Dearest Rita. Love to you and to everyone. How I miss you all in these bad times. It's dreadful, isn't it, with the war taking so many lives, not to be able to speak, to clasp hands, to reassure each other? I pray each day for Sasha and for Dmitri. I trust they both are safe.

She might, from her tone of voice, have been extending her sister's greetings and hopes to a flock of chickens.

Lenka shifted heavily in her chair, the smallest sarcastic smile twitching at her lips. No-one, not even Anna, could bring themselves to pray for Donovalov.

I keep abreast as much as is possible with what is happening there with you. Guy has a contact in the Embassy in London – a very kindly man, Count Boris Stelyetsin – who keeps us informed, and of course the papers here keep us in touch with our allies in this war against the German aggressors. There were pictures the other day, of a patriotic march upon Nevsky Prospekt. I have to admit that it was such a shock to see that familiar street that a tear came to my eye. I searched and searched to see if any of you were there, though I knew as I did it how silly I was being!

For ourselves, sadly, the news is not good. Guy's health is slow to improve – if I were honest I would admit that it does not improve at all. I have taken on most of the responsibility for the business, which is no trial I assure you, and keeps me busy, which is a blessing. There's war work as well of course though down here in the country, where we spend a good deal of our time, that seems at the moment to consist of little but what the vicar's wife calls 'our little sewing bees' and a constant speculation as to where and when the first Zeppelins will raid. I and Robert (our gardener, a dear good friend) are very busy destroying our extravagant and pretty flower garden in order to plant vegetables. I hope you there in the city (isn't it strange to think of dear Petersburg as 'Petrograd'? I can't seem to get used to it at all!) won't be subject to too many shortages if this beastly war drags on?

Darling Rita, I hope all's well with you. Sasha seems to have done well for himself – Boris says that to be at Baranovici with the Grand Duke is to be at the very heart of the Russian war effort. In England the spirit is very good, though no-one now thinks it will be easy. But we will prevail, our two countries together, and then your loving sister Anna will be back to kiss your cheek and hold your hand and laugh as we used to. Much love to all the family – is there any news of Katya? I haven't heard from her for months. Is she with you in Petrograd, or has she gone with Jussi to Finland? – and please give Mama a hug and a kiss from me. I know how difficult a time it's been for her. Tell her I'll write very soon. Love too to Lenka, and to the children, and to Dmitri, 'Talia and their small brood. Just think, a whole tribe of children who've never met their Aunt Anna! Pray God the war ends soon and we can be together again.

Margarita was reading very rapidly now, scant interest in her voice.

Much love and God's true blessing on you all, Anna.

Briskly she folded the paper.

Varya's pretty handkerchief flickered. 'Poor Anna.'

'Why is she poor?' Margarita's mouth was set in a small, sulky line. For some reason the letter from her sister, with its breath of events and concerns beyond the snowlocked confines of war-constricted Petrograd, had unsettled her. This reading had produced again, as it had when first she had read it, a small, indefinable stirring of restless resentment that she found herself hard put to explain. 'Why is she poor?' she asked again.

'In a foreign land. Far from her family, her home. And at such a time!' Varya was indignant.

'England, surely, is her home now?' Zhenia, used to her sister's irrational outbursts, pulled upon the bell cord. 'We'll take tea, shall we? Of course it's her home. She doesn't sound unhappy.'

'Of course she does! She's missing her family! It's apparent in every line she writes!'

'We're all missing our families.' Zhenia stood, collectedly tidied her knitting. 'It's part of the burden of war. Even having Katya just such a short distance away in Finland is a far greater worry than it normally would be. It's strange. War seems to have made distances greater. And bonds more loving.'

337

Lenka shifted her bulk in the armchair. Her face was expressionless. Margarita had wandered back to the window, stood looking out, taking no further part in the conversation. She had a photograph at home, that Anna had sent her, of her sister's house in the place called Sussex. A rambling, pretty house, not grand like a palace nor forbidding or romantic like a · castle, but a small, flower-set jewel of a house, a dacha in a lush, tree-filled countryside. And they had an apartment in London, overlooking the city's river Thames. London! And she'd been to Paris. Several times! And to Florence, and to Rome – poor Anna indeed!

'Trust Anna,' Lenka said, 'to be able to worry about us all at a very great and very safe distance.'

'Of course she's worried about us!' Varya failed entirely to hear the heavy sarcasm in Lenka's voice. 'Of course she is! What better daughter, what better sister, could anyone ever have asked for than Anna?'

Adages about absences and fond hearts, Zhenia thought, wryly, could truly have been coined for Varya.

Inconsequentially, tired of the conversation, noting only the grating sound of her sister's voice, so familiar and so wearing, Margarita found herself wondering suddenly if Lenka knew of the visits that Pavel Petrovich Donovalov had taken to paying to the tiny apartment behind the Liteini Prospekt. The recollection brought the usual small tremble of unease. The man had the strangest eyes. He sat, drank tea, asked after Sasha. Asked all the time after Sasha. But that wasn't why he came. She knew it. No man came to that apartment simply to ask about Sasha. And for every second he was there those awful eyes watched her. Made her feel – she lifted her head sharply, pushing the thought away.

'What better sister indeed?' Lenka asked, quietly.

'I still think,' Zhenia said, moving her chair a little closer to the stove, clearing a space around the samovar for the tea glasses, 'that your little Tonia is her very image. Varya, don't you remember Anna at that age?'

The small, tinkling crash arrested them all. Tonia stepped back, hands clasped firmly behind her back.

With a sharp cry Zhenia stepped forward, dropped,

shimmering striped skirts billowing about her, reached out a hand, withdrew it.

The tiny bright shards of crystal glittered upon the carpet. The little bird lay still and silent.

'I'm sorry,' Tonia said, expressionlessly. 'I dropped it.'

Katya moved, for what seemed like the hundredth time, from the dark window to the stove and then, within a moment, back again, plain woollen skirts swishing about the tiled floors. 'You're sure he said today?'

'Today. He said today.' Kaarlo sat apparently unconcerned, the inevitable knife, needle-sharp, in his hand, paring his nails. His dirty stockinged feet were lifted to the warm stove.

'Then where is he? Where in the name of God is he?' All day she had contained herself, all day she had told herself to remember the circumstances in which Jussi travelled, not to pin her hopes on that one laconic message. Today, he had said; but that could mean tomorrow, or the next day, or – chilling, unthinkable thought – never. 'Where *is* he?' she repeated, urgently, more to herself than to her companion.

Kaarlo shrugged. 'Could be anywhere between here and –' he caught himself, glanced at her '– and the coast. At least we know he got across the ice. Don't worry. Jussi will make it.' His reassurance was not personal, bore no warmth. It was a statement of fact. In Kaarlo's eyes the day that Jussi failed would be the day the world collapsed and burned to a cinder.

Katya stood for a little while longer looking out into the darkness.

'Draw the blinds,' Kaarlo said. 'Close the shutters. You'll draw their attention.'

'I'd rather put out the lights.'

The young man moved impatiently. 'Put them out then. But don't stand there like a bloody beacon attracting every sodding Russian soldier within miles to the door.'

Without comment she extinguished the lamps. She was beyond responding to his provocation. She took her stand by the darkened window again, renewed the litany that ran in her head like weary feet on a treadmill. *Dear God, let him be safe. I'll give anything, do anything, just so you make him safe.*

339

*Please. Don't take him from me. I'll do anything. Anything.
I'll go to church – I'll* build *a bloody church. With my bare
hands. But please! – don't let him come to harm.*

'Is there tea?' Kaarlo asked.

'In the kitchen.' She did not turn. Her voice was calm.

He muttered something.

'Make it yourself,' she said, crisply.

She remembered, suddenly, the first time she and Jussi had
made love. Turned restlessly, walked to the stove again, stood
looking at the pretty shining tiles that surrounded it, colourless
in the darkness, yet gleaming in reflected light.

Walked back to the window. *Jussi! I hope you're listening,
in that daft head of yours. I'll never forgive you if you let
yourself be killed. You hear me? I'll haunt you. Oh, Lord!* Even
in such extremity, amusement lifted at the nonsense of such a
notion. *I'll force you to haunt me. There! You won't enjoy that,
I promise you!*

'Where's the blasted tea?'

'Where the blasted tea should be. In the blasted box on the
blasted table.'

She remembered other times, other lovemaking, beside the
lake. In the lake. She remembered their bodies, shining and cold
and slick with water. She remembered too the blithe and happy
St Petersburg nights, after their return to the city, before the
coming of war had blighted everything and catapulted Jussi still
further into this dangerous game he insisted on playing. She
remembered the graceless deceptions, the shared laughter, and
above all the love. The silly, astounding, frightening love. She
had not known it was possible that one's whole happiness, one's
very life, could rest in the hands of another. *Jussi, you stupid,
brainless idiot of a man – where are you?* She couldn't trust
him to take care of himself, that was the problem. The stories
Kaarlo had told! By God, she'd kill him – if he walked through
the door at this minute, she'd kill him!

In the deserted street beyond the window, beneath the low
overhang of the eves of one of the painted wooden houses, the
shadow of a shadow moved, cast a goblin shade upon the snow
for a moment and was gone. She narrowed her eyes, trying to
probe the darkness. Kuopio lay in uneasy silence beneath its

winter shroud. At the outbreak of war all pretence that Russia was not an occupying power had been abandoned. The Finnish Parliament – the Diet – had been summarily dismissed. Russian troops had been billeted everywhere. The Tsar's Secret Police were suddenly much in evidence. Finland's own young men had not been mobilized into the Russian armies, for their Russian masters did not trust them, and with good reason. Yet these same young men were not, on the whole, to be found at home twiddling their thumbs; some indeed were not to be found at all. Under the darkness of the bitter northern winter a secret war was being waged. Shadows slipped through the silent forests, in ones, in twos, in threes; the swish of skates was heard upon the misty, frozen lakes and rivers. Ski tracks appeared and were blown away before morning. Bridges fell. Trains were derailed. The odd Russian soldier, unwise enough to wander the apparently deserted forest alone, disappeared. Information was passed, quietly, from ear to ear beneath the very noses of the ever-suspicious Russians. Letters were sent, and cryptic telegrams, many from Stockholm where so many Finns had friends and relatives; it was natural, was it not, to communicate with such in times of trouble? Jussi had made three trips to Stockholm in the past four months, taking the perilous but apparently well-organized route across the ice of the Gulf of Bothnia, slipping through the Russian guard at night and striking out across the white wilderness of frozen ocean to Sweden. She did not know the purpose of these trips, though recently she had begun to suspect, and neither Jussi nor any of the others had chosen completely to confide in her; she was, after all, a Russian still. Jussi's light-hearted declaration that what she did not know could not worry her did not fool her; the one thing she had had to come to terms with very early in their life together – the one thing that, tartly and with clarity, her sister-in-law Elisabet had taken quite unnecessary pains to point out to her on their return to St Petersburg – was that his love for his country would always outweigh his love for her. That particular passion was too long-held to be superseded by another. He would die for her, she supposed, if it were necessary; but not as readily as he would die for his country. It was a knowledge with which she lived day and night, a constant companion, a crow perched heavily upon her shoulder waiting for any chance to peck at her brain.

And now, today, he was due back, back at her side, safe for a few short weeks.

But he had not arrived.

A glimmer of light caught her eye. She leaned forward. Lit by guttering torchlight a patrol of Russian soldiers was coming down the road towards the house. They looked huge, great bears of men in their greatcoats and fur hats, their heavy boots trampling the fresh fall of snow. The winter windows were in; she could hear nothing. Tensely she stood and watched them come. Their long rifles were slung across their shoulders, collars were turned up; grotesque shadows stretched and capered upon the snow.

Kaarlo appeared at the kitchen door, silent and watchful.

On they came, a dozen or so men, straight towards the house.

Her hands were cold, and clenched to fists. When she tried to relax them she could not.

Even as they trudged on past the house, without so much as a glance in the direction of the window where she stood in darkness, she still could not hear anything. The double panes, as always, worked well, keeping out sound as well as cold. She took a breath, her first for several long seconds. And then she saw it – again, a shadow amongst shadows – a movement, sensed rather than seen – a fleeting glimpse of a tall, familiar figure, hunched and shapeless in fur.

'He's coming,' she said, nervelessly calm. 'He's gone round the back. Open the door, Kaarlo.'

Moments later he was there, in the room, cold-flushed, very much alive, grinning, shaking off the frozen furs, his arms about her, cracking bones, before she could exclaim at the bloody gash on his forehead, the dirty, reddened bandage on one of his hands. She clung to him in total silence, feeling him, breathing the scent of him, her face crushed against the filthy shirt, hearing his heartbeat, wanting quite simply never, never to let him go. She heard the quick exchange, in their mother tongue, above her head between Jussi and Kaarlo, understood a little – for difficult as it was she was learning his language – cared nothing in that moment for what they said. Until this moment she truly had not realized how very much she had feared for him. Dear

God, was that what happened? Was it to become worse each time?

'Well, chicken, what's this?' Gently he put her from him, looked down into her face. 'Tears?'

'Of pain,' she said, collectedly. 'You nearly broke my back, you great clumsy Finn.'

'The company is set up?' Kaarlo was saying.

Jussi was looking at Katya with clear, pale, searching eyes. 'It's set up,' he said, almost absently. 'Yes.'

'And – the raw materials? The consignments are getting through all right?'

'Of course they are. I told you they would. Our friends are nothing if not efficient.' The steady eyes had not moved from Katya.

'What happened?' Kaarlo asked.

'What?'

'Your head, numbskull. Your hand. Did you cut yourself shaving?'

'Ah. No. A skirmish, that's all. Nothing serious.' He smiled a very little. 'Not for us, anyway.' Jussi lifted a dirty hand and touched Katya's face, a fleeting, almost tentative touch. 'Kaarlo. I have a suggestion.'

'What's that?'

'Go.' The bright, tired eyes, turned suddenly to his friend, took the edge from the word. 'I'll see you tomorrow. You'll hear everything then, I promise. It's been a very long day. It's been several long days as a matter of fact. I need rest.'

Kaarlo pushed himself away from the wall. Dark eyes flicked sardonically from Jussi to Katya and back again. 'Rest,' he said, straight-faced. 'Yes. I can see that.'

'Out, Kaarlo.' Wearily Jussi reached for Katya, rested his face for a moment on her soft hair. 'Someday I'll do the same for you.'

For a moment longer the other man stood, then he shrugged and reached for the filthy sheepskin jacket that had more than once tempted Katya to a bonfire. 'Unlikely,' he said. At the door he paused. 'Just reassure me,' he said. 'All's well?'

Jussi's look was level. 'All's well. I promise you. There are still –' he paused '– reservations. No, Kaarlo!' The other man had turned, hands outstretched. 'I'll not discuss it tonight! Tomorrow. Tomorrow will do.'

'The separate peace shit?'

Tired, exasperated, Jussi ran his hand through too long hair, dirtied and tangled by the wearing of his battered fur hat. 'Yes. Of course. Be reasonable. They have to try.'

'And us? What about us?'

Calmly Jussi let Katya go, stepped towards his friend. 'We are where we always were, Kaarlo.' A long arm shot out, a bloodstained, grimy hand gripped an equally grimy collar. His smile was wide and friendly. 'Suomi is the nut in the cracker. The cheese in the mouse trap. The scorpion – under – the rock.' As he spoke he propelled the other man, twice his bulk if not as tall, into the kitchen. 'Any help we might receive –' he paused by the table to pick up Kaarlo's hat and set it gently upon his head '– will not be because we are lovable, nor because we deserve it, nor because there is a just God in his heaven, but because we are useful. And at this moment –' he pinned the unresisting Kaarlo to the wall beside the back door, let go of his collar to button his coat '– it is our good fortune to be, potentially, more useful than ever before.' He stepped back. 'Off you go, Kaarlo. And pray for our Little Father the Tsar. Pray harder than you've ever prayed for anything. Believe it or not in that precious, stubborn, stupid man lies our salvation. Now, out!'

Grinning, Kaarlo quite deliberately reached up and ruffled Jussi's already wild hair, not avoiding the crust of blood that split the hairline. Jussi could not prevent himself from flinching away. Kaarlo bunched his fist, crunched it none too gently into the other man's chest. 'Till tomorrow, then.'

'Till tomorrow. And remember – pray for the Tsar.'

Kaarlo's reply, perhaps fortunately, was beyond Katya's grasp of the language.

'One day,' she said quietly into the silence after the door had shut, 'I'm going to feed rat poison to that man.'

'He'd thrive on it.' Jussi turned. In the comparatively bright light of the kitchen she could see now just how awful he looked. There were deep shadows beneath his eyes and at least a day's growth of beard on the lantern jaw. The weal upon his head showed dark, the skin blue-black about it.

Ignoring the turning of her heart Katya surveyed him with lucid exasperation. 'What in the world did I do,' she asked the ceiling, thoughtfully, 'to deserve this?'

He thought for a moment. 'Must have been something pretty bad.' Neither made a move towards the other. Yet as their quietly smiling eyes met a warmth filled the simple room about them, as close and as intimate as a touch.

'Look at you.' She took two small, graceful steps into his arms, laid her head very lightly upon his chest, her lifted arms about his neck. 'I wouldn't give you houseroom if I weren't married to you.'

She felt his laughter, through his body. Felt his exhaustion too.

'I suppose I must award the returning warrior the prize he most desires?' She tilted her head to look at him.

His arms tightened about him. 'Sounds reasonable. Even promising.'

'It's a shame it's so small.' The tone was innocence itself.

He waited, refusing to rise to the bait.

She cupped his rough chin in her two still-soft hands. 'The sauna,' she said. 'You're a Finn. I'd go so far as to say that you're the most Finnish Finn it's ever been my misfortune to come across. Surely the first thing any good Finn would want under the circumstances is a sauna? It's ready. It's been ready all day.'

For the barest moment he allowed her to suffer. Then he bent to kiss her. 'Second,' he said. 'The sauna comes second.'

They made love on the couch beside the stove; not fiercely, as she had so often imagined in his absence, but in a manner that suited the tenderness, and in Jussi's case, the exhaustion, of the moment. It was a slow and lovely act of joining; lying in the darkness, Jussi's head a dead weight upon her breast, the reflections of the snow-world beyond the window glimmering upon the ceiling, Katya found her face wet with tears, her emotions such a tangle that she could not herself discover if they were of happiness or of sorrow.

Later she bathed the nasty cut on his head and tended the wound on his hand. He brushed aside her questions. While he took his sauna at last she cooked fish in creamy egg sauce,

345

checked on the pan of *ternin maito* that baked gently in the oven, filling the air with its spicy cinnamon smell.

'God in heaven. I leave a Russian termagant and come home to a Finnish housewife.'

She turned. He leaned in the doorway, dressed in a shabby bathgown, the shaggy, too-long hair damp and clinging to his head, his fair skin flushed and shining. His face was full of amusement.

'Not in the least,' she said. 'I'm a Countess, remember? I've had three maids and five footmen preparing this feast all day. They were going to wait at table too, but I decided you were too disreputable to be seen. One must always put on a show for the servants, you know. Your head's bleeding again.'

'Is it?' He put an absent hand to his forehead, winced a little as his exploring fingers did indeed come away stained with blood.

'Sit down. I'll plaster it for you again. It's that damned steam. I'm sure it must be awfully bad for you. Almost certainly thins the blood.'

He sat down, flinched a little beneath her brisk ministrations.

'Don't say it. As a nurse I'd make a good vet. Kaarlo's already told me.'

'What else has Kaarlo told you?'

The movement of her fingers stilled for a moment, then busied again. 'Not much. You know Kaarlo.' She stepped back. 'Jussi – you have to trust me, you know. Sooner or later.'

He smiled, very gently, put out his hand to link his fingers with hers. 'Yes. I do know. But later, Katya, later. For now, can we not simply enjoy the moment?'

She leaned to kiss him lightly. 'And the food. I'll murder you if you don't enjoy the food. I've been practising for weeks. It's the only thing I can cook.'

'I'm starving. I'll eat anything.'

'Really?' she smiled, sugar-sweet. 'How very flattering. I find that I wish I'd cooked you whaleblubber. I'll bet you didn't get that in Stockholm?'

They made love again later, upstairs beneath the sloping eaves in the big, comfortable bed that Katya had dressed with the crispest and prettiest linen she could find, and this time their loving was fierce, savage and not in the least light-hearted. Afterwards Jussi lay for a very long time, sprawled across her, so still that she thought he must have gone to sleep where he lay; but at last, with a long-drawn breath he rolled off her, onto his back. She felt him stretch, settle himself into the feathers of the mattress with a sigh that was almost a groan of pleasure. His hand reached for hers and she took it, holding it lightly with both her own, resting upon her breast. Silence settled about them. His breathing was regular and quiet. But yet she knew he was awake.

'Jussi?'

She sensed his hesitation, the temptation to feign sleep. 'Yes?'

'You haven't been to Sweden, have you?'

His stillness held a different quality now. He withdrew his hand, gently. 'Yes. I have.'

'But not only to Sweden.' It was not a question.

The bedclothes rustled a little as he moved. 'No. Not only to Sweden.'

She waited, but he said no more. 'It's Germany, isn't it?' she asked at last, very quietly. 'You've been to Germany.'

She felt movement again, saw the faint pale oval of his face in the darkness above her as he leaned on his elbow to look at her. 'Yes,' he said.

There was a very long silence.

'Katya,' Jussi said, 'listen to me. We've tried the others – you know it. We get sympathy. Understanding, even. We get words. Kind words. Soft words. But we get no help. Both Britain and France agree that Finland should be independent; but they'll do nothing – nothing! – about it. They'll not move against their ally, nor do anything to weaken Russian arms. Very well; we understand that. But this is our war too. And in war, friends and allies are where you find them. Katya, a whole generation of our young men have never served in the Russian army; we have no training, no military skills, no weapons. The Germans have agreed – are on the point of agreeing – to raise, arm and train a battalion. A battalion of young Finns. To come back to fight for Finland. For her independence.'

'But, Jussi! – the Germans? We're at *war* with the Germans!'

She saw the faint movement as he shook his head. 'No, Katya.' His quiet voice was grim. 'We are not at war with the Germans. The Russians are at war with the Germans.' He lay back upon the pillows. There was another long silence. 'The enemy of my enemy is my friend,' he added, at last, softly. 'And I will use any weapon he puts into my hand.'

'The "company",' she said. 'The – "raw materials" that Kaarlo spoke of?'

'We are negotiating under cover of a company set up in Stockholm. The raw materials are the men we're smuggling across the ice to Sweden, and thence to Germany.'

Later still, lying wide-eyed in the darkness she said, 'Why did you say the Germans are on the point of agreeing? Has something held it up? Was – was this what Kaarlo meant – a separate peace? Between Russia and Germany?'

'Yes.' She could tell from his voice that despite his exhaustion he was no nearer sleep than she was herself. 'If the Germans could close down the Eastern Front with separate peace negotiations they could concentrate their whole might upon the Western Allies. Until he loses all hope of that the Kaiser won't risk the Tsar's good will by arming insurgents behind his back.'

Katya thought of Dmitri, of Sasha, of other young friends and relatives under arms in far places. 'And is it likely to happen?'

'A separate peace? No.' Jussi's voice was positive. 'No, Katya. While the Tsar lives the war will go on. And Germany will arm and train our Finnish Battalion. I'm certain of it.'

'And – this battalion will fight? Fight against the Tsar's army?'

'Yes. The battalion will come back to Finland and will fight.'

'And – you'll be a part of it.'

'Yes. Of course.'

'Yes. Of course.' She echoed his words in a soft, desolate voice.

He reached for her, drew her to his shoulder, stroked her hair. It was a very long time before either of them slept.

CHAPTER SEVENTEEN

Dmitri Shalakov was killed in the summer of 1915, during the disaster of what became known as the Great Retreat, as the Tsar's battered armies were pushed inexorably from the line of the Eastern Front deep into the heartland of Russia. Dima's family never discovered the manner of his death, nor where the human remains of the young man whose second son was born six weeks after his death had been buried, if indeed they had been buried at all. Perhaps, for their peace of mind, it was just as well; there was no easy death to be had on those battlefields. Most of those that fell in that debacle received scant ceremonial. Dima's was simply one small tragedy in the midst of a much greater one; few of the hard-pressed, often inexperienced field officers caught up in the bloody shambles of the Retreat were able to observe the niceties; shell-shocked and exhausted, they had little time or energy left for the living, let alone for the dead.

The year was a catastrophe for Russian arms. Casualties were measured in millions, and at least another million were captured by or surrendered to the enemy. Poland was abandoned. Steadily, amidst shaming scenes of slaughter, extortion and brutality inflicted upon the civilian and refugee populations by the frightened and ill-disciplined retreating soldiers, the Russian armies were pushed back, forced to a stand at last once again upon the sacred soil of Russia herself. The cavalry, the best-armed and best-led pride of the Tsarist forces, found themselves worse than useless in the grim business of trench warfare and against the iron might of modern arms. There was simply no part for them to play; but with their aristocratic connections, their assumption of superiority and their insistence upon priority they clogged up the military machine and stretched the already sketchy and ill-organized supply services to breaking

349

point. And all to no effect. In this war no personal valour, no courageous charge, no gallant self-sacrifice could make up for a lack of field artillery, a shortage of shells and of rifles – in many cases infantrymen going into battle had to rely on the rifles and ammunition of their fallen comrades. Facing a modern, well-equipped and well-trained army the Russians had no properly efficient transport system, no aerial support, no well-organized modern communications system. Sabres and swords had become outdated overnight, and those that trusted to them died in their thousands, or fled in confusion. As an incompetent and factionalized Russian High Command squabbled, intrigued, and sent out a stream of contradictory orders a swathe of misery and death was cut through Eastern Europe; vast areas of Russian territory were abandoned to the enemy; the Germans were stopped at the very gates of Riga, and Petrograd herself was threatened. Desertions assumed massive proportions; regiments on occasion surrendered as a unit, officers and men together. Under such circumstances the death of one nameless, faceless conscript could easily pass with no impact upon anything or anyone but his own family.

As the Germans advanced and as the Russian armies were forced back, step by step towards Riga and finally towards Petrograd, the city was flooded with refugees. Men, women and children, dispossessed, desperate, often starving or sickly, were herded together in filthy wooden barracks or filled to overflowing the already overcrowded slums of the city. As summer turned to autumn and the ever-present spectre of the Russian winter hovered threateningly upon the horizon there was talk of starvation and of epidemic. Spirits were low and tempers high; discontent was rife. Where was the Little Father, the Tsar? What of his sacred duty to protect his suffering people? Most knew, with a bleak nod and a cautious sideways glance, the answer to those questions; the Tsar was ruled by the hated Empress, who was ruled in her turn by the debauched and degenerate Rasputin – and whilst that state of affairs persisted the people, threatened with starvation and oppression, their sons dying by the million for a cause they did not understand, could expect no help, no protection.

And in the teeming breeding-grounds of the Vyborg and other

working-class districts of the capital, the agents of sedition did their whispered, perilous work, establishing committees, organizing forbidden meetings, fomenting strikes and unrest. Whilst the Generals fought each other with every bit as much energy and rather more efficiency than they fought the enemy, whilst the Tsar vacillated, caught in his weakness between his strong-willed wife, his ministers and his conscience, in the city slums the seeds of hatred, fear and anger were assiduously and skilfully cultivated in a soil all too receptive and fertile.

Sasha arrived in Petrograd on leave – his second in the course of the war so far – on a brisk, clear, early-autumn day that went some way to disguising the dourness and squalor of the once-lovely city. He was tired, hungry and depressed. Quite apart from the constant stress of fear that was his permanent companion and to which he had become almost accustomed, the journey – despite a pass personally signed by the General and a purse well-filled – had been a nightmare. He felt filthy. The train that had lumbered so painfully slowly across the vast and dusty plains to the city had been packed with wounded; every inch of space in compartment, in corridor, in goods van or baggage-rack had been taken up by armless, legless, eyeless men. Bandages and blood; suppurating wounds. Patient nurses, overworked doctors, and the stubble-darkened, pallid faces of the wounded, resigned and stoic; he had turned his face from them all, refusing to look, refusing to feel, refusing above all his own guilt, deeply but insecurely buried. But he could not ignore the smell; it was in his nostrils now, clung to his clothes and to his skin. He thought of the apartment behind the Liteini; small, quiet, calm. He thought of warm and fragrant water, of Margarita's quick, light-hearted smile, her soft skin and perfumed hair, of one short week's peace and release from fear, and quickened his steps.

Margarita had visitors; two of them. One was a young captain of the Semenov Regiment of the Tsar's Own Guards, whom Sasha knew very slightly, the other, from his uniform, an ensign in one of the Cossack regiments whom he had never seen before.

He stood by the open door, fighting exhaustion, disappointment and the too-quick, dangerous stirrings of anger. Margarita presided straight-backed, composed and bewitchingly pretty, over the samovar that bubbled upon the table. The two men sat upon overstuffed armchairs, shining boots crossed at the ankles, tea glasses small in large, well-manicured hands, the relaxed and comfortable atmosphere clearly bespeaking a familiarity with their surroundings that did nothing for Sasha's already chancy temper. They were handsomely turned out, uniforms pristinely clean and smart, brass and leather gleaming. Their hats and gloves lay neatly side by side upon the small table beneath the window. The two fresh faces turned at Sasha's entrance, and both men scrambled to their feet, a certain embarrassment in the hasty movement as it dawned upon them who this unexpected arrival must be. Margarita, on the other hand, smiled calmly and charmingly and made no move whatsoever, as if the unheralded homecoming of a husband whom she had not seen for the best part of six months was a matter that could not be allowed to ruffle the small ceremonies of her tea party. 'Sasha,' she said, a shade too brightly, 'good heavens! How unexpected! How nice.' She tilted her chin, fluffy fair hair gilded by the light of the sunlit window behind her. Her voice was light, and gave absolutely no hint of the turmoil that the sudden entrance of this lean, unsmiling man that was her husband had brought. She proffered a smooth cheek, waited for him to cross the room, bend and kiss her. "Lexis, be a dear and fetch another glass, would you? Sasha – you'll take tea? 'Lexis brings it every week, or we'd be drinking ground acorns by now! I do find this beastly war a trial!' She cocked her head, smiling, apparently blandly unaware of his displeasure, or of the awkward atmosphere his sudden coming had produced. 'Sasha, my darling, whatever have you been doing to yourself? You look as if you've slept for a week in your clothes –'

'As a matter of fact I haven't slept at all in the past forty-eight hours.'

She patted the hand that rested upon her shoulder. 'Poor Sasha,' she said, lightly and with no discernible trace of sympathy. 'Now – let me introduce you – you remember Alexis Konstantinovich, don't you? And this handsome young man is the Count Devanovov – Mikhail to his friends.' She smiled brilliantly up into the young man's face.

'I think,' the young Count mumbled, eyes flicking to Sasha's unimpressed face and away, 'that with your permission, Margarita Victorovna, we should perhaps take our leave.' With his silent companion he gathered gloves and cap. Then he lifted his head and looked directly into Sasha's face. His eyes were troubled; he could not, Sasha estimated, have been more than eighteen years old. 'You've come from the Front?'

Sasha shook his head. 'From Stavka.' In a small, nervy gesture he rubbed the back of his hand across his mouth. His skin still smelled disgustingly of the hospital train. 'Which is most certainly,' he added dourly, 'as dangerous and exhausting as any battlefield since General Alexeyev took over.'

The boy smiled, a small, nervous twitch of a smile. 'He's an uncle of mine. I know what you mean. He used to terrify me. Still would, I suspect.'

'A new broom,' Sasha said, 'sweeping clean.' He did not want to think about it, let alone talk about it. Not now. In fact right now he discovered he wanted nothing so much as to take these two handsome, neatly-shaven, well-fed young men and to pitch them down the stairs, neck, crop and shining buttons.

'I think – perhaps it was necessary? The reorganization?' the boy said, hesitantly.

'I think perhaps it was.' Sasha walked firmly to the door, held it open invitingly. 'I'm sorry. Another time perhaps? It's been a very long journey.'

Margarita watched, silent, her expression unreadable.

'Of course, of course!' Stumblingly they took their leave, bending over Margarita's hand – the man Alexis for just a second too long in Sasha's opinion – and left.

'Well.' Sasha turned, leaning against the door, his hand still on the knob. 'I'm glad to see my pretty wife isn't pining away in my absence –'

'Well, darling, of course I'm not! What would you expect?' With a graceful movement she stood and came to him, leaning lightly against him, her hair brushing his cheek, her lips as light as thistledown upon his. Before he could hold her she was gone. 'Goodness, Sasha, how you smell! Petra? Petra!'

The door to the kitchen opened and a small, frightened, non-descript face peered in.

Margarita flicked her fingers. 'Clear the glasses, please. And then draw a bath for the master. Supper will be for two.'

The girl mumbled something, cast a fearful glance first at her mistress and then at the strange, travel-stained man who stood in the other doorway, before scurrying like a frightened mouse to the table.

Sasha waited until the door closed behind her. His eyes were riveted to Margarita. The soft curves of youth were gone from her face; she held herself now with the confidence of a lovely woman who knows the power she wields. Her bright, curly hair was piled in that carefully artless way that still suited her so. Long earrings dangled from her ears, swinging against her slender neck, about which she had tied a narrow length of velvet ribbon, from which a tiny golden heart depended; a trinket which he did not recognize. She was wearing a gown he had not seen before, of heavy rose satin trimmed with rich ivory lace, high at the neck, very close-fitting about her breasts and her slender waist. But not for him. The thought brought hurt and anger in about equal measure. Disturbed and unhappy, nerves strung almost to breaking point, he watched her as she moved about the room, and suddenly the truly unstudied, feminine grace of her movements, the flare of her hips beneath the rich, swagged material caused an unexpected surge of a primitive physical arousal that caught him unawares and set his heart pounding. This woman was his. It was her duty to give herself, his right to take her. It took a singular effort of will to remain standing where he was, to force from his mind the thought of stripping the armour of that shining dress from her body, of overpowering her, hurting her, compelling her to copulate with him there and then, with no ceremony, upon the floor of this room that suddenly seemed to belong to strangers. To overmaster her. Would that bring an easing of the pain? For one short space of time to bury himself, his terrors, his dishonour in that vulnerable, soft, female flesh? To vanquish her weakness with his strength?

She turned, unruffled, unaware. 'Why didn't you let me know

354

you were coming? I should not have been so –' she lifted long fingers, let them subside gracefully '– unprepared.'

'I couldn't. The reorganization, you know? I've been posted. The opportunity for leave simply came up and I took it. I'd have been here long before any message.' His words were stilted; the sudden surge of lust had left the warmth of shame in his cheeks. He had not moved from the open doorway, where he leaned against the doorjamb, watching her. 'Letters are taking weeks. I only just got your last one. About your brother. I'm sorry. How's Natalia taken it?'

Margarita made a small, impatient gesture. 'Oddly. She's absolutely obsessed with the wretched –' she stopped herself '– with the new baby. You know she had another little boy? Oh, no, of course not. He was born a few weeks ago. She called him Dmitri, of course. A little morbid, don't you think?'

He shrugged, tiredly, again rubbed the back of his hand across his mouth. 'It would seem natural, under the circumstances.'

'Would it? Oh – perhaps so.' She dismissed the subject of her brother's death and her sister-in-law's agony with a brisk flick of her hand.

Sasha leaned, hands in pockets, watching her, still. 'And the rest of the family? Your mother? What's happening to the business? I assume that someone's running the shop?'

She lifted her shoulders. 'Everyone's fine. Well, we don't see a lot of Lenka –' She hesitated, wondering whether to mention the fact that she had in fact seen rather more of her brother-in-law than of her sister, decided against it. 'Mama is still – well – you know. Difficult. Actually –' she smiled, brightly '– she's getting rather fat.'

'Fat?' Sasha was surprised.

'Mm.' Margarita rearranged an ornament upon the mantel-piece, turned. 'She's eating rather a lot. Chocolates and things. When she can get them, that is.'

Sasha pushed himself upright. 'And the shop?'

'Oh, Volodya's running that.' She shook her head a little. 'Oh, of course, I forgot, I don't think you ever knew him. Vladimir Pavelovich Yamakov. A violin maker, a protégé of Uncle Andrei's. He's been invalided out of the army – a leg wound.' She laughed a little. 'Strange to have him back. He was rather sweet on Anna, actually. We all thought –' She stopped. 'Goodness, how long ago it all seems.' Her voice was very light.

'I don't think I ever met him.'

'No. Probably not.' She was moving inconsequentially about the room, twitching this, touching that, not looking at him. 'Will you take tea before you bathe?' He might have returned from a day's shooting. 'Oh, wretched girl! I keep telling her –' The magnificent toy theatre he had bought her after the miscarriage stood still in pride of place upon the sideboard. Margarita, face absorbed, bent her head to it, rearranging the figures.

Watching her, the warmth of desire, of need, still heated his tired body. He came up behind her, his arms about her before she was aware of him. 'In a moment,' he whispered. 'In a moment, my love – tea – baths – food – the world – all in a moment. But – now –' His mouth was on her face, her ear, her smooth, cool neck, his hand rough on her breast. 'Oh, God, you can't know how I've –'

'Sasha!' She sounded truly shocked, and her struggles were not counterfeit. Outraged, she beat at him with her small fists. 'Sasha, stop it! Petra – she's in the kitchen!'

'And there she'll stay if she has any sense.' He tightened his grip, bending her body to his, his mouth on hers, warm and urgent.

She stiffened in his arms, her mouth twisted under his. She tore her head loose from the grip of his hand. 'Stop it! Stop it, I say! Sasha, please! Don't be – don't be so disgusting!'

Painfully aroused, all anger gone, he was aching for her now – ready to beg her – for her softness, her loving, her heartfelt surrender, that might, somehow, ease the tensions and the fears. He released her and stepped back.

Breathing heavily, face flushed unbecomingly, she smoothed her skirt, not looking at him. 'I think – perhaps a bath first, wouldn't you agree?' she asked, her voice almost normal. 'And then we'll have supper, and you can tell me all that's happened.' She was busying herself about the room again, moving cushions back to where they had been before, flicking nonexisting dust from shining surfaces.

'Margarita,' he said.

She turned. Looked at him. Saw, as she had seen before, a

356

disturbing stranger. The dark, still-handsome face was no longer young. It had thinned and hardened, it was difficult to hold with any serenity the gaze of the haunted eyes. She shook her head a little, dumb with fright; and her fear showed in her wide eyes. There had been changes enough in the world about her in these past terrifying months without this. With all her self-centred little heart she wished him away from here, far away, back into the world of make-believe, where he was her handsome knight, bravely and steadfastly defying danger, her shield from afar, undemanding. This dishevelled, distressed, urgent, aggressively male flesh-and-blood man was more than she could take with no warning, no chance to prepare. 'Later,' she said, almost choking on the word. 'Later, Sasha, I promise. But not now – please – not now.'

They made love in darkness and almost in silence, Margarita frantic that Petra, asleep on her pallet in the kitchen, should not hear them. Afterwards, Sasha lay for a long time, naked and still beside her, looking into the darkness, trying not to think of her mouth closed against his, of the rigid rejection implicit in every tense line of her smooth body as he had caressed and entered her, of her turned head, of the sense of total isolation that had overcome him at the moment of climax. Of her turned back afterwards, the relief in her long drawn breath. He'd had more loving, more warmth, from the camp-following whores who'd tested his coins with their teeth before grinning and lifting their skirts. The tears that brimmed and finally ran down his cheeks were cold.

In the distance, faint and menacing, he fancied he heard gunfire.

He turned on his side, shivering, the blankets pulled to his ears.

And allowed into his thoughts, as he did at his most desperate moments, his salvation, his Valentina; courageous, down-to-earth, laughing and warm. Valentina and her poetry, her fiercely argumentative nature; the passion of her loving. Valentina; thin as a boy, far from beautiful, intransigently independent. His love.

She lay not much more than a mile from him. Who lay with

her tonight? Did she ever think of the young man who had saved her from the Cossack horsemen? Had she forgotten him?

No. Oh, no. Of that he was certain. As sure as the coming of death, as sure as his hope of heaven, Valentina would not have forgotten him.

Margarita lay rigid, her back to him, feigning sleep.

The leave was not a success. They visited friends and family. They promenaded in the parks and beside the river. He took her for tea at the Europa, and to a performance of the Imperial Ballet at the Narodni Dom. He spent money that would have fed them for a month on a meal at the Villa Rhode, on the Islands, where they were entertained by Tzigane musicians and dancers, the leader of whom, to her great pleasure, took an especial shine to Margarita, serenading her soulfully as she sipped the house's second best and strictly illegal champagne. But they did not – could not – talk; and their lovemaking was always the same; hurried, silent, unsatisfactory and always under cover of darkness, an activity that Margarita endured rather than enjoyed, and never, ever, instigated. Neither did she ask a single question about his life, his experiences, or his fears. And in return he volunteered nothing, not even the information that the new posting was back to active service, that this was the reason for his unexpected leave, the last favour his General had been able to afford him. Effort was being made at last to reform the aristocratic 'officers' club' of the Stavka; there were no more easy billets. Sasha was being sent to Riga, where the Russian forces were still stubbornly holding out. He sweated at night, thinking of it. But he did not tell Margarita.

It was on the fourth day that they quarrelled.

Sasha had been morose and nervy all day. Four precious days were gone; there were only four left – four days and four nights before he faced the terror again. Four days of empty conversation, of empty lovemaking, of an empty mind and heart. He could not stand the thought.

They were supposed to be going to supper, with friends, at a small restaurant still rumoured to have a cellar full of fine French wines and a proprietor who was ready, for a price, to flout the war-time law prohibiting the sale of alcohol and allow his customers to sample them. Margarita sat at her small dressing table, taming with practised fingers the curling mass of her hair and piling it gracefully onto her head. She had not for a moment contemplated the more practical and less time-consuming shorter hairstyles that were becoming the vogue. She was still dressed in the filmy robe, belted at the waist, that she wore before she dressed. The rose-coloured satin was laid across the bed. Happy as always to be going out, always an adventure, always an opportunity to see and to be seen, she applied herself to her task, her face attractively flushed, her eyes shining with excitement. Sasha stood in the shadows, watching her, a glass of vodka, his second and now only half full, in his hand.

'You're more beautiful than ever,' he said.

She raised her eyes to look at him in the candlelit mirror. Her flush of pleasure was entirely natural, her happiness at the compliment entirely unstudied. 'Thank you.' She had grown used to his changed looks, his rather quieter demeanour. She had in fact to her own surprise come to realize, in face of the covert glances of other women, that in some strange way he had become more, not less, attractive. The slightly shabby uniform that at first had offended her had, she had been startled to see, been treated as a badge of honour by others. She smiled at him, with genuine, if shallow, warmth. If he could just contrive to be a little less – intense – a little less physical – the blush grew, hotly, in her face. She reached for her swan's-down powderpuff, was so intent upon her reflection that she did not notice his approach until he was behind her, tall in the shadows for all his slightness of build, strong hands clamped uncomfortably hard upon her shoulders. She shifted a little, shaking herself free. Smiled uncertainly into the deeply shadowed face. Her stomach shifted, churning uncomfortably. She knew that look. Surely – oh surely! – he would not make his horrible demands on her now? She was bathed and clean, perfumed, her hair arranged to pretty perfection. In God's name, why must he spoil it? What did he want of her? It was Petra's night off. They were alone in the apartment. She had so desperately hoped he would not take advantage of that, at the very least not until later.

He laid his hand against her cheek, felt the softness of her skin against the flat, calloused palm. 'Rita,' he said, softly. 'Darling. Why don't we stay here tonight?'

She smiled, brightly, into the mirror, a muscle in her jaw jumping. 'Don't be silly, Sasha dear. We've made arrangements. The others –'

'Won't miss us.' He leaned closer, eyes bright and probing. She hated the excitement she could see in them, feel in the urgent warmth of his body, so close to hers. 'I could go to the little café down the road, bring something back. You wouldn't need to dress – you're so beautiful just as you are – we'll eat here, just the two of us. We'll talk –'

'Well, goodness –' uneasily she moved, leaning closer to the mirror, away from him, ostentatiously rearranging a curl '– we can talk at the restaurant, can't we? And what, for heaven's sake, have we been doing all day? Sasha, please, don't do that – you're disarranging my hair –'

'For God's sake!' He straightened, violently, the vodka slopping from his glass.

'Sasha, do be careful!' In her panic and in her effort to control it her voice came out as cold as the first night of ice upon the river. She might have been talking to an ill-behaved child. 'You've splashed vodka on my robe –'

His hand, the fiercely strong hand of a horseman, and one who could curb the most recalcitrant of mounts, was suddenly, agonizingly, about her right wrist. She felt the bones give painfully under the pressure. Instinctively, difficult though it was, she knew not to struggle. She held herself still, her body arched rigidly against him. 'Did I now?' His voice was very quiet. His grip did not relax. 'Well. Should I suck it dry? Perhaps that at least is something I should get for my money? And my name?'

'I don't know what you mean.' Her voice, despite her effort at control, was a breath of pain. Yet still, with an understanding that was primeval in its depth, she did not struggle.

'Of course you don't.' Slowly he was forcing her body backwards against him, her back arched against his raised knee. With the hand that still held the glass, quite gently despite the brutal grip of his other hand, he bared her breasts. The candlelight flickered on the smooth skin, the darkened, raised nipples. The vodka glass was poised and steady. His face was expressionless. With a hand still savagely gentle he rubbed the glass against the bared teats, ran it, cold and hard, down the open front of the robe to rest on her belly. She sobbed, once, turned her head from him and was still. 'In Vladivostok I went to a brothel,' he said, reflectively, 'where for good coin you could drink your liquor from any receptacle you wished – the more imaginative the better – it was a most entertaining evening.' The glass tilted. The clear liquid splashed upon her breasts. He bent his head, licked the stuff from her skin, sucked it as it dripped from the taut nipples.

She lay against him, ice-cold and rigid, aware of nothing but disgust and shock and a humiliation so deep it could never be forgiven.

He lifted his head.

There was a long moment of still silence.

He let her go, very suddenly, throwing her from him, turning away from her.

Shivering she sat up, pulling her robe around her, hunching her shoulders against him.

In the lamplit shadows of the room he was moving, with the sharp and violent movements of anger. It took a few shocked minutes before she was recovered enough to understand. 'What – what are you doing?'

He had thrown off his evening suit, tossed it in a heap upon the floor, had pulled on a pair of old corduroy trousers and was dragging his battered English shooting jacket from its hook in the wardrobe. 'I'm going out.'

She turned, aghast. 'You can't! We've made arrangements!'

'Unmake them.' Stone-faced, he was ramming his arms into the jacket, shrugging it onto his shoulders.

She stood up. In her whole life she had never felt such an overwhelming fury. 'Stop this! This minute! Do you hear me? Take those stupid clothes off! We are dining with the Melaknikovs. They are expecting us. I will not have you –'

'You won't have me. Full stop.' He rummaged in the pocket of his suit, transferred a handful of notes and coin. 'So why should you care what I do or where I go?' He turned to the door.

She barred his way like a fury. 'You can't! *You can't!*'

'Stop me,' he said, very calmly and with an intonation that, for all her anger, made her step sharply back from him.

In the quiet that followed her eyes, fierce upon his, suddenly sharpened. 'You're going to her, aren't you?' It was a statement rather than a question.

He did not answer.

'*Aren't you?*'

There was no need, no point, in questioning the pronoun. 'It's none of your business,' he said.

'I think it is.'

'I don't give a bugger's arse what you think.' It was quite deliberate, as brutal as his grip upon her arm that had raised welts that already were turning blue.

Still she barred the way. 'You're disgusting. You're – you're drunk – filthy!'

'All the more reason to be rid of me, I'd have thought.'

'You're mad.'

He sighed, ostentatiously, waiting.

She was in tears now, her face distorted. 'Sasha, why can't you be nice to me? Why can't we be like we used to be? Why can't you just – just love me without constantly touching – pawing –'

He shrugged. 'Because I'm disgusting. And filthy. Because I'm a man, for Christ's sake. Margarita, are you going to let me out of that door or do I have to use the window?' The sudden calm was unnatural.

'You're not going to that woman. I won't let you.'

'Oh?'

'You're not leaving me, Sasha. You can't! Remember what happened last time! Remember what I went through!'

He pushed past her and out through the door. As he ran down the stairs her voice pursued him. 'I'll make you pay for this, Sasha! I'll make you pay!'

Blinded by anger, driven by need, he hardly remembered the journey across the city.

He walked very fast down towards the river, swung aboard a clanking yellow tram, stood swaying amongst the silent, poorly dressed passengers as it crossed the bridge, rattled through drab streets, past looming factories and depressing tenements. One

362

thought and one thought only filled his mind; let her be there. Please, God, just let her be there. Let me find her. Just once more. And let her be as I remember her.

Alone in the apartment behind the Liteini Prospekt Margarita cried herself in a passion of fury to exhaustion, beating her fists upon the pillows that were crumpled and drenched with tears.

When the storm had eased she turned to lay on her back, small sobs still catching in her throat, staring into the lamplit shadows.

He was hateful! Hateful!

She brooded upon revenge. How most could she hurt him, as he had hurt her? Should she leave? Desert him, as he deserved? Wouldn't he be frantic with worry if he came back to an empty apartment, not knowing where she was, what had happened to her? Wouldn't he be sorry, then?

She could not admit, even to herself, that she did not know, could not predict how this new, changed Sasha would react.

There was, too, another consideration. Suddenly in control of herself she found herself thinking, long and hard. They'd had news that Sasha's mother had been poorly. Margarita had sent suitably caring messages, had ensured that the two women closeted at Drovenskoye understood that it was impossible for her to travel in such dangerous times and then had spent long and happy hours constructing daydreams about the future. She had conjured into her mind the house, the servants, the estate; had as determinedly shut from her memory the recollection of shabbiness, of penny-pinching, of neglect. She had lovingly reconstructed her dream of becoming a great lady. The Lady of Drovenskoye, gracious and beautiful. Loved – worshipped – by all. No-one was going to take that from her. She sat up now, drew her knees to her breast, her arms wrapped about them, one hand nursing her bruised and painful wrist, eyes narrowed. No. She wouldn't leave Sasha. She'd never leave him. But she'd bring him to heel, see if she didn't! He could not have changed so very much. She'd handled him before, and she'd do it again. And God help him if he tried to fight her. There were things he could give her that no-one else could; and who would grace better his home and his life? Sasha was hers, her prince, her

363

salvation. *Of course I'm sure. I made him up. I invented him.*

It was the beastly war, of course. He was overwrought. Not himself. He'd come back to her. Certainly he would.

In the meantime – just in case – she must think, constructively and clearly. She needed weapons, any that might come to hand; and once she found them, if necessary she would use them.

It took Sasha a full hour to find the apartment block in which Valentina lived; he had reckoned without the dreary sameness of the roads, the corners, the buildings of this depressing and overcrowded part of the city. Even when he stood at last in the gloomy corridor outside what he hoped was her door he was not entirely sure of himself. He had been certain, downstairs, that he had recognized the grimy lobby, the broken, filthy tiles of the floor; now his confidence deserted him. He hesitated for a long moment, then lifted his hand and rapped sharply with his knuckles upon the battered door.

Nothing happened.

He rapped again, loudly, urgently, willing her to be there.

There was no movement, no sign of life.

He swore, intensely and viciously, a searing stream of blasphemy that was all he could think of to keep the tears from his eyes. In fury he punched at the door, hurting his knuckles, turned, leaning against it, head tilted backwards.

'Not there. She's not there.'

He jumped. The door opposite had opened a crack. A gaunt old woman peered with black, button eyes from the shadows. 'Not there,' she said again, and the door began to close.

Sasha was across the corridor in a flash, his foot slamming against the closing door. 'But – wait – she does live here? This is Valentina's room?' He had not realized until now that he had never discovered her full name. 'Valentina!' he said again, urgently, 'she lives here?'

The old woman grunted. It could have meant anything.

Sasha exerted his strength against the door. Grumbling, the woman gave way. Her dirty face was vindictive and distrustful.

Sasha scrabbled in his pocket, brought out a coin. 'Valentina? She lives in that room?'

The beady eyes were fixed upon the coin. 'Yes. On and off.'

'Do you know where she is now?'

Narrow, shawled shoulders lifted in a shrug. A dirty, shaking hand reached for the coin.

Sasha held on to it for a moment. 'Do you know when she'll be back?'

Another shrug. 'Sooner or later, I daresay.' The coin was spirited from his fingers and disappeared into the ragged skirt. He stepped back. The door closed.

He stood for a moment, looking at it, face sombre. Then he turned back to Valentina's door, leaned against the wall beside it, slid down upon his haunches and set himself to wait.

He was dozing when he heard the voices; two of them, one a man's, sharp and concise, and the other the voice, light and clear, that he had heard so often in his head in these past mad months.

'All right, all right! If you all insist. Though, honestly, Lev, I – ' Valentina stopped.

Sasha stood, very carefully, painfully slowly and with no great grace. His right leg was dead as a doornail and he was chilled to the bone. He said nothing.

Valentina stood at the top of the stairs, her hand on the chipped banister, struck to stillness and silence by the sight of him. She was staring, wary and afraid, as if he were some sprite sprung from the air to startle her. Her companion, a shabby young man with a lean, intense face, looked from one to the other, faintly enquiring, faintly suspicious, wholly displeased.

Valentina turned to him. 'Er – Lev – if – if you don't mind?' Her voice had cracked a little oddly. She cleared her throat.

He raised deliberately uncomprehending brows.

'It seems – I have a visitor.' Valentina gestured.

There was a flicker in the young man's dark face, a shadow of anger that as swiftly disappeared. 'You were to deliver something to me,' he said, his voice flat.

'I – yes – of course – just come in. I'll get them.' She led the way to the door. She did not look at Sasha. Her companion did, long and hard. Sasha glared back belligerently. At this moment the devil himself could have challenged his right to be here, and

Sasha would have fought him; and it showed in his eyes.

The young man, Lev, hunched his shoulders, barged in front of Sasha, following Valentina into the room where she was bending over the table lighting a small oil lamp. Sasha followed, moved into the shadows, stood quiet and watching. He had not said a word.

Valentina pulled open a drawer. 'Here.' She pulled out a sheaf of leaflets and thrust them at the other man. 'That's all that's left, I'm afraid. Vasha's got some more, I think, if you need them. But be careful.'

'You're telling me to be careful?' Caught with her in the warm circle of lamp light the young man emphasized the pronouns very slightly, and smiled, easy and mocking. Valentina's own answering smile flashed like a gleam of sunlight in the shadowed room. The small moment of intimacy set Sasha's teeth on edge. He forced his hands, which had bunched into fists at his side, to relax; found a moment to reflect that lately his reactions were too swift, too violent. He pushed from him the sudden recollection of Margarita's rigid, frightened face.

'You'll do as we suggested then?' The young man was insistent.

Valentina nodded, the smile still lingering. 'Yes.'

'You promise?' His relief was obvious.

'I promise.'

'When? When will you come?'

She hesitated only for a moment. Her dark glance flicked to Sasha and away. 'Tomorrow. If you really think it's necessary.'

'I do. We all do.'

There was a moment's silence. 'Then all right, I'll come. I promise,' Valentina said, gently.

'Right.' The young man hunched his shoulders, shoved his hands into his pockets, sent a sudden glowering glance at Sasha.

Valentina stepped across to him and kissed his cheek, lightly. 'I'll see you tomorrow, Lev. I promise.'

He growled something and turned. She escorted him to the door. Sasha heard the murmur of conversation, Lev's voice still sharp and unhappy, Valentina's reassuring. There was a moment's silence that could only have been a kiss, then the

366

door shut and Valentina moved once more back into the pool of light cast by the lamp.

She leaned her two hands upon the battered table that stood between them and watched him, levelly, for a very long time.

'I'm sorry,' he said at last, suddenly uncertain, 'I shouldn't have come.'

'No.' Her voice was very quiet. 'You shouldn't.' She was not smiling. Her sharp, intelligent face was drawn taut with something that for a moment he mistook for anger.

'I – had to see you.' Stupid, empty words. Hands spread helplessly before him he stepped forward, into the circle of light.

She moved as he did, was around the table and into his arms almost before he had taken that first step. If anything her grip was fiercer than his, her mouth wilder and more demanding. He wrapped long arms about her, folding her tightly to him, feeling the moulding of her body to his; knowing its surrender and its needs. They murmured to each other; silly, meaningless words that bore no relationship whatsoever to the fierce greed of their bodies. They coupled there, standing up, awkward, with her skirts about her waist and his trousers kicked about his feet; whose hands had unfastened which hook, which button, tugged at which tape or belt, neither could have said. They laughed then in real amusement, each pulling the other towards the comparative comfort of the couch, tumbling onto its sagging length, laughing again aloud at its protests, wrapping arms and legs about each other as if in this tangle of limbs they could find safety for their love.

But, of course, they could not.

Later, naked and lying together, they were quiet.

Valentina lifted a tousled brown head. 'Would you like a drink?'

'A concoction of Lev's?'

'Vodka. The real thing. Though yes,' she hesitated, lifted a bare shoulder, 'Lev brings it.'

'Good for Lev. You're sure he didn't make it himself?'

'I'm sure.' She climbed over him, fought off his hands with a grin, stood tall and naked in the lamp light. 'Not that he couldn't. Lev can do most things.'

'Is that right?'

'That's right.' The words were calm. She moved about the room collecting glasses and a bottle, came back to the couch, settled down upon the floor beside him.

'So.' He could not quite keep the edge from his voice. 'Just who is Lev?'

She paused in the pouring of the drinks. Lifted her eyes to his. 'A friend,' she said, simply. 'An old friend and a good one.'

'A very good one?'

Her eyes were unwavering. 'A very good friend indeed. How's your wife?'

For a startled moment he was silent. Then, in response to her grin he laughed. 'Well. But not as versatile as is your Lev.'

'I wouldn't expect her to be.' She was collected, containing her laughter. 'Not many people are.' She toasted him, eyes sparkling wickedly. 'Drink up. You won't get better than this out of the Tsar's own cellars.'

He allowed his own eyes to widen. 'That's where it comes from?'

'That's where it comes from.'

He did not know whether to believe her or not. He sipped the liquor. It was fiery and aromatic and exploded halfway down his throat like a bomb.

'That's not the way you're supposed to drink it,' she said. Naked, she was sitting back on her heels watching him with eyes that made no attempt to hide their hunger, their pleasure at the sight of him. 'Even I know that.'

He leaned onto his elbow, clinked his glass with hers. 'Go on, then. Show me.'

She laughed, a small explosion of sound. 'I can't! I'd choke to death!'

'What kind of a man are you?' Easily he tilted his head, tossed the vodka down in one draught. Threw himself back, arms spread, in mock ecstasy.

Before he could move she was over him, the short, swinging hair brushing her cheeks and his, her long-fingered, rough hands pinioning his arms. Very, very slowly she lowered her mouth to his. Kissed him, lightly. Ran her tongue swiftly along his lower lip. The tips of her breasts brushed his body. 'Would you like another?' she asked, politely.

'Yes. Please.'

'Now? Or later?'

'Later,' he said.

Her mouth tasted sweetly of vodka; they laughed at first, and wrestled like children. But it ended – as between them, sooner or later, it was bound to end – in tears.

'Don't!' he said, kissing her, rubbing his own cheek against hers. 'Don't cry. Please.'

'I'm not.'

'It's raining, then.'

'Yes.' She pushed him from her. 'It's raining. The Tsar would like to know if you'd like another glass of his vodka?'

He thought for a moment, head cocked. 'Please convey my respects to His Imperial Majesty and inform him there's nothing I'd like better.'

She turned a tear-drenched, innocent smile upon him, bright as a rainbow. 'Nothing?'

'Nothing I could manage at this particular moment.'

They wrapped themselves in blankets and applied themselves to the vodka. 'I hope you don't want to eat,' she said. 'I've nothing here, I'm afraid.'

He eyed her, speculatively. Grinned suddenly, teasing. 'I could turn cannibal.'

She shuddered, shook her head in quick repulsion. 'Don't!'

Too late he remembered the stories; the starving villages, the flesh-sellers who moved through the forests. The endless cycle of famine, the awful recourse to human flesh. He put his arms about her. 'I'm sorry.'

'It's all right. It's just – one of those things that –' she hesitated, drew the blanket tighter about her body '– that repulses me. So very much.'

'Yes. I know.'

There was a moment's silence. 'No-one should have to suffer so,' she said, her voice very low. 'No-one!'

He'd never really thought of it. 'No,' he said. 'No, they shouldn't.'

She leaned her head against him. 'I always think – what would I do? A starving child. A dying husband. The chance to feed them –' She shuddered again. 'Nothing changes, does it?

There's no hope. It's only luck. The worst of lotteries. Where you're born. Who you're born to. You in your pretty palace –'

He made a small, derisive sound.

'– me to my enlightened, earnest –' she hesitated for a moment, laughed '– grindingly boring family.' It was the closest she had ever come, through all their meetings, to self-revelation. He lifted his head, looking at her, interested. She laid a hand upon his face and pushed him back. 'It isn't fair. It has to change.'

'And you think you can change it?'

'Yes.' The word was sharp and unequivocal. She sipped her vodka, thoughtfully, held it in her mouth, savouring the warmth. Caught his eye upon her. Leaned forward, blanket slipping, to share it. 'Yes,' she said, a little later, as if there had been no interruption. 'Sasha, surely you can see you can't treat ninety per cent of the population like animals? All right – they aren't, strictly, serfs any more. They aren't actually owned like animals, as they used to be. But where's the difference, truly? They have no say in their own affairs. They're exploited to the gain of others. They have no hope and no future, neither for themselves nor for their children. They're flogged and chained and murdered if they protest. They're dying now like flies in a war that is none of their making –'

She stopped. Sasha, almost brushing her aside, had sat up, abruptly, the blanket falling from his pale shoulders. The long curve of his back looked oddly fragile. He reached for the bottle, poured himself a generous measure, tossed it back. 'Isn't everyone?'

She was too painfully attuned to him to miss the note in his voice. 'Yes.' She laid a hand and then a cheek upon his cool shoulder. 'Yes. Of course. I know. I'm not belittling that. I'm sorry.'

'You know?' He closed his eyes for a long, agonized moment. 'You know?' he repeated, more softly, almost to himself.

In silence for a long moment she stayed, her head resting upon his tense shoulder. Then, 'No,' she said, softly, 'of course I don't know. Tell me.' She waited. 'Can you?'

It took a long and terrible time. They both cried, sometimes together, sometimes alone. He would not hear her urgent reassurances. 'I'm a coward, Valentina. A craven. I can't stand it. I don't know what to do.'

She was holding him, stemming his tears with her fingers, with the palm of her hand. There was nothing she could say, and both of them knew it. 'I love you,' she said. 'I love you. I love you.'

'I ran away. I betrayed their trust. I'll do it again. I know it.'

'Perhaps –' She stopped, helpless.

'No.'

'You don't believe in what you're doing,' she said, staunchly.

He turned a quiet face to her. The burden had been eased, at least a little. 'No. I don't. But then, I don't know what I do believe in. And if I did, I'd never have the courage to fight for it. I'm not like you.'

'Nonsense. You stopped the Cossack horse. You saved my life.'

'On impulse. Think yourself lucky I hadn't time to think.' His lips twitched, wryly. Then, in the dimming light, his face convulsed. 'Suffering Jesus,' he said, his voice suddenly dying as if in panic in his throat, 'I don't know how I'm going to go back.'

She held him, and they made love again, and then slept at last, sprawled and tangled uncomfortably together upon the creaking couch.

She woke him, whispering. 'Sasha? Sasha!'

He moaned, shook his head, burrowed beneath the blanket.

'Sasha! Wake up! It's four o'clock!'

He mumbled something totally incomprehensible.

'Sasha!' She pushed him away from her, struggled to a sitting position. 'Wake up, do! You have to go home! It's four o'clock!'

He pushed himself upright, shaking his tousled head. 'What?'

'It's four o'clock,' she said patiently. 'Presumably at some time or another you have to go home. Wouldn't it be better to arrive before daylight? And I'm a working girl, you know. I can't lie abed like the gentry.' She laughed a little, but her heart was not in it.

He sat in silence, his head in his hands.

'You have to go, my love,' she said.

He dressed, hastily and awkwardly, by the light of a candle stub. She watched him in silence.

'I can come again?' he asked, urgently.

She shook her head. Looked at her spread hand, that was hardened and grained with dirt. 'I won't be here.'

He was beside her in a second, hands fierce on her shoulders. 'What do you mean? *What do you mean?*'

'I promised Lev. You heard. They think I'm in   some kind of danger. I've agreed to move. Tomorrow. To a – to a secret address.'

He looked at her, bewildered. 'Secret from me?'

She said nothing.

'What are you doing?' he asked, very quietly. Then, with more emphasis, 'Valentina? What are you doing that's so dangerous that you have to hide?'

It was a long time before she lifted her eyes to his. 'It isn't your business,' she said, quietly. 'I'm sorry, Sasha. But it's true. It's best you don't know.'

'You don't trust me?'

She spread helpless hands. She was not too far from exhaustion.

'I have only three more days. Before I –' He took a small, sharp breath '– before I go back. You won't let me see you in that time?'

Her expressive face showed every emotion. 'How can I not?' she asked, at last, through the tears that slipped tiredly down her face.

'Where will you be?'

'Don't write it down,' she said. 'At least don't do that. I'll tell you. Memorize it. And don't come tomorrow – oh, my love, it isn't that I don't want you to –' he had made a quick, almost despairing gesture '– but believe me, I can't. Thursday. Come Thursday. Come early, if you can. I'll cook a meal. We'll have the evening, and as much of the night as you can manage.'

'Tell me the address,' he said. 'Tell me how to come to you.'

Margarita was asleep in the wide bed when he got home. Wearily, fully dressed, he settled onto the couch. When dawn came up he still lay there, open-eyed and sleepless.

'Sasha?'

He turned his head. Margarita stood in the shadows by the door. Her voice was perfectly calm. Any trace of tears or distress was gone. 'Come to bed, please. Petra will be here within the hour. We don't want her to find you sleeping there, do we?' She turned and left him.

He struggled to his feet, went into the bedroom. She turned her back as he began to undress. 'Margarita,' he said.

She shook her head, sharply. 'No, Sasha. Don't say anything. There's no need. I don't want to talk about what happened last night. In fact I absolutely won't talk about it. I trust to your honour that you will never behave in such a manner again. Beyond that, there's nothing to say. Now, I think perhaps you should get some sleep. We're due at Aunt Zhenia's for lunch at twelve.'

He endured the day. He endured Zhenia's well-meant and solicitous but exhausting attentions, endured Varya's pale, plump, demanding presence, endured Mischa's back-slapping bonhomie.

'A bad business, my boy, a bad business indeed. But you know what they say – it's an ill wind that blows no good at all – there's money to be made, there's no denying that, good money to be made.'

And in his mind he found himself reciting, like a charm, the address Valentina had given him.

'Poor Natalia – she's taken it very badly, you know –'

He nodded. Said nothing. Across the room Margarita's bright eyes watched him.

'– gone completely to pieces. Strange, she always seemed such a capable girl – the kind to stand up against the worst –'

'Dima had the worst,' he found himself saying, his voice suddenly loud. 'No matter what you think. No matter what you say. Dima had the worst.'

Flustered, Zhenia reached for a tray of cakes. 'Why yes, of course. We realize that, Sasha my dear. Of course we do. Please, do have another of these – we were so very lucky to get the sugar.'

Sasha shook his head. 'Thank you. No.'

'I'll have another of those, Zhenia dear.' Varya's small hand snatched the tray that her sister had been about to put back onto the table. 'Though I must say I've tasted better. What a trial this war is.' She appealed to her son-in-law, sulky-faced. 'Nothing tastes the same as it used, does it? Absolutely nothing.'

They escaped at last. Walked in silence through the drab streets back to the apartment. There was a chill in the wind that came off the river. 'The Melaknikovs sent a message,' Margarita said, as they climbed the stairs to the front door. 'They have a table at the P'tit Chat tonight. They asked us to join them.'

He said nothing.

'I said yes.' Every line of her body was tense. Her mouth was set in an unhappy line.

He shrugged. 'All right.'

She glanced at him. 'You haven't any other plans?' She pulled a small, bitter face. 'I shouldn't like to disrupt them if you have.'

He turned to face her. 'Tomorrow,' he found himself saying. 'I have other plans for tomorrow. A friend from before the war – I met him last night – he lost a leg at Tannenberg.'

She stared at him, through level, narrowed eyes.

He forced himself on. Why, oh why was he lying? To protect himself? To protect Valentina? Even in some strange way to protect Margarita herself? Or was it simply a habit into which he had fallen and from which he could not extricate himself? He did not know. 'We got drunk together. We thought we might do it again tomorrow.'

'How nice for you.' Her voice was very cold.

He helped her from her cloak, handed it to the silent Petra who had appeared from the kitchen.

She turned a cool shoulder. 'Your suit needs brushing before you put it on,' she said. 'I left it on the floor for rather a long time last night.'

He fled to Valentina the following night; he had been able to think of nothing and no-one else all day. Even the thought of his imminent return to the Front was swamped by his need to see her. For the first time he wished the hours away, even though he knew that each fleeting minute took him closer to the nightmare that awaited him in Riga.

Margarita made no comment, no protest. She was sitting upon a low chair, skirts spread gracefully about her, the toy theatre upon a table in front of her, apparently absorbed in some project entirely her own. To his surprise she even lifted a cool, careless cheek to be kissed as he left, her eyes still upon the bright little scene before her. 'Do be careful, Sasha dear. Don't get too drunk.'

'I won't.' In his urgency there was no place for shame. He kissed her, picked up his jacket, ran swiftly down the stairs to the front door.

He did not see, as he stepped into the street, the urchin who emerged from the shadows behind him, a very shadow himself – Sasha's shadow – who, with Margarita's roubles in his pockets and more promised, followed unobtrusively in his every footstep.

Some days later, as Sasha's train sped south carrying him back to the fields of death, an uncomfortable meeting took place in a small and dingy office in the Ministry of the Interior.

'Gone? What do you mean, gone?'

The small, shabbily-dressed man who stood before the desk of Pavel Petrovich Donovalov moved uneasily from foot to foot. 'Just gone, Pavel Petrovich. The bitch has disappeared.'

Lenka's husband steepled his fingers. His desk was very tidy; he was obsessive about it. Papers were stacked in militarily precise piles, trays were set exactly at right angles to the edges of the desk, pencils and pens were ranged as if on parade. He lifted his eyes.

The other man, flinching a little, looked away. 'I'm sorry, Pavel Petrovich. I didn't realize it was that important. There are so many jobs on the go at the moment.' His voice was as aggrieved as he dared to make it.

'And every one of them –' Donovalov's voice was chill as he interrupted '– every single one of them is important. You fool, Kutya!'

'Yes, Pavel Petrovich.'

'Damned subversives!' Donovalov's voice was low. He banged the desk with the heel of his hand. The man Kutya jumped, blinking. 'With their bloody committees, their troublemaking. Trouble? I'll give them trouble! We're at war, Kutya.' His voice was still quiet. Kutya sweated under the malevolence of the other man's eyes. 'These are traitors. Death is what they deserve. Death is what will come to them. *But not if bloody incompetents like you bungle every sodding job you're given!*' The words were not loud, yet the blistering rancour of them brought a sheen of sweat to the small man's face.

'Yes, Pavel Petrovich. I'm sorry.'

'Sorry? You're sorry? You lose our only lead to the Barjov Group – a lead we've been nursing for months, no, *years* – to a group that now, only now, is coming out into the open with its filthy subversions – and you're – *sorry?*'

'Yes, Pavel Petrovich.' The words were barely audible.

There was a long silence. Donovalov's level eyes did not blink as he surveyed the other man. Then, 'Get out,' he said, disgustedly. 'Send Salkov in.'

'Yes, Pavel Petrovich.' Shaking with relief and sick with hatred the small man scurried to the door. There he stopped. 'Oh – one thing, Pavel Petrovich?'

Donovalov raised weary eyes from the piece of paper he had picked up. 'What is it? You need the lavatory?'

'No, Pavel Petrovich. It's just – I forgot to say – the man turned up. You know? The one you were interested in. Tall, dark, a scar on his face –'

Donovalov had stilled absolutely. His eyes sharpened. 'You're sure?'

'Oh yes, I'm sure. I saw him myself. It was the day before –' he swallowed '– the day before the bitch went to ground.'

It was so long before the man at the desk reacted that Kutya, shrugging a little, left the room, closing the door carefully behind him.

'Was it indeed?' Donovalov asked the silence, thoughtfully. 'Was it – indeed?'

CHAPTER EIGHTEEN

By the autumn of 1915 Germany had agreed, in principle, and
with reservations that were to cause much anguish to those
whose hopes were pinned upon the promise, to train a battalion
of two thousand young Finns and to arm them with rifles,
machine guns and ammunition. The military equipment was
not to be German, but materials captured from the Russian
armies on the Eastern Front.

Under the circumstances it was of course all but impossible
to keep the project entirely secret. The prosaic telegram that
informed the anxious Finnish patriots of their success after
much delicate negotiation – 'Send two thousand copies of
ordered book immediately' – was sent to a bookseller in Helsinki. And whilst that was not intercepted and immediately
recognized by the authorities as the triumphant message it actually was, the Russian Government was far from unaware of
what was happening in Finland; how could it not be? Disaffection was widespread and deep-rooted. The movement for independence had been gathering strength for years. It would have
been a truly insensitive and unintelligent occupying power –
which was the way that many Finns were beginning openly to
describe their Russian 'protectors' – that did not recognize the
ripening time for outright rebellion.

Jussi Lavola, his sister, his band of comrades and – to her
own surprise – his Russian wife were in the thick of it all. It
was not the easiest job in the world to smuggle hundreds of
able-bodied young men from Finland to Sweden and thence
from Sweden to Germany, under the eyes, ears and guns of an
occupying army and in the teeth of a war that was tearing
Europe to shreds. And the opposition was brutal. The authorities clamped down mercilessly on anyone involved in or simply
suspected of being connected with the freedom movement.

Russian soldiers and their officers and members of the secret police were billeted all over Finland, from Helsinki itself to the wastes of the arctic tundra. An already massively repressive regime became more so. Upon the flimsiest of evidence – sometimes upon no evidence at all – men and women were arrested, shot, or deported to Siberia. Yet still the young men escaped, slipping through the almost impenetrable forests, striking north to Lapland and the arctic circle to cross the Swedish frontier by land or smuggled upon fishing boats – and, too, upon smaller, swifter vessels that had known these routes well before there was flesh and blood contraband to be run from frontier to frontier – across the Gulf of Bothnia.

And then, as autumn advanced into winter and the waters froze, other routes were opened up. More direct; more dangerous.

'Do you have to go?' Katya kept her voice calm, almost light. It had become habit to her, at even the most dire of times, not to fuss. She had learned from experience that it made no difference; in such matters, much as she knew he had come to love her, there was no deflecting Jussi once he had made up his mind. 'You've only been home two days. You're still exhausted.'

Jussi was sitting at the table, wolfing down bread, cheese and beer. 'I told you, *Kulda*, I must. There's no-one else. Paavo's in Lockstedt negotiating with the German Command – God, the excuses they can come out with the minute we want any concrete commitment to anything! – and Armas –' He stopped.

'I know. Armas is dead. Heimo told me.' Katya stood with her back to him, calmly rolling bandages and packing them into a sturdy rucksack, which was all the luggage her husband would carry on his perilous journey. Meat, cheese and bread were already methodically packed. 'And so is Kosti Puhakka. And the young man who was here last month – what was his name? Otto something? He's been taken, hasn't he?'

'Yes. Don't worry. He won't betray us.'

She turned at last, met his eyes. 'I don't worry. Not about that,' she said.

Elisabet, seated by the stove darning a pair of heavy socks for her brother, glanced up, looked from one to the other, ostentatiously turned her back, giving them at least a little privacy.

Jussi had pushed his plate away and stood up. Katya moved quietly to him and stood within the warm circle of his arms, her fair head laid upon his chest. He said nothing, holding her to him, stroking her hair.

She closed her eyes. Concentrated every smallest atom of her being into this moment. For this was the fear she lived with; that he would one day leave, and she would never see him, feel him warm and live against her, again. 'Be careful,' she said at last.

'I'm always careful. I promise you. I have far too much to lose not to be.'

'Do you know how long you'll be gone?'

'No. A couple of weeks, perhaps. But it could be longer.'

'Elisabet and I are going to Helsinki at the end of the week. We've nearly fifty thousand marks to deliver to headquarters.'

His arms tightened about her. 'I don't like you doing that.'

'Don't be silly, Jussi,' Elisabet said tartly from her seat by the stove. 'We're perfectly safe. Who would ever suspect the two of us? Respectably married women, one Russian born, the other Russian by marriage, both ready to tell anyone who'll listen what we think of these dreadful subversives who are undermining good Russian Government and turning the country into a bear garden – no, Jussi. Don't worry about us. We organize the collecting of the money; it's only right that we should be the ones safely to deliver it. You fight your way and we fight ours. Money may not sound romantic but it's every bit as important as your precious battalion, you know.'

'I know. You're doing a wonderful job. But I still –' Jussi stopped as the door was flung open and Kaarlo, snow on his shoulders and on his fur cap, came into the room, stamping his feet against the cold. Pikku Kulda was still the safe haven it had always been; they set no lookouts about it.

'We can't take the Kemi route,' he said, with no preamble. 'It's finished. Closed.'

Katya felt every muscle in Jussi's body tighten. He put her from him. 'What happened?' His voice was very quiet.

'Looks as if a Russian agent infiltrated the network. When the last lot got to the Osula – you remember, the inn at Kemi, where we stayed?'

379

Jussi nodded.

Kaarlo's voice was grim. 'A detachment of Russian police was waiting for them. Cut them to pieces by all accounts. Three dead, all but one of the others captured.'

'Anyone we knew?'

'Toivo Aarkenan. He's dead. The innkeeper – Heiskanen, wasn't it? He's been taken too. The route's gone for good.' Kaarlo's voice was brusque. 'So, what do we do?'

'Another route lost. And another guide. Well, we have to go, there's no question of that.' Jussi perched upon the table, leg swinging, eyes very thoughtful. 'There are seven men waiting for us in the forest north of Kajaani. We can't leave them there.'

'Why not go via Vaasa? The Gulf's well frozen. The camp's established – I was out there last week with Toivo. We both know the route. Why not go that way?'

'Camp?' Elisabet asked, intrigued. 'In the middle of the Gulf?'

Jussi nodded. 'A tent. Shelter. It's a long trip across the ice. It's too much to expect the men to try to make it in one go. It's shelter, and a place to rest, that's all. It has a stove and fuel, provisions, warm clothes, that sort of thing.'

'The lads have christened it the Kaiser Wilhelm Hotel,' Kaarlo said, grimly humorous. 'But it's a hotel that's very particular about its guests. Russians aren't welcome.' His dark eyes flickered to Katya. She pulled a gargoyle face and sniffed dismissively. She had long ago ceased to worry about Kaarlo's gibes. Kaarlo laughed.

'All right.' Jussi pushed himself away from the table. 'That's the way we'll go. You've provisions?'

'Outside.'

'Then we leave at once. Katya, my camouflage jacket isn't here?'

'In the cupboard.' With quiet and quick efficiency Katya fetched the thin white jacket that he would wear over his heavy clothes to cross the ice. She finished packing the rucksack, stood back to let his stronger fingers pull the stiff leather straps tight.

'Kaarlo,' Elisabet said. 'Come and look at the lake.'

He stared at her, blankly. 'The lake?'

380

'The lake.' Firmly she reached up and took hold of the ear that stuck out from beneath his cap. 'Come – and look – at the lake!' She spoke very slowly, as if to a half-wit.

'Ah.' Suddenly comprehending, he looked at Jussi and Katya; smiled with yellow teeth. 'Ah! Yes. The lake.'

'God Almighty,' Elisabet said, with feeling, as she towed him to the door. 'Dear God Almighty. And upon this does my country's freedom depend!'

The door shut behind them. Katya and Jussi surveyed each other, the same rueful, unhappy yet amused smile mirrored upon both faces. 'Will we ever get any time together?' Katya asked, softly.

'Yes.' The word was positive. 'I promise you. Soon. This one last trip and then it will be easier. There are others now, many others. I won't have to make the trip much more. Now, tell me you'll be careful when you go to Helsinki.'

'I will. Of course I will. And you promise me – faithfully! – that you won't take unnecessary risks.'

He laughed then, opened his arms to her. 'Of course I won't. Don't worry, *pikku Kulda* –' he knew how she loved those small words – little darling – the same name given to the house where they had discovered their love '– the devil isn't ready for me yet.'

'Don't!' she said, against his chest. 'Don't say that!'

She kept back the tears until she stood at the door with Elisabet, watching the two men cross the snowy clearing to disappear down the narrow track into the forest. And even then she would not acknowledge her distress. Briskly she turned back to the warm room, began to tidy away the remains of her husband's meal.

Elisabet watched her, noted the wash of tears upon her cheeks, saw the hard-bitten lip. 'What is it, Katya?' Her usually sharp voice was oddly, tentatively gentle. They were still not close; the suspicion and hostility that had marked their early relationship had long been buried in the absolute essential need for mutual trust. If they could not be counted bosom friends at least their relationship now was characterized by confidence and by respect. Katya did not usually behave so when Jussi left. 'Katya?' she asked again.

'Nothing,' Katya said. 'It's nothing. I'm tired, that's all. I'm sorry.'

The words sounded banal and stupid in her own ears. She saw Elisabet's eyes still very sharp upon her. For a moment she was tempted, then put the temptation from her. How could she say, 'I'm expecting his child and he doesn't know it?' How could she say, 'It's changed me! I'm not brave any more! It isn't exciting any more! I'm afraid for him! Afraid for myself!' And above all how could she put into words the dreadful doubts – she veered from the word premonitions – that had settled upon her like vultures upon a carcass as she had watched his tall, lean figure striding across the clearing beside the shorter, stockier Kaarlo? How could she say, 'This time I truly fear I will never see him again'?

She straightened her back, rubbing at it absently with her hand. 'My mother,' she said, apparently inconsequentially, looking into space, into a childhood that suddenly seemed far, far away, 'always used to make us sit down together before we set off on a journey. Neither she nor my aunt would dream of going anywhere without sitting down for a minute or so first.' She bent again, gathered the plates, eyes still blinded with tears. 'Silly, isn't it?'

The Russian patrol picked up their trail not far from the coast, north of Vaasa.

'We should go back?' one of the men in the party asked, nervously.

'The buggers are behind us,' Kaarlo said drily, trudging steadily through a fresh fall of snow and into a rising wind, iron-shod boots crunching rhythmically as he walked. 'Going back doesn't seem to be exactly the most sensible thing to do in those circumstances, does it?'

'I mean –' The young man stumbled, righted himself. 'I mean –'

'I know what you mean,' Kaarlo said, repressively and with enough edge to his voice to still any argument.

'They're a way behind,' Jussi said, reassuringly. 'They don't know the terrain. We do. We'll lose them amongst the islands before we hit the open ice.'

The other man muttered something, caught Kaarlo's fierce eye and subsided.

Some time later Kaarlo came up close to Jussi, glancing over his shoulder to where the others ploughed doggedly in their tracks. His voice was very quiet. 'They're getting closer. I just caught a glimpse up on the hill there. At least a couple of the bastards are on horseback.'

'Yes. I know.' Jussi glanced up at the sky. 'If only the wind would lift. Or that damned snowfall had come later.'

Kaarlo grunted, hitched his rifle higher onto his shoulder.

'They can't actually be sure,' Jussi said, speaking as quietly as had his companion. 'They've presumably found our tracks. They can't be absolutely certain that we're who they suspect we are. They won't shoot until they're sure, I think. Until they actually catch up with us. Or until we do something to confirm their suspicions.'

'Should we split up?'

Jussi shook his head decisively. 'That's the last thing we can do. Only you and I know where we are or how to get where we're going. Only you and I are armed. Two smaller, weaker groups would be just as easily tracked and far easier to take once they'd caught up with us. No. We stick together.'

'They'll know for sure once we head out over the ice towards the islands.'

'Yes,' Jussi said. 'I know they will.'

The snowstorm struck like a gift from heaven, just as they reached the barren coast and struck out across the ice of the gulf. One moment the scattered islands loomed about them in the dim winter light, held firm in the rough grey shackles of the frozen sea; the next they were gone, lost in a dizzying curtain of white. Jussi glanced at Kaarlo, caught the grimly exultant, yellow smile from within the depths of the other man's hood. 'Stay together,' he said, reaching into his pocket for his compass. 'And for God's sake keep going. If we push on we'll lose them, for sure.'

'If they haven't already turned back.' Kaarlo's tone expressed exactly his contempt for their pursuers. 'Fucking Russians.' He spat into the snow.

'Shouldn't we – wait a little?' It was the same man who had

spoken before. Nervously defiant, he avoided Kaarlo's disgusted eye.

'No. We wait. They wait. We all wake up a few yards from each other. Not an appealing thought, is it? We go on. But for Christ's sweet sake watch where you're putting your feet. The ice is as safe as it ever is, but there are always holes.'

That concentrated their minds with marvellous effect. In silence they followed him into the storm.

It did not last long. Jussi was aware, with slightly sinking heart, that it had not lasted long enough. It had given them a chance, certainly, but if the Russian patrol had decided, as they had, to push on towards the west –

'Shit,' Kaarlo said, very calmly.

Jussi turned. The last flurries of snow still gusted across the ice. They had left the islands behind them. They were in a wasteland, a rough, bright desert of frozen ocean. And, as if the devil himself had crooked a finger to entice the covering storm away, the clouds were clearing. A pale sky shone to the west, and fickle sunshine – treacherous sunshine, however short-lived – lit the cold world with heartless, slanting light.

On the horizon, steady and clear, curiously magnified in the sudden brightness, the pursuers trudged relentlessly on, the two horses, with their riders, walking tall and quiet beside them.

'We can see them –' Kaarlo said.

'– which means that they can see us,' Jussi finished, grimly.

'Wh-what are we going to do?' A young man with a pinched, cold face hitched his rucksack higher onto his shoulders in a reflexive, nervous gesture and turned to Jussi, his pale blue eyes frightened.

'We push on,' Jussi said.

And, 'We kill the horses,' said Kaarlo, in all but the same breath.

The two men exchanged a swift, amused smile that held in its sudden gleam the recklessness of camaraderie. 'We push on,' Jussi repeated, and grinned. 'And as soon as they're close enough – we kill the horses.'

'But then what?' The man with the frightened eyes was not so easily calmed.

'Jesus, Vannemo, do shut up,' one of the other men said, shortly, his own uncertainty betrayed only by the slight tremor in his voice.

Jussi thought for a moment, his eyes narrowed upon the small, oncoming figures. 'We have two rifles,' he said.

'Three,' said another voice, quietly. A tall young man in a sleeveless wolf-skin jacket unslung his long bundle from his shoulder. 'I wasn't sure if I could bring it. I'm a hunter. My rifle and I are good friends. We didn't take kindly to being parted.'

'You said you had snowshoes in there!' another voice said, aggrievedly.

The tall young man smiled. 'So I did. And so I have. And the rifle.'

Jussi nodded. 'Right. Three rifles. Between nine of us.'

'There are only seven of them,' someone pointed out, hopefully.

'All armed to the teeth.' Kaarlo hefted his rifle in his hand. 'And two of them mounted. Officers at a guess.'

Jussi was watching the oncoming group, eyes narrowed against the light. 'Kaarlo's right. The horses are the thing. So. We push on. We find a defensible position – an ice-wall, perhaps, it doesn't take much – and those of us that are armed will stay behind to hold up our friends out there. The others push on to the camp. It isn't far now. We kill the horses, to slow them to our own pace.'

'And as many sodding Russians as we can manage as well,' put in Kaarlo, equably.

'And then, hopefully, we'll catch you up. There are some weapons at the camp – I'm not sure what, they come and go. But there's always something. We can make a stand there if necessary. Give our Russian friends something of a surprise. Agreed?'

There was a mumble that could have meant anything.

'Right.' Pleasantly Jussi smiled into each pair of anxious eyes. 'Well done. Now, come on – the further we can go before they're in range the better chance we have.'

'They'll break,' Kaarlo said, conversationally, as they settled themselves behind a rearing outcrop of ice that was embedded in the vast white plain of the frozen gulf. 'Not the best packages we've ever delivered.'

Jussi glanced quickly at their silent companion, crouched near them, his long rifle leaning beside him.

'Don't mind me,' the young man said, and almost responded to Jussi's quick smile, albeit with no more than an answering twitch of his lips.

'They'll be all right.' Jussi lifted a hand to shield his eyes against the painful glare of the light and focused upon the figures that moved in the slanting sunshine, implacably closer with every second. 'Wait till they meet Max.'

Kaarlo snorted with what might have been laughter.

'Who's Max?' their companion asked, mildly.

'The best damned commander any Finn could ask for,' Jussi said. He had unslung his rifle, taken out his *puukko*, the sharp dagger-like knife they all carried, and was chipping with calm concentration at an ice ledge. 'Major Maximillian Bayer. The best bloody Finn of us all. Except that he's German. They're coming.' He levelled the rifle, steadied by the niche in the ice wall.

Kaarlo had narrowed keen, long-sighted eyes. 'Now,' he said.

One horse went down in the first staccato volley. The other reared, stung, and danced upon the ice. Its rider flung himself from the saddle. Kaarlo picked him off as he ran. 'Take the other horse,' Jussi said to their unknown companion, and calmly the young man stood, steadied his weapon.

'Down, you silly bastard!' Kaarlo shouted.

The one shot and then the other sounded in one long echo. The second horse fell, as if poleaxed. The young rifleman was flung yards by the bullet that caught him, to lie spread-eagled, bloody, lifeless in the snow.

'Shit,' Kaarlo said.

Jussi said nothing.

There was a moment's charged silence. Then Kaarlo moved a little. 'Two down,' he said, calmly. 'At least one an officer.'

'And the horses gone.' Jussi settled himself as best as he was able, crouched uncomfortably behind the dubious shelter of the ice.

'At least now they can't move any faster than we can.' Kaarlo was reloading his rifle. A bullet rebounded, singing, a few inches from his face. 'Fucking Russians,' he muttered, more viciously than usual.

Jussi was looking to the west. In the distance their charges ploughed through the difficult terrain, dark, distant specks in that merciless brightness. 'At least they're getting a move on.'

The yellow grin again, subversive, derisive. 'Wouldn't you?'

There was a moment's deceptive silence. The stillness of the icy wastes was absolute. Then a frenzy of shots shattered it.

Kaarlo was swearing, steadily, his voice low. His rifle was rock-still. 'Got you!' he said, undisguised satisfaction in his voice.

'They're outflanking us.' Jussi was sliding back from the ice wall. 'There may only be four of them left, but they're not stupid and they're much better armed.' As if to prove his point a bullet sang close to his head and instinctively he ducked.

'How far are we from the camp, would you say?'

'Not far. The others must be there by now.'

'Sun's going. It'll be dark soon. Best to make a run for it?'

The sharp, stained grin was the only answer.

Almost they made it. So close that a minute, perhaps two, would have made the difference. It was in the last dash that Jussi, who had stayed back to cover Kaarlo's final retreat to the camp, was caught in the sharp and crackling hail of bullets that sent him jerking into the air like a ghoulish puppet to land sprawled in an ungainly heap on the suddenly hideously stained ice.

Kaarlo, howling, turned. Charged back across the ice to where Jussi lay. A volley of wildly discharged bullets from the camp kept the pursuit at bay. 'Holy Mother,' Kaarlo said as he hauled the shrieking Jussi upright. 'We'd do better to deliver these stupid bastards to the Russians! I'd rather have them on their side than ours! Hold on, man! Hold on!'

As Kaarlo began to haul him to safety Jussi gave one more animal-like scream, and fainted. Blood marked their scrambling path back to where the others waited; blood fresh and bright, and in terrible quantity. In the tent Kaarlo worked, ripping the material from the shattered legs, tearing open the shirt to reveal the bubbling, bloody chest. Jussi made a small sound. His eyes flickered open.

'I'll take him.' One of the recruits, a small man muffled in sheepskin, knelt beside him. 'You go and help the others. They need you. I've had training. Let me try.'

'Try?' Kaarlo's face was tight with shock and with pain. 'You'd better do bloody better than try.'

The other man eyed the groaning Jussi and said nothing. Kaarlo grabbed his rifle and went outside.

For the moment all was quiet. He sidled up beside one of the young recruits. The man was steadying a heavy Russian revolver – one of the captured weapons that had been left at the camp in case of just such an emergency – against an outcrop of ice.

'Where are they?' Kaarlo asked.

'Two over there – behind that low ice wall, see? And the others over to the right. I think we might have got another of them. Injured at least.' The man's voice was commendably cool. 'We've managed to pin them down for the moment.'

'Right.' Kaarlo eyed the darkening sky. 'If we can keep them there while your mate in the tent patches Jussi up then we might have a chance.'

The other man, who had seen Jussi's wounds, as they all had, as Kaarlo had dragged him in, eyed his companion doubtfully, but said nothing.

Something moved next to the ice wall. Unhurriedly, Kaarlo took aim. The crack of his rifle echoed across the ice.

'Got him!' the other man said, excitedly. 'By God, you got him!'

Kaarlo said nothing.

'Three left.' The words were spoken almost like a prayer.

Quiet minutes passed.

'Kaarlo?'

Kaarlo turned. The man who had offered to attend to Jussi had crawled to his side. 'He wants to see you.'

Jussi was propped against a packing case. His face was bleached and drawn with pain, his eyes heavy with it. His rough jacket had been draped about his shoulders to keep the cold out, almost hiding the bandages that covered his chest, bandages through which the bright blood was already seeping. A blanket covered his shattered legs.

From outside the canvas tent came the sound of a shot, and then another.

'We're holding them off?' Jussi asked.

Kaarlo swallowed, blinked rapidly. 'Yes. There are three, maybe four of them left. If we can hold them until dark –'

Jussi shifted a little, took a shallow, painful breath. 'Yes. That was what I wanted to talk to you about.'

'You mean, they left him there?' Katya stared at Heimo in horror. 'Kaarlo – he *left Jussi there?*'

'Katya, he had no alternative.'

'What do you mean, no alternative?' Katya's voice was rising, outraged, edged with hysteria. 'Of *course* he had an alternative! He left a wounded man – his friend, or so he always pretended – alone – in the middle of the ice – surrounded by Russian soldiers – Heimo, I don't believe what you're saying. *I don't believe it!*'

Heimo, exhausted, dangerously close to tears himself, took an uncertain breath and cleared his throat. 'Katya – please – calm yourself. Listen to me –'

'Listen? Listen to what?' Her voice was suddenly, caustically calm. 'Listen to your excuses? To Kaarlo's excuses? There are none. What he did was inexcusable. I'll never forgive him. I pray God he'll never forgive himself.'

'He won't,' Heimo said, quietly.

'Then why? Why did he do it?'

'Katya, listen to me! Kaarlo was on active duty. His commanding officer – Jussi – gave him a direct order. He couldn't disobey it. Don't you see that? He couldn't!'

'Playing at soldiers,' Katya said, bitterly.

There was a long moment's silence. 'Is that what you think we're doing?' Heimo asked, at last.

Katya had turned away from him. She did not for a moment reply, but stood, head bowed, arms crossed tightly over her breast, as if in some way to contain the pain. At last she shook her head, briefly. 'No. Of course not. I'm sorry. It's just –' She stopped, shoulders hunched, her teeth clamped into her lip.

Heimo watched her in helpless sympathy. He lifted a hand, dropped it again. Every tense line of her body rejected any such advance. 'He tried,' he said, after a moment, grimly continuing the tale he had set himself to tell. 'The men who were with them testified to that. Please believe it, Katya. He flatly refused the order.' He waited. She gave no sign she had heard. 'Jussi threatened to shoot him where he stood.'

Still she said nothing.

'Night was closing in. Jussi insisted – and he was right – that their duty was to get the men they had with them to safety. He ordered Kaarlo to take them on, to leave him to defend the camp, to hold up the pursuit. Kaarlo offered to stay with him. Jussi refused. The recruits would never have made it on to Sweden without a guide. Katya, he was right. It was the only way.'

'They should never have left him,' Katya said quietly, stubbornly. 'They should have taken him with them.'

'No.' This time Heimo stepped across to her, turned her gently to face him, his hands on her shoulders, his kindly face stricken with a grief almost as great as hers, a grief he made no attempt to hide. 'He was too badly injured, Katya. Jussi knew it. Kaarlo knew it. He'd lost an enormous amount of blood. His legs –' He stopped. 'They had no sledge. Even if they had, the journey would probably have killed him. And the Russians were hunting them. Katya – they couldn't have saved him. It would simply have meant that they would all have died, or been taken. Jussi gave the only order possible. And Kaarlo had no option but to obey. And it worked. They all got through. Thanks to Jussi.'

'I should be happy about that?' Katya pulled herself free of his hands, walked to the table, sat, elbows on the table, staring into space with eyes that were wide and unblinking. Then with a sudden movement she dropped her face into her cupped hands. Yet still there were no tears; just the dreadful tension of grief that held her in a grip of iron, relentless and harsh.

'I'm so very, very sorry.' The pitifully inadequate words were very quiet.

'Yes. Thank you,' she said coldly, lifting her head.

'Kaarlo –' He hesitated.

'Where is he?'

'Still at Lockstedt, with the battalion. He wanted to come himself.'

'Tell him not to.' The words were brusque. 'Not now. Not ever. I don't want to see him.'

'Katya –'

Fiercely she flung up her head to look at him. Her face blazed. 'I tell you I don't want to see him! Tell him to stay away. You hear me, Heimo? *I won't see him!* You say that Jussi threatened to kill him if he didn't leave? Well tell him this – if he comes near me *I'll* kill him, for doing it. I swear it.'

'Katya, that simply isn't fair –'

'Fair?' Bleakly she grimaced. 'What's fair, Heimo? That Kaarlo's alive and Jussi's dead? That I'll never see my husband again? That he died without ever knowing that I'm carrying his child?' Her voice choked suddenly in her throat.

'God in heaven,' Heimo said.

'Is he? I doubt it. At the moment – I doubt it.' She took a long breath, closing her eyes, which stung and burned and yet still remained dry as the sands of the desert. She rubbed the tips of her fingers against her aching brow.

'Is there something I can get you? Someone I can call?'

'No. Thank you. I'm all right.' She sighed again, and at last relaxed. 'I'm sorry, Heimo. I know how bad this is for you. And I'm sorry I lost my temper –'

He made a small, dismissive gesture. 'Katya –'

'– but please, I'd like to be alone now. Quite alone. I have to think.'

He hesitated. 'You're sure?'

'Quite sure.' She came to him, lifted her face to his, kissed his cheek. 'Thank you.'

He hugged her to him for a moment, suddenly and fiercely. She felt the sobs that wracked his huge frame; and even that did not break through the chill, silent wall of shock that girded her own heart. Quiet at last, he let her go. She stood calm as he palmed the tears from his face with the heels of his hands, groped in his pocket for a handkerchief. Then, 'Just one thing?' she said.

'Yes?'

Her eyes were very bright and very steady upon his face. 'You are – absolutely sure? There can be no mistake? If Kaarlo and the others left?' She let the sentence hang in mid-air.

He shook his head. 'No. Don't think it, Katya. He was terribly injured. Even if the patrol captured him – if they didn't kill him – Kaarlo's convinced he could not have survived the journey back across the ice. And anyway –'

'And anyway, Jussi would not have allowed himself to be captured. I know.' Katya nodded.

He took his leave, kissing her again, squeezing her hand. She leaned tiredly for a long time against the door she closed behind him. 'Jussi,' she said, very quietly. 'Jussi.'

And still, strangely, the relief of tears was denied her.

The long, overcrowded train crawled through the bitter winter's night. The railway line ran through white-cloaked forests, empty and still, frozen into a brittle landscape that gleamed with an eerie beauty in the bright, chill light of the moon. The air, sharp as a knife, fairly glittered with cold.

Within the filthy carriages the walls and windows ran with condensation, and the air was foul. Sasha huddled into his corner, his aching head turned to the crack in the blind, beyond which he could see the blank and streaming window. He could catch no glimpse of the passing countryside. He was sweating beneath his clothes, his skin itched, his bladder was filled to bursting. There could be no question of trying to use the lavatory; as was the case throughout the train, the one provided within this carriage had long become so unendurably clogged with filth as to be unusable. The more hardy souls – or perhaps the more desperate – had taken to making for the front of the train, waiting until its crawling pace slowed almost to a stop – an all too frequent event – jumping into the snow in order to use the cover of the forest to relieve themselves, then scrambling back aboard before the battered, overstrained monster picked up speed again. Sasha slid his hand behind the blind, rubbed at the streaming window. For a second, blurred by the ice on the outside of the glass, he caught a smudged glimpse of the frozen world through which they passed. Those who did not make it back aboard the train – and there must have been some

392

– would be lucky to survive the night. And the halt, the lame and the sick who made up most of the passenger complement lay or sat in their own ordure, with no help, no hope and no pity offered them. The stench was intolerable; it clogged the nostrils and clung to the tongue.

He shifted uncomfortably in his seat. He'd have to risk it. Petrograd was still many hours away.

Even as he thought it the train shuddered and slowed, brakes grinding. 'Suffering Son of God.' A man in the bloodied uniform of a cavalryman laid his head back against the seat, shutting his one good eye. 'Not again?' The patch over his other eye had slipped, revealing the edge of a raw and empty gash. Sasha gritted his teeth and looked away.

The train slowed, carriages clanking, and stopped, the distant engine hissing steam. Outside, someone shouted.

'Open the window,' someone said.

Happy to breathe clear air, Sasha stood, opened the window, stuck his head out into the biting, literally breathtaking cold.

'What's the imbecile saying?' the cavalryman asked.

Sasha listened. The guard was making his way up the train, scrunching through the knee-deep snow by the side of the line, shouting. Windows were opening, and then doors, as men climbed from the hot train into the bitter cold of the night and stood shivering, huddled into their coats, breath steaming about them.

'What is it?' Sasha called.

The guard glanced up. 'We've run out of fuel, Excellency,' he said, brusquely. 'All able-bodied men into the forest. We need logs.'

'What we need,' someone said, very clearly from behind Sasha, 'is some sort of bloody organization in this bloody stinking war.'

Sasha shrugged into his greatcoat, jammed his hat on his head, jumped onto the track, flexed his tingling legs, and along with almost every other of the men who had left the train at the guard's call, relieved himself upon the bank, shielding himself carefully from the cold. The one-eyed cavalryman had jumped down beside him, joined him companionably at the bank. The urine hissed and steamed into the snow. 'If you ran a brothel the way they're running this war,' the one-eyed man said, mildly, 'we'd all be on our backs and the girls –' The rest of the sentence was lost as the engine expired finally in an anguished shriek of steam. The guard plodded back past them. 'Hatchets and saws in the tender, hatchets and saws in the tender. Form groups of four. One torch to each group. Meet at the front of the train.'

Sasha muttered a vague reply to his companion and turned away, hunching against the cold, collar turned up around his face. He had come this far with safety, further than, in those first desperate hours, he had ever believed he could possibly make it. His initial flight had been an instinctive, animal thing. A need to escape. There had been neither logic nor hope attached to it. But God – or the devil – had been with him and now, unbelievably, Petrograd lay only a few tantalizing hours away. He was really beginning to believe he had a hope of reaching the city. Once there he could disappear; the place was crawling with deserters, was a seething antheap of refugees and displaced people. In Petrograd he would be safe. They'd never find him. They'd never be able to force him to go back. He would not jeopardize his chances now by an offhand exchange, the possibility, however remote, of recognition.

He picked up his hatchet, trudged off into the forest with the other men. The still winter silence was shattered. For three hours they worked like fiends. Sasha found himself hauling the makeshift sledges of cut wood back to the train, stacking it in the tender. He was hungry and he was cold. But in an odd way the unexpected physical work soothed him. When at last he climbed wearily back into his carriage and dropped into his seat his closed eyes and steady breathing were no sham. As the train pulled slowly away, wheels moving rhythmically along the tracks, Sasha slept.

His last thoughts were of Valentina. But his uneasy dreams, oddly, were of a raging and implacable Margarita.

Margarita was out when her brother-in-law Donovalov first called upon her. 'Said it was most important, he did.' Petra shuffled her feet, cuffed her nose.

Margarita winced. 'For goodness' sake, girl! How often must I tell you not to do that? What did he want?'

'Didn't say.' The girl, as always, was surly. She knew no other defence for her own shortcomings. 'Said he'd be back this afternoon.'

Margarita turned to the mirror, lifted her arms with the practised grace that could deceive the most knowing watcher into believing it to be natural, removed the pin from her hat, handed the pretty, feathered thing to the girl who stood behind her. 'When this afternoon?'

'Didn't say. Just this afternoon.'

Margarita tutted. She had not enjoyed her day. The city had become impossible. Queues and shortages. Filthy, squalid streets. And, too, an odd feeling of menace about the city that had once been so graceful, so light-hearted. As she had passed along the Liteini a man – a ruffian – had stepped into her way and thrust a leaflet at her. When she had refused to take it he had muttered to her, as she had pushed past him, words that had only some seconds later registered in her brain. 'Take it, bitch. See what's in store for you.' Her skin crawled now, as it had then, at the thought of it. Why didn't they clear such scum from the streets? Why weren't they where they belonged, in the army, fighting for their country? How had it happened that Petrograd – oh, how she hated the name! – had become, it seemed, the midden of the nation, attracting to itself the thousands, the hundreds of thousands, of displaced, malcontent, desperate people that this dreadful war had produced?

'Tea, Petra, please,' she said. 'And in God's name don't tell me we have no sugar.'

Her brother-in-law came to the little apartment as the early winter twilight was closing in. Margarita was reading a magazine. She looked up as Donovalov was announced by a Petra who scuttled, the moment the words were pronounced, back into the cupboard of a kitchen, which was her refuge.

'Pavel Petrovich.' Gracefully Margarita extended her small hand. 'You came earlier, I believe. I'm sorry I was away from home. Please, won't you sit down? And would you care for tea?'

Donovalov hesitated. This was an interview to be savoured. A pretty butterfly, laid upon the board, the long pin poised above it. The thought amused him. Aroused him. He lingered upon it in his mind. 'Thank you, Margarita Victorovna, no. And I'll stand – ' he hesitated for a fraction of a second ' – if you don't mind?'

'Of course not. Why should I mind?'

She did mind. She did not know why, but she minded very much indeed. Something about the man's face, the intent and secretive eyes sent a small chill through her body; yet the room was warm, perhaps overly so. Margarita could no more bring herself to preserve fuel than she could conserve those other bodily comforts that were becoming more and more difficult to obtain. A box of chocolates, bestowed by a sympathetic – inevitably male – friend, must be eaten at once. Two spoonfuls of sugar must sweeten her tea; it must be two, or none. Now was all she understood. Tomorrow was a concept, had little reality as time. 'Why should I mind?' she asked again, and tilted her head to look at him, aware that the lamp upon the table glared too fully upon her, casting unflattering shadows.

He stood, tall and narrow-shouldered, his back to the warm stove. His face was in shadow, yet oddly that very fact emphasized its character; and its character was cruelty, pure and simple. Cruelty not simply in the slanting black eyes, nor in the sharp, rodent-like features – warmth, humour, would have softened that face, would have brought it to humanity; even, perhaps, made it attractive – but in the underlying character of the man, which suddenly and undisguisedly confronted her. For one, small, uncharacteristically selfless moment the woman in her found herself thinking; in God's sweet name, how was Yelena wed to this man?

She cleared her throat delicately, straightened her back, hands clasped in her lap. 'You're well, Pavel Petrovich?' The words dropped into the silence like stones thrown, tentatively, by a child.

He ignored them. When he spoke his voice was gentle, intimate, almost caressing. 'Where is Sasha, Margarita? Is he here?'

She stared at him. Laughed a little. Shook her head. 'Sasha? Here?' The dread was growing. 'Why – why should he be here?'

Donovalov was the master of the small silence. 'Because he's deserted, Margarita,' he said at last, his tone very soft, very reasonable. 'He has deserted his men and his command. He has disgraced himself, and you. He has run away. And he's here. In Petrograd.'

She looked at him for a very long time. Even breath seemed suspended. Then, 'No,' she said, quietly and positively. 'No, Pavel Petrovich. That can't be so. You've made a mistake.'

'No mistake, my dear.' Never had his address been so personal, never his menace so obvious. 'Where is he, Margarita? You know? Surely, you know?'

'It's a mistake,' she said again, woodenly.

He took a slow, overly patient breath. Let the quiet deepen about them.

Margarita's hands, clasped as they had been upon her lap, were fused together, white-knuckled, white-nailed, the tendons standing clear of the smooth skin. 'It's a mistake,' she said again, purposefully, stubbornly. And the self-deception almost worked. She lifted her head defiantly, met his eyes.

They did not waver. 'No mistake,' he repeated. 'Your husband was engaged in action near Mogil'ov. His men were cut off. He left them. It was his bad luck that enough of them survived to report it. He ran away, Margarita. We've had reports since. There's no doubt that he's in Petrograd. He's a coward and a traitor. An officer who has deserted his men.'

'I don't believe you,' she said. She stood, agitatedly, facing him. *'I don't believe you!'*

'Believe me, my dear. It's true.'

In her heart, suddenly, she did not doubt it. She stared at him, mute.

'He's here. In Petrograd.' He stepped towards her, drawing her to him with that fearful, reptilian attraction that lured even as it repelled. 'You're sure you don't know where?'

'No,' she said.

He spread mock-apologetic hands. 'Do you mind if I look around the apartment?' His smile was as unpleasant as it had been in the whole of the interview. 'A formality, you understand. We know he isn't here.'

Humiliation sickened her. 'Look if you like.'

Cursorily he pushed open doors. Surveyed rooms. Insultingly neither opened cupboards nor searched for any kind of secret place. Came back into the sitting room. 'Where is he, Margarita?'

Her mind was a complete, shocked blank. She felt as she had felt when, as a child, she had been thrown from a sledge and hit her head upon a log. She remembered now the daze, the odd, disembodied feel of it. She could not think. She said nothing.

He knew his victims well. Satisfied, he could leave her. It was more than a strong possibility that she did not in fact know where her despicable, handsome, aristocratic bastard of a husband was. But if she knew – if she suspected – sooner or later she would tell him.

He had already noted the brand new instrument that hung upon the wall by the door. 'You have a telephone, I see?'

'Yes.' The look she cast was defiant, challenging him to ask how she had come by such an expensive toy.

He did not bother to pass comment. He took a notebook and the stub of a pencil from his pocket, scribbled a number upon a page, tore it from the book. Laid it upon the table. 'If you think of anything, remember anything, that might help us?' He glanced at her. She avoided his eyes. Her face was as cold and as still as an icefield. 'Just telephone me on this number. You'll get no-one but me, I promise. And – of course – anything you might have to tell me will be considered as absolutely confidential.'

She said nothing.

He turned to go. Stopped by the sideboard that stood next to the door. The miniature, brilliant-coloured, pasteboard theatre stood where it always had. He surveyed it in silence. Behind him, Margarita made not a sound. She might herself have been one of those stiffly-poised cardboard figures.

He reached a finger, flicked sharply at the small, bright prince who smiled so emptily at his two-dimensional princess. The figure teetered, then fell, face down, upon the stage. 'A pity,' Donovalov said. 'A very great pity.'

For a very long time after he had gone Margarita barely moved. Then, with a sudden brisk step and a swirl of skirts she walked into the bedroom. At the dressing table she bent, pulling open a small drawer, rummaging impatiently through the contents, straightening at last with a small, folded scrap of paper in her hand.

She turned, walked back into the sitting room and over to the table, where she laid the paper beside that other, which Donovalov had left, smoothing them both flat.

On the one, a telephone number. And on the other an address. An address supplied by an urchin, bought for a few roubles.

She sat carefully upon one of the chairs that was pulled to the table, arranging her skirts fastidiously. Drew the pieces of paper towards her. Smoothed them again, meticulously, carefully.

An address. A telephone number.

Of course I'm sure – I made him up – I invented him.

A pity. A very great pity.

A little under two hours later, Margarita picked up the telephone.

CHAPTER NINETEEN

The news in England, during that spring of 1916, was dominated not by events in Russia but by the fighting at Verdun. After an autumn and winter of stalemate the Germans had launched an offensive at the end of February callously designed literally to bleed the battered and battle-weary French forces to death. The Allies were caught by surprise, and the punishment was devastating. Yet, incredibly, the French did not, as the Germans had so confidently expected, break. For week after week and then for month after exhausted month they stubbornly held the line, despite catastrophic losses in men and arms. By early March the landscape around Verdun had been reduced to a lunar nightmare; no tree stood, no building survived, the very structure of the earth was destroyed. Men fought knee-deep in mud and filth, the wounded died in shellholes flooded with melted ice-water. Attack and counter-attack was mounted. The fighting was ferocious, through two months, three months and then four. Land was captured, almost yard by yard, and lost again within hours. Thousands upon thousands of men died in a vicious struggle that gained nothing for either side. One hundred thousand shells filled with phosgene gas rained upon the defenders; the poisoned fog seeped across the land, sinking into cellars and dugouts; men choked and died and were buried where they lay. Yet still the French held and still it continued.

Aware that their allies could not sustain such savage punishment for much longer, the British High Command conceived a plan to divert at least some of the pressure from the wounded and weary French. They planned a campaign on the Somme, to be launched at the beginning of July, and to be preceded by the greatest bombardment the world had ever seen.

Unfortunately for the planners, and far more so for the men

who were to be involved in the attack, this massive bombardment was not the only dreadful record that would be set in those first days on the battlefields of the Somme.

Very little of this was reported in the newspapers that Anna read to her husband each day. The casualty lists grew, the Zeppelins raided with apparent impunity, the public were exhorted to greater and greater endeavours to support the war effort; but on the whole the really bad news was kept from them. It was not considered to be in the public interest – perhaps it truly was not in the public interest – to tell the tragic truth.

Guy was dying. Anna knew it; was sadly certain that he knew it too. By the early spring of 1916 they had moved, at Anna's own insistence, from the country, and from Sythings, the house they both so much loved, to London, to a house in Portland Place, to be near Guy's specialist. But it could only be a matter of time, and there was little anyone could do. Her husband was an old man, and his heart was tired. She devoted her days to his comfort and happiness. She had much to thank him for, and these were her thanks.

She had also, as she had written to Margarita, begun to take an active interest in the business. Though for obvious reasons it was less profitable than it had been in peacetime yet still it prospered, quietly. Even in times such as these there was a place for music. The Portland Place house was just around the corner from the shop, which was in Wigmore Street, and, during the walks that Guy very sensibly insisted that she took, she quite often called in. Horace Parker, the manager who had taken over from the younger man who had been conscripted into the forces, was a dull but competent man; it amused her to see how he scurried to meet her each time she arrived. She was also astute enough to realize that he was a man who needed a guiding hand. With an interest that quite surprised her, she took it upon herself to guide him, with Guy's solid and sensible advice behind her.

Guy watched, and smiled tiredly, satisfied.

Anna went, too, to the workshop in Soho. And, as she stood unnoticed in the doorway at the top of a long, narrow flight of steps, was utterly taken aback at the fierce surge of homesickness that flooded her; an emotion she was to experience in the same degree and with as much surprise on each subsequent visit. She was looking into a scene that was as familiar to her as her own face in the mirror. Here were the padded work-benches, set beneath the windows as they were in her father's workshop, though in scale this was much greater. Here were the tools, the rows of bottles, the half-made instruments, the polishing cloths, the shavings upon the floor and the racks of violins and violas, finished and half-finished, hanging from the ceiling. Instruments were propped against the wall, or lay upon the benches and tables. Small boxes were set upon the benches full of bits and pieces of pegs and bridges, carved scrolls and tiny slivers of wood that could have been anything; here was the controlled chaos of creativity that she remembered so well. And above all, here was the smell; the elusive smell of the wood, the varnish, the polish, that was utterly unmistakable. Had she been blindfolded she would have known the nature of the place in which she stood. And had she been blindfolded she would, against all sense, have expected to hear Andrei's voice, the sound of his laughter.

'Mrs de Fontenay –' An elderly man looked up and saw her standing in the doorway, laid aside the instrument upon which he was working, came towards her, wiping his hands upon his canvas apron. This was Albert Thompson, craftsman and long-time manager of the workshop. He knew his own worth. He was not too discomposed at this unexpected visit. '– Good afternoon. I'm sorry, I didn't know –'

Anna shook her head. 'No, no, Albert. Don't worry. To be truthful I didn't know I was coming myself. An impulse, you understand?'

'Of course. Of course. You know young Peter, here?' Anna nodded, smiling. 'Young' Peter was a good couple of years older than she was herself. Indeed most of the men who awkwardly acknowledged her greetings were far from young. The young men were at war, their skilled hands being put to other less peaceable pursuits than these. 'And this is Harry Stewart. A good lad, is Harry. Got good hands.'

The boy, no more than nineteen or twenty, blushed with pleasure and shifted upon his stool. His empty trouser leg was tucked and pinned neatly at the knee.

'What are you making?' Anna stood beside him at the workbench.

'A viola, Ma'am.' His strong, varnish-stained fingers delicately held a chisel half the size of a box of matches. The sight of those stained fingers brought another strange and painful twist of memory; Andrei's long finger had been stained just so as it had rested upon a sheet of music as her uncle had bent close to her, explaining a phrase, a breath of emotion in the music that she was attempting to play.

'You'd like a cup of tea, Ma'am?'

'Yes please, I would. If it isn't too much trouble?'

She stayed for longer than she had intended, though nobody seemed to mind. After that first painful rush of nostalgia it was good to be back in this atmosphere that she remembered so well. At Albert's invitation she tested the violin he had just finished, and pronounced it a beautiful instrument.

'And beautifully played, Ma'am, if I might venture such an opinion.'

She smiled, ruefully. 'Not as well as it might be, Albert. Nowhere near as well as it might be!' She was truly unaware of the effect that her still-accented English had upon her listeners. They gazed at her, rapt.

'I do hope I haven't disrupted your afternoon?' she asked as she left.

'Not at all, Ma'am. We're delighted to see you. Any time.'

She told Guy that evening where she had been, and he smiled. 'I wondered how long it would take you to find your way down there.'

'You don't mind?'

'Why should I mind, my dear? And as for the shop, I think it an excellent idea that you should drop in from time to time. We can safely leave the running of the workshop to Albert, but to be honest with you I'm not so sure of Parker. It won't do him any harm to have you call in on him every now and again.'

Anna leaned forward to pour tea. The tea cups were pretty; bone china, patterned with roses, and the teapot, jug and sugar-bowl matched them. The room, too, was lovely, all rose and cream, the furniture light and elegant, tall windows opened to a tiny walled garden and the scents of an English spring. In six years she had grown so used to English ways that she rarely thought of the customs of her homeland. Yet now, perhaps because of the memories the afternoon had brought, she found herself thinking of a steaming samovar, the tea glasses waiting, a snow-covered world beyond the window, a skyline of golden onion domes and slender spires –

'I went somewhere else, too.' She set his tray over his legs, put the tea cup upon it.

He was watching her, his eyes, which despite illness and age had faded only a little from their brilliant blue, calm and loving. These few years she had given him had been the most precious of a long and enjoyable life. He had thought to help her, and Andrei, and had in fact been himself presented with the most precious gift of all. He recognized her restlessness – indeed had recognized it before she had herself – and understood it. It would not be long, he knew, before it could be assuaged. A very little while more at his side, and then she would be free. 'Oh? Where was that?'

She took her tea cup to the window, stood, tall, lean-framed and elegant in forest-green silk, looking out into the tiny walled garden. The bright hair had been cut short and cleverly shaped. Her high-boned face, which had never been pretty but equally had never been less than interesting, was now arresting and attractive, still without coming anywhere near any ideal of conventional beauty. 'I went to the Russian church in Welbeck Street. You know – the Embassy Chapel.'

He sipped his tea, the effort involved in keeping his hands steady greater than he would admit, even to himself.

'It was astonishing.' Her voice was very quiet, there was a far-away look in her eyes. 'I had forgotten how very beautiful – how very different – our Russian churches are.'

'And the music,' he said.

She turned, smiling. 'Ah yes. The music. Your charming, calm, civilized churches have little like it, do they?'

'No. They don't.' He did not comment upon nor question the pronouns she had used.

She put her cup back onto the tray. 'Would you like me to read to you?'

'No, thank you.' He laid his head back upon the pillow and smiled. 'I should like you to play for me, Anna Victorovna.'

It was summer when he died, and the dreadful shambles of the Somme was at its height. This was not a catastrophe that could be kept from the people. On that first terrible day, the first day of July, the stark figures had spoken for themselves and would not be silenced. Whole regiments were gone, and with them whole families, whole villages, whole networks of relationship. Men had joined together, served together and then, terribly, were massacred together. The so-called 'Pals' battalions had proved a disaster in this gruelling modern war in which thousands – hundreds of thousands – could die in a day. The country was in mourning.

Guy died two weeks after the start of the campaign on the Somme. Unlike those young men who perished in France beneath the gun he died peacefully and quietly – a fate many at that time would envy him – and, predictably, his affairs were in perfect order. Anna sat, pale and utterly composed, and listened to lawyers and solicitors, accountants and advisers. Friends called with their commiserations, and she thanked them, served tea, sherry or ten-year-old Scotch, according to their needs and habits. She said very little. She even, in those first few days, thought very little. She felt oddly removed from those about her, who with the best of intentions fussed and tried to cosset her. She did not need to be cosseted, though politely she accepted the help of others when it was forced upon her. She found herself perfectly capable of organizing the funeral, of coping with the small, everyday tasks that demanded her attention, perfectly well able to understand the not-too-complicated matters of the Will, the inheritance and the business, which was now hers. What she could not do, it seemed, was to feel. Guy was gone; she had known it would happen, had, with his understanding and encouragement, prepared herself for it; perhaps with altogether too much success. Now there was nothing to do but to endure; endure the knowledge that something warm and enchanting had gone from her life and would never return. A gaping hole had been torn in the fabric of her world. She rather wished that people would simply leave her alone to adjust, to come to terms with a suddenly, shockingly, empty life.

She did not cry at the funeral. Or perhaps she couldn't. She wasn't sure.

In the weeks before Guy's death she had taken as a matter of habit on the way back from the shop to visiting the Russian church in Welbeck Street. On occasion she herself questioned her motives in doing so; was she truly in this place to worship, or was she simply revisiting a childhood long past, long lost, yet somewhere still remembered, somehow still yearned for?

For some time after Guy's death, without really understanding why, she knew she was avoiding the place; but then one afternoon, after a visit to the shop, she found herself standing on the pavement in Welbeck Street. She did not remember taking any conscious decision; it was as if her feet had carried her there entirely of their own accord.

The church was empty; unusually so. She stood very quiet and still in the womb of this sacred place, with its flickering candlelight, its icons, its overwhelming silence. The air was impregnated with incense and the smell of the candles; a smell that was like the very breath of her young life. Images flickered in her mind. Her grandfather. Her family. Andrei. The wide and sweeping countryside of her homeland, the great, slow-moving rivers, the domes and spires of the cities. And, too, suddenly she found herself remembering Guy. Not the sick man she had nursed for so many months – not even the attentive and observant English gentleman of Sythings – but Guy, as she first had known him. The Guy in the photograph that had stood upon Andrei's sideboard. The Guy she had liked and respected from the first time she laid eyes upon him. The Guy who had, in the apartment in St Petersburg, listened to her music with a look of wonder on his face. The Guy who had taken her to the opera. Suddenly that night gleamed in her memory, clear as if it had been yesterday. The dress – her first grown-up dress. The Italian Opera. They had performed 'La Bohème', and she had cried – oh, heavens, how she had cried! – and he had given her his handkerchief. Then he had taken her to the restaurant on the Islands – the name escaped her for the moment – and had told her to hold up her head as she crossed the dance floor to go to the ladies' room. Not, in fact, the least important advice he had ever given her. She laughed suddenly at the recollection, and then at last she was crying. Not noisily, nor passionately, but simply and quietly, the tears running unchecked and uncheckable down her face, dripping into the expensive lace of her collar. Guy was gone. For ever. What would she do without him? Without his wit and his laughter, without his protection? Without his love?

She thought it odd that, having remained dry-eyed for so long, once the tears had started she found it all but impossible to stop them. She dried her eyes before she left the little church, but found them overflowing again as she walked down the busy streets towards Portland Place. Briskly she walked, and as briskly the tears fell. No-one took the slightest notice; this was London, after all, and London in the summer of 1916, at that. It was not so very unusual to see tears upon the streets of a capital at war.

She did not come to her decision lightly; certainly not as arbitrarily as she knew it seemed to others that she had. Nor did she contemplate its implementation without misgiving. But the moment she made it, it became a compulsion. No objections, no obstacles would divert her.

She wanted to go home.

Not for ever. England had claimed her, she had a life and responsibilities here that she could not – indeed had no wish to – abrogate. But a large part of her heart, perhaps more truly her soul, still belonged to Russia, and she had been away far, far too long. Guy had recognized her homesickness before she had herself. Over the past months, compounded by very real worry for her family, from whom she had not heard for months, it had been growing. Only the need to stay with Guy had kept her from going before; now nothing held her.

She wanted to go home.

She made the final decision sitting at the table in the small but elegant dining room of the Portland Place house, listening to an animated young man talk about Petrograd, from which he had just returned. He had been brought to the house by an old friend from the Russian Embassy, who knew Anna had family in the city. Anna had invited them both to dine. She sat now, elbows on table, chin in hand, food all but untouched, her eyes fast upon the young man, her brain, after the years of silence, tuning in to his rapid Russian speech.

'Shortages are getting worse. The queues for bread get longer each day – I saw whole streets full of queuing people. There's much talk of profiteering. The people are angry – the war isn't going well, our losses have been enormous, the Generals fight and squabble amongst themselves. And the Empress –' the young man spread expressive hands '– she's very unpopular.'

'She always was, surely?' Anna asked, quietly.

He nodded. 'That's true. But now –' He shrugged a little. 'She's truly loathed. It's said she traffics with the enemy. That she and the Nameless One influence the Tsar to such an extent that –'

'The what?'

The young man laughed. 'Sorry. Force of habit. People in the city are so superstitious about the man they won't even mention his name.'

'Rasputin, you mean?'

'Yes. Every sin is laid at his door. You'd think him the devil himself if you could hear the way they speak of him. And the Empress is being tarred with the same brush –'

'– and through her the Tsar.' Count Boris Stelyetsin rubbed his short, neat beard thoughtfully.

'Yes.'

'I suppose the people have to have someone to blame?' Anna nodded to the manservant who stood beside the wine table, indicating that he should replenish the gentlemen's glasses. 'If things are as bad as you say they are?'

'They're worse, Anna Victorovna, far worse, I promise you. The city is overcrowded, all but swamped with refugees, with wounded, even with deserters. And with peasants who are flocking in from the countryside, where already there's famine. Shortages in the city are desperate, and can only get worse. Food, medicines, clothes, fuel. I dread the thought of what winter will bring. The summer has been a bad one – grey and rainy, with hardly a day's sunshine. The people are hungry, and there's unrest amongst the workers –'

'Enough, Grigor Petrovich!' The older man held up a hand. 'Don't frighten Anna Victorovna!'

'I'm not frightened,' Anna said, with sober truth. 'Tell me more, Grigor Petrovich.'

He told her more, painting a picture of a city, of a country, in complete disarray, of a people being pushed perilously close to the edge of anarchy by hardship and by a monarch and an administration that appeared neither to care about nor to understand what was happening under their noses. He told of the agitators, of the strikes and the marches, of the riots. Of the mutinous mutterings in the food queues and in the ranks of the ill-led, ill-equipped army. He told of a vicious repression and of the people's hatred for the Tsar's Secret Police. He painted a vivid picture of a city in which life became more difficult, more exhausting and more uncertain every day.

'And the journey, Grigor Petrovich?' Anna asked, mildly. 'How did you get to Petrograd and back?'

The young man did not see his older companion's sudden frown. 'Via Newcastle, Anna Victorovna. To Sweden, on to Finland and then to Petrograd. The North Sea crossing is the riskiest part of course – you'll remember Lord Kitchener was drowned just a couple of months ago when his ship hit a mine. But the Hun have been relatively quiet in that part of the world since Jutland.'

'So it isn't an impossible journey?'

He laughed. 'Oh, no. Far from it. People do it all the –' The young man stopped, startled by a sharp cough from the Count, who was watching Anna with growing concern upon his affable face.

Anna faced him, calmly, smiling. 'Dear Boris, something tells me I'll need a friend at the Embassy if I'm to contemplate such a trip?'

The younger man's jaw dropped.

In his agitation the older almost choked on his wine. 'Absolutely not, Anna Victorovna! I utterly forbid it!'

She shook her head, still calm, still smiling. 'You can't forbid it, Boris. You know it. And if you won't help me I shall simply keep on banging on doors until I find someone who will. Guy had many contacts and much influence. I'll find someone, I

409

assure you. But I should prefer it to be a friend. I should prefer it to be you.'

'It's madness, Anna! Complete madness! There's a war on!'

'I know it.'

'Petrograd is a dangerous place.'

Her face was sober. 'I know that, too. I know it even better after Grigor Petrovich's graphic description. Grigor, my family are in Petrograd. I haven't heard from any of them for months. I don't know where they are or what's happened to them. I intend to find out.' Guy, had he been there, would have noted the sudden stubborn set of her sharp jaw.

The Count was not going to give up so easily. 'My dearest Anna – you can't –'

She would not allow him to continue. 'Grigor, I can. And I will. There's hardship and there's want in Petrograd – what a very ugly name that is! And one thing I do know; in such circumstances money can be a very potent weapon. And I have money now, Boris. Would you expect me to stand by whilst my family starve, or worse, without my even trying to help? No. The only question to be answered, the only point to be discussed is – will you help me, or must I search out someone else? I assume one needs passes and things?'

Grigor spluttered with sudden laughter.

The Count surveyed her helplessly. 'Yes, Anna. One does need passes. And things.'

'And you can get them for me?' She was relentless.

'I –'

Composedly watching him she folded her hands and her lips and let the silence lengthen. Grigor was still grinning.

'I could, yes,' he said at last, reluctantly.

'And will you?'

He made one last try. 'Anna, my dear, why don't you simply send the money to your family? I promise – I swear! – I'll make sure it reaches them.'

She shook her head. 'That isn't good enough, Boris, and you surely know it. I have to go myself. I'm certain you can see that?' The strange, empty life that a few days before had threatened to overwhelm her was receding. Here was action, here was a purpose. 'So, please, will you help me?'

He leaned back in his chair, his hands resting upon the table, his eyes upon hers. 'Do I have any choice in the matter?'

She smiled and shook her head. 'No. You don't.'

Only once did she regret that decision, and that was not during the long-drawn-out process of obtaining her travel documents, her tickets, the permission for this, that and the other that naturally attended such a journey in wartime and that took, incredibly, a full six months to complete. Impatience was her constant companion, and exasperation with the mills of officialdom that ground so exceedingly slow and so exceedingly small, but never doubt. Her only moment of regret came during the violent February North Sea crossing, when, in a claustrophobic cabin, clinging to her bunk and vomiting into a bucket in company with two other women and a small, miserable child, she came to the conclusion that she would not survive the journey.

Grigor Petrovich, heading back to the Russian Office of Foreign Affairs and detailed by Count Stelyetsin to escort Anna to Petrograd – the coincidence of dates, Anna suspecting, having much to do with the slowness with which her application to travel to Russia had been serviced – had no such problems.

'I've seen worse, Anna Victorovna,' he assured her, cheerfully, when at last she joined him on deck, pale and none too happy, as they approached the Swedish coast. 'I've seen worse. Take a good breath of this air. That will do the trick.'

The shoreline had appeared, frozen and decked in snow. The clouds were clearing. A low sun slanted light from the horizon. Anna stared. 'I had forgotten,' she said, quietly.

He smiled, understanding. Turned, his back to the rail, his coat collar pulled up about his face. He, like Anna, was wearing a fur hat and heavy gloves. He looked down at her, his eyes interested. 'You're not afraid?' he asked.

She smiled, wryly. 'Three hours ago I was terrified. But now? No. What can Petrograd throw at me that the North Sea didn't?'

He did not smile. 'Things have changed since our conversation around your dining table. Very much for the worse.'

'I know they have. All the more reason for me to go.' The news that had been coming out of Russia in the past months

411

had been all bad. The Russian army, ill-led, ill-supplied, ill-trained, was just a step from complete demoralization. There were reports of officers refusing to lead their men into battle for fear of being shot in the back. In Petrograd it had, in October, taken four Cossack regiments to restore order after a bout of factory strikes in which soldiers took the side of the strikers and fired on police. One hundred and fifty soldiers had been executed. All winter the strikes and demonstrations had continued, as temperatures had dropped to minus forty degrees, as bread and fuel had disappeared almost entirely from the shops and the markets, and as the price of food had risen from between forty to sixty per cent. Inflation had risen to seven hundred per cent. Starvation prowled the streets of the city and the fields and lanes of the countryside alike. Widespread famine and brutal losses at the Front were combining to produce the sullen growlings of a storm. 'All the more reason,' Anna repeated.

'The last reports from the city were very confused.' He leaned easily upon the rail, watching her. Nauseously Anna averted her eyes from the shifting, angrily swelling sea. 'The Tsar has postponed the next session of the Duma, I heard that just before I left London. There have been demonstrations. Violent demonstrations. Petrograd has been described as a powder keg awaiting the match.'

Anna conquered her stomach and lifted her head. 'That's why I'm here, Grigor,' she said. 'My family are in Petrograd. Where else should I be?'

It was a long journey from Stockholm, around the frozen gulf to Haparanda and the Finnish–Swedish frontier. Yet not for a moment did Anna tire. The view, after the late, northern sunrise, from the window of the train kept her spellbound. The soft green countryside of Sussex had receded in her memory, distant as a recollected dream. These were the landscapes, the snow-scapes, of her childhood. When they arrived at Haparanda, just after noon, the sun, risen a couple of hours before, still hung low on the southern horizon, sliding sideways across the sky and casting rainbow beams between low islands of snow-cloud. The frontier crossing was just fifteen miles from the Arctic Circle; the air was cold and clear.

The formalities at the customs post seemed to take for ever; civil as the Swedish officers were, Anna was impatient. 'What on earth is going *on*? Why can't we cross the river?'

'Smugglers,' Grigor said. 'There's a fortune to be made if you're ready to take the risk.'

Anna tapped a sharp fingernail upon the table at which they sat. 'Well, surely, they can see that *we* aren't smugglers?'

He smiled at her indignation. 'If it were that easy, they'd be out of a job,' he said.

They drove at last across the river towards Torneo. On an island that marked the frontier, in the middle of the river, they were stopped again. Here was the outpost of the Russian Empire; represented in this instance by a few roughly-built wooden houses, a sprawling warehouse and barracks, and an enclosure with high paling fencing that looked like a miniature prison camp. They were treated with courtesy by an officer eager to practise his English upon Anna, required to fill out an elaborate and so far as Anna could see entirely unnecessary questionnaire, and then were kept waiting for an hour whilst the thing was processed. Anna took one look at the packed and squalid little restaurant and declined a glass of tea. But at last they were allowed to join their hired sledge to drive through the cold, crisp air on across the river towards the low hilly coastline of Finland. Long lines of freight sledges moved steadily across the snow-covered ice. Amongst the roofs of Torneo Anna glimpsed the gilded domes of a Russian church, set bright against the darkly-wooded slopes. At the station their luggage was checked yet again; and at last, only three hours behind schedule – a positive triumph of organization – they were on the move again, the long train pulling into the early winter dusk, heading down the length of Finland towards the Russian frontier and the city that Anna still thought of as St Petersburg.

The trip was exhausting. If the packed train stopped once it stopped a hundred times, snorting and wheezing. Uncomfortably Anna dozed, and woke, dozed and woke again in the cramped compartment. There were no sleepers available. Suddenly the stress of the past few days caught up with her; she seemed to have been travelling for ever. And towards what? The sharp teeth of fear nibbled in the darkness. Her snatched sleep was disturbed by turbulent dreams.

They breakfasted in the darkness of a northern dawn, grateful for tea and rough bread rolls. And slowly they rolled south. They passed through Kuopio still in darkness.

'I have a cousin who I think must live somewhere around here,' Anna said. And found herself remembering; Katya, vivid and laughing – the lessons with Monsieur Drapin, the poor pompous little man so disconcerted by Katya's mischief – the light-hearted days, the walks, arm in arm, along the banks of the Fontanka. Where in God's name had it all gone? What madness had overtaken the world that had vanquished youth and put in its place death and destruction?

'Sorry?' Grigor leaned across the narrow aisle towards her.

She turned her head, not letting him see the sudden brightness of her eyes. 'I said I have a cousin who married a Finn. She lived somewhere around here, I believe. I was just wondering where she is now.' Safe, surely? Of all of them Katya must certainly be safe. She was always the lucky one.

Wearily Anna leaned her head against the cold glass, peered through the frosted window into the lightening sky and wondered if Katya ever thought of those days in St Petersburg, and of her quiet cousin, who had caused her so much mirth.

Katya was not in Kuopio; she was in Helsinki. And at that moment the last person on her mind was her cousin Anna, comfortably settled in England with her rich and elderly husband. Katya was pulling the small sledge that contained, amongst other things, her three-month-old son very carefully indeed along the snowy sidewalk, towards a house that stood by the market place on the quayside. The baby was wrapped like an Eskimo and settled deep into furs, against the bitter cold.

There were Russian soldiers everywhere, standing around braziers at street corners and crossroads, stamping their feet, their breath clouding the air about them, talking no doubt, at least whilst their officers were not listening, of the strange and violent events taking place in their homeland, rumours of which, ever growing, reached this near-neighbour of Petrograd very quickly. Small platoons marched the dirty, impacted snow of the arrow-straight streets, guns slung upon their shoulders, greatcoats buttoned against the cold. There was little traffic. Those Finnish civilians who braved the streets walked as hurriedly as conditions would allow, heads down, intent above all upon not attracting attention. With the news of the Lockstedt Battalion inevitably reaching Russian ears, repression had descended upon Finland with a vengeance during this gloomy winter. House-searches and arrests were an everyday occurrence. Men and women were imprisoned, exiled, or worse on the merest suspicion of sympathy with the independence movement. The route to Sweden had become harder and harder to work. Many people had given up hope; the prospects for freedom seemed dimmer than they had ever been. But still a nucleus of fighters worked doggedly on. The battalion was training. Sooner or later they would come back to fight for Finland. They had to believe that; for if they did not then men and women had suffered and died for nothing, and Finland was entangled for ever in the Russian chains.

Activity had certainly not stopped, despite the increased difficulties and dangers. Quite apart from the small but determined groups of men and women who had been working from the beginning to raise money, to recruit men and to supply armaments, already small groups of trained men had slipped back from Germany into Finland to help organize resistance, but the odds against them were enormous; to some eyes, overwhelming. To make matters worse the unrest that was sweeping Russia like a storm had to a certain extent, perhaps inevitably, seeped across the border. The situation was confused and very dangerous. Katya, pulling her precious burden behind her, kept her head down and her face averted as she passed a group of soldiers gathered about a brazier on the quay. She was nearly there. The task was almost done. Just a few more minutes and they would both be safe –

'What's this then?'

She froze, her heart in her throat. A huge man, rifle swinging casually from his shoulder, had detached himself from the group and was coming towards her. 'Where are you going, my pretty, on this cold morning? What brings you out with such a little one in weather such as this?'

He spoke Russian, with the accent of the Ukraine. She replied in the same language, as crisply as she could. Already she had learned that in such circumstances her nationality was her best protection. 'To the house of my sister-in-law. The one over there, on the corner. She's unwell. I have soup for her, and bread.'

'Very charitable, I'm sure.' He bent to peer into her face in the half-light. As she had expected, the sound of her voice had disconcerted him. 'You're no God-forsaken Finn, I know?'

'No. I'm not. I'm as Russian as you are. Now, if you don't mind –' she pulled at the sledge, which swung a little, snagged upon a ridge of ice '– I don't want my little boy kept out in the cold for longer than is necessary.'

''Course not.' The big man bent to set the sledge to rights, grinned into the tiny, sleeping face that was nestled in furs. 'There's a sight that takes me back! I remember mine when they were this age. Nine I've got. Nine strong sons to work for me in my old age!' He grinned broadly, showing the rotten teeth of a man who sucked his tea through sugar lumps. 'Good thing about them when they're so little – they can't answer you back!' He laughed heartily.

Katya smiled, thinly, in acknowledgement, pulled again on the rope. Again the sledge stuck, tilting a little, weighted as it was with the stolen armaments that Katya was delivering to the partisans who awaited her in Elisabet's house.

'Here.' The soldier bent as if to lift the narrow vehicle bodily over the obstruction, grunted as Katya, with a small cry, fell against him, knocking him off balance.

'Oh, I'm so sorry – I slipped.' She wrestled with the rope. The sledge slid free, hissing against the packed grey ice. Katya grabbed the wooden side to steady it, reached in to tuck the baby tight and safe into the furs.

The soldier laughed again. 'Here. I'll take him. It isn't far. Give me something to do. Hanging round street corners with my arse freezing off – if you'll pardon the phrase – isn't my idea of soldiering, I can tell you.' He reached for the rope.

Katya held on to it. Fear was so close she could feel it, brushing her like the wings of the bats that swooped the summer night of Pikku Kulda. 'I – no, please – I can manage – I couldn't possibly put you to the trouble –'

'It's no trouble.' Genially he wrenched the rope from her hand, set off with the sledge towing heavily behind him, calling to his companions as he went. There was nothing Katya could do but follow. Nothing she could do but pray. Small Jaakko mewed in his furs like a kitten. God help us, Katya thought, God help us both if Kaarlo is watching from the window, with his finger upon a trigger.

Those few short yards were the longest she had ever had to cover. Outside the house she took the rope with nerveless fingers, thanked him politely.

'You want the sledge lifted up the steps?'

She was beyond panic now. Lucidly she smiled, shook her head. 'No, thank you. It can as easily stay there.' She bent to the sledge, carefully extricated the baby. Stood with the child in her arms as the soldier executed a sloppy half-salute, turned away and stomped through the snow back to his companions.

She heard the door open behind her. Sensed Elisabet's light steps approaching. Katya stood quite still, clutching the child, frozen to the spot.

'Well, well.' Elisabet's voice verged on amusement. 'Nothing like arriving in style. I had to stop Kaarlo from blowing his head off.'

Katya swallowed. 'Don't.'

Cheerfully Elisabet reached for the baby. 'Come, Jaakko, my darling, come to Aunt Lissi.' She turned towards the house. 'Kaarlo can fetch the sledge.'

'No!' Katya was galvanized. She ran up the steps quickly, catching her sister-in-law at the top. 'Wait for a little. We'll have to let it stay for the moment at least. I said I was going to leave it there. If he noticed, he might become suspicious.' The release from tension was telling. Her voice was edged with laughter that was not far from hysteria. 'He – he wanted –' she choked back a small splutter of laughter '– he wanted to carry it in for me!'

'You should have let him,' Elisabet said. 'It would have saved us a job.'

In the room upstairs several familiar faces were waiting, one of them Kaarlo's.

'That was a fine trick,' he growled.

Katya cast a repressive glance but did not bother to respond. Jaakko, divested of his bulky outside garments, was cooing and smiling in his most beguiling way at his Aunt Lissi. Katya resisted the impulse to snatch him back, to hold him tightly to her, to prove to herself that he was whole and unharmed.

'How many?' A tall man who was standing by the stove walked to the window, peered down onto the quay below, and the gathered soldiers.

'Four rifles, three pistols, and some ammunition,' Katya said, shortly. 'There'll be more ammunition in a week or so. You've heard about the mutiny?'

Kaarlo scowled. The tall man nodded. 'Yes. A bad business by all accounts.'

'If the bloody Hun had left Bayer in charge –' Kaarlo began.

The tall man cut him off. 'We all know that, Kaarlo. But they didn't, and that's an end.'

Elisabet had for once allowed her attention to wander from her small nephew. 'What exactly happened?'

The tall man shrugged, a little tiredly. 'The battalion was sent to the Front a couple of months ago, as you know.'

'Bloody cheek.' A small dark man who until now had been silent lifted his head, eyes glowing angrily. 'The battalion was raised to fight for Finland, not to do Germany's dirty work.'

Katya sniffed. 'Is that coffee I smell?'

Elisabet smiled, derisively. 'We'll make a Finn of you yet, my girl. Russians are supposed to drink tea, didn't you know that?'

The wrangling behind them went on. Katya had heard it many times before.

'– the men need more than training – they need real experience under fire. It's perfectly logical that they should have been sent to the Front. For God's sake, how long do you think the Germans would put up with a battalion of that strength taking up time, barrack space, money and effort, and eating their heads off to boot, in the vague hope that one day they might be useful in nipping the flanks of the Russians? The bloody German army isn't a charitable institution you know! We always knew this could happen –'

'I still think –'

'A Finn was killed,' a girl Katya did not know said. 'Killed by a German officer. Isn't that right?'

'It seems so, yes.'

The anger in the room was tangible.

'Listen. All of you.' The tall man spread his hands placatingly. 'There are rights and wrongs on both sides –'

'There speaks a Finn,' someone muttered, mocking but not unaffectionate.

'The men are impatient. They don't want to be fighting Russians in Poland, they want to be fighting them here, in Finland.'

'Hear, hear!'

'They're a very long way from home and conditions are hard. But –' he held up a finger, preventing further comment '– whether they like it or not – whether we like it or not – they're a Jaeger battalion under German command, until they come back home to Finland. That was the agreement. And German officers don't take kindly to a fighting battalion that thinks it can hold a meeting and elect a committee every time anyone gives an order. They refused an order. That's mutiny. A man was shot. It's over and done and there's an end to it.'

There was a moment's silence, then a voice asked, 'And the troubles in Petrograd? What's to come of that? Is it good for us or bad? There were more riots last night. I heard that more army units have defected to the people – it sounds like chaos over there.'

'Who knows?' Erik turned again to the window, stood looking down at the still, snow-bound quayside. 'The first thing any sensible revolutionary government would do is to make peace with the Germans.'

No-one needed to be told what that would mean for them, for their battalion, still held fast in Germany, or in the long run for their country. The conversation that ensued was low-voiced and troubled.

'Difficult times,' Elisabet said, her voice flat and quiet, handing Katya a steaming cup of coffee. 'Drink it slowly. It's the last.'

And, 'Difficult times indeed,' Katya agreed.

Elisabet deftly relieved her of the baby. 'Your mother's still with you?' she asked, in that same neutral tone of voice; though the blue glance that Katya caught above her child's head was sharp.

Katya sighed, unable – unwilling was perhaps the better word – to play silly, timewasting games. 'Yes, Elisabet, my mother is still with me. And I'm sorry if it inconveniences you.' She glanced about her, corrected herself wryly. 'Us. But she came from the goodness of her heart. And she's a great help. She doesn't suspect anything, I promise. She believes that Jussi's death was a hunting accident.'

Elisabet made a tiny, bitter face.

Katya nodded. 'Yes. The irony of that had occurred to me, too. It's what it was, isn't it? But no accident.'

Elisabet laid her face upon the baby's head.

Katya saw Kaarlo approaching. 'Elisabet,' she said, and there was in her voice the faintest thread of appeal that brought her sister-in-law's eyes sharply to her. 'Please, don't make a fuss about mother. She poses no danger, I promise you. If she knew what I was doing – and she doesn't, I know it – she'd never betray me.' She watched the other woman steadily, over the soft, fair head of Jussi's son. 'I truly believe that Jussi would not have begrudged me the comfort of my mother, nor my mother the joy of her grandson.'

Into the small silence Kaarlo said from behind her, gruffly, 'I'll get the sledge in and emptied. You'll want to be getting on home.'

He offered to walk the mile or so back to the small but comfortable house in the district of Kamppi that she shared with her mother. She refused with a smile and a shaken head. 'I'm perfectly safe, Kaarlo. It's best I go alone, or our friends outside might be suspicious.'

He shrugged and returned to the others. Elisabet tucked the furs around the baby very carefully before handing him to Katya. 'Take care. Get him home quickly. It's very cold.'

Katya found herself thinking as she took her leave and went to the front door that neither Elisabet's nor Kaarlo's concern was for her. She hugged Jaakko to her. She could not blame them. To anyone who had loved Jussi, this child was more than precious. She tried always, often through irritation, to remember that.

She was tucking the baby back into the sledge when Elisabet joined her. The other woman stood, waiting, until she had finished and straightened and was pulling on her gloves. 'Katya?'

Katya glanced at her in question.

'I just wanted to say –' Elisabet stopped, oddly awkward, almost defensive.

Katya waited.

'I just wanted to say – we know what you risk, and for a country and a cause not your own. And – we do appreciate it.' The words came out in a rush. 'Jussi would have been proud of you. I know it. We all know it.'

There was a small, surprised and slightly unnerving silence. Katya blinked. 'I know it too,' she said, quietly, at last. 'That's why I do it.'

She thought about that as she trudged along the icy sidewalks towards home. It was the simplest of truths. Only one thing had Jussi loved better than he had loved her, and that was his country. He had fought and he had died to free Finland from the manacles of repression. Now he had a son, and in her heart and soul she had never felt herself to have a choice; the least she could do was to continue that fight, in Jussi's name. To make sure that Jaakko grew up in the free and independent country for which his father had made that last and terrible sacrifice.

She was tired when she reached the house. She lifted the small sledge – relatively light now that it contained no more than her small baby – up the steps that had been neatly swept clear of snow, set it down in the porch, carefully lifted the sleeping baby from it. The wooden front door opened into the pleasant, square hall, light and bright and smelling of polish. The house was warm and cosy. 'Aili?' she called. 'Mama? Anyone home?' She unwrapped the still soundly sleeping Jaakko from the encumbering furs, dropped them onto a polished bench that stood by the wall, kicked off her boots.

There came the sharp tapping of footsteps upon the wooden floor of the parlour. The door opened. Zhenia stood, looking at her daughter with an expression upon her face that all but stopped Katya's heart. 'Mama! Mama – whatever's wrong?' She hurried to her. Stopped.

Through the open doorway, over her mother's shoulder, she saw the comfortable and familiar parlour, clean and neat as the rest of the house, enamelled stove shining in the corner against a background of blue and white tiles and pastel-painted walls, the rug-scattered wooden floor polished to a mirror-like shine, sofas and chairs bright with cushions set about the well-proportioned room.

And in one of them Jussi sat, haggard-faced, lean as ever, fair hair flopping untidily over his eyes.

Jussi. Alive.

For a long, paralysed moment she did not take a breath.

'Katya,' her mother said, and stopped, biting her lip, stepping back from the door.

There were two others in the room, men she did not know. Katya did not even spare them a moment's attention. Very slowly, very carefully, carrying her sleeping child, she walked towards the seated figure. 'Jussi?' she asked, into the silence. 'It's you?'

He smiled. Lifted both his hands. He did not stand, and as she neared him she understood why. 'Jussi,' she said again, and sank to her knees beside him, still clutching the sleeping Jaakko.

Jussi cupped her face in his long hands, that were in memory so strong but now oddly smooth and soft. The hands of an invalid. His strained and tired face was the loveliest thing she had seen in her entire life. 'Jussi!' she said again, as if it were the only word she could say, or would ever say again.

Behind her she heard the sound of her mother's tears.

She lifted the baby. Sleeping still, his innocent face was like a flower, the sweep of dark lashes upon his smooth, rounded cheek perfectly symmetrical, irresistibly beautiful. Gently Katya laid him in his father's arms. 'I called him Jaakko,' she said.

He grinned, a shadow of that old, feckless smile. 'Not Ivan? Not Boris?' Tears lit his eyes to a brighter blue than she remembered.

'No. Nor Vladimir nor Nicholai. I can't think why.'

He shifted the child to his other arm, reached for her, pulled her to him.

The feel of him, so close, convinced her at last. He was real. He was here. She saw and accepted the cruel thing that had happened to him; the right leg stiff and awkward, the left not there at all, in its place a cruelly truncated stump. But this was Jussi, her Jussi, alive and come back to her, and to his son.

The fragile strength to which she had unswervingly clung for months seeped from her. Like a child she laid her head upon his lap and cried as she had never allowed herself to cry when she had believed him dead.

The explanations came later, after the euphoria had waned a little and conversations could be held without tears.

Within an hour of Kaarlo and the others leaving Jussi at the camp another small group of recruits had arrived, making for the same sanctuary. The already demoralized remnants of the Russian patrol had been taken in the rear, and entirely by surprise. Jussi had not had to fire a shot. Which was just as well since by the time his rescuers found him he had slipped into a deep coma and was half frozen to death.

'And me supposed to be playing the hero,' he added, his voice caustic. 'What a joke.'

'Don't be so daft,' Katya said. 'Go on.'

Since for obvious reasons none of them carried identification, and since the group that found him came from a different part of the country, no-one knew who the injured man might be, except that he was clearly a Finn, and as clearly a partisan. In any case he was so very close to death that shelter and care were the priority; names and explanations could wait. They sledged him on across the ice to Sweden, truly astonished that he survived the journey. There they left him in the care of a sympathetic household, to fight his own fight, to live, or to die.

'And there I lay,' Jussi said, 'like the Sleeping Beauty –'

'Sleeping what?' Katya asked.

'– for longer than I care to remember.'

Katya still sat on the floor beside him, her hand in his, unwilling to lose physical contact with him. She turned her head to look at him. 'How long?' she asked. 'How long were you unconscious?'

There was a small and acute silence.

She waited, all laughter suddenly and swiftly fled.

Jussi said nothing.

'Well?' she asked again, at last, calmly, determined upon an answer. Knowing with sudden certainty what he had done to her. To all of them. To himself.

He did not, directly, answer her question. 'When I woke up,' he said, 'I was not – quite as I had been.' His free hand, resting upon the stump of his leg, curled slowly to a fist.

Katya waited to see if he would say more. 'And – how long ago was that?' she asked at last, very quietly. 'When did you realize?'

'That I was a cripple?' The word was obviously chosen with bitter deliberation. He turned clear eyes upon her. 'Five months ago.'

'Five –' she bit the word off, disentangled her fingers from his, sat back on her heels, watching him. Lamp light gilded her hair, which was still wild and uncombed since she had thrown her hat aside, to a halo bright as sunshine. 'You didn't try to contact us.'

'No.'

'Why not?'

He shook his head, helplessly.

She considered, carefully, trying to reason when her heart was raw with shock and hurt. Fighting sudden fury. 'You didn't know about the baby.' The words were very quiet, very careful.

'No.'

'If you had – would it have made a difference?'

'Yes.' The word was so swift, so sure, that it could not be doubted.

'So.' She lifted her chin. 'Why didn't you let us know where you were?'

'I couldn't,' he said, simply. 'I had to think.'

'*Think about what?*' The violence in her own voice shocked her to silence. She turned her head sharply from him, angrily fighting tears. 'I'm sorry.'

She sensed his movement, resisted the strength of his hand

for a moment before she allowed him to draw her around to face him again. The onlookers, caught unwillingly in this sudden, emotional storm stood helpless witness to something that should have been – that was – intensely private.

'No. It's I who am sorry,' he said quietly. His hand rested upon the stump of his leg. 'I have no excuse, can ask no forgiveness. I can only say that – at the time – I thought it best.'

'Best to have me – to have others who love you – think you dead?'

'Yes.' The word was utterly uncompromising.

'You were wrong,' she said, fiercely.

'Yes. I know. Now, I know.'

There was a small, searching silence. Katya took a quiet breath. 'What changed your mind?'

'You did,' he said.

'I?' The bright and lively face he had remembered so well during these past tortured months, so used to laughter, so impatient of sobriety and sorrow, had changed, he saw suddenly, matured to something far more precious than simple beauty. There were dark shadows beneath the eyes that could not be attributed simply to her recent tears. The bones stood stark through the fine, fair skin. 'I did? How?'

'I dreamed of you. And I knew I had to come home.'

The hand that rested upon the stump was moving, restless, rubbing back and forth.

Katya reached a hand and stopped the nervous movement.

There was a long moment of silence. From another part of the house came the sound of an aggrieved wail. Collectedly Katya stood, palmed the tears away, bent to kiss her husband's cheek. 'I must go to see to the baby – Aili can't cope with him when he gets into a temper.'

With difficulty Jussi smiled. 'I'd have guessed it.'

'And I,' Zhenia said briskly, sniffing, 'must find Cook who appears to have hidden herself with Finnish discretion in the kitchen and arrange for dinner, before we all starve to death.'

In the hall Katya stopped for a moment, her hand on her mother's arm. 'Mama – I'm sorry about all this – it must be such a shock, and terribly confusing. I'll explain, I promise.'

'Explain?' her mother asked, mildly, tears banished, fair

eyebrows cocked, in her eyes that faint look of exasperation that only a muddle-headed offspring can engender. 'Whatever can you mean?'

There was a long moment in which the only sounds were the murmur of conversation from the room behind them and the faint crying of the baby from upstairs. 'You know,' Katya said, astonishment leaching all other emotion from her voice. 'Mama? You *know*?'

'Certainly I know. At least some of it. For goodness' sake, Katya –' the same affectionate exasperation showed in the tartness of her tone '– do you think I'm blind? And deaf too? Or simply stupid?'

'Why no, of course not –'

'Because I would have had to be all three not to know that something was going on in this house.'

'Why didn't you *say*?'

Her mother smiled, wryly. Katya flushed to the roots of her hair.

'Katya, darling, why didn't *you*?' Zhenia asked, with gentle asperity, and to Katya's relief was robbed of her reply by a sharp knocking upon the door.

Katya got there first. Elisabet stood on the doorstep, usually serene face animated. 'Katya, there's news from Petrograd – what news! Oh, good morning, Zhenia Petrovna.' She flew across the threshold, divesting herself of fur coat, hat, gloves as she came, and fairly bursting with excitement. 'It's happened! Revolution! Revolution in Russia! There've been huge demonstrations – strikes – riots. Battles on the streets of Petrograd! God knows how it will end, but they say –' She stopped, suddenly realizing that her momentous news was not quite creating the excitement nor the impression she had expected. 'It's revolution!' she said again, eagerly. 'The people have risen against the Tsar.' Puzzled, she looked from one to the other. 'Well, don't you *care*? Aren't you going to *say* anything? What's the matter?'

Katya, back on the edge of tears, was smiling, widely and with unselfish affection. She stepped forward, threw her arms about Jussi's sister and hugged her tightly, something that in the years they had known each other she had never done before.

426

'Nothing's the matter, Elisabet. Nothing. On the contrary. And yes – your news is exciting. Astounding. But we have news of our own, Lissi. Wonderful news of our own. Come – come and see.'

CHAPTER TWENTY

The city in which Anna and her travelling companion arrived on that afternoon of 25 February 1917 was in turmoil.

On the previous day, in a culmination of the most serious social unrest the city had seen in years, there had been a general strike which had inevitably degenerated into violence and to bloody clashes on the streets. Shops, houses and government offices had been looted and wrecked, and in some cases fired, with indiscriminate and impartial fury. Death, too, had been even-handed in this upheaval: students and workers had been shot and cudgelled to death as they marched; but this time vengeance was being taken in full, and all over Petrograd the roughest and most brutal justice was being meted out to those against whom the mobs and their leaders harboured a grudge. In the streets and boulevards the barricades were up. The armed forces were in uproar; men who just the day before had obeyed without question their officers' commands to shoot unarmed demonstrators were today listening to other arguments and defying authority to take to the streets themselves. Whole regiments had defected – with their arms – to the people, at times murdering their officers as they went. Yet many of the rank and file wavered still; enough, certainly, to threaten to reduce the city to a bloody battleground if they could not be persuaded to join the rebels. Confusion reigned; no-one knew truly what was happening. Not the Generals who had consistently refused to listen to warnings of the possibility of revolt, not the Tsar himself, far away in Mogilev and still naively believing the reports of officers too frightened to tell him the truth, nor his furious and outraged Empress, trapped in the palace at Tsarskoe, utterly refusing to believe the evidence of her eyes and ears. Not even the Duma that was now in open rebellion, nor any citizen from the richest and most powerful down to the lowest street-sweeping urchin. The city was chaos. A few days before, in an attempt to head off possible trouble, the Government had ordered the arrest of the Menshevik leaders, whom they saw as the greatest threat to political and social stability; a mistake they were to rue. With these relatively moderating influences under lock and key the way was open to their rivals for the leadership of the workers; those who advocated the extremes of revolution. Bolsheviks and Socialist Revolutionaries now manned the barricades, delivered impassioned speeches to the regiments and whipped up the fury of a people pushed at last to violence by disillusion, by constant betrayal and by hunger.

In the ensuing confusion Petrograd was swept by rumour, as a forest by fire, and the city was as chancy and unstable as a powder keg in a burning waggon.

As they alighted from the train at the Finland Station Anna and Grigor were already aware that dramatic and dangerous events had overtaken them; they had seen the conflagrations in the city from the windows of the train, heard the gossip and speculation that had swept from carriage to carriage ever since they had passed the frontier. Containing her unease Anna stood, hands clasped in the warm shelter of her fur muff, watching as Grigor supervised the unloading of their trunks. The huge station buzzed with subdued and anxious talk. People milled around uncertainly, or stood grouped about huge piles of luggage, master or mistress and servant together, all equally unsure, all equally afraid. 'What do you suppose we should do?' Anna asked, calmly. Very faintly she heard a distant crackle that could only be gunfire. Heads turned, listening. 'The man over there said there are no sledges – indeed no transport of any kind.'

Grigor's young face was grim. 'Look, if I stack the luggage here, by this pillar, will you stay by it whilst I discover what's happening?'

'Of course.' Nearby, a frightened-looking woman was trying to pacify a small crying child.

The ten minutes he was away seemed like as many hours. The look on his face as he pushed through the crowd towards her was not comforting.

They had travelled a long way together; he paid her the

429

compliment of complete honesty. 'There's nothing,' he said. 'No sledges, no cars. The trams aren't running. So far as I can see it's as you said; there's no transport of any kind.'

'What's happening in the city?'

'No-one seems exactly to know. Everyone's got a different story. But it certainly seems that the Duma has turned on the Tsar, and is trying to take control. The people have taken to the streets. Half the army's gone over to the rebels. The situation's totally confused.' He stood suddenly uncertain, watching her. She could almost feel the weight of responsibility he felt that he carried as her escort. He looked all at once quite touchingly young and unsure of himself. 'There's sporadic fighting all over the city, especially around the Liteini District, where the barracks are.'

As if on cue there came again the distant spattering of gunfire, like pebbles thrown sharply against glass. A woman, elegant in expensive furs, was crying, her husband patting her shoulder awkwardly, her young maid staring, frightened and open-mouthed.

'Well, we can't stand here all day, that's for sure,' Anna said, still stubbornly calm. 'What are the alternatives?'

'I'm not sure. Without transport –'

'We walk,' she finished for him, apparently unruffled. 'And what, then, of our luggage? We certainly can't carry it.'

He thought for a second. The moment of uncertainty had passed. Spurred by Anna's own outward composure he was crisp and efficient again. 'Wait. I'll see what I can do.'

He was back quicker this time, accompanied by a heavily-built man in station uniform. 'That's it,' Grigor said, pointing at the far from inconsiderable pile of luggage.

'Yes, Excellency.' The man did not move, but stood, waiting.

Grigor shook his head. 'Oh, no. We get the luggage safely stowed first. Then you get the money.'

The man eyed him for a moment, insolently. Then he lifted a shoulder and turned away.

'Hey!' Grigor grabbed his arm. 'Where the devil do you think you're going?'

With a gesture that just a few days before would have been unthinkable the man shook the detaining hand from his sleeve.

Slanting, coal-black eyes surveyed Grigor with calm hostility.

For one moment Grigor stared back in sheer astonishment. Then he shrugged. The moment did not call for heroics. 'All right. Half now, and half afterwards.' He produced a folded note, which disappeared into the other man's pocket, then stooped himself to pick up two of the smaller suitcases. 'Can you manage the black one? Or perhaps the small brown?' he asked Anna.

'I can manage them both.' She struggled upright, a bag in each hand. 'Where are we going?'

'The station master has requisitioned some rooms and is storing passengers' luggage. At a price, of course – a quite extortionate price, as a matter of fact. But I don't see that we have any choice. At least it should be safe until we can send someone to pick it up. I've dropped every name I can think of, including the British Ambassador's.' His quick and boyish smile was suddenly less strained. 'You have an overnight bag?'

'Yes. The one I packed for the train.'

'Right. We'll take that with us, and anything else –' he glanced at the impassive face of the porter and decided against the word 'valuable' '– anything else you might need. Then I'll get you to your hotel – unless you'd rather make for the Embassy?'

'The British Embassy?' Anna shook her head firmly. 'No. They'd be just as likely to try to pack me straight up and send me back to England. I'll make contact later. When I've found my family.'

Half-heartedly he opened his mouth to say something, changed his mind and shut it again. He had been in Anna de Fontenay's company for long enough to know when not to argue. 'Right. Let's get this safely stowed and we'll be on our way.'

Anna nodded briskly, both her confident smile and her imperturbable calm every bit as bogus as his. 'I just hope they haven't burned down the hotel. I'm dying for a proper bath.'

'At least we don't have to go through the centre of the city,' Grigor said, ten minutes later as they made their way in bitter cold up the bleak and eerily quiet road that led from the station. A dirty yellow tram stood abandoned upon the lines in the middle of the street, its windows broken, its interior wrecked. A sullen glow marked the sky above the grimy stucco buildings behind it. 'Your hotel is on the Voskresenskaya. We only have to cross the river, it isn't far. Most of the trouble is beyond, in the city itself I think. Let's hope the bridges are clear.'

They trudged on in silence, feet crunching upon dirty snow. The glow in the sky was brighter. A woman hurried past them, head and shoulders huddled into her shawl. They drew into a dark doorway at the sound of horses' hooves; a detachment of cavalry trotted briskly past, heading towards the bridge, and the city. Anna's feet had lost all feeling; the shoes she had worn to travel in had never been intended for wear in solid-packed, frozen snow. She was shivering with cold despite her expensive coat, hat and muff. Grigor glanced at her worriedly and increased his pace a little. 'It isn't far now.'

She smiled reassuringly. 'Don't worry, a little cold won't kill me. You forget, Grigor Petrovich, I'm a Russian – and no aristo-crat, either. I've been cold before.' Strangely, the tartly cheerful edge in her voice was this time not forced. Despite the danger, despite the cold, she found herself acknowledging a stirring of excitement, of anticipation, that would not be denied. The initial shock absorbed, she was beginning to realize that, how-ever demoralizing the circumstances, she was back in St Petersburg – Petrograd – at last. The city did not look as she remembered it – torn posters fluttered upon drab walls, shops were boarded up, the dreary streets were desolate and empty – yet still, after all, once it had been home. And if the homecom-ing was not quite as she had planned it, then that could not be helped, and must be survived. War had come, and now, appar-ently, revolution; but the city had seen both before – indeed, within her own lifetime – and would no doubt see them again. She determinedly crushed misgivings. Despite the unfortunate and slightly unnerving circumstances, she had not the slightest doubt that she had done the right thing in coming; quite the contrary. The sense of fate that was so much a characteristic of so many of her countrymen had not entirely passed Anna by. The urge that had brought her home at such a time was not without reason, of that she was certain; she would trust to God and to her own common sense – not necessarily in that order –

to work out the future. First she would find her family; all else must stem from that. For now it was enough that she was here, and hopefully could be of some help to them. England stood behind her, safe and secure, a refuge and a protection. And anyway – the trouble would blow over. It always had before.

Despite her companion's anxious urging she paused on the bridge and looked down upon the vast expanse of the silent, frozen river. The palaces that lined the southern bank were unusually dark and quiet, most of them shuttered and closed against a threat until now unimagined and unimaginable. On the other bank the vast bulk of the Fortress reared against the sky, the Imperial Standard fluttering above it as it always had. She remembered, suddenly, that afternoon with Katya – the fires upon the banks, the laughter, the gay music of sleigh bells, the graceful figures of the skaters.

'Anna Victorovna – please! We should hurry!' Her young escort was looking nervously up and down the length of the all but deserted bridge. Behind them the rattle and roar of a convoy of lorries could be heard approaching. Ahead lay the broad sweep of the Liteini, leading to the heart of the city and to the large barracks area. A sudden sustained rattle of gunfire echoed again, recalling her brusquely from the calm and stable past to the astonishing present.

'Of course. I'm coming.' She turned her back upon the wide, frigid expanses of the Neva and hurried after him across the bridge.

Grigor set down her bags and surveyed the dingy room in helpless apology. 'I'm sorry. It truly seems to be all that's available. I couldn't even bribe anything better out of them. The city's bursting at the seams. This is part of the servants' quarters, I think. But I honestly believe you're lucky to get a room at all.'

Anna surveyed the tiny, drab room; the wallpaper, of a colour so faded as to be unrecognizable, hung in some places in ragged strips from the walls; the furniture, such as it was, was a jumble of worn and shabby cast-offs; the whole smelt unappetizingly of damp and of something that reminded her unpleasantly of cabbage stew. 'So much for my bath!' she shrugged, wryly. 'Don't worry. It will do. At least it's warm. And I shan't be here

433

for long. Just until I find out where Mama is living.' She walked to the window, looked down into the dirty narrow street beyond. As she watched, a man with a rifle slung over his shoulder moved from a darkened doorway on the opposite side of the road, scurried warily along the shadowed street and disappeared.

'If you should need me – if I can be of any assistance,' Grigor was saying behind her, 'please don't hesitate to contact me. You have my number at the Foreign Office?'

She turned, smiling. 'Yes. And thank you, Grigor, thank you for everything.'

'It was nothing.' He came to join her at the window. The sky above the crowded buildings still flickered with lurid light. 'They said downstairs that the worst of the fighting so far has been about the barracks in the Liteini District.' His brow was furrowed. 'My mother and my sisters live not far from there –' His voice trailed to silence.

She touched his arm in immediate contrition. 'Oh, my dear, how selfish I've been! Here I am monopolizing your time when of course you have your own family to worry about! You must go, at once.'

He hesitated, obviously torn.

She leaned to drop a light, friendly kiss upon his cheek. 'Go,' she said, gently. 'You've been too good already. Please. I insist. I promise you I'll be all right.'

He needed no more bidding. Courteously but in relieved and understandable haste he made his farewells and left her.

It took less than an hour for Anna to become so restive that she thought she might scream. The depressing room was silent, all sound muffled by the winter windows. It was oppressively hot and smelled disgusting. From the window she could see nothing. A slightly nervous venture into the public rooms downstairs discovered most of them to have been turned into dormitories, lined with bunks and packed with luggage. People, almost all men, milled busily about the lobby, too intent upon their own affairs to bother with hers. She drank a glass of weak tea at a small table in the corner, which she shared with a morose man who answered her questions in surly impatience whilst scribbling hasty notes in a small book, which he covered jealously with his arm, as if he suspected her of spying on him.

Yes, it seemed that much of the army, to say nothing of a great section of the population, had turned against the Tsar and taken the side of the Duma. The Pavlovski Regiment had turned yesterday, there were reports of others today. Yes, the rioting had been bad – more savage, more organized yet more destructive than he had ever known it – and yes, many people were said to have died, on both sides. Discovering her ignorance, he warmed to his subject a little. Strikes and demonstrations in these past few weeks had brought the city close to a standstill, the strikers and demonstrators had taken to rioting and looting, and they had been suppressed with thorough brutality. Now, suddenly, the boot was well and truly on the other foot, and the bloodlust of the crowds was up. It was not just the people who were dying now, but those they considered their enemies; the police, the Tsar's Government officials, the officers who had ordered their men to fire upon unarmed civilians – it was all very bad for business. He relapsed into his ill-tempered silence.

'I need to go to my mother's apartment,' Anna said, steadily, watching him, her thin fingers wrapped around her tea glass. 'Over the river – the Venskaya – are the streets safe enough, do you think?'

He took an impatient breath, lifted his eyes to hers, then relented. He leaned upon his elbows, his face close to hers. She tried not to recoil from his breath. 'My dear lady, of course they aren't safe. But you ask me is it possible? Yes, it's possible. Most of the trouble is on the main streets and squares. The Liteini is barricaded, the Nevsky too in places, but – if you know the city?'

'I do,' she said.

He nodded. 'Then it's possible to avoid trouble,' he said, and determinedly and finally returned his attention to his notebook.

Anna thought about that. She could not – she absolutely could not! – stay here in solitary and lonely ignorance until something happened to restore order to the city. She could not remain in that dreadful little room for one minute longer than was necessary. She had to find out what was happening to her family, and her parents' apartment – she faltered upon that, surprised at the trick her memory had played her – her mother's apartment – seemed to be the best place to start.

435

'Though if I were you –' The evil breath was in her face again. The man had stood, was bending above her, his face not unfriendly, 'I'd find something to cover those fancy clothes. Just a precaution, you understand?' He cocked a knowing eyebrow and left her.

Instinctively she did understand, and did not miss the irony. Anna Victorovna Shalakova, the ordinary girl who had walked the streets of St Petersburg in perfect safety, had become Anna de Fontenay, a lady of some means and substance. How very much things must have changed in the city if that could be considered a change for the worse.

There were maids, still, in the Hotel de la Quay, and one was ready to sell her soul, never mind her cloak and boots, for the money that Anna offered her.

An hour later Anna left the hotel under cover of the early-evening darkness and set off along the quay, westwards, in the direction of the Winter Palace and the Nevsky Prospekt.

As she had been advised, she tried to steer clear of the main streets and squares. She was not, as she had expected, alone. Everyday life, as always in the face of prodigious events, had to go on. Others too were hurrying about their business, or simply standing around watching, waiting, animatedly arguing. Every street corner had its small group of observers, smoking, talking, stamping their feet against the cold; to Anna's surprise she heard laughter, and excitement in the voices. History was being made and the people of Petrograd were making it. Groups of soldiers disputed noisily, amongst themselves and with anyone else who would listen, brandishing their guns and bayonets as they talked. The occasional uniformed horseman clattered past, to the hoots and derision of the crowds.

No-one took the slightest notice of Anna.

She stood in the shadow of a wall, watching, as a mixed bunch of soldiers and ill-dressed young men marched past in ragged order. All carried weapons of one kind or another, and Anna recognized in astonishment amongst them the uniform of the famed Semeonovsky Regiment of the Tsar's own Guards. At the end of one street a detachment of Cossacks had been cornered by a shouting crowd. In vain a purple-faced officer screamed at his men to charge; the mounted soldiers sat their horses, ignoring him, until one bent, straight-armed, to hand his weapon to a man in the crowd. A roar went up. Almost hysterical, the young officer levelled his pistol at the rebellious soldier's head. The roar this time was of a different and terrifying nature. Anna watched, horrified, as the officer was dragged from his terrified, rearing horse down into the furious mob, as if into the maw of a hungry animal. She heard his scream as she turned away, aghast, hurrying on.

The incident had shaken her. For the moment she too had been seduced by the heady feeling of excitement that pervaded these streets; yet the violence that lurked beneath the surface was truly terrifying. Thankful for the shabby cloak she wore, she drew it tighter about her and turned the corner into the Nevsky.

Luck was with her. For two or three hundred yards the wide avenue was empty. Further on there was a crowd, with torches, and she could see the tumbled obstruction of a barricade. Further on still she saw the glimmer of fire. The shopfront by which she stood was shattered, the interior looted. A chair lay broken upon the pavement. She hesitated for a long moment, heart beating very fast. She had to cross that wide expanse of road; then she could slip into the sidestreets again and be safe.

A group of young men, shabbily dressed, buffeted past her, laughing and shouting. One of them carried a bayonet, another an officer's sword. She drew back from their path. One cannoned into her, knocking her against the wall. She steadied herself. A convoy was driving towards them and towards the barricade; two long, shining limousines, small red flags fluttering upon their bonnets, young men with rifles standing upon the running boards and lying upon the roofs, followed by a lorry full of students and workers, armed to the teeth, waving and shouting as they went. The group on the pavement ran into the road, swarmed onto the truck, hauled on board by willing hands. The convoy roared on towards the barricade, where a banner-waving crowd awaited it, and comparative quiet fell.

Anna took a breath, wrapped the cloak tightly about her, ducked her head and picked her way across the slippery packed snow of the wide thoroughfare.

No-one shouted. No shot sounded. Somewhere an engine revved violently, and died. The smell of smoke was strong on the cold air and the dirty snow was specked with black fire fragments that floated about her, smudging upon her skin and her clothes. Then she was in the shadows again, and safe. She slipped into a sidestreet, her confidence growing.

The confidence was not entirely well-placed. In her anxiety to get away from the main thoroughfare she had taken an unfamiliar turning; in minutes she was lost. It had been so very long since she had walked these streets, and at that never in such distracting circumstances. She spent ten minutes in trying to find her bearings and her way down to the river; another five in hurrying through these quieter streets until at last she came to the familiar corner and turned into the Venskaya to find herself at last outside the apartment building and then the door that she remembered so well.

The street was empty and quiet. Somewhere not too far distant what sounded like a fully-fledged battle had broken out. Machine-gun fire rattled, punctuated by the sharper shots of rifle and small arms. It was full dark now, a full dark lit to rosy hue by the reflection of fire in the sky. She stood at the foot of the steps that led to the door, memories flooding. It was here she had first seen Andrei, slim and slight, the mop of silver hair like a halo about his head, his angel's smile lighting his face as he came to greet them.

Briskly she ran up the steps, pushed the door open.

Stopped, staring.

The building, though never particularly impressive or elegant, had always been clean and presentable, its tenants on the whole civil and self-respecting. Now it was a shambles. The door to what had been Andrei's apartment was all but off its hinges. The room beyond, empty in the guttering light of an ill-tended oil lamp, was squalid and untidy, the remains of a meal still on the table. The stairs were even filthier, words and slogans were scrawled upon the walls, and the smell was ghastly. She looked up to the door that had been the Shalakovs'. It too was daubed with a slogan in a language she did not recognize. Surely – surely! – her mother could not still be living here?

The building was very quiet; unnaturally so. Presumably

most of the occupants were out in the streets watching, or partaking in, the fun. Very slowly she mounted the stairs and tapped upon the door. The doorbell hung broken and rusty. The muffled sounds of battle still sounded from outside. She knocked again, louder. Someone spoke from inside. The door opened a crack to reveal a young woman, sullen-faced and wary-looking, a child in her arms and another at her skirts.

'I'm sorry,' Anna said. 'I'm looking for Varya Petrovna Shalakova – she used to live here?'

The woman looked at her in blank incomprehension.

'Shalakova,' Anna said again.

The woman shook her head violently, tried to close the door.

Anna put out her hand. 'Please, I only want –'

The woman all but snarled at her, spat something in a language that Anna half-recognized as eastern European – Polish, she thought, but could not be certain, and slammed the door in her face.

There was no point in staying, in attempting to argue. Her mother was not here; patently had not been here for some time; she must surely then still be with her sister in the mansion on the Fontanka. Gritting her teeth, Anna asked herself why she hadn't started at the Fontanka in the first place.

She almost ran from the defiled building and back into the ravaged streets of Petrograd.

It astonished her how rapidly it was possible to become accustomed to the sights and sounds of violence. She hurried through the streets within earshot of what in some parts of the city had become a full-blown battle as the remnants of the regiments still loyal to the Tsar fought on against the rebels and the military reinforcements that had defected to the side of the people. Perhaps fortunately she was not to know that this was not the only violence loose in the city that night. The hunt was up for those who had enforced repression for so long; no policeman was safe, nor any officer suspected of old loyalties, nor anyone associated with the Tsar's hated Interior Ministry. Buildings were stormed, taken, and purged; police stations and the District Courts of Justice set ablaze. Old scores were settled with relentless and savage efficiency.

At the very moment that Anna emerged once more into the Nevsky Prospekt and realized with a jolt that she was no more than a stone's throw from her father's shop, Pavel Petrovich Donovalov was being dragged, struggling like a demon, from his hiding place in the cellars beneath the Ministry a mile or so away and hauled to where an open-backed lorry stood parked beneath the balcony of the building opposite. To cheers a noosed rope snaked down, swung empty and ominous beside another that bore the obscene fruit of an earlier hunt. Donovalov's demented struggles increased – for a single moment he tore himself free; stood panting with terror within a solid ring of faces; faces in which no scrap of human sympathy, no vestige of compassion showed. He screamed as they took him. By the time that Anna, drawn as by a magnet to the place she had loved so well, stood on the ruined threshold of her father's shop, the dancing flames of revolution lighting the wreckage within, Lenka's husband was engaged in his final, mortal struggle, choking slowly and terribly to death as he swung, his last sight those hate-filled faces, the last sound to penetrate the agony of his dying the fierce, animal howl of the mob.

Anna stepped into the shop. Glass crunched beneath her heavy boots, setting her teeth on edge. The destruction was absolute. There was not a pane of glass, not a mirror, that was not smashed or shattered. Someone had tried to set fire to the counter; the solid wood had defied the flame but still smouldered balefully and the stink of it pervaded everything. Cabinets were splintered, shelves pulled down. Anything movable and useful had been looted. One chair remained, drunken upon three legs, in the corner. Even the sweeping staircase had been damaged, the mahogany banisters and handrail, substantial as they had been, chopped to matchwood.

Outside, a convoy of lorries roared noisily past, gears grinding. A volley of shots sounded. Upon the barricade a little further up the road people were singing, against the background of machine-gun fire.

Within the odd, enclosing silence of the wrecked building she walked carefully to the shadowed staircase, stood listening. All was quiet. Slowly, stepping gingerly, she began to mount the stairs.

The workshop too was gutted. She had not expected less. She stood for a very long time in the gap where the door had been, confronting the senseless destruction. Even in the half-light she could see it. The workbenches were smashed, their padding hanging in ribbons. The instruments and the tools were gone. Again, cupboards and shelves had been ripped from the walls. Debris littered the floor. And in that debris, cast down and stove in by a booted foot, an unvarnished and unstrung violin lay, mute and beyond any repair. Unsteadily she moved through the wreckage, bent to pick up the poor, shattered thing. And froze, as behind her in the flickering darkness she heard a sound. The crunching of a foot upon shattered glass. And then, slowly and steadily, footsteps mounting the stairs.

She glanced around her at the room, lit by the fitful flare of a fire on the opposite side of the street. Nowhere. Nowhere to hide –

'Anna Victorovna?' It was a male voice; quiet, reassuring. 'Is it you?'

She straightened to face the door.

He was a tall, narrow-shouldered man in an overcoat that, like almost every other article of clothing she had observed since her arrival in Petrograd, had seen better days. As she faced him he snatched the shapeless fur hat from his head. Faded fair hair fell over a wide brow. Pale, tranquil eyes searched her face in the treacherous, flickering light.

She knew him. She frowned. She knew that face –

He waited.

Then, 'Volodya!' she said. 'It's Volodya, isn't it?'

He smiled, bowed his head.

'Oh,' it was a small sound, compounded of relief and bewilderment, 'oh, I am so pleased to see you!'

He shambled, limping heavily, across the floor towards her. She still held the shattered violin. Very gently he took it from her, tossed it into a corner. 'I saw you in the street,' he said. 'I was coming to check on the shop.' He looked around. Watching him she saw his pain. There was a long moment of silence.

She tried very hard but with minimum success to laugh. 'And you recognized me?'

'Oh, but of course!' The reply was remarkably swift. 'Of course I recognized you.'

She moved a foot amongst the wreckage upon the floor. 'Why? Why did they do this?'

He shook his head.

'Senseless,' she said.

He said nothing for a long while. Then, 'They take what they want,' he said, softly, 'and they break what they don't understand, I think.'

'Like children?'

'Perhaps.'

They shared a small, thoughtful silence. 'Dangerous children,' Anna said then, bleakly.

Her companion did not reply.

She lifted her head. 'Mama – you know where she is?'

He smiled. 'Of course. She's at your aunt's apartment on the Fontanka. She's quite safe. I've just come from there. I thought you knew. She's been there since your father's death.' The words were calm, held sympathy but no embarrassment nor awkwardness.

Anna nodded. 'I should have thought of it. I did think of it. But, stupidly perhaps, I went to the old apartment first.'

'Ah.' He took her arm, helped her back to the doorway. 'The whole building's been taken over by refugees –'

'So I discovered.' Reaction dried Anna's throat suddenly. She coughed a little.

'So much of the city has been.' Still holding her arm he guided her, his own steps uneven but his strong grip steady, along the dark landing to the stairs. 'Be careful, Anna Victorovna, the stairs are dangerous.'

The formality of his address was absurd. She turned to tell him so. 'Please, Volodya –' She stopped. Swallowed. 'Anna, do call me –' the pent up emotion she was battling erupted in an undignified, hiccoughing sob '– do call me Anna –' Her knees gave way beneath her. Entirely unable to prevent herself she sank, crouching upon the stairs, her face bowed to her hands, and the tears came. For a few minutes she sobbed, passionately, noisily, allowing confusion and shock to overwhelm her. Nothing was as she had hoped, nothing was as she had expected. She had come home to destruction, to anarchy and to fear. Had come home to this, a familiar shrine desecrated.

She sensed him as he lowered himself, a little awkwardly, one leg stiff in front of him, to the stair beside her. Felt his arm about her shaking shoulders. He said nothing, made no attempt to quieten her, simply held her, comfortingly, and let her cry.

It was over almost as suddenly and as surprisingly as it had begun. She blew her nose, loudly, scrubbed at her eyes, lifted her head. 'I'm sorry. That was unforgivable.' Tiredly she took a long breath, calming herself. Through the shattered windows came the steady clatter of hooves, as a regiment of cavalry cantered by, steadily and with purpose. The noise of the gunfire had not abated.

He was watching her gravely, the pale eyes tranquil and untroubled as she remembered them. He shook his head. His arm was still about her. 'Natural,' he said. 'Quite natural.'

They sat so, each leaning upon the other for a moment; a moment of human warmth, of companionship in a perilous world.

'You would like me to take you to your mother?' he asked, at last.

She knuckled the last of the tears from her eyes. Nodded.

He took her hand, pulled her to her feet. 'Come.'

The trip was not without its alarms. Obviously practised, he kept her from the worst of it, but still they were stopped over and again by snipers, by officious groups of workers and students with red armbands and cockades in their caps, by skirmishes and by hastily erected barricades. Volodya calmly talked them through the checkpoints and barricades – indeed in several places he was readily recognized. 'You seem to know everyone!' Anna smiled, at one point, intrigued that the quiet and shy young man she had known should show such command of a difficult and dangerous situation. He shook his head, glanced at her, returning her smile. 'Not everyone,' he said, and would say no more. Vladimir Pavelovich Yamakov, Anna found herself thinking with a small twist of amusement, was undoubtedly that rarely encountered breed, a man of few words.

Normally it would have taken less than half an hour to walk from the shop to the mansion apartment on the Fontanka; the roundabout route they were forced to take, their progress made more difficult not just by the uproar in the streets but by the fires that had been set by the insurgents, took at least twice that. As they made their way at last along the banks of the canal an excited young man galloped by on a captured Cossack pony, shouting that the Fortress had fallen. Nearby, soldiers and workers were gathered outside a tall house, jeering and pointing, occasionally firing with more enthusiasm than accuracy in the general direction of the roof. Anna paused to watch. Volodya, with no ceremony, caught her arm and hauled her away. As he did so a shot rang out and one of the soldiers was flung backwards to sprawl bloodily against the wall, screaming. Another shot followed, and another, each finding its mark. The prey that had been hunted into that house was not about to surrender meekly to the cavalier mercies of the mob.

'Come. Quickly.' Guiding her firmly, remarkably agile despite his uneven stride, Volodya made a last, limping dash to the house. They ran up the shallow flight of steps to the huge revolving door that used to swing so easily but which now creaked protestingly as he threw his weight against it.

The foyer, which had always seemed so splendid to Anna, was unlit and unnervingly silent, an absurd oasis of peace and false tranquillity. The stairs curved gracefully upwards into darkness. Still holding her hand, Volodya made confidently towards them, their feet making no sound on the thick pile of the carpet.

'Where is everyone?' Absurdly Anna found herself whispering, as if afraid to wake the echoes that hung in the shadows above them.

'Most of the residents have cut and run.' They began to mount the stairs. Volodya too kept his voice low. 'Many people in this building have cause to fear the changes that are taking place out there.'

Anna stopped, staring at him, her eyes wide. This was something that simply had not occurred to her. Still holding her hand he stopped too, watching her. 'Uncle Mischa?' she asked.

He nodded. 'He left some days ago. No-one knows where he is. And your aunt's in Helsinki with her daughter.'

'Katya. She's still in Finland?'

'Yes. You heard her husband was killed in an accident?'

It was just one more shock, one more horror in a day of them. Anna shook her head. 'No. No, I hadn't heard that.'

They were mounting the stairs again, slowly. 'She had a little boy, three or four months ago. Your aunt's been with her since then.'

'And Mama?'

They had reached the door of the apartment. He stopped. 'She's been living here alone. Anna –'

She had her hand on the door handle. He put out his own to restrain her, seemed about to say something. She looked at him, surprised. Then with something that was almost a shrug he stepped back, the hand dropping from hers.

She opened the door.

The huge apartment, which Anna remembered as always full of people, always full of noise, of light, of laughter, of quarrelsome talk, was still and cold and oppressively quiet. One lamp burned upon the table in the spacious entrance hall, its light gleaming upon the lovely wood, the heavy, expensive drapes, the tall mirrors.

'Where is everyone?' She was whispering again. Anna cleared her throat, tried to speak normally. 'Where are the servants?'

Volodya was frowning a little. 'I don't know. I was here just a few hours ago; some had left, certainly, but not all.'

'Where's Mama?' Anna's heart was beating so violently that she could barely breathe.

'This way.' Volodya, with the most natural of movements, held his hand to her again. Equally naturally she took it and let him lead her across the polished floor of the entrance hall into the corridor that ran behind the ballroom along which Anna remembered the family bedrooms had been situated.

There was a sharp and frightening rattle of gunfire from the street outside.

The corridor was entirely unlit.

Volodya, his movements becoming more urgent, went back to the table and picked up the lamp. Anna, sensing his anxiety, hurried behind him to a door at the far end of the corridor.

He tapped upon it. 'Varya Petrovna? Are you there?' He pushed open the door.

'Volodya? Is that you?' The voice was peevish, querulous. 'Where have you been? Where is everyone? Why haven't the lamps been lit?'

There was a brief and appalled moment's silence. Anna was standing in the shadowed shelter of the doorway looking at the grotesque figure that half-sat, half-reclined in an armchair next to the stove that heated the room in contrast to the rest of the apartment to the temperature of a hot-house. Small, bright eyes sunk in pallid flesh gleamed in the flickering, moving light cast by Volodya's lamp. For a frightful moment Anna was reminded of nothing so much as a massive and fleshy spider crouched in the corner of a web.

Varya shifted a little, heaving herself more upright in the chair, moving her swollen legs upon the footstool, peering into the shadows. 'Who *is* that? Volodya? Is it you? In the name of God, what is going on? What is all that dreadful noise? Did you bring my chocolates? Who's that with you? Volodya? Do you have someone with you?'

It took as great an effort of will as Anna could ever remember having to muster to step forward, smiling, hands outstretched. 'It's me, Mama. It's Anna.'

CHAPTER TWENTY-ONE

Once the demon of violence and anarchy had been let loose upon the city it proved, not surprisingly, all but impossible to capture and confine it again. Not even after the unthinkable had happened and the Tsar had abdicated, just three days after Anna's arrival at the apartment on the Fontanka, did the disturbances cease. Confusion reigned not only in the streets and amongst the common people but in the halls of political power and amongst those whose actions and ambitions had brought this chaos into being; and who now fought each other grimly for control not simply of the city but of a mighty nation. Most members of the Duma were dismayed by the abdication; certainly they had fought to curb the power of the throne but never had they desired or foreseen this outcome, especially not whilst the country was still embroiled in a bitter and exhausting war. The Petrograd Soviet on the other hand had wanted and worked for exactly this – and having so astonishingly achieved its aim now turned its dangerous attentions upon other targets, not least the Duma itself. The bourgeois Provisional Committee of the Duma might be a constitutionally elected body, and therefore consider itself the legitimate government of the country; but it was the Soviet revolutionary committee that represented the workers that on the whole held sway over the people, and the rebel army and navy, and who therefore truly ruled the city with its anarchic orders and decrees. Yet even now few observers, outside or inside Russia, really believed that these extremist groups could win the day; it was widely held certain that in the end good sense would prevail and a moderate, middle-class government would come in to being. Some did not even rule out the possibility of a constitutional monarchy, though to anyone familiar with the excesses of Romanov rule to date this seemed an unlikely outcome.

Meanwhile, as the two sides fought bitterly and with mortal intent for power, and as the Soviet itself was split into Menshevik, Bolshevik and Socialist Revolutionary components who often hated each other quite as much as – if not more than – they hated the opposition, anarchy continued to stalk the streets of the city. The bloodlust of the mob was aroused; there were old scores to settle. And settled they all too often were, with a brutal thoroughness.

Anna was astonished at how quickly it was possible to become used to living with violence. Not that she ventured out too often in those first few days; Volodya, quiet and unruffled, came and went with news and supplies whilst she spent most of her time in the apartment, caring for her mother, who all too soon had come to appreciate the advantage of having a pair of willing hands to wait upon her. The Bourlovs had never been a family particularly to command loyalty from their staff; many of the servants were gone, and those few who remained did so either from fear or from necessity. The streets were a perilous place for the timid, and lodgings were all but impossible to find in this overcrowded city. But the contagion of the streets could not be avoided and there was a new and resentful edge of insolence in their service, especially that of the younger ones; there were one or two with whom Anna felt positively ill at ease. The kitchen servants had deserted almost en masse; what food was to be had appeared on the table ill-cooked and unappetizing – a fact about which Varya complained loudly, scathingly and incessantly.

'Mama, please! We're lucky to be eating at all!'

'Lucky? To eat this – this pig swill?' Varya shovelled a huge spoonful of lumpy potato into her mouth. Anna averted her eyes. 'In my opinion the cook should be flogged.'

Anna laid down her knife and fork, pushed her plate away.

'Where's Volodya?' Varya eyed Anna's rejected lunch. 'Didn't he say he'd come this morning?'

'He said he'd come when he could,' Anna said. 'It's very difficult for him –' She stopped talking as, from somewhere in the city, there came a crackling burst of gunfire.

Varya looked up nervously, clutching her napkin close to her mouth.

Anna, as always, was touched by her fear. She reached out a reassuring hand. 'It's all right, Mama. Nothing to worry about.'

A sudden tear slid down the plump, pale cheek. 'Nothing? You call it nothing when we live in constant danger of being murdered in our beds? Or, God save us, of worse?' She made a hasty sign of the cross. 'If those fiends should take it into their heads to attack us, who is there to defend us?'

'Mama –'

'No-one. No-one at all.' Agitatedly she twisted the napkin into a rag.

'Mama, there's nothing to fear. Why should they attack us? We aren't aristocrats. No-one knows us. Why should they want to hurt us?' In actual fact Anna was as aware as was her mother of the danger of living in such an apartment, owned by such a family; Mischa Bourlov might not have been an aristocrat but he was a prominent and wealthy businessman and had made enemies.

'Volodya should stay here. That's what he should do. He should stay here. To protect us.' The noise had subsided. Varya was recovering her equilibrium. 'Aren't you going to eat that?'

Anna shook her head, wordlessly passed her plate across the table. She had been here for four days, yet still she was shocked each time she looked at the grotesque figure of her mother. The tiny frame was enveloped in flesh – so much so that she had difficulty in moving. Her days were spent in the armchair by the stove or here at the table, propped by cushions for comfort. For a great part of the time she dozed; when she did not, she ate. At the start of the war Zhenia Bourlova had, in the manner of a man laying down a cellar full of wine as a precaution, hoarded chocolates; boxes and boxes and boxes of them. These were Varya's stay and comfort. Surrounded by her romances and heaps of battered pre-war magazines, she ate chocolate with unflagging appetite. It had already occurred to Anna to worry about what might happen when the far from inexhaustible supply ran out.

Varya demolished what was left upon her daughter's plate. 'He should stay here,' she said again, returning to her earlier point with that relentless tenacity that Anna remembered so well. 'We need a man here.'

'We do very well alone, Mama,' Anna said, a little shortly. 'We can hardly demand that Volodya – ah, that must be him –' The doorbell had shrilled.

They waited a moment. The bell jangled again. 'I'll go,' Anna said.

'Damned servants!' Varya muttered. 'Wait till Mischa comes home. I'll see to it he dismisses the whole idle bunch of them!'

Smiling exasperatedly, Anna strode out into the hall. 'Volodya!' she said, as she opened the door. 'Thank goodness! Mama's acting the dowager duchess again –' She stopped. There was a startled moment of silence. Then, 'Lenka,' she said, faintly. 'Lenka – is it you?'

Her sister stood as if rooted to the spot. Her clothes were shabby, an old shawl covered her head. Her wide shoulders were stooped, her body heavy, but her face was unmistakable.

'Lenka!' Anna said again, and stepped to her, arms outstretched. 'Oh, I'm so pleased to see you! I was going to come to find you as soon as the streets were safe –'

Lenka stood rigid within the encircling arms, making not the slightest attempt to return her sister's kiss. 'They're safe enough,' she said.

Anna stepped back, rebuffed.

Lenka walked past her into the apartment. Turned. 'So you've come back at last.' Pale, acrimonious eyes swept the other woman from head to foot, missing nothing. 'Very smart,' she said, drily.

'Lenka – for heaven's sake!'

'Who is it, Anna?' Varya's voice was querulous. 'Don't stand out there talking where I can't hear you!'

'It's Lenka, Mama.' Anna watched her sister turn and enter the dining room, fighting a hurt so strong that it surprised her. In all these years Lenka had never answered one of her letters; so why should she be surprised at this fresh rejection? Yet she was; surprised and deeply pained.

Lenka bent and brushed her lips against her mother's cheek; a token kiss only. Varya turned her head a little, drawing away slightly, her small mouth tight.

Anna sighed. Nothing had changed. As always, with Lenka had come into the room a sullen tension that could trigger temper and beget argument as a storm cloud could beget thunder and lightning.

'So.' Lenka had straightened, was shrugging out of her threadbare coat and shawl, watching Anna over their mother's head. 'You've picked a fine time to visit. Might I ask to what we owe the honour?'

Anna controlled a surge of anger; and still the open hostility in her younger sister's eyes hurt her more than she would have admitted. 'I was – worried about you all. We had reports in England about the shortages – the difficulties – I thought I might be able to help.'

'Ah, yes. The shortages. The difficulties.' The twist to Lenka's mouth was caustic. She strode back to the door, went back out into the hall to throw her coat and shawl onto a chair.

'It's money she's come for!' Varya hissed, too loudly. 'You mark my words. It's always money!'

'Mama!' Anna tried in vain to hush her.

Lenka came back into the room, walked to the stove, rubbing her hands together. 'Well, then. Here you are. And life's treated you well, from the look of it.'

Anna was silent, looking at her.

Lenka turned. Her face was bitter. 'Lucky Anna,' she said, her voice totally devoid of expression.

'I hope it isn't money you've come for, Lenka,' Varya said, peevishly. 'My little nest egg is quite gone – and now the shop is wrecked.' The easy tears squeezed from her eyes. She dabbed at them delicately with her napkin.

Lenka had paled.

'That's absolutely outrageous, Mama!' Anna said, rapidly. 'Lenka has obviously come out of concern for you –'

'As a matter of fact,' Lenka said, cutting flatly across her sister's attempt to defend her, 'I've come to tell you the news. The good news. That my pig of a husband is dead.'

Varya made a small, outraged sound.

Lenka ignored her. She was watching Anna, her eyes like flint.

'Dead?' Anna asked, faintly. 'In – in the war, you mean?'

'No. At the end of a rope. Outside his lair in the Ministry, I gather.'

The chill of it, the look in her sister's eyes, made Anna's stomach roil unpleasantly. 'You mean – he was –?' She swallowed a sudden rush of saliva.

'The mob hanged him.' Lenka let the shocked silence extend; still her eyes had not left Anna's. And still those eyes held an inimical hostility and now, seeing her sister's squeamish reaction to her news, a trace of contempt. 'Justice was done,' she said. 'If I'd have been there, I'd have helped them.'

'Lenka!'

She shook her head fiercely. 'Don't "Lenka!" me, Anna! What do you know? What do you know of anything? Ask her –' she flung out a hand to point a steady, grimy finger at Varya '– ask her what kind of man it was you let them hand me over to!'

Distressed, Anna glanced at her mother. Varya, her face venomous, scowled at her empty plate.

'Ask her if I should be mourning the pig! Do you want the filthy details? Do you want to know what I and others have suffered from this man while you've been swanning around with your ancient Prince Charming in your country house in England – playing the fiddle – beguiling the natives – spending your rich old husband's money?' There was no mistaking now the depth of loathing in her calm voice.

'Lenka, stop it!' Anna was appalled. Had her sister been hysterical she might have been able to accept the viciousness; but this cold, deliberate attack – the open desire to inflict pain – had taken her completely by surprise, and she was unable to disguise her shock and hurt.

Lenka, seeing it, almost smiled. 'All right,' she agreed almost affably, 'I'll stop.' She looked from one to the other, grimacing in disgust as her mother continued stubbornly to glare at her plate.

'No need to have worried about you after all, then, Mama,' she said. 'With darling Anna here to look after you no doubt you'll survive better than most.' She turned on her heel, strode to the door.

'She always was an ungrateful and ill-mannered brat,' Varya said to the empty air above her plate.

Anna ran after her sister, caught her in the hall as she buttoned her coat and snatched her shawl from the table. In

452

contrast to her controlled tone throughout the exchange her movements were fierce, and full of anger. 'Lenka, please! Don't go like this! Won't you stay? Won't you explain what's wrong between us?'

Lenka turned, undisguised astonishment in her face. 'What's wrong? *What's wrong between us?* Are you pretending you don't know? Are you pretending to forget what you did? Have you so conveniently forgotten? The promises you made and had no intention of keeping? The way you abandoned me to –' she jerked her head in the direction of the dining room '– to *them* and their plans to be rid of me?'

'Lenka – I didn't know! I didn't understand!'

Her sister stepped very close to her. 'Oh, yes, Annoushka! You knew! You understood! You knew what *you* wanted! You understood what was best for *you*!' The finger she pointed was like a steady, levelled knife. 'You could have helped me. You could have stopped them. You always told me you'd look after me, remember? Remember your promises? I'd have done anything, Anna. I'd have come with you – worked for you – *anything*! But you abandoned me. I tell you this, my dearest sister; you'd have done better to have taken a razor and cut my throat!' She held her sister's appalled eyes for one harsh moment before turning abruptly away, pulling the shawl up over her head.

'Lenka, no! Can't you see? It wasn't like that! It wasn't!' Anna was almost in tears. Even now, all these years later, she knew she would not be able to bring herself to break faith with Andrei and tell this harsh and bitter woman the true reason for her flight. Not now. Not like this. Not when it might be used as a weapon against her. Against Andrei's memory. 'It's – it's irrational still to think like that!'

At the door Lenka turned. Her face was implacable. 'To you perhaps. Not to me.'

The silence was absolute. Anna stood still as a statue for a long moment. Then she took a shaky breath. 'I'm sorry. I'm truly sorry. I had no idea how much you hated me.'

Lenka said nothing, her face as still and cold as ice.

'But please –' Anna fumbled in the small purse she carried at her waist. 'Won't you take this? For the children, at least?' Tentatively she held out a small sheaf of notes.

Lenka remained by the door for a moment. Then, calmly, she walked to her sister, took the money from her fingers; tore it to shreds and let the pieces drift like spinning snowflakes to the floor before turning back to the door, where she stopped for a moment, looking back over her shoulder. 'If you're so anxious to help,' she said, the words flat and laced with contempt, 'go and see Natalia. She's the one who needs it.'

Anna nodded. 'All right, I will. And – Margarita?' she asked, hesitantly.

Lenka shrugged. 'Who knows?'

'She's still at the same apartment? Mama is so very vague, she doesn't seem to know what's –'

'Mama knows nothing,' Lenka said, heavily sardonic, 'because Mama doesn't want to know anything. She never did. She never will.' She held her sister's eyes for one long last moment. 'Hasn't life taught you anything, stuck in that ivory tower of yours?' And with no farewell she was gone, her slow, heavy steps echoing upon the wooden flooring before being muffled by the carpet of the sweeping stairs.

Someone in the street shouted, and a heavy lorry rattled by.

Anna shut the door and leaned against it, her eyes tight shut.

Volodya acceded to Varya's request that he move into the apartment with them with an alacrity that, for Anna, was mildly alarming.

'You have no-one else to consider?' she asked, cautiously.

He shook his head. 'No-one.'

'We – wouldn't want to put you out –'

'Not at all. It's a sensible suggestion.' He eyed her with a gleam of humour in his narrow, pleasant face. 'If you have no objections, of course, Anna Victorovna?'

'No,' she said. 'No. Of course not.'

'Right.' He pulled himself up from the chair. 'I'll have to make a few arrangements. I'll come tomorrow, if that's all right.' He did not wait for her to agree. 'Have you heard the latest news?'

She shook her head.

'They're handing out bulletins in the street. The Soviet is calling for a separate peace.'

'They want to stop the war?' Anna's eyes were wide.

'That's right.'

'Will they be able to, do you think?'

He shrugged. 'Who knows? The Duma wants to carry on, but this war's unpopular enough by any measure. The army is a shambles. They say men are killing their officers rather than go into battle. The troops here in Petrograd are refusing flatly to go to the Front. Discipline's broken down entirely.' He pulled on his coat, turned to take her by the shoulders. 'Anna, make sure you lock the door after me when I go. There have been some bad disturbances in the city again. Don't take any chances.'

'I – I was going to try to find Natalia today. Lenka said she needed help.'

He shook his head. 'Not yet. Leave it for another couple of days. Then I'll come with you.'

She nodded, more relieved than she cared to admit. She had not looked forward to walking the streets alone. 'And you'll come tomorrow?'

'I'll come tomorrow.'

It was not, as it happened, the best of timing. For the soldiers came looking for Mischa Bourlov that very day, just an hour or so after Volodya had left.

As if by magic that morning the last of the servants had gone, disappeared apparently into thin air and several small pieces of silver and china spirited away with them. It did not occur to Anna to place any sinister interpretation upon that; it had been bound to happen, sooner or later.

'A few mouths less to feed,' she said, 'and a couple of stoves less to keep going.' She was manhandling a bucket of logs into Varya's sitting room. 'We're getting rather low on fuel. I was anyway going to suggest that it might be best if we just heat this room, and perhaps your bedroom – what in the name of God is that?' Startled, she almost dropped the bucket.

The crashing at the door came again. No knock, this, but a steady, thumping smash, as of an axe, or a hammer.

Varya screamed.

'Mama – calm yourself – Mama!' Anxiously, her own heart in her mouth, Anna ran to her mother.

455

From the direction of the hall came the sound of splintering wood, and a man's voice, raised. Varya was sobbing, almost choking with fear. *'Mama, please!'* In her own anxiety Anna nearly shook her. 'Calm yourself! Here –' She wrapped a shawl about the shaking shoulders. 'No-one will hurt you. I promise.'

There came a last crash from the hall as the door flew back against the wall. 'Anyone here?' The voice was rough.

Varya had subsided, trembling, her eyes upon the door.

The temper that Anna had believed to be long tamed sprang full-blown and raging to her aid. She was in the hall and facing them before she had had a moment to think.

'How dare you! How *dare* you! You – you ruffians! The door has a perfectly good bell. If you had rung it I would have opened it! Are you animals that you have to behave so and frighten a poor old lady half to death?' There were seven or eight of them, all armed, all dressed in a ragtag excuse for a uniform, all with red bands around their arms. One or two hung back, looking at least a little shamefaced. The others were not impressed.

'You're the Bourlov girl?' one asked. He was tall and thin with a day's growth of beard. A fearful array of weaponry was strung about his person.

'No, I am not!' Anna snapped. 'I am Mikhail Mikhailovich's niece, Anna de Fontenay. And, I might add, a British subject. And I warn you I shall protest in the strongest possible terms to the authorities about this outrage!'

If she had hoped to impress or intimidate, she had failed dismally. 'Bourlov is here?' the man asked coldly.

'Of course he isn't. He hasn't been here for months. There's only me, and my mother, Varya Petrovna Shalakova, my uncle's sister-in-law.'

The tall man nodded curtly at his men. 'Search the place.'

'I tell you he isn't here!' Anna was forced to step back as the men pushed past her into the apartment. Almost immediately, from the drawing room, came the sound of a crash. Anna turned to run into the room. The tall man's hand clamped painfully upon her shoulder, preventing her.

'Where is he, your uncle?'

She struggled to free herself. 'I don't know. Let me go!'

His other hand caught her wrist, bending it backward, the bones grating. She let out a small scream of pain.

'Where is he?' he asked again, his voice unemotional.

'I tell you I don't *know*! How should I? I've only been in the city for a week!'

Doors slammed. There came the crash of splintering china. Varya's voice quavered, hoarse with terror. 'Anna? Anna!'

'It's my mother,' Anna said. 'Please, she's frightened – let me go to her.'

He held her for a moment longer, then released her, all but throwing her from him. She flew through the apartment to her mother's sitting room. Varya was trembling, her bloated face chalk-white with fear. 'Anna? What's going on?'

'It's all right, Mama.' Anna fought to keep her own voice level. 'They won't hurt us. They're looking for Uncle Mischa.'

'Mischa? Mischa? What do they want him for?'

'Because he's an enemy of the people, Grandma,' a voice said from the door. The tall man had followed Anna and stood watching them both, scratching his unshaven face. 'An enemy of the people,' he repeated, as if the phrase much satisfied him.

'That's ridiculous,' Anna said, from beside her mother's chair.

He sent her an unfriendly glance.

'He doesn't seem to be here, Comrade Smolonov.' One of his henchmen had come into the room. Anna's eyes widened. The man was quite openly carrying a silver dish, tucked under his arm, and his pockets bulged.

Smolonov's eyes narrowed, travelling about the room. He walked to the window, peered behind the curtains. Opened a large cupboard.

'You've forgotten to look under the table,' Anna said tartly, through lips tight with rage. 'And would you mind asking this – gentleman –' she sent a withering look at the unconcerned soldier '– to put the silver back where it belongs?'

Smolonov walked to her, stood very close, reached a hard hand to grip her face, tilting it so that he could look directly into her eyes. 'The silver, Madame de Fontenay,' he said softly, emphasizing the title mockingly, '*is* where it belongs.' His grip upon her jaw was cruel. The soldier looked on, entertained. 'If

Bourlov returns,' Smolonov continued, quietly, 'advise him to give himself up. We'll find him. Sooner or later. Tell him that.'

Anna said nothing, stood rigid, his body pressed against hers. Others of the company were coming to the door now, all reporting no sign of the criminal Bourlov, all quite openly carrying looted pieces of plate, china or jewellery. They lounged about the doorway, enjoying the fun, their comments and advice becoming increasingly salacious and explicit. Smolonov held her for just long enough for real fear to take hold, and despite her efforts to show upon her face. Then, malice in his eyes, he let her go. 'Not my type,' he said, dismissively. 'Thin as a rake and with a head like a carrot? I'd as soon fuck a matchstick.'

'Hand her on, then, Comrade,' a dirty-faced young man with rotten teeth said eagerly from the door. 'I like 'em thin – an' I don't care what colour, either.'

'You don't care what bloody species, Barski,' an older man said, acidly; and there was a sudden, almost good-natured roar of laughter.

'Out,' Smolonov said.

They trooped out, clattering across the polished floors in their rough, heavy-nailed boots. One of them, as they went, swept a tall Chinese vase from a table. It smashed noisily upon the floor, and those behind crunched through the pretty, fragile fragments.

At the door Smolonov turned, sketched a derisive salute. 'Grandma. Madam Matchstick.' And then he followed his men. All the doors were left standing open. They heard the clatter of footsteps, the talk and the laughter as they went down the stairs and through the great door out into the street.

The silence after they had gone was absolute.

'Don't you think,' Varya said at last with quite astounding calmness and presence of mind, 'that you should try to shut the outer door?'

'Yes, Mama. Of course.'

Anna dragged herself from the room; down the corridor, into the magnificent reception hall. Through open doors she could see the devastation; nothing, it seemed, had escaped. A whirlwind – a hurricane – could not have done more damage. Mirrors and furniture were splintered and smashed. Anything that could be moved had gone. The outer door stood open, its lock demolished. No-one had come to help nor to enquire. Most of the other apartments stood empty; the inhabitants of those that did not knew better than to involve themselves in such matters as this.

Anna rammed the door shut and dragged a heavy table in front of it. Then she walked into the drawing room, which had always been her favourite.

It was wrecked. Broken china and glass littered the floor, delicate chairs and tables were overthrown and turned to matchwood. The mindless vandalism had even extended to the pictures; each one was neatly slashed, corner to corner, by the sharp point of a knife.

No room had escaped. She wandered from one to another, all but stunned by the disaster and by the incredible suddenness of its happening; in the lovely little ballroom at last she stopped. Here again, senseless destruction had been wreaked upon furniture and fittings. Gilded chairs and tables were wrecked, mirrors cracked and splintered, great gouges had been torn even in the polished floor. She wandered, her footsteps echoing, across the ruined room, stood for a moment at the balcony window, looking out onto the canal, her mind a tired and shocked blank. Then she turned, and by a trick of memory she was for a split second back in this room when it was filled with talk and with laughter, with music and with the vivid colour of ball gown and uniform. She had filled this lovely place with her music, and the great Scriabin himself had listened, rapt. She saw Katya again, laughing as she flitted through her father's guests, mischief in her eyes. *'Anna, darling – what on earth are you doing drinking that beastly stuff?'* The shattered room blurred and swam. How long ago? Eight years? Nine? It might have been another life. Another world.

'Anna?' Her mother's voice quavered a little, uncertain and edged with temper. 'Anna, where are you?'

She used her fingertips to wipe away all trace of tears. 'I'm here, Mama. Here.'

It was undeniably comforting to have Volodya move into the apartment with them. The shy, talented and tongue-tied youth

459

that Anna remembered had come through his own trials to emerge a calm and dependable man, still reserved, still undemonstrative but a reassuring and competent companion in such bemusingly unstable times. He rarely spoke of himself. If the leg that had been shattered by a bullet at Tannenberg gave him pain he never complained of it. He was unfailingly good-tempered, even when Varya was at her peevish worst; indeed Volodya seemed the only one who could coax her out of her ill-tempers. After the episode with the soldiers Anna was more than glad to have him there. Together, as best they could, they cleared up the mess.

'So many lovely things,' Anna said, sadly. 'Simply smashed. Ruined. Why did they do it? Why?'

Volodya shook his head. His face was grim. 'Who knows? It's a kind of madness, I think. God alone knows where it will end.'

Anna was kneeling on the floor, in her hands the shards of a Dresden china bowl. She bowed her head, blinking back tears. 'I could understand, I think, if they wanted to take it – to have it for themselves – but to ruin it, for no reason – to destroy it utterly –' She could not go on. In trying to control the sudden lift of tired fear and grief that threatened to overcome her she clutched convulsively at the pieces in her hand, felt a small, fierce pain in her finger.

Very quietly he knelt beside her, took the razor-sharp slivers from her hands. Tears were running down her face. A bright bead of blood stood upon her finger, broke in a scarlet thread across her skin and dripped upon the floor.

'Silly girl,' he said, gently. 'Look what you've done.'

'It doesn't matter,' she said, helpless to stop the flooding tears. 'What does it matter?'

'It matters to me,' he said.

She lifted her face, thin, tear-stained and dirt-smudged beneath the tangled thatch of hair.

There was a moment of quiet. Anna it was who broke the odd, still silence. She turned her head away sharply, lifted her bleeding finger to suck the blood away. 'What will happen,' she asked quietly after a moment, her voice calmer, 'if men like those take over the country?'

His large, pale eyes were still steadily upon her. 'As I said. God alone knows.'

She turned to him again, looking at him squarely, searching in that open, honest face for some kind of reassurance. 'I'm frightened,' she said, the words spoken before she could prevent it.

For a moment she thought he would take her in his arms, hold her, comfort her. For a moment she most desperately wanted it. Then he smiled a little, shook his head ruefully. 'So am I, Anna,' he admitted, quietly. 'So am I.'

'Anna?' Varya's voice shrilled, echoing across the empty rooms. 'Anna – where are you?'

It was two days before Varya would consent to being left alone for an hour or so whilst Anna and Volodya went to find Natalia and the children.

'Why can't one of you stay with me?' she demanded for the hundredth time. 'Why must you both go? Supposing they come again? What will I do if they come again?' Her voice was shrill.

'Mama, please!' Anna, dressed in her plainest coat, a woollen shawl about her head, dropped to her knees beside her mother's chair. 'We've been through this so many times. The streets are still dangerous. Volodya won't let me go alone –'

'Then why can't he go? Why can't you stay here?'

'Because I'm hoping to persuade Natalia to bring the children here. It would be so much easier – so much more sensible. But she hardly knows Volodya. I'm not sure she'd trust him. I have to go, Mama, I have to.' Quite apart from anything else, danger or no, Anna felt she would go entirely mad if she did not get some air and some exercise, to say nothing of a brief respite from her mother's tongue. Guilt made her brisk. She stood up. 'You'll be all right, Mama, I promise. We won't be gone for long.'

Determinedly she turned to leave. Varya settled back into her chair, grumbling, reached for a half-empty box of chocolates that stood on the table beside her. Anna wrinkled her nose. The very air smelled, sickly sweet, of chocolate. It sometimes physically nauseated her when she walked into the room. She had reached the door when she heard her mother say,

461

pathetically, 'Holy Mother, what an inconsiderate child you are! Your poor, martyred father must be turning in his grave to see you leave me here like this, defenceless –'

Anna fought a temper that was, with confinement, becoming chancier every day. 'Mama, you know that isn't fair! I'm going to get Natalia and the children. Think how lovely that will be for you.'

Her mother poked amongst the chocolates. Paper crackled. 'I hope you'll be able to keep them quiet, that's all,' she said. 'Your poor Mama isn't a well woman, Anna, you know that. Young children can be very noisy – very disruptive.'

Anna stared at her. 'Mama, these are Dmitri's children – your grandchildren! Lenka said that Natalia – Dmitri's widow! – is in trouble. Are you – you're surely not? – saying you don't *want* them here?'

The bright, sunken eyes flickered to Anna's face, faintly defiant. Anna despite all efforts could not control her expression. Her mother's fat, white face crumpled. 'Dmitri!' she wailed. 'How could you speak your brother's name so callously? Don't you know it breaks my heart to hear it? My poor, martyred Dima!'

Anna gritted her teeth. Closed the door with infinite care and not a sound behind her.

Volodya took one look at her face as she joined him on the landing outside the apartment and wisely held his tongue.

The streets, carpeted in a new and heavy fall of snow, were, after all, quite calm; no-one paid the slightest attention to Volodya and Anna. And although everywhere about them was evidence of the violence of the past days – burned buildings, broken windows, bullet-pocked walls – some semblance of normality appeared to be returning to the city. People went about their business, wrecked and burned-out trams had been cleared from the streets and some were running again, some brave – and lucky – shopkeepers had even opened their shops. Every wall and fence, even some windows, had been covered with the pasted-up bulletins that had kept the populace informed during this past amazing week. Anna, interested despite herself, stopped to read some of them.

*'UPRISING OF THE TROOPS – on 27 February there passed
over to the revolutionary people the following military units:
Volynian, Preobrajensky, Litovsky, Keksholmsky and Sapper
regiments.*

*On the side of the revolutionary people are nearly 25,000
from the military ranks.'*

This was followed by an account of a delegation from the
said military ranks to the Duma to *'enquire about the position
occupied by the representatives of the people'*. Here too was a
copy of the telegram dispatched to the headquarters of the Tsar
by the Duma three days before the abdication: *'The situation
is serious. In the capital is anarchy. The Government is paralysed. Transportation, the supply of provisions and fuel have
come to complete disorder. Dissatisfaction is growing general.
On the streets is occurring disorderly shooting –'*

'It still doesn't seem possible,' Anna said, wondering.

There were terse accounts of arrests, lists of those arrested
or of those representatives of the people in the Duma who had
supported the revolution, accounts of battles and of stormy
meetings. The incredible pace of the revolution was illustrated
by the speed with which key positions in the capital had been
taken by the people. *'CAPTURE OF THE ARSENAL AND
CHIEF ARTILLERY HEADQUARTERS,'* Anna read. *'CAP-
TURE OF "THE CROSSES" PRISON AND LIBERATION OF
POLITICAL PRISONERS. THE FALL OF THE FORTRESS OF
PETER AND PAUL.'*

'Have you seen this one?' Volodya asked.

Anna moved to where he stood, read aloud the bulletin he
pointed out. *'DESTRUCTION OF THE SECURITY DIVISION.
The Security Division was destroyed and burned down. All
archives and political matters were destroyed.* Lenka's husband?' she asked.

He nodded.

It had begun to snow again. She pulled her shawl closer about
her head as they walked on. At a street corner Volodya bought
a copy of the newspaper *Izvestia* and tucked it into the pocket
of his overcoat. 'We can read it when we get home. It helps if
you know what's going on.'

A column of soldiers tramped by, red armbands flashing as

their arms swung in less than perfect unison. They were led by a man dressed as they were, except for a red sash across his chest. No officer rode with them, resplendent in uniform. Anna and Volodya watched them pass as they waited to cross the road. On the opposite pavement a huge queue had formed, snaking along the icy pavement and around a corner out of sight. A sign above the shop showed it to be a bakery. Men and women came from the door hugging the precious bread to them, eyeing their fellow citizens suspiciously, as if they feared robbery at any moment. Anna hesitated. 'Shouldn't we try to get a loaf each?'

Volodya considered the length of the queue. 'Your mother's alone. I don't think we can afford a two-hour wait. She's likely to get very nervous if we leave her for too long. I'll come out and see what I can find tomorrow.'

It was bitterly cold. The people in the queue huddled against the wall or stamped their feet upon the pavement in a vain effort to keep warm. Anna felt a sudden lift of something close to shame. It was the first time it had even occurred to her to think of what Volodya had been going through to keep them supplied with food. 'We both will,' she said.

Not all the tram services had been reinstated. It took them nearly an hour to reach Natalia's apartment on the far side of the river, on the outer edges of the working-class area of the city.

When the door of the apartment opened Anna found herself staring at the girl who surely must be her sister-in-law in dismay. She had not expected Natalia to be unchanged; who in heaven's name was? But never had she been prepared for this.

The emaciated, brown-haired woman looked from one to the other, her expression blank, and a little hostile. 'Yes?'

'Natalia?' Anna asked, doubtful despite herself.

Natalia peered at her. Her eyes were red-rimmed and painful-looking. Some small recognition flickered in her tired face. 'Who are you?'

'It's Anna. Natalia – Anna! Dima's sister,' she added in desperation as those abstracted, red-rimmed eyes still showed sign neither of warmth nor of welcome.

'Anna,' Natalia said. She frowned a little, as if in concentration. Behind her Anna could see two children, hovering, hands clasped, as still and as tense as was their mother. The older was a girl with a mop of fair curls that clustered lank and greasy about her face. The boy was small, dark and timid, looking the very image of Anna's brother as she remembered him as a child.

She tried again. 'Natalia, it's me, it's truly Anna,' she repeated, very quietly. 'I've come –' She hesitated, unsure of what to say in face of this strange, passive unsurprise. 'Look, please – mayn't we come in? Then I can explain.'

A small grimace, that might have been an attempt at a smile, flickered upon the all but skeletal face. Natalia stepped back. 'Anna!' she said. 'Of course. Goodness me, what a surprise! Come in.'

As they stepped forward the little boy drew back, fearfully. His sister, holding his hand, hauled him back again to stand beside her. She was watching the strangers with a wary interest, laced well with suspicion.

'You must be Natasha?' Anna asked, gently. 'And this is Nicholai?'

The child did not answer, but glanced at her mother.

Natalia appeared to have recovered herself a little. 'Yes,' she said. ''Tasha – Nikki – this is your Aunt Anna.'

Still they said nothing.

'I'm sorry.' Natalia waved a bony, distracted hand. 'They see so few people, I'm afraid their manners are not of the best.'

'Aunt Anna,' 'Tasha said, suddenly daring, 'you sent us letters. From –' she thought for a moment, frowning '– from England.'

'That's right.' Anna smiled. The child, still wary, smiled back. Anna turned back to Natalia. 'You remember Volodya, who has been running the workshop for Mama?'

'I – yes, I do, I think. But Anna, how in the world?' Natalia stopped, stiffening. From the inner room came a small sound, the barest breath. 'The baby!' she said, and lifting her drab skirts fairly flew to the door, leaving her guests where they stood.

Anna and Volodya exchanged glances.

'It's the baby,' 'Tasha explained, solemnly, as if that were all that needed to be said.

From within the inner room came the soft whisper of mother

to child, 'There, there, my darling, my dearest little one. Don't cry. Don't cry, precious one. You know how it distresses Mama if you cry –'

'You'd better come in,' 'Tasha said, with practical clarity, and led the way.

The room was uncomfortably warm, ill-furnished and as neat and clean as a prison cell. In one corner were two pallet beds and a cot, in another a table, upon which bubbled a cheap samovar, and two chairs. In the third corner was an altar; at least that was what Anna supposed it to be until she saw that it was actually a small table surmounted by a shelf upon which stood rank upon rank of photographs, all draped or ribboned in black, and all of the same subject. The largest stood in pride of place in the centre of the table; Dmitri in his uniform, stiffly and awkwardly posed, his face set in an expression of wooden and unsmiling severity. Before the icon that was set above the table a tiny flame glimmered. Two very battered armchairs were set beside the stove.

Natalia, holding her shawl-wrapped child, turned to greet them. 'Please, do come in. I'm sorry, I've little to offer I'm afraid. But 'Tasha will make tea – well, what passes for tea these days.'

The little girl was already busying herself at the table.

The child in Natalia's arms lay against her shoulder, hardly moving. Natalia held him gently, rocking him as she moved. 'Please, do sit down.'

Anna and her companion lowered themselves into the battered armchairs.

'I'm afraid I've had to burn most of the furniture,' Natalia said with perfect calm. 'It's Dimochka, you see. He isn't strong. He must be kept warm. I find it impossible to heat more than one room, so we live in here, as you can see.'

Anna accepted tea in a chipped glass from the solemn 'Tasha. 'Natalia – that's what we've come about. Mama is living in the Bourlov apartment on the Fontanka. There's plenty of room, and it's very comfortable – and it would be much easier if we were all together, to take turns to go out to buy food. Please, Natalia – come and stay with us for a while?' Her eager words trailed to nothing.

466

Natalia was shaking her head, very firmly. 'I'm sorry, Anna, no. We couldn't possibly do that. 'Tasha, pour some tea for me into the tin mug, please, that's a good girl.'

The little girl, who had been standing watching and listening with an expression of such eager intentness that it took a moment for her mother's words to register, threw one swift pleading glance at Anna then trotted back to the table.

'But Natalia, in heaven's name, why? You'd be so much better off with us –'

'No.' The word was adamant. 'I told you, Anna. We can't.'

'But why ever not?'

Natalia was fussing with the baby, who Anna now saw was in fact a child of more than a year old; he mewed a little, unhappily, as his mother settled him upon her lap. 'It's not possible,' Natalia said, 'in case Dmitri comes.'

There was a moment's difficult silence.

'Natalia –' Anna began.

The haggard face lifted. Dull brown eyes looked suddenly fiercely into Anna's. 'He might,' Natalia said, a small defiance in her voice, 'Anna, he might! I know what you're thinking, but we don't know for certain that he's dead, do we? There was no – no body. No funeral. No end to it, you see. And strange things happen in war. Mistakes are made. Mistakes are often made. Others have turned up, you know. The boy upstairs – he came back, long after his parents had been told he was dead.'

'Natalia, it's been nearly eighteen months!'

'He might,' she said again, stubbornly. 'I don't know that he's dead. Don't you think I'd know? Know in my heart – if he were dead? No. We have to stay here. In case Dima comes.'

'Mama,' little 'Tasha said, pleadingly.

'No, 'Tasha.' Her mother did not even look at her, her attention wholly upon the child on her lap. 'We stay here. Or Papa won't know where to find us.'

Anna exchanged a glance with Volodya. Very slightly he shrugged, shook his head.

'He'll come to see his little Dimochka,' Natalia said, very quietly. 'You see if he doesn't. And then the poor little fellow will brighten up, won't you, my lamb? Now,' she turned, bizarrely brightly, to Anna, as if they were exchanging pleasantries across tea and cakes in Varya's parlour, 'do tell me – what in the world are you doing here? Your last letter reached us, oh, it must be a year or so ago –'

Volodya tried once more. 'Might it not be better for the little chap to be in the Fontanka apartment with us?' he asked. 'There'd be others to help you care for him.'

Natalia cast him a look of patient dismissal. 'No,' she said, firmly. 'Thank you. Now, Anna?'

They stayed for perhaps an hour before, with darkness falling, they took their leave. To Anna's last plea that she accompany them, or at least think about it, Natalia simply shook her head again. 'I told you. We have to stay. We have to be here if he comes.'

'You could – you could leave a note – a message –'

'Don't be silly, Anna. Do you think that if we left this apartment, poor as it must seem to you, it would stay empty for as much as a day? Folk have a nose for such things. There'd be two or three families in here at the shake of a lamb's tail. And what would happen to my message then? No. We must stay.'

'At least she accepted the money,' Anna said later, a little gloomily, as they trudged through the darkening, snowy streets. 'That's something, I suppose.'

Volodya took her arm, helping her across the wide, icy pavement of the bridge. Beneath them the snow-shrouded river gleamed in the fast failing light. Ahead of them was the Winter Palace; over it, a sight still to amaze, streamed a huge red flag. In the great open space of the Palace Square soldiers drilled and columns of trucks and lorries lumbered through the snow. A detachment of Cossacks, red pennants flying, trotted past them over the bridge.

'I'll see if I can get some supplies to them,' Volodya said.

'That's kind. Thank you.'

Something in her tone drew his glance sharply to her face. 'What's wrong?'

She shrugged, dispiritedly, then none too successfully glanced a small smile at him. 'An unworthy attack of self-pity, I'm afraid,' she admitted. 'I came with such very good intentions, but – apart from Mama, I suppose – what good am I doing? It doesn't really seem to matter if I stay or go, does it?'

His hand was still firmly upon her elbow. Surprisingly steadily despite his limp he steered her past a group of rowdy young men and back onto the pavement. His words were lost in their noisy laughter.

She turned her head. 'I'm sorry?'

'I said "It matters to me",' he said, smiling, and bent lightly to kiss her cheek, his lips cool and undemanding against her skin, before once again he took her arm and resumed his brisk, uneven step. 'That's the second time I've said it. I think.' He gave another small, shyly amused smile.

Taken utterly by surprise she stumbled a little.

'I'm sorry,' he said, in a matter-of-fact tone, 'I suppose I shouldn't have done that.'

Her breath came back and she laughed a little, shrugging, her depression lifting. 'I don't actually see why not,' she said, after a moment.

The rest of the journey was completed in a thoughtful and companionable silence.

In bed that night, wrapped against the cold, her feet snug against a stone hot-water bottle, she remembered that kiss in those last, dreamily quiet moments before she slept. It had been a kindly gesture. But then Volodya was a kindly man. A very kindly man indeed. And he liked her; she knew it. 'It matters to me,' he had said. Twice. She smiled to herself in the darkness, warm and on the edge of sleep.

She woke up in blind panic to the absolute certainty that someone was in the room.

She lay rigid, listening, frightened half to death. It came again; the creak of a floorboard, and with it a breath of icy air from an open window. Petrified, she stared into the darkness; felt rather than saw the shadow that loomed above her. Before she could draw her fear-shackled breath to scream a hand had clamped hard upon her mouth. 'It's all right! Please, it's all right! I won't hurt you, I promise. Just don't scream – please don't scream.' The voice, low and urgent, close to her ear was as familiar as her own father's had been. Terror fled. She stopped struggling, lay still beneath the strong hand. The light of a small torch brightened the gloom and flickered to her face. 'Anna!' her uncle gasped. 'Holy Mother! Anna! Of all people! What in the name of God are you doing here?'

She sat up. 'Uncle Mischa!' she said. 'Oh, dear Uncle Mischa!' She flung her arms about his neck, buried her face in the strong warmth of his shoulder. He held her very tightly, his cheek resting upon her tousled hair.

'Little Anna!' he said, gently. 'Hush, darling, I didn't mean to frighten you. But the key wouldn't work. I had to find a way in – your window was the easiest.'

'We changed the lock,' she whispered, her voice hoarse, and muffled by his heavy coat. 'Volodya did it. After the soldiers came. They broke the door down –'

He drew back, holding her still by the shoulders, looking at her sombrely in the faint light of the torch. 'Soldiers? There have been soldiers here?'

'Yes. A few days ago. Looking for you.'

'Ah.' His hands dropped from her shoulders. He rubbed a hand tiredly across his eyes. 'I thought that might be the case.'

'Uncle Mischa, you can't stay! They're hunting for you! They called you – an enemy of the people.'

He laughed a little, grimly, at that. 'Bloody right they are too, if they count themselves the people,' he said, and his voice, though muted, was as she had always known it, confident and glimmering with humour. He stood up, tall in the darkness. 'Anna my dear, you're right. I can't stay. In fact I didn't intend to. Had my key worked I would have been here and gone with no-one any the wiser. I'm sorry to have given you a fright. Sorrier still that there's little time to talk. There's something I've come to collect, then I must go.'

'Where?' She was scrambling from bed as she talked, throwing her heavy woollen bedgown around her shoulders. 'Where are you going? What have you come for? Can I help?'

'Oh, Anna.' There was an undisguised catch in his voice as he held his arms open to her once more. 'How the sight of you – the sound of your voice – takes me back! You and my little Katya, what an irresistible pair you made. How very serious you were, how grave! And how disgracefully light-minded my charming Katya!' There was the smallest of silences. Mischa swallowed, audibly. 'She loved you dearly, you know. As a sister; though the little devil may never have shown it. She'll be so pleased to know that I've –' He stopped abruptly.

'Katya?' she asked, swiftly. 'You're going to Katya? Oh, Uncle Mischa – how is she? And her little boy? I was so sorry to hear about Jussi's accident.'

Her uncle lifted helpless hands, spoke in a rapid whisper. 'Anna, there's so much to tell and no time to tell it. Listen, I have a minute only. One thing I can tell you. Jussi isn't dead. Ssh!' He lifted a sharp finger at her exclamation. 'He was badly injured. Crippled. But they're together again, in Helsinki. You've heard of the trouble in Finland?'

'A little.'

'They're involved in it. Heavily involved. I can say no more than that. And they have a route out of the country, via Sweden.'

'That's where you're going?'

'Yes. To England, perhaps, or America. There's no place for me here now.' His voice held an edge of bitterness. 'Anna, I don't know what you're doing here, and I haven't time to find out, but take my advice and get out whilst you can. The trouble has only just begun, believe me. If you stay you'll suffer for it. Tell me – you aren't alone here?'

'No. Mama is here, and Volodya, who used to run the shop for her –'

He glanced at her sharply. 'Don't let them hold you, Anna, don't let any of them hold you. Take your practical uncle's advice; get out while you can. Now, I'll fetch what I came for – and then, Annoushka, perhaps you'll let your old uncle out of the front door to prevent him breaking a leg, or worse, in an undignified scramble down the drainpipe that in desperation got him up here!'

He was walking quietly to the door. Her bare feet already chilled to the bone, Anna followed. 'Uncle Mischa – the soldiers – they took everything!'

In the light of the torch he carried she saw the faint shake of his head, sensed his smile. 'We'll see, shall we?'

He led the way into the ballroom. She felt his anger as the

tiny beam of the torch played upon the destruction. 'We cleared it as best we could,' she said, almost apologetically.

He did not reply, but strode towards the far wall, played the torch upon the ornate, smashed mirrors, counting under his breath. 'One – two – there, the third –' He moved swiftly to a mirror, which was cracked from top to bottom, ran his hands deftly along the ornate frame. 'Ah!' There came a tiny click, and a whirring sound. A panel next to the mirror slid open revealing a small, solid door set into the wall. Mischa had a key in his hand. He glanced over his shoulder, smiling at Anna's surprised face, before he opened the concealed safe.

Perhaps five minutes later she escorted him to the front door and opened it cautiously. The building towered about them in utter silence, the stairwell was dark and still. 'Uncle Mischa – please be careful.'

'I will, my Anna – you know I will. Don't worry.' Mischa was carrying the small yet bulky linen bag he had taken from the safe. At the open door he stopped, fumbling with the cord that tied it. 'Anna, take this – you might need it.'

'It's all right, Uncle. I have plenty of money, I promise you.'

'It's good to have money,' he said. 'It's even better to have insurance. Take it. And Anna, remember what I said: get out before things get any worse.'

She did not reply to that, but let him thrust several small objects into her hand, clung to him as he engulfed her in a bearhug that said more than words. As he turned to go she touched his arm. 'Uncle Mischa – give all my love to Katya.'

'I will, my dear. Be sure I will.'

For a big man he moved extraordinarily quietly. He was gone before she knew it, and the stairwell was empty. She closed the door silently, stood for a moment listening. The apartment, for all its sleeping occupants, seemed with Mischa's going to be cold, dark and utterly empty. Not wanting to wake the others, she groped her way back to her icebox of a bedroom, closed the door and lit the tiny night-lamp she kept by her bed. Leaning to it, she opened her clenched hand. Lying in the palm were three items of jewellery; an ornate ring, set with rubies, a pendant of gold and gleaming sapphire, and a brooch, a magnificent thing of gold and aquamarine set within a bed of diamonds whose skilfully cut facets reflected the feeble rays of the lamp in dazzling – and valuable – fire.

Clutching them still, she climbed into the chilled bed, pushed them for the time being under her pillow. She would find a place of safe-keeping for them tomorrow.

It was a very long time before she slept.

The timing of her first visit to Margarita was dictated by the degree of unrest still prevailing in the city. For two days it was too dangerous to venture out. On the third day, however, even Volodya thought it safe enough for her to go to find her youngest sister. It was with real excitement that she set off towards the Liteini and Sasha's and Margarita's apartment.

The first moments of astonishment and delight could not have been more as she had hoped. Margarita showed every sign of pleasure at seeing her, asked non-stop questions – and characteristically barely waited to hear the answers – as she made tea. Yet Anna thought there was an edge of strain in the light voice, the too-bright laughter.

'Me? Why I'm very well of course.' Margarita pirouetted, smoothing the waist of her pretty dress. 'Can't you see it? Just driven absolutely to *distraction* by all this foolish revolution nonsense. Why can't everyone just settle down and enjoy themselves again, that's what I want to know. Sasha?' She looked up at her sister's question, blue eyes limpid. 'Oh, he was fine last time I heard – letters take such ages of course – more tea?'

Certainly it was obvious that she was in no immediate need of help, financial or otherwise. Of all of them, indeed, Rita seemed to have fared the best. Her shelves were stocked, her small apartment warm and comfortable.

Anna could not, then, quite understand the obscure feeling of unease that dogged her as she took her leave and made her way back to the Fontanka.

Volodya was waiting for her; he too had been busy and produced, with the air of a magician bringing rabbits from hats, tea, sugar and fresh-baked bread. He eased off her shoes and chafed her cold feet. He listened to her account of her visit to her sister and with sensible words calmed her disquiet. He drew laughter from her as he told of an incident in the bread queue

473

that morning, and grateful thanks at the news that he had suggested to Varya that Natalia's two children, 'Tasha and Nikki, might come to stay for a few days, and had persuaded from her the reluctant agreement that Anna herself had been utterly unable to extract.

In the cold kitchen as she tried to express her thanks, he kissed her. And, gratefully and with real affection, she kissed him back.

That night, he came to her bed. In such strange and confusing times it was good not to be alone.

CHAPTER TWENTY-TWO

Margarita pushed impatiently through the excited crowds, uncaring of the growled complaints and hard looks occasioned by her ready use of elbow and shoulder. The man who stood upon a chair and harangued the throng punched the air with his fist as he spoke.

'And I tell you, comrades, that we did not fight and die in the streets – in these very streets – for the right to continue a Tsarist Imperialist war –'

'Bloody Bolshevik,' a man muttered as Margarita passed, and she dodged with practised speed as another standing nearby lunged at the speaker, grabbing him by the collar. 'And what's wrong with the Bolsheviks, my Menshevik friend?'

She reached the edge of the gathering. The whole of the Liteini was blocked by the meeting.

'– what good have our sacrifices done us? *Our* sacrifices, comrades, not the sacrifices of the petty bourgeois who sit on their fat behinds around a table and call themselves a parliament! *Our* sacrifices! What good has it been, tell me that! The people still starve, still die for nothing under the filthy guns of tyranny –'

'Mind where you're going, girl!' A man caught her arm. She snatched it away; saw the speculative look in his eye as he took in her fashionable dress and hat, the cloud of golden hair. Damn it that she could have been so stupid as to leave her brown cloak in Vassili's room! Unseasonally warm as the April day was, the enveloping garment was disguise and protection in these dangerous days. She slid swiftly into the crowd like a fish into water, leaving the man staring after her.

'I tell you this, comrades: you have more in common with the workers of Germany, the poor bloody bastards who suffer as you suffer, and die as you die, than with those that seek to rule you now – traitors all, to the revolution and to the people –'

She was almost at the crossroads. Hampered by her slim, hobbled skirt she hurried along the pavement. Swore under her breath as, suddenly, from a nearby turning a large group of men – yes, and some women too, she noted with disdain – erupted into the main street and advanced on the Bolshevik meeting, staves and cudgels in hand.

'Listen as your comrades at the Front are listening!' The impassioned voice echoed still behind her, bouncing from the walls of the buildings that lined the wide thoroughfare. 'They don't want to fight this war – they are *refusing* to fight this war! They are deserting – deserting by the thousands – by the hundreds of thousands. You know it! You know them! These are the brave lads who are standing up for their rights, and for the rights of every one of us. Now that Comrade Lenin is back with us –'

'Look out!' someone shouted.

Margarita plastered herself up against the wall as the grim-faced oncoming marchers broke into a determined trot, pouring past her and ploughing into the outer edges of the meeting, weapons raised.

She lifted her skirts and sped the last few yards, turned into the familiar street, shrieks and screams of anger, outrage and pain dying behind her.

She ran up the stairs to the apartment, fumbling in her bag for her key as she went. 'Damned hooligans! Barbarians! God-forsaken apes, the lot of them!' She swung herself briskly up and around the painted banister post onto the landing. A woman was coming out of one of the doors. She turned as she heard Margarita's coming. For a moment they were eye to eye. Then the other woman – dark-clad and fat as a priest, Margarita thought contemptuously – stepped back, drawing her skirts aside, pursed her mouth, openly insulting, making as if she would spit.

Margarita, smiling viciously, gestured obscenely with her fingers.

And then saw Anna, waiting at the front door of the apartment.

She watched the other woman down the stairs, turned and

sauntered defiantly towards her sister. She looked, Anna thought, quite exceptionally beautiful; thinner than she used to be, her face fine-boned and taut, the wide blue eyes a blaze of bright colour beneath the mass of her hair. Beautiful, yes; but not happy. 'Fat bitch,' she said, casually, as she reached to fit the key into the lock. 'Fine neighbours I've got!'

'Margarita!' Anna said, unhappily.

'Oh, do stop it, 'Noushka. Come in or stand there, but don't lecture me. I'm not in the mood.' She snatched her hat from her head and tossed it onto the table.

Anna followed her into the apartment. No sign of deprivation here. Despite the warmth outside the stoves glowed with heat; the paint was fresh, a new set of curtains decked the windows.

Margarita walked to the window, stood looking down into the street. She said nothing.

Irritatingly Anna felt every bit as awkward as she knew her young sister was hoping she would. 'I – we – haven't heard from you for a week or so. Mama – asked me to check that you were all right –'

Margarita turned, her sudden smile seraphic. 'No she didn't, Anna, don't talk such nonsense. Mama doesn't care whether any of us lives or dies. It was you who wanted to know if I was all right.'

Anna shrugged.

Margarita walked to the table, opened a silver box, took out a cigarette and lit it, taking a long, satisfied pull at it before throwing back her head to blow the smoke theatrically into the air. 'I'm all right,' she said, lightly.

'You are?' Her sister's voice was openly, tartly sceptical.

'Yes. As all right as anyone can be, that is, who has just heard that a bunch of bastard peasants has burned down her country home.' She drew on the cigarette again, watching her sister. 'Are the English peasants prone to fire-raising, Anna? Are you sure your precious Sythings is safe?'

'Oh, Rita, I'm so sorry. Drovenskoye is gone? I'd heard reports – it's been very bad in the countryside they say.' Anna stepped towards her sister, hand outstretched, and stopped as Margarita turned, avoiding her. 'Your mother-in-law? And Sasha's sister? Are they safe?'

477

Margarita turned to look at her through a cloud of smoke. 'I've no idea,' she said, coolly.

Anna surveyed her sister helplessly. In the half a dozen times they had met since her return to Petrograd she had never once come near to breaking this bright and brittle shell with which Margarita had armoured herself. 'Does Sasha know?'

Margarita lifted a shoulder.

'Have you heard from him?'

The swift irritation that any reference to her husband seemed to occasion flickered in Margarita's face. 'Of course I haven't heard from him. I've told you – how ever many times have I told you? – he's at the Front. How the devil do you think he'd find time to write with things as they are? They're saying whole regiments are refusing to fight, that men are executing their officers, have you heard? The whole thing's a shambles. If Sasha's in one piece I doubt if his priority would be to write to me!'

'No. I suppose not.'

Margarita leaned to the window again, peering down into the street. 'There's more trouble out there. They're breaking up a meeting.'

'There's been trouble all over the city.'

'I don't understand in the least what's going on. I thought they wanted to get rid of the Tsar? Well, they've got rid of him. What the hell are they all fighting for now?'

'Power,' Anna said, bleakly. 'The revolution isn't over, Rita. It's only just started. The Socialists aren't satisfied with sharing power with the Duma. They aren't going to stand by and let the Duma reap the benefit of what they see as their victory. Volodya says they won't be satisfied until they've taken complete control.'

'Ah,' Margarita said, lightly spiteful, 'if Volodya said it, it must be so.'

Anna ignored the silly and obviously deliberate provocation; she had in these past weeks realized that Margarita the woman was little different to Margarita the child: to rise to her bait was to encourage her to even more outrageous behaviour. She had joined her sister at the window. Beneath them a group of men ran past, shouting and waving heavy staves. One of them had a pistol that he was firing wildly into the air.

478

'But why are they fighting amongst themselves?' Margarita asked after a moment, a sudden flash of real interest in her voice. 'That lot down there are all Socialists, aren't they? Yet they seem to hate each other more than they ever hated the Tsar!'

'The same answer, I suppose; power. Whoever takes control of the people will in the end, they think, take control of the country. Since the man Lenin came back –'

'Who exactly is he?' Margarita had finished her cigarette. She wandered to the table, stubbed it with thoughtful deliberation into an ashtray.

'A Bolshevik leader. The Bolshevik leader, I suppose you could say. One of the most dangerous men in the country, Volodya says. He's been in exile in Switzerland. He's stirring up the most terrible trouble.'

'Well.' Margarita had reached the end of her attention span. She stretched, bored. 'As long as they leave me alone I don't much care what they do. Now, Anna, I'm really terribly sorry – it's absolutely lovely to see you, of course, but I am rather rushed at the moment. I have a visitor coming, a friend –'

Their eyes met, one pair questioning, the other defiant. Then, 'Of course,' Anna said, brightly, gathering her handbag and gloves. 'I won't hold you up. I just wanted to check that all was well.'

'It is,' Margarita said.

At the door Anna paused, looking down at her smaller, slighter sister. 'Rita,' she began.

Margarita was too quick for her. 'Don't,' she said, swiftly, 'don't lecture me, Anna. Just don't. We all have our own way of coping with things, isn't that right? This is mine.'

'Yes. I'm sorry. But, Rita, do try to come to see Mama just occasionally?'

Margarita shrugged unenthusiastically. 'All right. I'll try.'

She closed the door behind her sister with a sigh of relief, went back into the small parlour. A bottle of vodka stood upon the sideboard. She splashed a generous tot into a glass and tossed it back with one movement. Then as she lifted her head she caught sight of her own face in a small mirror that hung upon the wall. She stood for a long moment, her movements arrested, absolutely still, before turning fiercely away and reaching for the silver cigarette box.

Anna arrived back at the apartment, later that afternoon, dog tired and with aching feet, a loaf of bread and a few potatoes the prize for over two hours of queuing.

'Anna, where have you been? You leave me alone here for hours on end. It isn't fair, you know, it really isn't fair! And where's Volodya? I don't see why you need both go out at the same time?'

Wearily Anna stood in the hall, eyes closed. Then she straightened her shoulders, walked down the hall to the parlour. 'I'm sorry, Mama. There was a shop with some bread – I didn't think I should miss the chance. And everything takes so long – there's so much trouble in the streets again.'

'Trouble in the streets! Trouble in the streets!' Varya grumbled. 'They need a good flogging, that's what they need! It was never like this in the old days! In the good days of the Tsar! God's judgement on us all, that's what it is, you mark my words. God's judgement! Anna, do light the stove, for goodness' sake. And where are my chocolates?'

Anna bit her lip hard for a moment, then with precariously held patience said, 'Mama, I've told you – we can't light the stove. We're very low on fuel. And there's hardly any to be had. We must conserve what we have. It really isn't that cold, you know. I'll get you a rug, if you like, to put across your knees. And as for the chocolates, I gave you your allowance before I went out – it was supposed to last you the day.'

'Allowance! The very thought!' The white jowls wobbled pathetically. 'I don't ask for much, Anna – your poor Mama doesn't ask for much, but how you can be so cruel as to deny me –'

'Mama! I've told you! There are hardly any left! If you gobble them all up now you'll have none, none at all.'

'Don't shout at me, Anna! There's no need for that!' The inevitable tears were squeezing from Varya's eyes and running down her plump cheeks. 'Oh, the shame! The shame and the pity of it! That my own daughter should treat me so!'

Anna, her patience fled, muttered a short, sharp and uncompromising answer to that as she stamped down the long passageway to the scullery that she and Volodya were using as a kitchen. The huge, wrecked, empty apartment was oppressive around her. They had spoken of trying to leave it, of finding somewhere smaller and easier to manage, but in present circumstances such plans were all but impossible. There was not a square inch of room in the city that was not already crammed with people. Her one half-hearted attempt to lobby a harassed Embassy official in the faint hope that he might be able to help with the problem had brought exactly the response she had expected; the British Embassy was not, understandably, interested in its citizens' housing problems. It was interested in getting as many of those citizens as possible out of the disturbed city and back to Britain and to safety; when Mrs de Fontenay was ready to consider that option they would be all too eager to help.

She leaned for a moment, tiredly, against the sink. Not, she thought, wryly, that the thought of England, of lovely Sythings and of safety did not become, with each passing day, a more attractive temptation to the said Mrs de Fontenay. But how could she go? Having come in the first place to offer help, how could she now run away, leave Mama – Natalia – the children – in such uncertain circumstances and with absolutely no guarantee of their safety? And Volodya. There was, too, now, the problem of Volodya. Dear, devoted Volodya, who undoubtedly loved her: and with whom she now found herself, to her private dismay, inextricably involved. It was not that she did not enjoy his warm and gentle lovemaking; she did. She enjoyed it very much indeed. Their snatched moments together in the quiet darkness after Varya had finally given in and allowed herself to sleep were perhaps the most precious of the day. Nor did she fail to appreciate how much they all owed him, how far they had come to depend on him. But she was all too honestly aware that she did not love him. She was very fond of him. She respected him. She used him, as a shield and a prop. But she did not love him.

She sighed, hugely.

The doorbell rang, brief and shrill.

481

Her heart jumped to her throat. 'Damn!' she said, out loud. 'Who the devil's that?'

'Anna? Anna, there's someone at the door!' Varya's voice was frightened.

'Yes, I know, Mama. Don't worry. It's all right.' The reassuring words were automatic, their conviction totally spurious. She went into the hall and opened the door with a dry mouth and her heart pounding in her throat.

A tall fair man stood upon the landing. He was dressed in working-man's clothes, a cap jauntily upon his lank, over-long hair. His smile was charming. 'You are Mrs de Fontenay?' he asked, courteously, and then, at her bewilderment, his smile expanding, 'Anna? Katya's cousin Anna?' His Russian was heavily accented. The accent was Finnish.

Anna stepped back. 'Yes. Yes! Oh, do come in! You've come from her? You've come from Katya?'

He nodded, smiling at her excitement, reached into his breast pocket and brought out a thick envelope which he proffered her. 'My name is Heimo. Heimo Puhakka. I have the honour of being your cousin's friend. I have some messages for you, and this letter.' He smiled his charming smile again. 'A letter so long I fear it will take you a week to read it!' He broke off, suddenly, coughing dryly.

Anna clutched the grubby envelope. 'She's well? And Jussi? And Uncle Mischa – he reached Helsinki safely? Oh, of course he must have or you wouldn't know I was here. Come in, come in – let me take your coat.'

As he stepped into the hall he was overtaken again by a choking bout of throaty coughing. He put his hand out to the wall to steady himself.

'You're not well!' Anna said, with swift concern.

Too breathless to deny it in words he shook his head, reassuringly. But Anna could see now the brightness of fever in his face. The hand that touched hers was dry and hot.

'Anna? Anna, who is it?'

'It's a friend, Mama. A friend of Katya's.' Full of worry, she watched as the tall young man with the gentle smile pushed himself away from the wall and determinedly steadied himself. 'Come in,' she repeated briskly. 'Come in at once and sit down.

I'll make you something warm to drink, something to soothe your throat.'

The cough rasped harshly again. 'I'm sorry,' he said. 'A little cough, that's all –' and sank to his knees, his head in his hands.

By the time Volodya came home Anna's guest was tucked into bed and sleeping restlessly, his breathing harsh. Volodya stood, frowning, in the doorway. 'Anna, you're sure this is a good idea?'

Anna had spent a long time talking to Heimo before his illness had finally and utterly felled him. 'You think it a better idea to turn him out onto the streets to take his chances? Perhaps to die?' The words were crisp. She had foreseen careful Volodya's objections. 'We have no choice. He's very sick. Come – come and read Katya's letter. What adventures! Trust Katya to be in the thick of things!' With brisk movements and a repressive expression that spoke louder than any words she shut the door and led the way back into the scullery.

'There's insurrection in Finland,' he said, leaning on the door, watching her as she hauled out her bag of potatoes.

'I know there is,' she said, shortly. 'Read Katya's letter. You'll find out all about it.'

'Anna, that man is an enemy of the Russian Government –'

She turned on him, fiercely. 'That man is Katya's good friend, Volodya,' she snapped. 'And that's good enough for me.'

'If they should find out –'

'Who should find out? Why should they find out? And what else do you suggest? Volodya, I tell you the man is sick!' She turned back to her potatoes. The silence was heavy. She stopped, turned to him. 'You want to peel the potatoes?'

He shook his head, sheepishly.

'Then go and do something else,' she said composedly and turned back to her task. 'Try reading Katya's letter. It might make you think twice about who is an enemy and who a friend.'

Heimo's fever rose. Anna sat with him throughout the long night, sponging him with cold water, trying to make him drink, praying when all else seemed to be failing.

'We need a doctor,' she said when Volodya crept in to join her as the first pale light of dawn touched the sky.

'A doctor? Are you mad?'

483

She said nothing.

The man in the bed thrashed restlessly, muttering. His fair skin glowed drily and painfully bright.

'What would you rather?' Anna asked at last, tiredly. 'That he died here? How, pray, would you explain that?'

The doctor was a small, plump and nervous man. Anna distrusted him on sight. Yet his examination of the patient was brisk and professional, and he did have some medicines, at a price.

'*How much?*' Anna gasped.

'I'm sorry. It is the market price. Inflation, you know.'

'Greed more like it.' Anna thrust the money at him. It was true that each time she went to the bank the money she drew out bought less and less and lasted for a shorter and shorter time. Heimo muttered confusedly, and not in Russian.

The doctor's face was bland. 'The market price,' he said again. 'Even doctors have to live.'

The fever subsided a few hours later, though whether due to the drugs, to Anna's ministrations or to the simple workings of a healthy constitution it was impossible to tell. Exhausted Heimo lay upon fresh pillows in the bed that had seen Katya's conception, and smiled a tired but still infectious smile. 'Look at this. A bed fit for a king.'

'Fit for a friend of Katya's, certainly,' Anna said. 'Lie still, do! We have little, I'm afraid, to tempt an invalid appetite, but I have potatoes and a little butter. Could you manage a spoonful?'

She sat with him as he ate, left him to sleep, then returned when he awoke.

'You've been so very kind,' he said. His fair skin was cool now, the ugly flush gone. His eyes were calm. He still coughed a little, but it was less harsh, less obviously painful. 'I'm so very sorry to have inflicted this upon you. I hadn't realized – a cold, I thought, just a cold. The journey was perhaps a little longer, a little more difficult, than I had expected.' He grinned, faintly. 'We go from dodging the Tsar's patrol boats to dodging those of the Provisional Government. Perhaps I preferred the Tsar's. At least, I never had to swim for it before!'

'So that was what happened?'

484

He spread expressive hands.

'Katya's letter wasn't damaged.'

'Neither were the others I carried. There are ways to protect such things.'

Anna leaned forward, her elbows on the bed. 'Are you tired? Can you talk?'

'For as long as you wish.'

'Then tell me – tell me about Finland – about Katya.'

Heimo's presence was, perhaps inevitably, a cause of friction between cautious Volodya and an Anna who, despite these past months, had become dangerously used to living in a more open society.

'He stays for as long as he needs to.'

'Every moment he stays is a danger to us all. To you. To me. To your mother.'

She turned from him in disgust.

'Anna, please, be sensible!'

'Volodya,' she said, coldly and she well knew unjustly, over her shoulder, 'be a little brave. Just a little.'

That night in bed she tried to make it up to him, knowing how she had hurt him. They lay in silence after their love-making, his head upon her shoulder. 'I'm sorry, my dear,' she said, softly, and the apology fell emptily into the silence that engulfed them.

He turned his head to kiss her breast. But he said nothing.

Later they talked. 'He's almost better,' Anna said. 'A day or two and he'll be gone.'

She sensed his smile. 'It's jealousy,' he said, 'pure jealousy. I want you to myself.'

The soldiers came looking for him the next day. This time they had the courtesy to ring the front doorbell; by which time Heimo, nothing if not alert, having seen them enter the building, was on his way out of the servants' door on the back landing.

'But won't they have the back of the building guarded?' Anna asked anxiously.

'Don't worry – I shan't go down, but up. Where there's a roof

485

there's usually a way across it.' He caught her hand. 'Anna, thank you. I know what you've done for me.'

'It's nothing.'

'You call saving my life nothing?' He shook his head. 'Now, don't forget – if you need us, you know where we are. You've memorized the Helsinki address?'

'Yes.'

He dropped a quick kiss on her cheek.

'God speed!' she said. 'And be careful! Give all my love to Katya!'

There was one last flash of that smile, and he was gone.

The soldiers searched, noisily and carelessly, and found nothing. They declined to tell her the source of their suspicions that she was harbouring 'an enemy of the people'.

'That bloody doctor,' Volodya said, after they had gone.

Anna was scraping about with a pair of tongs in the cold ashes of the stove. 'I suppose so. Well, Heimo's gone, and so have they. Ah –' She pulled out a package, shaking it free of ash. 'Here it is. Katya's letter.'

'Anna! You were supposed to have destroyed it! What if they had found it?'

'Well, they didn't, did they?' Anna blew the fine ash from the paper.

'Anna? Anna! Anna, where are you?'

Anna raised her eyes to heaven. 'Here, Mama. Coming, Mama.'

In the dangerous and disturbed weeks that followed Anna took to visiting Natalia and her children very frequently. She had come to be very fond of the two children, especially the little girl 'Tasha; and 'Tasha and her brother, bereft of any real warmth or tenderness from a mother who was all but obsessed with their small, ailing brother, returned her affection in full. Since Natalia still adamantly refused to leave the apartment Anna made sure that what supplies her money and Volodya's contacts could provide were shared between the two households. Life was getting harder with each day that passed. After the violent riots and the mass demonstrations in April against the Provisional Government's determination to honour their obligations to their allies and continue the war, the city seethed, faction and counter-faction fighting bitterly for advantage, the streets of the city their battleground. At the beginning of May a Coalition Government was formed, that included both the Duma deputies and some Socialists, though no Bolsheviks. But the apparent co-operation was never anything but a farce, and unrest and anarchy continued to stalk the city. Food became scarcer, and more expensive, by the day. There were massive and violent demonstrations against the Government. At the Front the Russian army was nearly disintegrating; up to a million men deserted in that year of 1917, and discipline had broken down entirely. No-one doubted that worse was to come. As the month of June approached preparations were laid for more demonstrations, more challenges to the power of the Government. Quarrelsome committees and Bolshevik Soviets took charge of factories, workplaces and regiments. There were stories of disaffection in the Baltic Fleet. Once again, Petrograd was a powder keg, and this time it was the Bolsheviks, led by the man known as Lenin, that held the match, poised to light the fuse.

On a warm and placid day in late May Anna and Volodya sat in the sunshine upon a bench in the Tauride Gardens, behind the palace that was the seat of the Duma, relishing a moment's peace and privacy. For once the city was quiet. Anna, driven to distraction by her mother's demands, had been desperate to get out, if only for an hour or so. In the cause of her own sanity she had produced almost the last of Zhenia's store of chocolates, dumped them into Varya's lap, and, with Volodya, had fled into the open air. She sat, face tilted to the sun, eyes closed, for a long, still moment. Volodya watched her, smiling faintly. A swan glided lazily across still, shining water.

At last Anna sighed, opened her eyes, settled back against the seat. 'That's better!' She breathed deeply again. 'Funny how nothing seems so bad in the sunshine!'

They sat for several minutes in an easy silence, watching the water birds and the glitter of the sunshine through the trees. A mother and three small children strolled by. The eldest boy was inexpertly bowling a large hoop that all at once escaped him, wobbled wildly and fell, clattering, beside Volodya. He bent to right it, sent it bowling back towards the child. The mother smiled her thanks. Volodya watched the child's renewed and dogged efforts to control his toy with amused and affectionate eyes.

Anna turned to look at him, her eyes thoughtful. 'You like children, don't you?'

'Yes. Yes, I do.'

'And yet – you never married?'

'No.' The word was quiet.

She held his eyes for a moment, then, uncomfortable, looked away.

'The only girl I ever wanted ran away and married someone else,' he said, lightly.

She shook her head vehemently. 'Volodya –' She stopped, at a loss for words.

'It's all right,' he said, calmly, and reached a hand to cover hers. 'It has to be said, doesn't it? Anna, I know. I know you don't love me. You didn't then, and you don't now. It isn't your fault.'

'I do!' she said. 'I do love you! But –'

'But not in the way that I love you. Not in the way I would wish you to love me.'

For one brief moment she remembered; remembered the blaze, the wonder, the agony of her feelings for Andrei. The warm depth of her love for Guy. 'No,' she said. And then, 'I'm sorry,' she added.

'No need to be. I told you. It isn't your fault.'

'It feels as if it is.'

He shook his head.

The silence this time was long, and not quite as easy.

'Volodya, I don't know what to do,' Anna said at last. 'I don't know what to do for the best; for you, for the others – for myself.'

'You must go of course,' he said, very promptly. 'As soon as possible. There's nothing else you *can* do in the end. You have another life. A safe and happy life. You should go back to it.'

'Save myself? Forget everyone else?' She rubbed her forehead a little tiredly with her fingertips. 'I sometimes find myself wondering – why did I come? It's so hard to remember what it was like. What on earth did I think I was going to be able to *do*? Waltz in – tidy everyone up – spend a few roubles – waltz back out again!'

'You do yourself an injustice.'

'Do I?' she asked, bleakly unreassured. 'Oh, Volodya, it all seemed so *simple* then. And it isn't. It isn't simple at all. It's all such a muddle, isn't it? A horrible, messy – dangerous! – *muddle*.'

He caught her shoulders firmly, turned her to face him. 'Anna, there's one thing you must face. We are lost. Russia is lost. What is to come will be as bad as if not worse than what has gone before. You have to go back to England. You have to save yourself.'

'You want me to go?'

'I want you to be safe. I want you to be happy.'

She turned away from him, shaking her head. 'I don't know. I don't *know*!'

'Come. You're overwrought. Let's walk a little way.' He held out his hand.

They walked in silence.

'Nothing's as I had expected, as I had hoped,' Anna said, quietly, as they came out onto the embankment of the Neva. 'Mama – Natalia and her poor weakling of a baby – God alone knows what's got into Margarita. And then – Lenka.' She stopped walking, her eyes distant on the busy scene before her. 'Volodya, why should Lenka still hate me so, after all this time?' It was a question that haunted her.

He watched with her for a moment the wide, busy waterway that divided the city. Grey naval ships were anchored on the bank opposite the Winter Palace, near the Fortress, tugs and civil traffic ploughed through the wide, slow-moving waters. 'I don't know. I didn't know any of you well enough to know exactly what went on.'

Impulsively she turned to him, touched his arm. 'I want to go and see her. I want to try to explain.'

'Now?'

She shrugged a little. 'Why not? If trouble starts again I may not get another chance.'

* * *

The apartment building where Lenka had a room was typical of many in the overcrowded industrial suburbs of the city. It was dark, depressing and none too clean. The alleyway outside was squalid. Despite the warmth of the day the air within the heavy walls was chill and damp, and the smell was stomach-turning.

Volodya hesitated by the door, looking at Anna enquiringly. Anna took a breath; nodded. He rapped, sharply.

The door opened almost immediately. A girl perhaps seven or eight years of age peered in the half-light. 'Yes?'

Anna stood struck to silence. The youngster was tall, and very thin. The wiry halo of her hair was lit to fire by the light of a flickering lamp upon the wall behind her. Her skin was pale and freckled, her nose straight, her mouth wide.

'Yes?' the girl asked again, sharply. 'What do you –' She stopped abruptly, looking at Anna, her face registering the same shock, and then almost immediately a flame of fierce anger. She reached to slam the door.

Volodya moved his foot and the door jammed against it. 'Is your mother here?'

'Who is it, Tonia?' Lenka's voice was hoarse. The words were followed by a fit of coughing.

'Lenka, it's me,' Anna said, very clearly, her eyes riveted, appalled, upon the hate-filled look that the child who from appearances might have been mistaken for her own had fixed upon her.

There was a moment of silence, followed by movement. Lenka appeared behind her daughter; a Lenka thinner and gaunter than Anna remembered her, wrapped in an ancient dressing gown, a handkerchief clutched in her hand. 'What do you want?'

'To talk. Please, Lenka.'

'Anna, there is nothing to talk about. I'm not well. Please go.' There was nothing of the old sullen strength of will; she looked simply exhausted, her eyes dark-ringed.

'Let me help you,' Anna said.

'No.' There was no weakness in that. 'We're all right. Just go away.'

'Who is it, Mama?' A little boy had come up behind her,

490

wrapped his hand in the worn skirt of her gown, his thumb in his mouth, bright eyes upon Anna.

'It's a wicked witch,' Tonia said, loudly, 'who's come to gobble you up.'

The dark eyes widened.

'That will do, Tonia,' Lenka said, none too severely. She was breathing heavily, the sound of it loud in the quiet.

'Five minutes,' Anna said. 'That's all I ask. Five minutes to talk. To let me try to explain.'

Tonia, thin and agile as a monkey, had ducked beneath her mother's arm and stood, blazing with protective fury in front of her and the bemused little boy. 'Go away!' she shouted. 'Go away, witch! Leave us alone!'

'Tonia –' Anna put out a hand to her. The child struck it aside.

'*Tonia!*' The sudden effort was too much for Lenka. Coughing all but choked her.

The child was beside her in a moment, arm about her waist. 'Mama, Mama! You mustn't cough! Come – come and sit down.'

Lenka allowed herself to be pushed into a patched armchair, its horsehair stuffing bulging through its threadbare covering. She was struggling to contain the fit of coughing.

Anna and Volodya followed them into the room. Watched as Tonia, competent and gentle as a woman three times her age, fetched a tin cup of water from the table, helped her mother guide it to her lips. Then she straightened, her arm across her mother's shoulders, and faced the intruders defiantly. 'I know who you are,' she said. 'And we don't want you here. Go away.'

Lenka's silence was every bit as eloquent as her daughter's impassioned words.

'She's right, Anna,' she said at last, with a slow and difficult dignity that brought the sudden burning of tears to Anna's eyes. 'It's too late. Go away.'

Anna came to kneel beside her sister. Steadfastly she ignored the child's eyes, so like her own and yet fiercely and openly hostile as, like a distrustful animal's, they followed her every movement. 'All right. I'll go. But Lenka – you aren't well. Let me help you. You need food, medicines?'

491

'No!' the child snapped, loathing in her face and in her voice.

'Quiet, Tonia!' The effort of raising her voice brought on another bout of coughing. Lenka doubled up.

'Now look what you've done!' Tonia was there again, with a supporting arm, her fingers tender in her mother's tangled hair, glaring at Anna above the bent head.

Lenka wiped her mouth, reached out to take her daughter's hand in a firm grip. 'Just a few roubles,' she said to Anna, 'for the children, you understand. Be still, Antonia!'

The child subsided, glowering.

'Here.' Anna pulled out her purse, pressed it into Lenka's hand. 'And there's more –'

'No.'

'Very well. But remember, Lenka, if you need anything – anything at all! – send for me and I'll come. I promise you.'

Lenka lifted a haggard face. 'You promised me something very like that once before,' she said, very softly.

Once in the dingy streets, which not even the light from the soft May sky could beautify, Anna walked briskly, blindly and in silence for a full five minutes before her companion caught at her hand and stopped her. 'Anna.'

She turned to him. Tears reddened her eyes, slicked her cheeks, dripped from the sharp line of her jaw. 'Don't say anything, Volodya,' she said. 'Just don't say anything at all.' And she turned and hurried on through the dreary, embattled streets and the long, pearly dusk of the summer's evening.

What came to be known as Petrograd's June Days brought crisis once more to the streets of the city. As always the origins of the trouble were confused; there were demonstrations and counter-demonstrations and the confrontations were fierce. Forbidden by the Government to march, the Bolsheviks at first conceded defeat, then with savage enterprise and no mean organization proceeded to take over the Government's own demonstrations, turning out in massive force, leaving no doubt in anyone's mind as to who was winning this battle for the heart and mind of the working man. The simple slogan of the Soviets, 'Peace, Land and Bread!', appealed directly and forcefully to a population tired of the war, tired of oppression and all but exhausted by hunger. When it became clear that the Government was withstanding this fresh surge of pressure, tempers again rose to explosion point; there were strikes and demonstrations; workers' delegations from seventy-four factories met to demand the immediate transfer of power from the Provisional Government to the Petrograd Soviet. Thirty-five thousand men downed tools to march in support of their Bolshevik leaders. The First Machine Gun Regiment, ordered by a nervous Government to quit the city and transfer itself to the Front, obliged by sending ten units to fight the Germans whilst keeping twenty in Petrograd for more pressing battles. Other regiments ignored their orders altogether. The soldiers, and their arms, once again began to join the workers on the streets.

By early July it was obvious that events had moved too fast; the mass of the people had run all but beyond the control of those who had sought to manipulate them. The Bolshevik leadership tried to stop the increasingly violent protests and were themselves ignored and vilified. Workers poured into the capital, and twenty thousand sailors from Kronstadt prepared to sail upriver and into the city. For two days the Tauride Palace was besieged by demonstrators calling for the resignation of Prince Lvov's Government and the handing of power to the Soviet Executive Committee. Yet still the people themselves were divided and there were bitter clashes between rival factions.

Anna had become almost used to it by now; the massed marches, the waving banners, the inevitable violence, the fires, the barricades, and the forums that formed on almost every street corner, arguing and shouting, debating furiously, never so far as she could see coming to any conclusion. Life had to go on. Food must be found, contact maintained with the family, arrangements made with the bank for more funds. Plainly dressed and using common sense in her choice of routes she walked the streets unmolested. Like many others her only choice seemed to be to live from day to day, until some sort of order came out of the chaos; then she would make her decision. She spent a great deal of time with Natalia and the children; her sister-in-law was only too pleased to have her care for and entertain the two older children, whom she sometimes took back to the Bourlov apartment for days at a time, whilst Natalia devoted herself to the frail Dimochka. Anna had not attempted to visit Lenka again, though Volodya had taken supplies and money – both of which Lenka had flatly refused to accept. Margarita no-one had seen since the beginning of the disturbances two or three weeks before.

'I might try to pop in on her after I've been to see Mr Lawson at the bank,' Anna said to Volodya on the day that he had come in with a precious chicken, a bag of even more precious onions and the news that the Bolshevik leadership were, with the exception of Lenin and a few close associates who had fled the city, under arrest.

Volodya swung Nikki, who was perched astride his shoulders, to the floor. 'I wish you'd wait until I could come with you.'

'Don't be silly. There's no real risk.' She laughed as the agile little boy launched himself again at Volodya.

'Another ride, Uncle 'Lodya! Another ride!'

'You're in more danger here from the look of it.' She settled a small straw hat upon the wiry mass of her hair. 'Goodness, if there's one thing I truly miss it's a decent hairdresser! Just look at me! I look like a hedgehog!'

'A hedgehog! A hedgehog!' Nikki crowed, elevated once more to the heights.

'Don't be silly, Aunt Anna.' 'Tasha was loyally indignant. 'Of course you don't!'

'Anna? Anna, are you there?' At the sound of Varya's voice all four of them stilled, almost guiltily.

'Don't worry. I'll go,' Volodya said.

'Thanks.' She kissed his cheek lightly, beneath the bright, interested eyes of the two children. 'I won't be long. It's a formality, I think.' She grimaced a little. 'I want formally to ask for some more of my own money and Mr Lawson wants formally to lecture me on the advisability of returning to England.'

'He's right.'

'That's as may be.' She waved from the door. 'Be good, you two.'

'What about Uncle 'Lodya?' 'Tasha asked.

'Yes. Him too. You'll look after him for me, won't you? Don't let him misbehave?'

'Tasha giggled.

'Anna!' Varya shrieked.

'Go,' Volodya said.

The interview with Mr Lawson of the Anglo-Russian Bank went much as she had foreseen.

'Mrs de Fontenay, in view of the unrest, and given the quite terrifying scale of inflation in the country at present –'

Anna, taking just enough time to register with some amusement that it was the rate at which she was spending money that was concerning the man just as much as any personal danger she might be in, stopped listening. At the end of the lecture she smiled, at her most charming. 'Thank you, Mr Lawson. I shall of course consider what you've told me very carefully. Very carefully indeed. Now, if I may collect my money?'

The news of the arrests of the Bolshevik leaders had fired much excited discussion and a fair amount of disquiet in the streets. The inevitable noisy meeting was taking place in the Liteini. Anna squeezed through the animated participants. Soldiers, workers and students of both sexes, and a few sailors from the Kronstadt fleet that had anchored in the river, shouted each other down with a fine disregard for sense or courtesy. Almost all of them carried arms of one kind or another, and many wore the red armbands of revolution. Anna picked her way through the remains of a barricade, skirted about the burned-out remains of a tramcar – sometimes she thought it a wonder that there was a tram left in working order in the whole of the city – and turned the corner into Margarita's street.

The building was quiet, the landing empty.

Anna rapped sharply at the door.

Nothing happened.

She knocked again; and when it became evident that Margarita was not there, disappointed, she turned to leave. Stopped. The smell of cigarette smoke was strong. Strong and fresh. She knocked again, louder. 'Rita? Rita, are you there?'

She heard, distinctly, a muffled cough.

'Rita, it's Anna. Oh, do come on, Margarita – what are you doing?' She rapped again.

'Go away, Anna.'

She stared at the door.

As if she had willed it so, it opened, just a little. 'Anna, go away,' Margarita said, tiredly. She leaned against the door jamb, cigarette in hand. The air of the dark little hallway behind her was thick with pungent smoke. Her hair was a tangle, her eyes heavy. She wore a crumpled scarlet satin evening dress, brazenly low-cut, and her feet were bare.

'Rita, darling – whatever is wrong?'

Margarita turned away, walked back into the apartment, leaving the door swinging open behind her.

Anna followed, closing the door.

The pretty little parlour was untidy. A vodka bottle stood upon the table, a half-empty glass beside it. Margarita turned to face her sister as she followed her into the room, defiantly picked up the glass and emptied it at a swallow. 'Want one?'

'No. Thank you.'

'Of course not. No. Of course not.' Margarita turned and wandered to the sideboard. Set amongst the clutter stood the little theatre that Sasha had bought her. It stood neglected now, the tiny characters piled in a heap upon the stage. With careful, over-steady fingers she began idly to sort them, picking them out one by one, standing them in a row along the edge of the sideboard, pushing them into a straight line with the tip of her finger.

Anna waited for as long as she humanly could. 'Margarita,' she said, when she could stand the tense silence no longer. 'What is it? What's the matter? What's happened?' She stood watching her sister in concern. 'Is it – Rita, dear – is it Sasha?' Margarita laughed at that, sudden and shrill. 'Yes!' she said, 'I suppose you could say that! Yes, it's Sasha!'

Try as she might she could not stop the trembling.

How in the name of God had they found out, Vassili and the others? How had they discovered what she had done?

Almost unaware of her sister's eyes upon her, she saw again those faces, those distorted and terrifying faces, endured again the disgust, the violent obscenities. How could they have turned against her so? They were her friends. Her only friends. Vassili's handsome face had been ugly in its rage. 'Tell me! Tell me! Tell me it's a lie!' His hands, that had gentled and loved her, had been savage as he shook her. She had thought, for a moment, that he might kill her. Why? For God's sake, why? She was Sasha's wife; yet not one of them had thought twice about cuckolding the man they now declared to be their blood brother. Betrayal? Who were they – any of them – to talk of betrayal? A tear – not the first she had shed in the long hours since she had dragged herself home the night before – ran almost unnoticed down her cheek.

'He's dead?' Anna's voice was gentle.

She turned. 'Yes,' she said, blankly. 'Of course he's dead.' She looked round, vague and distracted, for her cigarettes.

'Oh, my dear, I'm so sorry.'

'I can't find – ah, there they are.' She picked up the packet from the table, struck a match to light it, shook the flame out. Whore, they had called her. Treacherous whore. An easy weapon to reach for, that. And who had made her so? Had she whored alone? Bastards, every one of them; heartless, brutal bastards. She remembered how they had manhandled her, remembered the probing, twisting fingers, and felt sick.

'How did it happen?' Anna asked, her quiet voice distant through the strange rushing sound in Margarita's ears. 'Do you know? Did they tell you?'

Margarita's control snapped. She turned on her sister in sudden and mindless fury. 'For God's sake, Anna, stop talking to me as if I'm a child who's heard her favourite toy's broken! Of course I bloody know! They stood him up against a wall and they shot him!'

There was a short, appalled silence.

'I told them where to find him,' Margarita said, perfectly steadily. 'Him and that bitch on heat that he was sniffing around. And they found them. Found them both. Together. It's a bloody shame they didn't shoot them together too. They exiled her. Sent her off to Siberia. I hope she's dead! I hope she died slowly, and I hope it hurt! I hope –' She broke off. She was shaking visibly.

'Sasha – was executed?' Anna asked, slowly.

'Yes, Anna. Sasha was executed. He deserted! Brave, beautiful Sasha deserted! He was a coward! He ran away! And he ran not to me but to her – to her! So I told them where he was, and they shot him, and I'm glad! You hear me? I'm glad!' The tears came in sudden, huge, choking sobs. She cried loudly, her mouth open like a child's. 'And now they've found out and they hate me – they called me names – they did horrible things to me – the pigs! The stinking pigs!'

'Who did?' Anna's voice was remarkably calm. Her eyes were not.

'Sasha's friends – my friends.' Margarita stopped at that, suddenly realizing what she had said, and to whom she had said it. The sobbing subsided. She pulled at the tablecloth to wipe at her nose and face. Several small ornaments fell to the floor, clattering and rolling.

'I – I don't think I have this right, Margarita.' Anna rubbed at her forehead. 'You aren't – you aren't honestly telling me – you betrayed Sasha? He deserted – and you –' She stopped. She looked, and felt, genuinely ill.

Margarita turned away from the look in her sister's eyes. 'I'm not sorry,' she said. 'You won't make me feel sorry.'

'When? When did this happen?'

Margarita shrugged. 'I don't know. Months ago. Months and months ago. Now go away, Anna. For God's sake, go away.'

'How could you do such a thing?' Shock had robbed Anna of any grace or courtesy. Pure undisguised horror was in the question. She could do nothing to prevent it.

'Go away,' Margarita repeated.

'Months ago?' The words were only just sinking in. 'You said months ago? And all this time you – you've been pretending –' Words finally failed.

'Go away! Get out! I don't want you here!'

Anna backed away from her, very slowly. Then, abruptly, she turned and all but ran from the room. Margarita heard the slamming of the front door; it echoed like a pistol shot in her head long after the sound of her sister's stumbling footsteps had died.

Left alone, Margarita wandered the room, touching this,

handling that, her face vacant. She took a vase from the shelf and dropped it, watching it explode and splinter at her feet. She picked up the vodka bottle, took a mouthful, choked a little, pulled a face, put the bottle back upon the table. Walked to the sideboard.

The cardboard figures stood in line, smiling fixedly and inanely into space.

She picked up the figure of the prince, traced with her finger the tiny, rakish scar upon the cardboard cheek. Then with deliberate movements she reached for the matches, struck one, and set it to the figure's feet. The bright material flared and curled, began to burn.

Margarita smiled. With no haste she set the burning figure in the centre of the stage, stood and watched as the flames licked and glowed about it.

Then she turned, and without bothering to shut the doors behind her walked out of the apartment and down the stairs into the street.

Comrade Sergei Krakovski had had a good day. He'd helped derail a tram and he'd brained a Menshevik. He'd also consumed, along with his fellows, a great deal of vodka kindly donated by the owner of a shop they'd come across in the Nevsky, and he was ready for anything. He was a brute of a man, big as a bear, a man who worked with iron and was proud of it. 'Ashkenov?' he said, frowning in disbelief, 'Kurakin? Do you see what I see?'

A woman was walking towards them. A vision. She walked with dainty steps, the folds of her scarlet skirt held high above the pavement, disclosing incongruously bare and dirty feet. The golden mass of her uncombed hair fell in tangled curls upon her naked shoulders. The dress was cut so low that it all but exposed her nipples. She smiled, dazzlingly, as she approached. Stopped. 'Gentlemen? May I pass?' She lifted her chin, eyes wide and challenging.

They moved forward, surrounding her with their rank male smell, with the animal sound of their breathing. She did not move, but stood still, straightening her shoulders and arching her back a little, deliberately provocative.

Krakovski reached a huge hand roughly to fondle the nearly bared breast. 'And if we say no, little whore?'

She let him pull the dress down to her waist. Smiled into their faces.

Kurakin gawked. The man Ashkenov turned his head, sniffing. 'There's a fire down the street –'

'There's a fire right here,' Krakovski growled. 'And I'm going to be the first to put it out.'

'Who says so?'

Without taking his eyes from Margarita, Krakovski bunched his great iron fist under the other man's nose. 'My good right hand says so. Wait your turn. Come, little lady. Here, in the doorway. That's right! Up with it. Sweet Jesus! Watch this, lads – this is the way it's done – that's right, girl – Christ, yes! – that's the way!'

CHAPTER TWENTY-THREE

'Mrs de Fontenay.' The man across the desk regarded her gravely over the tips of his steepled fingers. 'I must repeat that we are advising all British passport holders to leave the city as soon as possible.'

Anna shook her head. 'I can't. Not yet.'

He affected not to have heard her. He was a small man, meticulously neat, and she knew from past experience not unkind, but at this moment he looked drawn and harassed, and she had already sensed that his temper was short. 'You must know how grave the situation is, and becoming more so by the minute. The latest attempt by the Bolsheviks to take over the city has been defeated; but that isn't to say that they won't try again. Each time it happens the unrest and disturbances get worse and the chance of very real civil violence increases. I'm afraid that I don't see Mr Kerensky being able to pull this particular chestnut from the fire. To add to the confusion there is a strong rumour of a counter-revolutionary coup by a section of the army. Anything can happen in the next few months, Mrs de Fontenay – absolutely anything! Not least, of course, that Petrograd could fall into German hands.'

'Surely not?' Anna was shocked.

'It's not the most distant possibility.' He leaned forward. 'Mrs de Fontenay, I implore you – get out now, whilst you can, and whilst we are still able to facilitate your going. The situation here can only worsen. There are epidemics and famine in the city, the political situation is a shambles. Petrograd, and Russia, is falling apart. Anarchy, Mrs de Fontenay, that's what we'll be facing in a very few weeks, I assure you. Anarchy.'

'I thought –' Anna stopped. 'They've arrested the Bolshevik leaders, haven't they? Won't that stop any further trouble?'

'Stop it? It will foment it! The Bolsheviks have wormed

themselves into every position of power amongst the people. The Soviet has gone over to them almost entirely. They promise the earth – bread, peace, land. Bread, peace and land, indeed!' His voice was wearily angry. 'Promises, such promises! You mark my words, they'll turn out to be as bad as the worst of them. It's democracy they're fighting against now. What the Bolsheviks are fighting for is simply another dictatorship. The same oppression, the same cruelty, the same crushing of freedom. I tell you, Mrs de Fontenay –' he rested his head upon his hand for a brief moment '– I despair of this country. I truly do.'

'It's my country,' she said, very quietly.

He lifted his head, looked at her levelly. 'Yes. I realize that. And there's the rub, isn't it? You have to make a decision, Mrs de Fontenay. And it has to be soon. The situation is too desperately uncertain for me to be able to give you any guarantees for the future. It is even conceivable that a time will come when your British citizenship will be more threat than protection. If the Germans come – or if the Russian Government makes a separate peace – you will be an enemy alien. Think about it, Mrs de Fontenay. Please think about it. We are anxious to get as many people away whilst we still can. My own family is gone.'

Anna picked up her gloves and pulled them on, reached for her handbag and stood up. 'But mine, Mr Thompson, is not.'

He sighed, stood, extended a hand. 'No. I do realize that. And I understand your reluctance to leave them. But, believe me, Mrs de Fontenay, I know what I'm saying. Things are going to get worse. Far worse. And the violence is by no means over. Please – if you change your mind – do get in touch with me. I'll be pleased to make the arrangements.'

She inclined her head politely. 'Thank you.' At the door she hesitated. 'If I decided to go – it would have to be alone? My family – I couldn't take them with me?' She knew before he shook his head what his answer would be; knew, too, what a wild and silly scheme it was, even to contemplate. Natalia would not leave the apartment; what chance of persuading her to leave Petrograd? Varya could no more face a journey to England than she could grow wings and fly there, and as for Lenka –

'No, Mrs de Fontenay. I'm sorry. The authorities in both

countries are getting stricter and stricter. It would pose enormous problems, and could take years. I don't believe we have that amount of time. I'm sorry,' he said again.

She nodded, unsurprised. 'Well. Thank you anyway for your advice, Mr Thompson. I'll think about it.'

He hurried to open the door for her. As she passed him he laid a hand upon her arm. 'Another word of advice, Mrs de Fontenay, if I may?'

She waited.

'The next time you draw money from the bank, don't let them give you paper roubles. They will be all but worthless in a matter of weeks. Gold, Mrs de Fontenay – take it in gold.'

She nodded. 'Thank you. If I can I will.'

'Get to the bank soon. You're with the Anglo-Russian?'

'Yes.'

'Mr Stoddart will see to it for you.'

'Thank you.'

She walked home through streets that shimmered in August heat; on impulse, with Mr Thompson's grim warnings still fresh in her ears, she stopped at the bank to make the arrangements he had recommended. At least they wouldn't be short of money; though like almost everyone in the city they were short of everything else. There were simply no supplies to be had, except, inevitably, on the black market and at extortionate prices. Bread rationing had not helped; what point in rationing a commodity that had all but disappeared from the shops? They, like most others, were reduced to one meal a day, and that not always as nourishing as it should be. There was no question now of eating for enjoyment, of choosing one thing over another; it was the stark business of survival that drove them from shop to shop, from one black market contact to another. Anna worried about the children; the baby Dmitri was sick again – Natalia's other two children 'Tasha and Nikki were practically living with them at the Bourlov apartment now, and were constantly on the move. Delighted by the unaccustomed space they raced about the huge rooms like a pair of over-active puppies, and were forever hungry. Every day upon the streets she saw the thin, gaunt-faced children who begged or stole what they could to keep body and soul together. Great, empty, hungry

503

eyes followed her wherever she went; 'Tasha and Nikki would not suffer so. She would do anything – anything! – before she would allow that to happen to the two children who had come to mean more to her than she was ready to admit, even to herself.

She knew the moment she saw Volodya's face as she stepped through the door that something had happened. The children, as always, launched themselves upon her, hugging and kissing her, clamouring to know where she had been, who she had seen, what was going on in the city. Volodya came into the hall behind them. In his hand he held a grubby envelope.

'What is it?' she asked over 'Tasha's fair head.

'Lenka,' he said. 'She's sent you a note.'

Anna straightened, disentangled herself from small, clinging hands. 'Lenka?' she asked, disbelieving. '*Lenka* has sent a note?'

'Yes. A neighbour delivered it. I had to give her the last half loaf before she'd let me have it.'

Anna all but snatched the note, ripped it open, scanned the two briefly scrawled lines. 'I have to go out,' she said. 'Lenka needs me.'

'I suspected that might be it.' Volodya was reaching for his cap and overcoat. 'I'll come with you.'

'No!' The word was sharp; too sharp, she knew. 'No, Volodya,' Anna said again, more placatingly. 'I'd rather you didn't. In the first place we can't leave Mama with the children. And in the second –' she looked back down at the note '– in the second, I feel this is something I have to do alone.' She avoided his mild, questioning eyes. Not for anything would she admit that she was frightened; frightened of what might lie behind this unexpected approach, afraid to have anyone else witness what might only be another and perhaps more cruel rejection. Whatever Lenka wanted, whatever she wished to say to her, Anna's wary instincts told her it was best faced alone. 'Please, I'll be all right. The streets are comparatively quiet today. It's too damned hot; not even the students have got enough energy to cause trouble.'

'Volodya's showing us how to make a violin,' 'Tasha was saying, eagerly. Volodya, some weeks before, had visited the wrecked shop and salvaged what he could of the materials from the workshop. More from a need to do something than in any hope of selling it, he had begun to make an instrument; it had been soothing to them both in these past weeks to sit together as he worked, lovingly cutting, smoothing and planing the wood, carving the intricate scroll.

Anna tugged at the tangled curls. 'Watch well, my love. You won't find a better teacher.' She looked up, caught Volodya watching her. She turned away sharply, obscurely distressed by the look in his open, friendly face. 'Lenka's note sounds urgent. I'll go straight away. Volodya – there's soup left from yesterday, and some cheese in the cupboard. Did you really give away the last of the bread?'

He shrugged. 'Almost the last. There's a little left. Enough for the children.'

'I'll see what I can do when I'm out.' She kissed the children swiftly. 'All right, all right, I won't be long, I promise. Look after Uncle Volodya for me, won't you? Don't let him misbehave.'

There were the usual voluble, scruffy groups on street corners, still endlessly debating, though perhaps in the enervating heat marginally less passionately than usual. What on earth they found to talk about, Anna found herself thinking with a sudden weary spurt of anger, she could not imagine. What were grown men doing standing around on street corners and arguing when their wives and families were starving? What was more important than the search for food, the security and health of the children? What in heaven's name did these people *want*? She doubted that they knew themselves. There were, as always, soldiers everywhere, their uniforms shabby, guns slung sloppily upon their shoulders. They slouched in the shade of the buildings, leaned against the remnants of the last lot of barricades to block the city's streets, marched in ragged formation or drove past in noisy trucks and lorries. Anna was used to it all. She walked through the dingy streets of the once-beautiful city quickly, head bent, avoiding all eyes.

She noticed the stench first, foul and stomach-stirring, hanging about the stairs and landings like a reeking fog. She put her handkerchief to her nose. Somewhere a child was crying, thinly, exhaustedly, a sound to wrench the heart. She climbed the worn stairs to Lenka's room. The door to the single, filthy toilet on the landing stood open; the foetid air stank like an open sewer. It took all Anna's strength of will not to gag.

She pushed open the door. 'Lenka? It's Anna. Lenka, are you there?'

It took a moment for her eyes to adjust to the gloom within. Here too the smell was so dreadful that it was difficult to breathe without choking.

Lenka lay on a narrow truckle bed on the far side of the room, rough blankets heaped upon her. The girl Tonia was crouched beside her. On the floor was a bowl of water and the child was with careful concentration soaking and wringing out small pieces of flannel, bathing her mother's brow with infinite and intent gentleness. She looked up as Anna entered, and her expression changed with fearsome suddenness. Coming to her feet like a small, fierce, startled animal, she glared at her aunt, placing herself protectively between her mother and the new-comer. Her small brother, a child, Anna thought, of three or perhaps four years, huddled in a shabby armchair, eyes huge, his thumb in his mouth, watching in silence.

'What do you want?' Tonia snapped. 'Go away. We don't want you here. We don't want to see you.'

'Your mother sent for me,' Anna said quietly. Once again the startling resemblance between this child and herself struck her forcibly. Even in this dim light, the sharp-boned, pointed face beneath its mop of wiry hair could be seen to be the very image of her own. She wondered if the child herself knew it.

'No!' Tonia snapped. Her pale eyes were too big; the bones of her face stood out, fragile and sharp in the faint light. 'No, she didn't! She couldn't have –'

'Tonia,' Lenka said from the bed, her voice so weak and exhausted that the sound barely carried to where Anna stood, 'be quiet, child.'

'But, Mama, you must be still! You must rest!' In a flash the child was crouched beside her again. Her voice was urgent; desperate.

'Lenka, what is it? What's the matter?' Anna stepped forward, was warded off by the fierce and furious glance Tonia sent her.

'Typhoid.' The word was tired and flat. Lenka turned her head upon the pillow to look at her sister. Anna flinched from the sight of that face. It was drawn and agonized; the eyes sunken and shadowed with pain.

'No,' Tonia said firmly. 'Not typhoid, Mama.'

Lenka gripped her daughter's small hand. 'If God wills it, Tonia,' she said softly, and then, with an effort lifting her voice a little, 'Anna – '

'Yes?' Despite the hostility of the child Anna dropped to her knees beside Lenka. She took her sister's hand; it burned in hers like a brand.

Lenka shifted suddenly in the bed, her face a spasm of pain, her hands lifted to press in agony to her head, her lip caught in her teeth, to prevent her from crying out. 'God!' she said. 'Oh, God!'

'Hush, Mama, hush, dear Mama.' Tonia was wringing out the flannel again, laying it upon her mother's burning forehead, murmuring endearments as she might to a child. She turned a sudden, frightened face to Anna, her hostility for the moment overwhelmed by her terror for her mother. 'I don't know what to do for her! I don't know how to make her better!'

Lenka, weak as she was, snatched her hand from Anna's and reached to her daughter. 'You're doing everything you can, my darling. You're doing right. Tell her, Anna.'

'If it is typhoid – ' Anna hesitated. If it were typhoid then in these conditions and given Lenka's weakened constitution there could be little hope no matter what anyone did. 'You're right to try to keep her temperature down.'

'But then she gets cold, so very cold – she shivers, as if she's in the street in winter – ' The brave child was fighting tears. They trembled in her voice and stood in her eyes. Furiously she dashed them away.

Anna said nothing. The symptoms were classic.

'It's all over the city,' Lenka said. She had calmed a little. Her eyes were steady. 'A woman died in the street yesterday.'

'I'll get a doctor,' Anna said.

Lenka laughed harshly. Winced in pain.

507

'I will. There must surely be one somewhere near?'

Lenka shook her head upon the filthy, crumpled pillow. 'Don't be ridiculous. A doctor? You won't get a doctor anywhere near here. He'd be afraid of catching something.' The words were derisive.

Anna stood up. 'Nevertheless, I'll find one somewhere.'

'No!' Lenka's voice was wearily obstinate. 'No! Listen to me.'

'But, Lenka, we must get you well.'

'Whether I get well or not is in the hands of God,' Lenka said. 'Anna, it's the children –'

Anna felt the child who crouched beside her stiffen, caught from the corner of her eye the quick movement as the small head lifted sharply.

'– I want you – to take the children –'

'No,' Tonia said.

'– can't feed or care – for them –' The exhausted, anguished voice was getting fainter by the moment.

'*No!*'

'It isn't – just this –' Lenka gestured at her wasted body. Beneath the inadequately thin covering of the dirty blankets Anna could clearly see the outline of the painfully distended belly. Lenka convulsed again in pain.

'I won't go,' Tonia said, very calmly, not to her mother but to Anna, her haunted eyes fierce. 'You won't make me. You can't make me. I won't go. I won't leave her.'

'Tonia –'

'No, Mama. No. I'm staying with you. You can't make me go. She can take him –' the child jerked her head at the little boy who still crouched silently in the armchair, watching them all with eyes almost blank with pain and fright '– good riddance I say, he's nothing but a nuisance. But I'm staying.'

Anna shook her head helplessly.

Lenka lifted herself from the pillow, eyes blazing. 'Anna, you promised! You promised you'd help if I asked.'

'I will! Of course I will!'

'Then *take the children*! Forget me – God will take me or not as he sees fit. But the children, Anna – the children! They haven't eaten in days! Take them – feed them – care for them – until I can –' She could not finish. The furious spark of energy

508

died and she collapsed in sudden silent agony upon the pillow.

Anna turned to face the child Tonia. Turned to look into her own childhood face, distorted with intransigent anger and hatred, her own eyes, blazing with fear and defiance. 'No!' the child all but spat. 'I won't come with you! I won't! I won't leave Mama.'

'Listen – Tonia, please – listen.' Anna reached out pleading hands. Tonia shook them off as fiercely as if they had been the grasping claws of nightmare. Anna found herself shaking. On the bed Lenka, despite herself, moaned softly in pain. Anna put her hands to her own head, forcing herself to think. 'Tonia, your Mama is right – this is no place for either of you –'

'No!'

'Will you *listen*!' For one moment furious temper flared. They glared at one another. Then Tonia, outgunned for the moment at least, subsided, sulkily, and let Anna speak. 'What I suggest is this. First, I'll take the little boy – what's his name?'

'Stepan.'

'Stepan. I'll take Stepan with me, back to the apartment. Your cousins 'Tasha and Nikki are there – they'll help care for him for now. Then I'll find a doctor, and I'll come back. Once your mama is better then you can both come to join us. How does that sound?'

'Anna,' Lenka whispered, agonized, 'no! Take Tonia – you promised –'

Anna spread helpless hands. 'Lenka – I can't! The child simply won't come! I can't shackle her and drag her through the streets!'

Tonia had settled upon the floor beside the pallet again. 'I'll take care of you, Mama. We don't need her. We don't need anyone.' Her back was turned resolutely upon Anna, and upon her own small brother.

Lenka closed her eyes in a gesture of defeat. 'You promised!' she said, bleakly, to Anna.

'Lenka – I'll take Stepan. I'll leave him with Volodya and the others. Then I'll bring a doctor back to you – when you're better you can all come to the apartment.'

Lenka turned her face from her. Tonia tilted her small, fierce white face to look at her aunt. 'She doesn't want to live with you,' she said, calmly. 'She hates you. She's told me. Lots of times.'

The room was oppressive, the stench of Lenka's illness overpowering; yet the weight of this child's hatred was worse. Anna stood with leaden heart, defeated and helpless. Then she walked to the silent child who crouched in the armchair. 'Come, Stepan,' she said, gently, reaching her arms to him. 'Come to Aunt Anna. We'll go and see 'Tasha and Nikki, shall we?'

He shrank back, thumb still jammed in his mouth, eyes wide with terror.

'Come, now.' She picked him up. He was rigid, his slight frame a tense weight in her arms. 'Say goodbye to Mama and Tonia – you'll see them again soon.'

Tonia did not even bother to turn her head. Lenka lay like death, her eyes closed. Stepan buried his head in Anna's shoulder, the small body, desperately light and undersized for his age, curled into a taut, defensive ball.

'I'll be back soon,' Anna said. For all the notice mother or daughter took she might just as well not have spoken. At the door she remembered something. Balancing Stepan awkwardly on one arm she felt in her bag for her heavy purse, extracted a few of the coins she had picked up from the bank that morning. 'Tonia, take these – you might at least be able to buy some food to see you through until I get back with the doctor.'

At the sound of the chink of coins Tonia's bright, dirty head came round quickly. She scrambled to her feet, snatched the money from Anna with no thanks then went back to her vigil at Lenka's bedside.

'Aren't you going to say goodbye?' Anna asked uncertainly, her heart aching for the little boy in her arms.

'Goodbye, Stepan,' Tonia said, heartlessly, not turning round.

'Goodbye.' As Lenka opened her eyes the tears were released. They ran down the creases of her haggard face and into her hair. 'Remember, Stepan, be a good boy.'

Anna could bear no more. Clutching the child who now sobbed heartbrokenly in her arms she all but ran from the room.

There was no doctor to be found; at least, there was no doctor that Anna could find who was willing to risk life and limb to go into the area where Lenka lived in order to treat an almost certainly dying victim of the typhoid epidemic that was sweeping the city. The most she got for her gold was a tired and discouraging shake of the head and a bottle of medicine of dubious worth to a woman already debilitated by want and starvation.

'I'll fetch them both,' Volodya said, reassuringly. 'If I have to carry the pair of them I'll get them back here, don't worry. I'll go first thing in the morning.'

'The morning? But, Volodya!'

'Anna, my love, it's too late now. The city isn't safe at night, you know it. One more night won't hurt. Then we'll get them back here, safe and sound, you'll see.'

Anna spent a haunted night. In the big bed beside her Stepan shivered and whimpered desolately like a young animal deserted by its mother. He would not allow her to touch him but curled about a small, soft silken pillow he had taken from one of the chairs, burying his face in it if anyone spoke to him. She had not been able to coax a single word from him since she had brought him away from that terrible room, though he had eaten with steady and voracious appetite anything edible that had been put in front of him. Heavy-eyed, she rose in the morning and hurried Volodya away on his errand.

He came back late in the morning, sombre-faced and alone.

'Dead? Lenka's dead?' Anna whispered, trembling. 'But, Volodya – she can't be! She was alive! Yesterday – she was alive!'

'I'm sorry,' Volodya said. 'Anna, I'm so sorry.'

'You saw her? You really saw her? You're sure?' Urgently she caught his sleeve. The hurt and the misunderstandings, the betrayals and the wasted love – it was all still there, all still waiting to be resolved. 'She can't be dead!' she burst out, shaking her head. 'She can't be!'

'Anna, I saw her.' Volodya's eyes were darkened by the memory of it. The finding of that emaciated, stinking corpse in a room that smelled of death and corruption was not to be easily forgotten.

'And Tonia? The little girl?' Anna glanced about distractedly, as if the child might appear from behind the curtains or under the table, 'Where is she? Why isn't she with you?'

He took her by the shoulders, holding her, wanting to take her in his arms, deterred by the fierce and shocking force of her grief that held her rigid, that repulsed all comfort, that for the moment even denied her the ease of tears. 'Anna – she wasn't there. She'd gone. I asked everywhere. No-one had seen her. No-one knew where she'd gone.'

'But she can't just have disappeared into thin air! She must be somewhere!' Torn by her own guilt she lashed out at him. 'Volodya, how can you have been so stupid as to leave without finding her? Someone must have come – taken her to comfort her –'

'Anna, no! I tell you I asked everywhere. Hardly anyone even knew the child. Hardly anyone, come to that, seemed to know Lenka, not even her closest neighbours.'

'Then where is she? Where's Tonia?' The words were anguished. If it were indeed true that Lenka was dead, then all recompense, all atonement, was in the child. And she was gone. Gone, Anna knew with a heartbreaking certainty, because Lenka's daughter would go anywhere, face anything rather than turn to her mother's detested sister.

'She can't have gone far.' He was gently reasonable. 'She's been through a dreadful experience – seeing her mother die –'

Anna flinched from that, covering her face with her hands, seeing that fierce, loving, sharp little face, remembering the tender care in the small hands.

'– she's probably hiding somewhere. She's very young and she's had a terrible shock. But she knows where to find us. She'll come, Anna, you'll see. In a day or so, she'll come.'

Anna dropped her hands, shook her head. 'No. She won't come.' A small sound caught her attention. She turned. 'Stepan,' she said, softly.

The child's elfin face was expressionless. The enormous eyes held uncertain, flickering shadows of grief and fear. When Anna held out her hands he stepped backwards, clutching his cushion, watching her, but did not have the confidence to turn and run.

In a single step Anna was beside him, had caught the unresponsive child to her, hugging child and cushion together, fiercely, burying her face in the tangled dark curls of his hair.

'Anna?' Varya called. 'Anna, where are you?'

*   *   *

The final upheaval, which brought about the violent death of any hopes of democracy in Russia, came at the end of that October. Between Lenka's death and this last bloody convulsion seven or eight weeks passed; weeks of hardship, tension and uncertainty. The country drifted like a rudderless ship in stormy seas. An attempted counter-coup led by the royalist General Kornilov was defeated only after his march upon Petrograd came perilously close to success. And meanwhile the war ground disastrously on as the German forces moved, an armoured and efficient nemesis, ever closer to the capital; a capital in which the fighting between the factions of the so-called Government was savage enough to constitute a full-blown war in itself. There was too another menace; in the south and east the White armies, loyal to the Tsar, were mustering their considerable strength with the support of those Western powers who were desperate to keep the German armies pinned down along the Russian Front.

In the city hunger, deprivation and disease wracked a despairing and overcrowded population. As summer became autumn in a country beset by war and by civil strife, a country in which even the most basic discipline and organization had collapsed, things could only go from bad to worse. Winter was again approaching, and with it the spectre of worse hardship, of real starvation.

In the apartment on the Fontanka it was becoming harder and harder to keep the children clothed and fed. And meanwhile the obstinate, fruitless, depressing search for the missing Tonia went on. Margarita too had disappeared after the fire that had destroyed her apartment. And though Anna knew that in a city teeming like an antheap with displaced people any attempt to find someone who quite clearly had no intention of being found was doomed to failure from the start, yet still she felt she had to try. It was a weary and heartbreaking task. And, often as she told herself that she was not alone in being exhausted, hungry, constantly fearful, constantly nerve-strung, it rarely helped to ease the burden. It was a time to dim even the brightest of spirits.

She took to dreaming of Sythings.

Standing stoically for hours on end in yet another queue, or lying too worried and too tired to sleep by Volodya's side she perfected the art of withdrawing to her own safe and secret world. She walked the tranquil woods and gardens, listened to the birdsong and the music of the little fountain. In her imagination she roamed from room to room in the house, each dearly familiar piece of furniture, each ornament, each picture as clear in her mind as if she stood physically before them. And always these enchanted wanderings ended in the music room, with its great, gleaming piano, its music stands, its comfortable furniture, its wide French windows onto the terrace. And her violin, in its scuffed leather case, lying still where she had left it last, silent and waiting. Once she dreamed so vividly of that room and instrument that she woke with desolate tears streaming down her face. Struggling to control them, she was aware of Volodya awake beside her. Wordlessly he reached for her, drew her to him to cry soundlessly against his shoulder. He did not ask her why she cried. And she, ashamed, did not tell him. But Volodya was a sensitive man, and he loved her: he knew what lay behind the shadows in her eyes.

The political situation in the city meanwhile grew more confused and volatile every day. The war had been unpopular; now it was detested. Kerensky and his Liberals had had their supporters, even amongst the mass of the workers; now patience had run out and they were reviled as useless and worse than useless. The rumours grew and persisted of a White army gathering to the south; gathering to murder the people, to reinstate the deposed Tsar, to bring back the bad old ways. An army, what's more, that was backed by foreigners; the mere thought was enough to bring bile to the mouth of any true Russian. It was at the end of October that the seething pot boiled over; and armed revolution came again to Petrograd.

'What on earth's happening?' An anxious Anna was waiting in the hallway of the apartment when Volodya came in, having been watching for him from the balcony window.

Volodya unwound his scarf and unbuttoned his coat. His clothes were shabby, his face thin; none of them had had enough to eat for weeks, and what there was both Anna and Volodya tended to give to the children. Even Varya had lost weight.

'The Provisional Government has fallen. The Bolsheviks have taken the Winter Palace and the Fortress. It's said they control the Post Office, the Telephone Exchange and all the stations. Red Guards are everywhere. They're arresting people; there's been some looting.' He passed a tired hand through his hair.

Anna watched him, concern in her face. 'It's no more serious than usual, is it?' she asked, uncertainly. 'I mean – it's all happened before – it won't affect us, will it?'

'I don't know. I just don't know. The Bolsheviks are true fanatics, Anna. Anyone who isn't for them is accounted against them.' He cast a sombre look about the despoiled but still obvious grandeur of the apartment. 'I wish we weren't living here. Perhaps we should look for somewhere else.'

'But why? Why should we? What harm are we doing?'

He shook his head, wearily.

'Volodya, I don't understand what's happening. Why shouldn't we be here? What are you afraid of?'

He took her hands in his. 'Anna –'

'What's that?' Anna turned her head. There was shouting outside in the street. They both ran across the ruined ballroom to the balcony. Men were running in the streets. 'Cossacks! Cossacks marching on the city! The traitors Krasnov and Kerensky are bringing Cossacks to Petrograd! The city is besieged!'

'Look, Aunt Anna, look at the aeroplane! What's it doing?' Nikki had joined them, excitement on his face. Anna looked up. A small aeroplane was swooping over the city, showering the streets with pamphlets that whirled and fluttered in the air like snow. 'I'll get one!' Before they could stop him Nikki had darted back into the apartment. A moment later they saw him slip out into the street, pick up one of the pamphlets and scurry back up the steps. 'There! Read it, Aunt Anna, tell us what it says.'

Anna smoothed the paper. '*Citizens of Petrograd, I call upon you to save the city from anarchy, from tyranny and famine, to save Russia from the indelible shame to which a handful of ignorant men, bought by Kaiser Wilhelm's gold, are trying to subject her. The active army looks upon these criminals with*

515

horror and contempt. Their acts of vandalism and pillage, their crimes, the German mentality with which they regard Russia – stricken down but not yet surrendered – have alienated them from the entire people.' She looked up. 'Is that right, do you think? Are the Bolsheviks in the pay of the Germans?'

Volodya shrugged. 'Who knows? Come now – come in and close the windows. We can do nothing but wait. If Kerensky really has got an army at his back then the Bolsheviks could collapse in a matter of days. We'll just have to wait and see.'

But in the event it was not the Bolsheviks who collapsed but Kerensky and his army, mainly because most of his soldiers deserted to their comrades in the city as soon as they got close enough to do so. On 1 November, the day after Red Guards had inflicted heavy losses on the White army of General Krasnov at Pulkovo Heights, on the outskirts of Petrograd, a truce was arranged and the General promised to have Kerensky arrested and handed over to the Bolsheviks. The former head of the Provisional Government escaped just moments before the Cossacks came to take him; but he was finished, and so was his attempt – the first, and many feared the last, in Russia – at something close to a liberal democratic government. The Bolsheviks were in control of the capital, and also of Moscow. In several other parts of the vast country, however, Bolshevik takeovers had come to nothing; and with the active help and participation of Tsarist Russia's Western allies the White army was readying itself to fight back; civil war loomed, and anti-foreign fervour reached fever pitch.

Fanaticism stalked the city now, triumphant. All too clearly Anna saw the reason for Volodya's disquiet on the day of the Bolshevik takeover. The decree known as 'Order Number One' was issued, abolishing all ranks in the armed forces – the main effect of which, predictably, was that what small degree of discipline had been left in the army and the navy disappeared completely, officers no longer had control over the troops and the men deserted by the thousand and poured back from the Front to the already chaotic cities. Unpopular officers were 'tried' and shot with no ceremony. Anarchy reigned. Throughout November and into December the new Government consolidated its grip on the city and on its population. Property was confiscated. Varya's last pathetic possession, the wrecked shop on the Nevsky, was taken from her. No citizen was allowed to draw more than ten roubles a day from any bank, and no money could be transferred abroad. Ration cards were issued, but only to workers. So far as the new 'People's Government' was concerned, anyone else could starve. Any personal property could be confiscated; jewellery, furniture, money, anything that caught the eye or attracted the interest of the Red Guard, and there was no redress. 'Take everything!' Lenin told his audiences of students and workers. 'Take everything, because everything is yours! Country places, land, houses, banks, securities. Take them because they belong to you – take them because they are yours!' And take them they did. The pendulum had swung from one extreme to the other and a deprived and tyrannized people took its revenge for the years of oppression. In the ensuing weeks, as always, the innocent suffered along with the guilty.

In early December Lenin brought into being the All Russia Extraordinary Commission for the Suppression of Counter Revolution, known generally by its acronym CHEKA; Donovalov, had he been alive, would have recognized the organization, which was to become the most powerful body in Lenin's Russia. The country once more had its Secret Police.

The money Anna had had transferred from England was lost when the banks were nationalized, though not before she had managed to withdraw a fair amount in gold. They hoarded the coins, hiding them with Mischa's pieces of jewellery beneath the floorboard in the bedroom they shared, eking it out from week to week. And as winter grasped the city with skeletal fingers Anna's thoughts, no matter how hard she fought against it, turned more and more often to England; to Sythings, safe and lovely in its green valley, to comfort, and to an end of fear. To a normality that had never before seemed precious, but that now seemed worth all the fortunes of the world. Despite the negotiations going on between the Soviet Government and the Germans, the British Embassy was still open. She had her passport. The way was still open. But only for her. It would be difficult to leave her mother – though in truth her feelings for

Varya were more of duty than love – and even more so to leave Volodya, of whom she was very fond. But the children. Here was the thread, no, the chain of steel, that held her. How could she abandon the children? Lively 'Tasha, laughing Nikki, and, most loved of all, the painfully quiet and withdrawn Stepan, Lenka's son. She could not leave them. It was out of the question. And so – watched, had she but realized it, by a painfully aware and equally painfully silent Volodya – she once again put off making a decision. Something would happen; life surely could not continue to be so hard? Once things settled she would see what she could do about getting them all to safety.

The Red Guards came to the apartment three days before Christmas.

Volodya had obtained work in a factory in the Vyborg, as much to get a precious ration card as anything else. Despite the new Bolshevik ruling that no employee should be required to work for more than eight hours a day – a rule entirely disregarded by the committees and workers' Soviets that had taken over the old private businesses – he spent long hours at the factory and came home exhausted. He was sitting in an armchair in the kitchen by the only stove in the apartment they could afford to light, his head nodding as Varya directed a barrage of complaints and grievances at his all but sleeping form. Nikki and 'Tasha were kneeling on chairs by the table doing a jigsaw puzzle. Small Stepan, quiet and withdrawn, sat upon the floor near the stove, hugging his cushion – now a little the worse for wear – and stared into space. Anna, sitting at the table with the other children to share the light from the one oil-lamp that was burning as she patched a pair of trousers for Nikki watched Stepan with troubled eyes. 'Steppi? Do you want to come and help with the jigsaw?'

Stepan did not raise his eyes to look at her. He shook his head. She sighed and went back to her mending. She had long since discovered that trying to force the child to join in with the activities of others did not work; for a quiet child he was capable of the most fearsome tantrums. She turned to the other two. 'I thought perhaps we might go and see your mama tomorrow. We'll take some of the potatoes Volodya bought.

And I've a little honey that might help with the baby's cough
– what in the name of God is that?'

The knocking on the door was thunderous. 'Open up! Open
up, there!'

Volodya started awake, sitting bolt upright. The children had
frozen, suddenly pale. Stepan buried his face in the grubby
cushion.

'I'll – I'll go,' Anna said, unsteadily. 'Stay here, children.
Don't worry –'

The crashing came again. 'Open up!'

Varya whimpered.

'It's all right, Mama.' As steadily as she could manage, Anna
stood, laid her mending upon the table.

Volodya followed her into the hall.

A group of uniformed men stood at the door, bands of red
about their arms and caps. They pushed in as soon as she turned
the key. Beyond them Anna could see others, running up and
down the wide staircase, banging on doors, putting shoulders
and feet to those that were not immediately opened. Somewhere a woman was crying, a thin, pathetic whine of terror.

'What do you want?' she asked, her voice shaking a little
despite all her efforts.

The leader of the group was a thin man with a face marred
and pitted by the ravages of smallpox. He wore rimless glasses,
behind which his eyes were pale and entirely devoid of warmth.
'We're requisitioning the building, comrade. You have ten
minutes.'

'You're – what?' She looked at him blankly. From the upstairs
gallery came the sounds of violence; a man shouted angrily, a
woman screamed.

The cold eyes flicked to her and away again, dismissively.
'We're requisitioning the building. Removing it from the owner-
ship of the criminal bourgeoisie. Property belongs to the people.'
His voice was completely expressionless. He walked to the
drawing-room door, peered in. 'You have ten minutes,' he
repeated, over his shoulder.

'Ten minutes to what?' Stunned by the suddenness of it,
Anna's brain was barely working. 'What are you talking about?'

'Ten minutes to pack up and leave. You may take a suitcase

each – we'll search them, of course. No valuables; all property belongs to the people. To try to take more than purely personal possessions will be treated as theft.'

From somewhere in the building came the sound of a crash, and then gunfire. The man did not bat an eyelid. 'Ten minutes,' he said.

'But – we have children – an old lady – we *can't –*'

The chill, venomous eyes turned to her again. 'Then you leave as you are,' he said, calmly. 'As I said. The building is requisitioned.' He jerked his head at the men who accompanied him. They barged past Anna, almost knocking her from her feet. 'Come. Hurry up.'

A door crashed. Varya screamed. Anna could hear Stepan whimpering. Volodya, at a glance from Anna, left at a run. She turned back to the Red Guard. 'The children?' she asked, very quietly. 'You'd turn the children out into the street, at this time of night, in these temperatures?'

The marked face was unfriendly. 'Bourgeois whelps,' he said. 'It will do them no harm to experience what others have had to experience before them.'

There was no point in arguing; there was nothing to be done. All around them in the building was the sound of protest, the sound of destruction, of violence. The children must be kept safe at all costs. Head high, she walked past him. In the kitchen she joined the others. 'Come, children, we must leave. 'Tasha, will you take the boys and help them pack? We'll go to your mama. It will be all right – don't worry. No-one will hurt you. Mama, I'll pack a bag for you. Volodya, you'll help Mama to prepare?' Varya had not been out of the apartment for months; the simple task of heaving her to her feet and dressing her would take as long as the ten minutes they had been allowed.

Anna hurried to the bedroom she shared with Volodya. Blessedly it was empty. With thundering heart she prised up the floorboard and reached into the hole for the small bag of gold coins that was their lifeline.

Heavy footsteps sounded in the hallway.

She laid the floorboard back, threw the rug over it.

The door opened. 'Comrade Vassalov says you must go.' The young soldier could not have been more than eighteen years old. Very calmly Anna opened drawers, threw clothing, toiletries and a couple of precious books into a case, straightened to face him. 'You should be ashamed,' she said, quietly. 'Does your mother know of the war you fight? A war against helpless women and children?'

The boy flushed furiously, then caught her by the arm. 'Get on!' he said.

The others were gathered in the hall. Small 'Tasha's face was tearmarked. Upon the floor beside her lay the wreckage of Volodya's violin, casually smashed to matchwood. Varya too was crying, tears running down her fat white cheeks and dripping from her chin. Her shoulders heaved. 'Don't make such a fuss, Grandma,' one of the young soldiers said, uneasily. 'You've somewhere to go, haven't you?'

'What's it to you if she has or she hasn't?' Anna asked, tartly, her tamped-down anger rising. 'What's it to you if she freezes to death in the streets? She's an enemy of the people, isn't she? Look at her – you can see it.'

'Enough.' Vassalov pointed to the bags. 'Search them.'

The young soldier poked into the bags. Anna's fingers closed over the small bag of coins in her pocket. The soldier snatched Stepan's pillow. 'What's this?'

The child shrieked, a sound of pure, agonized anger. 'It's mine! It's mine!'

Anna whirled and launched herself at the man who was about to tear open the pillow. 'For God's sake – it's the child's only possession!'

The bag of coins fell to the floor with a chinking thud that drew all eyes.

'Well, well,' Vassalov said, stooping and sweeping the small bag into his hand. He straightened, weighing it in his palm, his eyes on Anna. She returned the look defiantly. The man smiled, and tucked the little bag into his greatcoat pocket, his eyes never leaving hers, daring her to challenge him.

'Thief,' she said, savagely quiet.

His hand moved swiftly, the mark of it was on her cheek almost before she realized what was happening. She rocked on her heels; felt blood in her mouth.

Volodya started forward. Anna put out a restraining hand.

'No! It's what he wants. Don't give him the satisfaction.'

Vassalov smiled. Stepped to the door and opened it with scornful courtesy. The rest of the building was shrouded in a sudden, ominous quiet. An elderly couple shuffled their way past the door and slowly and painfully down the wide staircase from which the luxurious carpet had long been looted.

Anna slung one of the children's bags upon her shoulder, picked up her own case, hitched Stepan's slight weight upon her hip and led the way out of the Bourlov apartment, head high and without looking back. Knowing with a satisfaction that was as savage as any anger that at least the few but valuable pieces of jewellery that Mischa had given them were safely sewn into the tattered cushion that Stepan still clutched as if it were his only lifeline.

CHAPTER TWENTY-FOUR

Natalia's apartment was miserably overcrowded, but it was a roof, and at first that was enough.

But not for long.

Inevitably the stresses and strains of so many people living in three chill, cramped rooms in a city that seemed in the grip of a nightmare began to tell. The older children, used to the space of the Bourlov apartment, very quickly became fractious; they were fretful and quarrelsome. The adults' nerves – especially the women's, since Volodya at least had the doubtful advantage of going to the factory each day – were strung almost to breaking point. Despite Anna's constant tramping the streets there was little food and less fuel; as a place to live the city of Petrograd had become all but unendurable. Anna was out at five each morning, often coming home empty-handed and frozen to the bone in the late afternoon. Varya complained constantly. The children fought amongst themselves, or occasionally joined forces to defy the adults. And worst of all, little Dmitri, deprived now even of the rest and quiet he needed, failed, visibly, before their eyes. The child lay in his mother's arms, unmoving, his eyes lacklustre, his small face wizened and shrunken like that of an elderly monkey. Natalia nursed him for long hour by long hour whilst 'Tasha and Nikki squabbled and fought about her and Stepan huddled into a corner clutching his cushion and watching the world with confused and fear-filled eyes. With Volodya away all day it fell to Anna to attempt to cope with the everyday problems of running the apartment, with the temper and tantrums of her mother and the two older children alike, with Natalia's fears and small Stepan's terrors, as well as the arduous task of marketing. She sold the ruby ring and, accompanied often by 'Tasha, whose liveliness and quick temper were the usual cause of friction in the small household, she queued for hours in bitter cold for bread, for potatoes, for milk for the ailing Dmitri. There were other worries growing; with the Bolsheviks on the point of signing a separate peace treaty with the Germans, her British nationality as she had been warned was threatening to become more of a liability than a protection. Her contacts with the Embassy had, until recently, been quite open, and since an unsuccessful attempt upon Lenin's life at the beginning of January the CHEKA was more active than ever. If the Bolsheviks started rounding up alien nationals they would have little trouble in finding her.

The short, bitter days and the long dark nights passed in a miserable and anxious succession. A sense of hopelessness invested not just Anna and her small, struggling family, but, it seemed, the whole of the population of the city. Whilst the victorious revolutionaries still dashed about the streets in their requisitioned, flag-bedecked limousines and the Bolshevik grip on the government of the country became ever more vice-like, whilst officers, politicians and members of the old aristocracy, no matter how inoffensive, were arrested, imprisoned and often executed, their homes and palaces looted and wrecked, the ordinary people, as ever, froze and starved, the old and the young prey to disease and famine, their babies dying at the breast. They stood in line interminably for food and for fuel. They stoically saw their children die.

'Why do we let it happen? What's the matter with us? Why are we so – so damnably *Russian*?' Anna asked one January night in despair. Exhaustedly she dropped her head into hands that were swollen and inflamed by chilblains. 'Who has won and who has lost in this – glorious revolution?' The last two words were spoken with a bitter emphasis. 'The bad old Russia is dead, they tell us – but what does the new have to put in its place? The same chains, but of a different colour! The same tyranny! The same terror! How much more say do any of us have in our own lives? What great freedoms have we achieved by all this bloodshed and upheaval? None! And still we shuffle from queue to queue, grateful for a crust here, a handful of kindling there! Still the weak suffer and die as we stand and watch! A new repression has taken over from the old and we can do nothing about it! Nothing! I hate it all! Oh, how I hate it!' Tired and overwrought, at last entirely unable to control herself, she burst into a sudden passion of tears.

Varya and Natalia watched her in silence, taken aback by the outburst from one who had until now, of all of them, been a mainstay of strength and relative good-humour. Dmitri slept, as always, in his mother's arms, his breathing difficult. The other children were tumbled like sleeping puppies upon a mattress in the far corner of the room: the unheated bedrooms were too cold to use.

Volodya came to Anna, put a quietening hand upon her shoulder. Her hold upon her strained emotions vanquished, she was sobbing unrestrainedly into her hands, repeating the same phrase over and over, like a tired and confused child, the words too broken by tears to be clearly heard. Gently he reached to her, held her to him. She could feel the stark bones of him through the rough material of his shirt, the calluses on his craftsman's hands.

She quietened. Sniffed. Pulled away from him to knuckle her eyes, shamefaced. 'I'm sorry.'

'What were you saying, Anna?' he asked, very softly, after a moment.

She glanced at him then looked away, shaking her head. 'Nothing. Nothing! I'm tired, that's all – so very tired!'

'Tell me, Anna.' He was quietly persistent. 'Tell me! What were you saying?'

Her mouth set in a miserable, stubborn line. She shook her head.

He caught her shoulder, shook her a little. 'Anna! Say it!'

Her fragile hold upon herself broke once more. She glared at him through tears. 'I said, I want to go home!' she shouted, appalled to hear the words, entirely incapable of stopping herself. 'I said, I hate it here! *I want to go home! Home – you hear me? Home!*' She stopped, her hand to her mouth, anguished. One of the children stirred, and was still.

The words had fallen into a sudden, deathly silence. Varya's face closed like a trap, her eyes narrowed upon her daughter. Natalia glanced at the children asleep in the corner, then looked down at the sleeping Dmitri, rocked him a little, gently.

Volodya sat back on his heels with a quick, small breath. The silence was absolute.

'I'm sorry!' Anna said. 'I'm sorry! I'm sorry – I didn't mean it – I didn't! You shouldn't have made me say it! It's only that I'm so tired –'

'Of course you are. We all are,' Volodya said, mildly. 'And you did mean it. Of course you did – why shouldn't you? You have a life, a good life, waiting for you in England. The longer you leave it the harder it will be to get out of the country. Sooner rather than later now you'll have to leave. We all understand that.'

Anna stared at him.

'You've done everything you could. Everything anyone could possibly have expected of you. But things have changed. Now –' He turned a little away from her, his face schooled against pain. He had waited and watched for this moment. No weakness of his must be allowed to hinder his plans for Anna. '– now, truly, there is little more you can do. You're just another mouth to feed – you, and Steppi.' He sensed her sudden movement, brought his eyes back to hers. 'You do want to take the child with you, don't you?'

She was watching him in astonishment. 'Yes,' she said, faintly. 'Yes, of course I do. If it's possible.'

'It's possible,' he said, quietly. 'There are ways. And we're luckier than most – we have the contact with Katya and Jussi in Helsinki.'

'Never!' Varya heaved herself upright in her chair, sitting straight as a ramrod, her eyes fierce with anger and with fear. 'You'd desert us, Anna? Now? You'd leave us to fend for ourselves, helpless as we are? You should be shamed to think it! If you can go – and the child – why can't we all?'

Anna bowed her head, the small flame of hope that had been kindled by Volodya's calm words snuffing out like a blown match, leaving darkness. 'Mama, I'm sorry – you're right, of course.'

'No,' Volodya said, quietly but in a voice that held an edge of steel. He looked at Varya.

The light of the single lamp shone upon her white, bloated

face. Beside herself with rage and terror she glared back at him defiantly. 'Anna has no right –' she began.

'Anna has every right,' he interrupted very firmly. 'Anna had every right to stay safely in England in the first place; but she didn't. She had every right to run like a rabbit at the first sign of trouble – but she didn't do that, either. She could have left us at any time, no-one could have blamed her, but she didn't. Not while she thought she could help. We all owe her more than we can ever repay.' He kept his eyes pointedly upon Varya. 'Now the situation has changed. She can no longer help us. Worse; whilst she stays in the city her British nationality is likely to become a positive danger to her. And through her to us. If there's a possibility that she can leave, and young Stepan with her – and I know there is, for I have already made –' with one wary eye on Anna's astounded face he hesitated upon the word 'arrangements' '– enquiries – then she should go. In God's good name!' Abruptly he flung his hands wide in a sudden, angrily helpless gesture. '*Someone* should survive this shambles and attempt to be happy!'

Natalia lifted her head. Looked from Anna to Volodya and back again. 'Anna,' she said, 'Volodya's right.' Her voice was surprisingly firm. 'You must go.'

'But –' Anna stopped, put her hand to her head.

'Volodya and I have spoken about it.' Very carefully Natalia settled the shawl more comfortably about her sleeping child's face, resumed her rhythmic rocking. Lifted her head, pale-faced. 'I agree with him. You mustn't stay. The longer you leave it the more difficult and dangerous it will become. But, Anna, I have a favour to ask. A huge favour. Too huge, I suppose. If you think it too difficult – if you feel you can't –' She paused, biting her lip. Her red-rimmed eyes were steady and pleading. 'Anna, I want you to take the children,' she said. ''Tasha and Nikki. I want you to take them with you.'

'Natalia, what are you saying?' Varya's voice was edged with hysteria. 'Has everyone run mad? Anna's going nowhere! She's to stay here, with us!'

'No, Mama! No.' Astoundingly Natalia would not allow herself to be shouted down. 'Volodya's right. Anna is the only one of us who has a chance to get out. She should take it and go. I only ask – though I know I have no right – that she gives my children the chance to go with her.' The words spoken, she was suddenly quite calm. 'I can neither support nor look after them. God knows what will happen to them here. I have the little one – he takes so much of my time.' She looked down at the child who slept in her arms, turned back to Anna. 'They'll have a better chance and a better life with you. Will you take them?'

Anna was struck wordless.

'And what of me?' Varya demanded. 'Who consults me in all this? Ungrateful child, Anna! What of me? Will you take your poor mama to England with you – to your riches and your fancy house?'

'No, Mama, she will not.' It was Natalia who spoke again, still calm, still perfectly composed. 'The journey will not be easy. There will be dangers and difficulties enough without your adding to them. It is enough if Anna is willing to take the children. To take you would be to put them all at risk. No, Mama, you stay here with us. The children must be kept safe.' She looked back at Anna. 'You will take the children?' For the briefest of moments her voice betrayed her, ragged with grief and the pain of imminent loss.

Anna swallowed. 'Yes, Natalia. Of course I'll take them. If you're sure?'

'I'm sure.'

'And if there really is a way?' Anna looked back at Volodya.

'There's a way,' he said. 'I've made some contacts – spoken to some people. If you are to go you should make it soon, whilst the ice is still safe –'

'The ice?' Anna stared in surprise, confused at the suddenness of it all. 'You mean – the Gulf? But – don't you think – with the children – the train?'

Volodya shook his head. 'Out of the question, my love. To try to travel to Helsinki by train would be far too dangerous – a woman alone, with children and with no protection. God alone knows what might happen. And, too, the situation in Finland is just as unsettled as it is here – there's talk of armed uprising – the borders are as closely watched as any in the country. Your papers are British; the children have none at all. Even if the authorities let you go, they well might not allow the children to travel with you. No. The only way is Katya's way.' He smiled a little. 'You'll be in very grand company. The Gulf smugglers have fine customers nowadays. Many who are used to travelling a lot softer are pleased enough now with a rough sledge and a passage to freedom. And where aristocrats and their smuggled treasures can go, you and three small children can surely follow. It shouldn't be too difficult; and once you get to Helsinki, and to Katya and Jussi, you'll be at least a step closer to freedom. There are still routes open from there to Sweden – and there the Embassy will help you.'

Anna watched him for a long moment. 'You've been planning this?' she asked, suddenly.

He nodded composedly. 'Yes.'

'For how long?'

He shrugged.

'Without consulting me?'

'Yes.'

'Might I ask why not?' For all her relief, for all the sudden lightening of her heart at the hope, however slight, of freedom, she was obscurely resentful.

He took her hand. His smile was rueful. 'If you think about that for a moment you'd answer it yourself,' he said. 'I had to wait. I had to wait for the right moment. If I had suggested it to you even a matter of days ago you would have been outraged. You would totally have refused to contemplate it. Isn't that true?'

She hesitated. Then, 'I – suppose so. Yes.'

'So. I simply laid what plans I could and waited. Now, we need money, of course – we'll sell the brooch your uncle left you – and I need a couple of days to set things up. Friday, I think. That should give us time.'

'Friday,' she said, bemusedly.

He smiled, that mild and quiet smile of his. 'Friday. That is, of course, if you haven't any other arrangements made for the day?'

They reached the edge of the Gulf in darkness. Volodya had laid the plans well; palms had been greased, permits written, they had left the city with no great alarms. It was here on the dark

529

fringes of the frozen wastes of the Gulf that the danger started; there was no bribing the Bolshevik guards of Kronstadt, on the lookout for fleeing aristocrats and their transportable goods and valuables, which could as easily disappear into their captors' pockets as into the coffers of the revolutionary government. The children, wrapped in almost every item of clothing they possessed, had been carefully briefed and warned. In so much terror of discovery were they that not a word had passed even lively 'Tasha's lips since they had set out from the city in the ramshackle sledge that Volodya had hired. 'Tasha's and Nikki's farewells to their mother had been said before they left. Only Anna had cried. Natalia's strength had been channelled into the saving of her children; the decision taken, she refused to grieve to see them go.

The children were settled now into the small, fast sledge with its restless horses whose hooves were muffled with rags, which was to take them across the ice. Volodya kissed them all swiftly. 'Be good. Do as Aunt Anna tells you. Good luck, my darlings.'

'Tasha clung to him wordlessly for a moment. Nikki was too interested in the horses to think of anything else. Stepan clutched his cushion and wormed his hand from his mitten so that he could suck his thumb.

Anna faced Volodya on the icy shore. It was a dark night, with no moon. The only illumination was a guttering torch stuck into the seat beside the driver, a light that would be extinguished before they reached the danger of the Kronstadt fortresses. Its flicker threw shadows across their faces. The driver muttered, impatient to be gone.

Anna could find nothing to say. She stepped into his arms, laid her head upon his breast. 'I'm sorry,' she said at last, and lifted her face to his.

He smiled at her. 'If you had loved me,' he said, 'I'm not sure I could have let you go. So perhaps it's just as well that you didn't.'

She lifted her head. 'You could have come with me.'

She sensed the shake of his head. 'No. My place is here. Natalia – your mother –'

'– are my responsibilities, not yours!' The agony of torn

loyalties that she had suffered in the past days sounded in her voice.

'No. Don't think it. The decision is made. Go. And – be happy. Take care of the children. They are our link. Their safety and happiness is what you give me in place of love.'

She blinked, the cold air stinging her eyes.

He kissed her, gently.

Turning to leave him, she stopped. 'Volodya – you won't stop looking for Tonia? And poor Margarita?'

'Of course not. If it's possible to find them I will. Now go, Anna. Hurry.'

If there had been moonlight she might have seen his tears as she stepped into the sledge and as in ghostly silence it slid into darkness. But there was not. He waited a long time, until the only sound was the rustle of the icy wind amongst the frozen trees and battered reeds of the marshy shore. Then, tiredly, he climbed back into the empty sledge and turned it back towards the city.

CHAPTER TWENTY-FIVE

They slipped past the searchlights in the hour after midnight. Anna could feel small Stepan tense and trembling beside her. She put an arm about the child's shoulders; he turned his face into the fur of her coat, his thumb in his mouth, eyes tight shut against the eerie glow.

And then they were through, the sweeping lights throwing ghostly shadows upon the ice wastes and dark skies behind them. The driver whipped up the tough little horses and they sped on, towards the coast of Finland, safe at least for the moment.

In the relief from tension, lulled by the smooth, swift movement and the warmth of the dirty furs in which like small squirrels they nested, the children slept.

Anna did not.

Huddled against the bitter wind of their flight, the little boy curled tight against her, not daring to move her numbed arm in case she disturbed him, she looked into the cold and empty darkness, alone with her thoughts: of the past, and of the future. She felt no sadness at leaving Petrograd; the city she had once loved no longer existed. The sadness that lay heavily upon her was due wholly to the thought of those she had left behind in that miserable and uncertain prison of a place.

Her mother, poor Varya, bitterly deprived of those things which for all of her life she had taken for granted, never now to achieve those things to which she had so hopelessly aspired.

Volodya, brave and kind. Alone again, as he had been before her coming.

Natalia and her poor weakling child who surely would not survive the winter.

Margarita. Where was Margarita, who had betrayed her husband, her prince, to death in spite and hatred of another woman?

And Lenka. Lenka: dead and beyond torment, yet haunting her sister still. That Lenka should have died before the wounds of the past could be healed had hurt beyond measure; that Lenka's daughter, Anna's own image, had run to the foul and dangerous streets of the city rather than come to her was a burden of grief and of guilt that she would carry for ever. Her arm tightened around Stepan. She had him. And the other two children. Not hers. Never hers. But a trust; a trust she would not betray. Nothing would stop her from getting them to safety, from bringing them home to Sythings. Here was the future. Here was her reparation to Lenka, and yes, as he had himself said, to Volodya. As the little sledge sped on through a sudden driving flurry of snow gradually she felt her spirits lighten. If all went as had been planned there would be someone waiting on the other shore to take them to Helsinki. Once there, Katya would help, she was sure. Others had done it – the journey was perilous, but certainly not impossible. They were going home. All of them.

It was not, of course, as it turned out, anywhere near that simple.

They arrived at the village of Virojoki, just inside the Finnish borders, in the early hours of the morning.

There was no-one to meet them.

'The man Petersen has gone,' the sledge-driver said, brusquely, rejoining them after a quick trip into the village. 'A day ago.'

'But –'

'Helsinki's fallen. The Reds have taken it. The Government has gone north. To Vaasa, to Mannerheim –'

She had heard the name. 'Mannerheim? The General?'

The driver executed an ironic salute. 'Commander-in-Chief of the Finnish White Army. For what that's worth.' He was leaning into the sledge, rapidly unloading their pathetically few possessions. He avoided her eyes. 'It's civil war. The Russian army was supposed to have pulled out two or three weeks ago. It hasn't. It's supporting the Reds. It's all over but the shouting if you ask me.' He reached for the last of the bags. The children were watching, wide-eyed and uncertain.

Anna grasped his arm. 'But, please! Wait a moment! What – what are we supposed to do?'

He shook his head. 'Take your chances like the rest of us, lady,' he said, baldly. 'I was paid to get you here. You're here. I'm sorry, but that's the end of that. I'm not getting myself tangled in anything else.'

Oddly, the shock and disappointment were so great that they steadied her to an almost nerveless calm. 'Wait. You can't possibly simply dump us here and leave us. At least tell us where to go – who to talk to – to find another guide. You must know this place well enough for that?'

He looked at her for a moment, his weathered face closed and granite-hard, and she thought he would refuse even that. Then he said, 'All right. I know someone, yes. But I promise nothing, you understand? Come.'

They climbed stiffly from the sledge, 'Tasha holding her small, sturdy brother's hand, though whether to support him or to comfort herself would be difficult to say. Anna gave her a quick, encouraging smile, took Stepan's cold little hand in her own, bent to pick up a bag.

God in heaven – supposing she were to be stranded here, in the middle of nowhere, with these three small, helpless creatures?

'All right, Stepan, you can carry your cushion if you wish, but don't let go of it whatever you do! I can't hunt all over Finland for it if you lose it!' She kept her voice light. Then, 'There's been fighting?' she asked the man.

'Not much. Not yet. But there will be. The Reds just walked into Helsinki by all accounts – no-one tried to stop them. The Government had already left, and anyone of any importance had gone with them, to the north. But it won't be that easy from now on, I'll wager.'

Anyone of any importance. Did that include Katya and Jussi? She did not know.

They trudged over rutted, frozen snow along the one, narrow, straggling street of the village. There were few lights. The small wooden houses crouched, huddled and quiet in the darkness. Only the smell of woodsmoke hinted at life behind the blank and shuttered windows. It was bitterly cold.

'Here.' The man had stopped outside what looked like a very large shed. A glint of light showed beneath the door.

From somewhere very close a sharp voice snapped a challenge. Startled, Anna caught her breath, felt Stepan's hand clutch at hers in a spasm of fear. She pulled him closer to her. The challenge had been in Finnish, a language Anna did not understand. Their guide muttered a quick reply. A tall shadow detached itself from the deeper darkness. The two men spoke, briefly and rapidly. The tall shadow carried a gun.

Then the guard stood back, jerking his head.

Anna walked past him to the door.

Their entrance stopped a noisy conversation dead in its tracks. They stood, Anna and her three small charges, clustered by the door, the children leaning into Anna's skirts, Stepan's thumb firmly and nervously in his mouth.

Every eye turned to them.

'What's this?' someone demanded into the silence, in Russian.

In the quiet Anna realized with a jolt that their reluctant guide, true to his word, had dumped the bags and left them. The question was addressed to her, and the tone was not friendly. She took a breath and lifted her head. She was aware of the smoke-hazed and dim interior of what looked like a fisherman's shed. A hurricane lamp hung low from the rafters, illuminating draped nets, stacked oars, a small upturned rowing boat, two battered benches and a table, and upwards of a dozen men, rough-dressed, hard-faced, all of them looking at her, their expressions ranging from surprise to downright and wary hostility. All were armed. Two rifles lay upon the table.

'Gentlemen, I'm sorry.' Her brain was suddenly ice-cold and clear. She drew the children around her, Stepan in front, her hands upon his shoulders, his wide eyes fear-filled over the clutched cushion as he shrank back against her. It was a tableau, she thought, that surely must touch at least one heart? 'We've come over the ice from Petrograd.' She was amazed at the coolness of her own voice. 'A guide was supposed to be waiting here to take us on to Helsinki, where we have friends –'

No-one spoke.

'The man's name was Lars Petersen.'

'He left yesterday,' someone volunteered in heavily-accented Russian.

'Yes, I know. The sledge-driver told me. Please, we have to get to Helsinki. The children are cold and tired. Frightened, too. Is there someone who can help us?' She paused, weighed advantage against risk, and then added, 'I can pay.'

'You'll get no-one to take you to Helsinki, lady.'

She looked at the speaker, an older man, grizzled and moustachioed, who sat upon the upturned boat, elbows on knees, a long pipe smoking in his hand. He did not, she thought, look altogether unsympathetic.

She addressed herself to him. 'There's been some kind of trouble?'

A man at the back of the room laughed, short and sharp. 'Nothing like there's going to be, lady. Tell her, Toivo.'

The older man nodded. 'The Reds took over Helsinki yesterday. The Government's gone north. There's fighting to the east of the city, we've heard. Cutting us off. The place is crawling with Red patrols. No-one knows what's happening. It's too dangerous to move at the moment.'

'But I have to get to Helsinki,' she said, doggedly.

The man Toivo moved his shoulders expressively and apparently dismissively. But still she thought she saw some small gleam of benevolence in the shrewd and narrowed eyes as he looked at Stepan.

'The children,' she said, gambling on that look, 'I have to get them to safety.'

'You should have thought of that before you started.' The young voice, speaking from the shadows, was hostile and impatient.

'In God's name, what's the woman doing here?' demanded another. 'What's it to do with us?'

The older man held up a gnarled, tranquil hand. The palm was leather-hard and ingrained with dirt. 'Wait.' He lifted his eyes from the children to Anna's face. 'I've told you. There's fighting between here and the city. No-one will take you to Helsinki. You were hoping to leave the country from there?'

She nodded wearily. 'To go to England. I have an English

passport. I'm taking the children –' She stopped, shaking her head a little.

'Hey, Toivo – if she could get to Helsinki the Swedish Legation might help her,' a voice called from the back of the room.

Someone laughed, a small harsh laugh. 'And if she could transport herself to Rome then no doubt the Pope could be of some assistance,' a voice said, drily helpful.

Everyone began speaking at once, a babble of Russian and Finnish.

'For Christ's sake!' A tall, dark man with an angry scar on his cheek banged the table. 'What the hell is this? A kindergarten?'

The man beside him riposted shortly and presumably sharply to the point in Finnish. There was a muffled explosion of laughter.

The man called Toivo held up his hand again, spoke quietly. The noise subsided. He turned to Anna, spoke again in Russian. 'To get you to Helsinki would be very difficult,' he said. 'At least for the next few days, until we establish some kind of communication with our friends in the city. I suppose, however, that it might be possible for you to stay here in the village for a few days – I assume you have money for board and lodging?'

Anna nodded.

'Until things settle a little. You say you have contacts in Helsinki?'

'Yes. The Lavolas. They –' She stopped. There had been an unmistakable stir of sound in the room at the name. Heads lifted. Eyes sharpened. A dark and stocky young man with a forbidding face stepped suddenly away from the wall and into the harsh circle of light thrown by the hurricane lamp. 'Lavola?' he asked, very softly. 'What do you know of Lavola?'

She could not for her life tell if the reaction had been friendly or hostile. She hesitated. Then, 'That's who I'm looking for,' she said. 'Jussi Lavola. And his wife, Katya. She's my cousin –'

'Your name?' The sharp words cut across hers.

Still not knowing if she spoke to friend or foe, she looked at him helplessly. The dark face gave no answers. She held his eyes. 'Anna de Fontenay,' she said, firmly. The chance had to be taken. Pressed against her heavy skirts she could sense Stepan's fear. 'Tasha stood, straight and frail as a flower, grasping her brother's hand. 'My mother is sister to Katya's. My father was Victor Valerievich Shalakov.'

Subtly his face had changed. There was a moment's silence. The men looked from one to the other, obviously awaiting the young man's reaction, still uncertain.

He stepped forward, hand outstretched. 'I know of you,' he said, gruffly. 'You once looked after a friend of mine. He told me of it. Welcome to Suomi.'

The relief was enormous. Tiredness overwhelmed her. Her mind groped past the puzzling words to their import. 'You'll take us, then? You'll take us to Helsinki?'

Kaarlo shook his head. 'I'm sorry. Jussi and Katya are no longer in Helsinki. They've gone north, to join General Mannerheim.'

They sat later about a warm stove in a nearby house. The children had been fussed and fed and tucked together into a huge feather bed by Toivo's wife, whose spic-and-span home this was.

Toivo sat now holding his peace and sucking his pipe, listening to Kaarlo as the young man spoke. 'Jussi was too well-known by then to stay in Helsinki with the Reds coming. He took Katya and the baby and left the city three days ago. They'll be in Vaasa by now. Jussi's helping to negotiate with the Germans for the return of the Finnish regiment from Lockstedt.' He scowled ferociously. The Germans' continued reluctance to release the Finnish Jaegers to fight for their homeland, as had been promised, was the source of much anger and bitterness in Finland. 'I and some of the others are going to join them as soon as we can.'

'And Uncle Mischa, Aunt Zhenia? Katya's parents? Are they with them?'

He shook his shaggy head. There was a pistol in his belt. His knee-high boots were scuffed and worn. Even in the warmth of the room he had not taken off the filthy sleeveless sheepskin jacket. He looked, Anna thought, disconcertedly, an absolute bandit. 'They left some months ago. Gone off to America. Katya could have gone too, with the child.' He shrugged, but his mouth quirked to something close to a grin. 'She wouldn't.

Threatened Jussi to break his head if he tried to make her.'

That sounded reassuringly like Katya. Anna smiled. 'And your friend Heimo? He's in Vaasa too?'

A spasm of something too ferocious to be termed mere pain showed for a second upon the usually impassive face. 'No. Heimo isn't in Vaasa. Heimo's dead.'

'Oh!' Anna saw a sudden, startlingly clear picture of a mild, smiling, intelligent face, heard the light and pleasant voice. 'Oh, I am so sorry!'

'He was killed in a skirmish just before Christmas.' Kaarlo's voice betrayed nothing, but his right hand, resting upon his knee, had knotted to a fist. Anna saw him look at it, saw the strong, stubby fingers uncurl slowly, as if the movement required enormous effort. 'He told me about you,' Kaarlo said, abruptly, the tone brusque. 'Told me how you looked after him.'

'It was nothing.'

'Heimo didn't think so.' Kaarlo stood up, went to the stove, lifted the lid and hefted a couple of logs into it. Turned. 'Neither do I.'

Toivo shifted a little, took his pipe from his mouth, stared pensively at it. 'So how do we get the lady and the children out of Finland?'

In the silence Anna looked from one to the other, waiting. Neither man looked at her.

'Perhaps we could get her into Helsinki,' Kaarlo said at last, with no great conviction.

'Who would I go to now?' she asked. 'If Katya and Jussi are gone?'

Kaarlo shook his head, gloomily.

'Borge back there mentioned the Swedish Legation.' Toivo tamped his pipe down thoughtfully. 'He's right. They've helped many refugees.'

'Why would they help me? Even supposing we could get to them? A Russian, British by marriage, and with a gaggle of children I can't actually prove I have guardianship over?' Anna asked, bleakly. The circumstances of her flight with the children had already been explained.

'Mm. The situation is a little irregular, I suppose. And the Swedes, it must be said, can be a bit sticky about such matters.'

539

Anna was watching Kaarlo. Kaarlo, studiously, was not watching her.

'Kaarlo?' she asked.

He glanced at her. Looked away. Began to shake his head long before she had opened her mouth.

'When you go north to join Jussi and Katya – would you take us with you?'

'No.'

'Kaarlo, please? We can't stay here for ever. Won't you please help us?'

'You don't know what you're asking. What you'd be letting yourself in for. It's two hundred and fifty miles of wild country. We'll be travelling through –' He stopped abruptly, his voice drowned by a thunderous knocking on the outer door.

Toivo rose swiftly to his feet. A wicked-looking blade had appeared in Kaarlo's hand as if by magic. Anna stood tensely, watching the door. The knocking came again. Toivo's plump wife appeared in the bedroom doorway, hands clasped anxiously before her. 'Toivo?'

He motioned her to silence. Gestured to Kaarlo. Silently Kaarlo moved to the door, stood with his back to the wall beside it, knife at the ready.

'Toivo! Toivo? Open up! It's Erik! Toivo – you hear me? Open up!'

The woman let out a small gasp of relief. 'Erik, it's Erik – let him in.'

Toivo opened the door. A young man stumbled into the room, his face beneath the shaggy fur of his hat ablaze with excitement. 'Toivo, have you heard? Have you heard the news? God bless him! God bless the man!'

'What man? What news? Erik, are you drunk? What are you talking about?'

The young man calmed a little, stood breathing heavily, looking from face to face, suddenly savouring the moment.

Kaarlo stepped back into the middle of the room to join them, gestured with the knife. 'Well?'

'Last night –' the shining eyes travelled again from one to the other, rested at last upon the older man. He spoke quietly now, and very clearly '– last night Mannerheim and his men

540

disarmed almost every Russian garrison in the south of Ostro-bothnia. With hardly the loss of a single life.'

'How?' It was Kaarlo, sharp and obviously disbelieving. 'How could he do such a thing? The Jaegers aren't home yet, Manner-heim has only a handful of troops. The Russian garrisons must number in thousands.'

'He surprised them. Outmanoeuvred them – fooled them completely! He cut the rail and telephone links, isolated the garrisons, gulled the Russians into thinking that each one was under threat from a massive attack. The situation's confused enough already – half the garrisons don't know what they're supposed to be doing – most of them surrendered meekly as lambs. We've captured rifles, machine guns, mortars, ammu-nition – the whole area is in White Finnish hands.'

'And in Carelia?' Toivo asked quietly.

'They're fighting. It's fierce, so they say. Reports are confused.'

'So. It's begun,' Kaarlo said. He swung away from them, exul-tation in his eyes, smacked a fist into his palm. 'Really begun. At last!'

Toivo was at the sideboard where stood a bottle and some small glasses. He poured the liquor, handed the glasses around, lifted his own in a toast. 'To free Suomi.'

And, 'To free Suomi!' roared Kaarlo. In one swift movement he swallowed the drink at one draught and before anyone could guess his intention had flung his glass to smash against the metal stove.

Fragments flew everywhere.

'Kaarlo!' shrieked Toivo's wife, understandably outraged.

Kaarlo grinned like a wolf.

'Heavens. And here was I,' Anna said, mildly, 'under the impression that only the barbarian Russians did that?'

Kaarlo's eventual agreement to take them north with him was nothing if not reluctant. They were to travel across country, a small band of them, on skis. The addition of a sledge for Anna and the children was a complication he was not happy to con-template.

'We'll be no trouble, I promise,' Anna urged. 'Please, Kaarlo, we can't stay here – there's no knowing what might happen.

It's quiet now, but fighting's breaking out everywhere – we could find ourselves in the middle of a battlefield. Kaarlo, for the children, please! Just get us to the coast, and we can make arrangements to get across to Sweden. These last few miles, Kaarlo – please help us.'

Kaarlo scowled. Nikki, leaning against his knee, peered up into his face. 'I'll help, Uncle Kaarlo. I'll carry your knife, if you'd like.' To Kaarlo's overt embarrassment but Anna suspected secret pleasure, the child had taken to him, following him about, hanging upon his every word, even imitating, perhaps unconsciously, his pugnacious, rolling gait. The day before Nikki had begged Anna to cut out the arms from his small fur coat. Only the direst of threats had kept the garment whole. 'I'll look after Aunt Anna and the others. You won't have to worry about us.'

'Tasha gave a sisterly snort.

Kaarlo bent and swept the little boy onto his knee; an incongruous sight, Anna thought, but a promising one.

'All right,' he said, after a moment. 'Providing the others agree, we'll take you. We leave as soon as it's dark tomorrow afternoon.'

'Hooray!' Nikki threw up his arms, putting himself in imminent danger of a tumble. 'We're going with Kaarlo! We're going with Kaarlo! I'm going to kill a Red Guard!'

Kaarlo swung him, squealing, high in the air, held him suspended. 'You're going to do no such thing, sonny. You're going to obey orders and stay as quiet as a bloody mouse, you hear?'

Nikki giggled, 'Yes.'

Kaarlo thumped him ungently back down on the ground, thrust his dark face close to the boy's. 'Yes – what?'

'Yes, sir!' Nikki said, grinning.

'And what are you going to do?'

'I'm going to stay as quiet as a bloody mouse, sir!'

Anna raised exasperated brows.

Kaarlo threw her his wolfish grin. 'Tomorrow. Be ready. And don't make me regret it. Cause any trouble, and we leave you right where you are, there and then.'

Anna believed him.

*　*　*

They travelled in darkness through a country in which rumour and counter-rumour flew. There was fighting around Kuopio. The northern town of Oulu was in flames. The Reds were pressing on in the east. The Reds were being held in the east. The Jaegers had landed. The Jaegers were still twiddling their thumbs and polishing their empty rifles in Lockstedt. The Bolsheviks in Petrograd were ready to concede terms to the Germans. The Germans were refusing to negotiate. Russian troops were to be withdrawn from Finland. The Bolsheviks were sending reinforcements to their Finnish comrades.

The small party moved quietly and steadily north-west, through endless and trackless forest, along frozen waterways, over snow-blanketed lakes. The men travelled expertly on skis, Anna drove the children in a small, unsprung wooden sledge pulled by a stocky, rough-coated little pony. It was country that Kaarlo knew well. They slept at isolated farms and hamlets, grateful after a bitter night's hard travelling for a plate of stew and a place in front of a stove to sleep. Sometimes, in the wilderness of forest and lake, Kaarlo deemed it safe to travel by day, and they made better progress. Any road or railway was approached with caution. Once they stood hidden in the pine-shadows as an armoured division ploughed past them on a main highway. Kaarlo's jaw was tight as he watched them. Anna found herself praying, with a trace of real urgency, that he would resist the temptation to take on the Russian army with a knife, single-handedly. In a village fifty miles or so north of the important industrial town of Tampere, Kaarlo and his friends met up with another group, partisans, Anna suspected, on some mission of sabotage. Her suspicions were confirmed when Kaarlo announced that they would break their journey here for a couple of days. 'The horse needs rest, and so do the children.'

'And?' Anna asked, her voice caustic.

He shrugged.

That night Anna and the children watched as their companions strapped on pistols, sheathed knives, pulled on heavy jackets. 'Where are you going?' Nikki asked, excitedly. 'Are you going to kill Bolsheviks?'

'No, little friend.' One of the men tousled his hair. 'We're going to play trains.'

Anna heard them come back perhaps four hours later, heard the whispers, the quiet laughter, and slept at last. Whatever they had done, they had done safely. The next day they moved on again. At mid-morning they came to a railway line. Anna reined the pony in. Kaarlo took its head, laughing, leading it across the tracks. 'No need to look for trains, Anna. There aren't any. Not today.'

They left the lakeland behind them. Now almost all was forest, mile after endless mile of it. The going was difficult. The children were bored. Anna was exhausted.

'You want to stop?' Kaarlo asked, maliciously solicitous after she had sworn at the inoffensive and gallant little pony for the third time in half an hour.

'No.'

He grinned, tucked his head down, ploughed on.

It snowed. Snowed as if it would never stop. They found refuge in a friendly farmhouse, a farmhouse occupied only by women. Mother and daughters made them welcome. The men-folk were with General Mannerheim – 'Bless the man's soul!' – and at least here there were some reliable tidings. In the west two more towns had surrendered to the Whites, and the supply line to friendly Sweden, so important to the rebels, was secured. The focus of the struggle at the moment appeared to be the town of Vilppula, north of Tampere, where a tiny garrison of Whites was under attack by an overwhelming number of Russians and Red Finns.

'They've beaten them off twice,' the woman said, calmly, ladling out salt fish soup. 'They'll come through, you'll see. The Godless Bolsheviks won't win here.'

'Tell me,' Anna asked, later, as she stood by the window with Kaarlo watching the snow that blew in gusts across the small cleared fields of the farm, 'this war – is it Finn against Russian? Or is it Finn against Finn? Just how strong is your support amongst the population?'

Kaarlo hunched his shoulders almost to his ears, scowled his familiar scowl. Not to be intimidated, she watched him, waiting for an answer.

'There are Finns, are there not,' she persisted, 'who are fighting for the Bolsheviks – fighting to remain with Russia?'

He turned a suddenly savage face. 'There are always traitors. There are always crawling, gutless cowards that prefer a known master to the perils of freedom. And, yes, there are Finns who have been as readily gulled by these – Bolsheviks –' he spat the word in vicious disgust '– as have the Russian people.'

'So, it is a civil war?'

He pushed himself away from the window. 'It is a war for independence. And we shall win it. Now, get some sleep. We leave tomorrow, snow or no snow.'

Two-thirds of their journey was done, now. Less than a hundred miles lay between them and their destination. Anna had lost count of the days. The children slept, and squabbled, and slept again. The wind bit at her cheeks, her eyes became red-rimmed and sore. The men pushed on for the most part in silence. For the first time they missed the village towards which they were heading and had to spend an uncomfortable night in the open, in a hastily-constructed tent-like cabin made from furs and hurriedly-cut branches. Breakfast that morning was meagre. Anna and the children ate it huddled uncomfortably in the comparative warmth of the tent.

'I'm hungry,' 'Tasha announced, plaintively. 'And I smell horrible.'

'So are we all, and so do we all,' Anna replied, grimly, breaking her own portion of bread into three pieces. 'Here. Don't eat it all at once.'

'I think I've got fleas,' Nikki said in an interested voice.

'Oh, do shut up, Nikki –'

'Are we nearly there?' It was Stepan, suddenly, who so rarely said a word that three pairs of eyes turned to him, astonished. His cushion was tucked under his arm as always, his small face was pinched with cold, his mouth trembled. 'Oh, please, Aunt Anna – are we nearly there?'

The question struck them all to a sudden choking silence. 'Tasha blinked. Nikki's face turned very red. Anna reached for Stepan and hugged him to her. As always he lay rigid against her, neither resisting nor returning her embrace. 'Yes, darling, truly yes. It won't be long now.' She felt tired tears rising in her own eyes. 'You've all been very brave, so very brave. Just a little while longer, my pets, just a day or two longer.'

'Tasha curled herself around to lay against Anna's side. 'Tell us about England, Aunt Anna. Tell us about Sythings. Will we really be allowed to have dogs, and ponies of our own? Is there really a garden as big as a park?'

It was a favourite game, and one which Anna played with every bit as much fervour as did the children. Talking about England, talking about Sythings, made it feel close, and real; even made it seem possible that one day she might actually see it again.

It was the following day that they ran into the white-coated ski patrol. Anna, seeing them as they emerged from the trees, hauled on the reins to turn the pony and flee. Kaarlo it was who saw the insignia and armbands. 'No, Anna, no! It's all right – they're friends! Friends!' He was in amongst them then, shaking hands, accepting cigarettes – they had run out two days before – exchanging news.

'We can strike out for the road now. We're safe. They've held Vaasa. Mannerheim's there.'

They struggled into the battered, busy town the following day. Evidence of its takeover by the military – Anna found out later there were two thousand men stationed in the town – was everywhere. Men drilled in the streets and squares, volunteers who were pouring in from the countryside to support the charismatic Mannerheim and to fight at last for the independence of their country. Small cavalry columns trotted by, field guns and armoured cars ploughed noisily along the neat and usually quiet thoroughfares.

They took leave of their companions on the edge of the town. All the young men were here to volunteer and were anxious to be gone. They shook hands and mumbled good wishes, kissed the children. Anna watched as they set off talking and laughing excitedly, skis over their shoulders, before with Kaarlo leading the pony they turned towards the centre of town. Kaarlo too was impatient to don uniform and regularize at last his participation in his country's battle, but he had offered, to Anna's surprise, to escort them to the address where they hoped to find Jussi and Katya first.

The last fraught moment of these anxious days came when they reached the house and Kaarlo pulled the doorbell. Neither spoke. The thought was in both their minds. Much had happened in the past weeks. There must be at least as much chance that the Lavolas had left the city than that they had stayed.

And then the door was open and Katya was there, a bright-faced child astride her hip, her eyes first, delightedly, upon Kaarlo and then in growing recognition and utter disbelief upon Anna. 'Anna! My God! It is Anna, isn't it? *Anna!* It can't be!'

There was so very much to talk about. They had not met since Anna's wedding. They talked all day and, with the exhausted children and the overexcited Jaakko bathed and safely asleep in bed, half the night.

'So,' Jussi said at last, 'you'd like help to get to Sweden?'

'Is it possible?' Anna, despite her happiness and relief, was battling fatigue. The skin of her face was chapped and sore, and she ached all over.

'Of course it is. Jussi will fix it. Jussi can fix almost anything,' Katya laughed. She sat on the floor beside Jussi in his wheeled chair, her arm leaning on his good leg. She was thinner than Anna remembered her, and the smile she recalled so vividly was neither quite so ready nor so carefree. There was no surprise in that; much had happened since those days in the schoolroom in the Bourlov apartment. Those days a lifetime ago when they had been friends, and the world about them had been safe and secure. She watched as Katya lifted her head to smile again at her husband, saw the warmth in his face as he looked down at her; and felt the faintest twinge of envy. Despite Jussi's terrible disability and the short temper she had already seen it could occasionally produce, despite the bloodshed and danger about them, they had each other and they had Jaakko, flesh of their flesh, child of their love.

'Rest here for a couple of days,' Jussi was saying. 'You've had a hard time, and the children need to recuperate before you go on. The supply lines are open to Sweden. They're perfectly safe. We'll get you out.'

*   *   *

547

They crossed the frozen Gulf of Bothnia two days later. Jussi himself drove the sledge, part of a column that plied freely between the liberated west coast of Finland and friendly Sweden. At Umea they boarded the train for Stockholm. In Stockholm there was a British Embassy; friends, help and safety.

On the third day of March 1918, the day that the Bolshevik Government of Russia finally signed a punitive peace treaty with Germany in the city of Brest-Litovsk, Anna and the children sailed for Newcastle, and for home.

INTERLUDE: 1918–1925

The men of the erstwhile 27th Royal Prussian Jaeger Battalion finally reached their homeland a few days before Anna and the children sailed from Stockholm. For a week they had known that the German High Command had at last officially agreed to their return to Finland. For a week they waited; until, on 13 February 1918, the battalion was disbanded as a German fighting unit and the men, who had waited three long, tough years for this, were told they could go home. They were also told as a final and potentially disastrous twist of the two-faced diplomacy that had dogged them for all of those years that their uniforms and their arms must stay in Germany.

The years of planning and of hope might have been crushed at that one stroke. The only Independent Finland that Lenin and his Bolsheviks were ready to recognize was a Red Independent Finland; and to that end units of Russian soldiers were pouring into the country to support the Finnish Reds, to 'liberate' the people and to ensure they stayed in the Russian fold. Whilst Mannerheim and his fighters with skill and with courage held onto the advantage he had so brilliantly engineered the month before, he was desperately short both of trained men and of arms. The well-trained, properly-armed Jaegers, dispersed between the hastily assembled battalions of the White Finnish army, were essential to his plans; he knew that victory, if it might be gained, must come quickly. The longer the fighting continued, the stronger established became the Government in Petrograd and the more likely was the successful negotiation of a separate peace with Germany. That achieved, Lenin would be free to turn his full energy upon crushing the rebellion.

It was the integrity of the Jaegers' German field officers, in contrast to the political duplicity of their masters, that saved the day in the end. Orders were orders, and the orders were that

549

the Finns were to board the two ships that awaited them in the port of Libau as civilians. No orders were given, however, to patrol the streets of the town, nor to supervise the embarkation of these newly-made civilians. It was with little surprise that a certain Captain Ausfeld woke in the chill of the morning of 14 February to discover that the men he had trained, and whose cause he had come so firmly to support, had during the night spirited aboard the transport ships *Arcturus* and *Castor* not just themselves but their weapons and their uniforms. Jubilantly, and armed for combat, the young men of Finland were going home; and from the bow of each ship flew, for the first time, the gold and blue Lion Banner of Finland.

The Treaty of Brest-Litovsk, which brought peace to the Eastern Front, was signed two weeks later. But the joyfully-greeted homecoming of the Jaegers had by then put new and determined life into the fight for Finland. The struggle throughout the March of 1918 was bitter. Many died. There were betrayals and atrocities, as in war there always are. The wood-built towns and villages of Finland were in flames. But as so often the spirit of independence, no matter how long held to a glimmer by repression, once exposed to the fresh air of freedom burned stronger and brighter than the inimical flame that consumed building and forest. The Russian troops that bolstered the strength of the Finnish Red Guards, confused and debilitated already by war and revolution, were undisciplined and demoralized. Mannerheim's Finns were not. Outnumbered and outgunned, yet they possessed the weapons of will and determination. The decisive battle – the battle for Tampere – came at the beginning of April. It was bitterly fought, and one of the longest and bloodiest of the war. By 10 April the Red armies were in retreat – a shambles of a retreat, its path marked by fire and indiscriminate death.

On 29 April the Red Western army was all but destroyed at Viipuri; and a few days later the war was at an end. On 16 May the victorious White army, led by the Jaegers, marched through the streets of a liberated Helsinki, and Suomi was free.

Just over a month later, civil war broke out in Russia; a civil war that was to prove perhaps the bloodiest and most hate-filled in the blood-drenched history of the country. In July the Tsar, his wife and their five children were brutally murdered in Ekaterinburg; they were not the only, simply the best-known, victims of the indiscriminate brutality inflicted by both sides on the other in the savage struggle. No-one knew then, nor ever discovered, how many people died in the slaughter that followed, the so-called Terror. For the peasants and the poorest of the people it hardly mattered that Lenin was as systematically murdering Mensheviks, Socialist Revolutionaries and Anarchists in his bid for total power as he was the detested Whites who supported the Tsar. For simple folk, no matter who fought, who won, or who lost, the problems were the same as they always had been. Quite apart from the bloodletting, hardship, famine and epidemic killed an estimated seven million people between 1918 and 1920. By 1922 the Bolsheviks, now called the Communists, had a stranglehold upon Russia.

And, ironically, it was in the spring of that same year that Lenin had his first stroke. The second felled him in December, and the third the following March, leaving him half-paralysed and speechless. Ten months later he died.

There were many who truly mourned the passing of a visionary – and inevitably in the case of such a man, such a catalyst in so many people's lives, there were perhaps as many who did not. But any rejoicing was premature. For looming in the shadows, awaiting his moment, was a man who had watched, planned and ruthlessly manoeuvred in anticipation of this hour. A man who, despite Lenin's own opposition and distaste, had manipulated himself into an all but unassailable position of power, and who stood now, the prize within his grasp. Over the next few years the monstrous Josef Stalin mercilessly eliminated, one by one, any who opposed him: the true Terror had begun.

Meanwhile, in the West, in November 1918, the War To End All Wars at last ended, leaving Europe battered and exhausted, a generation of young men wiped out, the lives of many of the survivors wrecked. But life, as ever, was not to be denied by tragedy. As the decade ended and the new era of the Twenties was ushered in, frenetic gaiety became the order of the day, at least for some. By then Alcock and Brown had flown the Atlantic non-stop, and civilian airships were catching the popular imagination, their wartime past forgiven if not forgotten. The first regular broadcasting station was started in Pittsburgh and jazz and the pursuit of noisy pleasure swept the western world like an epidemic.

In a Germany bitter, sore and resentful at the punitive terms of the Treaty of Versailles, the National Socialist Party was founded.

Anna and the children arrived at Sythings in the late spring of 1918. Resilient as only children can be, 'Tasha and Nikki settled into their new life as if born to it. Even withdrawn Stepan, who for some time, still silent, still undemonstrative, clung to Anna as if she were the only stable thing in a world gone mad about him, did at last begin to respond to the peace, security and comfort with which Anna surrounded and anxiously protected him. Mistrustful at first, flinching fearfully from anything he did not understand, yet gradually as the months and then the years went by the unseen wounds apparently healed. Only the worn and threadbare cushion that lay always upon his bed and which he stubbornly refused to allow anyone to touch – the mere suggestion was enough to send him into a rage that left him white-faced and shaking, and even the tormenting 'Tasha learned when to let well alone – testified to the continued existence of old terrors, old hurts.

Anna watched, and waited, and hoped. She loved all three of them as if they had truly been her own; but in her secret heart, this was her most precious child.

News from Russia itself was scant. If Volodya wrote, Anna never received his letters, and those she wrote to him simply, it seemed to her, disappeared into an empty void; she never knew if he received them. It did not take long to occur to her that even to have such letters addressed to them could constitute a danger to those she had left behind; after a year, reluctantly, she stopped writing.

It was with Katya in Finland that she established swift and regular contact. It was from Katya that they heard, almost a year after the event, of the death of baby Dmitri in the 'flu epidemic of the summer of 1918. Anna cried a little; neither 'Tasha nor Nikki did. It was as if the slate of their early lives had been wiped clean; their mother, Dmitri, their grandmother,

Volodya, were shadowy figures from a past in young minds long gone and best forgotten. The human race survives so. Anna had employed a tutor to teach them English, and as soon as they were able, which had been remarkably quickly, had found a good local school for them. They were altogether too involved with tadpoles and newts, with puppies and kittens, with school friends and the *Boys'* or *Girls' Own Paper* to be concerned with an uneasy yesterday that became more distant and hazy as time slipped by. Nikki developed a passion for the internal combustion engine. 'Tasha wanted to be an actress. Then an opera singer. And then a nurse in a pretty uniform. Then she was given a pony and the world revolved around that. Steppi gave as little away of his ambitions as of anything else. Like any other family they squabbled and fought on occasion like demons, supported each other with fierce single-mindedness in the face of outside attack. Judging the first, precarious bridge to have been crossed, Anna began to pick up the threads of her own life, surprised and joyful to discover that friends made in those years with Guy were still there, and still friends. She started again to invite to the house the writers, artists and musicians who had made up their circle before the war and who to her delight needed little or no persuasion to make Sythings their meeting place again. As they grew the children became a part of these gatherings.

She worried, as any mother would, at the thought of their going away to school. Given their less than ordinary background she feared to part them from her and from Sythings, though the conventions of the time and place demanded it. She need not have concerned herself. 'Tasha it was, in 1923, who led the campaign to be allowed to go away to school as, she insisted dramatically, every other person in the world had been allowed to do but her. Nikki weighed in eagerly behind her. His main passion – apart from the filthy bits of engine that were permanently spread across the floor of his room – was sport. A chap really couldn't get anywhere without going to a school with a decent cricket pitch. And where the others led Steppi – and, Anna discovered within a day of his leaving, with an absurd mixture of tears and laughter, his battered cushion – would doggedly and unflinchingly follow. The first term without them was a strange one for Anna; the fledglings were, if not flown, at least spreading tentative wings. She said so in her next letter to Katya.

In that case, Katya answered promptly and with crisp relief, she could do them all a favour and give houseroom to a young musician who had fled the repression and terror of Stalin's Russia and taken refuge with the Lavolas, whose Helsinki home had become, over the past years, a haven for such refugees. The route across the ice was still open to those who dared to take it. For some strange reason this boy's heart was set upon England (Katya had already passed on what she described as 'several stray parcels' to her parents in the United States). He was also a promising violinist. What more appropriate resting place for such a package than Sythings?

It was with a stirring of excitement that Anna agreed. Two weeks later – having set off, Anna noted with affectionate exasperation, long before her letter to her cousin agreeing to the proposition could possibly have arrived – the young Sergei Ivanovich Stavlov appeared on her doorstep. Six months later, Sergei having found a place in Anna's heart and then in the Guildhall School of Music and Drama, an intense and difficult piano virtuoso arrived; a young man whose anti-social habit of sleeping all day and playing impassioned piano music all night made it a positive relief when he was invited to join an orchestra in Manchester. Anna, with visits in mind, was mildly sorry that the orchestra was not in New York. And then, in the winter of 1925, Katya herself came at last, escorting a prize – a young composer snatched, so Katya would have it, from the very jaws of Stalin's secret police.

Anna never forgot that day. With typical panache and no warning – although it later transpired that she had spent two days in London to break the journey – Katya arrived, complete with 'guest' and brought with her into the quiet house the bright aura of laughter and warmth that Anna so well remembered. It was termtime. The children were away. Astonished and delighted greetings and the sketchiest of news exchanged, and the somewhat fraught young man Katya had brought with her installed a little suspiciously in the guest suite, the cousins faced each other, suddenly silent, suddenly still, across the warmth of a glowing fire. Katya, restless, turned, held her glass to the firelight, watched as its depths glowed ruby red.

'What is it?' Anna asked.

Katya took a long breath. 'Anna – I'm sorry – there's no easy way to say it. Your mother is dead.'

Anna did not move. Dreamlike impressions drifted across her mind. A skein, a tangled web of images. A delicate, bright-eyed doll: 'Anna? Anna, my shawl? Where's my shawl? You know I mustn't –'

'And Volodya,' Katya said, expressionless.

Anna's head jerked up. 'Volodya?'

There was a brief silence. Katya lifted her hands. Dropped them. Even sombre and close to tears, even with the faint lines of strain about eyes and mouth that had been the first thing Anna had noticed when they had met, she was still magnetically attractive. Still imbued with that verve and inner warmth that would attract attention wherever she went. 'He was taken,' she said.

'Taken?'

Katya turned to look at her. 'You don't know what it's like, Anna. You can't.'

'But – taken? What does it mean?'

Katya shrugged. 'Gone. Disappeared.'

'But *why*? What had he done?'

Katya shook her head.

'Natalia?' Anna asked.

'She's gone too. I've tried, through friends, but I haven't been able to trace her.'

There was a long moment of quiet.

'Gone,' Anna said. And lifted her head.

Around her the house stood quiet, warm and sheltering. From the music room came a sudden and unexpected ripple of sound.

'Boris has found the piano,' Katya said, and laughed a little. 'The piano – and freedom.' She cast a sudden, sardonic, infinitely compassionate look upon Anna. 'Be careful. A free Boris bears watching.'

And, 'Oh, Katya,' Anna said through laughter and sudden tears, 'I am so very glad to see you!'

EPILOGUE: SUMMER 1928

'When is Aunt Katya actually due to arrive with this new protégé of hers?' 'Tasha was sitting upon the garden table, long
bare legs swinging. She was dressed for tennis, her fair hair
caught back in a fashionable bandau that well suited the strong,
Slavic bone structure of her face. As she spoke she spun a racquet in her hand, back and forth, flipping it with a quick, fidgety
movement. 'Tasha was and always would be a blaze of exhausting energy, Anna thought, watching her. Just being near her was
enough to tire the faint of heart.

'Some time this afternoon or evening, I suppose. You know
Katya. The boat should have docked yesterday, but it won't
occur to her to let us know exactly when she'll be here.'

'I like Aunt Katya. She's fun.' 'Tasha reached for a cake,
wolfed it with unladylike speed and relish. Her mass of fair hair
and blue eyes were Margarita's, but any resemblance between
the two stopped sharply there. 'Tasha was tall, strong and ath-
letically built, straightforward in character, impatient and
blunt-spoken. No, there was little true similarity between
'Tasha and her Aunt Margarita.

'Have you seen Nik?' Restlessly the girl slipped from the
table and prowled the terrace, swinging her racquet. 'He
promised me a game, and now the beast has disappeared.'

Anna, her face shaded by a large, tattered straw hat, flicked
the pages of her magazine. The sun was very warm, the sounds
of the garden muted in the heavy, quiet air. 'He was in the
music room with Sebastien last time I saw him.'

'Huh.' The sound came close to a snort. 'Good old Sebastien.
Of course. I might have known. Clicked his fingers, did he?
Honestly, what the bloody wonderful Sebastien – sorry –' the
word was automatic rather than apologetic as Anna lifted a
sharp, questioning glance '– what the undoubtedly wonderful

Sebastien has that the rest of us lack is entirely beyond me.'
She took a quick swipe, with mortal intent, at an inoffensive
passing fly.

The courteous though far from unfriendly distance their
handsome young guest had preserved between himself and the
boisterous 'Tasha might have something to do with it, Anna
thought, not without sympathy. 'He's a very nice young man.'
Her voice was neutral, her eyes upon her magazine. 'And he's
the most promising young pianist any of us have come across
for a very long time.'

'Oh, I grant you that. No-one could hold his piano playing
against him, not even a Philistine like me.' 'Tasha grinned suddenly. 'It's the Crown Prince of Ruritania charm that I can't
stand.'

'Don't be graceless, 'Tasha.' Anna kept her voice detached
and cool, furious with herself at the faint burning she could feel
colouring her cheeks. She had hoped, vainly, that she might
outgrow this mortifying tendency to glow like a firefly at the
slightest and silliest thing. She turned her head, tipping the
wide brim of the hat, hoping that the unobservant 'Tasha would
not notice the blush that was unbecoming, she well knew, in
more ways than one. 'That's exactly what most girls would like
about him, I should think.'

'Tasha snapped a dead head from a rose bush and served it
neatly into the middle of the lawn. 'Maybe so,' she said, lightly,
shrugging. 'Personally I don't go for the Rudolph Valentino
looks and the cloak across the puddle manners. Right, I'm off
to find Nikki. A promise is a promise and I'm dying for a game.
Oh – Step asked me to tell you he'd be up in the woods. If you
want him or if Aunt Katya does arrive, just blow the whistle.'

Anna laughed. 'I will.'

She watched her niece stride off into the house, then strolled
down the steps and along the path to the fountain. The Crown
Prince of Ruritania. She had to laugh. Trust 'Tasha. There was
no faulting the aptness of the tart description.

Sebastien had come to Sythings a couple of months before.
He had come, as they all did, from Katya, son of a French mother
long dead and a talented father who had fallen foul of the
CHEKA. He was a tall, dark-haired and good-looking lad about

twenty years of age; a boy, only a few years older than 'Tasha herself – and yet, oddly, it was difficult to think of him so. His background, his grave and courteous manners, above all his talent, gave an impression of a maturity beyond his years.

When he first arrived he had been exhausted, thin as a rail and convalescing from illness and from the terrors through which he had lived and about which he politely but very firmly refused to speak. Two months of Sussex peace and sunshine – to say nothing of Sussex country food – had brought a bright colour to him, put strength and vigour into his frame and made his smile more ready. Musically he was a prodigy; he was too a child who had been brought up amongst adults, in an intimate situation made more intense by persecution and in an atmosphere perhaps too rarefied for his own good. This unusual background was presumably what had produced the rather intriguing mixture of extreme and vulnerable youth and strange, perceptive maturity that despite her good sense Anna found so intriguing. Despite the trials through which he had lived his good temper seemed unassailable, his temperament peaceable, veiling the depths that could be glimpsed through his music; for it was the music of angels. It was his music, of course, that had so attracted her to the young man.

Always she told herself this, insisting against the clear memory of the first, instant lurch of her heart when she had seen him, the later delight in his company. It was absurd to think for a moment that anything beyond his talent, the draw of his complicated personality, had attracted her. But yet these past weeks had been so very special. It had been so long since she had woken in the morning with excitement and anticipation in her heart, so long since she had looked for one face, one smile when she entered a room or walked in the garden. Ridiculous. Such thoughts were utterly ridiculous. She knew it. The boy was at least fifteen or sixteen years her junior. There could be nothing between them. Or so she had thought until last night.

She stood now, pensive beside the fountain. For those first four or five weeks they had been in the house alone, apart from the servants. It had seemed a perfectly proper arrangement. He was after all barely older than the children she thought of as her own. And to all outward appearances, to the very letter indeed, all proprieties had been observed. She had not known then – and did not know now – if he had sensed, despite all her efforts, how he had stirred her. She had quite fervently hoped not. She still did.

The years since Russia, she considered, had been kind to her. First there had been Guy. Now she had her music, she had Sythings and she had her children. Life could have worked out very differently, and she knew it. In her heart still she grieved for her homeland and for her compatriots. Who would not? She had had too, of course, in these past ten years lovers of various standing, various enthusiasm and for various reasons, though not many, and never close enough to hurt. But never in all these years had anyone touched her as Sebastien had. Distantly, though always she had denied it to herself, he had reminded her of Andrei.

It had been the first time she had picked up her grandfather's violin to play to Sebastien's accompaniment that the real rapport had begun to grow between them. It had been the most magical evening, begun in laughter, ending in a very real and shared passion of understanding and excitement. The musical partnership had been close to perfection, and both had known it.

From then on she had, to her credit, been very careful.

The children had come home; the house had filled with noise, with activity, with constant comings and goings, inconsequential quarrels, and tennis parties. Katya had announced by letter her arrival with yet another refugee, this one, she promised, the greatest prize of them all.

With pleasure and with joy Anna had watched Sebastien's love of Sythings and of the family grow.

After that first evening they played often together, either contentedly alone or for others, and each time it was the same; from the first note a mutual passion, a wordless communication shared by no-one else. As for that other warmth he aroused in her, it was a secret, a small secret she shared with no-one, least of all with Sebastien. She was certain he had no inkling of her tender feelings for him.

Until last night, when he had kissed her.

They had been here, by the fountain. They had dined well, the evening was fine and warm, and at 'Tasha's insistence they had opened another bottle of champagne in place of coffee. Stepan had walked into the garden with them, remote yet friendly, drifting off, as he always at some point did, his presence melting into his absence between one moment and the next.

'I like Step,' Sebastien had said, quietly.

And, 'Yes. So do I,' Anna had said, and turned, unwary. 'Of all of them he's –' and had stopped, too close to him.

His young face had been shadowed, the light from the house shifting like starlight in his eyes. With no warning he had bent to her and kissed her, on the lips, a long, soft, tentative kiss. And startled and delighted she had stood quite still, her face lifted to his. And then he had left her, walking swiftly, gauchely graceful, across the lawn.

She had stayed there – here – by the fountain for a long time. She had heard the young voices, the laughter, the sound of the gramophone. She had tried to untangle her thoughts and her emotions, and had failed. Now, with a sudden movement, she pulled off her hat, lifted her face to the sun. One inappropriate love in life was surely enough? Two could only be thought ridiculous.

'They're here! Aunt Katya's here!' 'Tasha's voice floated across the garden. She heard the sound of a car's engine.

Nikki appeared on the terrace. 'Aunt Anna? They're here, they've arrived – I've yelled for Step, he's coming.' He dived back into the house.

She ran across the lawn and around the house. On the sanded drive by the front door the battered local taxi stood. Katya was the centre of a tangle of laughing young people.

'Aunt Katya! Gosh, how lovely you look!' 'Tasha elbowed her way to her smaller aunt's side, gave her a bearhug that left Katya gasping and knocked her hat askew.

'Oh, God, 'Tasha, you're like a flipping octopus! Let Aunt Kat get some breath!'

Anna had stopped, struck to immobility, watching. The second occupant of the taxi had clambered from the car and stood surveying the noisy proceedings with a reserved and wary eye. She was tall, thin and untidy, and she carried a cheap violin case scuffed at the corners and in general very much the worse for wear.

The sun gleamed upon wiry, marigold hair.

Katya had extricated herself from the enthusiasm of the young and, turning, had seen Anna.

'Anna, darling – well, here we are as you see.' Katya positively gleamed with pleasure, turned to hold a hand to her companion, drawing her forward. Pale eye met pale eye, the one hostile, the other in dawning understanding.

'It's Tonia,' Katya said. 'You didn't guess, did you? I so much wanted it to be a surprise – Anna, it's Tonia. Lenka's girl –'

Guess? She had not remotely considered the idea that Katya's latest escapee might be Lenka's daughter. The shock was all but overwhelming.

'Tonia.' Anna moved forward, hands outstretched. 'Tonia. Oh my dear, it's so very good to see you here.'

The thin, pale face was closed, defensive. Purposefully the girl held out her hand, forestalling any attempt that Anna might make to embrace her. 'Thank you.'

There was a small and slightly difficult silence. Then, 'Aren't you a cousin or something?' 'Tasha enquired. They had all, at some unnoticed point, lapsed easily into Russian. A common habit when outsiders were not around.

'Well of course she is.' Katya turned, waved a hand to where the taxi driver was unloading her cases. 'Nikki, Step, give me a hand with these, would you? And where's my lovely Sebastien?'

'He's coming,' Nikki said. 'Ah, there he is.' He raised his voice. 'Hey, Seb! Here's Aunt Katya – come on, you slowcoach!'

Sebastien, from the top of the steps, smiled his bright and tranquil smile, ran swiftly to them to fling his arms about Katya and hug her. She extricated herself after a moment, put him from her, surveyed him with approving eyes. 'Goodness me, how well you look!' She linked arms with him, turned to follow the boys and 'Tasha up the steps. Everyone was talking at once.

'I'm sorry,' Tonia said to Anna. 'I know I shouldn't have come. I won't stay long, I promise. Just until I can find somewhere.'

She spoke haltingly. It took a moment for the words to sink in. Anna stared at her.

'I had to get out – I had to go somewhere – Aunt Katya was my only contact.' The small, closed face looked wretchedly tired.

'Tonia, please, don't!' Anna felt the old, familiar stirring of distress. 'Of course you must stay. As long as you like. Please believe me – I'm so glad you came –'

The noisy entourage had reached the top of the steps where Mrs Barton the housekeeper now stood to add her greetings to her favourite guest.

'Thank you,' Tonia said, the words polite and empty as the thanks of a child told by adults that she should be grateful. 'You're very kind.'

She turned and walked up the steps, straight-backed and shabby, every tense line of her body, the lift of her chin, rejecting warmth.

Anna watched her with heavy heart, remembering the child who had faced her in that dreadful room, defying her, refusing her help and her friendship; poisoned by her mother's hatred of a sister she believed had betrayed her. She shook her head. Surely – surely! – something must have changed? The girl couldn't still nurse a grievance carried since childhood?

'Anna?' Sebastien had reappeared on the steps above her. His young face had lost its smile. He looked grave, a little tense. She stopped, lifting her head to him, smiling, about to hold out her hand as she normally would. Something in his face stopped her. 'Sebastien?'

She knew before he spoke what he would say. Had known, she supposed, since that moment last night when he had left her by the fountain. She waited, smiling as he wanted her to smile, mild, understanding, a touch of amusement, vaguely aunt-like.

He could not meet her eyes; he looked truly wretched. 'I'm so very sorry. So very ashamed. Last night – the champagne I think –' He hung his head, his smooth young cheeks flushed. 'I have no excuse. I can't think what came over me. I don't know how to apologize. To have done such a thing –' he bit his lip '– it was truly unforgivable, I know.'

From inside the house came a shout of laughter.

'Last night?' she asked, her voice determinedly light. 'Why, my dear, whatever happened last night that you should be so ashamed of?' She smiled an affectionate smile, slipped her arm through his, as she might with Stepan or Nikki, guiding him back up the steps.

He hung back. 'Please. Don't be kind. I feel so dreadful about it. I wouldn't blame you – couldn't blame you – if – if you wished me to leave?' He turned on her a look of real misery. 'To have repaid your hospitality so. What must you think of me?'

Anna's smile remained firmly in place. 'Silly boy. I think of you exactly as I did before. As you say, a little too much champagne – there's no blame in that once in a while. And as for the other –' She stopped, looking up at him, willing her voice to the bright warmth of pure friendship, 'Why, I was quite flattered! An old lady like me? Why shouldn't I be? Come now –' she laughed a little, teasing, ignoring the odd, leaden feeling in her heart '– don't spoil it! It was quite the prettiest compliment anyone's paid me in ages. Now,' she added briskly, before he could answer, 'come along, let's get back to the others. I don't know if you realize quite what a red-letter day this is for us all. Tonia is my sister's child, you know – we lost touch with her in Petrograd ten or eleven years ago. It's so exciting to see her here.'

The first days were very difficult. After the initial excitement had worn off, after the youngsters had given up making allowances for this strange, withdrawn, sometimes sullen cousin of theirs, after they had stopped trying to coax her out of her shell and left her firmly to her own devices it fell often to Anna to try to break through the wary reserve, to tempt the girl to relaxation and to laughter. To absolutely no avail.

'It's no good,' she said to Katya, a week or so after their arrival, 'I simply can't get through to her. Oh, she isn't overtly rude, I don't mean that. On the contrary she's always excessively, quite wearyingly, polite. It's just – it's as if there's a wall between us. A wall she won't even let me peep over, let alone pull down.'

'You've tried to talk to her?' Katya asked. They were sitting on the terrace with tea. The three youngsters and Sebastien were engaged in a cut-throat game of croquet at the far end of the garden. Tonia was nowhere to be seen. 'About what happened, between Lenka and you?'

Anna nodded. 'Tried's the word. She simply refuses to talk about it. Very politely of course.' She sighed, heavily, then into the silence added, 'She's so much like her, isn't she? Like Lenka, I mean? So – difficult – so unhappy all the time. If only there were something we could do to show her –' She trailed off, frustrated.

'There's one person who could,' Katya said, and leaned forward. 'More tea?'

There was a small silence. 'No thank you,' Anna said. And then, 'Sebastien, you mean?'

'Of course. The poor girl's crazy about him. Hadn't you noticed? She follows him around like a little puppy. Not that one can blame her of course.'

Anna turned to watch the young folk laughing and squabbling on the lawn. 'I had noticed, I suppose. Yes. But Katya, isn't that even more dangerous? Isn't it likely to make her even more unhappy?' She turned her eyes from the fountain that played prettily in the centre of the lawn. Sipped her tea. That episode was over and forgotten, by a relieved Sebastien at least. The thought was wry. He had all too eagerly accepted her 'forgiveness' for his lapse.

'It rather depends, doesn't it – may I have another of Mrs Barton's delicious biscuits please? – on how Sebastien feels about it?'

Anna turned her head. 'What do you mean?'

Katya shrugged. 'He doesn't seem to mind. The way she follows him about, I mean. He seems perfectly happy in her company.'

'Well he would, of course. He's a very kind young man. He wouldn't want to hurt her feelings.'

'Perhaps not. I heard them playing together the other day. I'm no expert as you know, but they sounded pretty good to me. That's got to be the basis of something, hasn't it?'

'Yes. Yes, I suppose it has.' Anna's voice was quiet.

Katya turned to look at her. 'How good is she? Tonia, I mean? You'd know better than any of us.'

Anna waited a moment before she answered. 'From what I've managed to hear,' she said at last, 'she shows promise. She needs more training of course. But,' she shook her head, 'it's hard for me to tell. You must have noticed she won't play in front of me? I only ever hear her from behind closed doors.'

Katya leaned forward and patted her hand. 'Don't worry, my dear. She'll come round. She's been through so much. We can't expect her to change in a week.'

'No. I suppose not. Now,' briskly and deliberately Anna changed the subject, 'the houseparty next weekend. Did you want me to get in touch with the Bradburys? You remember – the portrait painter and her husband, they were here last year – they were asking after you just a couple of weeks ago. I'm sure they'd love to see you again.'

The summer days were warm and long. Doors and windows stood open to the air and the sunshine. On the afternoon after her conversation with Katya, Anna came down the curving staircase to hear from behind the music-room door the sound of a violin.

She hesitated at the foot of the stairs, her hand on the post. Turned to walk away. Stopped, listening. The Bach Concerto in E Major. One of her own favourites, played with a lilting precision that held her for a moment of real and disinterested pleasure. Impulsively she turned and walked to the music-room door.

Tonia did not hear her entrance. The girl was absorbed in the music, hair fallen in an untidy tangle across her eyes. For a moment Anna was tempted to withdraw quietly and leave her to it, but the slight movement she made attracted Tonia's attention. The music stopped abruptly, a fragile thread broken by intrusion. The thin arms lowered, the violin hung by her side. Her chin came up. She did not smile.

'I heard you from outside,' Anna said, with no preamble. 'You were playing so well. Won't you continue?'

It was the first time she had bluntly invited a straight rejection. Calmly she walked to the table that stood by the open French windows and reached to rearrange, quite unnecessarily, the vase of summer flowers that stood upon it.

From behind her, after a long moment's quiet, the violin

565

began to play. Anna did not turn, but stood looking out into her lovely garden, listening. Many thoughts came to her, and many memories; but one in particular, a small, haunting and vivid picture of a girl she had thought long forgotten; a girl as pale, as intense and she supposed as awkward as the one who played in the room behind her. Herself at Tonia's age, devastated because her dream of music had been taken from her by her father.

Yet he had given her something else.

The last note died. She turned. The girl was watching her with the old unapproachable, half-defiant look. A look Anna saw in a sudden moment of utter clarity that, despite all her efforts, could not disguise the fear of rejection, the palpable yearning behind it. 'That was truly lovely,' she said.

Tonia half-turned, dropping her eyes, lifted the battered violin to rub at it with her sleeve.

Anna crossed the room to where her own violin rested in the same scuffed case in which it had first travelled from Moscow to St Petersburg all those long years ago. 'Have you seen this?'

Tonia shook her head. Could not resist coming closer as Anna unsnapped the catch and lifted the instrument out. She turned. The girl's eyes were fixed, unguarded, upon the violin. 'Your great-grandfather made it,' Anna said. 'It's a wonderful instrument.'

The girl put out a bony hand and, very gently, laid the back of her knuckles upon the shining wood before snatching her hand away.

'Would you like to play it?' Anna asked.

'I –' Tonia swallowed. Stiff-necked pride battled irresistible temptation. Temptation won. She reached for the instrument.

Anna held on to it for only a fraction of a second too long before she relinquished it into the younger girl's hand.

Tonia held it with disciplined delicacy, weighing it in her hands, turning it this way and that, watching as the burnished wood caught the light. Then, carefully, she lifted it and tucked it beneath her chin.

Anna turned and walked to the window again. Stepan and Sebastien were walking across the lawn towards the house. She saw Sebastien's exaggerated gestures as he talked, saw Stepan's slow, and to Anna who remembered so well the terrified, brow-beaten child he had been, perfectly lovely smile.

Behind her the music lifted once more; Mozart's Fourth Concerto, one part of her brain automatically noted; evocative, gently passionate, perfect for the day. She saw Sebastien stop, turn his head quickly towards the music room before, after saying something and lifting a quick hand in farewell to his companion, turning to walk swiftly and lightly towards the terrace and the open French windows.

Anna watched him come.

Silhouetted in the doorway he stopped. 'Anna?' Then, 'Tonia! It's you?'

Tonia had stopped playing. Her face was bright as a poppy. She nodded. Eagerly Sebastien came to her. 'Play it again – no! – I have a better idea. Come.' He pulled her towards the piano, shuffled through the music that was strewn upon the table beside it. 'Ah, here, the Beethoven – the Kreutzer, you know it?'

'I – yes, I know it.'

'It's my favourite. Come. Let's try it.' He was already settling himself at the piano.

Anna stood all but forgotten.

He played a few notes, loosening his fingers. Tentatively Tonia drew the bow across the strings of her great-grandfather's violin.

No, Anna thought, very determinedly, pushing away an impulse that, once lodged in her mind, refused to be ignored. No. That would be too much.

Sebastien, face grave and intent now, lifted a finger then nodded. Once again the bow touched the strings, as a little uncertainly Tonia began to play.

'Wait,' Anna interrupted, suddenly and sharply, as Sebastien was poised to play the first resonant chord. 'I'm sorry. Just a moment.'

She hurried to a long cabinet that stood at the far end of the room and without giving herself time to think reached for the long, slender case that lay upon it. She stood in the shadows, the open case in her hand, feeling the surprised eyes of the two

youngsters on her back. Then she turned and walked to Tonia.
'I thought –' She offered the bow. 'Your great-uncle Andrei
made it. Try it. See what you think.'

Tonia laid down the bow she held and took the one that Anna
offered. Her face, usually so tense and drawn, softened as she
lifted it, drew it with gentle pressure across the strings. 'It's
wonderful. Perfect –'

'I always thought so,' Anna said.

She turned and walked out into the sunshine, leaving them
there. The sound of violin and piano drifted out behind her.
With slow and careful steps she walked from the terrace
to where a small stone seat was set beneath an ancient apple
tree.

She sat there, very still, for a very long time.

'Anna? Why here you are. I've been looking everywhere. See,'
ice clinked musically against glass, 'I've brought us both a rather
naughty drink. Champagne and fruit juice. It is such a very
lovely day – Anna? Are you all right?' Katya settled herself
beside her, a tall glass held out.

'Yes. I'm fine. Thank you.' Anna took the drink.

Katya cocked her head, listening. 'Ah.' Her eyes brightened.
'Sebastien and Tonia?'

Anna nodded.

'How beautifully they play together,' Katya said,
thoughtfully.

'Yes. Don't they?'

The music filled the air, piano and violin weaving enchanted,
precise and passionate patterns like the swooping flight of birds
in the summer's sky.

'Sebastien and Tonia,' Katya said again, after a moment, the
intonation a little different, the tone delighted and amused.
'Well. Stranger things have happened, I suppose.'

Anna held the cool, beaded glass to her flushed cheek.
'Strange are the ways of God,' she said.

'Good Lord!' Katya gave a soft laugh. 'It's years since I heard
that saying. That old woman of yours – what was her name?
Irina? Irisha? – used to say it all the time, didn't she?'

'Yes,' Anna said. 'She did. And she was right.'

'Tasha's voice lifted, laughing, from the tennis court on the other side of the hedge. A bird sang into the sunshine from the branch above them.

Across the lawn the music drifted, timeless and beautiful.